Troup-Harris Regional Library
LAGRANGE MEMORIAL LIBRARY
115 Alford Street
LaGrange, GA 30240

D0221537

L G gift
7/08
420 KA
ALE

THE ORIGINS AND DEVELOPMENT OF THE ENGLISH LANGUAGE

The
Origins and
Development
of the
English
Language

Fifth Edition

John Algeo

Thomas Pyles

THOMSON

WADSWORTH

Australia   Canada   Mexico   Singapore   Spain   United Kingdom   United States

The Origins and Development of the English Language, Fifth Edition
John Algeo, Thomas Pyles

Publisher: Michael Rosenberg
Acquisitions Editor: Stephen Dalphin
Development Editor: Lynn McGarvin
Senior Production Editor: Lianne Ames
V.P., Director of Marketing: Elana Dolberg
Executive Marketing Manager: Carrie Brandon
Manufacturing Manager: Marcia Locke

Compositor: WestWords
Project Manager: Jami L. Darby
Photo Manager: Sheri Blaney
Cover Designer: Diane Levy
Text Designer: WestWords
Printer: Quebecor World

Cover Image: © *Stapleton Collection/CORBIS*

Copyright © 2005, 1993, 1982, 1971, 1964 by
Thomson Wadsworth, a part of the Thomson
Corporation. Thomson Wadsworth, Thomson,
and the Thomson logo are trademarks used
herein under license.

All rights reserved. No part of this work covered
by the copyright hereon may be reproduced or
used in any form or by any means—graphic,
electronic, or mechanical, including photocopy-
ing, recording, taping, Web distribution or information storage and retrieval systems—without
the written permission of the publisher.

Printed in the United States of America.
2 3 4 5 6 7 8 9 10 07 06 05 04

For more information contact Thomson
Wadsworth, 25 Thomson Place, Boston,
Massachusetts 02210 USA, or you can visit our
Internet site at http://www.wadsworth.com

For permission to use material from this text or
product, submit a request online at
http://www.thomsonrights.com
Any additional questions about permissions
can be submitted by email to
thomsonrights@thomson.com

ISBN: 0-155-07055-X

PCN: 2003114840

PREFACE

This fifth edition of a book Thomas Pyles wrote more than forty years ago preserves the outline, emphasis, and aims of the original. The focus of the book is on the internal history of the English language: its sounds, grammar, and word stock. As in earlier editions, the first three chapters are introductory, treating language in general as well as the pronunciation and orthography of present-day English. The succeeding central six chapters are the heart of the book, tracing the history of the language from prehistoric Indo-European days through Old English, Middle English, and early Modern English up to the present time. The final three chapters deal with vocabulary—the meaning, making, and borrowing of words.

The book continues to focus on the facts of language rather than any of the various contemporary theoretical approaches to the study of those facts. The presentation is that of fairly traditional grammar and philology, so as not to require students to master a new theoretical approach at the same time they are exploring the intricacies of language history.

The entire book has, however, been revised for helpfulness to students and ease of reading. In the process, a number of changes have been made. Somewhat more emphasis has been put on external history—the events in the lives of English speakers that have affected the language. The central historical chapters have been introduced by a list of dates and events of moment to the development of the language. The information has been updated where appropriate, new examples have been cited in many places (although effective older ones have not been avoided), many new items have been added to the bibliography, and the glossary has been revised for clarity and accuracy. Suggested readings have been added at the end of each chapter. And an index of persons, places, and topics has also been added. Footnotes have been dispensed with by incorporating discursive information into the text and by using the MLA-recommended in-text reference system of author and short title when needed. Numerous other minor changes have been made that should serve the interests and convenience of students.

All of the debts acknowledged in earlier editions are still owing in this one. This edition has, however, also benefited from the critiques of five very knowledgeable readers, whose suggestions I have tried to follow wherever I could: Robert M. Correale, Shirley D. Laird, Daniel J. Ransom, and two anonymous reviewers. Carmen Acevedo Butcher has assisted very helpfully in proofing. My wife, Adele S. Algeo, has worked with me at every step of the revision, and of her I can gratefully adapt the words Tom Pyles used of his wife, Becky: she is my dearest friend and most perceptive critic, who assists in innumerable and invaluable ways.

John Algeo

CONTENTS

6 THE MIDDLE ENGLISH PERIOD (1100–1500) **123**

7 THE EARLY MODERN ENGLISH PERIOD (1500–1800): SOCIETY, SPELLINGS, AND SOUNDS **153**

xii CONTENTS

1 LANGUAGE AND THE ENGLISH LANGUAGE

AN INTRODUCTION

The English language has had a remarkable history. When we first catch sight of it in historical records, it is the **speech** of some none-too-civilized tribes on the continent of Europe along the North Sea. Of course, it had a still earlier history, going back perhaps to somewhere in eastern Europe or western Asia, and before that to origins we can only speculate about. From those murky and undistinguished beginnings, English has become the most widespread language in the world, used by more peoples for more purposes than any other language on Earth. How the English language changed from being the speech of a few small tribes to becoming the major language of the world, and in the process itself changed radically, is the subject of this book.

Whatever language we speak—English, Chinese, Hindi, Swahili, or Arapaho—helps to define the community we belong to. But the fact that we can talk at all, the fact that we have a language, is inextricably bound up with our humanity. To be human is to use language, and to talk is to be a person. As the biologist and author Lewis Thomas remarks:

> The gift of language is the single human trait that marks us all genetically, setting us apart from the rest of life. Language is, like nest-building or hive-making, the universal and biologically specific activity of human beings. We engage in it communally, compulsively, and automatically. We cannot be human without it; if we were to be separated from it our minds would die, as surely as bees lost from the hive. (*Lives of a Cell* 89)

The language gift that is innate in us is, of course, not English or indeed any specific language. It is instead the ability to learn and to use a human language. When we say, "Bread is the staff of life," we do not mean any particular kind of bread—whole wheat, rye, pumpernickel, French, matzo, pita, or whatever sort. Rather we are talking about the kind of thing bread is, that which all bread has in common. So also, when we say that language is the basis of our humanity, we do not mean any particular language—English, Spanish, Japanese, Tagalog, Hopi, or **Ameslan** (the sign language of the deaf). Rather we mean the ability to learn and use any such particular language systems, an ability that all normal human beings have. This ability is language in the abstract, as distinct from individual language systems like English or any of the others.

1

A DEFINITION OF LANGUAGE

We can define **language** as a system of conventional vocal signs by means of which human beings communicate. There are six important terms in this definition, each of which is examined in some detail in the sections below. They are *system, signs, vocal, conventional, human,* and *communicate.* On the following pages we consider what these words mean and what they imply about the nature of language.

LANGUAGE AS SYSTEM

Perhaps the most important word in the definition of *language* is **system**. We speak in patterns. A language is not just a collection of words, such as we find in a dictionary. It is also the rules or patterns that relate the words to one another.

Every language has two levels to its system—a characteristic that is called **duality of patterning**. One of these levels consists of meaningful units—for example, the words and word parts such as *Adam, like, -d, apple,* and *-s* in the sentence "Adam liked apples." The other level consists of units that have no meaning in themselves, although they serve as components of the meaningful units—for example, the sounds represented by the letters *a, d,* and *m* in the word *Adam.*

The distinction between a meaningful word (*Adam*) and its meaningless parts (*a, d,* and *m*) is important. Without that distinction, language as we know it would be impossible. If every meaning had to be represented by a unique, unanalyzable sound, only a few such meanings could be expressed. We have only about 35 basic sounds in English; we have hundreds of thousands of words. Duality of patterning lets people build an immensely large number of meaningful words out of only a handful of meaningless sounds. It is perhaps the chief characteristic that distinguishes true human language from the simpler communication systems of all non-human animals.

The meaningless components of a language make up its **sound system**, or **phonology**. The meaningful units are part of its **lexis**, or **vocabulary**, and its **grammatical system**, or **morphosyntax**. All have patterning. Thus, according to the sound system of Modern English, the consonant combination *mb* never occurs at the beginning or at the end of any word. As a matter of fact, it did occur in final position in earlier stages of our language, which is why it was necessary in the preceding statement to specify "Modern English." Despite the complete absence of the sounds *mb* at the ends of English words for at least 600 years, we still insist—such is the conservatism of writing habits—that the *b* be written in *lamb, climb, tomb, dumb,* and a number of other words. But this same combination, which now occurs only medially in English (as in *tremble*), may well occur in final or even in initial position in the sound systems of other languages. Initial *mb* is indeed a part of the systems of certain African languages, as in the Efik and Ibibio *mbakara* 'white man,' which became *buckra* in the speech of the Gullahs—black Americans living along the coastal region of Georgia and South Carolina who have preserved a number of words and structural features that their ancestors brought from Africa. It is notable that the Gullahs simplified the initial consonant combination of this African word to conform to the pattern of English speech.

The lexis or vocabulary of a language is its least systematic aspect. Grammar is sometimes defined as everything in a language that can be stated in general rules, and lexis as everything that is unpredictable. But that is not quite true. Certain combinations of words, called **collocations**, are more or less predictable. *Mild* and *gentle* are words of very similar meaning, but they go with different nouns: "mild weather" and "gentle breeze" are somewhat more likely than the opposite combinations ("mild breeze" and "gentle weather"). A case of the flu may be *severe* or *mild;* a judgment is likely to be *severe* or *lenient.* A "mild judgment" would be a bit odd, and a "lenient case of the flu" sounds like a joke. Some collocations are so regular that they are easily predictable. In the following sentence, one word is more probable than any other in the blank: "In its narrow cage, the lion paced back and _____." Although several words are possible in the blank (for example, *forward* or even *ahead*), *forth* is the most likely. Some combinations are completely predictable: "They ran ____ ____ fro." *Fro* is normal in present-day English only in the expression "to and fro." The tendency of certain words to collocate or go together is an instance of system in the vocabulary.

In the grammatical system of English, a very large number of words take a suffix written as *-s* to indicate plurality or possession. In the latter case, it is a comparatively recent convention of writing to add an apostrophe. Words that can be thus modified in form are nouns. They fit into certain patterns in English utterances. *Alcoholic,* for instance, fits into the system of English in the same way as *duck, dog,* and *horse:* "Alcoholics need understanding" (compare "Ducks need water"), "An alcoholic's perceptions are faulty" (compare "A dog's perceptions are keen"), and the like. But it may also modify a noun and be modified by an adverb: "an alcoholic drink," "somewhat alcoholic," and the like; and words that operate in this way are called adjectives. *Alcoholic* is thus either an adjective or a noun, depending on the way it functions in the system of English. The utterance "Alcoholic worries" is ambiguous because our system, like all linguistic systems, is not completely foolproof. It might be either a noun followed by a verb (as in a newspaper headline) or an adjective followed by a noun. To know which interpretation is correct, we need a context in which to place the expression. That is, we need to relate it to a larger system.

Grammatical Signals

The grammatical system of any language has various techniques for relating words to one another within the structure of a sentence. Six kinds of signals are especially important.

1. Words can be put in various categories called **parts of speech**, of which there are four major ones in English: **noun, verb, adjective,** and **adverb.**

Some words belong primarily or solely to one part of speech: *child* is a noun, *seek* is a verb, *tall* is an adjective, and *rapidly* is an adverb. Other words can function as more than one part of speech; in various meanings, *last* can be any of the four major parts. English speakers move words about pretty freely from one part of speech to another, as when we call a book that is enjoyable to read "a good read," making a noun out of a verb. Part of knowing English is knowing how words can be shifted about in that way and what the limits are to such shifting.

2.   A word's part of speech is sometimes signaled by its form, specifically by an **affix**—a beginning or ending—used with it. The **prefix** *en-* at the beginning of a word, as in *encipher, enrage, enthrone, entomb, entwine,* and *enwrap,* marks the word as a verb. The **suffix** *-ist* at the end, as in *dentist, geologist, motorist,* and *violinist,* marks the word as a noun. English also has a small number of **inflectional suffixes** (endings that mark distinctions of number, case, person, tense, mood, and comparison). They include the plural *-s* and the possessive *'s* used with nouns (*boys, boy's*); the third person singular present tense *-s,* the past tense and past participle *-ed,* and the present participle *-ing* used with verbs (*aids, aided, aiding*); and the comparative *-er* and superlative *-est* used with some adjectives and adverbs (*slower, slowest*). **Inflection** (the change in form of a word to mark such distinctions) may also involve internal change, as in the singular and plural noun forms *man* and *men* or the present and past verb forms *sing* and *sang.* A language that depends heavily on the use of inflections, either internal or suffixed, is said to be **synthetic**; English used to be far more synthetic than it now is.

3.   When a language uses inflections, they are often interconnected by **concord**, or **agreement**. Thus in "The bird sings" and "The birds sing" there is subject-verb concord (it being merely coincidental that the signal for plural in nouns happens to be identical in form with the signal for singular in third person present tense verbs). Similarly, in "this day" both words are singular, and in "these days" both are plural; some languages, such as Spanish, require that all modifiers agree with the nouns they modify in number, but in English only *this* and *that* change their form to show such agreement. Highly synthetic languages, such as Latin, usually have a great deal of concord; thus Latin adjectives agree with the nouns they modify in number (*bonus vir* 'good man,' *bonī virī* 'good men'), in gender (*bona femina* 'good woman'), and in case (*bonae feminae* 'good woman's'). English used to have more such concord than it now does.

4.   **Word order** is a grammatical signal in all languages, though some languages, like English, depend more heavily on it than do others. "The man finished the job" and "The job finished the man" are sharply different in meaning, as are "He died happily" and "Happily he died."

5.   Minor parts of speech, also called **function words** (for example, articles, auxiliaries, conjunctions, prepositions, pronouns, and certain adverbial particles), are a kind of grammatical signal used with word order to serve some of

the same functions as inflections. For example, in English the indirect object of a verb can be shown by either word order ("I gave *the dog* a bone") or a function word ("I gave a bone *to the dog*"); in Latin it is shown by inflection (*canis* 'the dog,' *Canī os dēdi* 'To-the-dog a-bone I-gave'). A language like English whose grammar depends heavily on the use of word order and function words is said to be **analytic**.

    6. Prosodic signals, such as pitch, stress, and tempo, can indicate grammatical meaning. The difference between the statement "He's here" and the question "He's here?" is the pitch used at the end of the sentence. The chief difference between the verb *conduct* and the noun *conduct* is that the verb has a stronger stress on its second syllable and the noun on its first syllable. In "He died happily" and "He died, happily," the tempo of the last two words makes an important difference of meaning.

All languages have these six kinds of grammatical signals available to them, but languages differ greatly in the use they make of the various signals. Even a single language may change its use over time, as English has.

LANGUAGE SIGNS

    In language, signs are what the system organizes. A **sign** is something that stands for something else—for example, a word like *apple*, which stands for the familiar fruit. But linguistic signs are not words alone; they may also be either smaller or larger than whole words. The smallest linguistic sign is the **morpheme**, which is a meaningful form that cannot be divided into smaller meaningful parts. The word *apple* is a single morpheme; the word *applejack* consists of two morphemes (each of which can also function independently as a word); the word *apples* also consists of two morphemes, one of which (*-s*) can occur only as part of a word. Morphemes that can be used alone as words (such as *apple* and *jack*) are called **free morphemes**; those that must be combined with other morphemes to make a word (such as *-s*) are **bound morphemes**. The word *reactivation* has five morphemes in it (one free and four bound), as can be seen by analyzing it step by step:

    re-activation
      activate-ion
      active-ate
      act-ive

Thus the morphemes of this word are free *act* and bound *re-, -ive, -ate,* and *-ion.*

    A morpheme may have more than one pronunciation or spelling. For example, the regular noun plural ending has two spellings (*-s* and *-es*) and three pronunciations (an *s*-sound as in *backs,* a *z*-sound as in *bags,* and a vowel plus *z*-sound as in *batches*). Each of the spoken variations is called an **allomorph** of the plural morpheme. Similarly, when the morpheme *-ate* has added to it the morpheme *-ion* (as in *activate-ion*), the *t* of *-ate* combines with the *i* of *-ion* to become a *sh*-sound (so that we might spell the word "activashon"). Such allomorphic variation is typical of the morphemes of English, even though it is often not represented by the spelling.

Morphemes can also be divided into **base morphemes** and affixes. An affix is a bound morpheme that is added to a base morpheme. An affix may be either a prefix, which comes before its base (such as *re-*), or a suffix, which comes after its base (such as *-s, -ive, -ate,* and *-ion*). Most base morphemes are free (such as *apple* and *act*), but some are bound (such as the *insul-* of *insulate*). A word that has two or more bases (such as *applejack*) is called a **compound**.

In addition to being of word size (free morphemes) or smaller (bound morphemes), linguistic signs may also be larger than words. A combination of words whose meaning cannot be predicted from those of its constituent parts is an **idiom**. One kind of idiom that English has come to use extensively is the combination of a verb with an adverb, a preposition, or both—for instance, *turn on* (a light), *call up* (on the telephone), *put over* (a joke), *ask for* (a job), *come down with* (an illness), and *go back on* (a promise). From the standpoint of meaning, such an expression can be regarded as a single unit: to *go back on* is to 'abandon' a promise. But from the standpoint of grammar, several independent words are involved.

LANGUAGE AS SPEECH

Language is a system that can be expressed in many ways—by the marks on paper that we call writing, by hand signals and gestures as in sign language, by colored lights or moving flags as in semaphore, and by electronic clicks as in telegraphy. However, the signs of language—its words and morphemes—are basically vocal, or **oral-aural**, sounds produced by the mouth and received by the ear. If human communication had developed primarily as a system of gestures (like the American Sign Language of the deaf), it would have been quite different from what it is. Because sounds follow one another sequentially in time, language has a one-dimensional quality (like the lines of type we use to represent it in printing); gestures can fill the three dimensions of space as well as the fourth of time. The ears can hear sounds coming from any direction; the eyes can see only those gestures made in front of them. The ears can hear through physical barriers, such as walls, which the eyes cannot see through. Speech has both advantages and disadvantages in comparison with gestures; but on the whole, it is undoubtedly superior, as its evolutionary survival demonstrates.

Writing and Speech

Because writing has become so important in our culture, we sometimes think of it as more real than speech. A little thought, however, will show why speech is primary and writing secondary to language. Human beings have been writing (as far as we can tell from the surviving evidence) for at least 5,000 years, but they have been talking for much longer, doubtless ever since they were fully human beings. When writing developed, it was derived from and represented speech, albeit imperfectly, as we shall see in Chapter 3. Even today there are spoken languages that have no written form. Furthermore, we all learn to talk long before we learn to write; any human child who is not severely handicapped physically or mentally will learn to talk, and a normal human being cannot be prevented from doing so. It is as though we were "programmed" to acquire language in the form of speech. On the other hand, it takes a special effort to learn to write; in the past, many intelligent and useful members of society did not acquire the skill, and even today many who speak languages with writing systems never learn to read or write, while some who learn the rudiments of those skills do so only imperfectly.

To affirm the primacy of speech over writing is not, however, to disparage the latter. If speaking makes us human, writing makes us civilized. Writing has some advantages over speech. For example, it is more permanent, thus making possible the records that any civilization must have. Writing is also capable of easily making some distinctions that speech can make only with difficulty. We can, for example, indicate certain types of pauses more clearly by the spaces that we leave between words when we write than we ordinarily are able to do when we speak. *Grade A* may well be heard as *gray day,* but there is no mistaking the one phrase for the other in writing.

Similarly, the comma distinguishes "a pretty, hot day" from "a pretty hot day" more clearly than these are often distinguished in actual speech. But the question mark does not distinguish between "Why did you do it?" (I didn't hear you the first time you told me), with rising pitch at the end, and "Why did you do it?" (You didn't tell me), with falling terminal pitch. Nor can we show in writing the very apparent difference between *sound quality* meaning 'tone' and *sound quality* meaning 'good grade' (as in "The sound quality of the recording was excellent" and "The materials were of sound quality," respectively)—a difference that we show very easily in speech by strongly stressing *sound* in the first sentence and the first syllable of *quality* in the second. *Incense* 'enrage' and *incense* 'aromatic substance for burning' are likewise sharply differentiated in speech by the position of the stress, as *sewer* 'conduit' and *sewer* 'one who sews' are differentiated by vowel quality. But in writing we can distinguish these words only in context.

Words that are pronounced alike are called **homophones**. They may be spelled the same, such as *bear* 'carry' and *bear* 'animal,' or they may be distinguished in spelling, such as *bare* 'naked' and either of the *bear* words. Words that are written alike are called **homographs**. They may also be pronounced the same, such as the two *bear* words or *tear* 'to rip' and *tear* 'hurry' (as in "He's on a tear"), or they may be distinguished in pronunciation, such as *tear* 'a drop from the eye' and either of the other two *tear* words. **Homonym** is a term that covers either homophones or homographs, that is, a word either pronounced or spelled like another, such as all of the *bear/bare* and *tear* words.

Homophones are the basis of some nursery humor, as in the phrases "a bear/bare behind" and "a week/weak back," whose written forms rule out the slight possibility of ambiguity inherent in their spoken forms. But William Shakespeare was by no means averse to this sort of thing: puns involving *tale* and *tail, whole* and *hole, hoar* and *whore,* and a good many other homophones (some, like *stale* and *steal,* being no longer homophonous) are of rather frequent occurrence in the writings of our greatest poet.

The conventions of writing differ somewhat, but not really very much, from those of ordinary speech. For instance, we ordinarily write *was not, do not,* and *would not,* although we usually say *wasn't, don't,* and *wouldn't.* Furthermore, our choice of words is likely to differ occasionally and to be made with somewhat more care in writing than in ordinary, everyday speech. But these are stylistic matters, as is also the fact that writing tends to be somewhat more conservative than speech.

Representing the spellings of one language by those of another is **transliteration**, which must not be confused with **translation**, the interpretation of one language by another. Greek πῦρ can be transliterated *pyr,* as in *pyromaniac,* or translated *fire,* as in *firebug.* One language can be written in various **orthographies** (or writing systems). When the president of Turkey, Mustafa Kemal Pasha (later called Kemal Atatürk), in 1928 substituted the Roman alphabet for the Arabic in writing Turkish, the Turkish language changed no more than time changed when he introduced the Gregorian calendar in his country to replace the Islamic lunar one used earlier.

Gestures and Speech

Such specialized gestures as the indifferent shrug of the shoulders, the admonitory shaking of the finger, the lifting up of the hand in greeting and the waving of it in parting, the widening of the eyes in astonishment, the scornful lifting of the brows, the approving nod, and the disapproving sideways shaking of the head—all these need not accompany speech at all; they themselves communicate. Indeed, there is some reason to think that gestures are older than spoken language and are the matrix out of which it developed. When gestures accompany speech, they may be more or less unconscious, like the postures assumed by persons talking together, indicating their sympathy with each other's ideas (or lack of it, for example by crossed arms). The study of such communicative body movements is known as **kinesics**.

The various tones of voice that we employ optionally in speaking—the drawl, the sneer, the shout, the whimper, the simper, and the like—also play a part in communication (which we recognize when we say, "I didn't mind what he said, I just didn't like his tone of voice"). But they and the gestures that accompany speech are not language, but rather parallel systems of communication called **paralanguage**. Other vocalizations that are communicative, like laughing, crying, groaning, and yelping, usually do not accompany speech as tones of voice do, though they may come before or after it.

LANGUAGE AS CONVENTION

Writing is obviously **conventional** because we can represent the same language by more than one writing system. Japanese, for example, is written with kanji (ideographs representing whole words), with either of two syllabaries (writing systems that present each syllable with a separate symbol), or with the letters of the Roman alphabet. Similarly, we could by general agreement reform English spelling (soe dhat, for egzammpul, wee spelt it liek dhis). We can change the conventions of our writing system merely by agreeing to do so.

Although it is not so obvious, language itself—that is, speech—is also conventional. No one can deny that there are features shared by all languages—features that are natural, inherent, or universal. Thus the human vocal apparatus (lips, teeth, tongue, and so forth) makes it inevitable that human languages will have only a limited range of sounds. Likewise, since all of us live in the same universe and perceive our universe through the same senses with more or less the same basic mental equipment, it is hardly surprising that we should find it necessary to talk about more or less the same things in more or less similar ways.

Nevertheless, the systems that operate in the world's many languages are conventional and generally **arbitrary**; that is to say, there is usually no connection between the sounds we make and the phenomena of life. A comparatively small number of **echoic words** imitate, more or less closely, other sounds. *Bow-wow* seems to those of us who speak English as our native language to be a fairly accurate imitation of the sounds made by a dog and therefore not to be wholly arbitrary, but it is highly doubtful that a dog would agree, particularly a French dog, which says *gnaf-gnaf,* or a German one, which says *wau-wau,* or a Japanese one, which says *wung-wung.* In Norway cows do not say "moo" but *mmmøøø,* sheep do not say "baa" but *mæ,* and pigs do not say "oink" but *nøff-nøff.* Norwegian hens very sensibly say *klukk-klukk,* though doubtless with a heavy Norwegian accent. The process of echoing such sounds (also called **onomatopoeia**) is also conventional.

Most people think unquestioningly that their language is the best—and so it is for them, inasmuch as they mastered it well enough for their own purposes so long ago that they cannot remember when. It seems to them more logical, more sensible, more right—in short, more *natural*—than the way foreigners talk. But there is nothing really natural about any language, since all these highly systematized and conventionalized methods of human communication must be acquired. There is, for instance, nothing natural in our use of *is* in such a sentence as "The woman is busy." The utterance can be made just as effectively without that verb, and some languages do get along perfectly well without it. This use of *is* (and other forms of the verb *to be*) was, as a matter of fact, late in developing and has never developed in Russian.

To the speaker of Russian, it is thus more "natural" to say "Zhenshchina zanyata"—literally 'Woman busy'—which sounds to our ears so much like baby talk that the unsophisticated speaker of English might well (though quite wrongly) conclude that Russian is a childish tongue. The system of Russian also manages to struggle along without the definite article. As a matter of fact, the speaker of Russian never misses it—nor should we if its use had not become conventional with us.

To a naive English speaker, calling the organ of sight *eye* will seem to be perfectly natural and right, and those who call it anything else—like the Germans, who call it *Auge,* the Russians, who call it *glaz,* or the Japanese, who call it *me*— are likely to be regarded as unfortunate because they do not speak languages in which things are properly designated. The fact is, however, that *eye,* which we pronounce exactly like *I* (a fact that might be cited against it by a foreign speaker), is the name of the organ only in our present English linguistic system. It has not always been so. Londoners of the fourteenth century pronounced the word with two syllables, the vowel of the first syllable being that which we pronounce nowadays in *see* and the second like the *a* in *Ida.* If we chose to go back to King Alfred's day in the late ninth century, we should find yet another pronunciation and, in addition, a different way of writing the word from which Modern English *eye* has developed. The Scots are not being quaint or perverse when they say "ee" for *eye,* as in Robert Burns's poem "To a Mouse":

> Still thou art blest, compared wi' me!
> The present only toucheth thee:
> But och! I backward cast my e'e,
> On prospects drear!

The Scots form is merely a variant of the word—a perfectly legitimate pronunciation that happens not to occur in standard Modern English. Knowledge of such changes within a single language should dissipate the notion that any word is more appropriate than any other word except in a purely chronological and social sense.

Language Change

Change is the normal state of language. Every language is constantly turning into something different, and when we hear a new word or a new pronunciation or a novel use of an old word, we may be catching the early stages of a change. Change is natural because a language system is culturally transmitted. Like other conventional matters—such as fashions of clothing, cooking, entertainment, means of livelihood, and government—language is undergoing revision constantly; with language, such revision is slower than with some other cultural activities, but it is happening nonetheless.

There are three general causes of language change. First, words and sounds may affect neighboring words and sounds. For example, *sandwich* is often pronounced, not as the spelling suggests, but in ways that might be represented as "sanwich," "sanwidge," "samwidge," or even "sammidge." Such spellings look illiterate, but they represent perfectly normal, though informal, pronunciations that result from the influence of one sound on another within the word. When nearby elements thus influence one another within the flow of speech, the result is called **syntagmatic change**.

Second, words and sounds may be affected by others that are not immediately present but with which they are associated. For example, the side of a ship on which it was laden (that is, loaded) was called the *ladeboard,* but its opposite, *starboard,* influenced a change in pronunciation to *larboard.* Then, because *larboard* was likely to be confused with *starboard* because of their similarity of sound, it was generally replaced by *port.* Such change is called **paradigmatic** or **associative change**.

Third, a language may change because of the influence of events in the world. New technologies like the World Wide Web require new words like *google* 'to search the Internet for information.' New forms of human behavior, however bizarre, require new terms like *suicide bomber.* New concepts in science require new terms like *transposon* 'a transposable gene in DNA.' In addition, new contacts with persons who use speechways different from our own may affect our pronunciation, vocabulary, and even grammar. **Social change** thus modifies speech.

The documented history of the English language begins about A.D. 700, with the oldest written records. We can reconstruct some of the prehistory before that time, to as early as about 4000 B.C., but the farther back in time we go, the less certain we can be about what the language was like. The history of our language is traditionally divided into three periods: **Old English**, from the earliest records (or from the Anglo-Saxon settlement of England around A.D. 450) to about 1100; **Middle English**, from approximately 1100 to 1500; and **Modern English**, since about 1500. The lines dividing the three periods are based on significant changes in the language that happened about those times, but major cultural changes around 1100 and 1500 also contribute to our sense of new beginnings. These matters are treated in detail in Chapters 5 through 8.

The Notion of Linguistic Corruption

A widely held notion resulting from a misunderstanding of change is that there are ideal forms of languages, thought of as "pure," and that existing languages represent corruptions of these. Thus, the Greek spoken today is supposed to be a degraded form of Classical Greek rather than what it really is, a development of it. Since the Romance languages are developments of Latin, it would follow from this point of view that they also are corrupt, although this assumption is not usually made. Those who admire or profess to admire Latin literature sometimes suppose that a stage of perfection had been reached in Classical Latin and that every divergent development in Latin was indicative of steady and irreparable deterioration. From this point of view, the late development of Latin spoken in the early Middle Ages (sometimes called Vulgar, or popular, Latin) is "bad" Latin, which, strange as it may seem, was ultimately to become "good" Italian, French, Spanish, and so on.

Because we hear so much about "pure" English, it is perhaps well that we examine this particular notion. When Captain Frederick Marryat, an English novelist, visited the United States in 1837–8, he thought it "remarkable how very debased the language has become in a short period in America," adding that "if their lower classes are more intelligible than ours, it is equally true that the higher classes do not speak the language so purely or so classically as it is spoken among the well-educated English." Both statements are nonsense. The first is based on the captain's apparent notion that the English language had reached a stage of perfection at the time America was first settled by English-speaking people, after which, presumably because of the innate depravity of those English settlers who brought their language to the New World, it had taken a steadily downward course, whatever that may mean. One wonders also precisely how Marryat knew what constituted "classical" or "pure" English. It is probable that he was merely attributing certain superior qualities to that type of English that he was accustomed to hear from persons of good social standing in the land of his birth and that he himself spoke. Any divergence was "debased": "My speech is pure; thine, wherein it differs from mine, is corrupt."

Language Variation

In addition to its change through the years, at any given period of time, a language exists in many varieties. Historical or **diachronic** variation is matched by contemporary or **synchronic** variation. The latter is of two kinds: dialects and registers.

A **dialect** is the variety of a language associated with a particular place (Boston or New Orleans), social level (educated or vernacular), ethnic group (Jewish or African-American), sex (male or female), age grade (teenage or mature), and so on. Most of us have a normal way of using language that is an intersection of such dialects and that marks us as being, for example, a middle-aged, white, cultured, female Charlestonian of old family or a young, urban, working-class, male Hispanic from New York City. Some people have more than one such dialect personality; national politicians, for example, may use a Washingtonian government dialect when they are doing their job and a "down-home" dialect when they are interacting with the voters. Ultimately, each of us has a unique, personal way of using language, an **idiolect**, through which we can be identified by those who know us.

A **register** is the variety of a language used for a particular purpose: sermon language (which may have a distinctive rhythm and sentence melody and include words like *brethren* and *beloved,* which are seldom used otherwise), restaurant-menu language (which is full of "tasty adjectives" like *garden-fresh* and *succulent*), telephone-conversation language (in which the speech of the secondary participant is full of *umhum, I see, yeah, oh,* and such expressions), postcard language (in which the subjects of sentences are frequently omitted: "Having a wonderful time. Wish you were here."), and so on. Everyone uses more than one register, and the more varied the circumstances under which we talk and write, the larger number of registers we use.

The dialects we speak help to define who we are. They tell those who hear us where we come from, our social or ethnic identification, and other such intimate facts about us. The registers we use reflect the circumstances in which we are communicating. They indicate where we are speaking or writing, to whom, via what medium, about what subject, and for what purpose. Dialects and registers provide options—alternative ways of using language. And those options confront us with the question of what is the right or best alternative.

Correctness and Acceptability

The concept of an absolute and unwavering, presumably God-given standard of linguistic correctness (sometimes confused with "purity") is widespread, even among the educated. Those who subscribe to this notion become greatly exercised over such matters as split infinitives, the "incorrect" position of *only,* and prepositions at the ends of sentences. All these supposed "errors" have been committed time and again by eminent writers and speakers, so that one wonders how those who condemn them know that they are bad. Robert Lowth, who wrote one of the most influential English grammars of the eighteenth century (*A Short Introduction to English Grammar,* 1762), was praised by one of his admirers for showing "the grammatic inaccuracies that have escaped the pens of our most distinguished writers."

One would suppose that the usage of "our most distinguished writers" would be good usage. But Lowth and his followers knew, or thought they knew, better; and their attitude survives to this day. This is not, of course, to deny that there are standards of usage, but only to suggest that standards must be based on the usage of speakers and writers of generally acknowledged excellence—quite a different thing from a subservience to the mandates of badly informed "authorities" who are guided by their own prejudices rather than by a study of the actual usage of educated and accomplished speakers and writers.

To talk about "correctness" in language implies that there is some abstract, absolute standard by which words and grammar can be judged; something is either "correct" or "incorrect," and that's all there is to that. But the facts of language are not so clean-cut. Consequently many students of usage today prefer to talk instead about **acceptability**, that is, the degree to which users of a language will judge an expression as OK or will let its use pass without noticing anything out of the ordinary. An acceptable expression is one that people do not object to, indeed do not even notice unless it is called to their attention.

Acceptability is not absolute, but a matter of degree; one expression may be more or less acceptable than another. "If *I were* in your shoes" may be judged more acceptable than "If *I was* in your shoes," but both are considerably more acceptable than "If *we was* in your shoes." Moreover, acceptability is not abstract, but is related to some group of people whose response it reflects. Thus most Americans pronounce the past tense verb *ate* like *eight* and regard any other pronunciation as unacceptable. Many Britons, on the other hand, pronounce it as "ett" and find the American preference less acceptable. Acceptability is part of the convention of language use; in talking about it, we must always keep in mind "How acceptable?" and "To whom?"

LANGUAGE AS HUMAN

As noted at the beginning of this chapter, language is a specifically human activity. That statement, however, raises several questions. When and how did human beings acquire language? To what extent is language innate, and to what extent is it learned? How does human language differ from the communication systems of other creatures? We will look briefly at each of these questions.

Theories of the Origin of Language

The ultimate origin of language is a matter of speculation since we have no real information on the subject. The earliest languages of which we have any records are already in a high stage of development, and the same is true of languages spoken by technologically primitive peoples. The problem of how language began has naturally tantalized philosophical minds, and many theories have been advanced, to which waggish scholars have given such fancifully descriptive names as the pooh-pooh theory, the bow-wow theory, the ding-dong theory, and the yo-he-ho theory. The nicknames indicate how seriously the theories need be taken: they are based, respectively, on the notions that language was in the beginning ejaculatory, echoic (onomatopoeic), characterized by a mystic appropriateness of sound to sense in contrast to being merely imitative, or made up of grunts and groans emitted in the course of group actions and coming in time to be associated with those actions.

According to one theory, the early prelanguage of human beings was a mixture of gestures and sounds in which the gestures carried most of the meaning and the sounds were used chiefly to "punctuate" or amplify the gestures—just the reverse of our use of speech and hand signals. Eventually human physiology and behavior changed in several related ways. The human brain, which had been expanding in size, lateralized—that is, each half came to specialize in certain activities, and language ability was localized in the left hemisphere of most persons. As a consequence, "handedness" developed (right-handedness for those with left-hemisphere dominance), and there was greater manual specialization. As people had more things to do with their hands, they could use them less for communication and had to rely more on sounds. Therefore, increasingly complex forms of oral signals developed, and language as we know it evolved. The fact that we human beings alone have vocal language but share with our closest animal kin (the apes) an ability to learn complex gesture systems suggests that manual signs may have preceded language as a form of communication.

We cannot know how language really began; we can be sure only of its immense antiquity. However human beings started to talk, they did so long ago, and it was not until much later that they devised a system of making marks on wood, stone, and the like to represent what they said. Compared with language, writing is a newfangled invention, although certainly none the less brilliant for being so.

Innate Language Ability

The acquisition of language—that is, the mastery of any of the complicated linguistic systems by which human beings, and they alone, communicate—would seem to be an arduous task. But it is a task that normal children all over the world seem not to mind in the least. Even children in daily contact with a language other than their "home" language—the native language of their parents—readily acquire that second language, even to the extent of speaking it with a native accent. After childhood, however, perhaps in the teens, most minds undergo a kind of "hardening" with respect to learning a language. Young children seem to be genetically equipped with some sort of built-in "device" that makes the acquisition of languages possible. But after a while, that automatic ability atrophies, and the "device" closes down.

To be sure, children of five or so have not acquired all of the words they will need to know as they grow up or all of the grammatical constructions available to them. But they have rather fully mastered the system by means of which they will speak for the rest of their lives. The immensity of that accomplishment can be appreciated by anyone who has learned a second language as an adult. It is clear that, although every particular language has to be learned, the ability to acquire and use language is a part of our genetic inheritance and operates most efficiently in our younger years.

Do Birds and Beasts Really Talk?

Although language is an exclusively human phenomenon, some of the lower animals are physically just about as well equipped as human beings to produce speech sounds, and some—certain birds, for instance—have in fact been taught to do so. But no other species makes use of a system of sounds even remotely resembling human language.

In the second half of the twentieth century, a trio of chimpanzees, Sarah, Lana, and Washoe, greatly modified our ideas about the linguistic abilities of our closest relatives in the animal kingdom. After several efforts to teach chimps to talk had ended in almost total failure, it had been generally concluded that apes lack the cognitive ability to learn language. Some psychologists reasoned, however, that the main problem might be a simple anatomical limitation: human vocal organs are so different from the corresponding ones in apes that the animals cannot produce the sounds of human speech. If they have the mental, but not the physical, ability to talk, then they should be able to learn a language using a medium other than sound.

Sarah was taught to communicate by arranging plastic tokens of arbitrary color and shape into groups. Each of the tokens, which were metal-backed and placed on a magnetized board, represented a word in the system, and groups of tokens corresponded to sentences. Sarah learned over a hundred tokens and could manage sentences of the complexity of "Sarah take banana if-then Mary no give chocolate Sarah" (that is, 'If Sarah takes a banana, Mary won't give Sarah any chocolate'). Lana also used word symbols, but hers were on a typewriter connected to a computer. She communicated with the computer and through it with people, and they communicated with her in a similar way. The typed-out messages appeared on a screen and had to conform exactly to the rules of "word" order of the system Lana had been taught if she was to get what she asked for (food, drink, companionship, and the like).

Washoe, in the most interesting of these efforts to teach animals a language, was schooled in the gesture language used by the deaf, Ameslan. Her remarkable success in learning to communicate with this quite natural and adaptable system has resulted in a number of other chimpanzees and gorillas being taught some of the sign language. The apes learn signs, use them appropriately, combine them meaningfully, and when occasion requires even invent new signs or combinations. For example, one of the chimps, Lucy, made up the terms "candydrink" and "drinkfruit" to converse about watermelons.

The linguistic accomplishment of these apes is remarkable; nevertheless, it is a far cry from the fullness of a human language. The number of signs or tokens the ape learns, the complexity of the syntax with which they are combined, and the breadth of ideas that they represent are all far more restricted than in any human language. Moreover, human linguistic systems have been fundamentally shaped by the fact that they are expressed in sound. Vocalness of language is no mere incidental characteristic but rather is central to the nature of language. We must still say that only human beings have language in the full sense of that term.

LANGUAGE AS COMMUNICATION

The purpose of language is to communicate, whether with others by talking and writing or with ourselves by thinking. The relationship of language to thought has generated a great deal of speculation. At one extreme are those who believe that language is merely a clothing for thought and that thought is quite independent of the language we use to express it. At the other extreme are those who believe that thought is merely suppressed language and that, when we are thinking, we are just talking under our breath. The truth is probably somewhere between those two extremes. Some, though not all, of the mental activities we identify as "thought" are linguistic in nature. It is certainly true that, until we put our ideas into words, they are likely to remain vague, inchoate, and uncertain. We may all from time to time feel like the little girl who, on being told to express her thoughts clearly, replied, "How can I know what I think until I hear what I say?"

If we think—at least some of the time—in language, then presumably the language we speak must influence the way we think about the world and perhaps even

the way we perceive it. The idea that language has such influence and thus importance is called the **Whorf hypothesis** after the linguist Benjamin Lee Whorf.

Efforts have been made to test the hypothesis—for example, by giving to persons who spoke quite different languages a large number of chips, each of a different color. Those tested were told to sort the chips into piles so that each pile
contained chips of similar color. Each person was allowed to make any number
of piles. As might be predicted, the number of piles tended to correspond with
the number of basic color terms in the language spoken by the sorter. In English
we have eleven basic color terms (*red, pink, orange, brown, yellow, green, blue,
purple, black, gray,* and *white*), so English speakers tend to sort color chips into
eleven piles. If a language has only six basic color terms (corresponding, say, to
our *red, yellow, green, blue, black,* and *white*), speakers of that language will
tend to cancel their perception of all other differences and sort color chips into
those six piles. Pink is only a tint or light version of red. But because we have
different basic terms for those two colors, they seem to us to be quite distinct
colors; light blue, light green, and light yellow, on the other hand, are just
insignificant versions of the darker colors because we have no basic terms for
them. Thus how we think about and respond to colors is a function of how our
language classifies them.

Though a relatively trivial matter, color terms illustrate that the way we react
to the world corresponds to the way our language categorizes it. More complex
and important is the question of how many of our assumptions about things are
just reflexes of our language. In English, as in many other languages, we often
use masculine forms (such as pronouns) when we talk about persons of either
sex, as in "Everyone has to do his best." Does such masculine language influence our attitudes toward the equality of the sexes in other regards? In English
every regular sentence has to have a subject and a verb; so we say things like
"It's raining" and "It's time to go," with the word *it* serving as subject, even
though the meaning of that *it* is difficult to specify. Does the linguistic require-
ment for a subject and verb lead us to expect an actor or agent in every action,
even though some things may happen without anyone making them happen? The
implications of the Whorf hypothesis are far-reaching and of considerable philosophical importance, even though no way of confidently testing those implications seems possible.

OTHER CHARACTERISTICS
OF LANGUAGE

An important aspect of language systems is that they are "open." That is, a language is not a finite set of messages from which the speaker must choose. Instead,
any speaker can use the resources of the language—its vocabulary and grammatical patterns—to make up new messages, sentences that no one has ever said
before. Because a language is an **open system**, it can always be used to talk about

new things. Bees have a remarkable system of communication, using a sort of "dance" in the air, in which the patterns of a bee's flight tell other members of the hive about food sources. However, all that bees can communicate about is a nectar supply— its direction, distance, and abundance. As a consequence, a bee would make a very dull conversationalist.

Another aspect of the communicative function of language is that it can be displaced. That is, we can talk about things not present—about rain when the weather is dry, about taxes even when they are not being collected, and about a yeti even if no such creature exists. The characteristic of **displacement** means that human beings can abstract, can lie, and can talk about talk itself. It allows us to use language as a vehicle of memory and of imagination. A bee communicates with other bees about a nectar source only when it has just found such a source. Bees do not celebrate the delights of nectar by dancing for sheer pleasure. Human beings use language for many purposes quite unconnected with their immediate environment. Indeed, most language use is probably thus displaced.

Finally, an important characteristic of language is that it is not just utilitarian. One of the uses of language is for entertainment, high and low: for jokes, stories, puzzles, and poetry. From "knock-knock" jokes to *Paradise Lost,* speakers take delight in language and what can be done with it.

WHY STUDY THE HISTORY OF ENGLISH?

Language is an ability inherent in us. Languages such as English are particular systems that are developments of that ability. We can know the underlying ability only through studying the actual languages that are its expressions. Thus one of the best reasons for studying languages is to find out about ourselves, about what makes us persons. And the best place to start such study is with our own language, the one that has nurtured our minds and formed our view of the world, although any language can be useful for the purpose. A good approach to studying languages is the historical one. To understand how things are, it is often helpful and sometimes essential to know how they got to be that way. If we are psychologists who want to understand a person's behavior, we must know something about that person's origins and development. The same is true of a language.

Another reason for studying the history of English is that many of the irregularities of our language today are the remnants of earlier, quite regular patterns. For example, the highly irregular plurals of nouns like *man-men, mouse-mice, goose-geese,* and *ox-oxen* can be explained historically. So can the spelling of Modern English, which may seem chaotic, or at least unruly, to anyone who has had to struggle with it. The orthographic joke attributed to George Bernard Shaw, that in English *fish* might be spelled *ghoti (gh* as in *enough, o* as in *women,* and *ti* as in *nation*), has been repeated often, but the only way to understand the anomalies of our spelling is to study the history of our language.

The fact that the present-day pronunciation and meaning of *cupboard* do not much suggest a board for cups is also something we need history to explain. Why do we talk about *withstanding* a thing when we mean that we stand in opposition to it, rather than in company *with* it? If people are *unkempt,* can they also be *kempt,* and what does *kempt* mean? Is something wrong with the position of *secretly* in "She wanted to secretly finish writing her novel"? Is there any connection between *heal, whole, healthy, hale,* and *holy*? Knowing about the history of the language can help us to understand and to answer these and many similar questions. Knowledge of the history of English is no *nostrum* or *panacea* for curing all our linguistic ills (why do we call some medicines by those names?), but it can at least alleviate some of the symptoms.

Yet another reason for studying the history of English is that even a little knowledge about it can help to clarify the literature written in earlier periods, as well as some written rather recently. In his poem "The Eve of St. Agnes," John Keats describes the sculptured effigies on the tombs of a chapel on a cold winter evening:

> The sculptur'd dead, on each side, seemed to freeze,
> Emprison'd in black, purgatorial rails.

What image should Keats's description evoke with its reference to *rails*? Many a modern reader, taking a cue from the word *emprison'd,* has thought of the *rails* as railings or bars, perhaps a fence around the statues. But *rails* here is from an Old English word that meant 'garments' and refers to the shrouds or funeral garments in which the stone figures are clothed. Unless we are aware of such older usage, we are likely to be led badly astray in the picture we conjure up for these lines. In the General Prologue to his *Canterbury Tales,* Geoffrey Chaucer, in describing an ideal knight, says: "His hors were goode." Did the knight have one horse, or more than one? *Hors* seems to be singular, but the verb *were* looks like a plural. The knight did indeed have several horses; in Chaucer's day, *hors* was a word like *deer* or *sheep* that had a plural identical in form with its singular. It is a small point, but unless we know what a text means literally, we cannot appreciate it as literature.

In the remainder of this book, we will be concerned with some of what is known about the origins and the development of the English language. Chapter 2 examines the sound system of present-day English, a necessary preliminary to the later discussion of the many phonological changes that have affected our language during its history. Chapter 3 looks at the development of writing and at the orthographic conventions of present-day English. These preliminary matters out of the way, Chapters 4 through 9 trace the history of our language from prehistoric times, through the three periods mentioned above, to the present day. Finally, Chapters 10 through 12 examine the vocabulary of Modern English—its sources and its changes.

FOR FURTHER READING

Full bibliographical information for the works cited is in the Selected Bibliography, pp. 295–310.

General

Akmajian. *Linguistics: An Introduction.*
Cobley. *The Routledge Companion to Semiotics and Linguistics.*
Crystal. *The Cambridge Encyclopedia of Language.*
———. *The Cambridge Encyclopedia of the English Language.*
———. *A Dictionary of Language.*
Frawley. *International Encyclopedia of Linguistics.*
McArthur. *The Oxford Companion to the English Language.*
Robins. *General Linguistics.*

The Nature and Origins of Human Language

Aitchison. *The Seeds of Speech.*
Bickerton. *Language & Species.*
Carstairs-McCarthy. *The Origins of Complex Language.*
Corballis. *From Hand to Mouth.*
Ruhlen. *The Origin of Language.*

Language Acquisition

Baron. *Growing Up with Language.*
Blake. *Routes to Child Language.*
Bloom. *How Children Learn the Meanings of Words.*
Clark. *First Language Acquisition.*
Gleason. *The Development of Language.*
Karmiloff and Karmiloff-Smith. *Pathways to Language.*

Nonverbal Communication

Dimitrius and Mazzarella. *Reading People.*
Morris. *Gestures.*

Usage and Misconceptions

Bauer and Trudgill. *Language Myths.*

Animal Communication

Ford. *The Secret Language of Life.*
Morton and Page. *Animal Talk.*

Language and Thought

Lakoff. *Women, Fire, and Dangerous Things.*
Lee. *The Whorf Theory Complex.*
Whorf. *Language, Thought, and Reality.*

Language and Play

Crystal. *Language Play.*
Nilsen. *Humor Scholarship.*
Nilsen and Nilsen. *Encyclopedia of 20th-Century American Humor.*
Sherzer. *Speech Play and Verbal Art.*

2 THE SOUNDS OF CURRENT ENGLISH

Language is basically speech, so sounds are its fundamental building blocks. But we learn the sounds of our language at such an early age that we will be unaware of them without special study. Moreover, the alphabet we use has always been inadequate to represent the sounds of the English language, and that is especially true of Modern English. One letter can represent many different sounds, as *a* stands for as many as six different sounds in *cat, came, calm, any, call,* and *was* (riming with *fuzz*). On the other hand, a single sound can be spelled in various ways, as the "long *a*" sound can be spelled *a* as in *baker, ay* as in *day, ai* as in *bait, au* as in *gauge, e* as in *mesa, ey* as in *they, ei* as in *neighbor,* and *ea* as in *great.* This is obviously an unsatisfactory state of affairs.

Phoneticians, who study the sounds used in language, have therefore invented a phonetic alphabet in which the same symbols consistently represent the same sounds, thus making it possible to write sounds unambiguously. The **phonetic alphabet** uses the familiar Roman letters, but assigns to each a single sound value. Then, because there are more sounds than twenty-six, some letters have been borrowed from other alphabets, and other letters have been made up, so that finally the phonetic alphabet has one letter for each sound. To show that the letters of this phonetic alphabet represent sounds rather than ordinary spellings, they are written between square brackets, whereas ordinary spellings are italicized (or underlined in handwriting and typing). Thus *so* represents the spelling and [so] the pronunciation of the same word.

Phoneticians describe sounds and classify them according to the way they are made, so to understand the phonetic alphabet and the sounds it represents, you must know something about how sounds are produced.

THE ORGANS OF SPEECH

The diagram on page 23 represents a cross section of the head. It shows the principal organs by which speech is produced and a few other related ones. You can use this diagram together with the following discussion of sounds to locate the places where the sounds are made.

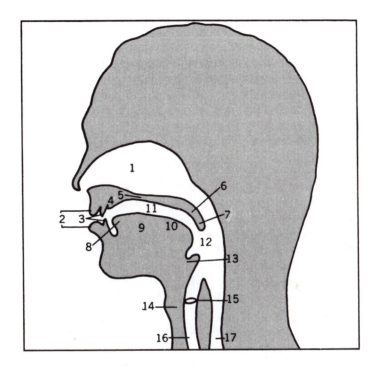

THE ORGANS OF SPEECH

1. Nasal cavity
2. Lips
3. Teeth
4. Alveolar ridge
5. Hard palate
6. Velum
7. Uvula
8. Tip of tongue
9. Front of tongue
10. Back of tongue
11. Oral cavity
12. Pharynx
13. Epiglottis
14. Larynx
15. Vocal cords and glottis
16. Trachea
17. Esophagus

CONSONANTS OF CURRENT ENGLISH

Consonants are classified according to their **place of articulation** (that is, where they are made) as labial (bilabial, labiodental), dental (interdental, alveolar, alveolopalatal), palatovelar (palatal, velar), or glottal. They are also classified by their **manner of articulation** (that is, how they are made) as stops, fricatives, affricates, nasals, liquids, or semivowels. For most of the consonants, it is also necessary to observe whether or not they have **voice** (vibration of the vocal cords). Voice can be heard as a kind of buzz or hum accompanying the sounds that have it.

The accompanying chart uses these principles of classification to show all the consonants of present-day English with illustrative words. A few other consonant symbols (without illustrative words) are also included; they represent sounds treated in later chapters.

Stops: The sounds [p], [t], and [k] are voiceless **stops** (also called **plosives** or **explosives**). They are so called because in making them the flow of the breath is actually stopped for a split second at some position in the mouth and is then released by an explosion of air without vibration of the vocal cords. If vibration or voice is added while making these sounds, the results are the voiced stops [b], [d], and [g].

When the air is stopped by the two lips, the result is [p] or [b]; hence they are called, respectively, the voiceless and voiced **bilabial** stops. Stoppage made by the tip of the tongue against the gums above the teeth (the alveolar ridge) produces [t] or [d]; hence these sounds are called, respectively, the voiceless and voiced **alveolar** stops. Stoppage made by the back of the tongue against the roof of the mouth produces [k] or [g]—respectively, the voiceless and voiced **palatovelar** stops.

The roof of the mouth is divided into the hard palate (called just palate for short) and the soft palate (or velum). You can feel these two parts by running the tip of your tongue back along the roof of the mouth; first, you will feel the hard bone under the skin, and then the roof will become soft and spongy. Depending on what vowels they are near, some [k] and [g] sounds are **palatal** (like those in *geek*) and others are **velar** (like those in *gook*).

Fricatives: For the sounds called **fricatives** (or **spirants**), a narrow opening is made somewhere in the mouth, so that the air must "rub" (Latin *fricare*) its way through instead of exploding through a complete obstruction as the stops do. The fricatives of present-day English are four pairs of voiceless and voiced sounds, plus one that is unpaired.

Labiodental [f] and [v] are produced with the lower lip against the upper teeth. **Interdental** [θ] and [ð] (as in *thigh* and *thy*) are produced with the tip of the tongue between the teeth or just behind the upper teeth; you may find these two sounds hard to tell apart at first because they are usually spelled alike and are not as important as some of the other pairs in identifying words. **Alveolar** [s] and [z] are made by putting the tip of the tongue near the alveolar ridge. **Alveolopalatal** [š] and [ž] (as in the middle sounds of *fission* and *vision*) are made by lifting the tip and front of the tongue toward the alveolar ridge and hard palate. These last four fricatives are also grouped together as **sibilants** (from Latin *sibilare* 'to hiss, whistle') because they have a hissing effect. The voiceless fricative [h] has very generalized mouth friction but is called a **glottal** fricative because when it is said very emphatically, it includes some friction at the vocal cords or glottis.

Affricates: The voiceless and voiced **affricates** are the initial and final sounds of *church* and *judge,* respectively. They begin very much like the stops [t] and [d], respectively, but end like the fricatives [š] and [ž]. They function, however, like single sounds in English, so the voiceless affricate is written [č] and the voiced affricate is written [ǰ].

Nasals: Consonants produced by blocking the mouth and letting the air flow through the nose instead are called **nasals**. They include the bilabial [m], with lips completely closed; the alveolar [n], with stoppage made at the gum line; and the palatovelar [ŋ] (as at the end of *sing* and *sung*), with stoppage made at the palate or velum.

PLACE OF ARTICULATION

	LABIAL		DENTAL			PALATOVELAR		GLOTTAL
	Bilabial	Labiodental	Interdental	Alveolar	Alveolo-palatal	Palatal	Velar	
Stops voiceless	p (**pup**), pʰ			t (**tat**), tʰ		k (**kick**), kʰ		
Stops voiced	b (**bub**), bʰ			d (**dad**), dʰ		g (**gig**), gʰ		
Fricatives voiceless		f (**few**)	θ (**thigh**)	s (**seal**)	š (**shun**)	ç	x	h (**hoe**)
Fricatives voiced	β	v (**view**)	ð (**thy**)	z (**zeal**)	ž (**vision**)		ɣ	
Affricates voiceless					č (**chug**)			
Affricates voiced					ǰ (**jug**)			
Nasals	m (**mum**)			n (**num**)				ŋ (**sing**)
Liquids lateral				l (**low**)				
Liquids retroflex				r (**row**)				
Semivowels						y (**ye**)	w (**we**)	

Liquids: The sounds [1] and [r] are called **liquids**. They are both made with the tip of the tongue in the vicinity of the alveolar ridge. The liquid [1] is called a lateral because the breath flows around the sides of the tongue in making it. The usual term for [r], retroflex 'bent back,' refers to the position sometimes assumed by the tongue in its articulation. The similarity in the articulation of [1] and [r] is indicated by their historical alternation, as in *Sally/Sarah, Kathleen/Katherine,* and the related words for 'star': *stella* (Latin) and *steorra* (Old English).

There is no single pronunciation of English—sounds vary greatly from one dialect to another. The liquid [r] is particularly unstable. In eastern New England, New York City, the coastal South, and the prestigious British accent called **RP** (for "received pronunciation"), [r] disappears from pronunciation unless it is followed by a vowel. So in those areas, *r* is silent in *farm,* "*far* distances," and "The distance is *far,*" but is pronounced in *faring.* In those same areas (except the American South), an [r] at the end of a word is pronounced if the next word begins with a vowel, as in "*there* is" and "*far* away." This [r] is called **linking *r*.** It is not used in the American South, where sometimes [r] is lost even between vowels within a word, as in *very* pronounced as "ve'y" and *Carolina* as "Ca'olina." Other varieties of American English—and many varieties of British English—preserve the [r] sound under most conditions.

Failure to understand that [r] is lacking before a consonant or in final position in standard British speech has led to American misinterpretation of such British spellings as '*arf* (for Cockney *half*), *cokernut* (for *coconut*), and *Eeyore,* Christopher Robin's donkey companion. *Eeyore,* which A. A. Milne, the creator of Christopher Robin and Winnie-the-Pooh, could just as well have spelled *Eeyaw,* is what [h]-less Cockney donkeys presumably say instead of *hee-haw.* Similarly, the New England loss of [r] motivates the spelling *Marmee* of Louisa May Alcott's *Little Women,* a spelling that represents the same pronunciation most Americans would spell as *mommy.*

Linking *r* gives rise by analogy to an unhistorical [r] sound called **intrusive *r*.** Those who say "Have no *fea(r)*" without an [r] but "the *fear* of it" with [r] are likely also to say "Have no *idea*" and "the *idear* of it." This intrusive *r* is common in the speech of eastern New England, New York City, and in British RP, as in "*law(r)* enforcement" and "*Cuba(r)* is an island." Because the American South has no linking *r,* it also has no intrusive *r.*

Semivowels: Because of their vocalic quality, [y] and [w] are called **semivowels**. In their manner of production, they are indeed like vowels (which are described below), the palatal semivowel [y] being like the vowels of *eat* or *it,* and the velar semivowel [w] like the vowels of *oodles* or *oomph.*

VOWELS OF CURRENT ENGLISH

Vowels are the principal sounds of syllables. In the accompanying chart, the vowels are shown according to the position of the tongue relative to the roof of the mouth (**high, mid, low**) and to the position of the highest part of the tongue (**front, central,**

back). The chart may be taken to represent a cross section of the oral cavity, facing left. Vowel symbols with keywords are those of present-day American English. Those without keywords represent less common vowels or those of older periods of the language, which are explained and illustrated below or in later chapters.

	FRONT	CENTRAL	BACK
HIGH	i (peat) ü ɪ (pit) ü	ɨ	u (pooh) ʊ (put)
MID	e (pate) ɛ (pet)	ə (putt, pert, sofa, motor)	o (Poe) ɵ ɔ (paw)
LOW	æː æ (pat)	a	ɒ ɑ (pot)

Some of the vowel symbols, especially [i], [e], and [ɑ], do not represent the sounds those letters usually have in current English spelling but rather approximately those that they stand for in Spanish, French, Italian, and German. Thus in transcribing Modern English words, we use [i] for the sound that is written *i* in other languages, although, except for words recently borrowed by English from these other languages (for example, *police*), the sound [i] is most frequently written *e, ee, ea, ie,* or *ei* in Modern English. We use [e] for the sound usually written *a* (followed by a consonant plus "silent *e*") or *ai* in Modern English (as in *bate, bait*). We use the symbol [ɑ] for "broad *a*," which often occurs in the spelling of English words before *r* and *lm* (as in *far* and *calm*); in *father, mama, papa,* and a few other words like *spa*; and in certain types of American English after *w* (as in *watch*). The most usual spelling of the sound [ɑ] in American English is, however, *o*, as in *pot* and *top*.

Of the vowels listed in the chart, [i], [ɪ], [e], [ɛ], and [æ] are called front vowels because of the positions assumed by the tongue in their articulation, and [u], [ʊ], [o], [ɔ], and [ɑ] are called back vowels for the same reason. Both series have been given in descending order, that is, in relation to the height of the tongue as indicated by the downward movement of the lower jaw in their articulation: thus [i] is the highest front vowel and [æ] the lowest, as [u] is the highest back vowel and [ɑ] is the lowest. All of these back vowels except [ɑ] are pronounced with some degree of rounding and protrusion of the lips and hence are called **rounded** vowels. Vowels without lip rounding (all of the others in Modern English) are called **unrounded** or **spread** vowels.

The symbol [ə], called **schwa**, represents the mid and central stressed vowels of *cut* and *curt* as well as the unstressed vowels in the second syllables of *tuba* and *lunar.* Those four vowels are acoustically distinct from one another, but differences between them do not serve to distinguish one word from another, so we can use the same symbol for all four sounds: [kət], [kərt], [tubə], and [lunər].

Some dialects of American English use a few other vowels: [a], [æ:], [ɨ], [ɵ], and [ɒ].

The vowel [a] is heard in eastern New England speech in *ask, half, laugh,* and *path* and in some varieties of Southern speech in *bye, might, tired,* and the like. It is intermediate between [ɑ] and [æ], and is usually the first element of a **diphthong** (that is, a two-vowel sequence pronounced as the core of a single syllable) as in *right* and *rout,* which we write, respectively, as [aɪ] and [aʊ].

Along the East Coast roughly between New York City and Philadelphia as well as in a number of other metropolitan centers, some speakers use clearly different vowels in *cap* and *cab, bat* and *bad, lack* and *lag.* In the first word of each of these and many other such pairs, they pronounce the sound represented by [æ]; but in the second word, they use a higher, tenser, and longer vowel that we may represent as [æ:]. Some speakers also use these two vowels to distinguish *have* from *halve* and *can* 'be able' from *can* 'preserve in tins.'

Some Americans pronounce the adverb *just* (as in "They've *just* left") with a vowel, namely [ɨ], which is different from that in the adjective (as in "a *just* person"), which has [ə]. It is likewise different from the vowels in *gist* (with [ɪ]) and *jest* (with [ɛ]). This vowel may also appear in *children, would,* and various other words.

In eastern New England, some speakers, especially of the older generation, use a vowel in *whole* that differs from the one in *hole.* This "New England short *o*" is symbolized by [ɵ] and is found also in *road, stone,* and other words. It is rare and is becoming more so.

British English has a lightly rounded vowel symbolized by [ɒ] in *pot, top, rod, con,* and other words in which Americans use the sound [ɑ] for the spelling *o.* This vowel also occurs in some American dialects.

Those who do not have these vowel sounds in their pronunciation obviously do not need the symbols to represent their own speech. It is wise, however, to remember that even in English there are sounds that you do not use yourself or that you use differently from others.

An increasingly large number of Americans do not distinguish between [ɔ] and [ɑ]. For them, *caught* and *cot* are homophones, as are *taught* and *tot, dawn* and *don, gaud* and *God, pawed* and *pod.* They pronounce all such words with either [ɔ] or [ɑ] or with a vowel that is intermediate between those two, namely the [ɒ] mentioned above.

Other Americans lack a phonemic contrast between two sounds only in a particular environment. For example, in the South, the vowels [ɪ] and [ɛ], although distinguished in most environments (such as *pit* and *pet*), have merged before nasals. Thus *pin* and *pen* are homophones for many Southerners, as are *tin* and *ten, Jim* and *gem,* and *ping* and the first syllable of *penguin.* The sound used in the nasal environment is usually [ɪ], though before [ŋ] it may approach [i].

Vowels can be classified not only by their height and their frontness (as in the vowel chart) but also by their tenseness. A **tense** vowel is typically longer in duration than the closest **lax** vowel and also higher and less central (that is, further front if it is a front vowel and further back if a back one). Tense vowels are [i], [e], [u], and [o]; the corresponding lax vowels for the first three are [ɪ], [ɛ], and [ʊ]. The "New England short *o*" is a lax vowel corresponding to tense [o]. For most Americans, the low and the central vowels do not enter into a tense-lax contrast. However, for those who have it, [æ:] (in *cab, halve, bag*) is tense, and the corresponding [æ] (in *cap, have, back*) is lax. Similarly, in standard British English, [ɔ] (in *caught, dawn, wars*) is tense, and the corresponding [ɒ] (in *cot, don, was*) is lax. In earlier times (as we shall see in Chapters 5 and 6), English vowels were either long or short; today that difference in duration has generally become a difference in tenseness.

In most types of current English, **vowel length** is hardly ever a distinguishing factor. When we talk about "long *a*," as in the first paragraph of this chapter, we are really talking about a difference of vowel quality, namely [e] usually spelled with the letter *a* (as in *fade* or *raid*), as distinguished from another vowel quality, namely [æ] also spelled with the same letter *a* (as in *fad*). But phonetically speaking, vowel length is primarily that—a difference in how long a vowel is held during its pronunciation—and any difference of vowel quality is secondary.

In current English, the length of vowels is determined primarily by neighboring sounds. For example, we distinguish *bad* from *bat, bag* from *back,* and *lab* from *lap* by the final consonants in those words, not by the longer vowel in the first of each pair. We tend to hold a vowel longer before a voiced consonant than before a voiceless one (as in *bad* versus *bat*), but that difference is secondary to and dependent on the voiced *d* versus the voiceless *t*.

Some speakers, as noted above, distinguish *can* 'preserve in tins' from *can* 'be able,' *halve* from *have,* and similarly *balm* from *bomb* and *vary* from *very* by length in the vowel of the first of each pair. But they may also have a difference of quality between the two vowels, with the first in each pair being higher, fronter, and tenser than the second. In southeastern American English, *bulb* (with no [l]) may be distinguished from *bub* by vowel length, and similarly *burred* (with no [r]) from *bud,* and *stirred* (with no [r]) from *stud.* In *r*-less speech, when [ɑ] occurs before etymological *r,* length may likewise be a distinguishing factor, as in *part* [pɑːt] and *pot* [pɑt]. In phonetic transcriptions, a colon is used to indicate vowel length when it is necessary to do so. Such distinctions need not concern most of us except in discussions of Old, Middle, and early Modern English, when vowel quantity was of considerably more importance.

A diphthong is a sequence of two vowels in the same syllable, as opposed to a **monophthong**, which is a single, simple vowel. Many English vowel sounds tend to have diphthongal pronunciation, most notably [e] and [o], as in *bay* and *toe,* which are usually pronounced in a way that might be written [eɪ] and [oʊ] if we wanted to record the secondary vowel. Normally, however, there is no need to do so. In parts of the United States, most vowels are sometimes diphthongized; thus *bed* may have a centralized **off-glide** (or secondary vowel): [bɛəd]. In keeping with our practice of writing only sounds that affect meaning, however, we will ignore all such diphthongal **glides**, writing as diphthongs only [aɪ] and [aʊ] in *my* and *now* and [ɔɪ] in *joy* and *coin.* Words like *few* and *cube* may be pronounced with a semivowel before the vowel, [fyu] and [kyub], or with a diphthong, [fɪu] and [kɪub]. The first pronunciation is more common.

In all three of the diphthongs [aɪ], [aʊ], and [ɔɪ], the tongue moves from the position for the first vowel to that for the second, and the direction of movement is more important than the exact starting and ending points. Consequently, the diphthongs we write as [aɪ] and [aʊ] may actually begin with vowels that are more like [ɑ], [æ], or even [ə]. Similarly, [ɔɪ] may begin with [ɒ] or [o] as well as with [ɔ]. The ending points are equally variable. The off-glide in [aɪ] and [ɔɪ] may actually be as high as [i] or as low as [ɛ] (and for [aɪ] it may disappear altogether, especially in parts of the South, being replaced by a lengthening of the first vowel, [aː]), and similarly the off-glide in [aʊ] may be as high as [u] or as low as [o]. Thus it is best to understand [aɪ] as a symbol for a diphthong that begins with a relatively low unrounded vowel and moves toward a higher front position, [aʊ] as representing a diphthong that begins the same way but moves toward a higher back rounded position, and [ɔɪ] as representing a diphthong that begins with a mid or low back rounded vowel and moves toward a higher unrounded front position. In a more detailed transcription, these differences could be represented, for example, in the word *white* as [ɑɛ], [aː], [əi], or various other possibilities. If we are interested in less detail, however, we can write [aɪ] and understand that digraph as representing whatever sound we use in words like *white.*

Vowels Before [r]

The sound [r] modifies the quality of a vowel that comes before it. Consequently, vowels before [r] are somewhat different from the same vowels in other environments. We have already noted that [ə] before [r], as in *curt* or *burst,* is different from [ə] in any other position, as in *cut* or *bust.* Similarly the [o] in *mourn* is not quite the same as that in *moan,* nor is the [ɑ] in *farther* quite the same as that in *father.* Such differences can be ignored, however, if we are interested only in writing differences of sound that are capable of making a difference in meaning.

Fewer distinctive vowels occur before [r] than elsewhere. In particular, for many speakers tenseness is not distinctive before [r]. Thus *nearer* and *mirror* may rime, with a vowel in the first syllables that is close to either [i] or [ɪ]. Similarly *fairy* and *ferry* may be identical, with either [e] or [ɛ], and *touring* and *during* may rime, with either [u] or [ʊ]. In all these variations, the lax vowel occurs more frequently. For most Americans nowadays, *hoarse* and *horse* are homophones. In their traditional pronunciation, *hoarse* has [o] (or [ɔ]) whereas *horse* has [ɔ] (or [ɒ]); the same difference of vowels was once made by most speakers in *mourning* and *morning,* *borne* and *born,* *four* and *for,* *oar* and *or,* and many other words. Today, for many speakers, these vowels have merged before [r], as a result of which many people misspell *foreword* as *forward* because they pronounce the two words alike.

In some American speech, especially of the lower Mississippi Valley and the West, there is no difference in pronunciation between *form* and *farm,* *or* and *are,* *born* and *barn,* or *lord* and *lard.* Some persons have [ɑ], some [ɔ], and others [ɒ] in all such words. There is much variation among speakers from various regions in the vowels they use before [r].

When [r] follows a vowel in the same syllable, a schwa glide may intrude, as in *near* [nɪr] or [niər]. The schwa glide is especially likely when the sentence stress and consequently a change of pitch fall on the syllable, as in "The time drew néar" with the glide versus "The time dréw near" without it.

STRESS

The most prominent syllable in a word has **primary stress**, indicated by a raised vertical mark at the beginning of the syllable in phonetic transcription or by an **acute accent** mark over the appropriate vowel symbol in normal orthography: [ˈsofə] or *sófa*, [əˈbaʊt] or *abóut*. For syllables bearing **secondary stress**, a lowered vertical mark is used in phonetic transcription and a **grave accent** mark in normal orthography: [ˈɛməˌnet] or *émanàte*. **Unstressed syllables** (which are sometimes said to carry "weak stress") are not marked in any way.

Unstressed Vowels

Although any vowel can be pronounced without stress, three are frequently so used: [i], [ɪ], and [ə]. There is a great deal of variation between [i] and [ɪ] in final position (as in *lucky, happy, city,* and *seedy*) and before another vowel (as in the second syllables of *various, curiosity, oriel,* and *carrion*). Old-fashioned pronunciation along the Eastern Coast uses [ɪ] in these positions, but the most common pronunciation in the United States is [i].

There is also a great deal of variation between [ə] and [ɪ] before a consonant. In the traditional pronunciation still used in British English and in some regions of the United States, [ɪ] occurs in the final unstressed syllable of words like *bucket* and *college,* and in the initial unstressed syllable of words like *elude* and *illumine.* Increasingly large numbers of Americans, however, use either [ə] or [ɪ] variably in such words, depending in part on the surrounding sounds, though with a strong preference for [ə]. A rule of pronunciation seems to be emerging that favors unstressed [ɪ] only before velar consonants (as in the first syllable of *ignore* and the final syllable of *comic* or *hoping*) and [ə] elsewhere. Thus, whereas the older pronunciation has [ə] in the second syllable of *stomach* and [ɪ] in the first syllable of *mysterious,* many speakers now reverse those vowels in the two words, ending *stomach* like *comic* and beginning *mysterious* like *mosquito.*

KINDS OF SOUND CHANGE

English words, as already observed, vary in their pronunciation, in part because sounds do not always change in the same way among different groups. Thus at one time all speakers of English distinguished the members of pairs like *horse-hoarse, morning-mourning,* and *for-four;* nowadays most probably do not. Because this change has not proceeded uniformly, the pronunciation of such words now varies.

Some changes of sound are very important and highly systematic. Two such changes, called the First Sound Shift and the Great Vowel Shift, are dealt with in Chapters 4 and 7, respectively. Other changes are more incidental but fall into several distinct categories. In this section we examine some of the latter kind, especially ones in informal and in nonstandard speech.

Assimilation: Sounds Become More Alike

A frequent sound change is **assimilation**, by which one sound becomes more like a neighboring sound. If *pancake* is pronounced carefully, as its parts would be when they are independent words, it is [pæn kek]. However, [n] is an alveolar sound, whereas [k] is a palatovelar; consequently, speakers often anticipate the place of articulation of the [k] and pronounce the word [pæŋ kek] with a palatovelar nasal. In addition to such partial assimilation, by which sounds become more alike while remaining distinct, assimilation may be total. That is, the sounds may become completely identical, as when *spaceship* changes in pronunciation from [spes šɪp] to [speš šɪp]. In such cases it is usual for the identical sounds to combine by the omission of one of them, as in [spešɪp]; a much older example is *cupboard,* in which the medial [p b] has become a single [b].

In speech with a moderately fast tempo, assimilation is very common. Thus, a slow pronunciation of "What is your name?" as [wət ɪz yʊr nem] in faster tempo may become [wəts yər nem], and in very fast tempo [wəčər nem], the latter two suggested by the spellings "What's yer name?" and "Whacher name?" The last also shows a particular kind of assimilation called **palatalization**. In the sequence [tsy] of "What's yer name?" the alveolar fricative [s] is assimilated to the following palatal semivowel [y], and the result is a palatalized [š], which combines with the preceding [t] to make the alveolopalatal affricate [č] of "Whacher name?" Such pronunciations, unlike the impressionistic spellings that represent them, are not careless or sloppy (much less substandard) but merely variants we use in speech that is more rapid and less formal than that using the unassimilated form. If we never used such assimilated forms in talking, we would sound very stilted indeed.

Dissimilation: Sounds Become Less Alike

The opposite of assimilation is **dissimilation**, a process by which neighboring sounds become less like one another. In the word *diphthong,* the sequence of two voiceless fricatives [fθ], represented by the medial *phth,* requires an effort to enunciate. Consequently, many speakers pronounce the word with medial [pθ], replacing fricative [f] with stop [p], as though the word were spelled *dipthong.* And consequently some of them do indeed misspell the word that way.

Another example of dissimilation is the substandard pronunciation of *chimney* as *chimley,* with the second of two nasals changed to an [l]. The ultimate dissimilation is the complete loss of one sound because of its proximity to another similar sound. A frequent example in present-day standard English is the omission of one of two [r] sounds from words like *cate(r)pillar, Cante(r)bury, rese(r)voir, terrest(r)ial, southe(r)ner, barbitu(r)ate, gove(r)nor,* and *su(r)prised.*

Elision: Sounds Are Omitted

The sentence used as an example of assimilation ("What's your name?") also exemplifies another kind of sound change: loss of sounds (**elision**) due to lack of stress. The verb *is* usually has no stress and thus often contracts with a preceding word by the elision of its vowel. A sound omitted by elision is said to be **elided**.

An initial unstressed vowel is also lost when *about* is pronounced *'bout* in a process known as **aphesis**. It is a specialized variety of a more general process, **apheresis**, which is the loss of any sounds (not just an unstressed vowel) from the beginning of a word, as in the pronunciation of *almost* in " 'Most everybody knows that." Loss of sounds from the end of a word is known as **apocope**, as in the pronunciation of *child* as *chile*. A common type of elision in present-day English is **syncope**—loss of a weakly stressed syllable from the middle of a word, as in the usual pronunciation of *family* as *fam'ly*. Indeed many words sound artificial when they are given a full, unsyncopated pronunciation. Like assimilation, syncope is a normal process.

Intrusion: Sounds Are Added

The opposite of elision is the **intrusion** of sounds. An intrusive [ə] sometimes pops up between consonants—for instance, between [l] and [m] in *elm* or *film,* [n] and [r] in *Henry,* [r] and [m] in *alarum* (an archaic variant of *alarm*), [s] and [m] in *Smyrna* (in the usual local pronunciation of New Smyrna Beach, Florida), [θ] and the second [r] in *arthritis,* and [θ] and [l] in *athlete.* A term for this phenomenon is **svarabhakti** (from Sanskrit), and such a vowel is called a svarabhakti vowel. If, however, you do not care to use so flamboyant a word, you can always fall back on **epenthesis** (**epenthetic**) or **anaptyxis** (**anaptyctic**). Perhaps it is just as well to call it an **intrusive schwa**.

Consonants may also be intrusive; for example, a [p] may be inserted in *warmth,* so that it sounds as if spelled *warmpth*; or a [t] may be inserted in *sense,* so it is homophonous with *cents*; and a [k] may be inserted in *length,* so that it sounds as if spelled *lenkth.* These three words end in a nasal [m, n, ŋ] plus a voiceless fricative [θ, s]; between the nasal and the fricative, many speakers intrude a stop [p, t, k] that is voiceless like the fricative but has the same place of articulation as the nasal (that is, the stop is **homorganic** in place with the nasal and in voicing with the fricative). There is a simple physiological explanation for such intrusion. To move directly from nasal to voiceless fricative, it is necessary simultaneously to release the oral stoppage and to cease the vibration of vocal cords. If those two vocal activities are not perfectly synchronized, the effect will be to create a new sound between the two original ones; in the examples under discussion, the vocal vibration ceases an instant before the stoppage is released, and consequently a voiceless stop is created.

Chimney, cited earlier as an example of dissimilation, has two other substandard variants with intrusion. The two nasals may be separated by an intrusive vowel (as though *chiminey*), or a consonant may intrude between the first nasal and the dissimilated [l] (as though *chimbley*).

Metathesis: Sounds Are Reordered

The order of sounds can be changed by a process called **metathesis**. *Tax* and *task* are variant developments of a single form, with the [ks] (represented in spelling by *x*) metathesized in the second word to [sk]—tax, after all, is a task all of us must meet. In present-day English, [r] frequently metathesizes with an unstressed vowel; thus the initial [prə] of *produce* may become [pər] and the opposite reordering can be heard in *perform* when pronounced as [prəfɔrm]. The metathesis of a sound and a syllable boundary in the word *another* leads to the reinterpretation of original *an other* as *a nother,* especially in the expression "a whole nother thing."

CAUSES OF SOUND CHANGE

The cause of a change of sound is often unknown. Two of the major changes already alluded to, namely the First Sound Shift and the Great Vowel Shift, are particularly mysterious. Various causes have been suggested for sound change— for example, that when people speaking different languages come into contact, one group learns the other's language but does so imperfectly, and thus carries over native habits of pronunciation into the newly acquired language. This explanation is known as the **substratum** or **superstratum theory** (depending on whether it is the language of the dominant group or that of the dominated group that is influenced).

A quite different sort of explanation is that languages tend to develop a balanced sound system—that is, to make sounds as different from one another as possible by distributing them evenly in **phonological space**. Thus, it is common for languages to have two front vowels [i, e] and three nonfront ones [u, o, ɑ]; it would be very strange if a language had five front vowels and no back ones at all, because such an unbalanced system would make poor use of its available resources. If, for some reason, a language loses some of its sounds—say, its high vowels—there would be an intrasystemic pressure to fill in the gap by changing some of the remaining sounds (for example, by making mid vowels higher in their articulation).

Changes like assimilation, dissimilation, elision, and intrusion are often explained as increasing the **ease of articulation**: some sounds can be pronounced together more smoothly if they are alike, others if they are different. Elision and assimilation both quicken the rate of speech, so the desire or need to talk at "fast" **tempo** (although more than speed is implied by tempo) would encourage both those processes. Intrusion can also help to make articulation easier. It and meta-thesis may result from our brains working faster than our vocal organs; consequently the nerve impulses that direct the movement of those organs sometimes get out of sync, resulting in slips of the tongue.

In addition to such mechanical explanations, some sound changes imply at least partial awareness by the speaker. The remodeling of *chaise longue* as *chaise lounge* because one uses it for lounging is **folk etymology** (264–5). The sounding of *comptroller* (originally a fancy, and mistaken, spelling for *controller*) with inter-nal [mptr] is a **spelling pronunciation** (51–3). These are matters that we will con-sider in more detail later.

Hypercorrection results from an effort to "improve" one's speech on the basis of too little information. For example, having been told that it is incorrect to "drop your *g*'s" as in *talkin'* and *somethin'*, the earnest but ill-informed self-improver has been known to "correct" *chicken* to *chicking* and *Virgin Islands* to *Virging Islands*. Similarly, one impressed with the elegance of a Bostonian or British pronunciation of *aunt* and *can't* as something like "ahnt" and "cahnt" may be misled into talking about how dogs "pahnt," a pronunciation of *pant* that will amuse any proper Bostonian or Britisher. Speakers have a natural tendency to generalize rules—to apply them in as many circumstances as possible—so in learning a new rule, we must also learn what limitations there are on its application. Another example of such **overgeneralization** is the use of the fricative [ž]. Although it is the most recent and most restricted of the English consonants, it seems to have acquired associations of exotic elegance and is now often used in words where it does not belong historically—for example, *rajah, cashmere,* and *kosher.*

As speakers use the language, they often change it, whether unconsciously or deliberately. Those changes become for the next generation just a part of the inher-ited system, available to use or again to change. And so a language varies over the years and centuries and may, like English, eventually become quite a different sys-tem from what it was earlier.

THE PHONEME

At the beginning of this chapter, some sounds were called the "same" and oth-ers "different." However, what are regarded as the same sounds may vary from language to language. In English, for instance, the vowel sound of *sit* and the vowel sound of *seat* are **distinctive**, and all native speakers regard them as differ-ent. Many pairs of words, called **contrastive pairs**, differ solely in the distinctive quality that these sounds have for us: *bit-beat, mill-meal, fist-feast,* and *lick-leak* are a few such pairs. But in Spanish this difference, so important in English, is of no significance at all; there are no such contrastive pairs, and hence the two vow-els in question are felt not as distinctive sounds but as one and the same. Native speakers of Spanish, when they learn English, are as likely as not to say, "I seat in the sit" for "I sit in the seat"—a mistake that would be impossible, except as a slip of the tongue, for native speakers of English.

What in any language is regarded as the "same sound" is actually a class of similar sounds that make up what is called a **phoneme**. A phoneme is the smallest distinctive unit of speech; it consists of a number of **allophones**, that is, similar sounds that are not distinctive. Thus, speakers of English regard as the "same sound" the sound spelled *t* in *tone* and *stone,* though a physically different sound is symbolized by the letter *t* in each of these words: in *tone* the initial consonant has **aspiration** [tʰ]; that is, it is followed by a breath puff, which you can clearly feel if you hold your hand before your lips while saying the word; in *stone,* this aspiration is lacking. The two physically different sounds both belong to, or are allophones of, the English *t* phoneme, which differs according to the phonetic environment in which it occurs. These allophones occur in what is called **complementary distribution**: that is to say, each occurs in a specific environment—in this instance, the unaspirated *t* occurs only after *s,* a position that the aspirated sound never occupies, so there is no overlapping of these two allophones. In other positions, such as at the end of a word like *fight,* aspirated and unaspirated *t* are in **free variation**: either may occur, depending on the style of speaking.

To put it in yet another way, in English there are no pairs of words whose members are distinguished solely by the presence or absence of aspiration of a *t* sound; hence, from a phonemic point of view, the two *t* sounds in English are the same because they are **nondistinctive**. They merely occur in different environments, one initially, the other after *s.* But the two sounds are phonemic in other languages: in Chinese, for instance, the difference between aspirated and unaspirated *t* is quite significant, and the aspiration or the lack of it distinguishes between words otherwise identical, just as *t* and *p* in English *tone* and *pone* do. Classical Greek had different letters for these sounds, θ for aspirated *t* and τ for unaspirated *t,* and the Greeks carefully differentiated them, whereas the Romans had only the unaspirated sound represented by Greek τ.

There are other allophones of the phoneme written *t.* For instance, in American English the *t* sound that appears medially in words like *item, little,* and *matter* is very like a [d]; or [t] and [d] in that position may even have become identical, so that *atom* and *Adam* or *latter* and *ladder* are pronounced alike. In a certain type of New York City speech, words like *bottle* have a **glottal stop** [ʔ], that is, a "catch" in the throat, instead of a [t]. In a word like *outcome,* the [t] may be **unreleased**: we pronounce the first part of the *t* and then go directly to the *k* sound that begins *come.*

It is usual to write phonemes within slanting lines, or **virgules** (also called **slashes**), thus /t/. In this book we ordinarily use a phonetic **broad transcription** enclosed in **square brackets**, showing only the particular characteristics of speech we are interested in and for the most part ignoring allophonic features such as the allophones of /t/ that have just been described. Such allophonic detail can be recorded in a **narrow transcription**, using special symbols such as [tʰ] for the *t* of *tone* and [t̺] for the *t* of *item*. Such detail is necessary, however, only for special purposes. Although phonetic broad transcriptions of speech are not in principle the same as phonemic transcriptions, in actual practice they do not differ much.

DIFFERING TRANSCRIPTIONS

The set of symbols we use to represent sounds depends on factors like convenience and familiarity, but it is essentially arbitrary. Dictionaries tend to use symbols closely aligned with conventional English spelling, although each dictionary makes its own alignment. This book uses a variant of the International Phonetic Alphabet (used for writing sounds in any language), adapted in certain ways by American dialectologists and linguists. Here is a list of some symbols used in this book, with variants you may find elsewhere:

ð	đ	**th**is	i	iy, iː	**peat**	o	ow, oʊ, oː, əʊ	**so**
š	ʃ	**sh**un	ɪ	i, ι	**pit**	ə	ʌ	**putt**
ž	ʒ	vi**si**on	e	ey, eɪ , eι, eː	**pate**	ər	ɝ, ɚ	**pert**
č	tš, ʧ	**ch**in	ɛ	e	**pet**	aɪ	ay, aι	**by**
ǰ	dž, ʤ	**j**ug	u	uw, uː	**fool**	aʊ	aw, aʊ	**bough**
y	j	**y**es	ʊ	u, ω, ʊ	**full**	ɔɪ	oy, ɔι	**boy**

Such differences in transcription are matters partly of theory and partly of style, rather than substantial disagreements about the sounds being transcribed. You need to be aware of their existence, so that if you encounter different methods of transcribing, you will not suppose that different sounds are necessarily represented. The reasons for the differences belong to a more detailed study than is appropriate here.

FOR FURTHER READING

General

McMahon. *An Introduction to English Phonology.*
Roach. *English Phonetics and Phonology.*
Wells. *Accents of English.*

American Pronunciation

Kenyon. *American Pronunciation.*

British Pronunciation

Gimson. *Gimson's Pronunciation.*

Pronouncing Dictionaries

Jones. *English Pronouncing Dictionary.*
Kenyon and Knott. *A Pronouncing Dictionary of American English.*
Upton, Kretzschmar, and Konopka. *The Oxford Dictionary of Pronunciation.*
Wells. *Longman Pronunciation Dictionary.*

3 LETTERS AND SOUNDS

A BRIEF HISTORY OF WRITING

Although talking is as old as humanity, writing is a product of comparatively recent times. With it, history begins; without it, we must depend on the archeologist. The entire period during which people have been making conventionalized markings on stone, wood, clay, metal, parchment, paper, or other surfaces to symbolize their speech is really no more than a moment in the vast period during which they have been combining vocal noises systematically for the purpose of communicating with each other.

IDEOGRAPHIC AND SYLLABIC WRITING

There can be no doubt that writing grew out of drawing, the wordless comic-strip type of drawing done by primitive peoples. The American Indians made many such drawings. It is not surprising that certain conventions should have developed in them, such as horizontal and vertical lines on a chief's gravestone to indicate, respectively, the number of his campaigns and the number of wounds he received in the course of those campaigns (Pedersen 143); the lines rising from an eagle's head were another convention indicating that the figure was the chief of the eagle totem, this in a "letter" from that chief to the president of the United States, represented as a white-faced man in a white house (Gelb 2). But such drawings, communicative as they may be once one understands their conventions, give no idea of actual words. Any identity of wording in their interpretation would be purely coincidental. No element even remotely suggests speech sounds or word order, and hence such drawings tell us nothing about the language of those who made them.

When symbols come to stand for ideas corresponding to individual words and each word is represented by a separate symbol, the result is **ideographic**, or **logographic**, writing. In Chinese writing, for example, every word originally had a symbol based not on the sound of the word but on its meaning.

Another method, fundamentally different, probably grew out of ideographic writing: the use of the **phonogram**, which is concerned with sound rather than with meaning. By a sort of punning process, pictures came to be used as in a **rebus**—that is, as if we were to draw a picture of a tie to represent the first syllable of the word *tycoon* and of a coon to represent the second. In such a method, we may see the beginnings of a **syllabary**, in which symbols, in time becoming so conventionalized as to be unrecognizable as actual pictures, are used to represent syllables.

FROM SEMITIC WRITING TO THE GREEK ALPHABET

Semitic writing, a second millennium B.C. development in Palestine and Syria, is the basis of our own and indeed of all **alphabetic writing**. It usually represented consonants only; there were ways of indicating vowels, but such devices were used sparingly. Since Semitic had certain consonantal sounds not found in other languages, the symbols for these sounds were readily available for use as vowel symbols by the Greeks when they adopted for their own use the Semitic writing system, which they called Phoenician. (To the Greeks, all eastern non-Greeks were *Phoenices,* just as to the Anglo-Saxons all Scandinavians were *Dene* 'Danes.') The Greeks even used the Semitic names of the symbols, which they adapted to Greek phonetic patterns: thus ʼ*aleph* 'ox' and *beth* 'house' became *alpha* and *beta* because words ending in consonants (other than *n, r,* and *s*) are not in accord with Greek patterns. The fact that the Greeks used the Semitic names, which had no meaning for them, is powerful evidence that the Greeks did indeed acquire their writing from the Semites, as they freely acknowledged having done. The order of the letters and the similarity of Greek forms to Semitic ones are additional evidence of this fact.

The Semitic symbol corresponding to *A* indicated a glottal consonant that did not exist in Greek. Its Semitic name was ʼ*aleph,* the initial apostrophe indicating the consonant in question. Because the name means 'ox,' the letter shape is thought to represent an ox's head, though interpreting many of the Semitic signs as pictorial characters presents as yet insuperable difficulties (Gelb 140–1). By ignoring the initial Semitic consonant of the letter's name, the Greeks adapted this symbol as a vowel, which they called *alpha. Beth* was somewhat modified in form to *B* by the Greeks, and from the Greek modifications of the Semitic names of these first two letters, the word *alphabet* is ultimately derived.

In the early days, the Greeks wrote from right to left, as the Semitic peoples usually did and as Hebrew is still written. But sometimes the early Greeks would change direction in alternate lines, starting, for instance, at the right, then changing direction at the end of the line, so that the next line went from left to right, and continuing this change of direction in alternate lines throughout. Solon's laws were so written. The Greeks had a word for the fashion—**boustrophedon** 'as the ox turns in plowing.' Eventually, however, they settled down to writing from left to right, the direction we still use.

The Greek Vowel and Consonant Symbols

The brilliant Greek notion (conceived about 3,000 years ago) of using as vowel symbols those Semitic letters for consonant sounds that did not exist in Greek gave the Greeks an **alphabet** in the modern sense of the word. Thus Semitic *yod* became *iota* (I) and was used for the Greek vowel *i;* at the time the symbol was taken over, Greek had no need for the corresponding semivowel [y], with which the Semitic word *yod* began. Just as they had changed *'aleph* into a vowel symbol by dropping the initial Semitic consonant, so also the Greeks dropped the consonant of Semitic *he* and called it *epsilon* (E), that is, *e psilon* ('*e* bare or stripped,' that is, *e* without the aspirate). Semitic *ayin,* whose name began with a voiced pharyngeal fricative nonexistent in Greek, became for the Greeks *omicron* (O), that is, *o micron* ('*o* little'). Semitic *heth* was at first used as a consonant and called *heta,* but the "rough breathing" sound it symbolized was lost in several Greek dialects, notably the Ionic of Asia Minor, where the symbol was then called *eta* (H) and used for long [e:].

The vowel symbol *omega* (Ω), that is, *o mega* ('*o* big'), was a Greek innovation, as was also *upsilon* (Y), that is, *u psilon* ('*u* bare or stripped'). *Upsilon* was born of the need for a symbol for a vowel sound corresponding to the Semitic semivowel *waw.* The sound [w], which *waw* represented, was lost in Ionic, as also in other dialects, and *waw,* which came to be called *digamma* because it looked like one letter gamma on top of another (F), ceased to be used except as a numeral—but not before the Romans had taken it over and assigned the value [f] to it.

Practically all of the remaining Semitic symbols were used for the Greek consonants, with the Semitic values of their first elements for the most part unchanged. Their graphic forms were also recognizably the same after they had been adopted by the Greeks. *Gimel* became *gamma* (Γ), *daleth* became *delta* (Δ), and so on. The early Greek alphabet ended with *tau* (T). The consonant symbols *phi* (Φ), *chi* (X), and *psi* (Ψ) were later Greek additions. A good idea of the shapes of the letters and the slight modifications made by the early Greeks may be obtained from the charts provided by Ignace Gelb (177) and Holger Pedersen (179). Gelb also gives the Latin forms, and Pedersen the highly similar Indic ones, Indic writings from the third century B.C. onward being inscribed in an alphabet adapted from the Semitic.

THE ROMANS ADOPT THE GREEK ALPHABET

The Ionic alphabet, adopted at Athens, became the standard for the writing of Greek, but it was the somewhat different Western form of the alphabet that the Romans, perhaps by way of the Etruscans, were to adopt for their own use. The Romans used a curved form of gamma (C from Γ), the third letter, which at first had for them the same value as for the Greeks [g] but in time came to be used for [k]. Another symbol was thus needed for the [g] sound. This need was remedied in time by a simple modification in the shape of C, resulting in G: thus C and G are both derived from Greek Γ. The C was, however, sometimes used for both [g] and [k], a custom that survived in later times in such abbreviations as *C.* for *Gaius* and *Cn.* for *Gnaeus,* two Roman names.

Rounded forms of *delta* (D from Δ), *pi* (P from Π), and *sigma* (S from Σ), as well as of *gamma,* were used by the Romans. They were not Roman innovations; all of them occur in Greek also, though the more familiar Greek literary forms are the angular ones. The occurrence of such rounded forms was doubtless due in early times to the use of pen and ink; the angular forms reflect the use of a cutting tool on stone.

Epsilon (E) was adopted without change. The sixth position was filled by F, the Greek *digamma* (earlier *waw*). The Romans gave this symbol the value [f]. Following it came the modified *gamma,* G. H was used as a consonant, as in Semitic and also in Western Greek at the time the Romans adopted it.

The Roman gain in having a symbol for [h] was slight, for the aspirate was almost as unstable a sound in Latin as it is in Cockney English; and ultimately, like Greek, Latin lost it completely. Among the Romance languages—those derived from Latin, such as Italian, French, Spanish, and Portuguese—there is no need for the symbol, since there is no trace of the sound, though it may be retained in spelling because of conservatism, as in some French and Spanish words—for example, French *heure* and Spanish *hora* 'hour' (but compare French *avoir* with Spanish *haber* 'to have').

Iota (I) was for the Romans both a semivowel and a vowel, as illustrated, respectively, by the two *i*'s in *iudices* 'judges,' the first syllable of which is like English *you*. The lengthened form of this letter, that is, *j,* did not appear until medieval times, when the **minuscule** form of writing developed, which used small letters exclusively. (In ancient writing only **majuscules**, that is, capital letters, were used.) The majuscule form of this newly shaped *i,* that is, J, is a product of modern times.

Kappa (K) was used in only a few words by the Romans, who, as we have seen, used C to represent the same sound. Next came the Western Greek form of *lambda,* L, corresponding to Ionic Λ. M and N, from *mu* and *nu,* require no comment. *Xi* (Ξ), with the value [ks], following Greek *nu,* was not taken over into Latin; thus in the Roman alphabet O immediately followed N. *Pi* (Π) having been adopted in its rounded form P, it was necessary for the Romans to use a tailed form of *rho* (P), as the early Greeks also had sometimes done, and thus create R. The symbol Q (*koppa*) stood for a sound that had dropped out of Greek, though the symbol continued to be used as a numeral in that language. The Romans used it as a variant of C in one position only, preceding V; thus the sequence [kw] was written QV—the *qu* of printed texts. *Sigma* in its rounded form S was adopted unchanged. *Tau* (T) was likewise unchanged. *Upsilon* was adopted in the form V and used for both consonant ([w], later [v]) and vowel ([u], [ʊ]).

The symbol Z (Greek *zeta*), which had occupied seventh place in the early Roman alphabet but had become quite useless in Latin because the sound it represented was not a separate phoneme, was reintroduced and placed at the end of the alphabet in the time of Cicero, when a number of Greek words were coming to be used in Latin. Another form of *upsilon,* Y, was also used in borrowed words to indicate the Greek vowel sound, which was like French *u* and German *ü. Chi* (X) was used with the Western Greek value [ks], the sound of Ionic X being represented in Classical Latin by CH, just as TH and PH were used to represent Greek *theta* (Θ) and *phi* (Φ) respectively. Actually these were accurate enough representations of the Classical Greek sounds, which most scholars agree were similar to the aspirated initial sounds of English *kin, tin,* and *pin.* The Romans in their transcriptions very sensibly symbolized the aspiration, or breath puff, by H. The sounds symbolized in Latin by C, T, and P apparently lacked such aspiration, as *k, t,* and *p* do in English when preceded by *s*—for example, in *skin, sting,* and *spin.*

Later Developments of the Roman and Greek Alphabets

Even though it lacked a good many symbols for sounds in the modern languages of Europe, the Roman alphabet was taken over by the various European peoples, though not by those Slavic peoples who in the ninth century got their alphabet directly from the Greek. Their alphabet is called **Cyrillic** from the Greek missionary leader Saint Cyril. Greek missionaries, sent out from Byzantium, added a number of symbols for sounds that were not in Greek and modified the shapes and uses of some of the letters for the Russians, Bulgarians, and Serbs, who use this alphabet. Those Slavs whose Christianity stems from Rome—the Poles, the Czechs, the Slovaks, the Croats, and the Slovenians—use the Roman alphabet, adapted by **diacritical marks** (for example, Polish *ć* and Czech *č*) and by combinations of letters (for example, Polish *cz, sz*) to symbolize sounds for which the Roman alphabet made no provision.

In various ways the Roman alphabet has been eked out by those who have adopted it. Such un-Latin sounds as the *o*-umlaut and the *u*-umlaut of German are written *ö* and *ü.* The superposed pair of dots, called an **umlaut** or **dieresis**, is used in many other languages also to indicate vowel quality and in old-fashioned English spellings like *preëminent* to indicate that two adjacent vowel symbols represent separate sounds. Other diacritical marks that have been used to extend the resources of the Latin alphabet are **accents**—the **acute, grave,** and **circumflex** (as, respectively, in French *résumé, à la mode,* and *rôle*). The **wedge** is used in Czech and is illustrated by the Czech name for the diacritic, *haček.* The **tilde** is used, for example, in *cañon,* borrowed from Spanish, and in Portuguese to indicate nasalized vowels, as in *São Paulo.* The **cedilla** is familiar in a French loanword like *façade.* Other less familiar diacritical markings include the bar of Polish *ł,* the circle of Swedish and Norwegian *å,* and the hook of Polish *ę.*

The Use of Digraphs

Digraphs (pairs of letters to represent single sounds), or even longer sequences like the German **trigraph** *sch,* have also been made use of to indicate un-Latin sounds, such as those that we spell *sh, ch, th,* and *dg.* In *gu,* as in *guest* and *guilt,* the *u* has the sole function of indicating that the *g* stands for the [g] of *go* rather than the [ǰ] that we might expect it to represent before *e* or *i,* as in *gesture* and *gibe.* The *h* of *gh* performs a similar useful function in *Ghent* to show that it is not pronounced like *gent,* but not in *ghost* and *ghastly.* English makes no use of diacritical marks save for the rare dieresis, preferring other devices, such as the aforementioned use of digraphs and of entirely different symbols: for example, English writes *man, men;* compare the German method of indicating the same vowel change in *Mann, Männer.*

Additional Symbols

Other symbols have sometimes been added to the Roman alphabet by those who adopted it. For example, the runic þ (called *thorn*) and ƿ (called *wynn*) were used by the early English, along with their modification of *d* as ð (called *edh*), all now abandoned as far as English writing is concerned. The þ and the ð were also adopted by the Scandinavians, who got the alphabet from the English, and are still used in writing Icelandic.

The **ligature** œ (combining *o* and *e*), which indicated a single vowel sound in post-Classical Latin, was used in early Old English for the *o*-umlaut sound (as in German *schön*). When this sound was later unrounded, there was no further need for œ in English. It was, however, taken over by the Scandinavians, who have long since given up the symbol, the Danes having devised ø and the Swedes using ö. It has been used in English in a few classical loanwords—for instance, *amœba* and *cœnobite,* more recently written with unligatured *oe* in British English. (American usage has simple *e* in these two words and others like them.)

For the vowel sound of *cat,* Old English used the digraph *ae,* later written prevailingly as ligatured æ, the symbol used for the same sound in the alphabet of the International Phonetic Association. This digraph they also got from Latin, in which the classical value (as in German *Kaiser,* from *Caesar*) had long before shifted to a vowel sound roughly similar in value to that which the English ascribed to it. The æ was called *æsc* 'ash,' the name of the runic symbol that represented the same sound, though the rune in no way resembled the Latin-English digraph. In Middle English times, beginning around 1100, the symbol went out of use. Today æ is used in Danish, Norwegian, and Icelandic. It occurs occasionally, with a quite different value, in loanwords of classical origin, like *encyclopædia* and *anæmia,* spelled *encyclopedia* and *anemia* in current American usage. (British English often has unligatured *ae* in such words.)

THE HISTORY OF ENGLISH WRITING

The Germanic Runes

When the Anglo-Saxons came to Britain, some of them were already literate in runic writing, but it was a highly specialized craft, the skill of rune masters. These Germanic invaders had little need to write, but when they did, which was certainly not very often, they used twenty-four **runes**, derived from their relatives on the Continent, to which they added six new letters. These runes in the beginning were associated with pagan mysteries—the word *rune* means "secret." They were angular letters intended originally to be cut or scratched in wood and were often used for inscriptions, charms, and the like.

The order of the runic symbols is quite different from that of the Roman alphabet. As modified by the English, the first group of letters consists of characters corresponding to *f, u, þ, o, r, c, g,* and *w*. The English runic alphabet is sometimes called **futhorc** from the first six of these. Despite the differences in the order of the letters, their close similarities to both Greek and Latin symbols make it obvious that they are derived partly from the Roman alphabet, with which the Germanic peoples could easily have acquired familiarity, or from some early Italic alphabet akin to the Roman alphabet.

The Anglo-Saxon Roman Alphabet

In the early Middle Ages, various script styles—the "national hands"—developed in those lands that had been provinces of the Roman Empire. But Latin writing, as well as the Latin tongue, had all but disappeared in the Roman colony of Britannia, which the Romans had of necessity practically abandoned even before the arrival of the English. With their conversion to Christianity, the English adopted the Roman alphabet (though they continued to use runes for special purposes). Although the missionaries who spread the gospel among the heathen Anglo-Saxons were from Rome and must have used an Italian style of writing, the manuscripts from the Old English period are in a script called the **Insular hand**, which was an Irish modification of the Roman alphabet. The Irish, who had been converted to Christianity before the English came to Britain, taught their new neighbors how to write in their style. A development of the Insular hand is still used in writing Irish Gaelic.

The Insular hand has rounded letters, each distinct and easy to recognize. To the ordinary letters of the Roman alphabet (those we use minus *j, v,* and *w*), the Anglo-Saxon scribes added several others mentioned earlier: the digraph æ, which we call **ash** after the runic letter *æsc*; the two runic letters þ **thorn** (for the sound [θ]) and *p* **wynn** (for the sound [w]), borrowed from the futhorc; and ð, the modification of Roman *d* that we call **edh**. Several of the Roman letters, notably *f, g, r, s,* and *t,* had distinctive shapes. *S* indeed had three alternate shapes, one of which, called **long s,** looks very much like an *f* in modern typography except that the horizontal stroke does not go through to the right of the letter. This particular variant of *s* (ſ) was used until the end of the eighteenth century except in final position, printers following what was the general practice of the manuscripts.

When the Normans conquered England in 1066, they introduced a number of Norman-French customs, including their own style of writing, which replaced the Insular hand. The special letters used in the latter were lost, although several of them, notably thorn and the long *s,* continued for some time. Norman scribes also introduced or reintroduced some digraphs into English orthography, especially *ch, ph,* and *th,* which were used in spelling words ultimately from Greek, although the last was also a revived spelling for the English sounds that Anglo-Saxon scribes had written with thorn and edh, and the first was pressed into service for representing [č]. Other combinations with *h* also appeared and are still with us: *gh, sh,* and *wh.*

Gradually the letters of the alphabet assumed their present number. *J* was originally a prolonged and curved variant of *i* used in final position when writing Latin words like *filii* that ended in double *i.* Since English scribes used *y* for *i* in final position (compare *marry* with *marries* and *married, holy day* with *holiday*), the use of *j* in English was for a long time more or less confined to the representation of numerals—for instance, *iij* for *three* and *vij* for *seven.* The dot, incidentally, was not originally part of minuscule *i,* but is a development of the faint sloping line that came to be put above this insignificant letter to distinguish it from the strokes of contiguous letters such as *m, n,* and *u,* as well as to distinguish double *i* from *u.* It was later extended by analogy to *j,* where, because of the different shape of the letter, it performed no useful purpose.

The history of the curved and angular forms of *u*—that is, *u* and *v*—was similar to that of *i* and *j.* Although consonantal and vocalic *u* in Latin had come to be sharply differentiated in sound early in the Christian era, when consonantal *u,* hitherto pronounced [w], became [v], the two symbols *u* and *v* continued to be used more or less interchangeably for either vowel or consonant. *W* was originally, as its name indicates, a double *u,* although it was the angular shape *v* that was actually doubled, a shape that we now regard as a different letter.

THE SPELLING OF ENGLISH CONSONANT SOUNDS

The words in the lists below will give some idea of the variety of ways our conventional spelling symbolizes the sounds of speech. What we think of as the normal or usual spellings are given first, in the various positions in which they occur (initially, medially, finally). Then, introduced by "*also*" come spellings that are relatively rare, a few of them unique. The words cited to illustrate unusual spellings have been assembled not for the purpose of stocking an Old Curiosity Shop of English orthography or to encourage in any way the popular notion that our spelling is chaotic— which it is not—but to show the diversity of English spelling, a diversity for which, as we shall see in subsequent chapters, there are invariably historical reasons. A few British pronunciations are included; these are labeled BE, for British English. Characteristically American pronunciations are labeled AE, for American English. Because there is variety in how speakers of English pronounce the language, some of the words will not illustrate the intended sounds for all speakers. For example, although *hiccough* usually ends in [p], being merely a respelling of *hiccup,* some speakers now pronounce it with final [f] under the influence of the spelling *-cough.*

Stops

[b] **b**i**b**, ru**b**y, ra**bb**le, e**bb**, tri**b**e; *also* cu**p**board, ras**p**berry, **bh**angra

[p] **p**u**p**, stu**p**id, a**pp**le, ri**p**e; *also* La**pp**, gri**pp**e, Cla**ph**am, hiccou**gh**

[d] **d**u**d**, bo**d**y, mu**dd**le, a**dd**, bri**d**e, ebbe**d**; *also* **bd**ellium, **dh**oti, Gan**dh**i

[t] **t**oo**t**, boo**t**y, ma**tt**er, bu**tt**, ra**t**e, hoppe**d**; *also* ciga**rett**e, **Th**omas, **pt**omaine, recei**pt**, de**bt**, sub**t**le, **phth**isic, indi**ct**, vic**t**uals, vel**dt**; *the sequence* [ts] *is written* z *in* s**ch**izophrenia *and* Mo**z**art, zz *in* me**zz**o (*also pronounced with* [dz])

[g] **g**a**g**, la**g**er, la**gg**ard, e**gg**; *also* **gu**ess, va**gu**e, **gh**ost, a**gh**ast, Hai**gh**, mort**g**age, *traditional but now rare* bla**ckgu**ard; *the sequence* [gz] *is written* x *in* e**x**alt *and* e**x**ist, *and* xh *in* e**xh**aust *and* e**xh**ilarate; *the sequence* [gž] *is written* x *in* lu**x**urious

[k] **k**i**t**, na**k**ed, ta**k**e, pi**ck**, ma**ck**erel, **c**ar, ba**c**on, musi**c**; *also* **q**uaint, pi**qu**et, **qu**eue, physi**qu**e, tre**k** (k *by itself in final position being rare*), chu**kk**er, **ch**asm, ma**ch**ination, s**ch**ool, stoma**ch**, sa**cqu**e, **kh**aki, gin**kg**o; *the sequence* [ks] *is written* x *in* fi**x** *and* e**x**it (*also pronounced with* [gz]) *and* xe *in* BE a**xe**; *the sequence* [kš] *is written* x *in* lu**x**ury (*also pronounced with* [gž]), xi *in* an**xi**ous, *and* cti *in* a**cti**on

Fricatives

[v] **v**al**v**e, o**v**er; *also* Sla**v**, Ste**ph**en, o**f**, *sometimes* schwa

[f] **f**i**f**e, i**f**, ra**ff**le, o**ff**; *also* so**f**ten, rou**gh**, tou**gh**en, **ph**antom, s**ph**inx, ele**ph**ant, Ral**ph**, Chekho**v**, *BE* lieu**t**enant

[ð] **th**en, ei**th**er, ba**th**e; *also* loa**th** (*also pronounced with* [θ]), e**dh**, eiste**dd**fod, **y**e (*pseudoarchaic spelling for* the)

[θ] **th**in, e**th**er, fro**th**; *also* **phth**alein, **chth**onian

[z] **z**oos, fi**zz**le, fu**zz**, oo**z**e, visa**g**e, pha**s**e; *also* fe**z**, posse**ss**, Quin**c**y (MA), **x**ylophone, **cz**ar, clo**th**es (*as suggested by the rime in Ophelia's song:* "Then up he rose, & don'd his clothes" *in* Hamlet 4.5.52); *it is still naturally so pronounced by many, who thus distinguish the noun* clothes *from the verb, whereas spelling pronouncers say the noun and verb alike with* [-ðz])

[s] **s**i**s**, perva**s**ive, vi**s**e, pa**ss**ive, ma**ss**, **c**ereal, a**c**id, vi**c**e; *also* **s**word, an**s**wer, **sc**ion, de**sc**ent, evane**sc**e, **sch**ism, **p**sychology, Tu**cs**on, faça**d**e, is**th**mus

[ž] *medially:* lei**s**ure, a**z**ure, delu**s**ion, equa**t**ion; *also initially and finally in a few recent borrowings especially from French:* **g**enre *and* rou**g**e (*the sound seems to be gaining ground, perhaps to some extent because of a smattering of school French, though the words in which it is new in English are not all of French provenience—for instance,* ada**g**io, ra**j**ah, Ta**j** Mahal, *and* ca**sh**mere) [š]   **sh**u**sh**, mar**sh**al; *also* **ch**amois, ma**ch**ine, ca**ch**e, mar**ti**al, pre**ci**ous, ten-**si**on, pa**ss**ion, fa**sh**ion, **s**ure, que**s**tion, o**ce**an, lu**sci**ous, nau**s**ea, cre**sc**endo, fu**chs**ia

[h]   **h**a, Mo**h**awk; *also* **wh**o, *school-Spanish* Don Qui**x**ote *as "Donkey Hoty,"* *recent* **j**unta (*though the word has since the seventeenth century been regarded as English and therefore pronounced with the beginning consonant and vowel of* junk), Mo**j**ave, **g**ila

Affricates

[ǰ]   **j**udge, ma**j**or, **g**em, re**g**iment, **G**eorge, sur**ge**on, re**g**ion, bu**dg**et; *also* exa**gg**er-ate, ra**j**, e**d**ucate, gran**d**eur, sol**d**ier, spina**ch**, congra**t**ulate (*with assimilation of the earlier voiceless affricate to the voicing of the surrounding vowels*)

[č]   **ch**ur**ch**, le**ch**er, but**ch**er, it**ch**; *also* **Ch**ristian, ni**ch**e, na**t**ure, **c**ello, **Cz**ech

Nasals

[m]   **m**u**m**, cla**m**or, su**mm**er, ti**m**e; *also* co**mb**, plu**mb**er, sole**mn**, govern**m**ent, paradi**gm**, *BE* progra**mm**e

[n]   **n**u**n**, ho**n**or, di**n**e, i**nn**, di**nn**er; *also* **kn**ow, **gn**aw, si**gn**, **mn**emonic, **pn**eumonia

[ŋ]   si**ng**, wri**ng**er, fi**ng**er, si**nk**; *also* to**ngue**, ha**n**dkerchief, *BE* charaba**nc**, *BE* restaura**nt**, Pago Pago

Liquids

[l]   **l**ape**l**, fe**l**on, fe**ll**ow, fe**ll**, ho**l**e; *also* **Ll**oyd, ki**ln**, Mi**ln[e]** (*the* n *of* kiln *and* Miln(e) *ceased to be pronounced in Middle English times, but pronunciation with* n *is common nowadays because of the spelling*)

[r]   **r**ea**r**, ba**r**on, ba**rr**en, e**rr**, ba**r**e; *also* **wr**ite, **rh**etoric, biza**rr**e, hemo**rrh**age, colonel

Semivowels

[w]   **w**on, **wh**ich (*a fairly large, if decreasing, number of Americans have in* wh-*words not* [w] *but* [hw]); *also* lang**u**ish, q**u**estion, **ou**ija, **O**axaca, h**u**arache, **Ju**an; *in* one, *the initial* [w] *is not symbolized*

[y]   **y**et, bull**i**on; *also* can**y**on, **ll**ama (*also pronounced with* [l]), La **J**olla, *BE* capercail**z**ie 'wood grouse,' *BE* bou**ill**on, **j**aeger, halleluj**ah**; *the sequence* [ny] *is written* gn *in* chi**gn**on *and* ñ *in* ca**ñ**on

THE SPELLING OF ENGLISH VOWEL SOUNDS

As with the consonants, words are supplied below to illustrate the various spellings of each vowel sound, although some of the illustrative words may have alternative pronunciations. Diphthongs, vowels before [r], and unstressed [i], [ɪ], and [ə] are treated separately.

Front Vowels

[i]   evil, cede, meter, eel, lee, eat, sea; *also* ceiling, belief, trio, police, people, key, quay, Beauchamp, Aesop, *BE* Oedipus, Leigh, camellia (*this word is exceptional in that the spelling* e *represents* [i] *rather than the expected* [ɛ] *before a double consonant symbol*), *BE for the Cambridge college* Caius [kiz]

[ɪ]   it, stint; *also* English, sieve, renege, been, symbol, build, busy, women, *old-fashioned* teat

[e]   acorn, ape, basin, faint, gray; *also* great, emir, mesa, fete, they, eh, Baal, rein, reign, maelstrom, *BE* gaol, gauge, weigh, *BE* halfpenny, *BE* Ralph (*as in act 2 of W. S. Gilbert's* H.M.S. Pinafore: *"In time each little waif / Forsook his foster-mother, / The well-born babe was Ralph— / Your captain was the other!!!"*), chef d'oeuvre, champagne, Montaigne, *AE* cafe, Iowa (*locally*), cachet, foyer, melee, Castlereagh

[ɛ]   bet, threat; *also BE* ate, again, says, many, *BE* Pall Mall, catch (*alternating with* [æ]), friend, heifer, Reynolds, leopard, eh, phlegm, aesthetic

[æ]   at, plan; *also* plaid, baa, ma'am, Spokane, *BE* The Mall, salmon, Caedmon, *AE* draught, meringue; *British English has* [ɑ] *in a large number of words in which American has* [æ], *such as* calf, class, *and* path

Central Vowel

[ə]   utter, but; *also* other, blood, does (*verb*), young, was (*alternating with* [ɑ]), pandit (alternating with [æ]), uh, ugh ([ə] *alternating with* [əg] *or* [ək]), twopence

Back Vowels

[u]   ooze, tooth, too, you, rude, rue, new; *also* to, tomb, pooh, shoe, Cowper, boulevard, through, brougham, fruit, *nautical* leeward, Sioux, rheumatic, lieutenant (*British English has* [lɛfˈtɛnənt] *or for a naval officer* [ləˈtɛnənt]), bouillon, rendezvous, ragout, *and alternating with* [ʊ] *in* room, roof, *and some other words written with* oo

Spellings other than with o, oo, *and* ou *usually represent the sequence* [yu] *initially* (**use**, **Eu**rope, **ewe**) *and after labial and palatovelar consonants:* [b] (b**u**reau, b**eau**ty), [p] (p**ew**, p**u**re), [g] (g**u**les, g**ew**gaw), [k] (c**ue**, q**ueue**, K**ew**), [v] (v**iew**), [f] (f**ew**, f**ue**l, f**eu**d), [h] (h**ue**, h**ew**, h**u**man; *the spelling of the Scottish surname* Home [hyum] *is exceptional*), *and* [m] (m**u**sic, m**ew**). *After dental consonants there is considerable dialect variation between* [u] *and* [yu]: [n] (n**u**clear, n**ew**s, n**eu**tral), [t] (t**u**ne, T**eu**ton), [d] (d**ew**, d**u**ty), [θ] (th**ew**), [s] (s**ue**, s**ew**er), [z] (res**u**me), [l] (l**ew**d, l**u**te). *After alveolopalatals* [š], [č], *and* [ǰ], *older* [yu] *is now quite rare.*

[ʊ] **oo**mph, g**oo**d, p**u**ll; *also* w**o**lf, c**oul**d, W**o**dehouse, w**o**rsted *'a fabric'*

[o] **o**leo, g**o**, r**o**de, r**oa**d, t**oe**, t**ow**, **owe**, **oh**; *also* s**ou**l, br**oo**ch, f**o**lk, b**eau**, chauff**eu**r, *AE* cantal**ou**pe, pic**o**t, th**ou**gh, ye**o**man, col**o**gne, s**ew**, coc**oa**, Phara**oh**, *military* prov**o**st

[ɔ] **a**ll, l**aw**, **awe**, c**au**se, g**o**ne; *also* br**oa**d, t**a**lk, **ou**ght, **au**ght, Om**a**ha, Ut**a**h, Ark**a**nsas, Mackin**a**c, *BE* M**a**rlborough ['mɔlb(ə)rə], *BE for the Oxford college* M**a**gdalen ['mɔdlɪn] (*the name of the Cambridge college is written* Magdalene, *but is pronounced exactly the same*), Gl**ou**cester, F**au**lkner, M**au**gham, Str**a**chan

[ɑ] **a**tman, f**a**ther, sp**a**, **o**tter, st**o**p (*the* [ɑ] *in so-called short-o words like* cl**o**ck, c**o**llar, g**o**t, *and* st**o**p *prevails in American English; British English typically has a slightly rounded vowel* [ɒ]); *also* s**o**lder, **ah**, c**a**lm (*because of the spelling, many Americans, mostly younger-generation ones, insert* [l] *in this word and others spelled* al, *for instance,* alms, balm, palm, *and* psalm), bur**eau**cracy, baccar**a**t, **e**nnui, kr**aa**l, **au**nt (*pronunciation of this word with* [ɑ], *though regarded by many as an affectation, is normal in African-American, some types of eastern American, and of course British English*)

Diphthongs

[aɪ] **i**ris, r**i**de, h**ie**, m**y**, st**y**le, d**ye**; *also* b**uy**, **I**, **eye**, **ay**, **aye**, p**i**, n**igh**t, h**eigh**t, **i**sle, **ai**sle, G**ei**ger, Van **Ey**ck, Van D**y**ck, k**ai**ser, m**ae**stro

[aʊ] h**ow**, h**ou**se; *also* b**ou**gh, Macl**eo**d, s**au**erkraut

[ɔɪ] **oi**l, b**oy**; *also* b**uoy** (*sometimes as* [buɪ] *in AE*), R**eu**ters (*English news agency*), B**ou**logne, p**oi**

Vowels plus [r]

[ɪ] *or* [i] m**e**re, **ea**r, p**ee**r; *also* p**ie**r, m**i**rror, w**ei**rd, l**y**ric

[ɛ], [e], *or* [æ] b**a**re, **ai**r, pr**a**yer, th**ei**r; *also* **ae**ronaut

[ə] **u**rge, **e**rg, b**i**rd, **ea**rn; *also* w**o**rd, j**ou**rnal, mass**eu**r, m**y**rrh; *in some words in which the* [r] *is followed by a vowel* (c**ou**rage, h**u**rry, th**o**rough, w**o**rry), *dialects have different syllable divisions, before or after the* [r]: [hər-i] *versus* [hə-rɪ] [ɑ] **ar**t (*some Americans have* [ɔ] *in these words*); *also* hea**r**t, se**r**geant, s**oi**ree ([wɑr] *for* oir *as also in other recent French loans*)

[ʊ] *or* [u] p**oor**, s**ure**, t**our**, j**ur**y, ne**ur**al; *also* B**oer**; poor *and* Boer *are often and* sure *is sometimes pronounced with the vowel* [o] *or* [ɔ]

[o] **oar**, **ore**; *also* f**our**, d**oor**; *many Americans, probably most nowadays, do not distinguish the vowels* [o] *and* [ɔ] *before* [r], *so for them, this and the next group are a single set, although historically the distinction was made*

[ɔ] **or**; *also* w**ar**, *AE* reserv**oir**

[aɪ] **fire**, **tyr**ant; *also* ch**oir** (*with* oir *representing* [waɪr])

[aʊ] fl**our**, fl**ower**; *also* d**owry**, c**oward**, s**auer**kraut

[ɔɪ] (*a rare combination*) c**oir**

Unstressed Vowels

[i] *or* [ɪ] *at the end of a word:* bod**y**, hone**y**; *also* Macaula**y**, speci**e**, Burle**igh**, Ral**egh** (*one spelling of Sir Walter's surname*), *BE* Cal**ais** ['kælɪ], recip**e**, guin**ea**, coff**ee**, *BE* ball**et** ['bælɪ], tax**i**, *BE* Carew, chall**is**, cham**ois**

   followed by another vowel: a**e**rial, ar**e**a; *also* Isra**e**l, Ephr**ai**m

[ɪ] *followed by a velar consonant:* **i**gnore, top**i**c, runn**i**ng

[ə] *or* [ɪ] *followed by a consonant other than a velar or* [r]: **i**llumine, el**u**de, bi**a**s, buck**e**t; *also* A**e**neas, myst**e**rious, misch**ie**f, forf**ei**t, bisc**ui**t, min**u**te (*noun*), marr**i**age, portr**ai**t, pal**a**ce, lett**u**ce, tort**oi**se, dact**y**l

[ə] *at the end of a word:* Cub**a**; *also* No**ah**, Goeth**e**, Edinb**urgh** [-brə]; *alternating with* [o] *in* pian**o**, bor**ough**, wind**ow**, bur**eau**, *and with* [i] *or* [ɪ] *in* Cincinnat**i**, Miam**i**, Missour**i**

   followed by a consonant other than [r]: bi**a**s, remed**y**, rum**i**nate, mel**o**n, bon**u**s, fam**ou**s; *also* Durh**a**m, for**ei**gn, Linc**o**ln, Aeschyl**u**s, Renai**ss**ance, auth**o**rity, *BE* blanc**m**ange

   followed by [r]: burs**a**r, butt**e**r, nad**i**r, act**o**r, fem**u**r; *also* glam**ou**r, Tourn**eu**r, cupb**oa**rd, av**oi**rdupois

SPELLING PRONUNCIATIONS AND PRONUNCIATION SPELLINGS

Many literate people attribute sounds to the letters of the alphabet. This is to put the cart before the horse, for, as should be perfectly clear by now, letters do not "have" sounds, but merely represent them. Nevertheless, literate people are likely to feel that they do not really know a word until the question "How do you spell it?" has been answered.

A knowledge of spelling has been responsible for changing the pronunciation of some words. When a word's spelling and pronunciation do not agree, the sound may be changed to be closer to the spelling. An example of such **spelling pronunciation** is [bed] rather than traditional [bæd] for *bade*.

The *t* in *often* became silent around the seventeenth century, as it did also in *soften*. But by the end of the eighteenth century, an awareness of the letter in the spelling of the first word caused many people to start pronouncing it again. Nowadays the pronunciation with [t] is so widespread that many Gilbert and Sullivan fans may miss the point of the *orphan–often* dialogue in *The Pirates of Penzance,* culminating in Major-General Stanley's question to the Pirate King, "When you said [ɔfən] did you mean 'orphan'—a person who has lost his parents, or 'often'—frequently?" This will make no sense to those who have restored the *t* in *often* (and keep the *r* in *orphan*). For the play's original audiences, who did not pronounce *r* before a consonant or the *t* in *often,* the words were homophones.

The compound *forehead* came to be pronounced [ˈfɔrəd], as in the nursery rime about the little girl who had a little curl right in the center of her forehead, and when she was good, she was very, very good, but when she was bad, she was horrid, in which *forehead* rimes with *horrid*. The spelling, however, has caused the second part of the compound to be again pronounced as [hɛd]. Reanalysis of *breakfast* as *break* plus *fast* would be parallel. Rare words are particularly likely to acquire spelling pronunciations. *Clapboard,* pronounced like *clabbered* until fairly recently, is now usually analyzed as *clap* plus *board;* the same sort of analysis might occur also in *cupboard* if houses of the future should be built without cupboards or if builders should think up some fancy name for them, like "food preparation equipment storage areas." A number of generations ago, when people made and sharpened their own tools much more commonly than now, the word *grindstone* rimed with *Winston*.

It is similar with proper names that we have not heard spoken. Our only guide is spelling, and no one is to be blamed for pronouncing *Daventry, Shrewsbury,* and *Cirencester* as their spellings seem to indicate they should be pronounced; indeed, their traditional pronunciations as [ˈdentrɪ], [ˈšrozbərɪ], and [ˈsɪsɪtə] or [ˈsɪzɪtə] have become old-fashioned even in England. In America, the Kentucky town of Versailles is called [vərˈselz] by those who live there, who care nothing for how the French pronounce its namesake.

The great scholar W. W. Skeat of Cambridge once declared, "I hold firmly to the belief . . . that no one can tell how to pronounce an English word unless he has at some time or other *heard* it." He refused to hazard an opinion on the pronunciation of a number of very rare words—among them, *aam, abactinal, abrus,* and *acaulose*—going on to say, "It would be extremely dishonest in me to pretend to have any opinion at all as to such words as these."

The relationship between writing and speech is so widely misunderstood that many people suppose the "best" speech is that which conforms most closely to the writing system, though this supposition has not yet been extended to such words as *through* and *night.* In our hyperliterate society, writing has begun to affect pronunciation more than it ever did before. This tendency is quite the reverse of what happened in earlier times, before English spelling became fixed, when writing was made to conform to speech.

On the other hand, when a word's spelling is changed to agree with its pronunciation, the result is a **pronunciation spelling** (Cassidy and Hall 1:xix). There are several types of these, apart from accidental misspellings, such as *perculate* for *percolate* or *nucular* for *nuclear.* Indeed, a number of presidents of the United States have favored the pronunciation "nucular" although presumably their secretaries have seen that the conventional spelling appears in their press releases. Even misspellings, however, can become standard forms of a word. Because it is now usually pronounced with initial [mə] rather than [mɪ], *memento* is sometimes spelled *momento,* even in edited publications. Consequently, *momento,* originally a misspelling, is now recorded in good dictionaries as a variant of the traditional spelling.

Other pronunciation spellings, like *spicket* (for *spigot*), are used to show a dialect pronunciation. Spellings like *sez* (for *says*) and *wuz* or *woz* (for *was*) are used in writing dialog to suggest that the speaker is talking carelessly, even though the pronunciations indicated by those respellings are the usual ones. Such literary use of unconventional spellings is called **eye dialect** because it appeals to the eye as dialect rather than to the ear.

Some respellings are deliberate efforts to reform orthography. The use of *dialog* (for older *dialogue*) a few sentences above is an example, as are *thru, lite,* and a variety of informal respellings favored by Internet users, such as *phreak, outta, cee ya* (see you), and *enuf.* Extreme examples are *U* 'you,' *R* 'are,' and *2* 'too.' These are visual puns like the older *IOU.*

WRITING AND HISTORY

Contemporary spelling is the heir of thirteen centuries of English writing in the Latin alphabet. It is hardly surprising, therefore, that our orthography has traces of its earlier history both in its general rules and in its anomalies. Whenever we set pen to paper, we participate in a tradition that started with Anglo-Saxon monks, who had learned it from Irish scribes. The tradition progressed through such influences as the Norman Conquest, the introduction of printing, the urge to reform spelling in various ways (including an impulse to respell words according to their etymological sources), and the recent view that speech should conform to spelling. Nowadays, in fact, we are likely to forget that writing, in the history of humanity or even of a single language like English, is relatively recent. Before writing there were no historical records of language, but languages existed and their histories can be in some measure reconstructed, as we shall see in the next chapter.

FOR FURTHER READING

Theory and Description of Writing Systems

Daniels and Bright. *The World's Writing Systems.*
Sampson. *Writing Systems.*

History of Writing

Fischer. *A History of Writing.*
Healey. *The Early Alphabet.*
Hooker. *Reading the Past: Ancient Writing.*
Man. *Alpha Beta.*

History of English Spelling

Venezky. *The American Way of Spelling.*

Contemporary Spelling

Carney. *A Survey of English Spelling.*

Spelling Reform

Haas. *Alphabets for English.*
Upward et al. *The Simplified Spelling Society Presents Cut Spelling.*

4

THE BACKGROUNDS OF ENGLISH

English, as we know it, developed in Britain and more recently in America and elsewhere in the former British Empire. But it was an immigrant language to Britain, coming there with the invading Anglo-Saxons in the fifth century. Before that, the ancestry of English was in the northeast part of the Continent, bordering on the North Sea. But long before that, it was a development of a much earlier speechway we call Indo-European, which was the source also of most of the other languages of Europe and many of those of south Asia. We have no historical records of those prehistoric Indo-European peoples, but we know something about them from comparing the languages that developed from the one they spoke.

INDO-EUROPEAN ORIGINS

Indo-European Culture

On the basis of cognate words, we can infer a good deal about the culture of the Indo-Europeans before the various migrations that carried them from their original homeland to many parts of Europe and Asia. Those migrations started at least by the third or fourth millennium B.C. and perhaps earlier. The Indo-Europeans' culture was considerably advanced. They had a complex sense of family relationship and organization, and they could count. They made use of gold and perhaps silver as well; copper and iron were not to come until later. They drank a honey-based alcoholic beverage whose name has come down to us as *mead*. Words corresponding to *wheel, axle,* and *yoke* make it perfectly clear that they used wheeled vehicles. They were small farmers, not nomads, who worked their fields with plows, and they had domesticated animals and fowl.

They had religious feelings, with a conception of multiple gods, including a Sky Father (whose name is preserved in the ancient Vedic hymns of India as Dyaus pitar, in Greek myth as Zeus patēr, among the Romans as Jupiter, and among the Germanic peoples as Tiw, for whom Tuesday is named). The cow and the horse were important to their society, wealth being measured by a count of cattle: the Latin word *pecus* meant 'cattle' but was the source of the word *pecūnia* 'wealth,' from which we get *pecuniary;* and our word *fee* comes from a related Old English

55

word *fēoh,* which also meant 'cattle' and 'wealth.' So we can say some things about the ancient Indo-Europeans on the basis of forms that were not actually recorded until long after Indo-European had ceased to be a more or less unified language.

The Indo-European Homeland

Conjectures differ as to the location of the original Indo-European homeland—or at least the earliest for which we have any evidence. Plant and animal names are important clues. The existence of cognates denoting trees that grow in temperate climates (*alder, apple, ash, aspen, beech, birch, elm, hazel, linden, oak, willow, yew*), coupled with the absence of such related words for Mediterranean or Asiatic trees (*olive, cypress, palm*); the similar occurrence of cognates of *wolf, bear, lox* (Old English *leax* 'salmon'), but none for creatures indigenous to Asia—all this points to an area between northern Europe and southern Russia as the home of Indo-Europeans before their dispersion, just as the absence of a common word for *ocean* suggests, though it does not in itself prove, that this homeland was inland.

The early Indo-Europeans have been identified with the Kurgan culture of mound builders who lived northwest of the Caucasus and north of the Caspian Sea as early as the fifth millennium B.C. (Gimbutas, *Kurgan Culture*). They had domesticated cattle and horses, which they kept for milk and meat as well as for transportation. They combined farming with herding and were a mobile people, using four-wheeled wagons to cart their belongings on their treks. They built fortified palaces on hilltops (we have the Indo-European word for such forts in the *polis* of place names like *Indianapolis* and in our word *police*), as well as small villages nearby. Their society was a stratified one, with a warrior nobility and a common laboring class. They worshipped a sky god associated with thunder; and the sun, the horse, the boar, and the snake also were important in their religion. They had a highly developed belief in life after death, which led them to the construction of elaborate burial sites, by which their culture can be traced over much of Europe. Early in the fourth millennium B.C., they began expanding into the Balkans and northern Europe, and thereafter into Iran, Anatolia, and southern Europe.

Other locations have also been proposed for the Indo-European homeland. Northern central Europe, between the Vistula and the Elbe, was favored earlier. Eastern Anatolia (the area that is modern Turkey and was the site of the ancient Hittite empire) is yet another proposal. Those who favor the latter trace the spread of Indo-European languages along with techniques of agriculture in quite early times to Greece and thence to the rest of Europe. The dispersal of Indo-European was so early that we may never be sure of where it began or of the paths it followed.

→ *How Indo-European Was Discovered*

Even a casual comparison of English with some other languages reveals degrees of similarity among them. Thus English *father* clearly resembles German *Vater* (especially when one is aware that the letter *v* in German represents the same sound as *f*), Dutch *vader,* Icelandic *faðir,* and Norwegian, Danish, and Swedish *fader.* Although there is still a fair resemblance, the English word is not quite so similar to Latin *pater,* Spanish *padre,* Portuguese *pai,* Catalan *pare,* and French *père.* Greek *patēr,* Sanskrit *pitar-,* and Persian *pedar* are all strikingly like the Latin form, and (allowing for the loss of the first consonant) Gaelic *athair* resembles the others as well. It takes no great insight to recognize that those words for 'father' are somehow the "same." When such widespread similarity is reinforced by other parallels among the languages, we are forced to look for some explanation of the resemblances.

The explanation—that all those languages are historical developments of a no longer existing source language—was first proposed more than 200 years ago by Sir William Jones, a British judge and Sanskrit scholar in India. The Indo-European hypothesis, as it is called, is now well supported with evidence from many languages: a language once existed that developed in different ways in the various parts of the world to which its speakers traveled. We call it **Proto-Indo-European** (or simply **Indo-European**) because at the beginning of historical times languages derived from it were spoken from Europe in the west to India in the east. Its "descendants," which make up the **Indo-European family**, include all of the languages mentioned in the preceding paragraph, as well as Russian, Polish, Czech, Bulgarian, Albanian, Armenian, Romany (Gypsy), and many others.

Nineteenth-century philologists sometimes called the Indo-European family of languages *Aryan,* a Sanskrit term meaning 'noble,' which is what at least some of the languages' speakers immodestly called themselves. *Aryan* has also been used to name the branch of Indo-European spoken in Iran and India, now usually referred to as Indo-Iranian. The term *Aryan* was, however, generally given up by linguists after the Nazis appropriated it for their supposedly master race of Nordic features, but it is still found in its original senses in some older works on language. The term *Indo-European* has no racial connotations; it refers only to a group of people who lived in a relatively small area in early times and who spoke a more or less unified language out of which many languages have developed over thousands of years. These languages are spoken today by approximately half of the world's population.

LANGUAGE TYPOLOGY AND LANGUAGE FAMILIES

In talking about a **language family**, we use metaphors like "mother" and "daughter" languages and speak of degrees of "relationship," just as though languages had offspring that could be plotted on a genealogical, or family-tree, chart. The terms are convenient ones; but, in the discussion of linguistic "families" that follows, we must bear in mind that a language is not born, nor does it put out branches like a tree—nor, for that matter, does it die, except when every single one of its speakers dies, as has happened to Etruscan, Gothic, Cornish, and a good many other languages. We speak of Latin as a dead language, but in fact it still lives in various developments as Italian, French, Spanish, and the other Romance languages. In the same way, Proto-Indo-European continues in all the various present-day Indo-European languages, including English.

Hence the terms *family, ancestor, parent,* and other genealogical expressions applied to languages must be regarded as no more than metaphors. Languages are developments of older languages rather than descendants in the sense in which people are descendants of their ancestors. Thus Italian and Spanish are different developments of an earlier, more unified Latin. Latin, in turn, is one of a number of developments of a still earlier language called Italic. Italic, in its turn, is a development of Indo-European. Whether or not Indo-European has affinities with other languages spoken in prehistoric times, and is hence a development of an even earlier language, sometimes called **Nostratic**, is moot. And whether all human languages can be traced back to a single original speech, **Proto-World**, is even more so; for we are quite in the dark about how it all began.

Earlier scholars classified languages as **isolating**, **agglutinative**, **incorporative**, and **inflective**, exemplified respectively by Chinese, Turkish, Eskimo, and Latin. The isolating languages were once thought to be the most primitive type: they were languages in which each idea was expressed by a separate word and in which the words tended to be monosyllabic. But although Chinese is an isolating and monosyllabic language in its modern form, its earliest records (from the middle of the second millennium B.C.) represent not a primitive language but actually one in a late stage of development. There is no evidence that our prehistoric ancestors prattled in one-syllable words.

Earlier scholars also observed, quite correctly, that in certain languages, such as Turkish and Hungarian, words were made up of parts "stuck together," as it were; hence the term *agglutinative* (etymologically 'glued to'). In such languages, the elements that are put together are usually whole syllables having clear meanings. The inflectional suffixes of the Indo-European languages were supposed once to have been independent words; hence some believed that the inflective languages had grown out of the agglutinative. Little was known of what were called incorporative languages, in which major sentence elements are combined into a single word.

The trouble with such a classification is that it was based on the now-discarded theory that early peoples spoke in monosyllables. Furthermore, the difference between agglutinative and inflective was not well defined, and there was considerable overlapping. Nevertheless, the terms are useful and widely used in the description of specific languages or even groups of languages. Objective and well-informed **typological classification** has been especially useful in showing language similarities and differences (Greenberg, *Language Typology*).

From the historical point of view, however, much more satisfactory is the **genetic classification** of languages, made on the basis of such correspondences of sound and structure as indicate relationship through common origin. Perhaps the greatest contribution of nineteenth-century linguistic scholars was the painstaking investigation of those correspondences, many of which had been noted long before.

NON-INDO-EUROPEAN LANGUAGES

Before proceeding to a more detailed discussion of the Indo-European group, we look briefly at those languages and groups of languages that are *not* Indo-European. Two important groups have names that reflect the biblical attempt to derive all human races from the three sons of Noah: the **Semitic** (from the Latin form of the name of his eldest son, more correctly called Shem in English) and the **Hamitic** (from the name of his second son, Ham). The term *Japhetic* (from Noah's third son, Japheth) once used for Indo-European, has long been obsolete. On the basis of many phonological and morphological features that they share, Semitic and Hamitic are thought by many scholars to be related through a hypothetical common ancestor, Hamito-Semitic, or **Afroasiatic**, as it is usually called now. There are also those who believe in an ultimate relationship between Semitic and Indo-European, for which evidence is suggestive but inconclusive.

The Semitic group includes the following languages in three geographical sub-groups: (Eastern) Akkadian, whose varieties include Assyrian and Babylonian; (Western) Hebrew, Aramaic (the native speech of Jesus Christ), Phoenician, and Moabitic; and (Southern) Arabic and Ethiopic. Of these, only Arabic is spoken by large numbers of people over a widespread area. Hebrew has been revived comparatively recently in Israel, to some extent for nationalistic reasons. It is interesting to note that two of the world's most important religious documents are written in Semitic languages—the Jewish scriptures or Old Testament in Hebrew (with large portions of the books of Ezra and Daniel in Aramaic) and the Koran in Arabic.

To the Hamitic group belong Egyptian (called Coptic after the close of the third century of the Christian era), the Berber dialects of North Africa, various Cushitic dialects spoken along the upper Nile (named for Cush, a son of Ham), and Chadic in Chad and Nigeria. Arabic became the national language of Egypt in the course of the sixteenth century, replacing Coptic in that role.

Hamitic is unrelated to the other languages spoken in central and southern Africa, the vast region south of the Sahara. Those sub-Saharan languages are usually classified into three main groups: **Nilo-Saharan**, extending to the equator, a large and highly diversified group of languages whose relationships to one another are difficult and in some cases impossible to establish; **Niger-Kordofanian**, extending from the equator to the extreme south, a large group of languages of which the most important belong to the Bantu group, including Swahili; and the **Khoisan** languages, such as Hottentot and Bushman, spoken by small groups of people in the extreme southwestern part of Africa. Various of the Khoisan languages use clicks—the kind of sound used by English speakers as exclamations and conventionally represented by spellings such as *tsk-tsk* and *cluck-cluck,* but used as regular speech sounds in Khoisan and transcribed by slashes or exclamation points, as in the !O!kung language, spoken in Angola.

In south Asia, languages belonging to the **Dravidian** group were once spoken throughout India, where the earlier linguistic situation was radically affected by the Indo-European invasion of approximately 1500 B.C. They are the aboriginal languages of India but are now spoken mainly in southern India, such as Tamil and Telegu.

The **Sino-Tibetan** group includes the various languages of China, such as Cantonese and Mandarin, as well as Tibetan, Burmese, and others. Japanese is unrelated to Chinese, although it has borrowed the Chinese written characters and many Chinese words. It and Korean are sometimes thought to be members of the Altaic family, mentioned below, but the relationship is not certain. Ainu, the language of the aborigines of Japan, is not clearly related to any other language.

A striking characteristic of the **Austronesian** languages is their wide geographical distribution in the islands of the Indian and the Pacific oceans, stretching from Madagascar to Easter Island. They include Malay, Maori in New Zealand, Hawaiian, and other Polynesian languages. The native languages of Australia, spoken by only a few aborigines there nowadays, have no connection at all with Austronesian, nor have the more than a hundred languages spoken in New Guinea and neighboring islands.

American Indian languages are a geographic rather than a linguistic grouping, comprising many different language groups and even isolated languages showing very little relationship, if any, to one another. A very important and widespread group of American Indian languages is known as the **Uto-Aztecan**, which includes Nahuatl, the language spoken by the Aztecs, and various closely related dialects. Aleut and Eskimo, which are very similar to each other, are spoken in the Aleutians and all along the extreme northern coast of America and north to Greenland. In the Andes Mountains of South America, **Kechumaran** is a language stock that includes Aymara and Quechua, the speech of the Incan Empire. The isolation of the various groups, small in number to begin with and spread over so large a territory, may account to some extent for the great diversity of American Indian tongues.

Basque, spoken in many dialects by no more than half a million people living in the region of the Pyrenees, has always been something of a popular linguistic mystery. It now seems fairly certain, on the basis of coins and scanty inscriptions of the ancient Iberians, that Basque is related to the almost completely lost language of those people who once inhabited the Iberian peninsula and in Neolithic times were spread over an even larger part of Europe.

An important group of non-Indo-European languages spoken in Europe, as well as in parts of Asia, is the **Ural-Altaic**, with its two subgroups: the Uralic and Altaic. **Uralic** has two branches: **Samoyed**, spoken from northern European Russia into Siberia, and **Finno-Ugric**, including Finnish, Estonian, Lappish, and Hungarian. **Altaic** includes several varieties of Turkish, such as Ottoman Turkish (Osmanli) and that spoken in Turkestan and Azerbaijan, as well as Mongolian and Manchu.

It is likely that some of these non-Indo-European families are distantly related to each other and to Indo-European. Joseph Greenberg has posited a linguistic stock called Eurasiatic, which includes Indo-European, Ural-Altaic, and other languages such as Etruscan, Korean, Japanese, Aleut, and Eskimo. But as with Nostratic and Proto-World, alluded to above, the evidence is not compelling, whereas that for Indo-European is.

The foregoing is by no means a complete survey of non-Indo-European languages. We have merely mentioned some of the most important groups and individual languages, along with some that are of little significance as far as the numbers and present-day importance of their speakers are concerned but that are nevertheless interesting for one reason or another. In *A Guide to the World's Languages,* Merritt Ruhlen lists 17 phyla, with nearly 300 major groups and subgroups of languages and about 5,000 languages, of which 140 are Indo-European. Although Indo-European languages are fewer than 3 percent of the number of languages in the world, nearly half the world's population speaks them.

MAIN DIVISIONS OF THE INDO-EUROPEAN GROUP

Of some Indo-European languages—for example, Thracian, Phrygian, Macedonian, and Illyrian—we possess only the scantiest remains. It is likely that others have disappeared without leaving a trace. Members of the following subgroups survive as living tongues: Indo-Iranian, Balto-Slavic, Hellenic, Italic, Celtic, and Germanic. Albanian and Armenian are also Indo-European but do not fit into any of these subgroups. Anatolian and Tocharian are no longer spoken in any form.

The Indo-European languages have been classified into **satem languages** and **centum languages**, *satem* and *centum* being respectively the Avestan (an ancient Iranian language) and Latin words corresponding to *hundred.* The classification is based on the development, in very ancient times, of Indo-European palatal *k.*

In Indo-European, palatal *k* (as in **kmtom* 'hundred') was a distinct phoneme from velar *k* (as in the verbal root **kwer-* 'do, make,' which we have in the Sanskrit loanword *karma* and in the name *Sanskrit* itself, which means something like 'well-made'). (An asterisk before a form indicates that it is a **reconstruction** based on comparative study of what can be assumed to have existed.) In the *satem* languages—Indo-Iranian, Balto-Slavic, Armenian, and Albanian—the two *k* sounds remained separate phonemes, and the palatal *k* became a sibilant—for example, Sanskrit (Indic) *śatam,* Lithuanian (Baltic) *šimtas,* Old Church Slavic *sŭto.* In the other Indo-European languages, the two *k* sounds became a single phoneme, either remaining a *k,* as in Greek (Hellenic) *(he)katon* and Welsh (Celtic) *cant,* or shifting to *h* in the Germanic group, as in Old English *hund* (our *hundred* being a compound in which *-red* is a development of an originally independent

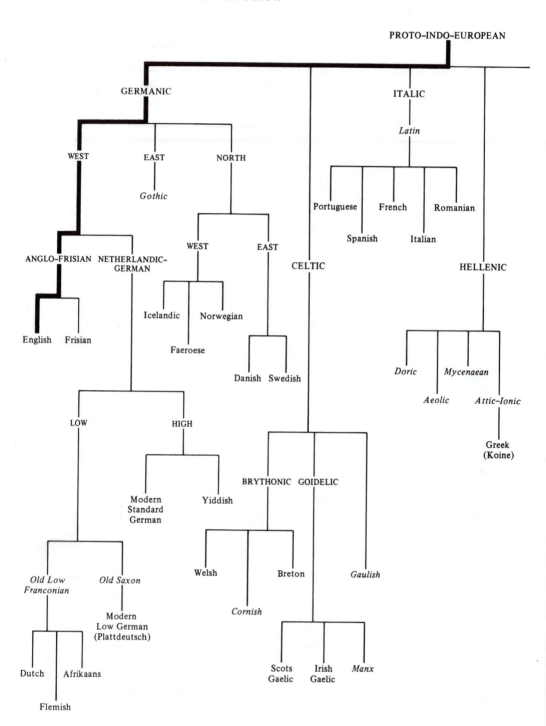

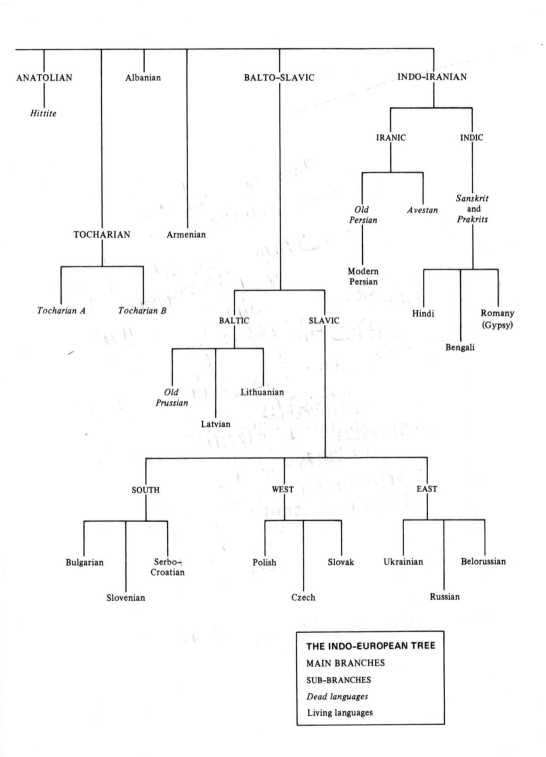

THE INDO-EUROPEAN TREE
MAIN BRANCHES
SUB-BRANCHES
Dead languages
Living languages

word meaning 'number'). In general, the *centum* languages tend to be spoken in the West and the *satem* languages in the East, although Tocharian, the easternmost of all Indo-European tongues, belonged to the *centum* group.

Indo-Iranian

The **Indo-Iranian** group (*Iranian* is from the same root as the word *Aryan*) is one of the oldest for which we have historical records. The Vedic hymns, written in an early form of Sanskrit, date from at least 1000 B.C. but reflect a poetic tradition stretching back to the second millennium B.C. Classical Sanskrit appears about 500 B.C. It is much more systematized than Vedic Sanskrit, for it had been seized upon by early grammarians who formulated rules for its proper use; the very name *Sanskrit* means 'well-made' or 'perfected.' The most remarkable of the Indian grammarians was Panini, who, at about the same time (fourth century B.C.) that the Greeks were indulging in fanciful speculations about language and in fantastic etymologizing, wrote a grammar of Sanskrit that to this day holds the admiration of linguistic scholars. And there were still other Indian writers on language whose work to preserve the language of the old sacred literature puts much of the grammatical writing of the Greeks and Romans to shame.

Sanskrit is still written by Indian scholars according to the old grammarians' rules. It is in no sense dead as a written language; its status is roughly comparable to that of Latin in medieval and Renaissance Europe.

Meanwhile, Indic dialects had developed, as we might expect, long before Sanskrit became a refined and learned language. They came to be known as Prakrits (a name that means 'natural,' thus emphasizing the "well-made-ness" of Sanskrit), and some of them—notably Pali, the religious language of Buddhism—achieved high literary status. From these Prakrits are indirectly derived the various non-Dravidian languages of India, the most widely known of which are Bengali, Hindi, Hindustani (a variety of Hindi, with mixed word stock), and Urdu, derived from Hindustani.

Romany (Gypsy) is also an Indic dialect, with many loanwords from other languages acquired in the course of the Gypsies' wanderings. When they first appeared in Europe in the late Middle Ages, many people supposed them to be Egyptians—whence the name given them in English and some other languages. A long time passed before the study of their language was to indicate that they had come originally from northwestern India. The name *Romany* has nothing to do with *Rome*, but is derived from the Gypsy word *rom* 'human being.' Likewise the *rye* of *Romany rye* (that is, 'Gypsy gentleman') has nothing to do with the cereal crop, but is a Gypsy word akin to Sanskrit *rajan* 'king,' as well as to Latin *rex,* German *Reich,* and English *regal* and *royal* (from Latin and French).

Those Indo-Europeans who settled in the Iranian Plateau developed a sacred language, Avestan, preserved in the religious book the Avesta, after which the language is named. There are no modern descendants of Avestan, which is believed by some to be the language of the Medes, whose name is frequently coupled with that of the Persians, most notably in the phrase "the law of the Medes and Persians, which altereth not" (Daniel 6.8). Avestan was the language of the sage Zarathustra—Zoroaster to the Greeks—many of whose followers fled to India at the time of the Muslim conquest of their country in the eighth century. They are the ancestors of the modern Parsis (that is, Persians) of Bombay. Old Persian is a different language from Avestan; it was the language of the district known to the Greeks as Persis, whose inhabitants under the leadership of Cyrus the Great in the sixth century B.C. became the predominant tribe.

Armenian and Albanian

Armenian and **Albanian**, as already mentioned, are independent subgroups. The first has in its word stock so many Persian loanwords that it was once supposed to belong to the Indo-Iranian group; it also has many borrowings from Greek and from Arabic and Syrian.

Albanian also has a mixed vocabulary, with words from Italian, Slavic, Turkish, and Greek. It is possibly related to the ancient language of Illyria in an Illyrian branch of Indo-European. Evidence of the ancient language is so meager, however, and modern Albanian has been so much influenced by neighboring languages that it is difficult to tell much about its affinities.

Tocharian

The **Tocharian** language had two varieties, called Tocharian A (an eastern dialect) and Tocharian B (a western dialect). The language is misnamed. When it was discovered at the end of the last century in some volumes of Buddhist scriptures and monastic business accounts from central Asia, it was at first thought to be a form of Iranian and so was named after an extinct Iranian people known to the ancient Greek geographer Strabo as Tocharoi. Later it was discovered that Tocharian is linguistically quite different from Iranian. Nevertheless, the name has stuck; the language itself has long been extinct.

Anatolian

Shortly after the discovery of Tocharian, another group of Indo-European languages was identified in Asia Minor. Excavations at the capital city of the Hittites (a people mentioned in the Old Testament and in Egyptian records from the second millennium B.C.) uncovered the royal archives. They contained works in a number of ancient languages, including one otherwise unknown. As the writings in the unknown tongue were deciphered, it became clear that the language, Hittite, was Indo-European, although it had been profoundly influenced by non-Indo-European languages spoken around it. Later scholars identified several different but related languages (Luwian, Palaic, Lydian), and the new branch was named **Anatolian**, after the area where it was spoken. One of the interesting features of Hittite is that it preserves an Indo-European "laryngeal" sound (translit-erated *h*) that was lost in all of the other Indo-European languages (for example, in Hittite *pahhur* 'fire' compared with Greek *pûr,* Umbrian *pir,* Czech *pýř,* Tocharian *por,* and Old English *fyr*).

Balto-Slavic

Although the oldest records of the Baltic and the Slavic languages show them as quite different, most scholars have assumed a common ancestor closer than Indo-European, called **Balto-Slavic**. The chief Baltic language is Lithuanian; the closely related Latvian is spoken in Latvia, to the north of Lithuania. Lithuanian is quite conservative phonologically, so that one can find a number of words in it that are very similar in form to cognate words in older Indo-European languages—for example, Lithuanian *Diẽvas* and Sanskrit *devás* 'god' or Lithuanian *platùs* and Greek *platús* 'broad.'

Still another Baltic language, Old Prussian, was spoken as late as the seven-teenth century in what is now called East Prussia, which was considered outside of Germany until the early years of the nineteenth century. Prussia in time became the predominant state of the new German Empire. The Prussians, like the Lithuanians and the Latvians, were heathens until the end of the Middle Ages, when they were converted at the point of the sword by the Knights of the Teutonic Order—a mili-tary order that was an outcome of the Crusades. The aristocracy of the region (their descendants are the Prussian *Junkers*) came to be made up of members of this order, who, having saved the souls of the heathen Balts, proceeded to take over their lands.

Slavic falls into three main subdivisions: East Slavic includes Russian, Ukrainian, and Belorussian, spoken directly to the north of the Ukraine. West Slavic includes Polish, Czech, the relatively similar Slovak, and Sorbian (or Wendish), a language spoken by a small group of people in eastern Germany; these languages have lost many of the early forms preserved in East Slavic. The South Slavic languages include Bulgarian, Serbo-Croatian, and Slovenian. The oldest Slavic writing we know is in Old Church Slavic (or Slavonic), which remained a liturgical language long after it ceased to be generally spoken.

Hellenic

In ancient times there were many **Hellenic** dialects, among them Mycenaean, Aeolic, Doric, and Attic-Ionic. Athens came to assume tremendous prestige, so its dialect, Attic, became the basis of a standard for the entire Greek world, a **koine** 'common (dialect),' which was ultimately to drive out the other Hellenic dialects. Most of the local dialects spoken in Greece today, as well as the standard language, are derived from Attic. Despite all their glorious ancient literature, the Greeks have not had a modern literary language until comparatively recently. The new literary standard makes considerable use of words revived from ancient Greek, as well as a number of ancient inflectional forms; it has become the ordinary language of the upper classes. A more natural development of the Attic koine is spoken by the masses and hence called *demotike.*

Italic

In ancient Italy, the main Indo-European language was Latin, the speech of Latium, whose chief city was Rome. Oscan and Umbrian have long been thought to be sister languages of Latin within the **Italic** subfamily, but now it appears they may be members of an independent branch of Indo-European whose resemblance to Latin is due to the long period of contact between their speakers. It is well known that languages, even unrelated ones, that are spoken in the same area and share bilingual speakers (in an association called a **Sprachbund**) will influence one another and thus grow more alike.

Whatever its relationship to Osco-Umbrian, Latin early became the most important language of the peninsula. As Rome came to dominate the Mediterranean world, spreading its influence into Gaul, Spain, and the Illyrian and Danubian countries (and even into Britain, where Latin failed to displace Celtic), its language became a koine as the dialect of Athens had been earlier. Spoken Latin, as has been noted, survives in the **Romance** languages. It was quite a different thing from the more or less artificial literary language of Cicero. All the Romance languages—such as Italian, Spanish, Catalan, Galician, Portuguese, French, Provençal, and Romanian—are developments of **Vulgar Latin** (so called because it was the speech of the *vulgus* 'common people') spoken in various parts of the Roman Empire in the early Middle Ages.

French dialects have included Norman, the source of the Anglo-Norman dialect spoken in England after the Norman Conquest; Picard; and the dialect of Paris and the surrounding regions (the Île-de-France), which for obvious reasons became standard French. In southern Belgium a dialect of French, called Walloon, is spoken. The highly similar varieties of French spoken in Quebec, Nova Scotia, New Brunswick, and Louisiana are developments of the dialects of northern France and are no more to be regarded as "corruptions" of standard (Modern) French than American English is to be regarded as a corruption of the present British standard. The Cajuns (that is, Acadians) of Louisiana are descendants of exiles from Nova Scotia, which was earlier a French colony called Acadia.

The speech of the old kingdom of Castile, the largest and most important part of Spain, became standard Spanish. The fact that Spanish America was settled largely by people from Andalusia rather than from Castile accounts for the most important differences in pronunciation between Latin American Spanish and the standard language of Spain.

Because of the cultural preeminence of Tuscany during the Italian Renaissance, the speech of that region—and specifically of the city of Florence—became the standard of Italian speech. Both Dante and Petrarch wrote in this form of Italian. Rhaeto-Romanic comprises a number of dialects spoken in the most easterly Swiss canton called the Grisons (German *Graubünden*) and in the Tyrol.

Celtic

Celtic shows such striking correspondences with Italic in certain parts of its verbal system and in inflectional endings that the relationship between them must have been close, though not so close as that between Indic and Iranian or Baltic and Slavic. Some scholars therefore group them together as developments of a branch they call Italo-Celtic.

The Celts were spread over a huge territory in Europe long before the emergence in history of the Germanic peoples. Before the beginning of the Christian era, Celtic languages were spoken over the greater part of central and western Europe. By the latter part of the third century B.C., Celts had spread even to Asia Minor, in the region called for them Galatia (part of modern Turkey), to whose inhabitants Saint Paul later addressed a famous letter. As the fortunes and the warlike vigor of the Celts declined, their languages were supplanted by those of their conquerors. Thus the Celtic language spoken in Gaul (Gaulish) gave way completely to the Latin spoken by the Roman conquerors, which was to develop into French.

Roman rule did not prevent the British Celts from using their own language, although they borrowed a good many words from Latin. But after the Angles, Saxons, and Jutes arrived—British (Brythonic) Celtic was more severely threatened. It survived, however, and produced a distinguished literature in the later Middle Ages, including the *Mabinogion* and many Arthurian stories. In recent years, Welsh (Cymric) has been actively promoted for nationalistic reasons. Breton is the language of the descendants of those Britons who, around the time of the Anglo-Saxon invasion of their island and even somewhat before that time, crossed the English Channel and settled in the Gaulish province of Armorica, naming their new home for their old one—Brittany. Breton is thus more closely related to Welsh than to long-extinct Gaulish. There have been no native speakers of Cornish, another Brythonic language, since the early nineteenth century. Efforts have been made to revive it: church services are sometimes conducted in Cornish, and the language is used in antiquarian re-creations of the Celtic Midsummer Eve rituals— but such efforts seem more sentimental than practical.

It is not known whether Pictish, preserved in a few glosses and place-name elements, was a Celtic language. It was spoken by the Picts in the northwestern part of Britain, where many Gaelic Celts also settled. These settlers from Ireland, who were called Scots (*Scotti*), named their new home Scotia, or Scotland. The Celtic language that spread from Ireland, called Gaelic or Goidelic, was of a type somewhat different from that of the Britons. It survives in Scots Gaelic, sometimes called Erse, a word that is simply a variant of *Irish*. Gaelic is spoken in the remoter parts of the Scottish highlands and the Outer Hebrides and in Nova Scotia; in a somewhat different development, it survived until recently on the Isle of Man (where it was called Manx).

In Ireland, which was little affected by either the Roman or the later Anglo-Saxon invasions, Irish Gaelic was gradually replaced by English. It has survived in some of the western counties, though most of its speakers are now bilingual. Efforts have been made to revive the language for nationalistic reasons in Eire, and it is taught in schools throughout the land; but this resuscitation, less successful than that of Hebrew in modern Israel, cannot be regarded as in any sense a natural development. In striking contrast to their wide distribution in earlier times, today the Celtic languages are restricted to a few relatively small areas abutting the Atlantic Ocean on the northwest coast of Europe.

Germanic

The **Germanic** group is particularly important for us because English belongs to it. Over many centuries, certain radical developments occurred in the more or less unified language spoken by those Indo-European peoples living in Denmark and the regions thereabout. **Proto-Germanic** (or simply **Germanic**) is the usual term for the relatively unified language—distinctive in many of its sounds, its inflections, its accentual system, and its word stock—which resulted from these developments.

Unfortunately for us, those who spoke this particular development of Indo-European did not write. Proto-Germanic is to German, Dutch, the Scandinavian languages, and English as Latin is to Italian, French, and Spanish. But Proto-Germanic, which was probably being spoken shortly before the beginning of the Christian era, must be reconstructed just like Indo-European, whereas Latin is amply recorded.

Because Germanic was spread over a large area, it developed marked dialectal differences leading to a division into North Germanic, West Germanic, and East Germanic. The **North Germanic** languages are Danish, Swedish, Norwegian, Icelandic, and Faeroese, the last named being very similar to Icelandic and spoken in the Faeroe Islands, in the North Atlantic about midway between Iceland and Great Britain.

The **West Germanic** languages are High German, Low German (*Plattdeutsch*), Dutch (and the practically identical Flemish), Frisian, and English. Yiddish developed from medieval High German dialects, with many words from Hebrew and Slavic. Before World War II, it was a sort of international language of the Jews, with a literature of high quality. Since that time, it has declined greatly in use, with most Jews adopting the language of the country in which they live; and its decline has been accelerated by the revival of Hebrew in Israel. Afrikaans is a development of seventeenth-century Dutch spoken in South Africa. Pennsylvania Dutch (that is, *Deutsch*) is actually a High German dialect spoken by descendants of early American settlers from southern Germany and Switzerland.

The only **East Germanic** language of which we have any detailed knowledge is Gothic. The earliest records in any Germanic language, aside from a few proper names recorded by classical authors, a few loanwords in Finnish, and some runic inscriptions found in Scandinavia, are those of Gothic. Almost all our knowledge of Gothic comes from a translation of parts of the New Testament made in the fourth century by Wulfila, bishop of the Visigoths, those Goths who lived north of the

Danube. There are also small fragments of two other books of the Bible and of a commentary on the Gospel of John. Late as they are in comparison with the literary records of Sanskrit, Iranian, Greek, and Latin, these remains of Gothic provide us with a clear picture of a Germanic language in an early stage of development and hence are of tremendous importance to the student of Germanic languages.

Gothic as a spoken tongue disappeared a long time ago without leaving a trace. No modern Germanic languages are derived from it, nor do any of the other Germanic languages have any Gothic loanwords. Vandalic and Burgundian were apparently also East Germanic in structure, but we know little more of them than a few proper names.

During the eighteenth-century "Age of Reason," the term *Gothic* was applied to the "dark ages" of the Medieval period as a term of contempt, and hence to the architecture of that period to distinguish it from classical building styles. The general eighteenth-century sense of the word was 'barbarous, savage, in bad taste.' Later the term was used for the type fonts formerly used to print German (also called *black letter*). Then it denoted a genre of novel set in a desolate or remote landscape, with mysterious or macabre characters and often a violent plot. Finally in recent generations it has been applied to an outré style of dress, cosmetics, and coiffure, featuring black and accompanied by heavy metal adornments and body piercing in unlikely parts of the anatomy. Thus the name of a people and a language long ago lost to history survives in uses that have nothing to do with the Goths and would doubtless have both puzzled and amazed them.

COGNATE WORDS IN THE INDO-EUROPEAN LANGUAGES

Words of similar form and of similar or often identical meaning in two languages are said to be **cognate**—that is, of common origin (Latin *co-* and *gnātus* 'born together'), and languages that have developed from a common ancestor are also called cognate. Thus the verb roots meaning 'bear, carry' in Sanskrit (*bhar-*), Greek (*pher-*), Latin (*fer-*), Gothic (*bair-*), and Old English (*ber-*) are cognate, all being developments of Indo-European **bher-*. Cognate words do not necessarily look much alike: their resemblance may be disguised by sound shifts that have occurred in the various languages of the Indo-European group. English *work* and Greek *ergon,* for example, are superficially unlike, but they are both developments of Indo-European **wergom* and therefore are cognates. Sometimes, however, there is greater similarity—for example, between Latin *ignis* and Sanskrit *agnis* from Indo-European **egnis* 'fire,' a root that is unrelated to the other words for 'fire' cited earlier.

The most frequently cited cognate words are those that have been preserved in a large number of Indo-European languages; some have in fact been preserved in all. These common related words include the numerals from one to ten, the word meaning the sum of ten tens (*cent-, sat-, hund-*), words for certain bodily parts (related, for example, to *heart, lung, head, foot*), words for certain natural phenomena (related, for example, to *air, night, star, snow, sun, moon, wind*), certain plant and animal names (related, for example, to *beech, corn, wolf, bear*), and certain cultural terms (related, for example, to *yoke, mead, weave, sew*). Cognates of practically all our taboo words—those monosyllables that pertain to sex and excretion and that seem to cause great pain to many people—are to be found in other Indo-European languages. Historically, if not socially, those ancient words are just as legitimate as any other words.

One needs no special training to perceive the correspondences between the following words:

LATIN	GREEK	WELSH	ENGLISH	ICELANDIC	DUTCH
ūnus	oinē[1]	un	one	einn	een
duo	duo	dau	two	tveir	twee
trēs	treis	tri	three	þrír	drie

[1] 'one-spot on a die'

Comparison of the forms designating the second digit indicates that non-Germanic *d* (as in the Latin, Greek, and Welsh forms) corresponds to Germanic *t* (English, Icelandic, and Dutch). A similar comparison of the forms for the third digit indicates that non-Germanic *t* corresponds to Germanic θ, the initial sound of *three* and *þrír* in English and Icelandic. Allowing for later changes—as in the case of θ, which became *d* in Dutch, as also in German (*drei* 'three'), and *t* in Danish, Norwegian, and Swedish (*tre*)—these same correspondences are perfectly regular in other cognates in which those consonants appear. We may safely assume that the non-Germanic consonants are older than the Germanic ones. Hence we may accept with confidence (assuming a similar comparison of the vowels) the reconstructions **oinos, *dwō,* and **treyes* as representing the Indo-European forms from which the existing forms developed. Comparative linguists, of course, have used all the Indo-European languages as a basis for their conclusions regarding correspondences, not just the few cited here.

INFLECTION IN THE INDO-EUROPEAN LANGUAGES

All Indo-European languages are **inflective**—that is, all have a grammatical system based on modifications in the form of words, by means of **inflections** (that is, endings and vowel changes), to indicate such **grammatical functions** as case, number, tense, person, mood, aspect, and the like. Examples of such inflections in Modern English are *cat-cats, mouse-mice, who-whom-whose, walk-walks-walked-walking,* and *sing-sings-sang-sung-singing.* The original Indo-European inflectional system is very imperfectly represented in most modern languages: English, French, and Spanish, for instance, have lost much of the inflectional complexity that once characterized them; German retains considerably more, with its various forms of the noun and the article and its strong adjective declension. Sanskrit is notable for the remarkably clear picture it gives us of the older Indo-European inflectional system; it retains much that has been lost or changed in the other Indo-European languages, so that its forms show us, even better than Greek or Latin can, what the system of Indo-European must have been.

Some Verb Inflections

When allowance is made for regularly occurring sound changes, the relationship of the personal endings of the verb in the various Indo-European languages becomes clear. For example, the present indicative of the Sanskrit verb cognate with English *to bear* is as follows:

SANSKRIT	
bharā-mi	'I bear'
bhara-si	'thou bearest'
bhara-ti	'he/she beareth'
bharā-mas	'we bear'
bhara-tha	'you (*pl.*) bear'
bhara-nti	'they bear'

The only irregularity here is the occurrence of -*mi* in the first person singular, as against -*o* in the Greek and Latin forms cited immediately below. It was a peculiarity of Sanskrit to extend -*mi,* the regular first person ending of verbs that had no vowel affixed to their roots, to those that did have such a vowel. This vowel (for example, the -*a* suffixed to the root *bhar-* of the Sanskrit word cited) is called the **thematic vowel**. The **root** of a word plus such a suffix is called the **stem**. To these stems are added endings. The comparatively few verbs lacking such a vowel in Indo-European are called **athematic**. The *m* in English *am* is a remnant of an Indo-European ending in such athematic verbs.

Leaving out of consideration for the moment differences in vowels and in initial consonants, compare the personal endings of the present indicative forms as they developed from Indo-European into the cognate Greek and Latin verbs:

GREEK	LATIN
pherō[1]	ferō
pherei-s	fer-s[3]
pherei[2]	fer-t
phero-mes (Doric)	feri-mus
phere-te	fer-tis
phero-nti (Doric)	feru-nt

[1]In Indo-European thematic verbs, the first person singular present indicative had no ending at all, but only a lengthening of the thematic vowel.

[2]The expected form would be *phere-ti.* The ending -*ti,* however, does occur elsewhere in the third person singular—for instance, in Doric *didōti* 'he gives.'

[3]In this verb, the lack of the thematic vowel is exceptional. The expected forms would be *feri-s, feri-t, feri-tis* in the second and third persons singular and the second person plural, respectively.

Comparison of the personal endings of the verbs in these and other languages leads to the conclusion that the Indo-European endings were as follows (the Indo-European reconstruction of the entire word is given in parentheses):

INDO-EUROPEAN	
-ō, -mi	(*bherō)
-si	(*bheresi)
-ti	(*bhereti)
-mes, -mos	(*bheromes)
-te	(*bherete)
-nti	(*bheronti)

The Germanic development of these personal endings are illustrated by the Gothic and early Old English forms:

GOTHIC	EARLY OLD ENGLISH
bair-a	ber-u, -o
bairi-s	biri-s
bairi-þ	biri-þ
baira-m	bera-þ[1]
bairi-þ	bera-þ
baira-nd	bera-þ

[1]From the earliest period of Old English, the form of the third person plural was used throughout the plural. This form, *beraþ,* from earlier **beranþ,* shows Anglo-Frisian loss of *n* before *þ.*

Germanic *þ* (that is, [θ]) corresponds as a rule to Proto-Indo-European *t.* Leaving out of consideration such details as the *-nd* (instead of expected *-nþ*) in the Gothic third person plural form, for which there is a soundly based explanation, it is perfectly clear that the Germanic personal endings correspond to those of the non-Germanic Indo-European languages.

Some Noun Inflections

Indo-European nouns were inflected for eight **cases**: nominative, vocative, accusative, genitive, dative, ablative, locative, and instrumental. These cases are modifications in the form of nouns, pronouns, and adjectives that show the relationship of such words to other words in a sentence. Typical uses of the eight Indo-European cases (with Modern English examples) were as follows:

nominative: subject of a sentence (*They* saw me.)

vocative: person addressed (*Officer,* I need help.)

accusative: direct object (They saw *me.*)

genitive: possessor or source (*Shakespeare's* play.)

dative: indirect object, recipient (Give *her* a hand.)

ablative: what is separated (He abstained *from it.*)

locative: place where (We stayed *home.*)

instrumental: means, instrument (She ate *with chopsticks.*)

The full array of cases is preserved in Sanskrit but not generally in the other descendant languages, which simplified the noun declension in various ways. The paradigms in the following table show the singular and plural of the word for 'horse' in Proto-Indo-European and five other Indo-European languages. Indo-European also had a dual number for designating two of anything, which is not illustrated.

INDO-EUROPEAN NOUN DECLENSION[1]

	INDO-EUROPEAN	SANSKRIT	GREEK	LATIN	OLD IRISH	OLD ENGLISH
Singular						
Nom.	*ekwos	aśvas	hippos	equus	ech	eoh
Voc.	*ekwe	aśva	hippe	eque	eich	
Acc.	*ekwom	aśvam	hippon	equum	ech n-[2]	eoh
Gen.	*ekwosyo	aśvasya	hippou	equī	eich	ēos
Dat.	*ekwōy	aśvāya	hippōi	equō	eoch	ēo
Abl.	*ekwōd	aśvād		equō		
Loc.	*ekwoy	aśve				
Ins.	*ekwō	aśvena				
Plural						
N./V.	*ekwōs	aśvās	hippoi	equī	eich	ēos
Acc.	*ekwons	aśvān(s)	hippous	equōs	eochu	ēos
Gen.	*ekwōm	aśvānām	hippōn	equōrum	ech n-[2]	ēona
D./Ab.	*ekwobh(y)os	aśvebhyas	hippois	equīs	echaib	ēom
Loc.	*ekwoysu	aśveṣu				
Ins.	*ekwōys	aśvais				

[1]There are a good many complexities in these forms, some of which are noted here. In Greek, for the genitive singular, the Homeric form *hippoio* is closer to Indo-European in its ending. The Greek,

WORD ORDER IN THE INDO-EUROPEAN LANGUAGES

Early studies of the Indo-European languages focused on cognate words and on inflections. More recently, attention has been directed to other matters of the grammar, especially word order in the parent language. Joseph Greenberg ("Some Universals of Grammar") proposes that the orders in which various grammatical elements occur in a sentence are not random, but are interrelated. For example, languages like Modern English that place objects after verbs tend to place modifiers after nouns, to put conjunctions before the second of two words they connect, and to use prepositions:

verb + *object:* (The workman) made *a horn.*

noun + *modifier:* (They marveled at the) size *of the building.*

conjunction + *noun:* (Congress is divided into the Senate) and *the House.*

preposition + *object:* (Harold fought) with *him.*

On the other hand, languages like Japanese that place objects before verbs tend to reverse the order of those other elements, placing modifiers before nouns, putting conjunctions after the second of two words they connect, and using postpositions. Most languages can be identified as basically either **VO languages** (like English) or **OV languages** (like Japanese), although it is usual for a language to have some characteristics of both types. English, for example, regularly puts adjectives before the nouns they modify rather than after them, as VO order would imply.

Winfred P. Lehmann (*Proto-Indo-European Syntax*) has marshaled evidence suggesting that Proto-Indo-European was an OV language, even though the existing Indo-European languages are generally VO in type. Earlier stages of those languages often show OV characteristics that have been lost from the modern tongues or that are less common than formerly. For example, one of the oldest records of a Germanic language is a runic inscription identifying the workman who made a horn about A.D. 400:

Latin, and Old Irish nominative plurals show developments of the pronominal ending *-oi,* rather than of the nominal ending *-ōs.* Celtic was alone among the Indo-European branches in having different forms for the nominative and vocative plural; the Old Irish vocative plural was *eochu* (like the accusative plural), a development of the original nominative plural *ekwōs.* The Greek and Latin dative-ablative plurals were originally instrumental forms that took over the functions of the other cases; similarly, the Old Irish dative plural was probably a variant instrumental form. The Latin genitive singular -ī is not from the corresponding Indo-European ending, but is a special ending found in Italic and Celtic (OIr. *eich* being from the variant *ekwī*).

[2]The Old Irish *n*- in the accusative singular and genitive plural is the initial consonant of the following word.

ek hlewagastiʀ holtijaʀ   horna tawido
I, Hlewagastir Holtson, [this] horn   made.

The order of words in sentences like this one (subject, object, verb) suggests that Proto-Germanic had more OV characteristics than the languages that evolved from it.

In standard Modern German a possessive modifier, as in *der Garten des Mannes* 'the garden of the man,' normally follows the word it modifies; the other order—*des Mannes Garten* 'the man's garden'—is possible, but it is poetic and old-fashioned. In older periods of the language, however, it was normal. Similarly, in Modern English a possessive modifier can come either before a noun (an OV characteristic), as in *the building's size,* or after it (a VO characteristic), as in *the size of the building,* but there has long been a tendency to favor the second order, which has increased in frequency throughout much of the history of English. In the tenth century, practically all possessives came before nouns, but by the fourteenth century, the overwhelming percentage of them came after nouns (84.4 to 15.6 percent, Rosenbach 179). This change was perhaps under the influence of French, which may have provided the model for the phrasal genitive with *of* (translating Fr. *de*).

When we want to join two words, we put the conjunction before the second one (a VO characteristic), as in *the Senate and people,* but Latin, preserving an archaic feature of Indo-European, had the option of putting a conjunction after the second noun (an OV characteristic), as in *senatus populusque,* in which *-que* is a conjunction meaning 'and.' Modern English uses prepositions almost exclusively, but Old English often put such words after their objects, using them as postpositions, thus:

Harold him wið gefeaht.
Harold him with fought.

Evidence of this kind, which can be found in all the older forms of Indo-European and which becomes more frequent the farther back in history one searches, suggests that Indo-European once ordered its verbs after their objects. If that is so, by late Indo-European times a change had begun that was to result in a shift of word-order type in many of the descendant languages. This kind of reconstruction depends not only on comparing languages with one another but also on comparing different historical stages of the same language, and it assumes that various kinds of word order are interconnected. For those reasons, it is less certain than the reconstruction of inflections and of vocabulary.

MAJOR CHANGES FROM INDO-EUROPEAN TO GERMANIC

One group of Indo-European speakers, the Germanic peoples, settled in northern Europe near Denmark. Germanic became differentiated from earlier Indo-European principally in the following respects:

1. Germanic has a large number of words that have no known cognates in other Indo-European languages. These could have existed, of course, in Indo-European but been lost from all other languages of the family. It is more likely, however, that they were developed during the Proto-Germanic period or taken from non-Indo-European languages originally spoken in the area occupied by the Germanic peoples. A few words that are apparently distinctively Germanic, given in their Modern English forms, are *broad, drink, drive, fowl, hold, meat, rain,* and *wife.* The Germanic languages also share a common influence from Latin, treated in Chapter 12 (272–3).

2. All Indo-European distinctions of tense and aspect were lost in the verb, except the **present** and the **preterit** (or past) tenses. This simplification of a more complex Indo-European verbal system (though it was not so complex as that which developed in Latin, Greek, and Sanskrit) is reflected in all the languages which have developed out of Germanic—in English *bind-bound,* as well as in German *binden-band,* Old Norse *binda-band,* and all the rest. No Germanic language has anything comparable to such forms as those of the Latin future, perfect, pluperfect, and future perfect forms (for instance, *laudābō, laudāvī, laudāveram, laudāverō*), which must be rendered in the Germanic languages by verb phrases (for instance, English *I shall praise, I have praised, I had praised, I shall have praised*).

3. Germanic developed a preterit tense form with a **dental suffix**, that is, one containing *d* or *t.* All Germanic languages thus have two types of verbs. Verbs that employ the dental suffix were called **weak** by Jacob Grimm because, being incapable of the type of internal change of *rise-rose* and *sing-sang* (which he called **strong**), they had to make do with suffixes, like *tug-tugged* and *talk-talked.* Although Grimm's terminology is not very satisfactory, it has become traditional. An overwhelming majority of our verbs add the dental suffix in the preterit, so it has become the regular way of inflecting verbs. Indeed, it is the only living way of doing so in English and the other Germanic languages, so new verbs form their preterit that way: *televise-televised, rev-revved, diss-dissed,* and so forth. Furthermore, many verbs that were once strong have become weak. Historically speaking, however, the vowel gradation of the strong verbs (as in *drive-drove, know-knew*) was quite regular, and some of the weak verbs are quite irregular. *Bring, think,* and *buy,* for instance, are weak verbs, as the dental suffix of *brought, thought,* and *bought* indicates; the vowel changes do not make them strong verbs. The suffix is the real test. No attempt at explaining the origin of this suffix has been wholly satisfactory. Many have thought that it was originally an independent word related to *do.*

4. All the older forms of Germanic had two ways of declining their adjectives. The **weak declension** was used chiefly when the adjective modified a definite noun and was preceded by the kind of word that developed into the definite article. The **strong declension** was used otherwise. Thus Old English had *þā geongan ceorlas* 'the young fellows (churls),' with the weak form of *geong,* but *geonge ceorlas* 'young fellows,' with the strong form. The distinction is preserved in present-day German: *die jungen Kerle,* but *junge Kerle.* This particular Germanic characteristic cannot be illustrated in Modern English, because in the course of its development English has lost all such declension of the adjective.

5. The "free" accentual system of Indo-European, in which the accent shifted from one syllable to another in various forms of a word, gave way to the Germanic type of accentuation in which the first syllable was regularly stressed. Exceptions were verbs like modern *believe* and *forget,* in which the initial syllable was a prefix. None of the Germanic languages has anything comparable to the shifting accentuation of Latin *vírī* 'men,' *virórum* 'of the men' or of *hábeō* 'I have,' *habḗmus* 'we have.' Compare the paradigms of the Greek and Old English developments of Indo-European **pǝtḗr* 'father':

	GREEK	OLD ENGLISH
Singular nominative	patḗr	fǽder
Singular genitive	patrós	fǽder(es)
Singular dative	patrí	fǽder
Singular accusative	patéra	fǽder
Singular vocative	páter	fǽder
Plural nominative	patéres	fǽderas
Plural genitive	patérōn	fǽdera
Plural dative	patrási	fǽderum
Plural accusative	patéras	fǽderas

In the Greek forms, the accent may occur on the suffix, the ending, or the root, unlike the Old English forms, which have their accent fixed on the first syllable of the root. Germanic accent is also predominantly a matter of **stress** (loudness) rather than **pitch** (tone); Indo-European seems to have had both types of accent at different stages of its development.

6. Some Indo-European vowels were modified in Germanic. Indo-European *o* was retained in Latin but became *a* in Germanic (compare Lat. *octo* 'eight,' Gothic *ahtau*). Conversely, Indo-European *ā* became Germanic *ō* (Lat. *māter* 'mother,' OE *mōdor*).

7. The Indo-European stops *bh, dh, gh; p, t, k; b, d, g* were all modified in what is called the **First Sound Shift** or **Grimm's Law**. These modifications were gradual, extending over long periods of time, but the sounds eventually appear in Germanic languages as, respectively, *b, d, g; f, θ, h; p, t, k.*

FIRST SOUND SHIFT

Grimm's Law

Because the First Sound Shift, described by Grimm's Law, is such an important difference between Germanic and other Indo-European languages, we illustrate it more fully by a series of forms consisting of a reconstructed Indo-European root or word (omitting the asterisk that marks reconstructed forms for convenience), the corresponding word from a non-Germanic language (usually Latin), and the corresponding native English word. (Only a single Indo-European root is given for each set, although the following words may be derived from slightly different forms of that root. Therefore, the correspondence between the two derived words and the Indo-European root may not be exact in all details other than the initial consonants.)

1. Indo-European *bh, dh, gh* (voiced stops with a puff of air or aspiration, represented phonetically by a superscript [ʰ]) became respectively the Germanic voiced fricatives, β, ð, ɣ, and later, in initial position at least, *b, d, g*. Stated in phonetic terms, aspirated voiced stops became voiced fricatives and then unaspirated voiced stops. These Indo-European aspirated sounds also underwent changes in most non-Germanic languages. Their developments in Latin, Greek, and Germanic are shown in the following table:

Indo-European	bh	dh	gh	(that is, [bʰ], [dʰ], and [gʰ])
Latin	f-	f-	h-	(initially; medially: -b-, -d- or -b-, -g-)
Greek	φ	θ	χ	(that is, [pʰ], [tʰ], [kʰ], transliterated *ph, th, ch*)
Germanic	b	d	g	

Unless these non-Germanic changes are kept in mind, the examples cited below will not make sense:

INDO-EUROPEAN *bh* / LATIN *f-*, GREEK *ph* / GERMANIC *b*

bhrāter / frāter / brother
bhibhru- / fiber / beaver
bhlē / flāre / blow
bhreg- / fra(n)go / break
bhudh- / fundus (*for* *fudnus) / bottom
bhāgo- / fāgus / beech
bhəg- / (*Gk.*) phōgein 'to roast' / bake

INDO-EUROPEAN *dh* / LATIN *f-*, GREEK *th* / GERMANIC *d*

dheigh- / fi(n)gere 'to mold' / dough
dhwer- / foris / door
dhē- / (*Gk.*) thē- 'to place' / do
dhug(h)ətēr / (*Gk.*) thugatēr / daughter

INDO-EUROPEAN *gh* / LATIN *h-*, GREEK *ch* / GERMANIC *g*

---

ghordho- / hortus / (*OE*) geard 'yard'
ghosti- / hostis / guest
ghomon- / homo / gome (*obsolete, but in* brideg(r)oom)
ghol- / (*Gk.*) cholē (> cholera) / gall
ghed- / (pre)he(n)dere 'to take' / get
ghaido- / haedus 'kid' / goat

2. Except when preceded by *s*, the Indo-European voiceless stops *p, t, k* became respectively the voiceless fricatives *f, θ, x* (later *h* in initial position):

INDO-EUROPEAN *p* / LATIN, GREEK *p* / GERMANIC *f*

---

pətēr / pater / father
pisk- / piscis / fish
pel- / pellis / fell 'animal hide'
pūr- / (*Gk.*) pūr / fire
prtu- / portus / ford
pulo- / pullus / foal
ped- / ped(em) / foot
peku- / pecu 'cattle' / fee (*cf. Ger.* Vieh 'cattle')

INDO-EUROPEAN *t* / LATIN *t* / GERMANIC *θ*

---

treyes / trēs / three
ters- / torrēre 'to dry' / thirst
tū / tū / (*OE*) þū 'thou'
ten- / tenuis / thin
tum- / tumēre 'to swell' / thumb (*that is,* 'fat finger')
tonə- / tonāre / thunder

INDO-EUROPEAN *k* / LATIN *k* (spelled *c, q*) / GERMANIC *h*

---

krn- / cornū / horn
kerd- / cord- / heart
kwod / quod / what (*OE* hwæt)
ker- / cervus / hart
kmtom / cent- / hund(red)
kel- / cēlāre 'to hide' / hall, hell
kap- / capere 'to take' / heave, have

3. The Indo-European voiced stops *b, d, g* became respectively the voiceless stops *p, t, k.*

INDO-EUROPEAN *b* / LATIN, GREEK, LITHUANIAN, RUSSIAN *b* / GERMANIC *p*

---

treb- / trabs 'beam, timber' (> [archi]trave) / (*archaic*) thorp 'village'
dheub- / (*Lith.*) dubùs / deep
abel- / (*Russ.*) jabloko / apple

The sound *b* was infrequent in Indo-European, and at the beginning of words extremely so. The foregoing have been proposed as cognates with *b* in noninitial position. Other certain examples are hard to come by.

INDO-EUROPEAN *d* / LATIN, GREEK *d* / GERMANIC *t*
---

dwō / duo / two
dent- / dentis / tooth
demə- / domāre / tame
drew- / (*Gk.*) drūs 'oak' / tree
dekm / decem / ten (*Gothic* taíhun)
ed- / edere / eat

INDO-EUROPEAN *g* / LATIN, GREEK *g* / GERMANIC *k*
---

genu- / genu / knee (*loss of* [k-] *is modern*)
agro- / ager 'field' / acre
genə- / genus / kin
gwen- / (*Gk.*) gunē 'woman' / queen
grəno- / grānum / corn
gnō- / (g)nōscere / know, can

Verner's Law

Some words in the Germanic languages appear to have an irregular development of Indo-European *p, t,* and *k*. Instead of the expected *f, θ,* and *x* (or *h*), we find *β, ð,* and *ɣ* (or their later developments). For example, Indo-European *pətḗr* (represented by Latin *pater* and Greek *patḗr*) would have been expected to appear in Germanic with a medial *θ*. Instead we find Gothic *fadar* (with *d* representing [ð]), Icelandic *faðir,* and Old English *fæder* (in which the *d* is a West Germanic development of earlier [ð]). It appears that Indo-European *t* has become *ð* instead of *θ*.

This seeming anomaly was explained by a Danish scholar named Karl Verner in 1875. Verner noticed that the Proto-Germanic voiceless fricatives (*f, θ, x,* and *s*) became voiced fricatives (*β, ð, ɣ,* and *z*) unless they were prevented by any of three conditions: (1) being the first sound in a word, (2) being next to another voiceless sound, or (3) having the Indo-European stress on the immediately preceding syllable. Thus the *t* of Indo-European *pətḗr* became *θ*, as Grimm's Law predicts it should; but then, because the word is stressed on its second syllable and the *θ* is neither initial nor next to a voiceless sound, that fricative voiced to *ð*.

Verner's Law, which is a supplement to Grimm's Law, is that Proto-Germanic voiceless fricatives became voiced when they were in a voiced environment and the Indo-European stress was not on the immediately preceding syllable. The law was obscured by the fact that, after it had operated, the stress on Germanic words shifted to the first syllable of the root, thus effectively disguising one of its important conditions. The effect of the position of stress on voicing can be observed in some Modern English words of foreign origin, such as *exert* [ɪg'zərt] and *exist* [ɪg'zɪst], compared with *exercise* ['ɛksərsaɪz] and *exigent* ['ɛksəǰənt]. The later history of the voiced fricatives resulting from Verner's Law is the same as that of the voiced fricatives that developed from Indo-European *bh, dh,* and *gh.*

The *z* that developed from earlier *s* appears as *r* in all recorded Germanic languages except Gothic. The shift of *z* to *r,* known as **rhotacism** (that is, *r*-ing, from Gk. *rho,* the name of the letter), is by no means peculiar to Germanic. Latin *flōs* 'flower' has *r* in all forms other than the nominative singular—for instance, the genitive singular *flōris,* from earlier *flōz-,* the original *s* being voiced because of its position between vowels.

We have some remnants of the changes described by Verner's Law in present-day English. The past tense of the verb *be* has two forms: *was* and *were.* The alternation of *s* and *r* in those forms is a result of a difference in the way they were stressed in prehistoric times. The Old English verb *frēosan* 'to freeze' had a past participle from which came a now obsolete adjective *frore* 'frosty, frozen.' The Old English verb *forlēosan* 'to lose utterly' had a past participle from which came our adjective *forlorn.* Both these forms also show the *s/r* alternation. Similarly, the verb *seethe* had a past participle from which came our adjective *sodden,* showing the [θ/d] alternation. In early Germanic, past participles had stress on their endings, whereas the present tense forms of the verbs did not, and that difference in stress permitted voicing of the last consonant of the participle stems and hence triggered the operation of Verner's Law.

The Sequence of the First Sound Shift

Although we cannot be sure of the chronology of the consonant changes described by Grimm and Verner, it is likely that they stretched over centuries. Each set of shifts was completed before the next began; the First Sound Shift was no circular process. The changes may have occurred in the following order:

1. Indo-European (IE) bh, dh, gh ⟶ (respectively) Germanic (Gmc) β, ð, ɣ
2. IE p, t, k ⟶ (respectively) Gmc f, θ, x (⟶ h initially)
3. Gmc f, θ, x, s ⟶ (respectively) Gmc β, ð, ɣ, z
   (under the conditions of Verner's Law)
4. IE b, d, g ⟶ (respectively) Gmc p, t, k
5. Gmc β, ð, ɣ, z ⟶ (respectively) Gmc b, d, g, r

WEST GERMANIC LANGUAGES

The changes mentioned in the preceding section affected all of the Germanic languages, but other changes also occurred that created three subgroups within the Germanic branch—North, East, and West Germanic. The three subgroups are distinguished from one another by a large number of linguistic features, of which we can mention six as typical:

1. The nominative singular of some nouns ended in *-az* in Proto-Germanic— for example, **wulfaz.* This ending disappeared completely in West Germanic (Old

English *wulf*) but changed to *-r* in North Germanic (Old Icelandic *ulfr*) and to *-s* in East Germanic (Gothic *wolfs*).

2. The endings for the second and third persons singular in the present tense of verbs continued to be distinct in West and East Germanic, but in North Germanic the second person ending came to be used for both:

OLD ENGLISH	GOTHIC	OLD ICELANDIC	
bindest	bindis	bindr	'you bind'
bindeþ	bindiþ	bindr	'he/she binds'

3. North Germanic developed a definite article that was suffixed to nouns—for example, Old Icelandic *ulfr* 'wolf,' *ulfrinn* 'the wolf.' No such feature appears in East or West Germanic.

4. In West and North Germanic, the *z* that resulted from Verner's Law appears as *r,* but in East Germanic as *s:* Old English *ēare* 'ear,' Old Icelandic *eyra,* but Gothic *auso.*

5. West and North Germanic had vowel alternations called mutation (treated in the next chapter); for example, in Old English and Old Icelandic, the word for 'man' in the accusative singular was *mann,* while the corresponding plural was *menn.* No such alternation exists in Gothic, for which the parallel forms are singular *mannan* and plural *mannans.*

6. In West Germanic, the *ð* that resulted from Verner's Law appears as *d,* but remains a fricative in North and East Germanic: Old English *fæder,* Old Icelandic *faðir,* Gothic *faðar* (though spelled *fadar*).

West Germanic itself was divided into smaller subgroups. For example, High German and Low German are distinguished by another change in the stop sounds—the **Second** or **High German Sound Shift**—which occurred comparatively recently as linguistic history goes. It was nearing its completion by the end of the eighth century of our era. This shift began in the southern, mountainous part of Germany and spread northward, stopping short of the low-lying northern section of the country. The *high* in High German (*Hochdeutsch*) and the *low* in Low German (*Plattdeutsch*) refer only to relative distances above sea level. High German became in time standard German.

We may illustrate the High German shift in part by contrasting English and High German forms, as follows:

Proto-Germanic *p* appears in High German as *pf* or, after vowels, as *ff* (*pepper-Pfeffer*).

Proto-Germanic *t* appears as *ts* (spelled *z*) or, after vowels, as *ss* (*tongue-Zunge; water-Wasser*).

Proto-Germanic *k* appears after vowels as *ch* (*break-brechen*).

Proto-Germanic *d* appears as *t* (*dance-tanzen*).

The Continental home of the English was north of the area in which the High German shift occurred. But even if this had not been so, the English language would have been unaffected by changes that had not begun to occur at the time of the Anglo-Saxon migrations to Britain, beginning in the fifth century. Consequently English has the earlier consonantal characteristics of Germanic, which among the West Germanic languages it shares with Low German, Dutch, Flemish, and Frisian.

Because English and Frisian (spoken in the northern Dutch province of Friesland and in some of the islands off the coast) share certain features not found elsewhere in the Germanic group, they are sometimes treated as an Anglo-Frisian subgroup of West Germanic. They and Old Saxon share other features, such as the loss of nasal consonants before the fricatives *f, s,* and *þ,* with lengthening of the preceding vowel: compare High German *gans* with Old English *gōs* 'goose,' Old High German *fimf* (Modern German *fünf*) with Old English *fīf* 'five,' and High German *mund* with Old English *mūð* 'mouth.'

English, then, began its separate existence as a form of Germanic brought by pagan warrior-adventurers from the Continent to the then relatively obscure island that the Romans called Britannia, which had up until a short time before been part of the mighty Roman empire. There, in the next five centuries or so, it was to develop into an independent language quite distinct from any Germanic language spoken on the Continent. Moreover, it had become a language sufficiently rich in its word stock, thanks largely to the impetus given to learning by the introduction of Christianity, that, as the philologist Kemp Malone put it, "by the year 1000, this newcomer could measure swords with Latin in every department of expression, and was incomparably superior to the French speech that came in with William of Normandy."

FOR FURTHER READING

General

Trask. *Dictionary of Historical and Comparative Linguistics.*
Watkins. *The American Heritage Dictionary of Indo-European Roots.*

History of Language

Fischer. *A History of Language.*
Janson. *Speak: A Short History of Languages.*

Nature of Language Change

Aitchison. *Language Change.*
McMahon. *Understanding Language Change.*

Indo-European Language

Baldi. *An Introduction to the Indo-European Languages.*
Beekes. *Comparative Indo-European Linguistics.*
Gamkrelidze and Ivanov. *Indo-European and the Indo-Europeans.*

Indo-European Homeland and Culture

Curtis. *Indo-European Origins.*
Day. *Indo-European Origins.*
Gimbutas. *The Kurgan Culture.*
Lincoln. *Myth, Cosmos, and Society.*
Mallory. *In Search of the Indo-Europeans.*
Renfrew. *Archaeology and Language.*

History of Linguistics

Dinneen. *General Linguistics.*
Robins. *A Short History of Linguistics.*
Seuren. *Western Linguistics.*

Historical Linguistics

Campbell. *Historical Linguistics.*
Fox. *Linguistic Reconstruction.*
Hock and Joseph. *Language History, Language Change, and Language Relationship.*
Lehmann. *Historical Linguistics.*
Trask. *Historical Linguistics.*

The World's Languages

Ruhlen. *A Guide to the World's Languages.*

Germanic Languages

Bennett. *An Introduction to the Gothic Language.*
Green. *Language and History in the Early Germanic World.*
Nielsen. *The Germanic Languages.*
Prins. *A History of English Phonemes: From Indo-European to Present-Day English.*

5 THE OLD ENGLISH PERIOD (449–1100)

The recorded history of the English language begins, not on the Continent, where we know English speakers once lived, but in the British Isles, where they eventually settled. During the period when the language was spoken in Europe, it is known as **pre–Old English**, for it was only after the English separated themselves from their Germanic cousins that we recognize their speech as a distinct language and begin to have records of it.

SOME KEY EVENTS IN THE OLD ENGLISH PERIOD

The following short chronological list is of some events during the Old English period that had significant influences on the development of the English language.

- 449 Angles, Saxons, Jutes, and Frisians began to occupy Great Britain, thus changing its major population to English speakers and separating the early English language from its Continental relatives.

- 597 Saint Augustine of Canterbury arrived in England to begin the conversion of the English by baptizing King Ethelbert of Kent, thus introducing the influence of the Latin language.

- 664 The Synod of Whitby aligned the English with Roman rather than Celtic Christianity, thus linking English culture with mainstream Europe.

- 730 The Venerable Bede produced his *Ecclesiastical History of the English People,* recording the early history of the English people.

- 787 The Scandinavian invasion began with raids along the northeast seacoast.

- 865 The Scandinavians occupied northeastern Britain and began a campaign to conquer all of England.

- 871 Alfred became king of Wessex and reigned until his death in 899, rallying the English against the Scandinavians, retaking the city of London, establishing the Danelaw, and securing the position of king of all England for himself and his successors.

- 991   Olaf Tryggvason invaded England, and the English were defeated at the Battle of Maldon.
- 1000   The manuscript of the Old English epic *Beowulf* was written about this time.
- 1016   Canute became king of England, establishing a Danish dynasty in Britain.
- 1042   The Danish dynasty ended with the death of King Hardicanute, and Edward the Confessor became king of England.

- 1066   Edward the Confessor died and was succeeded by Harold, last of the Anglo-Saxon kings, who died at the Battle of Hastings fighting against the invading army of William, duke of Normandy, who was crowned king of England on December 25.

HISTORY OF THE ANGLO-SAXONS

Britain Before the English

When the English migrated from the Continent to Britain in the fifth century, they found the island already inhabited. A Celtic people had been there for many centuries before Julius Caesar's invasion of the island in 55 B.C. And before them, other peoples, about whom we know very little, had lived on the islands. The Roman occupation, not really begun in earnest until the time of the Emperor Claudius (A.D. 43), was to make Britain—that is, Britannia—a part of the Roman Empire for nearly as long as the time between the first permanent English settlement in America and our own day. It is therefore not surprising that there are so many Roman remains in modern England. Despite the long occupation, the British Celts continued to speak their own language, though many of them, particularly those in the towns and cities who wanted to "get on," learned to speak and write the language of their Roman rulers. It was not until Britain became England that the survival of British Celtic was seriously threatened.

After the Roman legionnaires were withdrawn from Britain in the early fifth century (by 410), Picts from the north and Scots from the west savagely attacked the unprotected British Celts, who after generations of foreign domination had neither the heart nor the skill in weapons to put up much resistance. These same Picts and Scots, as well as ferocious Germanic sea raiders whom the Romans called Saxons, had earlier been a very considerable nuisance to the Roman soldiers and their commanders during the latter half of the fourth century.

The Coming of the English

The Roman army included many non-Italians who were hired to help keep the Empire in order. It is likely that the Roman forces in Britain in the late fourth century already included some Angles and Saxons brought from the Continent. Tradition says, however, that the main body of the English arrived later. According to the Venerable Bede's account in his *Ecclesiastical History of the English People,* written in Latin and completed around 730, almost three centuries after the event, the Britons appealed to Rome for help against the Picts and Scots. What relief they got, a single legion, was only temporarily effective. When Rome could or would help no more, the wretched Britons—still according to Bede—ironically enough called the "Saxons" to their aid "from the parts beyond the sea." As a result of their appeal, shiploads of Germanic warrior-adventurers began to arrive.

The date that Bede gives for the first landing, 449, cannot be far out of the way. With it the **Old English** period begins. With it, too, we may in a sense begin thinking of Britain as England—the land of the Angles—for, even though the long ships carried Jutes, Saxons, Frisians, and doubtless members of other tribes as well, their descendants a century and a half later were already beginning to think of themselves and their speech as English. (They naturally had no suspicion that it was "Old" English.) The name of a single tribe was thus adopted as a national name (prehistoric Old English **Angli* becoming *Engle*). The term **Anglo-Saxon** is also sometimes used for either the language of this period or its speakers.

These Germanic sea raiders, ancestors of the English, settled the Pictish and Scottish aggressors' business in short order. Then, with eyes ever on the main chance, a complete lack of any sense of international morality, and no fear whatever of being prosecuted as war criminals, they very unidealistically proceeded to subjugate and ultimately to dispossess the Britons whom they had come ostensibly to help. They sent word to their Continental kinsmen and friends about the cowardice of the Britons and the fertility of the island; and in the course of the next hundred years or so, more and more Saxons, Angles, and Jutes arrived "from the three most powerful nations of Germania," as Bede says, to seek their fortunes in a new land.

We can be certain about only a few events of these exciting times: the invading newcomers belonged to various Germanic tribes speaking a number of closely related and hence very similar regional types of Germanic; they came from the great North German plain, including the southern part of the Jutland peninsula (modern Schleswig-Holstein); and by the time Saint Augustine arrived to convert them to Christianity at the end of the sixth century, they held in their possession practically all of what is now known as England. As for the ill-advised Britons, their plight was hopeless; many fled to Wales and Cornwall, some crossed the Channel to Brittany, and others were ultimately assimilated to the English by marriage or otherwise; many, we may be sure, lost their lives in the long-drawn-out fighting.

The Germanic tribes that came first—Bede's Jutes—were led by the synonymously named brothers Hengest and Horsa (both names mean 'horse,' an important animal in Indo-European culture and religion, the men being reputed to be great-grandsons of Woden, the chief Germanic god, an appropriate genealogy for tribal headmen). Those first-comers settled principally in the southeastern part of the island, still called by its Celtic name of Kent. Subsequently, Continental Saxons were to occupy the rest of the region south of the Thames, and Angles, stemming presumably from the hook-shaped peninsula in Schleswig known as Angeln, settled the large area stretching from the Thames northward to the Scottish highlands, except for the extreme southwestern portion (Wales).

The English in Britain

The Germanic settlement comprised seven kingdoms, the Anglo-Saxon **Heptarchy**: Kent, Essex, Sussex, Wessex, East Anglia, Mercia, and Northumbria—the last, the land north of the Humber estuary, being an amalgamation of two earlier kingdoms, Bernicia and Deira. Kent early became the chief center of culture and wealth, and by the end of the sixth century its King Ethelbert (Æðelberht) could lay claim to hegemony over all the other kingdoms south of the Humber. Later, in the seventh and eighth centuries, this supremacy was to pass to Northumbria, with its great centers of learning at Lindisfarne, Wearmouth, and Jarrow (Bede's own monastery); then to Mercia; and finally to Wessex, with its brilliant line of kings beginning with Egbert (Ecgberht), who overthrew the Mercian king in 825, and culminating in his grandson, the superlatively great Alfred, whose successors after his death in 899 took for themselves the title *Rex Anglorum* 'King of the English.'

The most important event in the history of Anglo-Saxon culture (which is the ancestor of both British and American) occurred in 597, when Pope Gregory I dispatched a band of missionaries to the Angles (*Angli,* as he called them, thereby departing from the usual Continental designation of them as *Saxones*), in accordance with a resolve he had made some years before. The leader of this band was Saint Augustine—not to be confused with the African-born bishop of Hippo of the same name who wrote *The City of God* more than a century earlier. The apostle to the English and his fellow bringers of the Word, who landed on the Isle of Thanet in Kent, were received by King Ethelbert courteously, if at the beginning a trifle warily. Already ripe for conversion through his marriage to a Christian Frankish princess, in a matter of months Ethelbert was himself baptized. Four years later, in 601, Augustine was consecrated first archbishop of Canterbury, and there was a church in England. Later, Irish missionaries who had come from Iona to found a monastery at Lindisfarne made many converts in Northumbria and Mercia.

In the course of the seventh century, the new faith spread rapidly (though not without occasional backsliding); and by the end of that century, England had become an important part of Christendom. Christianity had come to the Anglo-Saxons from two directions—from Rome with Saint Augustine and from the Celtic Church with the Irish missionaries, who introduced their style of writing (the Insular hand). Therefore, for a time it was uncertain whether England would go with Rome or the Celts. That question was resolved at a synod held at Whitby in 664, where preference was given to the Roman customs of when to celebrate Easter and of how monks should shave their heads. Those decisions were symbolic of an alignment of the English Church with Rome and the Continent.

Bede, who lived at the end of the seventh century and on into the first third of the next, wrote about the Synod's work and in several ways contributed significantly to the growing cultural importance of England. He was a Benedictine monk who spent his life in scholarly pursuits and became the most learned person in Europe of his day. He was a theologian, a scientist, a biographer, and a historian. It is in the last capacity that we remember him most, for his *Ecclesiastical History,* cited above, is the fullest and most accurate account we have of the early years of the English nation.

The First Viking Conquest

The Christian descendants of Germanic raiders who had looted, pillaged, and finally taken the land of Britain by force of arms were themselves to undergo harassment from other Germanic invaders, beginning in the later years of the eighth century, when pagan Viking raiders sacked various churches and monasteries, including Lindisfarne and Bede's own beloved Jarrow. During the first half of the following century, other more or less disorganized but disastrous raids took place in the south.

In 865 a great and expertly organized army landed in East Anglia, led by the unforgettably named Ivar the Boneless and his brother Halfdan, sons of Ragnar Lothbrok (*Loðbrók* 'Shaggy-pants'). According to legend, Ragnar had refused his bewitched bride's plea for a deferment of the consummation of their marriage for three nights. As a consequence, his son Ivar was born with gristle instead of bone.

This unique physique seems to have been no handicap to a brilliant if rascally career as warrior. Father Ragnar was eventually put to death in a snake pit in York. On this occasion his wife, the lovely Kraka, who felt no resentment toward him, had furnished him with a magical snake-proof coat; but it was of no avail, for his executioners made him remove his outer garment.

During the following years, the Vikings gained possession of practically the whole eastern part of England. In 870 they attacked Wessex, ruled by Ethelred (Æðelræd) with the able assistance of his brother Alfred, who was to succeed him in the following year. After years of discouragement, very few victories, and many crushing defeats, Alfred in 878 won a signal victory at Edington over Guthrum, the Danish king of East Anglia, who promised not only to depart from Wessex but also to be baptized. Alfred was godfather for him when the sacrament was later administered.

Alfred is the only English king to be honored with the sobriquet "the Great," and deservedly so. In addition to his military victories over the Vikings, Alfred was a highly skilled administrator, reorganizing the laws and government of the kingdom and reviving learning among the clergy. His greatest fame, however, was as a scholar in his own right. He translated into English out of Latin Pope Gregory the Great's *Pastoral Care,* Orosius's history of the world, Boethius's *Consolation of Philosophy,* and Saint Augustine's *Soliloquies.* He was responsible for a translation of Bede's *Ecclesiastical History* and for the compilation of the *Anglo-Saxon Chronicle*—the two major sources for our knowledge of early English history. Alfred became the subject of folklore, some probably based on fact, such as the story that, during a bad period in the Danish wars, Alfred took refuge incognito in the hut of a poor Anglo-Saxon peasant woman, who, needing to go out, instructed him to look after some cakes she had in the oven. But Alfred was so preoccupied by his own problems that he forgot the cakes and let them burn. When the good wife returned, she soundly berated him as a lazy good-for-nothing, and the king humbly accepted the rebuke.

The troubles with the Danes, as the Vikings were called by the English, though there were Norwegians and later Swedes among them, were by no means over. There were further attacks, but these were so successfully repulsed by the English that ultimately, in the tenth century, Alfred's son and grandsons (three of whom became kings) were able to carry out his plans for consolidating England, which by this time had a sizable and peaceful Scandinavian population.

The Second Viking Conquest

In the later years of the tenth century, trouble started again with the arrival of a fleet of warriors led by Olaf Tryggvason, later king of Norway, who was in a few years to be joined by Danish King Svein Forkbeard. For more than twenty years there were repeated attacks, most of them crushing defeats for the English, beginning with the glorious if unsuccessful stand made by the men of Essex under the valiant Byrhtnoth in 991, celebrated in the fine Old English poem *The Battle of*

Maldon. As a rule, however, the onslaughts of the later Northmen were not met with such vigorous resistance, for these were the bad days of the second Ethelred, known as *Unrǣd,* that is, 'unadvised,' but frequently misunderstood as 'unready.'

After the deaths in 1016 of Ethelred and his son Edmund Ironside, who survived his father by little more than half a year, Canute, son of Svein Forkbeard, came to the throne. The line of Alfred was not to be restored until 1042, with the accession of Edward the Confessor, though Canute in a sense allied himself with that line by marrying Ethelred's widow, Emma of Normandy (the English preferred to call her Ælgifu), who thus became the mother of two English kings by different fathers: by Ethelred, of Edward the Confessor, and by Canute, of Hardicanute. (She was not the mother of Ethelred's son Edmund Ironside.)

As has been pointed out, those whom the English called Danes (*Dene*) were not all from Denmark. Linguistically, however, this fact is of little significance, for the various Scandinavian tongues were in those days little differentiated from one another. Furthermore, they were enough like Old English to make communication possible between the English and the Scandinavians. The English were perfectly aware of their racial as well as their linguistic kinship with the Scandinavians, many of whom had become their neighbors: the Old English epic *Beowulf* is exclusively concerned with events of Scandinavian legend and history. Approximately a century and a half after the composition of this literary masterpiece, Alfred, who certainly had no reason to love the Danes, interpolated in his translation of the history of Orosius the first geographical account of the countries of northern Europe in his famous story of the voyages of Ohthere and Wulfstan.

The Scandinavians Become English

Despite the enmity and the bloodshed, then, there was a feeling among the English that when all was said and done the Northmen belonged to the same "family" as themselves—a feeling that their ancestors could never have experienced regarding the British Celts. Whereas the earlier raids had been dictated largely by the desire to pillage and loot—even though a good deal of Scandinavian settlement resulted—the tenth-century and early eleventh-century invaders from the north seem to have been much more interested in colonization than their predecessors had been. This was successfully accomplished in East Anglia (Norfolk and Suffolk), Lincolnshire, Yorkshire, Westmorland, Cumberland, and Northumberland. The Danes settled down peaceably enough in time, living side by side with the English; Scandinavians were good colonizers, willing to assimilate themselves to their new homes. As John Richard Green eloquently sums it up, "England still remained England; the conquerors sank quietly into the mass of those around them; and Woden yielded without a struggle to Christ" (cited by Jespersen, *Growth and Structure* 58).

And what of the impact of this assimilation on the English language, which is our main concern here? Old English and Old Norse (the language of the Scandinavians) had a whole host of frequently used words in common, among others, *man, wife, mother, folk, house, thing, winter, summer, will, can, come, hear, see, think, ride, over, under, mine,* and *thine.* In some instances where related words differed noticeably in form, the Scandinavian form has won out— for example, *sister* (ON *systir,* OE *sweostor*). Scandinavian contributions to the English word stock are discussed in more detail in Chapter 12 (277–8).

The Golden Age of Old English

It is frequently supposed that the Old English period was somehow gray, dull, and crude. Nothing could be further from the truth. England after its conversion to Christianity at the end of the sixth century became a veritable beehive of scholarly activity. The famous monasteries at Canterbury, Glastonbury, Wearmouth, Lindisfarne, Jarrow, and York were great centers of learning where men such as Aldhelm, Benedict Biscop, Bede, and Alcuin pursued their studies. The great scholarly movement to which Bede belonged is largely responsible for the preservation of classical culture for us. It was to the famous cathedral school at York founded by one of Bede's pupils that Charles the Great (Charlemagne) turned for leadership in his Carolingian Renaissance, and especially to the illustrious English scholar Alcuin (Ealhwine), born in the year of Bede's death and educated at York.

The culture of the north of England in the seventh and eighth centuries was to spread over the entire country, despite the decline that it suffered as a result of the hammering onslaughts of the Danes. Luckily, because of the tremendous energy and ability of Alfred the Great, it was not lost, and Alfred's able successors in the royal house of Wessex down to the time of the second Ethelred consolidated the cultural and political contributions made by their most distinguished ancestor.

Literature in the Old English period was rich in poetry. Cædmon, the first English poet we know by name, was a seventh-century herdsman whose visionary encounter with an angel produced a new genre of poetry that expressed Christian subject matter in the style of the old pagan scops. The epic poem *Beowulf,* probably composed in the early eighth century (though not written down until much later), embodied traditions that go back to the Anglo-Saxons' origins on the Continent in a sophisticated blending of pagan and Christian themes. Its account of the life and death of its hero sums up the ethos of the Anglo-Saxon people and combines a philosophical view of life with fairy-story elements that still resonate, for example, in J. R. R. Tolkien's epic *Lord of the Rings.* Cynewulf was an early ninth-century writer who signed four of his poems by working his name, in runic letters, into their texts as a clue to his authorship.

Prose was not neglected either. The Venerable Bede's contributions to scholarship and literature in the early eighth century and King Alfred's in the late ninth are mentioned earlier in this chapter. Ælfric was a tenth- and early eleventh-century Benedictine monk who devoted himself to the revival of learning among both clergy and laity. He was the most important prose stylist of classical Old English. His saints' lives, sermons, and scriptural paraphrases were models for English prose long after his death and were the basis for the continuity of English prose through the years following the Norman Conquest under French domination. His grammar, glossary, and colloquy (a humorous dialog between teacher and pupil) were basic texts for education long after his death.

As for the English language, which is our main concern here, it was certainly one of the most highly developed vernacular tongues in Europe—for French did not become a literary language until well after the period of the Conquest. The English word stock was capable of expressing subtleties of thought elsewhere reserved for Latin. With English culture more advanced than any other in western Europe, the Norman Conquest, which ended the first period in the history of England and its language, amounted to a crushing defeat of a superior culture by an inferior one, as the Normans themselves were in time to have the good sense to realize—for they, like the Scandinavian invaders who had preceded them, were ultimately to become English.

Dialects of Old English

Four principal dialects were spoken in Anglo-Saxon England: **Kentish**, the speech of the Jutes who settled in Kent; **West Saxon**, spoken in the region south of the Thames exclusive of Kent; **Mercian**, spoken from the Thames to the Humber exclusive of Wales; and **Northumbrian**, whose localization (north of the Humber) is adequately indicated by its name. Mercian and Northumbrian have certain characteristics in common that distinguish them from West Saxon and Kentish, so they are sometimes grouped together as **Anglian**, since those who spoke these north-of-the-Thames dialects were predominantly Angles. The records of Anglian and Kentish are scant, but much West Saxon writing has come down to us, though probably only a fraction of what once existed. Old English dialect differences were slight as compared with those that were later to develop and nowadays sharply differentiate the speech of a lowland Scottish shepherd from that of his south-of-England counterpart.

Although standard Modern English is in large part a descendant of Mercian speech, the dialect of Old English that will be described in this chapter is West Saxon. During the time of Alfred and for a long time thereafter, Winchester, the capital of Wessex and therefore in a sense of all England, was a center of English culture, thanks to the encouragement given by Alfred himself to learning. Though London was at the same time an important and thriving commercial city, it did not acquire its cultural or even its political importance until later.

It is thus in West Saxon that most of the extant Old English manuscripts—all in fact that may be regarded as literature—are available to us. Fortunately, however, we are at no great disadvantage when we study the West Saxon dialect in relation to Modern English. Because differences in dialect were not great, Old English forms are usually cited from West Saxon rather than Mercian writings. Occasionally a distinctive Mercian form (labeled Anglian if it happens to be identical with the Northumbrian form) is cited as more obviously similar to the standard modern form than is the West Saxon form—for instance, Anglian *ald,* which regularly developed into Modern English *old.* The West Saxon form was *eald.*

The Old English to be described here is that of about the year 1000—roughly that of the period during which Ælfric, the most representative writer of the late tenth and early eleventh centuries, was flourishing. This development of English, in which most of the surviving literature is preserved, is called late West Saxon or classical Old English. That of the Age of Alfred, who reigned in the later years of the ninth century, is early West Saxon, though it is actually rather late in the early period. It is, however, about all that we know of the early West Saxon dialect from manuscript evidence.

The Old English period spans somewhat more than six centuries. In a period of more than 600 years, many changes are bound to occur in sounds, grammar, and vocabulary. The view of the language presented here is a snapshot of it toward the end of that period.

PRONUNCIATION AND SPELLING

Our knowledge of the pronunciation of Old English can be only approximate. The precise quality of any speech sound during the vast era of the past before phonographs and tape recordings can never be determined with absolute certainty. Moreover, in Old English times, as today, there were regional and individual differences, and doubtless social differences as well. At no time do all members of any linguistic community, especially an entire nation, speak exactly alike. Whatever were its variations, however, Old English differed in some striking ways from our English, and those ways are noted below.

Vowels

One striking difference between the Anglo-Saxons' pronunciation and ours is that vowel length was a primary distinction in Old English. Yet corresponding long and short vowels also doubtless differed somewhat in quality. In the spellings of Old English words, long vowels will be marked with a macron and short vowels left unmarked, thus: *gōd* 'good' versus *god* 'god.' In phonetic transcriptions, different vowel symbols will be used where we believe different qualities occurred, but vowel length will be indicated by a colon, thus for the same two words: [go:d] versus [gɒd].

The vowel letters in Old English were *a, æ, e, i, o, u,* and *y.* They represented either the long or short sounds, though sometimes scribes wrote a slanting line above long vowels, particularly where confusion was likely, for example, *gód* for [go:d] 'good,' but that practice was not consistent. The five vowel letters *a, e, i, o,* and *u* symbolized what are sometimes referred to as "Continental" values—approximately those of Italian, Spanish, German, and to some extent of French as well. The letter *æ* represented the same sound for which we use it in phonetic transcriptions: [æ]. The letter *y,* used exclusively as a vowel symbol in Old English, usually indicated a rounded front vowel, long as in German *Bühne,* short as in *fünf.* This sound, which has not survived in Modern English, was made with the tongue position of [i] (long) or [ɪ] (short) but with the lips rounded as for [u] or [ʊ] respectively. The sounds may be represented phonetically as [ü:] and [ü].

In the examples that follow, the Modern English form in parentheses illustrates a typical Modern English development of the Old English sound:

a as in *habban* (have)	*ā* as in *hām* (home)
æ as in *þæt* (that)	*ǣ* as in *dǣl* (deal)
e as in *settan* (set)	*ē* as in *fēdan* (feed)
i as in *sittan* (sit)	*ī* as in *rīdan* (ride)
o as in *moððe* (moth)	*ō* as in *fōda* (food)
u as in *sundor* (sunder)	*ū* as in *mūs* (mouse)
y as in *fyllan* (fill)	*ȳ* as in *mȳs* (mice)

Late West Saxon had two long diphthongs, *ēa* and *ēo,* the first elements of which were respectively [æ:] and [e:]. The second elements of both, once differentiated, had been reduced to unstressed [ə]. In the course of the eleventh century the [ə] was lost; consequently these long diphthongs became monophthongs that continued to be differentiated, at least in the standard pronunciation, until well into the Modern English period but ultimately fell together as [i:], as in *beat* from Old English *bēatan* and *creep* from *crēopan.*

Short *ea* and *eo* in such words as *eall* 'all,' *geard* 'yard,' *seah* 'saw' and *eoh* 'horse,' *meolc* 'milk,' *weorc* 'work' indicated short diphthongs of similar quality to the identically written long ones, approximately [æə] and [ɛə]. In early Old English, there were other diphthongs written *ie* and *io,* but they had disappeared by the time of classical Old English, being replaced usually by *y* and *eo,* respectively.

Consonants

The consonant letters in Old English were *b, c, d, f, g, h, k, l, m, n, p, r, s, t, þ* or *ð, w, x,* and *z.* (The letters *j, q,* and *v* were not used for writing Old English, and *y* was always a vowel.) The symbols *b, d, k* (rarely used), *l, m, n, p, t, w* (which had a much different shape, namely, *p*), and *x* had in all positions the values these letters typically represent in Modern English.

The sound represented by *c* depended on contiguous sounds. Preconsonantal *c* was always [k], as in *cnāwan* 'to know,' *cræt* 'cart,' and *cwellan* 'to kill.' If *c* was next to a back vowel, it indicated the velar stop [k] (*camp* 'battle,' *corn* 'corn,' *cūð* 'known,' *lūcan* 'to lock,' *acan* 'to ache,' *bōc* 'book'). If it was next to a front vowel (or one that had been front in early Old English), the sound indicated was the affricate [č] (*cild* 'child,' *cēosan* 'to choose,' *ic* 'I,' *lǣce* 'physician,' *rīce* 'kingdom,' *mēce* 'sword').

To be sure of the pronunciation of Old English *c,* it is often necessary to know the history of the word in which it appears. In *cēpan* 'to keep,' *cynn* 'race, kin,' and a number of other words, the first vowels were originally back ones (Germanic **kōpyan, *kunyō*), before which the palatalization of [k] resulting in Old English [č] did not occur. These vowels later changed into front ones under the influence of the following *y.*

Mutation is a change in a vowel sound brought about by a sound in the following syllable. The mutation of a vowel by a following *i* or *y* (as in the examples above) is called *i*-**mutation** or *i*-**umlaut**. In *bēc* 'books' from prehistoric Old English **bōci* and *sēcan* 'to seek' from prehistoric Old English **sōcyan,* the immediately following *i* and *y* brought about both palatalization of the original [k] (written *c* in Old English) and mutation of the original vowel. Thus, they were pronounced [be:č] and [se:čɑn]. For the latter word, Old English scribes frequently wrote *secean,* the extra *e* functioning merely as a diacritic to indicate that the preceding *c* symbolized [č] rather than [k]. Compare the Italian use of *i* after *c* preceding *a, o,* or *u* to indicate precisely the same thing, as in *ciao* 'goodbye' and *cioccolata* 'chocolate.'

In *swylc* 'such,' *ælc* 'each,' and *hwylc* 'which,' an earlier *ī* before the *c* has been lost; but even without this information, we have a guide in the pronunciation of the modern forms cited as definitions. Similarly we may know from modern *keep* and *kin* that the Old English initial sound was [k]. Unfortunately for easy tests, *seek* does not show palatalization (though *beseech* does) and the mutated plural of *book* has not survived.

The digraphs *cg* and *sc* were in post–Old English times replaced by *dg* and *sh,* respectively—spellings that indicate to the modern reader exactly the sounds the older spellings represented, [ǰ] and [š]—for example, *ecg* 'edge,' *scīr* 'shire,' *scacan* 'to shake,' and *fisc* 'fish.'

The pronunciation of *g* (usually written with a form like ȝ) also depended on neighboring sounds. In late Old English, the symbol indicated the voiced velar stop [g] before consonants (*gnēað* 'niggardly,' *glæd* 'glad, gracious'), initially before back vowels (*galan* 'to sing,' *gōs* 'goose,' *gūð* 'war'), and initially before front vowels that had resulted from the mutation of back vowels (*gēs* 'geese' from prehistoric Old English **gōsi, gǣst* 'goest' from **gāis*). In the combination *ng* (as in *bringan* 'to bring' and *hring* 'ring'), the letter *g* indicated the same [g] sound—that of Modern English *linger* as contrasted with *ringer*. Consequently, [ŋ] was not a phoneme in Old English, but merely an allophone of *n*. There were no contrastive pairs like *sin-sing* and *thin-thing,* nor were there to be any until the Modern English loss of [g] in what had previously been a consonant sequence [ŋg].

The letter *g* indicated the semivowel [y] initially before *e, i,* and the vowel *y* that was usual in late West Saxon for earlier *ie* (*gecoren* 'chosen,' *gēar* 'year,' *giftian* 'to give a woman in marriage,' *gydd* 'song'), medially between front vowels (*slægen* 'slain,' *twēgen* 'twain'), and after a front vowel at the end of a syllable (*dæg* 'day,' *mægden* 'maiden,' *legde* 'laid,' *stigrāp* 'stirrup,' *manig* 'many').

In practically all other circumstances, *g* indicated the voiced velar fricative [ɣ] referred to in Chapter 4 as the earliest Germanic development of Indo-European *gh*—a sound difficult for English-speaking people nowadays. It is made like [g] except that the back of the tongue does not quite touch the velum (*dragan* 'to draw,' *lagu* 'law,' *hogu* 'care,' *folgian* 'to follow,' *sorgian* 'to sorrow,' *swelgan* 'to swallow'). It later became [w], as in Middle English *drawen, lawe, howe,* and so on.

In Old English, [v], [z], and [ð] were not phonemes; they occurred only between voiced sounds. There were thus no contrastive pairs like *feel-veal, leaf-leave,*

thigh-thy, mouth (n.)–*mouth* (v.), *seal-zeal, face-phase,* and hence there were no distinctive symbols for the voiceless and voiced sounds. The symbols *f, s,* and *þ* (or *ð,*
used more or less interchangeably with it) thus indicated both the voiceless fricatives
[f], [s], [θ] (as in *fōda* 'food,' *lof* 'praise'; *sunu* 'son,' *mūs* 'mouse'; *þorn* 'thorn,' *pæð*
'path') and the corresponding voiced fricatives [v], [z], [ð] (between voiced sounds,
as in *cnafa* 'boy,' *hæfde* 'had'; *lēosan* 'to lose,' *hūsl* 'Holy Communion'; *brōðor*
'brother,' *fæðm* 'fathom'). Some scribes in late Old English times preferred to write
þ initially and *ð* elsewhere, but generally the letters were interchangeable. (Note that,
although the Old English letter *ð* could represent either the voiceless or voiced fricative, the phonetic symbol [ð] represents the voiced sound only.)

At the beginning of words, *r* may have been a trill, but after vowels in West Saxon
it was probably similar to the so-called retroflex *r* that is usual in American English.

Initial *h* was about as in Modern English, but elsewhere *h* stood for the velar
fricative [x] or the palatal fricative [ç], depending on the neighboring vowel—for
example (with [x]), *seah* 'saw,' *þurh* 'through,' *þōhte* 'thought' (verb); (with [ç]),
syhð 'sees,' *miht* 'might,' *fēhð* 'takes.' Of the sequences *hl* (as in *hlāf* 'loaf'), *hn*
(as in *hnitu* 'nit'), *hr* (as in *hræfn* 'raven'), and *hw* (as in *hwæl* 'whale'), only the
last survives, now less accurately spelled *wh,* and even in that combination, the [h]
has been lost in the pronunciation of many present-day English speakers. In Old
English, both consonants were pronounced in all these combinations.

The letter *z* was rare but when used, it had the value [ts], as indicated by the
variant spellings *miltse* and *milze* 'mercy.'

The doubling of consonant symbols between vowels indicated a double or long
consonant; thus the two *t*'s of *sittan* indicated the double or long [t] sound in *hot
tamale,* in contrast to the single consonant [t] in Modern English *hotter.* Similarly
ll in *fyllan* indicated the lengthened medial *l* of *full-length,* in contrast to the single or short *l* of *fully.* The *cc* in *racca* 'part of a ship's rigging' was a long [k], as
in *bookkeeper,* in contrast to *beekeeper,* and hence *racca* was distinguished from
raca 'rake,' and so on.

Handwriting

The writing of the Anglo-Saxons looked quite different from that of the present
day. The chief reason for the difference is that the Anglo-Saxons learned from the
Celts to write in the Insular hand (as noted in Chapter 3). The following sample of
that handwriting consists of the first three lines of the epic *Beowulf* as an Anglo-
Saxon scribe might have written it (with some concessions to our practices of using
spaces between words, punctuation, and putting each verse on a separate line):

> Hpǽꞇ, ƿe ᵹaꞃꝺeꞃa ꟾn ᵹeaꞃꝺaᵹum,
>
> þeoꝺcẏnꝛꞁᵹa, þꞃẏm ᵹeꝼꞃunon,
>
> hu ꝺa æþelꞟꞁᵹaꞃ ellen ꝼꞃemeꝺon!

A transcription of these lines into the modern alphabet and a translation of them
is at the end of this chapter.

Stress

Old English words of more than one syllable, like those in all other Germanic languages, were regularly stressed on their first syllables. Exceptions to this rule were verbs with prefixes, which were generally stressed on the first syllable of their main element: *wiðféohtan* 'to fight against,' *onbíndan* 'to unbind.' *Be-, for-,* and *ge-* were not stressed in any part of speech: *bebód* 'commandment,' *forsóð* 'forsooth,' *gehǽp* 'convenient.' Compounds had the customary Germanic stress on the first syllable, with a secondary stress on the first syllable of their second element: *lárhùs* 'school,' *híldedèor* 'fierce in battle.'

This heavy stressing of the first syllable of practically all words has had a far-reaching effect on the development of English. Because of it, the vowels of final syllables began to be reduced to a uniform sound as early as the tenth century, as not infrequent interchanges of one letter for another in the texts indicate, though most scribes continued to spell according to tradition. In general, the stress system of Old English was simple as compared to that of Modern English, with its many loanwords of non-Germanic origin, like *maternal, philosophy, sublime,* and *taboo.*

VOCABULARY

The vocabulary of Old English differed from that of later historical stages of our language in two main ways: it included relatively few loanwords, and the gender of nouns was more or less arbitrary rather than determined by the sex or sexlessness of the thing named.

The Germanic Word Stock

The influence of Latin on the Old English vocabulary is treated in Chapter 12 (273–4), along with the lesser influence of Celtic (276–7), and Scandinavian (277–8). The Scandinavian influence certainly began during the Old English period, although it is not apparent until later. Yet, despite these foreign influences, the word stock of Old English was far more thoroughly Germanic than is our present-day vocabulary.

Many Old English words of Germanic origin were identical, or at least highly similar, in both form and meaning to the corresponding Modern English words—for example, *god, gold, hand, helm, land, oft, under, winter,* and *word.* Others, although their Modern English forms continue to be similar in shape, have changed drastically in meaning. Thus, Old English *bréad* meant 'bit, piece' rather than 'bread'; similarly, *dréam* was 'joy' not 'dream,' *dreorig* 'bloody' not 'dreary,' *hláf* 'bread' not 'loaf,' *mód* 'heart, mind, courage' not 'mood,' *scéawian* 'look at' not 'show,' *sellan* 'give' not 'sell,' *tíd* 'time' not 'tide,' *winnan* 'fight' not 'win,' and *wiþ* 'against' not 'with.'

Some Old English words and meanings have survived in Modern English only in disguised form or in set expressions. Thus, Old English *guma* 'man' (cognate with the Latin word from which we have borrowed *human*) survives in the compound *bridegroom,* literally 'bride's man,' where it has been remodeled under the influence of the unrelated word *groom.* Another Old English word for 'man,' *wer,* appears today in *werewolf* 'man-wolf' and in the archaic *wergild* 'man money, the fine to be paid for killing a person.' *Tīd,* mentioned in the preceding paragraph, when used in the proverb "Time and tide wait for no man," preserves an echo of its earlier sense. Doubtless most persons today who use the proverb think of it as describing the inexorable rise and fall of the sea, which mere humans cannot alter; originally, however, *time* and *tide* were just synonyms. *Līc* 'body' continues feebly in compounds like *lich-house* 'mortuary' and *lych-gate* 'roofed gate of a graveyard, where a corpse awaits burial,' and vigorously in the *-ly* endings of adverbs (clearly, happily) and some adjectives (homely, manly); what was once an independent word has been reduced to a suffix marking parts of speech.

Other Old English words have not survived at all: *blīcan* 'to shine, gleam,' *cāf* 'quick, bold,' *duguþ* 'band of noble retainers,' *frætwa* 'ornaments, treasure,' *galdor* 'song, incantation,' *here* 'army, marauders (especially the Danes),' *leax* 'salmon' (*lox* is a recent borrowing from Yiddish), *mund* 'palm of the hand,' hence 'protection, trust,' *nīþ* 'war, evil, trouble,' *racu* 'account, explanation,' *scēat* 'region, surface of the earth, bosom,' *tela* 'good,' and *ymbe* 'around.' Some of these words continued for a while after the Old English period (for example, *nīþ* lasted through the fifteenth century in forms like *nithe*), but they gradually disappeared and were replaced by other native expressions or, more often, by loanwords. Old English also made extensive use of compounds that we have now replaced by borrowing: *āþwedd* 'oath-promise, vow,' *bōchord* 'book-hoard, library,' *cræftspræc* 'craft-speech, scientific language,' *dēorwurþe* 'dear-worth, precious,' *folcriht* 'folk-right, common law,' *galdorcræft* 'incantation-skill, magic,' *lustbære* 'pleasure-bearing, desirable,' *nīfara* 'new-farer, stranger,' *rīmcræft* 'counting-skill, computation,' *wiþerwinna* 'against-fighter, enemy.'

If Germanic words like these had continued to our own time and if we had not borrowed the very great number of foreign words that we have in fact adopted, English today would be very different.

Gender in Old English

Aside from its pronunciation and its word stock, Old English differs markedly from Modern English in having **grammatical gender** in contrast to the Modern English system of **natural gender**, based on sex or sexlessness. Grammatical gender, which put every noun into one of three categories (masculine, feminine, or neuter), was characteristic of Indo-European, as can be seen from its presence in Sanskrit, Greek, Latin, and other Indo-European languages. The three genders were preserved in Germanic and survived in English well into the Middle English period; they survive in German and Icelandic to this day.

Doubtless the gender of a noun originally had nothing to do with sex, nor does it necessarily have sexual connotations in those languages that have retained grammatical gender. Old English *wīf* 'wife, woman' is neuter, as is its German cognate

Weib; so is *mægden* 'maiden,' like German *Mädchen. Bridd* 'young bird' is masculine; *bearn* 'son, bairn' is neuter. *Brēost* 'breast' and *hēafod* 'head' are neuter, but *brū* 'eyebrow,' *wamb* 'belly,' and *eaxl* 'shoulder' are feminine. *Strengþu* 'strength' is feminine, *broc* 'affliction' is neuter, and *drēam* 'joy' is masculine.

Where sex was patently involved, however, this complicated and to us illogical system was beginning to break down even in Old English times. It must have come to be difficult, for instance, to refer to one who was obviously a woman—that is, a *wīf*—with the pronoun *hit* 'it,' or to a *wīfmann*—the compound from which our word *woman* is derived—with *he* 'he,' the compound being masculine because of its second element. There are in fact a number of instances in Old English of the conflict of grammatical gender with the developing concept of natural gender.

GRAMMAR, CONCORD, AND INFLECTION

Grammatical gender is not a matter of vocabulary only; it also has an effect on grammar through what is called **concord**. Old English, like Indo-European (although to a lesser extent) had an elaborate system of inflection for nouns, adjectives, and verbs; and words that went closely together had to agree in certain respects, as signaled by their inflectional endings. If a noun was singular or plural, adjectives modifying it had to be singular or plural as well; and similarly, if a noun was masculine or feminine, adjectives modifying it had to be in masculine or feminine forms also. So if Anglo-Saxons wanted to say they had seen a foolish man and a foolish woman, they might have said, "Wē sāwon *sumne dolne* mann ond *sume dole* idese," using for *sum* 'some' and *dol* 'foolish' the masculine ending *-ne* with *mann* and the feminine ending *-e* with *ides* 'woman.'

The major difference between the grammars of Old English and Modern English is that the language has become less inflective and more isolating. That is, Old English used more grammatical endings on words and so was less dependent on word order and function words than Modern English. These matters are discussed generally in Chapter 1 and are further illustrated below for Old English.

Inflection

As just noted, one of the principal grammatical differences between Old English and Modern English is the amount of inflection in the noun, the adjective, and also the demonstrative and interrogative pronouns. Personal pronouns, however, have preserved much of their ancient complexity in Modern English and even, in one respect, increased it.

Old English nouns, pronouns, and adjectives had four cases, used according to the word's function in the sentence. The **nominative** case was used for the subject, the complement of linking verbs like *bēon* 'be,' and direct address. The **accusative** case was used for the direct object, the object of some prepositions, and certain adverbial functions (like those of the italicized expressions of duration and direction in Modern English "They stayed there *the whole day,* but finally went *home*"). The **genitive** case was used for most of the meanings of Modern English *'s* and *of* phrases, the object of a few prepositions and of some verbs, and in certain adverbial functions (like the time expression of Modern English "He works *nights,*" in which *nights* was originally a genitive singular equivalent to "of a night"). The **dative** case was used for the indirect object and the only object of some verbs, the object of many prepositions, and a variety of other functions that can be grouped together loosely as adverbial (like the time expression of Modern English "I'll see you *some day*").

Adjectives and the demonstrative and interrogative pronouns had a fifth case, the **instrumental**, whose functions were served for nouns by the dative case. A typical example of the instrumental is the italicized phrase in the following sentence: "Worhte Ælfred cyning *lȳtle werede* geweorc" (literally 'Built Alfred King [with a] *little troop* [a] work,' that is, 'King Alfred with a *small troop* built a fortification'). The nominative of the expression for 'small troop' was *lȳtel wered;* the final *-e* marked the adjective as instrumental and the noun as dative, here functioning as instrumental. The concord of the endings of the adjective and noun also showed that the words went together. Because the instrumental was used to express the means or manner of an action, it was also used adverbially: "folc þe *hlūde* singeþ" ('people that *loud[ly]* sing').

Adjectives and adverbs were compared much like Modern English *fast, faster, fastest.* Adjectives were inflected for **definiteness** as well as for gender, number, and case. The **weak declension** of adjectives was used to indicate that the modified noun was definite—that it named an object whose identity was known or expected or had already been mentioned. Generally speaking, the weak form occurred after a demonstrative or a possessive pronoun, as in "se *gōda* dæl" ('that *good* part') or "hire *geonga* sunu" ('her *young* son'). The **strong declension** was used when the modified noun was indefinite because it was not preceded by a demonstrative or possessive or when the adjective was in the predicate, as in "*gōd* dæl" ('[a] *good* part') or "se dæl wæs *gōd*" ('that part was *good*').

NOUNS

Old English will inevitably seem to the modern reader a crabbed and difficult language full of needless complexities. Actually the inflection of the noun was somewhat less complex in Old English than it was in Germanic, Latin, and Greek and, naturally, considerably less so than in Indo-European, with its eight cases (nominative, accusative, genitive, dative, ablative, instrumental, locative, and vocative). No Old English noun had more than six distinct forms; but even this number will seem exorbitant to the speaker of Modern English, who uses only two forms for all but a few nouns: a general form without ending and a form ending in *-s.* The fact that three modern forms ending in *-s* are written differently is quite irrelevant; the apostrophe for the genitive is a fairly recent convention. As far as speech is concerned, *guys, guy's,* and *guys'* are all the same.

Old English had a large number of patterns for declining its nouns, each of which is called a **declension**. Only the most common of the declensions or those that have survived somehow in Modern English are illustrated here. The most important of the Old English declensions was that of the *a*-stems, so called because *a* was the sound with which their stems ended in Proto-Germanic. They corresponded to the *o*-stems of Indo-European, as exemplified by nouns of the Greek and Latin second declensions: Greek *philos* 'friend' and Latin *servos* (later *servus*) 'slave,' Indo-European *o* having become Germanic *a* (as noted in Chapter 4). The name for the declension has only historical significance as far as Old English is concerned. For example, Germanic **wulfaz* (nominative singular) and **wulfan* (accusative singular) had an *a* in their endings, but both those forms appeared in Old English simply as *wulf* 'wolf,' having lost the *a* of their stem as well as the grammatical endings *-z* and *-n*. The *a*-stems are illustrated in the table of Old English noun declensions by the masculine *hund* 'dog' and the neuter *dēor* 'animal.'

More than half of all commonly used nouns were inflected according to the *a*-stem pattern, which was in time to be extended to practically all nouns. The Modern English possessive singular and general plural forms in *-s* come directly from the Old English genitive singular (*-es*) and the masculine nominative-accusative plural (*-as*) forms—two different forms until very late Old English, when they fell together because the unstressed vowels had merged, probably as a schwa. In Middle English both endings were spelled *-es*. Only in Modern English have they again been differentiated in spelling by the use of the apostrophe. Nowadays, new words invariably conform to what survives of the *a*-stem declension—for example, *hobbits, hobbit's, hobbits'*—so that we may truly say it is the only living declension.

Neuter *a*-stems differed from masculines only in the nominative-accusative plural, which was without an ending in nouns like *dēor*. Such "endingless plurals" survive in Modern English for a few words like *deer*.

A very few neuter nouns, of which *cild* 'child' is an example, had an *r* in the plural. Such nouns are known as *z*-stems in Germanic but **r-stems** in Old English; the *z*, which became *r* by rhotacism, corresponds to the *s* of Latin neuters like *genus*, which also rhotacized to *r* in oblique (nonnominative) forms like *genera*. The historically expected plural of *child* in Modern English is *childer*, and that form indeed survives in the northern dialects of British English. In standard use, however, *children* acquired a second plural ending from the nouns discussed in the next paragraph.

An important declension in Old English was the **n-stem**. Nouns that follow this pattern were masculine (for example, *oxa* 'ox,' illustrated in the table) or feminine (such as *tunge* 'tongue'); the two genders differed only in the endings for the nominative singular, *-a* versus *-e*. There were also two neuter nouns in the declension, *ēage* 'eye' and *ēare* 'ear.' For a time, *-n* rivaled *-s* (from the *a*-stems) as a typical plural ending in English. Plurals like *eyen* 'eyes,' *fon* 'foes,' *housen* 'houses,' *shoen* 'shoes,' and *treen* 'trees' continued well into the Modern English period. The only original *n*-plural to survive as standard today, however, is *oxen*. *Children,* as noted above, has its *-n* by analogy rather than historical development. Similarly *brethren* and the poetic *kine* for 'cows' are post–Old English developments. The *n*-stem pattern is also sometimes called the **weak declension**,

OLD ENGLISH NOUN DECLENSIONS

	MASCULINE a-STEM	NEUTER a-STEM	r-STEM	n-STEM	ō-STEM	ROOT-CONSONANT STEM
	'hound'	'deer'	'child'	'ox'	'love'	'foot'
Singular						
Nom.	hund	dēor	cild	oxa	lufu	fōt
Acc.	hund	dēor	cild	oxan	lufe	fōt
Gen.	hundes	dēores	cildes	oxan	lufe	fōtes
Dat.	hunde	dēore	cilde	oxan	lufe	fēt
Plural						
N.-Ac.	hundas	dēor	cildru	oxan	lufa	fēt
Gen.	hunda	dēora	cildra	oxena	lufa	fōta
Dat.	hundum	dēorum	cildrum	oxum	lufum	fōtum

in contrast with the **strong declensions**, which have stems that originally ended in a vowel, such as the *a*-stems.

Somewhat fewer than a third of all commonly used nouns were feminine, most of them **ō-stems** (corresponding to the *ā*-stems, or first declension, of Latin). In the nominative singular, these had *-u* after a short syllable, as in *lufu* 'love' and no ending at all after a long syllable, as in *lār* 'learning.' They and a variety of other smaller classes of nouns are not further considered here because they had no important effect on Modern English.

Another declension whose nouns were frequently used in Old English and whose forms have contributed to the irregularities of Modern English consisted of the **root-consonant stems**. In early stages of the language, the case endings of these nouns were attached directly to their roots without an intervening stem-forming suffix (like the *-a, -r,* and *-n* of the declensions already discussed). The most striking characteristic of these nouns was the change of root vowel in several of their forms. This declension is exemplified by the masculine noun *fōt* 'foot,' with dative singular and the nominative-accusative plural forms *fēt.*

i-Umlaut

The vowel of a root-consonant stem changes because in prehistoric Old English several of its forms (which originally had the same root vowel as all its other forms) had an *i* in their endings, for *fōt:* dative singular **fōti* and nominative-accusative plural **fōtiz.* As mentioned above, anticipation of the *i*-sound caused **mutation** of the root vowel—a kind of assimilation, with the vowel of the root moving in its articulation in the direction of the *i*-sound, but stopping somewhat short of it. English *man-men, foot-feet* show the same development as German *Mann-Männer, Fuss-Füsse,* though German writes the mutated vowel with a dieresis over the same symbol used for the unmutated vowel, whereas English uses an altogether different letter. The process, which Jacob Grimm called **umlaut**, occurred in different periods and in varying degrees in the various languages of the Germanic group, in English beginning probably in the sixth century. The fourth-century Gothic recorded by Bishop Wulfila shows no evidence of it.

Vowel mutation was originally a phonetic phenomenon only; but after the endings that caused the change had been lost, the mutated vowels served as markers for the two case forms. Mutation was not in Old English a sign of the plural, for it was found also in the dative singular and not all plural forms had it. Only later did it become a distinctive indication of plurality for those nouns like *feet, geese, teeth, mice, lice,* and *men* that have retained mutated forms into Modern English. Modern English *breeches* is a double plural (OE nominative singular *brōc* 'trouser,' nominative plural *brēc*), as is the already cited *kine* (OE nominative singular *cū* 'cow,' nominative plural *cȳ* with the addition of the plural *-n* as in *oxen*).

Mutation is not limited to the nouns of this declension. Its effects can be seen also in such pairs as *strong-strength, old-elder,* and *doom-deem.* In all these pairs, the second word originally had an ending containing an *i*-sound (either a vowel or its consonantal equivalent [y]) that caused the mutation of the root vowel and was thereafter lost.

Modern Survivals of Case and Number

In all declensions, the genitive plural form ended in *-a.* This ending survived as [ə] (written *-e*) in Middle English in the "genitive of measure" construction, and its effects continue in Modern English (with loss of [ə], which dropped away in all final positions) in such phrases as *sixty-mile drive* and *six-foot tall* (rather than *miles* and *feet*). Though *feet* may often occur in the latter construction, only *foot* is idiomatic in *three-foot board* and *six-foot man. Mile* and *foot* in such expressions are historically genitive plurals derived from the Old English forms *mīla* and *fōta,* rather than the irregular forms they now appear to be.

The dative plural, which was *-um* for all declensions, survives in the antiquated form *whilom,* from Old English *hwīlum* 'at times,' and in the analogical *seldom* (earlier *seldan*). The dative singular ending *-e,* characteristic of the majority of Old English nouns, survives in the word *alive,* from Old English *on līfe.* The Old English voiced *f* between vowels, later spelled *v,* is preserved in the Modern English form, though the final vowel is no longer pronounced.

There are only a very few relics of Old English feminine genitives without *-s,* for instance, *Lady Chapel* and *ladybird,* for *Our Lady's Chapel* and *Our Lady's bird.* The *ō*-stem genitive singular ended in *-e,* which was completely lost in pronunciation by the end of the fourteenth century, along with all other final *e*'s of whatever origin.

The forms discussed in these paragraphs are about the only traces left of the Old English declensional forms of the noun other than the genitive singular and the general plural forms in *-s* (along with a few mutated plurals). One of the most significant differences between Old English and Modern English nouns is that Old English had no device for indicating plurality alone—that is, unconnected with the concept of case. It was not until Middle English times that the plural nominative-accusative *-es* (from OE *-as*) drove out the other case forms of the plural (save for the comparatively rare genitive of measure construction discussed above).

MODIFIERS

Demonstratives

There were two demonstratives in Old English. The more frequently used was that which came to correspond in function to our definite article and may be translated "the" or "that, those." Its forms were as follows:

	MASCULINE	NEUTER	FEMININE	PLURAL
Nom.	sē, se	þæt	sēo	þā
Acc.	þone	þæt	þā	þā
Gen.	þæs	þæs	þære	þāra
Dat.	þæm	þæm	þære	þæm
Ins.	þȳ, þon, þē	þȳ, þon, þē		

Genders were distinguished only in the singular; in the plural no such distinction of gender was made. The masculine and neuter forms were alike in the genitive, dative, and instrumental. There was no distinct instrumental in the feminine or the plural, the dative being used in that function instead. By analogy with all the other forms, sē/se and sēo were in late Old English superseded by the variants þē/þe and þēo.

The Modern English definite article the developed from the masculine nominative þe, remodeled by analogy from se. When we use the in comparisons, however, as in "The sooner, the better," it is a development of the neuter instrumental form þē, the literal sense being something like 'By this [much] sooner, by this [much] better.' The Modern English demonstrative that is from the neuter nominative-accusative þæt, and its plural those has been borrowed from the other demonstrative.

The other, less frequently used Old English demonstrative (usually translated 'this, pl. these') had the nominative singular forms þēs (masculine), þis (neuter, whence ModE this), and þēos (feminine). Its nominative-accusative plural, þās, developed into those and was confused with tho (from þā), the earlier plural of that. Consequently in Middle English a new plural was developed for this, namely these.

Adjectives

The adjective in Old English, like that in Latin, agreed with the noun it modified in gender, case, and number; but Germanic, as noted in Chapter 4, had developed a distinctive adjective declension—the **weak declension**, used after the two demonstratives and after possessive pronouns, which made the following noun definite in its reference. In this declension -an predominated as an ending, as shown in the following paradigms for se dola cyning 'that foolish king,' þæt dole bearn 'that foolish child,' and sēo dole ides 'that foolish woman.' Like the demonstratives, weak adjectives did not vary for gender in the plural.

WEAK SINGULAR ADJECTIVE DECLENSION

	MASCULINE	NEUTER	FEMININE
Nom.	se dola cyning	þæt dole bearn	sēo dole ides
Acc.	þone dolan cyning	þæt dole bearn	þā dolan idese
Gen.	þæs dolan cyninges	þæs dolan bearnes	þære dolan idese
Dat.	þǣm dolan cyninge	þǣm dolan bearne	þære dolan idese
Ins.	þȳ dolan cyninge	þȳ dolan bearne	

WEAK PLURAL ADJECTIVE DECLENSION

Nom., Acc.	þā dolan cyningas, bearn, idesa
Gen.	þāra dolra (or dolena) cyninga, bearna, idesa
Dat.	þǣm dolum cyningum, bearnum, idesum

The **strong declension** was used when the adjective was not preceded by a demonstrative or a possessive pronoun or when it was predicative. Paradigms for the strong adjective in the phrases *dol cyning* 'a foolish king,' *dol bearn* 'a foolish child,' and *dolu ides* 'a foolish woman' follow. The genders of the plural forms were different only in the nominative-accusative.

STRONG SINGULAR ADJECTIVE DECLENSION

	MASCULINE	NEUTER	FEMININE
Nom.	dol cyning	dol bearn	dolu ides
Acc.	dolne cyning	dol bearn	dole idese
Gen.	doles cyninges	doles bearnes	dolre idese
Dat.	dolum cyninge	dolum bearne	dolre idese
Ins.	dole cyninge	dole bearne	dolre idese

STRONG PLURAL ADJECTIVE DECLENSION

Nom., Acc.	dole cyningas	dolu bearn	dola idesa
Gen.	dolra cyninga	dolra bearna	dolra idesa
Dat.	dolum cyningum	dolum bearnum	dolum idesum

The comparative of adjectives was regularly formed by adding *-ra,* as in *heardra* 'harder,' and the superlative by adding *-ost,* as in *heardost* 'hardest.' A few adjectives originally used the alternative suffixes *-ira* and *-ist,* so consequently had mutated vowels. In recorded Old English they took the endings *-ra* and *-est* but retained mutated vowels—for example, *lang* 'long,' *lengra, lengest* and *eald* 'old,' *yldra, yldest* (Anglian *ald, eldra, eldest*). A very few others had comparative and superlative forms from a different root from that of the positive, among them *gōd* 'good,' *betra* 'better,' *betst* 'best' and *micel* 'great,' *māra* 'more,' *mǣst* 'most.'

Certain superlatives were formed originally with an alternative suffix *-(u)ma*—for example, *forma* (from *fore* 'before'). When the ending with *m* ceased to be felt as having superlative force, these words and some others took by analogy the additional ending *-est*. Thus double superlatives (though not recognized as such) like *formest, midmest, ūtemest,* and *innemest* came into being. The ending appeared to be *-mest* (rather than *-est*), which was even in late Old English times misunderstood as 'most'; hence our Modern English forms *foremost, midmost, utmost,* and *inmost,* in which the final syllable is and has long been equated with *most,* though it has no historical connection with it. Beginning thus as a blunder, this *-most* has subsequently been affixed to other words—for example, *uppermost, furthermost,* and *topmost.*

Adverbs

The great majority of Old English adverbs were formed from adjectives by adding the suffix *-e* (historically, the instrumental case ending)—for example, *wrāþ* 'angry,' *wrāþe* 'angrily.' This *-e* was lost along with all other final *e*'s by the end of the fourteenth century, with the result that some Modern English adjectives and adverbs are identical in form—for instance, *loud, deep,* and *slow*—though Modern English idiom sometimes requires adverbial forms with *-ly* ("He plunged deep into the ocean" but "He thought deeply about religious matters"; "Drive slow" but "He proceeded slowly").

In addition, other case forms of nouns and adjectives might be used adverbially, notably the genitive and the dative. The adverbial genitive is used in "He hwearf *dæges* and *nihtes*" 'He wandered of a day and of a night (that is, by day and by night),' in which *dæges* and *nihtes* are genitive singulars. The construction survives in "He worked nights" (labeled "dial[ect] and U.S." by the *Oxford English Dictionary*), sometimes rendered analytically as "He worked of a night." The usage is, as the *OED* says, "in later use prob[ably] apprehended as a plural," though historically, as we have seen, it is not so. The *-s* of *homewards* (OE *hāmweardes*), *towards* (*tōweardes*), *besides, betimes,* and *needs* (as in *must needs be,* sometimes rendered analytically as *must of necessity be*) is also from the genitive singular ending *-es*. The same ending is merely written differently in *once, twice, thrice, hence,* and *since.* Modern, if archaic, *whilom,* from the dative plural *hwīlum,* has already been cited, but Old English used other datives similarly.

Adverbs regularly formed the comparative with *-or* and the superlative with *-ost* or *-est* (*wrāþor* 'more angrily,' *wrāþost* 'most angrily').

PRONOUNS

Personal Pronouns

Except for the loss of the **dual number** and the old second person singular forms, the personal pronouns are almost as complex today as they were in Old

PRONOUNS **109**

English times. In some respects (particularly the two genitive forms of Modern English), they are more complex today. The Old English forms of the pronouns for the first two persons are as follows:

	SINGULAR	DUAL	PLURAL
Nom.	ic 'I'	wit 'we both'	wē 'we all'
Ac.-D.	mē 'me'	unc 'us both'	ūs 'us all'
Gen.	mīn 'my, mine'	uncer 'our(s) (both)'	ūre 'our(s) (all)'
Nom.	þū 'you (sg.)'	git 'you both'	gē 'you all'
Ac.-D.	þē 'you (sg.)'	inc 'you both'	ēow 'you all'
Gen.	þīn 'your(s) (sg.)'	uncer 'your(s) (both)'	ēower 'your(s) (all)'

The dual forms, which were used to talk about exactly two persons, were disappearing even by late Old English times. The second person singular (*th*-forms) and the second person plural nominative (*ye*) survived well into the Modern English period, especially in religious and poetic language, but they are seldom used today and almost never with traditional correctness. When used as modifiers, the genitives of the first and second persons were declined like the strong adjectives.

Gender appeared only in the third person singular forms, exactly as in Modern English:

	MASCULINE	NEUTER	FEMININE	PLURAL
Nom.	hē 'he'	hit 'it'	hēo 'she'	hī 'they'
Acc.	hine 'him'	hit 'it'	hī 'her'	hī 'them'
Dat.	him 'him'	him 'it'	hire 'her'	him, heom 'them'
Gen.	his 'his'	his 'its'	hire 'her(s)'	hire, heora 'their(s)'

The masculine accusative *hine* has survived only in southwestern dialects of British English as [ən], as in "Didst thee zee un?" that is, "Did you see him?" (*OED*, s.v. *hin, hine*).

Modern English *she* has an unclear history, but it is perhaps a development of the demonstrative *sēo* rather than of the personal pronoun *hēo*. A new form was needed because *hēo* became by regular sound change identical in pronunciation with the masculine *he*—an obviously unsatisfactory state of affairs. The feminine accusative *hī* has not survived.

The neuter *hit* has survived when stressed, notably at the beginning of a sentence, in some types of nonstandard Modern English. The loss of [h-] in standard English was due to lack of stress and is paralleled by a similar loss in the other *h*-pronouns when they are unstressed, as for example, "Give her his book," which in the natural speech of people at all cultural levels would show no trace of either [h]; compare also "raise her up" and "razor up," "rub her gloves" and "rubber gloves." In the neuter, however, [h] has been lost completely in standard English, even in writing, whereas in the other *h*- pronouns we always write the *h*, but pronounce it only when the pronoun is stressed. The genitive *its* is obviously not a development of the Old English form *his,* but a new analogical form occurring first in Modern English.

Of the third person plural forms, only the dative has survived; it is the regular spoken, unstressed, objective form in Modern English, with loss of *h-* as in the other *h-* pronouns—for example, "I told 'em what to do." The Modern English stressed form *them,* like *they* and *their,* is of Scandinavian origin.

In all of the personal pronouns except *hit,* as also in the interrogative *hwā* 'who,' considered in the next section, the accusative form has been replaced by the dative. In the first and second persons, that replacement began very early; for example, *mec,* an earlier accusative for the first person singular, had been lost by the time of classical Old English and its functions assumed by the original dative *mē.* A similar change had taken place in each of the first and second person paradigms and would later do so in the third person (except the neuter).

Interrogative and Relative Pronouns

The interrogative pronoun *hwā* 'who' was declined only in the singular and had only two gender forms:

	MASCULINE/FEMININE	NEUTER
Nom.	hwā	hwæt
Acc.	hwone	hwæt
Gen.	hwæs	hwæs
Dat.	hwǣm, hwām	hwǣm, hwām
Ins.	hwǣm, hwām	hwȳ

Hwā is the source of our *who, hwām* of *whom,* and *hwæt* of *what. Hwone* did not survive beyond the Middle English period, its functions being taken over by the dative. *Whose* is from *hwæs* with its vowel influenced by *who* and *whom.* The distinctive neuter instrumental *hwȳ* is the source of our *why.* Other Old English interrogatives included *hwæðer* 'which of two' and *hwilc* 'which of many.' They were both declined like strong adjectives.

Hwā was exclusively interrogative in Old English. The particle *þe* was the usual relative pronoun. Since this word had only a single form, it is a great pity that we ever lost it; it involved no choice such as that which we must make—in writing, at least—between *who* and *whom,* now that these have come to be used as relatives. Sometimes, however, *þe* was preceded by the appropriate form of the demonstrative *sē* to make a compound relative.

VERBS

Like their Modern English counterparts, Old English verbs were either **weak**, adding a *-d* or *-t* to form their preterits and past participles (as in modern *talk-talked*), or **strong**, changing their stressed vowel for the same purpose (as in modern *sing-sang-sung*). Old English had both several kinds of weak verbs and seven groups of strong verbs distinguished by their patterns of vowel change; and it had a considerably larger number of strong verbs than does Modern English. Old English also had a fair number of irregular verbs in both the weak and strong categories—grammatical irregularity being frequent at all periods in the history of the language, rather than a recent "corruption."

The **conjugation** of a typical weak verb, *cēpan* 'to keep,' and of a typical strong verb, *helpan* 'to help,' is as follows:

Present System

Infinitive

Simple	cēpan 'to keep'	helpan 'to help'
Inflected	tō cēpenne 'to keep'	tō helpenne 'to help'

Indicative

ic	cēpe 'I keep'	helpe 'I help'
þū	cēpest 'you keep'	hilpst 'you help'
hē, hēo, hit	cēpeþ 'he, she, it keeps'	hilpþ 'he, she, it helps'
wē, gē, hī	cēpaþ 'we, you, they keep'	helpaþ 'we, you, they help'

Subjunctive

Singular	cēpe 'I, you, he, she, it keep'	helpe 'I, you, he, she, it help'
Plural	cēpen 'we, you, they keep'	helpen 'we, you, they help'

Imperative

Singular	cēp '(you) keep!'	help '(you) help!'
Plural	cēpaþ '(you all) keep!'	helpaþ '(you all) help!'

Participle	cēpende 'keeping'	helpende 'helping'

Preterit System

Indicative

ic	cēpte 'I kept'	healp 'I helped'
þū	cēptest 'you kept'	hulpe 'you helped'
hē, hēo, hit	cēpte 'he, she, it kept'	healp 'he, she, it helped'
wē, gē, hī	cēpton 'we, you, they kept'	hulpon 'we, you, they helped'

Subjunctive

| Singular | cēpte 'I, you, he, she, it kept' | hulpe 'I, you, he, she, it helped' |
| Plural | cēpten 'we, you, they kept' | hulpen 'we, you, they helped' |

Past Participle

gecēped 'kept'   geholpen 'helped'

Indicative Forms of Verbs

The **indicative** forms of the verbs, present and preterit, were used for making statements and asking questions; they are the most frequent of the verb forms and the most straightforward and ordinary in their uses. The Old English **preterit** was used for events that happened in the past, and the **present tense** was used for all other times, that is, for present and future events and for habitual actions.

In the present indicative, the *-t* of the second person singular was not a part of the original ending; it came from the frequent use of *þū* as an **enclitic**, that is, an unstressed word following a stressed word (here the verb) and spoken as if it were a part of the stressed word. For example, *cēpes þū* became *cēpesþu*, then dissimilated to *cēpestu,* and later lost the unstressed *-u.*

Subjunctive and Imperative Forms

The **subjunctive** did not indicate person but only tense and number. The endings were alike for both tenses: singular *-e* and plural *-en.*

The subjunctive was used in main clauses to express wishes and commands: *God ūs helpe* '(May) God help us'; *Ne hēo hundas cēpe* 'She shall not keep dogs.' It was also used in a wide variety of subordinate clauses, including constructions in which we still use it: *swelce hē tam wǣre* 'as if he were tame.' But it also occurred in many subordinate clauses where we would no longer use it: *Ic heom sægde þæt hēo blīðe wǣre* 'I told them that she was happy.'

The **imperative** singular of *cēpan* and *helpan* was without ending, but for some verbs it ended in *-e* or *-a.* As in Modern English, imperatives were used for making commands.

Nonfinite Forms

In addition to their **finite forms** (those having personal endings), Old English verbs had four **nonfinite forms**: two infinitives and two participles. The simple infinitive ended in *-an* for most verbs; for some weak verbs, its ending was *-ian* (*bodian* 'to proclaim,' *nerian* 'to save'), and for some verbs that underwent contraction, the ending was *-n* (*fōn* 'to seize,' *gān* 'to go'). The inflected infinitive was a relic of an earlier time when infinitives were declined like nouns. The two infinitives were often, but not always, interchangeable. The inflected infinitive was especially used when the infinitive had a noun function, like a Modern English gerund: *Is blīðe tō helpenne* 'It is joyful to help,' 'Helping is joyful.'

The participles were used much like those of Modern English, as parts of verb phrases and as modifiers. The usual ending of the present participle was *-ende.* The ending of the strong past participle, *-en,* has survived in many strong verbs to the present day: *bitten, eaten, frozen, swollen.* The ending of weak past participles, *-d* or *-t,* was, of course, the source for all regular past participle endings in Modern English. The prefix *ge-* was fairly general for past participles but occurred sometimes as a prefix in all forms. It survived in the past participle throughout the Middle English period as *y-* (or *i-*), as in Milton's archaic use in "L'Allegro": "In heaven ycleped Euphrosyne . . ." (from OE *geclypod* 'called').

Weak Verbs

There were three main classes of weak verbs in Old English. The three classes can be illustrated by citing the principal parts for one or two verbs of each class. **Principal parts** are forms from which the whole conjugation can be predicted:

	INFINITIVE	PRETERIT	PAST PARTICIPLE
Class I	fremman 'to do'	fremede 'did'	gefremed 'done'
	cēpan 'to keep'	cēpte 'kept'	gecēped 'kept'
Class II	endian 'to end'	endode 'ended'	geendod 'ended'
Class III	habban 'to have'	hæfde 'had'	gehæfd 'had'
	secgan 'to say'	sægde 'said'	gesægd 'said'

Many of the weak verbs were originally causative verbs derived from nouns, adjectives, or other verbs by the addition of a suffix with an *i*-sound that mutated the stem vowel of the word. Thus, *fyllan* 'to fill, cause to be full' is from the adjective *full,* and *settan* 'to set, cause to sit' is from the verb *sæt,* the preterit singular of *sittan.* Other pairs of words of the same sort are, in their Modern English forms, *feed* 'cause to have food,' *fell* 'cause to fall,' and *lay* 'cause to lie.'

Strong Verbs

Most of the other Old English verbs—all others, in fact, except for a few very frequently used ones discussed in the next two sections—formed their preterits by a vowel change called **gradation** (also called **ablaut** by Jacob Grimm), which was perhaps due to Indo-European variations in pitch and stress. Gradation is by no means confined to these strong verbs, but it is best illustrated by them. Gradation should not be confused with mutation (umlaut), which is the approximation of a vowel in a stressed syllable to another vowel (or semivowel) in a following syllable. Although there are roughly similar phenomena in other languages, the type of mutation we have been concerned with is confined to Germanic languages. Gradation, which is much more ancient, is an Indo-European phenomenon common to all the languages derived from Proto-Indo-European. The vowel differences reflected in Modern English *ride-rode-ridden, choose-chose, bind-bound, come-came, eat-ate, shake-shook,* which exemplify gradation, are thus an Indo-European inheritance.

Like the other Germanic languages, Old English had seven classes of strong verbs. The differences among these classes were in the particular vowel alternations in their principal parts, of which there were four. Like the Modern English preterit of *be,* which distinguishes between the singular *I was* and the plural *we were,* most strong verbs had differing stems for their singular and plural preterits. Had that number distinction survived into present-day English, we would be saying *I rode* but *we rid,* and *I fond* but *we found.* Sometimes the old singular has survived into current use and sometimes the old plural (and sometimes neither, but a different form altogether). Examples, one of each of the seven strong classes and their main subclasses, with their principal parts, follow:

		INFINITIVE	PRETERIT SINGULAR	PRETERIT PLURAL	PAST PARTICIPLE
Class I		wrītan 'write'	wrāt	writon	gewriten
Class II	(1)	clēofan 'cleave'	clēaf	clufon	geclofen
	(2)	scūfan 'shove'	scēaf	scufon	gescofen
	(3)	frēosan 'freeze'	frēas	fruron	gefroren
Class III	(1)	drincan 'drink'	dranc	druncon	gedruncen
	(2)	helpan 'help'	healp	hulpon	geholpen
	(3)	ceorfan 'carve'	cearf	curfon	gecorfen
Class IV		beran 'bear'	bær	bǣron	geboren
Class V	(1)	sprecan 'speak'	spræc	sprǣcon	gesprecen
	(2)	gifan 'give'	geaf	gēafon	gegifen
Class VI		scacan 'shake'	scōc	scōcon	gescacen
Class VII	(1)	cnāwan 'know'	cnēow	cnēowon	gecnāwen
	(2)	hātan 'be called'	hēt	hēton	gehāten

The change from *s* to *r* in the last two principal parts of the class II (3) verb *frēosan* was the result of Verner's Law. The Indo-European accent was on the ending of these forms rather than on the stem of the word, as in the first two principal parts, thus creating the necessary conditions for the operation of Verner's Law. The consonant alternation is not preserved in Modern English.

Preterit-Present Verbs

Old English had a few verbs that were originally strong but whose strong preterit had come to be used with a present-time sense; consequently, they had to form new weak preterits. They are called **preterit-present verbs** and are the main source for the important group of modal verbs in Modern English. The following are ones that survive as present-day modals:

INFINITIVE	PRESENT	PRETERIT
āgan 'owe'	āh	āhte (*ought*)
cunnan 'know how'	cann (*can*)	cūðe (*could*)
magan 'be able'	mæg (*may*)	meahte (*might*)
*mōtan 'be allowed'	mōt	mōste (*must*)
sculan 'be obliged'	sceal (*shall*)	sceolde (*should*)

Although not a part of this group in Old English, the verb *willan* 'wish, want,' whose preterit was *wolde*, also became a part of the present-day modal system as *will* and *would*.

Anomalous Verbs

It is not surprising that very commonly used verbs should have developed irregularities. *Bēon* 'to be' was in Old English, as its modern descendant still is, to some extent a badly mixed-up verb, with alternative forms from several different roots, as follows (with appropriate pronouns):

(ic) eom *or* bēo	'I am'
(þū) eart *or* bist	'you (sg.) are'
(hē, hēo, hit) is *or* bið	'he, she, it is'
(wē, gē, hī) sindon, sind, sint, *or* bēoð	'we, you, they are'

The forms *eom, is,* and *sind(on)* or *sint* were from an Indo-European root *es-, whose forms *esmi, *esti, and *senti are seen in Sanskrit *asmi, asti,* and *santi* and in Latin *sum, est, sunt.* The second person *eart* was from a different Indo-European root *er-, with the original meaning 'arise.' The Modern English plural *are* is from an Anglian form of that root. The forms beginning with *b* were from a third root *bheu-, from which came also Sanskrit *bhavati* 'becomes' and Latin *fuī* 'have been.' The preterit forms were from yet another verb, whose infinitive in Old English was *wesan* (a class V strong verb):

(ic) wæs

(þū) wǣre

(hē, hēo, hit) wæs

(wē, gē, hī) wǣron

The alternation of *s* and *r* in the preterit was the result of Verner's Law. The Old English verb for 'be,' like its Modern English counterpart, combined forms of what were originally four different verbs (seen in the present-day forms *be, am, are, was*). Paradigms that thus combine historically unrelated forms are called **suppletive**.

Another suppletive verb is *gān* 'go,' whose preterit *ēode* was doubtless from the same Indo-European root as the Latin verb *ēo* 'go.' Modern English has lost the *ēode* preterit but has found a new suppletive form for *go* in *went,* the irregular preterit of *wend* (compare *send-sent*). Also irregular, although not suppletive, is *dōn* 'do' with the preterit *dyde* 'did.'

It is notable that *to be* alone has preserved distinctive singular and plural preterit forms (*was* and *were*) in standard Modern English. Nonstandard speakers have carried through the tendency that has reduced the preterit forms of all other verbs to a single form, and they get along very nicely with *you was, we was,* and *they was,* which are certainly no more inherently "bad" than *you sang, we sang,* and *they sang*—for *sung* in the plural would be the historically "correct" development of Old English *gē, wē, hī sungon.*

SYNTAX

Old English syntax has an easily recognizable kinship with that of Modern English. There are, of course, differences—and some striking ones—but they do not disguise the close similarity between an Old English sentence and its Modern English counterpart. Many of those differences have already been treated in this chapter, but they may be summarized as follows:

1. Nouns, adjectives, and most pronouns had fuller inflection for case than their modern developments do; the inflected forms were used to signal a word's function in its sentence.

2. Adjectives agreed in case, number, and gender with the nouns they modified.

3. Adjectives were also inflected for "definiteness" in the so-called strong and weak declensions.

4. Numbers could be used either as we use them, to modify a noun, as in *þrītig scyllingas* 'thirty shillings,' or as nominals, with the accompanying word in the genitive case, as in *þrītig rihtwīsra,* literally 'thirty of righteous men.' Such use of the genitive was regular with the indeclinable noun *fela* 'much, many': *fela goldes* 'much [of] gold' or *fela folca* 'many [of] people.'

5. Old English used the genitive inflection in many circumstances that would call for an *of* phrase in Modern English—for example, *þæs īglandes micel dæl* 'a great deal of the island,' literally, 'that island's great deal.'

6. Old English had no articles, properly speaking. Where we would use a definite article, the Anglo-Saxons often used one of the demonstratives (such as *se* 'that' or *þes* 'this'); and, where we would use an indefinite article, they sometimes used either the numeral *ān* 'one' or *sum* 'a certain.' But all of those words had stronger meanings than the Modern English definite and indefinite articles; thus frequently Old English had no word at all where we would expect an article.

7. Although Old English could form verb phrases just as we do by combining the verbs for 'have' and 'be' with participles (as in Modern English *has run* and *is running*), it did so less frequently, and the system of such combinations was less fully developed. Combinations using both those auxiliary verbs, such as *has been running,* did not occur in Old English, and one-word forms of the verb (like *runs* and *ran*) were used more often than today. Thus, although Old and Modern English are alike in having just two inflected tenses, the present and the preterit, Old English used those tenses to cover a wider range of meanings than does Modern English, which has frequent recourse to verb phrases. Old English often relied on adverbs to convey nuances of meaning that we would express by verb phrases; for example, Modern English "He had come" corresponds to Old English *Hē ǣr cōm,* literally 'He earlier came.'

8. Old English formed passive verb phrases much as we do, but it often used the simple infinitive in a passive sense as we do not—for example, *Hēo hēht hine lǣran* 'She ordered him to be taught,' literally 'She ordered him to teach,' but meaning 'She ordered (someone) to teach him,' in which *hine* 'him' is the object of the infinitive *lǣran* 'to teach,' not of the verb *hēht* 'ordered.' Another Old English alternative for the Modern passive was the indefinite pronoun *man* 'one,' as in *Hine man hēng* 'Him one hanged,' that is, 'He was hanged.'

9. The subjunctive mood was more common in Old English. It was used, for example, after some verbs that do not require it in Modern English, as in *Sume men cweðaþ þæt hit sȳ feaxede steorra* 'Some men say that it [a comet] be a long-haired star.' It is also used in constructions where conservative present-day usage has it: *swilce hē wǣre* 'as if he were' or *þēah hē ealne middangeard gestrȳne* 'though he [the] whole world gain.'

10. Old English had a number of **impersonal verbs** that were used without a subject: *Mē lyst rǣdan* '[It] pleases me to read' and *Swā mē þyncþ* 'So [it] seems to me.' The object of the verb (in these examples, *mē*) comes before it and in the second example gave rise to the now archaic expression *methinks* (literally 'to me seems'), which the modern reader is likely to misinterpret as an odd combination of *me* as subject of the present-day verb *think.*

11. The subject of any Old English verb could be omitted if it was implied by the context, especially when the verb followed a clause that expressed the subject: *Hē þē æt sunde oferflāt, hæfde māre mægen* 'He outstripped you at swimming, [he] had more strength.'

12. On the other hand, the subject of an Old English verb might be expressed twice—once as a pronoun at its appropriate place in the structure of the sentence and once as a phrase or clause in anticipation: *And þā þe þǣr tō lāfe wǣron, hī cōmon to þæs carcernes dura* 'And those that were there as survivors, they came to that prison's door.' This construction occurs in Modern English but is often considered inelegant; it is frequent in Old English.

13. The Old English negative adverb *ne* came before (rather than after) the verb it modified: *Ic ne dyde* 'I did not.' Consequently it contracted with certain following verbs: *nis* (*ne is* 'is not'), *nille* (*ne wille* 'will not'), *næfþ* (*ne hæfþ* 'has not'); compare the Modern English contraction of *not* with certain preceding verbs: *isn't, won't, hasn't.*

14. Old English word order was somewhat less fixed than that of Modern English but in general was similar. Old English declarative sentences tended to fall into the subject-verb-complement order usual in Modern English—for example, *Hē wæs swīðe spēdig man* 'He was a very successful man' and *Eadwine eorl cōm mid landfyrde and drāf hine ūt* 'Earl Edwin came with a land army and drove him out.' However, declarative sentences might have a pronoun object before the verb instead of after it: *Se hālga Andreas him andswarode* 'The holy Andrew him answered.' (Notice also the order of objects in the sentences in numbered paragraph 8 above.) When a sentence began with *þā* 'then, when' or *ne* 'not,' the verb usually preceded the subject: *Þā sealde se cyning him sweord* 'Then gave the king him a sword'; *Ne can ic nōht singan* 'Not can I nought sing (I cannot sing anything).' In dependent clauses the verb usually came last, as it does also in German: *God geseah þā þæt hit gōd wæs* 'God saw then that it good was'; *Sē micla here, þe wē gefyrn ymbe spræcon* . . . 'The great army, which we before about spoke . . . .' Old English interrogative sentences had a verb-subject-complement order, but did not use auxiliary verbs as Modern English does: *Hæfst þū ænigne gefēran?* 'Hast thou any companion?' rather than 'Do you have any companion?'

15. Although Old English had a variety of ways of subordinating one clause to another, it favored what grammarians call **parataxis**—the juxtaposing of clauses with no formal signal of their relationship other than perhaps a coordinating conjunction. These three clauses describe how Orpheus lost his wife Eurydice in an Old English retelling of the Greek legend: *Ðā hē forð on ðæt leoht cōm, ðā beseah he hine under bæc wið ðæs wīfes; ðā losode hēo him sōna* 'Then [when] he forth into that light came, then looked he him backward toward that woman; then slipped she from him immediately.'

There are a good many other syntactic differences that could be listed; if all of them were, the resulting list would suggest that Old English was far removed in structure from its modern development. But the suggestion would be misleading, for the two stages of the language are much more united by their similarities than divided by their differences.

OLD ENGLISH ILLUSTRATED

The first two of the following passages in late West Saxon are from a translation of the Old Testament by Ælfric, the greatest prose writer of the Old English period. The opening verses from Chapters 1 and 2 of Genesis are printed here from the edition of the Early English Text Society (O.S. 160), with abbreviations expanded, modern punctuation and capitalization added, some obvious scribal errors corrected, and a few unusual forms regularized. The third passage is the parable of the Prodigal Son (Luke 15), edited by Walter W. Skeat (*The Holy Gospels in Anglo-Saxon, Northumbrian, and Old Mercian Versions*), also slightly regularized. The fourth passage consists of the opening and closing lines of the epic poem *Beowulf.*

I. *Genesis 1.1–5.*
1. On angynne gescēop God heofonan and eorðan. **2.** Sēo
In [the] beginning created God heavens and earth.   The

eorðe wæs sōðlīce īdel and æmtig, and þēostra wǣron ofer ðǣre
earth was truly void and empty, and darknesses were over the

nywelnysse brādnysse; and Godes gāst wæs geferod ofer wæteru.
abyss's surface; and God's spirit was brought over [the] water.

3. God cwæð ðā: Gewurðe lēoht, and lēoht wearð geworht. **4.** God
God said then: Be light, and light was made.   God

geseah ðā ðæt hit gōd wæs, and hē tōdǣlde ðæt lēoht fram ðām
saw then that it good was, and he divided the light from the

ðēostrum. **5.** And hēt ðæt lēoht dæg and þā ðēostru niht: ðā
darkness.   And called the light day and the darkness night: then

wæs geworden ǣfen and morgen ān dæg.
was made evening and morning one day.

II. *Genesis 2.1–3.*
1. Eornostlīce ðā wǣron fullfremode heofonas and eorðe and
Indeed then were completed heaven and earth and

eall heora frætewung. **2.** And God ðā gefylde on ðone seofoðan dæg
all their ornaments.   And God then finished on the seventh day

fram eallum ðām weorcum ðe hē gefremode. **3.** And God geblētsode
from all the works that he had made.   And God blessed

ðone seofoðan dæg and hine gehālgode, for ðan ðe hē on ðone dæg
the seventh day and it hallowed, because he on that day

geswāc his weorces, ðe hē gescēop tō wyrcenne.
ceased from his work, that he made to be done.

III. *Luke 15.11–17, 20–24.*

11. Sōðlice sum   man hæfde twēgen suna.   **12.** Þā   cwæð se
Truly   a certain man had   two   sons.   Then said the

gingra   tō his fæder, "Fæder, syle mē mīnne dǣl   mīnre   ǣhte
younger to his father, "Father, give me my   portion of my   inheritance

þe   mē tō gebyreþ." Þā   dǣlde   hē him   his ǣhta.   **13.** Ðā
that me to belongs." Then distributed   he to him his inheritance. Then

æfter fēawum dagum ealle his þing   gegaderode se   gingra   sunu and
after a few   days   all   his things gathered   the younger son   and

fērde   wrǣclīce on feorlen   rīce and forspilde   þǣr his ǣhta,
journeyed abroad   in a distant land and utterly lost there his inheritance,

lybbende on his gǣlsan.   **14.** Ðā   hē hȳ haefde ealle āmyrrede, þā
living   in his extravagance. When he it   had   all   spent,   then

wearð mycel hunger on þām rīce and hē wearð wǣdla.   **15.** Þā   fērde
came a great famine on the land and he was   indigent.   Then went

hē and folgode ānum burhsittendum men þæs   rīces; ðā   sende hē
he and served a   city-dwelling man of that land; then sent   he

hine tō his tūne   þæt hē hēolde   his swīn.   **16.** Ðā   gewilnode hē
him to his estate that he should keep his swine.   Then wanted   he

his wambe gefyllan of   þām bēancoddum þe   ðā swȳn ǣton, and him
his belly   to fill   with the bean husks   that the swine ate, and to him

man ne sealde.   **17.** Þā   beþōhte hē hine   and cwæð, "Ēalā hū
no one gave.   Then thought he about himself and said, "Alas how

fela yrðlinga   on mīnes fæder hūse hlāf genōhne habbað, and ic
many farm workers in my   father's house bread enough have,   and I

hēr on hungre forwurðe! ... "   **20.** And hē ārās þā and cōm tō his
here in hunger perish! ... "   And he arose then and came to his

fæder. And þā   gȳt þā   hē wæs feorr   his fæder, hē hine geseah and
father. And when yet then he was far from his father, he him saw   and

wearð   mid mildheortnesse āstyred and ongēan hine arn and hine beclypte
became with compassion   stirred and toward him ran and him embraced

and cyste hine. **21.** Ðā cwæð his sunu, "Fæder, ic syngode on
and kissed him.   Then said his son, "Father, I sinned   against

heofon and beforan ðē. Nū ic ne eom wyrþe þæt ic þīn sunu bēo
heaven and before   thee. Now I not am worthy that I thy son be

genemned." **22.** Ðā cwæþ se fæder tō his þēowum, "Bringað hræðe
named."   Then said   the father to his servants, "Bring   quickly

þone sēlestan gegyrelan and scrȳdað hine, and syllað him hring on his
the   best   garments and clothe him, and give him a ring on his

hand and gescȳ tō his fōtum. **23.** And bringað ān fætt styric and ofslēað,
hand and shoes for his feet.   And bring   a fat calf and slay,

and uton etan and gewistfullian. **24.** For þām þes mīn sunu wæs dēad,
and let us eat and feast.   Because this my son was dead,

and hē geedcucode;   hē forwearð, and hē is gemēt."
and he came to life again; he was lost, and he is found."

IV. ***Beowulf, 1–3, 3178–82.***
Hwæt, wē Gār-Dena   in gēardagum,
Lo! we, of Spear-Danes,   in the old days,

þēodcyniga   þrym gefrūnon,
of the people's kings,   glory have heard,

hū ðā æþelingas   ellen fremedon!
how the princes   did valorous deeds!

. . . .

Swā begnornodon   Gēata lēode
So   lamented   the people of the Geats

hlāfordes hryre,   heorðgenēatas;
the lord's fall,   his hearth-companions;

cwædon þæt hē wære   wyruldcyninga
they said that he had been   of world-kings

manna mildest   ond monðwærust,
mildest of men   and kindest,

lēodum līðost   ond lofgeornost.
gentlest to people   and most eager for honor.

FOR FURTHER READING

General Historical Background

Black. *A History of the British Isles.*
————. *A New History of England.*
Morgan. *The Oxford History of Britain.*

Overviews

Hogg. *The Cambridge History of the English Language.* Vol. 1: *The Beginnings to 1066.*

History and Culture

Smyth. *King Alfred the Great.*
Stenton. *Anglo-Saxon England.*
Welch. *Discovering Anglo-Saxon England.*

Introductory Textbooks

Mitchell and Robinson. *A Guide to Old English.*
Quirk and Wrenn. *An Old English Grammar.*

Grammar

Campbell. *Old English Grammar.*
Faiss. *English Historical Morphology and Word-Formation.*
Fischer et al. *Syntax of Early English.*
Hogg. *A Grammar of Old English.*
Mitchell. *Old English Syntax.*

Lexicon

Barney. *Word-Hoard.*
Hall. *A Concise Anglo-Saxon Dictionary.*
Roberts and Kay. *A Thesaurus of Old English.*

6 THE MIDDLE ENGLISH PERIOD (1100–1500)

The dates for the beginning and end of the Middle English period are more or less arbitrary. By 1100 certain changes, which had begun long before, were well established, and the Norman Conquest had introduced changes that were dramatically to affect the use of English. The consequences of those changes justify our use of the adjective *middle* to designate the language in what was actually a period of transition from the English of the early Middle Ages—Old English—to that of the earliest printed books, which, despite certain superficial differences, is essentially the same as our own.

The changes that occurred during this transitional, or "middle," period may be noted in every aspect of the language: its sounds, the meanings of its words, and the nature of its word stock (many Old English words being replaced by French ones). During the Middle English period there were such extensive changes in pronunciation, particularly of unaccented inflectional endings, that grammar too was profoundly altered. Many of the grammatical distinctions of the Old English period disappeared, thereby producing a language that is structurally far more like the one we speak.

SOME KEY EVENTS IN THE MIDDLE ENGLISH PERIOD

Among the events during the Middle English period that had significant influence on the development of the English language are those listed below.

- 1066   The Normans conquered England, replacing the native English nobility with Anglo-Normans and introducing Norman French as the language of government in England.
- 1204   King John lost Normandy to the French, beginning the loosening of ties between England and the Continent.
- 1258   King Henry III was forced by his barons to accept the Provisions of Oxford, which established a Privy Council to oversee the administration of the government, beginning the growth of the English constitution and parliament.

- 1337   The Hundred Years' War with France began and lasted until 1453, promoting English nationalism.
- 1348–50   The Black Death killed an estimated one-third of England's population, and continued to plague the country for much of the rest of the century.
- 1362   The Statute of Pleadings was enacted, requiring all court proceedings to be conducted in English.
- 1381   The Peasants' Revolt led by Wat Tyler was the first rebellion of working-class people against their exploitation; although it failed in most of its immediate aims, it marks the beginning of popular protest.
- 1384   John Wycliffe died, having promoted the first complete translation of scripture into the English language (the Wycliffite Bible).
- 1400   Geoffrey Chaucer died, having produced a highly influential body of English poetry.
- 1476   William Caxton, the first English printer, established his press at Westminster, thus beginning the widespread dissemination of English literature and the stabilization of the written standard.
- 1485   Henry Tudor became king of England, ending thirty years of civil strife and initiating the Tudor dynasty.

THE BACKGROUND OF THE NORMAN CONQUEST

Almost at the end of the Old English period, the great catastrophe of the Norman Conquest befell the English people—a catastrophe more far-reaching in its effects on English culture than the earlier harassment by the Scandinavians.

After the death without heirs of Edward the Confessor, the last king in the direct male line of descent from Alfred the Great, Harold, son of the powerful Earl Godwin, was elected to the kingship. Almost immediately his possession of the crown was challenged by William, the seventh duke of Normandy, who was distantly related to Edward the Confessor and who felt that he had a better claim to the throne for a number of tenuous reasons.

The Norman Conquest—fortunately for Anglo-American culture and civilization, the last invasion of England—was, like the earlier harassments, carried out by Northmen. Under the leadership of William the Conqueror, they defeated the English and their hapless King Harold at the battle of Hastings in 1066. Harold was killed by an arrow that pierced his eye, and the English, deprived of his effective leadership and that of his two brothers, who had also fallen in the battle, were ignominiously defeated.

William and the Northmen whose *dux* he was did not come immediately from Scandinavia but from France, a region whose northern coast their not-very-remote Viking ancestors had invaded and settled as recently as the ninth and tenth centuries, beginning at about the same time as other pagan Vikings were making trouble for Alfred the Great in England. Those Scandinavians who settled in France are commonly designated by an Old French form of *Northmen,* that is, *Normans,* and the section of France that they settled and governed was called Normandy.

The Conqueror was a bastard son of Robert the Devil, who took such pains in the early part of his life to earn his surname that he became a figure of legend—among other things, he was accused, doubtless justly, of poisoning the brother whom he succeeded as duke of Normandy. So great was his capacity for rascality that he was also called Robert the Magnificent. Ironically, he died in the course of a holy pilgrimage to Jerusalem.

Robert's great-great-grandfather was Rollo (*Hrólfr*), a Danish chieftain who was created first duke of Normandy after coming to terms satisfactory to himself with King Charles the Simple of France. In the five generations intervening between Duke Rollo and Duke William, the Normans had become French culturally and linguistically, at least superficially—though we must always remember that in those days the French had no learning, art, or literature comparable to what was flourishing in England, nor had they ever seen anything comparable, as they themselves were willing to admit, to the products of English artisans: carving, jewelry, tapestry, metalwork, and the like.

English culture changed under French influence, most visibly in the construction of churches and castles, but it retained a distinctively English flavor. The **Norman French** dialect spoken by the invaders developed in England into **Anglo-Norman**, a variety of French that was the object of amusement even among the English in later times, as in Chaucer's remark about the Prioress, that "she spoke French quite fair and neatly—according to the school of Stratford-at-Bow, for the French of Paris was unknown to her."

THE REASCENDANCY OF ENGLISH

For a long time after the Norman Conquest, England was trilingual. Latin was the language of the Church, Norman French of the government, and English of the majority of the country's population. The loss of Normandy in 1204 by King John, a descendant of the Conqueror, removed an important tie with France, and subsequent events were to loosen those ties that remained. By the fourteenth century, a number of events came together to promote the use of English. The Hundred Years' War, beginning in 1337, saw England and France bitter enemies in a long, drawn-out conflict that gave the deathblow to the already moribund use of French in England. Those whose ancestors were Normans eventually came to think of themselves as English.

In addition, the common people had begun to exercise their collective power. The Black Death, or bubonic plague, perhaps reinforced by pneumonia, raged during the middle of the fourteenth century, killing a third to a half of the population. It produced a severe labor shortage that led to demands for higher wages and better treatment of workers. The Peasants' Revolt of 1381, led by Wat Tyler and sparked by a series of poll taxes (fixed taxes on each person), was largely unsuccessful, but it presaged social changes that were centuries in being fulfilled.

Meanwhile, John Wycliffe had challenged the authority of the Church in both doctrinal and organizational matters and spawned a movement called Lollardy, which translated the Bible into English and popularized doctrines that anticipated the Reformation. The fourteenth century also saw the development of a mystical tradition in England that carried through to the early fifteenth century and included works still read, such as Richard Rolle's *Form of Perfect Living,* the anonymous *Cloud of Unknowing,* Walter Hilton's *Scale of Perfection,* Juliana of Norwich's *Revelations of Divine Love,* and even the emotionally autobiographical *Book of Margery Kempe,* more valuable for its insights into medieval life than for its spiritual content. Four cycles of mystery plays, which dramatized the history of the world as recorded in Scripture, and various morality plays such as *Everyman,* which allegorized the human struggle between good and evil, were the forerunners of the great English dramatic tradition from Shakespeare onward.

The late fourteenth century saw a blossoming of alliterative and unrimed English poetry that was a development of the native tradition of versification stretching back to Anglo-Saxon times. The most important work of that revival was William Langland's *Piers Plowman,* which echoes much of the intellectual and social ferment of the time. Another important work was the *Morte Arthure,* an alliterative account of the life and death of King Arthur that anticipated other works on the subject, from Sir Thomas Malory's *Le Morte Darthur* (printed by William Caxton in 1485), through Alfred Lord Tennyson's *Idylls of the King* (1859–88), to Alan Jay Lerner and Frederick Loewe's musical *Camelot* (1960, film 1967) and, in theme if not in plot and characters, the *Star Wars* series. The most highly regarded of the alliterative poems was *Sir Gawain and the Green Knight,* which combines courtly romance, chivalric ideals, moral dilemma, and supernatural folklore. Its anonymous author is known as the *Pearl* poet, from the title of another work he wrote.

Geoffrey Chaucer, the greatest poet of Middle English times and one of the greatest of all times in any language, wrote in both French and English, but his significant work is in English. By the time Chaucer died in 1400, English was well established as the language of England in literary and other uses. By the end of the fourteenth century, public documents and records began to be written in English, and Henry IV used English to claim the throne in 1399.

FOREIGN INFLUENCES ON VOCABULARY

During the Middle English period, Latin continued to exert an important influence on the English vocabulary (Chapter 12, 274–5). Scandinavian loanwords that must have started making their way into the language during the Old English period become readily apparent in Middle English (277–8), and Dutch and Flemish were also significant sources (285–6). However the major new influence, and ultimately the most important, was French (279–81).

The impact of the Norman Conquest on the English language, like that made by the earlier Norse-speaking invaders, was largely in the word stock, though Middle

English also showed some instances of the influence of French idiom and grammar. A huge number of French words were ultimately to become part of the English vocabulary, many of them replacing English words that would have done for us just as well. Suffice it to say that, as a result of the Conquest, the English lexicon acquired a new look.

Compare the following pairs, in which the first word or phrase is from an Old English translation of the parable of the Prodigal Son (cited at the end of the last chapter), and the second is from a Middle English translation (cited at the end of this chapter):

æhta	catel	'property'
burhsittende man	citeseyn	'citizen'
dæl	porcioun	'portion'
dælde	departide	'divided'
forwearð	perischid	'perished'
gælsa	lecherously	'lechery, lecherously'
genōh	plente	'enough, plenty'
gewilnode	coueitide	'wanted, coveted'
gewistfullian	make we feeste	'let us feast'
mildheortness	mercy	'mercy'
rīce	cuntre	'country'
þēow	seruaunt	'servant'
wræclīce	in pilgrymage	'abroad, traveling'

In each case, the first expression is native English and the second is, or contains, a word borrowed from French. In a few instances, the corresponding Modern English expression is different from either of the older forms: though Middle English *catel* survives as *cattle,* its meaning has become more specific than it was; and so has that of Middle English *pilgrymage,* which now refers to a particular kind of journey. However, most of the French terms have continued essentially unchanged in present-day use. The French tincture of our vocabulary, which began in Middle English times, has been maintained or even intensified in Modern English.

MIDDLE ENGLISH SPELLING

Consonants

Just as French words were borrowed, so too were French spelling conventions. Yet some of the apparent innovations in Middle English spelling were, in fact, a return to earlier conventions. For example, the digraph *th* had been used in some of the earliest English texts—those written before 900—but was replaced in later Old English writing by þ and ð; during the Middle English period, *th* was gradually reintroduced, and during early Modern English times printers regularized its use.

Similarly, *uu,* used for [w] in early manuscripts, was supplanted by the runic wynn, but was brought back to England by Norman scribes in a ligatured form as *w.* The origin of this symbol is accurately indicated by its name, *double-u.*

Other new spellings were true innovations. The Old English symbol ȝ (which we transliterate as *g*) was an Irish shape; the letter shape *g* entered English writing later from the Continent. In late Old English, ȝ or *g* had three values, as we have seen (97). In Middle English times, the Old English symbol acquired a somewhat different form, ȝ (called yogh), and was used for several sounds, notably two that came to be spelled *y* and *gh* later in the period. The complex history of these shapes and the sounds they represented is illustrated by the spellings of the following five words:

	GOOSE	YIELD	DRAW	KNIGHT	THROUGH
OE:	gōs [g]	geldan [y]	dragan [ɣ]	cniht [ç]	þurh [x]
ME:	goos [g]	ȝelden [y]	drawen [w]	cniȝt [ç]	þurȝ [x]
		or yelden		*or* knight	*or* thurgh

The symbol yogh (ȝ) was also used to represent *-s* or *-z* at the ends of words in some manuscripts, such as those of the *Pearl* poet, perhaps because it resembles *z* in shape. It continued to be written in Scotland long after the English had given it up, and printers, having no ȝ in their fonts, used *z* for it—as in the names *Kenzie* (compare *Kenny,* with revised spelling to indicate a pronunciation somewhat closer to the historical one) and *Menzies.* The newly borrowed shape *g* was used to represent not only [g] in native words but also the [ǰ] sound in French loanwords like *gem* and *age,* that being the sound represented by *g* before *e* and *i* of French in earlier times.

The consonant sound [v] did not occur initially in Old English, which used *f* for the [v] that developed internally, as in *drifen* 'driven,' *hæfde* 'had,' and *scofl* 'shovel.' Except for a very few words that have entered standard English from Southern English dialects, in which initial [f] became [v]—for instance, *vixen,* the feminine of *vox* 'fox'—no standard English words of native origin begin with [v]. Practically all our words with initial *v* have been taken from Latin or French. No matter how familiar such words as *vulgar* (Latin), *vocal* (Latin), *very* (French), and *voice* (French) may be to us now, they were once regarded as foreign words—as indeed they are, despite their long naturalization. The introduction of the letter *v* (a variant of *u*) to indicate the prehistoric Old English development of [f] to [v] was an innovation of Anglo-Norman scribes in Middle English times: thus the Middle English form of Old English *drifen* was written *driven* or *driuen.*

When *v,* the angular form of curved *u,* came to be used in Middle English, scribes followed the Continental practice of using either symbol for either consonant or vowel; as a general rule, though, *v* was used initially and *u* elsewhere, regardless of the sound indicated, as in *very, vsury* (*usury*), and *euer* (*ever*), except in the neighborhood of *m* and *n,* where for the sake of legibility *v* was frequently used for the vowel in other than initial position.

Ch was used by French scribes, or by English ones under French influence, to indicate the initial sound of *child,* which in Old English had been spelled simply with *c,* as in *cild.* Following a short vowel, the same sound might also be spelled *cch* or *chch;* thus *catch* appears as *cache, cacche,* and *cachche.*

In early Old English times, *sc* symbolized [sk], but during the course of the Old English period the graphic sequence came to indicate [š]. The *sh* spelling for that sound was an innovation of Anglo-Norman scribes (OE *sceal*—ME and ModE *shall*); the scribes sometimes used *s, ss,* and *sch* for the same purpose.

Middle English scribes preferred the spelling *wh* for the phonetically more accurate *hw* used in Old English times, for example, in Old English *hwæt*—Middle and Modern English *what.*

Under French influence, scribes in Middle English times used *c* before *e* and *i* (*y*) in French loanwords—for example, *citee* 'city' and *grace*—with an earlier French value of this symbol [ts], later becoming [s]. In Old English writing, *c* never indicated [s], but only [k] and [č]. Thus, with the introduction of the newer French value, *c* remained an ambiguous symbol, though in a different way: it came to represent [k] before *a, o, u,* and consonants, and [s] before *e, i,* and *y. K,* used occasionally in Old English writing, thus came to be increasingly used before *e, i,* and *y* in Middle English times (OE *cynn* 'race'—ME *kin, kyn*), leaving *c* to represent [s] in that position, as in *certain.*

French scribal practices are responsible for the Middle English spelling *qu,* which French inherited from Latin, replacing Old English *cw,* as in *quellen* 'to kill,' *queen,* and *quethen* 'to say,' which despite their French look are all native English words (in Old English, respectively, *cwellan, cwēn,* and *cweðan*).

Also French in origin is the digraph *gg* for [ǰ], supplanting in medial and final positions Old English *cg* (OE *ecg*—ME *egge*), later written *dg(e),* as in Modern English *edge.*

Vowels

To indicate vowel length, Middle English writing frequently employed double letters, particularly *ee* and *oo,* the practice becoming general in the East Midland dialect late in the period. These particular doublings have survived into our own day, though, of course, they do not indicate the same sounds as in Middle English. As a matter of fact, both *ee* and *oo* were ambiguous in the Middle English period, as every student of Chaucer must learn. One of the vowel sounds indicated by Middle English *ee* (namely [ɛ:]) came generally to be written *ea* in the course of the sixteenth century; for the other sound (namely [e:]), *ee* was retained, alongside *ie* and, less frequently, *ei*—spellings that were also used to some extent in Middle English.

Double *o* came to be commonly used in later Middle English times for the long rounded vowel [ɔ:], the vowel that developed out of Old English long *ā.* Unfortunately for the beginning student, the same double *o* was used for the continuation of Old English long *ō.* As a result of this duplication, *rood* 'rode' (OE *rād*) and *rood* 'rood, cross' (OE *rōd*) were written with identical vowel symbols, though they were no more nearly alike in pronunciation ([rɔːd] and [roːd] respectively) than are their modern forms.

Because [ɛː] and [ɔː] are both lower vowels than [eː] and [oː] and thus are made with the mouth in a more open position, they are called **open** *e* and **open** *o*, as distinct from the second pair, which are **close** *e* and **close** *o*. In modern transcriptions of Middle English spelling, the open vowels may be indicated by a subscript hook under the letter: *ę̄* for [ɛː] and *ǭ* for [ɔː], whereas the close vowels are left unmarked except for length: *ē* for [eː] and *ō* for [oː]. The length mark and the hook are both modern scholarly devices to indicate pronunciation; they were not used by scribes in Middle English times, and the length mark is unnecessary when a long vowel is spelled with double vowel letters, as they indicate the extra length of the sound.

Final unstressed *e* following a single consonant also indicated vowel length in Middle English, as in *fode* 'food' and *fede* 'to feed'; this corresponds to the "silent *e*" of Modern English, as in *case, mete, bite, rote,* and *rule.* Doubled consonants, which indicated consonant length in earlier periods, began in Middle English times to indicate also that a preceding vowel was short. Surviving examples are *dinner* and *bitter,* as contrasted with *diner* and *biter.* In the North of England, *i* was frequently used after a vowel to indicate that it was long, a practice responsible for such modern spellings as *raid* (literally a 'riding,' from the OE noun *rād*), *Reid* (a long-voweled variant of *red,* surviving only as a proper name), and Scots *guid* 'good,' as in Robert Burns's "Address to the Unco Guid, or the Rigidly Righteous."

Short *u* was commonly written *o* during the latter part of the Middle English period if *i, m, n,* or *u* (*v, w*) were contiguous, because those **stroke letters** were made with parallel slanting lines and so, when written in succession, could not be distinguished. A Latin orthographical joke about "minimi mimi" ('very small mimes, dwarf actors') was written with those letters and consequently was illegible. The Middle English spellings *sone* 'son' and *sonne* 'sun' thus indicate the same vowel sound [ʊ] that these words had in Old English, when they were written respectively *sunu* and *sunne.* The spelling *o* for *u* survives in a number of Modern English words besides *son*—for example, *come* (OE *cuman*), *wonder* (OE *wundor*), *monk* (OE *munuc*), *honey* (OE *hunig*), *tongue* (OE *tunge*), and *love* (OE *lufu*), the last of which, if it had not used the *o* spelling, would have been written *luue* (as indeed it was for a time).

The French spelling *ou* came to be used generally in the fourteenth century to represent English long *ū*—for example, *hous* (OE *hūs*)—and sometimes represented the short *u* as well. Before a vowel, the *u* of the digraph *ou* might well be mistaken as representing [v], for which the same symbol was used. To avoid confusion (as in *douer,* which was a possible writing for both *dower* and *Dover*), *u* was doubled in this position—that is, written *uu,* later *w.* This use of *w,* of course, would have been unnecessary if *u* and *v* had been differentiated as they are now. *W* also came to be used instead of *u* in final position.

Middle English scribes used *y* for the semivowel [y] and also, for the sake of legibility, as a variant of *i* in the vicinity of stroke letters—for example, *myn homcomynge* 'my homecoming.' Late in the Middle English period there was a tendency to write *y* for long *ī* generally. *Y* was also regularly used in final position.

Middle English spelling was considerably more relaxed than present-day orthography. The foregoing remarks describe some of the spelling conventions of Middle English scribes, but there were a good many others, and all of them were used with a nonchalance that is hardly imaginable after the introduction of the printing press. Within a few lines, a scribe might spell both *water* and *watter, treese* and *tres* 'trees,' *nakid* and *nakyd* 'naked,' *eddre* and *edder* 'adder,' *moneth* and *moneþ* 'month,' *clowdes* and *cloudeʒ* 'clouds,' as did the scribe who copied out a manuscript of the Wycliffite Bible. The notion that every word has, or ought to have, just one correct spelling is relatively recent and certainly never occurred to our medieval ancestors.

THE RISE OF A LONDON STANDARD

Middle English had a diversity of dialects. Its Northern dialect corresponds roughly to Old English Northumbrian, its southernmost eastern boundary being also the Humber. Likewise, the Midland dialects, subdivided into East Midland and West Midland, correspond roughly to Old English Mercian. The Southern dialect, spoken south of the Thames, similarly corresponds roughly to West Saxon, with Kentish a subdivision.

It is not surprising that London speech—essentially East Midland in its characteristics, though showing Northern and to a less extent Southern influences—should in time have become a standard for all of England. London had for centuries been a large (by medieval standards), prosperous, and hence important city.

Until the late fifteenth century, however, authors wrote in the dialect of their native regions—the authors of *Sir Gawain and the Green Knight* and *Piers Plowman* wrote in the West Midland dialect; the authors of *The Owl and the Nightingale,* the *Ancrene Riwle,* and the *Ayenbite of Inwit* wrote in the Southern dialect (including Kentish); the author of the *Bruce* wrote in the Northern dialect; and John Gower and Geoffrey Chaucer wrote in the East Midland dialect, specifically the London variety of East Midland. Standard Modern English—both American and British—is a development of the speech of London. This dialect had become the norm for people of consequence and for those who aspired to be people of consequence long before the settlement of America by English-speaking people in the early part of the seventeenth century, though many of those who migrated to the New World obviously retained traces of their regional origins in their pronunciation, vocabulary, and to a lesser degree syntax. Rather than speaking local dialects, most used a type of speech that had been influenced in varying degrees by the London standard. In effect, their speech was essentially that of London, with regional shadings.

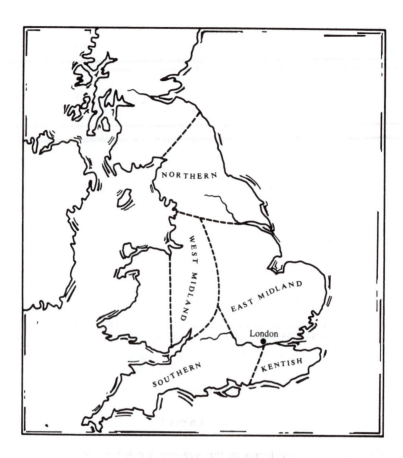

Thus it comes about that the language of Chaucer and of Gower is so much easier for us to comprehend at first sight than, say, the Northern speech (specifically
lowland Scots) of their contemporary John Barbour, author of the *Bruce.* In the following lines from Chaucer's *House of Fame,* for instance, an erudite eagle
explains to Chaucer what speech really is:

```
     Soune ys noght but eyre ybroken
     And every spech that ys yspoken,
     Lowde or pryvee, foule or faire,
     In his substaunce ys but aire;
  5  For as flaumbe ys but lyghted smoke,
     Ryght soo soune ys aire y-broke.
     But this may be in many wyse,
     Of which I wil the twoo devyse:
     Of soune that cometh of pipe or harpe.
 10  For when a pipe is blowen sharpe
     The aire ys twyst with violence
```

And rent. Loo, thys ys my sentence.
Eke, when men harpe strynges smyte,
Whether hyt be moche or lyte,
15 Loo, with the stroke the ayre to-breketh
And right so breketh it when men speketh:
Thus wost thou wel what thinge is speche.

Now compare Chaucer's English, so like our own, with that of the following excerpt from the *Bruce:*

Þan wist he weill þai wald him sla,
And for he wald his lord succour
He put his lif in aventur
And stud intill a busk lurkand
5 Quhill þat þe hund com at his hand,
And with ane arrow soyn hym slew
And throu the wod syne hym withdrew.

Scots needs to be translated to be easily understood:

Then he knew well they wished to slay him,
And because he wished to succor his lord
He put his life in fortune's hands
And stood lurking in a bush
5 While the hound came to his hand,
And with one arrow immediately slew him
And through the wood afterward withdrew himself.

Distinctively Northern forms in this passage are *slā* (corresponding to East Midland *slee*), *wald* (E. Midl. *wolde[n]*), *stud* (E. Midl. *sto[o]d*), *weill* (in which the *i* indicates length of the preceding *e*), *lurkand* (E. Midl. *lurking*), *quhīll* (E. Midl. *whȳl*), *āne* (E. Midl. *oon* [ɔːn]), *intill* (E. Midl. *intō*), and *syne* (E. Midl. *sith*). *Soyn* 'soon, immediately' is merely a matter of spelling: the *y,* like the *i* in *weill,* indicates length of the preceding vowel and not a pronunciation of the vowel different from that indicated by the usual East Midland spelling *sone.* The nominative form of the third person plural pronoun, *þai* 'they,' was adopted in the North from Scandinavian and gradually spread into the other dialects. The **oblique forms** (that is, nonnominative cases) *their* and *them* were not used in London English or in the Midland and South generally at this time, though they were common enough in the North. Chaucer uses *they* for the nominative, but he retains the native forms *here* (or *hire*) and *hem* as oblique forms. A Northern characteristic not illustrated in the passage cited is the *-es, -is,* or *-ys* verb ending of the third person singular and all plural forms of the present indicative (*he redys* 'he reads,' *thai redys* 'they read'). Also Northern, but not occurring in the passage, is the frequent correspondence of *k* to the *ch* of the other dialects, as in *birk-birch, kirk-chirche, mikel-michel* 'much,' and *ilk-eech* 'each.'

Throughout this chapter, the focus of attention is on London speech, which is the ancestor of standard Modern English, rather than on other dialects like that of the *Bruce*. Unless otherwise qualified, the term *Middle English* is used here to refer to the language of the East Midland area and specifically to that of London.

CHANGES IN PRONUNCIATION

Principal Consonant Changes

Throughout the history of English, the consonants have remained relatively stable, as compared with the notable vowel changes that have occurred. The Old English consonant sounds written *b, c* (in both its values in late Old English, [k] and [č]), *d, f* (in both its values, [f] and [v]), ʒ (in two of its values, [g] and [y]), *h* (in both its values, [h] and [x]), *k, l, m, n, p, r, s, t, þ* (*ð*), *w,* and *x* (that is, [ks]) remained unchanged in Middle English. Important spelling differences occur, however, most of them due to Anglo-Norman influence. They have been treated earlier in this chapter (127–9).

The more important changes in consonant sounds, other than the part played by *g* in the formation of new diphthongs (137), may be summarized as follows:

1. The Old English sequences *hl, hn,* and *hr* (*hlēapan* 'to leap,' *hnutu* 'nut,' *hraðor* 'sooner') were simplified to *l, n,* and *r* (*lēpen, nute, rather*). To some extent *hw,* written *wh* in Middle English, was also frequently reduced to *w,* at least in the Southern dialect. In the North, however, the *h* in this sequence was not lost. It survives to this day in some types of English, including the speech of parts of the United States. The sequence was frequently written *qu* and *quh* in Northern texts.

2. The Old English voiced velar fricative *g* after *l* or *r* became *w,* as in *halwen* 'to hallow' (OE *halgian*) and *morwe(n)* 'morrow' (OE *morgen*).

3. Between a consonant, particularly *s* or *t,* and a back vowel, *w* was lost, as in *sǭ* (OE *swā*) and *tō* 'two' (OE *twā*). Since Old English times it had been lost in various negative contractions regardless of what vowel followed, as in Middle English *nil(le)* from *ne wil(le), nǭt* from *ne wǭt, nas* from *ne was,* and *niste* from *ne wiste* (in which the *w* was postconsonantal because of elision of the *e* of *ne*). *Nille* survives in *willy-nilly.* A number of spellings with "silent *w*" continue to occur—for example, *two, sword,* and *answer* (early ME *andswarien*).

4. In unstressed syllables, *-ch* was lost in late Middle English, as in *-ly* (OE *-lic*). The form *ī* for the first person nominative singular pronoun represents a restressing of the *i* that alone remained of *ich* (OE *ic*) after this loss.

5. Before a consonant, sometimes with syncope of an unstressed vowel, *v* was lost in a few words like *hẹd* (by way of *hẹvd, hẹved,* from OE *hēafod*), *lǭrd* (*lǭverd,* OE *hlāford*), *hast, hath,* and *had* (OE *hæfst, hæfð,* and *hæfde*).

6. The Old English prefix *ge-* became *i-* (*y-*) as in *iwis* 'certain' (OE *gewiss*) and *ilimpen* 'to happen' (OE *gelimpan*).

7. Final inflectional *n* was gradually lost, as was also the final *n* of the unstressed possessive pronouns *mīn* and *þīn* and of the indefinite article before a consonant: compare Old English *mīn fæder* 'my father' with Middle English *mȳ fader* (but *mȳn eye* 'my eye'). This loss of *-n* is indirectly responsible for *a newt* (from *an ewte*) and *a nickname* (from *an ekename* 'an also-name'), where the *n* of the indefinite article has attached itself to the following word. In *umpire* (ME *noumpere*), *adder* (ME *nadder,* compare German *Natter* 'snake'), *auger* (ME *nauger*), and *apron* (ME *napron,* compare *napkin, napery* 'household linen') just the opposite has happened: the *n* of the noun attached itself to the article.

8. In the Southern dialect, including Kentish, initial *f, s,* and doubtless *þ* as well were voiced. It was noted as current in some of the Southern counties of England by Joseph Wright in his *English Dialect Grammar* (1905) and is reflected in such standard English words of Southern provenience as *vixen* 'she-fox' (OE *fyxe*) and *vat* (OE *fæt*).

9. Many words were borrowed from Old French (and much less frequently from Latin) beginning with [v] (for instance, *veal, virtue, visit*) and later with [z] (for instance, *zeal, zodiac*). As a result, these sounds frequently appeared in initial position, where they had not occurred in Old English.

10. Initial [θ] in words usually unstressed (for instance, *the, this, they*) was voiced to [ð].

11. With the eventual loss of final *-e* [ə] (140), [v], [z], and [ð] came to occur also in final position, as in *give, lose, bathe.*

As a result of the last four changes, the voiced fricatives, which in Old English had been mere allophones of the voiceless ones, achieved phonemic status.

Middle English Vowels

The Old English long-vowel sounds *ē, ī, ō,* and *ū* remained unchanged in Middle English although their spelling possibilities altered: thus Old English *fēt,* Middle English *fēt, feet* 'feet'; OE *rīdan,* ME *rīden, rȳden* 'to ride'; OE *fōda,* ME *fōde, foode* 'food'; OE *hūs,* Middle English *hous* 'house.'

Except for Old English *æ* and *y,* the short vowels of those Old English stressed syllables that remained short were unchanged in most Middle English speech—for example, OE *wascan* 'to wash,' ME *washen;* OE *helpan* 'to help,' ME *helpen;* OE *sittan* 'to sit,' ME *sitten;* OE *hoppian* 'to hop,' ME *hoppen;* and OE *hungrig* 'hungry,' ME *hungry.* The rest of the vowels underwent the following changes:

1. Old English *ȳ* [ü:] underwent **unrounding** to [i:] in the Northern and the East Midland areas. It remained unchanged, though written *u* or *ui,* in the greater part of the West Midland and all of the Southwest until the later years of the fourteenth century, when it was unrounded and hence fell together with the Northern and East Midland development. In Kent and elsewhere in the Southeast, the Old English sound became [e:]. Hence Old English *hȳdan* 'to hide' is reflected in Middle English in such dialect variants as *hīden, hūden,* and *hēden.*

2. In the Northern and East Midland areas, Old English *y* [ü] was unrounded to [ı], exactly as *ȳ* [ü:] was unrounded to [i:] in the same areas. In the Southeast it became *e;* but in the West Midland and the Southwest, it remained as a rounded vowel [ü], written *u*, until late Middle English times, when it was unrounded.

3. Old English *ā* remained only in the North (*hām* 'home,' *rāp* 'rope,' *stān* 'stone'), becoming [e:] in Modern Scots, as in *hame, rape,* and *stane*. Everywhere south of the Humber, *ā* became [ɔ:] and was spelled *o* or *oo* exactly like the [o:] that remained from Old English, as in *fo(o)de*. One can tell certainly how to pronounce a Middle English word so spelled by referring to its Old English form; thus, if the *o(o)* corresponds to Old English *ā* (ME *stoon*, OE *stān*), the Middle English sound is [ɔ:]; if the Old English word has *ō* (ME *mōne*, OE *mōna;* ME *root(e)*, OE *rōt*), the Middle English sound is unchanged. But there is an easier way for the beginning student of Middle English literature, who may not be familiar with Old English, and it is fairly certain: if the modern sound is [o], typically spelled *o* with "silent *e*" (as in *roe, rode*) or *oa* (as in *road*), then the Middle English sound is [ɔ:]. If, however, the Modern English sound is [u], [ʊ], or [ə], spelled *oo*, the Middle English sound is [o:], as in, respectively, Modern English *food, foot,* and *flood*, going back to Middle English [fo:də], [fo:t], and [flo:d].

There are, however, a number of special or exceptional cases. The Middle English [o:] of *twō,* as also of *whō* (OE *hwā*), developed from early Middle English [ɔ:] by assimilation to the preceding [w], which was then lost (as observed above in item 3 on consonant changes, 134). Thus Old English *twā* and *hwā* regularly became early Middle English [twɔ:] and [hwɔ:], which assimilated to later Middle English [to:] and [ho:], the sources of Modern English *two* [tu] and *who* [hu] (spelling preserves the now archaic forms from early Middle English).

Other exceptions are *gold* and *Rome*, which had [o:] in Middle English and [u] in early Modern English. Compare the proper name *Gould* and early rimes of *Rome* with *doom, room,* and so forth, in the poetry, for example, of Pope and Dryden. The earlier pronunciation of *Rome* is indicated by Shakespeare's pun in *Julius Caesar* 1.2.156: "Now is it Rome indeed, and room enough," which he repeats elsewhere. The change back to [rom] and [gold] has occurred in fairly recent times.

Brooch [broč] is an exceptional instance of *oo* as a spelling for [o] from Middle English [ɔ:]. A spelling pronunciation [bruč] is occasionally heard.

4. Old English [æ:] became Middle English [ɛ:]. Both [e:] and [ɛ:] were written *e* or *ee* in Middle English. In early Modern English times, *ea* was adopted as a spelling for most of those words that in the Middle English dialects spoken north of the Thames had [ɛ:], whereas those words that had in the same dialects [e:] usually continued the Middle English *e(e)* spelling. This difference in spelling is a great blessing to beginning students of Chaucer. By reference to it, they may ascertain that *swete breeth* in the fifth line of the General Prologue to the *Canterbury Tales* is to be read [swe:tə brɛ:θ]. The Modern English spellings *sweet* and *breath* here, as often, provide the clue to the Middle English pronunciation.

5. Old English short *æ* fell together with short *a* and came to be written like it in Middle English: Old English *glæd*—Middle English *glad*. In Southwest Midland and in Kentish, however, words that in Old English had short *æ* were written with *e* (for instance, *gled*) in early Middle English times—a writing that may have indicated little change from the Old English sound in those areas.

Changes in Diphthongs

The diphthongal system changed radically between Old English and Middle English. The old diphthongs disappeared and a number of new ones ([aɪ, eɪ, aʊ, ɔʊ, ɛʊ, ɪʊ, ɔɪ, ʊɪ]) developed:

1. The Old English long diphthongs *ēa* and *ēo* underwent **smoothing**, or **monophthongization**, in late Old English times (eleventh century), occurring in the twelfth century as [ɛ:] and (in the greater part of England) [e:], respectively. Their subsequent Modern English development coincided with that of [ɛ:] and [e:] from other origins. Thus post-eleventh-century Middle English *lęęf* 'leaf' [lɛ:f] develops out of Old English *lēaf,* and *seen* 'to see' [se:n] out of Old English *sēon.*

The short diphthongs *ea* and *eo* became by the twelfth century, respectively, *a* and *e,* as in Middle English *yaf* 'gave' from Old English *geaf* and *herte* 'heart' from Old English *heorte.*

2. In early Middle English, two new diphthongs ending in the off-glide [ɪ]— [aɪ] and [eɪ]—developed from Old English sources, a development that had in fact begun in late Old English times. One source of this development was the **vocalization** of *g* to *i* after front vowels (OE *sægde* 'said,' ME *saide;* OE *weg* 'way,' ME *wey*). Another source was the development of an *i*-glide between a front vowel and Old English *h,* which represented a voiceless fricative when it did not begin words (late OE *ehta* 'eight,' ME *eighte*). In late Middle English, the two diphthongs [aɪ] and [eɪ] fell together and became a single diphthong—presumably [aɪ]—as we know, for example, from the fact that Chaucer rimes words like *day* (which earlier had [aɪ]) and *wey* (which earlier had [eɪ]). When the off-glide followed *i,* it served merely to lengthen that vowel (OE *lige* 'falsehood,' ME *līe*).

3. Four new diphthongs ending in the off-glide [ʊ]—[aʊ], [ɔʊ], [ɛʊ], and [ɪʊ]—also developed from Old English sources. The vocalization of *g* (the voiced velar fricative) to *u* after back vowels contributed to the first two of these new diphthongs (OE *sagu* 'saw, saying,' ME *sawe;* OE *boga* 'bow,' ME *bowe*). Another source for the same two diphthongs was the development of a *u*-glide between a back vowel and Old English *h* (OE *āht* 'aught,' ME *aught;* OE *brohte* 'brought,' ME *broughte*). A third source contributed to all four diphthongs: *w* after a vowel became a *u*-glide but continued usually to be written (OE *clawu* 'claw,' ME *clawe;* OE *grōwan* 'to grow,' ME *growen;* OE *lǣwede* 'unlearned,' ME *lewed;* OE *nīwe* 'new,' ME *newe*). **Diphthongization** often involved a new concept of syllable division— for example, Old English *clawu* [kla-wʊ] but Middle English *clawe* [klaʊ-ə]. When the off-glide followed *u,* it merely lengthened it (OE *fugol* 'fowl,' ME *foul* [fu:l]).

4. Two Middle English diphthongs are of French origin, entering our language in the loanwords borrowed from the French-speaking conquerors of England. The diphthong [ɔɪ] is spelled *oi* or *oy,* as in *joie* 'joy' and *cloistre* 'cloister.' The diphthong [ʊɪ] is also written *oi* or *oy,* as in *boilen* 'to boil,' *poisen* 'to poison,' and *joinen* 'to join,' perhaps because of the substitution of *o* for *u* next to stroke letters, as noted above. Words containing the second diphthong have [əɪ] in early Modern English—pronunciations that have survived in nonstandard speech and are reflected in the dialect spellings *bile, pizen,* and *jine.* (E. J. Dobson 2:810–26 treats this complex subject at length.)

Other diphthongal developments are taken up in specialized grammars of Middle English. It was noted above that as the Old English diphthongs were smoothed into monophthongs, new diphthongs developed in Middle English. These have, in turn, undergone smoothing in Modern English (for instance, ME *drawen* [drauən], ModE *draw* [drɔ]). The process of smoothing still goes on: some inland Southern American speakers lack off-glides in [aɪ], so that "my wife" comes out as something very like [ma waf], and the off-glide may also be lost in *oil, boil,* and the like. On the other hand, new diphthongs have also developed: for instance, ME *rīden* [riːdən], ModE *ride* [raɪd]; ME *hous* [huːs], ModE *house* [haʊs]. Others have continued to develop: [ʊ] and [ɪ] off-glides occur in words like *boat* and *bait,* and some American dialects have glides in words like *head* [hɛəd] and *bad* [bæɪd].

Lengthening and Shortening of Vowels

In addition to the qualitative vowel changes mentioned above, there were some important quantitative changes, that is, changes in the length of vowels:

1. In late Old English times, originally short vowels were lengthened before *mb, nd, ld, rd,* and *rð.* This **lengthening** frequently failed to maintain itself, and by the end of the Middle English period it is to be found only with *i* and *o* before *mb* (*clīmben* 'to climb,' *cǭmb* 'comb'); with *i* and *u* before *nd* (*bīnden* 'to bind,' *bounden* 'bound'); and generally before *ld* (*mīlde* 'mild,' *yēlden* 'to pay, yield,' *ǭld* 'old,' *gōld* 'gold'). Reshortening has subsequently occurred, however, in some words—for instance, *wind* (noun), *held, send, friend;* compare *wind* (verb), *field, fiend,* in which the lengthening survives. If another consonant followed any of the sequences mentioned, lengthening did not occur; this fact explains Modern English *child-children* (OE *cild*–nominative-accusative plural *cildru*).

2. Considerably later than the lengthenings due to the consonant sequences just discussed, short *a, e,* and *o* were lengthened when they were in **open syllables,** that is, in syllables in which they were followed by a single consonant plus another vowel, such as *bāken* 'to bake' (OE *bacan*). In Old English, short vowels frequently occurred in such syllables—for example, *nama* 'name,' *stelan* 'to steal,' *þrote* 'throat,' which became in Middle English, respectively, *nāme, stęlen, thrǫte.* This lengthening is reflected in the plural of *staff* (from ME *staf,* going back to OE *stæf*): *staves* (from ME *stāves,* going back to OE *stafas*). Short *i* (*y*) and *u* were likewise lengthened in open syllables, beginning in the fourteenth century in the North, but these vowels underwent a qualitative change also: *i* (*y*) became *ē,* and *u* became *ō*—for example, Old English *wicu* 'week,' *yvel* 'evil,' *wudu* 'wood,' which became, respectively, *wēke, ēvel, wōde.* This lengthening in open syllables was a new principle in English. Its results are still apparent, as in *staff* and *staves,* though the distinction between open and closed syllables disappeared in such words with the loss of final unstressed *e,* as a result of which the vowels of, say, *staves, week,* and *throat* now occur in closed syllables: [stevz], [wik], and [θrot].

3. Conversely, beginning in the Old English period, originally long vowels in syllables followed by certain consonant sequences were shortened. The consonant sequences that caused **shortening** included lengthened (doubled) consonants but naturally excluded those sequences that lengthened a preceding vowel, mentioned above under item 1. For example, there is shortening in *hidde* 'hid' (OE *hȳdde*), *kepte* 'kept' (OE *cēpte*), *fifty* (OE *fīftig*), *fiftēne* (OE *fīftȳne*), *twenty* (OE *twēntig*), and *wisdom* (OE *wīsdōm*). It made no difference whether the consonant sequence was in the word originally (as in OE *sōfte,* ME *softe*), was the result of adding an inflectional ending (as in *hidde*), or was the result of compounding (as in OE *wīsdōm*). The effects of this shortening can be seen in the following Modern English pairs, in which the first member has an originally long vowel and the second has a vowel that was shortened: *hide-hid, keep-kept, five-fifty,* and *wise-wisdom.* There was considerable wavering in vowel length before the sequence *-st,* as indicated by such Modern English forms as *Christ-fist, ghost-lost,* and *least-breast.*

4. Vowels in unstressed syllables were shortened. Lack of stress on the second syllable of *wisdom* accounts for its Middle English shortening from the Old English *dōm.* Similarly, words that were usually without stress within the sentence were subject to vowel shortening—for example, *an* (OE *ān* 'one'), *but* (OE *būtan*), and *not* (OE *nāwiht*).

5. Shortening also occurred regularly before two unstressed syllables, as reflected in *wild-wilderness, Christ-Christendom,* and *holy-holiday.*

Leveling of Unstressed Vowels

As far as the grammar of English is concerned, the most significant of all phonological developments in the language occurred with the falling together of *a, o,* and *u* with *e* in unstressed syllables, all ultimately becoming [ə], as in the following:

Old English	*Middle English*
lama 'lame'	lāme
faran 'to fare,' faren (past part.)	fāren
stānes 'stone's,' stānas 'stones'	stǭnes
feallað 'falleth'	falleth
nacod 'naked'	nāked
macodon 'made' (pl.)	mākeden
sicor 'sure'	sēker
lengðu 'length'	lengthe
medu 'liquor'	mẹde

This **leveling**, or **merging**, was alluded to in the last chapter, for it began well before the end of the Old English period. The *Beowulf* manuscript (ca. A.D. 1000), for instance, has occurrences of *-as* for the genitive singular *-es* ending, *-an* for both the preterit plural ending *-on* and the dative plural ending *-um* (the *-m* in *-um* had become *-n* late in the Old English period), *-on* for the infinitive ending *-an,* and *-o* for both the genitive plural ending *-a* and the neuter nominative plural ending *-u,* among a number of such interchanges pointing to identical vowel quality in such syllables. The spelling *e* for the merged vowel became normal in Middle English.

Loss of Schwa in Final Syllables

The leveled final *e* [ə] was gradually lost in the North in the course of the thirteenth century and in the Midlands and the South somewhat later. Many words, however, continued to be spelled with *-e,* even when it was no longer pronounced. Because a word like *rīd(e)* (OE *rīdan*) was for a time pronounced either with or without its final [ə], other words like *brīd(e)* (OE *brȳd*) acquired by analogy an optional **inorganic *-e*** in both spelling and pronunciation. That this historically unjustified [ə] was pronounced is indicated in a good many lines of verse, such as Chaucer's "A bryde shal net eten in the halle" (*Canterbury Tales,* E 1890), in which the scansion of the line of iambic pentameter requires "bryde" to have two syllables. There was also a **scribal *-e*,** which was not pronounced but merely added to the spelling for various reasons, such as filling out a short line, in the days before English orthography was standardized.

In the inflectional ending *-es,* the unstressed *e* (written *i, y,* and *u* in some dialects) was ultimately lost except after the sibilants [s], [z], [š], [č], and [ǰ]. This loss was a comparatively late development, beginning in the North in the early fourteenth century. It did not occur in the Midlands and the South until somewhat later.

In the West Saxon and Kentish dialects of Old English, *e* was usually lost in the ending *-eð* for the third person singular of the present indicative of verbs. It is hence not surprising to find such loss in this ending in the Southern dialect of Middle English and, after long syllables, in the Midland dialects as well, as in *mākth* 'maketh' and *bērth* 'beareth,' as also sometimes after short syllables, as in *comth.* Chaucer uses both forms of this ending; sometimes the loss of [ə] is not indicated by the spelling but is dictated by the meter.

The vowel sound was retained in *-ed* until the fifteenth century. It has not yet disappeared in the forms *aged, blessed,* and *learned* when they are used as adjectives. Compare *learnëd woman, the blessëd Lord,* and *agëd man* with "The woman learned her lesson," "The Lord blessed the multitude," and "The man aged rapidly." (In "aged whiskey," the form *aged* is used as a past participle—one could not say "very aged whiskey"—in contrast to the adjectival use in *agëd man.*) And the vowel of *-ed* is still retained, of course, after *t* or *d,* as in *heated* or *heeded.*

CHANGES IN GRAMMAR

Reduction of Inflections

As a result of the merging of unstressed vowels into a single sound, the number of distinct inflectional endings in English was drastically reduced. Middle English became a language with few inflectional distinctions, whereas Old English, as we have seen, was relatively highly inflected, although less so than Germanic. This reduction of inflections was responsible for a structural change of the greatest importance.

In the adjective—for instance, the Old English weak forms (those used after the demonstratives)—the endings *-a* (masculine nominative) and *-e* (neuter nominative-accusative and feminine nominative) fell together in a single form as *-e.* Thus an indication of gender distinguishing the masculine form was lost. Middle English *the ǭlde man* (OE *se ealda man*) has the same adjective ending as *the ǭlde tāle* (OE feminine *sēo ealde talu*) and *the ǭlde sword* (OE neuter *þæt ealde sweord*). The Old English weak adjective endings *-an* and *-um* had already fallen together as *-en* and, with the loss of final *-n,* they also came to have only *-e.* The Old English genitive plural forms of the weak adjective in *-ena* and *-ra,* after first becoming *-ene* and *-re,* were made to conform to the predominant weak adjective form in *-e,* though there are a very few late survivals of the Old English genitive plural in *-ra* as Middle English *-er,* notably in *aller* (OE *ealra*) and related forms. Thus the five singular and plural forms of the Old English weak adjective declension (*-a, -e, -an, -ena,* and *-um*) were reduced to a single form ending in *-e,* with gender as well as number distinctions completely obliterated. For the strong function, the endingless form of the Old English nominative singular was used throughout the singular, with a generalized plural form (identical with the weak adjective declension) in *-e:* thus (strong singular) *grēǫt lord* 'great lord' but (generalized plural) *grēǫte lordes* 'great lords.'

To describe the situation more simply, Middle English monosyllabic adjectives ending in consonants had a single inflection, *-e,* used to modify singular nouns in the weak function and all plural nouns. Other adjectives—for example, *free* and *gentil*—were uninflected. This simple grammatical situation can be inferred from many of the manuscripts only with difficulty, however, because scribes frequently wrote final *e*'s where they did not belong.

Changes resulting from the leveling of vowels in unstressed syllables were considerably more far-reaching than what has been shown in the declension of the adjective. For instance, the older endings *-an* (infinitives and most of the oblique, or non-nominative, forms of *n*-stem nouns), *-on* (indicative preterit plurals), and *-en* (subjunctive preterit plurals and past participles of strong verbs) all fell together as *-en.* With the later loss of final inflectional *-n* in some of these forms, only *-e* [ə] was left, and in time this was also to go. This loss accounts for endingless infinitives, preterit plurals, and some past participles of strong verbs in Modern English, for instance:

Old English	Middle English	Modern English
findan (inf.)	finde(n)	find
fundon (pret. pl.)	founde(n)	found
funden (past part.)	founde(n)	found

It was similar with the Old English -as nominative-accusative plural of the most important declension, which became a pattern for the plural of most nouns, and the -es genitive singular of the same declension (OE *hundas* 'hounds' and *hundes* 'hound's' merging as ME *houndes*). So too the noun endings -eð and -að (OE *hæleð* 'fighting man,' *mōnað* 'month') and the homophonous endings in verbs (OE *findeð* 'he, she, it finds,' *findað* 'we, you, they find')—all ended up as Middle English -eth.

Loss of Grammatical Gender

One of the important results of the leveling of unstressed vowels was the loss of grammatical gender. We have seen how this occurred with the adjective. We have also seen that grammatical gender, for psychological reasons rather than phonological ones, had begun to break down in Old English times as far as the choice of pronouns was concerned (101), as when the English translator of Bede's Latin *Ecclesiastical History* refers to Bertha, the wife of King Ethelbert of Kent, as *hēo* 'she' rather than *hit,* though she is in the same sentence designated as *þæt* (neuter demonstrative used as definite article) *wīf* rather than *sēo wīf.*

In Old English, gender was readily distinguishable in most nouns: masculine nominative-accusative plurals typically ended in -as, feminines in -a, and short-stemmed neuters in -u. In Middle English, on the other hand, all but a handful of nouns acquired the same plural ending, -es (from OE -as). This important development, coupled with the invariable *the* that supplanted the Old English masculine *se,* neuter *þæt,* and feminine *sēo* along with all their oblique forms (106), effectively eliminated grammatical gender as a feature of English.

NOUNS, PRONOUNS, AND ADJECTIVES

The Inflection of Nouns

To cite a further instance of how the structure of English was affected by the leveling of unstressed vowels, among nouns the Old English distinctive feminine nominative singular form in -u fell together with the nominative plural form in -a, that is, singular *denu* 'valley' and plural *dena* 'valleys' both became for a while Middle English *dẹne.* It was similar with the neuter nominative-accusative plurals in -u and the genitive plurals in -a: all came to have the same -e ending. What further happened with *dẹne* happened to most other nouns that had not formed their nominative-accusative plurals in -*as* in Old English and has been alluded to before: namely, the -*es* that was the Middle English reduced form of this ending was made to serve as a general plural ending for such words (for example, singular nongenitive *dẹne*, general plural *dẹnes*). In like fashion, the genitive singular ending -*es* was extended to nouns that had belonged to declensions lacking this ending; thus the genitive singular and the general plural forms of most nouns fell together and have remained that way ever since: Old English genitive singular *speres* and nominative plural *speru* became Middle English *spẹres,* Modern English *spear's, spears;* and Old English genitive singular *tale* and nominative plural *tala* became Middle English *tāles,* Modern English *tale's, tales.*

A few *s*-less genitives—feminine nouns and the family-relationship nouns ending in -*r*—remained throughout the period (as in Chaucer's "In hope to stonden in his lady grace" and "by my fader kyn") and survived into early Modern English, along with a few nouns from the Old English *n*-stem declension. Sometimes the genitive -*s* was left off a noun that ended in *s* or that was followed by a word beginning with *s*. The same omission, for the same phonological reason, accounts for the occasional modern loss of the genitive -*s* in "Keats' poems, Dickens' novels," when these are not merely matters of writing. Solely a matter of writing is the occasional modern "for pity sake," which indicates the same pronunciation in conversational speech as "for pity's sake."

The few nouns that did not conform to the pattern of forming the plural by suffixing -*es* nevertheless followed the pattern of using the nominative-accusative plural as a general plural form. They include those that lack -*s* plurals today—for example, *oxen, deer,* and *feet.* There were also in Middle English a number of survivals of weak-declension plurals in -*(e)n* that have subsequently disappeared—for example, *eyen* 'eyes' and *fọọn* 'foes.' The -*(e)n* was even extended to a few nouns that belonged to the *a*-stem strong declension in Old English—for example, *shoon* 'shoes' (OE *scōs*). A few long-syllabled words that had been neuters in Old English occurred with unchanged plural forms, especially animal names like *sheep, deer,* and *hors.* However, the most enduring of these alternative plurals are those with mutation: *men, feet, geese, teeth, lice,* and *mice.*

During the Middle English period, then, practically all nouns were reduced to two forms, just as in Modern English—one without -*s* used as a general nongenitive singular form, and one with -*s* used as a genitive singular and general plural form. The English language thus acquired a device for indicating plurality without consideration of case—namely, the -*s* ending, which had been in Old English only one of three plural endings in the strong masculine declension. It also lost all trace of any case distinctions except for the genitive, identical in form with the plural. English had come to depend on particles—mainly prepositions and conjunctions— and word order to express grammatical relations that had previously been expressed by inflection. No longer could one say, as the Anglo-Saxon homilist Ælfric had done, "Þās gelæhte se dēma," and expect the sentence to be properly understood as 'The judge seized those.' To say this in Middle English, it is necessary that the subject precede the verb, just as in Modern English: "The dēme ilaughte thọs."

Personal Pronouns

As we have noted, simplification occurred in other categories as well. Only the pronouns retained (as they still do) a considerable degree of the complexity that characterized them in Old English. These words alone preserved distinctive subject and object case forms, except for the neuter pronouns *(h)it, that, this,* and *what,* which even in Old English had not differentiated the nominative and accusative. The distinction in form between accusative and dative, however, disappeared in all the pronouns (as it had already in late Old English for those of the first and second persons). Consequently, in Middle English we can speak only of an **objective form** of the pronouns, just as we do in Modern English.

The dual number of the personal pronouns virtually disappeared in Middle English. Such a phrase as *git būtū* 'you two both,' occurring in late Old English, indicates that even then the form *git* had lost much of its idea of twoness and needed the reinforcement of *būtū* 'both.' There was a great deal of variety in the remaining Middle English forms, of which those in the following table are some of the more noteworthy.

	SINGULAR	PLURAL
First Person		
Nom.	ich, I, ik	wē
Obj.	mē	us
Gen.	mī; mīn	our(e); oures
Second Person		
Nom.	thou	yē
Obj.	thee	you
Gen.	thī; thīn	your(e); youres
Third Person		
Nom.	hē	hī, they, thai
Obj.	him, hine	hem, heom, them, thaim, theim
Gen.	his	her(e), their(e); heres, theires
Nom.	shē, hō, hyō, hyē, hī, schō, chō, hē	
Obj.	hir(e), her(e), hī	
Gen.	hir(e), her(e); hires	
Nom.	hit, it	
Obj.	hit, it	
Gen.	his	

The dialects of Middle English differed in the forms they used for the pronouns. For example, *ik* was a Northern form corresponding to *ich* or *I* elsewhere. The nominative forms *they* or *thai* (and other spelling variants such as *thei* and *thay*), which were derived from Scandinavian, prevailed in the North and Midlands. The corresponding objective and genitive forms *them, thaim, theim,* and *their* were used principally in the North during most of the Middle English period. The native nominative form *hī* remained current in the Southern dialect, and its corresponding objective and genitive forms *hem, heom,* and *here* were used in both the South and Midlands. Thus in Chaucer's usage, the nominative is *they* but the objective is *hem* and the genitive *here.* Ultimately the Scandinavian forms in *th-* were to prevail; in the generation following Chaucer, they everywhere displaced the native English forms in *h-* except for unstressed *hem,* which we continue to use as *'em.*

The Old English third person masculine accusative *hine* survived into Middle English only in the South; elsewhere the originally dative *him* took over the objective function. The feminine accusative *hī* likewise survived for a while in the same region, but in the later thirteenth century it was supplanted by the originally dative *hir(e)* or *her(e)* current elsewhere in objective use. The feminine pronoun had a variety of nominative forms, one of them identical with the corresponding masculine form—certainly an awkward state of affairs, forcing the lovesick author of the lyric "Alysoun" to refer to his sweetheart as *hē,* the same form she would have used in referring to him (for example, "Bote he me wolle to hire take" means 'Unless she will take me to her'). The predominant form in East Midland speech, and the one that was to survive in standard Modern English, was *shē.*

The genitive forms of the personal pronouns came in Middle English to be restricted in the ways they could be used. A construction like Old English *nǣnig hira* 'none of them' could be rendered in Middle English only by *of* plus the objective pronoun, exactly as in Modern English. The variant forms of the genitive first and second persons singular—*mīn, mī; thīn, thī*—preceding a noun were in exactly the same type of distribution as the forms *an* and *a;* that is, the *-n* was lost before a consonant (135). Following a noun, the forms with *-n* were invariable (as in the rare construction "baby mine," as also when the possessives were used nominally as in Modern English "That book is mine," "Mine is that book," and "that book of mine"). By analogy with this unvarying use of the forms in *-n* as nominals, *hisen, heren, ouren, youren,* and *theiren* arose. From the beginning, their status seems to have been much the same as that of their Modern English descendants *hisn, hern, yourn,* and *theirn.* The personal pronouns in *-r* developed new analogical genitive forms in *-es* rather late in Middle English: *hires, oures, youres,* and *heres* (Northern *theires*). These *-es* forms were used precisely like Modern English *hers, ours, yours,* and *theirs*—nominally, as in "The books on the table are hers (ours, yours, theirs)" and "Hers (ours, yours, theirs) are on the table."

Demonstrative Pronouns

Old English *se, þæt, sēo,* and plural *þā,* with their various oblique (nonnominative) forms, were ultimately reduced to *the, that,* and plural *thǭ.* However, inflected forms derived from the Old English declensions continued to be used in some dialects until the thirteenth century, though not in East Midland. *The,* which at first replaced only the masculine nominative *se,* came to be used as an invariable definite article. *That* and *thọ* were thus left for the demonstrative function. A different *the,* from the Old English masculine and neuter instrumental *þē,* has had continuous adverbial use in English, as in "The sooner the better" and "He did not feel the worse for the experience."

Thọ ultimately gave way to *thọs* (ModE *those*), from Old English *þās,* though the form with *-s* did not begin to become common in the Midlands and the South until the late fifteenth century. Chaucer, for instance, uses only *thọ* where we would use *those.* In the North *thās,* the form corresponding to *thọs* elsewhere, began to appear in writing more than a century earlier.

The other Old English demonstrative was *þes, þis, þēos.* By the thirteenth century, when gender distinction and some traces of inflection that had survived up to that time were lost, the singular nominative-accusative neuter *this* was used for all singular functions, and a new plural form, *thise* or *thēse,* with the ending *-e* as in the plural of adjectives, appeared. These developments have resulted in Modern English *that-those* and *this-these.*

Interrogative and Relative Pronouns

The Old English masculine-feminine interrogative pronoun *hwā* became in Middle English *whọ,* and the neuter form *hwæt* became *what.* Middle English *whọ* had an objective form *whọm* from the Old English dative (*hwām, hwǣm*), which had driven out the accusative (OE *hwone*), as happened also with other pronouns. Old English *hwæt* had the same dative form as *hwā,* but, as with other neuters, it was given up, so the Middle English nominative and objective forms were both *what.* In Old English, the genitive of both *hwā* and *hwæt* had been *hwæs;* in Middle English this took by analogy the vowel of *whọ* and *whọm:* thus *whọs.*

In Middle English, *whọ* was customarily used only as an interrogative pronoun or an indefinite relative meaning 'whoever,' as in "Who steals my purse steals trash," a usage that occurs first in the thirteenth century. The simple relative use of *who,* as in the title of Rudyard Kipling's story "The Man Who Would Be King," was not really widespread until the sixteenth century, though there are occasional instances of it as early as the late thirteenth. The oblique forms *whọs* and *whọm,* however, were used as relatives with reference to either persons or things in late Middle English, at about the same time that another interrogative pronoun, *which* (OE *hwylc*), also began to be so used. Sometimes *which* was followed by *that,* as in Chaucer's "Criseyde, which that felt hire thus i-take," that is, 'Criseyde, who felt herself thus taken.'

The most frequently used relative pronoun in Middle English is indeclinable *that.* It is, of course, still so used, though modern literary style limits it to restrictive clauses: "The man that I saw was Jones" but "This man, who never did anyone any real harm, was nevertheless punished severely." A relative particle *þe,* continuing the Old English indeclinable relative-of-all-work, occurs in early Middle English side by side with *that* (or *þat,* as it would have been written early in the period).

Comparative and Superlative Adjectives

In the general leveling of unstressed vowels to *e*, the Old English comparative ending *-ra* became *-re*, later *-er*, and the superlative suffixes *-ost* and *-est* fell together as *-est*. If the root vowel of an adjective was long, it was shortened before these endings—for example, *swēte, swetter, swettest*—though the analogy of the positive form, as in the example cited, frequently caused the original length to be restored in the comparative and superlative forms; the doublets *latter* and *later* show, respectively, shortness and length of vowel.

As in Old English, *ēvel* (and its Middle English synonym *badde*, of uncertain origin), *gōd, muchel* (*mikel*), and *lītel* had comparative and superlative forms unrelated to them etymologically: *werse, werst; bettre* or *better, best; mǫre, mǫst; lesse* or *lasse, lęste*. Some of the adjectives that in Old English had mutation in their comparative and superlative forms retained the mutated vowel in Middle English—for instance, *long, lengre* or *lenger, lengest; ǭld, eldre* or *elder, eldest*.

The simplification of the Old English adjective declensions has been discussed already (141).

VERBS

Verbs continued to conform to the Germanic division into strong and weak, as they still do. Although the vowels of endings were leveled, the gradation distinctions expressed in the root vowels of the strong verbs were fully preserved. The tendency to use exclusively one or the other of the preterit vowel grades, however, had begun, though there was little consistency: the vowel of the older plural might be used in the singular, or vice versa. The older distinction (as in *I sang, we sungen*) was more likely to be retained in the Midlands and the South than in the North.

The seven classes of strong verbs survived with the following regular gradations (although there were also many phonologically irregular ones). These gradation classes should be compared with those of the Old English forms (114):

	INFINITIVE	PRETERIT SINGULAR	PRETERIT PLURAL	PAST PARTICIPLE
Class I	wrīten 'write'	wrǫt	writen	writen
Class II	clēven 'cleave'	clęf	cluven	clǫven
Class III	helpen 'help'	halp	hulpen	holpen
Class IV	bęran 'bear'	bar	bēren	bǫren
Class V	sprękan 'speak'	sprak	sprēken	spręken
Class VI	shāken 'shake'	shōk	shōken	shāken
Class VII	hǫten 'be called'	hēt	hēten	hǫten

Although the seven strong verb patterns continued in Middle English, there were far more weak verbs than strong ones. Consequently, the weak *-ed* ending for the preterit and past participle came to be used with many originally strong verbs. Thus for a time some verbs could be conjugated in either way. Ultimately the strong forms were lost altogether in many other verbs. A few verbs, however, continue both forms even today, such as *hang-hung-hanged* and *weave-wove-weaved*.

Personal Endings

As unstressed vowels fell together, some of the distinctions in personal endings disappeared, with a resulting simplification in verb conjugation. With *finden* 'to find' (strong) and *thanken* 'to thank' (weak) as models, the indicative forms were as follows in the Midland dialects:

Present

	strong	*weak*
ich	fīnde	thanke
thou	fīndest	thankest
hē/shē	fīndeth, fīndes	thanketh, thankes
wē/yē/they	fīnde(n), fīndes	thanke(n), thankes

Preterit

ich	fǫnd	thanked(e)
thou	founde	thankedest
hē/shē	fǫnd	thanked(e)
wē/yē/they	founde(n)	thanked(e(n))

The verbs *been* 'to be' (OE *bēon*), *doon* 'to do' (OE *dōn*), *willen* 'to want, will' (OE *willan*), and *gǫǫn* 'to go' (OE *gān*) remained highly irregular in Middle English. Typical Midland indicative forms of *been* and *willen* follow:

Present

ich	am	wil(le), wol(le)[2]
thou	art, beest	wilt, wolt
hē/shē	is, beeth	wil(le), wol(le)
wē/yē/they	bee(n), beeth, sinden, ār(e)n[1]	wilen, wol(n)

[1]This Northern form is rare in ME.
[2]The forms with *o*, from the preterit, are late, but survive in *won't*, that is, *wol not*.

Preterit

ich	was	wolde
thou	wast, wēre	woldest
hē/shē	was	wolde
wē/yē/they	wēre(n)	wolde(n)

Developments of the following Middle English forms of the preterit present verbs are still in frequent use: *o(u)ghte* 'owed, was under obligation to,' *can* 'knows how to, is able,' *coude* (preterit of the preceding, ModE *could,* whose *l* is by analogy with *would*) 'knew how to, was able,' *shal* 'must,' *mōst(e)* (ModE *must*) 'was able to, must,' *may* 'am able to, may,' *mighte* (preterit of the preceding), *dar* (ModE *dare*), and *durst* (preterit of the preceding).

Participles

The ending of the present participle varied from dialect to dialect, with *-and(e)* in the North, *-ende* or *-ing(e)* in the Midlands, and *-inde* or *-ing(e)* in the South. The *-ing* ending, which has prevailed in Modern English, is from the old **verbal noun** ending *-ung,* as in Old English *leornung* 'learning' (that is, knowledge) and *bodung* 'preaching' (that is, sermon), from *leornian* 'to learn' and *bodian* 'to announce, preach.'

Past participles might or might not have the initial inflection *i-* (*y-*), from Old English *ge-;* the prefix was lost in many parts of England, including the East Midland, but frequently occurred in the speech of London as reflected in the writings of Chaucer.

WORD ORDER

Although all possible variations in the order of subject, verb, and complement occur in extant Middle English literature, as they do in Old English literature, much of that literature is verse, in which even today variations (inversions) of normal word order may occur. The prose of the Middle English period has much the same word order as Modern English prose. Sometimes a pronoun as object might precede the verb ("Yef þou me zayst, 'How me hit ssel lyerny?' ich hit wyle þe zigge an haste . . . ," that is, word for word, 'If thou [to] me sayest, "How one it shall learn?" I it will [to] thee say in haste . . . ,' or, in Modern English order, 'If thou sayest to me, "How shall one learn it?" I will say it to thee in haste . . . ').

In subordinate clauses, nouns used as objects might also precede verbs ("And we, þet . . . habbeþ Cristendom underfonge," that is, 'And we, that . . . have Christian salvation received'). In the frequently occurring impersonal constructions of Middle English, the object regularly preceded the verb: *me mette* '(it) to me dreamed,' that is, 'I dreamed'; *me thoughte* '(it) to me seemed.' *If you please* is very likely a survival of this construction (parallel to French *s'il vous plaît* and German *wenn es Ihnen gefällt,* that is, 'if it please[s] you'), though the *you* is now taken as nominative. Other than these, there are very few inversions that would be inconceivable in Modern English.

MIDDLE ENGLISH ILLUSTRATED

The first passage is in the Northern dialect, from *The Form of Perfect Living*, by Richard Rolle of Hampole, a gentle mystic and an excellent prose writer, who died in 1349. Strange as parts of it may look to modern eyes, it is possible to put it word for word into Modern English:

1. Twa lyves þar er þat cristen men lyfes: ane es called actyve lyfe,
Two lives there are that Christian men live: one is called active life,

for it es mare bodili warke; another, contemplatyve lyfe, for it es in mare
for it is more bodily work; another, contemplative life, for it is in more

swetnes gastely. Actife lyfe es mykel owteward and in mare travel,
sweetness spiritually. Active life is much outward and in more travail,

and in mare peryle for þe temptacions þat er in þe worlde.
and in more peril for the temptations that are in the world.

Contemplatyfe lyfe es mykel inwarde, and forþi it es lastandar
Contemplative life is much inward, and therefore it is more lasting

and sykerar, restfuller, delitabiler, luflyer, and mare
and more secure, more restful, more delightful, lovelier, and more

medeful, for it hase joy in goddes lufe and savowre in þe lyf
full of reward, for it has joy in God's love and savor in the life

þat lastes ay in þis present tyme if it be right ledde. And þat
that lasts forever in this present time if it be rightly led. And that

felyng of joy in þe lufe of Jhesu passes al other merites in erth,
feeling of joy in the love of Jesus surpasses all other merits on Earth,

for it es swa harde to com to for þe freelte of oure flesch and þe many
for it is so hard to come to for the frailty of our flesh and the many

temptacions þat we er umsett with þat lettes us nyght and day. Al
temptations that we are set about with that hinder us night and day. All

other thynges er lyght at com to in regarde þarof, for þat may na man
other things are easy to come to in regard thereof, for that may no man

deserve, bot anely it es gifen of goddes godenes til þam þat verrayli
deserve, but only it is given of God's goodness to them that verily

gifes þam   to contemplacion and til quiete for cristes   luf.
give them(selves) to contemplation and to quiet for Christ's love.

The following passages in late Middle English are from a translation of the Bible made by John Wycliffe or one of his followers in the 1380s. The opening verses of Chapters 1 and 2 of Genesis are based on the edition by Conrad Lindberg; the parable of the Prodigal Son (Luke 15) is based on the edition by Josiah Forshall and Frederic Madden. Punctuation has been modernized, and the letters thorn and yogh have been replaced, respectively, by *th* and *y, gh,* or *s.* These versions may be compared with the parallel passages in Chapters 5 and 8.

2.   Genesis 1.1. In the first made God of nought heuen and erth.   **2.** The erth forsothe was veyn withinne and voyde, and derknesses weren vp on the face of the see. And the spirite of God was yborn vp on the waters.   **3.** And God seid, "Be made light," and made is light.   **4.** And God sees light that it was good and dyuidide light from derknesses.   **5.** And clepide light day and derknesses night, and maad is euen and moru, o day.

3.   Genesis 2.1. Therfor parfit ben heuen and erthe, and alle the anournyng of hem.   **2.** And God fullfillide in the seuenth day his werk that he made, and he rystid the seuenth day from all his werk that he hadde fulfyllide.   **3.** And he blisside to the seuenthe day, and he halowde it, for in it he hadde seesid fro all his werk that God schapide that he schulde make.

4.   Luke 15.11. A man hadde twei sones.   **12.** And the yonger of hem seide to the fadir, "Fadir, yiue me the porcioun of catel that fallith to me." And he departide to hem the catel.   **13.** And not aftir many daies, whanne alle thingis weren gederid togider, the yonger sone wente forth in pilgrymage in to a fer cuntre; and there he wastide hise goodis in lyuynge lecherously.   **14.** And aftir that he hadde endid alle thingis, a strong hungre was maad in that cuntre, and he bigan to haue nede.   **15.** And he wente, and drough hym to oon of the citeseyns of that cuntre. And he sente hym in to his toun, to fede swyn.   **16.** And he coueitide to fille his wombe of the coddis that the hoggis eeten, and no man yaf hym.   **17.** And he turnede ayen to hym silf, and seide, "Hou many hirid men in my fadir hous han plente of looues; and Y perische here thorough hungir . . . ."   **20.** And he roos vp, and cam to his fadir. And whanne he was yit afer, his fadir saigh hym, and was stirrid bi mercy. And he ran, and fel on his necke, and kisside hym.   **21.** And the sone saide to hym, "Fadir, Y haue synned in to heuene, and bifor thee; and now Y am not worthi to be clepid thi sone."   **22.** And the fadir seide to hise seruauntis, "Swithe brynge ye forth the firste stoole, and clothe ye hym, and yiue ye a ryng in his hoond, and schoon on hise feet.   **23.** And brynge ye a fat calf, and sle ye, and ete we, and make we feeste.   **24.** For this my sone was deed, and hath lyued ayen; he perischid, and is foundun."

FOR FURTHER READING

General Historical Background

Black. *A History of the British Isles.*
————. *A New History of England.*
Morgan. *The Oxford History of Britain.*

Overviews

Blake. *The Cambridge History of the English Language.* Vol. 2: *1066–1476.*
Burrow and Turville-Petre. *A Book of Middle English.*

Grammar

Brunner. *An Outline of Middle English Grammar.*
Fischer et al. *Syntax of Early English.*

Dictionaries

Davis et al. *A Chaucer Glossary.*
Kurath and Kuhn. *Middle English Dictionary.*
Stratmann. *A Middle-English Dictionary.*

7 THE EARLY MODERN ENGLISH PERIOD (1500-1800)

SOCIETY, SPELLINGS, AND SOUNDS

The early Modern Period was a transformative one for both England and the English language. Most of the fifteenth century was a fallow period for English culture and language. But toward its end, events began to occur that were to spark developments culminating in what has been called England's most brilliant age, the Elizabethan and early Stuart periods (1558–1625).

SOME KEY EVENTS IN THE EARLY MODERN PERIOD

Among the events in the early Modern Period that laid the foundation for, or are symbolic of, changes of importance in the English language are those in the following list.

- 1476   William Caxton brought printing to England, thus both serving and promoting a growing body of literate persons. Before that time, literacy was confined to the clergy and a handful of others. Within the next two centuries, most of the gentry and merchants became literate, as well as half the yeomen and some of the husbandmen.
- 1485   Henry Tudor ascended the throne, ending the civil strife called the War of the Roses and introducing 118 years of the Tudor dynasty, which oversaw vast changes in England.
- 1497   John Cabot went on a voyage of exploration for a Northwest Passage to China, in which he discovered Nova Scotia and so foreshadowed English territorial expansion overseas.
- 1534   The Act of Supremacy established Henry VIII as "Supreme Head of the Church of England," and thus officially put civil authority above Church authority in England.
- 1549   The first *Book of Common Prayer* was adopted and became an influence on English literary style.
- 1558   At the age of 25, Elizabeth I became queen of England and, as a woman with a Renaissance education and a skill for leadership, began a

forty-five-year reign that promoted statecraft, literature, science, exploration, and commerce.

- 1577–80   Sir Francis Drake circumnavigated the globe, the first English-man to do so, and participated in the defeat of the Spanish Armada in 1588, removing an obstacle to English expansion overseas.
- 1590–1611   William Shakespeare wrote the bulk of his plays, from *Henry VI* to *The Tempest.*
- 1600   The East India Company was chartered to promote trade with Asia, leading eventually to the establishment of the British Raj in India.
- 1604   Robert Cawdrey published the first English dictionary, *A Table Alphabeticall.*
- 1607   Jamestown, Virginia, was established as the first permanent English settlement in America.
- 1611   The Authorized or King James Version of the Bible was produced by a committee of scholars and became, with the Prayer Book and the works of Shakespeare, one of the major examples of and influences on English literary style.
- 1619   The first African slaves in North America arrived in Virginia.
- 1642–48   The English Civil War or Puritan Revolution overthrew the monarchy and resulted in the beheading of King Charles I in 1649 and the establishment of a military dictatorship called the Commonwealth and (under Oliver Cromwell) the Protectorate, which lasted until the Restoration of King Charles II in 1660.
- 1660   The Royal Society was founded as the first English organization devoted to the promotion of scientific knowledge and research.
- 1670   The Hudson's Bay Company was chartered for promoting trade and settlement in Canada.
- ca. 1680   The political parties—Whigs (named perhaps from a Scots term for 'horse drivers' but used for supporters of reform and parliamentary power) and Tories (named from an Irish term for 'outlaws' but used for supporters of conservatism and royal authority), both terms being originally contemptuous—became political forces, thus introducing party politics as a central factor in government.
- 1688   The Glorious Revolution was a bloodless coup in which members of Parliament invited the Dutch prince William of Orange and his wife, Mary (daughter of the reigning English king, James II), to assume the English throne, resulting in the establishment of Parliament's power over that of the monarchy.
- 1702   The first daily newspaper was published in London, followed by an extension of such publications throughout England and the expansion of the influence of the press in disseminating information and forming public opinion.

- 1719   Daniel Defoe published *Robinson Crusoe,* sometimes identified as the first modern novel in English, although the evolution of the genre was gradual and other works have a claim to that title.
- 1755   Samuel Johnson published his *Dictionary of the English Language,* a model of comprehensive dictionaries of English.
- 1775–83   The American Revolution resulted in the foundation of the first independent nation of English speakers outside the British Isles. Large numbers of British loyalists left the former American colonies for Canada and Nova Scotia, introducing a large number of new English speakers there.
- 1788   The English first settled Australia near modern Sydney.

THE TRANSITION FROM MIDDLE TO MODERN ENGLISH

Despite vast changes in vocabulary and pronunciation, English speakers of the sixteenth century were unaware that they were leaving the Middle English period and entering the Modern. All such divisions between stages of the language's development are to some extent arbitrary, although they are based on clear and significant internal changes in the language—which may or may not be obvious to those living at the time—and correlate with external events in the lives of those who speak the language.

Expansion of the English Vocabulary

The word stock of English was expanded greatly during the early Modern period, partly to meet the need for new words to talk about new things, partly by a conscious design to improve and amplify the vocabulary, and partly as an automatic consequence of the extension of English outside the British Isles and the contact of English speakers with those of other languages.

During the Renaissance, an influx of Latin and Greek words (Chapter 12, 275–6) was associated with a vogue for **inkhorn terms,** so named from the fact that they were seldom spoken but mainly written (with a pen dipped into an ink container made of horn). The influence of the Classical languages has remained strong. French also continued to be a major source of loanwords into English (281–2), as it had been since the time of the Norman Conquest and has so remained up to our own time, especially in Britain, though less so in other parts of the English-speaking world in recent days. In addition, Spanish and Portuguese (283–4) became significant sources for borrowing words, especially from their colonial expansion in Latin America and elsewhere.

Many other languages contributed to the English vocabulary, especially as the period progressed and on into the late Modern period. Celtic (277) and Scandinavian (278–9) continued their influence, but new impulses came from

Italian (284–5) and German—both Low and High (285–7), including Yiddish (287–8). More far-flung influences were from the languages of Asia, Australasia, Africa, eastern Europe, Asia Minor, and the Americas (288–92).

Quite early in their history, the American colonies began to influence the general vocabulary with loanwords from both Amerindian languages and the languages of other European settlers in the New World. But also changes in the form, meaning, and use of English words originated in America and extended, sometimes under protest, to Britain (Chapter 9, 204–8). The first documented use of the word *lengthy* in the *Oxford English Dictionary* is by John Adams in his diary for January 3, 1759: "I grow too minute and lengthy." Early British reactions to this perceived Americanism are typified by a 1793 censorious judgment in the *British Critic:* "We shall, at all times, with pleasure, receive from our transatlantic brethren real improvements of our common mother-tongue: but we shall hardly be induced to admit such phrases as . . . 'more lengthy', for longer, or more diffuse."

Innovation of Pronunciation and Conservation of Spelling

The fifteenth century, following the death of Chaucer, marks a turning point in the internal history of English, especially its pronunciation and spelling, for during this period the language underwent greater, more important phonological changes than in any other century before or since. Despite these radical changes in pronunciation, the old spelling was maintained and, as it were, stereotyped. William Caxton, who died in 1491, and the printers who followed him based their spelling norm not on the pronunciation current in their day, but on the usage of late medieval manuscripts. Hence, though the quality of every single one of the long vowels had changed, the graphic representation of the newer values remained much the same as it had been for Middle English ones: for instance, though the [e:] of Middle English *feet, see, three,* and so forth had been raised to [i:], all such words went on being written as if no change had taken place. Consequently, the phonological value of many letters of the English alphabet changed drastically.

The influence of printers and that of men of learning—misguided though they frequently were—has been greater than any other on English spelling. Learned men preferred an archaic spelling; and, as we shall see, they further archaized it by respelling words etymologically. Printers were responsible for a further normalization of the older scribal practices. While it is true that early printed works exhibit a good many inconsistencies, they are nevertheless quite orderly as compared with the everyday writing of the time.

THE ORTHOGRAPHY OF EARLY MODERN ENGLISH

Here we consider briefly some of the spellings in early Modern English, in relation to both Middle English and our own later Modern English.

In a few words, especially *the* and *thee* but also a number of others, early printed books sometimes used *y* to represent the sounds usually spelled *th*. This substitution was made because the letter *þ* was still much used in writing English, but the early printers got their type fonts from the Continent, where the letter *þ* was not part of normal orthography. So they substituted for *þ* the closest thing they found in the foreign fonts, namely *y*. For example, *the* was sometimes printed *yᵉ*, and that same spelling was also used for the pronoun *thee*. The plural pronoun meaning 'you all,' on the other hand, was written *ye*. When the *e* was above the line, the *y* was always a makeshift for *þ*, and never to be interpreted as [y].

Writing letters superscript, especially the final letter of a word, was a device to indicate an abbreviation, much as we use a period. This convention lasted right through the nineteenth century, for example, in *Mʳ* for *Mr.* or *Genˡ* for *General*. Thus *yᵗ* was used as an abbreviation for *that*. The abbreviation *yᵉ* for *the* survives to our own day in such pseudo-antique absurdities as "Ye Olde Choppe Suey Shoppe," in which it is usually pronounced as if it were the same word as the old pronoun *ye*. Needless to say, there is no justification whatever for such a pronunciation.

The present use of *i* for a vowel and *j* for a consonant was not established until the seventeenth century. In the King James Bible (1611) and the First Folio (1623) of Shakespeare, for instance, *i* is used for both values; see, for instance, the passage from the First Folio at the end of this chapter, in which Falstaff's first name occurs as *Iack*. For a long time after the distinction in writing was made, however, the feeling persisted that *i* and *j* were one and the same letter: Dr. Johnson's *Dictionary* (1755) puts them together alphabetically, and this practice continued well into the nineteenth century.

It was similar with the curved and angular forms of *u*—that is, *u* and *v*—they too were originally used more or less indiscriminately for either vowel or consonant. But Continental printers came to use *v* and *u* for consonant and vowel, respectively, and by the middle of the seventeenth century English printers were generally making the same distinction. As with *i* and *j*, however, catalogues, indexes, and the like put *u* and *v* together well into the nineteenth century; in dictionaries *vizier* was followed by *ulcer*, *unzoned* by *vocable*, and *iambic* was set between *jamb* and *jangle*. Many modern editions of old texts substitute *j* and *v* for *i* and *u* when they indicate consonants, and *u* for initial *v* when it indicates a vowel, representing, for example, *iaspre*, *liue*, and *vnder* as *jaspre* 'jasper,' *live*, and *under*. Except for the two extended passages reproduced at the end of this chapter, those substitutions are made here when older writers are cited, as also in citations of individual words from older periods. The matter is purely graphic; no question of pronunciation is involved in the substitution.

The sound indicated by *h* was lost in late Latin, and hence the letter has no phonetic significance in those Latin-derived languages that retain it in their spelling. The influence of Classical Latin had caused French scribes to restore the *h* in the spelling of many words—for instance, *habit*, *herbage*, and *homme*— though it was never pronounced. It was also sometimes inserted in English words of French origin where it was not etymological—for instance, *habundance* (mistakenly regarded as coming from *habere* 'to have') and *abhominable* (supposed to be from Latin *ab* plus *homine,* explained as 'away from humanity, hence bestial'). When Shakespeare's pedant Holofernes by implication recommended this latter misspelling and consequent mispronunciation with [h] in *Love's Labour's Lost* 5.1.26 ("This is abhominable, which he would call abbominable"), he was in very good company, at least as far as the writing of the word is concerned, for the error had been current since Middle English times. Writers of Medieval Latin and Old French had been similarly misled by a false notion of the etymology of the word.

During the Renaissance, *h* was inserted after *t* in a number of foreign words—for instance, *throne,* from Old French *trone.* The French word is from Latin *thronus,* borrowed from Greek, the *th* being the normal Roman transliteration of Greek θ. The English respelling ultimately gave rise to a change in the initial sound, as also in *theater* and *thesis,* which earlier had initial [t]. It was similar with the internal consonant sound spelled *th* in *anthem, apothecary, Catherine* (the pet forms *Kate* and *Kit* preserve the older sound), and *Anthony* (compare *Tony*), which to a large extent has retained its historically expected pronunciation in British English, but not in American. The only American pronunciation of *Anthony* is with [θ], which is sometimes heard even in reference to Mark Antony, where the spelling does not encourage it. The *h* of *author,* from Old French *autor* (modern *auteur*), going back to Latin *auctor,* was first inserted by French scribes, to whom an *h* after *t* indicated no difference in pronunciation. When in the sixteenth century this fancy spelling began to be used in the English loanword, the way was paved for the modern pronunciation, historically a mispronunciation.

Certain Renaissance respellings ultimately effected changes in traditional pronunciations. *Throne* and *author* have already been mentioned. Another example is *schedule* (from Old French *cedule*), for which Noah Webster recommended the American spelling pronunciation with initial [sk], as if the word were a Greek loan. The present-day British pronunciation of the first syllable as [ʃɛd] is also erroneously based on the misspelling. The historically expected pronunciation would begin with [s].

Debt and *doubt* are likewise fancy **etymological respellings** of *det* and *dout* (both Middle English from Old French), the *b* having been inserted because it was perceived that these words were ultimately derivatives of Latin *debitum* and *dubitare,* respectively; similarly with the *c* in *indict* and the *b* in *subtle.* Those learned men responsible for such respellings perhaps thought to effect a change in pronunciation like that which Shakespeare's schoolmaster Holofernes recommended. In the passage referred to above, he speaks of those "rackers of ortagriphie [orthography]" who say *dout* and *det* when they should say *doubt* and *debt* (for to him, as to many after him, spelling set the standard for pronunciation). "*D, e, b, t,* not *d, e, t,*" he says, unaware that the word was indeed written *d, e, t* before schoolmasters like himself began tinkering with spelling. These etymological respellings have not so far affected pronunciation, but others have.

Rhyme and *rhythm* are twin etymological respellings. English had borrowed *rime* from Old French about the year 1200, but by 1560 scholars began to spell the word also as *rythme* or *rhythm* and then a bit later as *rhyme.* These respellings reflected the origin of the French word in Latin *rithmus* or *rythmus,* ultimately from Greek *rhythmos.* The *th* in the *rhythm* spelling came to be pronounced, and that form has survived as a separate word with the distinct meaning of 'cadence.' For the meaning 'repetition of sound,' the older *rime* spelling, which has continued alongside the fancy upstart *rhyme,* is better both historically and orthographically, and so is used in this book. Both are in standard use.

Comptroller is a pseudolearned respelling of *controller,* taken by English from Old French. The fancy spelling is doubtless due to an erroneous association with French *compte* 'count.' The word has fairly recently acquired a new pronunciation based on the misspelling. *Receipt* and *indict,* both taken from Anglo-French, and *victual,* from Old French, have been similarly remodeled to give them a Latin look; their traditional pronunciations have not as yet been affected, although a spelling pronunciation for the last is possible by those who do not realize that it is the same word as that spelled in the plural form *vittles. Parliament,* a respelling of the earlier *parlement* (a French loanword derived from the verb *parler* 'to speak'), has also fairly recently acquired a pronunciation such as the later spelling seems to indicate.

Another such change of long standing has resulted from the insertion of *l* in *fault* (ME *faute,* from Old French), a spelling suggested by Vulgar Latin *fallita* and strengthened by the analogy of *false,* which has come to us direct from Latin *falsus.* For a while the word continued to be pronounced without the *l,* riming with *ought* and *thought* in seventeenth-century poetry. In Dr. Johnson's day there was wavering, as Johnson himself testifies in the *Dictionary,* between the older *l*-less and the newer pronunciation with *l.* The eighteenth-century **orthoepists** indicate the same wavering. They were men who conceived of themselves as exercising a directive function; they recommended and condemned, usually on quite irrelevant grounds. Seldom were they content merely to record variant pronunciations. Thomas Sheridan, the distinguished father of a more distinguished son named Richard Brinsley, in his *General Dictionary of the English Language* (1780) decides in favor of the *l*-less pronunciation of *fault,* as does James Elphinston in his *Propriety Ascertained* (1787). Robert Nares in his *Elements of Orthoëpy* (1784) records both pronunciations and makes no attempt to make a choice between them. John Walker in his *Critical Pronouncing Dictionary* (1791) declared that to omit the *l* made a "disgraceful exception," for the word would thus "desert its relation to the Latin *falsitas.*" The history of the *l* of *vault* is quite similar.

Although such tinkering with the orthography is one cause of the discrepancy between spelling and pronunciation in Modern English, another and more important one is the change in the pronunciation of the tense vowels that helps to demark Middle from Modern English. This change, the most salient of all phonological developments in the history of English, is called the **Great Vowel Shift**.

THE GREAT VOWEL SHIFT

A comparison of the modern developments in parentheses in the chapter on Old English (96) shows clearly the modern representatives of the Old English long vowels. As has been pointed out, the latter changed only slightly in Middle English: [a:], in Old English written *a*, as in *stān,* was rounded except in the Northern dialect to [ɔ:], in Middle English written *o(o)*, as in *stoon.* But this was really the only particularly noteworthy change in quality. By the early Modern English period, however, all the long vowels had shifted: Middle English *ē*, as in *sweete* 'sweet,' had already acquired the value [i] that it currently has, and the others were well on their way to acquiring the values that they have in current English. The changes in the long vowels are summarized in the following table:

LONG VOWELS

LATE MIDDLE ENGLISH	EARLY MODERN ENGLISH		LATER ENGLISH	
[a:] name ⟶	[æ:] ⟶	[ɛ:] ⟶	[e]	name
[e:] feet ⟶	[i]	⟶		feet
[ɛ:] greet ⟶	[e]	⟶		great
[i:] ride ⟶	[əɪ]	⟶	[aɪ]	ride
[o:] boote ⟶	[u]	⟶		boot
[ɔ:] boot ⟶	[o]	⟶		boat
[u:] hous ⟶	[əʊ]	⟶	[aʊ]	house

In phonological terms:

1. The Middle English high vowels [i:] and [u:] were diphthongized, and then the vowel was centralized and lowered in two steps, to [əi], [aɪ] and to [əu], [aʊ].

2. Each of the Middle English mid vowels—both higher mid [e:] and [o:] as well as lower mid [ɛ:] and [ɔ:]—were raised one step, to [i] and [u] and to [e] and [o], respectively.

3. The low vowel [a:] was fronted to [æ:] and then raised in two steps through [ɛ:] to [e].

In early Modern English, vowel quality generally became more important than quantity, so length is shown with early Modern vowels only for [æ:] and [ɛ:], which alone were distinguished from short vowels primarily by length. The beginning and ending points of the shift can also be displayed diagrammatically as in the accompanying chart.

GREAT VOWEL SHIFT
Vowels without sample words are Middle English.
Vowels with sample words are Modern English.

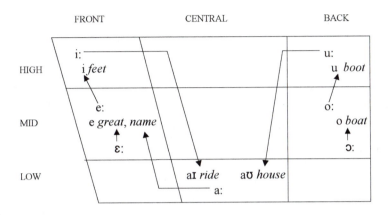

The stages by which the shift occurred and the cause of it are unknown. There are several theories, but as the evidence is ambiguous, they are best left to more specialized study. By some series of intermediate changes, long *ī*, as in Middle English *rīden* 'to ride,' became a diphthong [əi]. This pronunciation survives in certain types of speech, particularly before voiceless consonants. It went on in most types of English to become in the course of the seventeenth century [aɪ], though there are variations in pronunciation.

It was similar with Middle English long *ū*, as in *hous* 'house': it became [əu]. This [əu], surviving in eastern Virginia and in some types of Canadian English, became [aʊ] at about the same time as [əi] became [aɪ].

Middle English [o:], as in *ro(o)te* 'root,' became [u]. Laxing of this [u] to [ʊ] has occurred in *book, foot, good, look, took,* and other words; in *blood* and *flood* there has been unrounding in addition to laxing, resulting in [ə] in these two words. The chronology of this subsequent laxing and unrounding is difficult to establish, as is the distribution of the various developments. As Helge Kökeritz (*Shakespeare's Pronunciation* 236) points out, Shakespeare's riming of words that had Middle English long close *ō* gives no clue to his pronunciation, for he rimes *food* with *good* and *flood, mood* with *blood,* and *reprove* with *love* and *dove.* If these are not merely traditional rimes, we must conclude that the distribution of [u], [ʊ], and [ə] was not in early Modern English the same as it is in current English, and there is indeed ample evidence that colloquial English did vacillate a good deal. This fact is not particularly surprising when we remember that there is at the present time a certain amount of wavering between [u] and [ʊ] in such words as *roof, broom, room, root,* and a few others.

The development of Middle English [ɔ:] is straightforwardly to [o] as in Modern English *home* and *stone.* However, in a few words this [ɔ:] was laxed perhaps before the Great Vowel Shift could affect it—for instance, in *hot,* from Middle English *hǫ(ǫ)t.*

Middle English *ā* as in *name* and *ai* as in *nail* had by the early fifteenth century been leveled as [a:] and thus were affected alike by the Great Vowel Shift. The resultant homophony of *tale* and *tail* provided Shakespeare and his contemporaries with what seems to have been an almost irresistible temptation to make off-color puns (for instance, in *The Two Gentlemen of Verona* 2.3.52ff and *Othello* 3.1.6ff). The current pronunciation of such words—that is, with [e]—became normal in standard English probably in the early years of the eighteenth century. All these pronunciations may have existed side by side, however, just as **retarded** and **advanced pronunciations** may and do coexist in current English. (Some speakers today retain characteristics that, if they are noticed at all, are considered old-fashioned by younger-generation speakers, like *forehead* as [fɑrəd] or [fɔrəd] in contrast to ['fɔrˌhɛd].)

The development of Middle English [e:] to Modern [i] as in *three* and *kene* 'keen' is quite regular. Middle English [ɛ:] as in *heeth* 'heath,' however, had two developments in early Modern English. One is [e] as suggested by Falstaff's *raisin-reason* pun of 1598, in the passage cited at the end of this chapter, and many other such puns—for example, *abased–a beast,* and *grace-grease.* (The fullest treatment of Shakespeare's puns—sometimes childish, but frequently richly obscene—is in part 2 of Kökeritz's *Shakespeare's Pronunciation.*) But there is also convincing evidence that the present English vowel [i] in *heath* also existed in such words in early Modern English. The coexistence of two pronunciations pre-supposes that [e:] occurred in late Middle English times as a variant, perhaps dialectal, of [ɛ:]. Chaucer sometimes rimes close *e* words with words that in his type of English ordinarily had open *e,* indicating his familiarity with a pre-1400 raising of [ɛ:] to [e:] in some types of English. The present English vowel in such words as *meat* and *heath* is thus obviously, as H. C. Wyld (211) put it, "merely the result of the abandonment of one type of pronunciation and the adoption of another." Other authorities agree with Wyld's view—for instance, Kökeritz (*Shakespeare's Pronunciation* 194–209) and E. J. Dobson (2:606–16).

After about 1600, the polite pronunciation of words like *meat* and *heath* that continued Middle English [ɛ:] did not have the vowel [i], which we use for them, but rather [e], the vowel that survives to this day in the standard pronunciation of a few of them: *break, great, steak,* and *yea. Drain* (ME *draynen, dreynen,* from OE *drēahnian*), which is pronounced in standard English as its current spelling suggests, is yet another example, although a variant with [i] occurs in nonstandard usage. Many rimes from the seventeenth and eighteenth centuries testify to this pronunciation in words that today have only [i]—for instance, Jonathan Swift's "You'd swear that so divine a creature / Felt no necessities of nature" ("Strephon and Chloe"), in which the riming words are to be pronounced [kretər] and [netər], and "You spoke a word began with H. / And I know whom you meant to teach" ("The Journal of a Modern Lady"), in which the riming words are [eč] and [teč]. A few surnames borne by families long associated with Ireland, like *Yeats* (compare *Keats*), *Re(a)gan,* and *Shea,* have also retained the variant pronunciation with [e], which similarly occurs in *Beatty* in American speech.

The vowel variations in such words did not result from a new sound shift in Modern English of [e] to [i]. Middle and early Modern English [ɛ:], having reached [e], stopped there, although this [e] survives in the mere handful of words just cited. Pronunciation with [i] of these and all other such words had been a less prestigious option since the beginning of the Modern English period. This [i] pronunciation of words like *heath* was the regular development of the alternative late Middle English pronunciation mentioned above. As Dobson (2:611) points out, "Throughout the [early] ModE period there was a struggle going on between two ways of pronouncing 'ME ę̄ words'"; ultimately the [i] pronunciation was to win out, so that only a few words remain as evidence of the [e] sound that prevailed in fashionable circles from about 1600 to the mid-eighteenth century. The process was gradual, involving first one word, then another.

OTHER VOWELS

Final Unstressed Schwa

The loss of *e* [ə] at the end of words is just as widespread a change as the Great Vowel Shift. As already noted, however, this wholesale **apocopation**, as it is called, had occurred by the end of the fourteenth century and hence is not a modern change, though it is frequently so regarded, just as the leveling of all final vowels in inflectional syllables, frequently regarded as a Middle English change, actually began long before the date that is traditionally given for the beginning of the Middle English period. From early Modern spellings, as well as from poetic meter, the tendency to lose an unstressed -*e* seems also to have affected *the,* as in *th'earth* and the like.

Stressed Short Vowels

The stressed short vowels have remained relatively stable throughout the history of English. The most obvious changes affect Middle English short *a,* which shifted by way of [a] to [æ], and Middle English short *u,* which was unrounded and shifted to [ə], though its older value survives in a good many words in which the vowel was preceded by a labial consonant, especially if it was followed by *l*—for instance, *bull, full, pull, bush, push,* and *put* (but compare the variant *putt*).

It is evident that there was an unrounded variant of short *o,* reflected in late-sixteenth- and seventeenth-century spellings. Wyld (240–1) cites a number of examples of *a* for *o* in spellings, including Queen Elizabeth I's "I pray you stap the mouthes." This unrounding did not affect the language as a whole, but such doublets as *strop-strap* and *god-gad* remain to testify to its having occurred. Today [ɑ] is also found in the typical American pronunciation of most words that had short [ɔ] in Middle English (*god, stop, clock,* and so forth). Short *e* has not changed, except occasionally before [ŋ], as in *string* and *wing* from Middle English *streng* and *wenge,* and short *i* remains what it has been since Germanic times.

SHORT VOWELS

LATE MIDDLE ENGLISH	EARLY MODERN ENGLISH	LATER ENGLISH
[a] that	⟶ [æ]	⟶
[ɛ] bed	⟶	⟶
[ɪ] in	⟶	⟶
[ɔ] on, odd	⟶	[ɔ] or [ɑ]
[ʊ] but	⟶ [ə]	⟶

Diphthongs

The Middle English diphthongs had a tendency to monophthongize. For example, [aʊ] in *lawe* and [ɔʊ] in *snow* were monophthongized to [ɔ] and [o], respectively. The early fifteenth-century merger of [æɪ] in *nail* with [a:] as in *name* has already been mentioned; the subsequent history of that diphthong was the same as that of the long vowel with which it merged.

The Middle English diphthongs [ɛʊ] and [ɪʊ], written *eu, ew, iu, iw,* and *u* (depending to some extent on when they were written), merged into [yu]. As we saw in Chapter 2, this [yu] has tended to be reduced to [u] in such words as *duty, Tuesday, lute,* and *stews,* in which it follows an alveolar sound. The [y] has been retained initially (*use* as distinct from *ooze*) and after labials and velars: *b* (*beauty* as distinct from *booty*), *p* (*pew* as distinct from *pooh*), *m* (*mute* as distinct from *moot*), *v* (*view* as distinct from the first syllable of *voodoo*), *f* (*feud* as distinct from *food*), *g* (the second syllable of *argue* as distinct from *goo*), *k* (often spelled *c* as in *cute* as distinct from *coot*), and *h* (*hew* as distinct from *who*). After [z] this [y] ultimately gave rise by mutual assimilation to a new single sound [ž] in *azure, pleasure,* and the like. Similarly, the earlier medial and initial [sy] in *pressure, nation, sure,* and the like has become [š], though this was not a new sound, having occurred under other circumstances in Old English.

The Middle English diphthong [ʊɪ], occurring almost exclusively in words of French origin, such as *poison, join,* and *boil,* was written *oi* rather than *ui* because of the substitution of *o* for *u* next to stroke letters like *m, n,* and in this case *i* (Chapter 6, 130). The first element of this diphthong underwent the shift to [ə] along with other short *u*'s. The diphthong thus fell together with the development of Middle English *ī* as [ɔɪ], both subsequently becoming [aɪ], so that the verb *boil*, from Old French *boillir* (ultimately Lat. *bullīre*) and the etymologically quite distinct noun meaning 'inflamed, infected sore,' which is of native English origin (OE *bȳl*, occurring in Middle English as *bȳle* or *bīle*), have both become current nonstandard [baɪl]. Many rimes in our older poetry testify to this identity in pronunciation of the reflexes of Middle English *ī* and *ui*—for instance, Alexander Pope's couplet "While expletives their feeble aid to join; / And ten low words oft creep in one dull line." The current standard pronunciation of words spelled with *oi* for etymological *ui* is based on the spelling. The folk, however, preserve the pronunciation with [aɪ] (Kurath and McDavid 167–8, maps 143–6).

The quite different Middle English diphthong spelled *oi* and pronounced [ɔɪ] is also of French origin, going back to Latin *au*, as in *joie* (ultimately Lat. *gaudia*) and *cloistre* (Lat. *claustrum*). It has not changed significantly since its introduction.

DIPHTHONGS

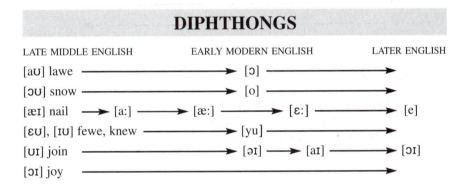

LATE MIDDLE ENGLISH	EARLY MODERN ENGLISH	LATER ENGLISH
[aʊ] lawe ⟶	[ɔ] ⟶	
[ɔʊ] snow ⟶	[o] ⟶	
[æɪ] nail ⟶ [a:] ⟶ [æ:] ⟶	[ɛ:] ⟶	[e]
[ɛʊ], [ɪʊ] fewe, knew ⟶	[yu] ⟶	
[ʊɪ] join ⟶	[əɪ] ⟶ [aɪ] ⟶	[ɔɪ]
[ɔɪ] joy ⟶		

Quantitative Vowel Changes

Quantitative changes in the Modern English period include the lengthening of an originally short vowel before voiceless fricatives—of [æ] as in *staff, glass,* and *path* to [æ:], which in the late eighteenth century was replaced by [ɑ] in standard British English; most forms of American English, however, keep the unlengthened [æ]. Similarly, short *o* was lengthened in *soft, lost,* and *cloth;* that lengthened vowel survives in American English as [ɔ], compared with the [ɑ] of *sot, lot,* and *clot,* which comes directly from an earlier short *o* without lengthening. Short [ɔ] also lengthened before [g], as in *dog,* compared with *dock.* In *dog* versus *dock,* the lengthening has resulted in a qualitatively distinct vowel in most varieties of American English, [ɔ] versus [ɑ]. The earlier laxing of [u] to [ʊ] in *hood, good,* and so forth has already been referred to in connection with the development of Middle English [o:] in the Great Vowel Shift. In *mother, brother, other,* and *smother,* originally long vowels were shortened (with eventual modification to [ə]). *Father* and (in some types of speech) *rather,* with originally short vowels, have undergone lengthening, for what reason we cannot be sure—quite contrary to the shortening that occurred in *lather* and *gather.*

EARLY MODERN ENGLISH CONSONANTS

The consonants of English, like the short vowels, have been rather stable, though certain losses have occurred within the Modern English period.

The Old English and Middle English voiceless palatal fricative [ç], occurring next to front vowels and still represented in our spelling by *gh*, disappeared entirely, as in *bright, sigh,* and *weigh.* The identically written voiceless velar fricative [x], occurring next to back vowels, either disappeared, as in *taught, bought,* and *bough,* or became [f], as in *cough, laugh,* and *enough.* These changes occurred as early as the fifteenth century in all England south of the Humber, though there is evidence that, still in the later part of the sixteenth century, old-fashioned speakers and a few pedants retained the sounds or at least thought that they ought to be retained (Kökeritz, *Shakespeare's Pronunciation* 306).

In the final sequence *-mb,* the *b* had disappeared in pronunciation before the beginning of the Modern English period, so the letter *b* could be added after final *m* where it did not etymologically belong, as in *limb.* There was a similar tendency to reduce final *-nd,* as in *lawn,* from Middle English *laund;* confusion seems to have arisen, however, because a nonetymological *-d* has been added in *sound* and *lend* (ME *soun* and *lene*), though in the latter word the excrescent *d* occurred long before the Modern English period.

The *l* of Middle English preconsonantal *al* was lost after first becoming a vowel: thus Middle English *al* and *au* fell together as *au,* ultimately becoming [ɔ] (as in *talk* and *walk*) or [æ] before *f* and *v* (as in *half* and *salve*) or [ɑ] before *m* (as in *calm* and *palm*). The *l* retained in the spelling of these words has led to spelling pronunciations, particularly when it occurs before *m;* many speakers now pronounce the *l* in words like *calm* and *palm,* and seem to more traditional speakers to be making a special effort to do so. The *l* of *ol* was similarly lost before certain consonants by vocalization, as in *folk, yolk, Holmes,* and the like.

A number of postvocalic *l*'s in English spelling were added because the ultimate Latin sources of their words had an *l,* although it had disappeared in French, from which the words were borrowed; ultimately those added *l*'s came to be pronounced from the new spellings. The *l* in the spelling of *falcon* was thus restored from the Latin etymon (ME *faucon,* from Old French, in which the vocalization to [ʊ] also occurred). A football team known as the *Falcons* is everywhere called [fælkənz], a pronunciation widely current for the bird long before the appearance of the team. The spelling has as yet had little if any effect on the pronunciation of the name of the writer William Faulkner. Perhaps if his name had been written *Falconer,* which amounts to the same thing, the spelling pronunciation might in time have come to prevail. As noted above, the *l* in *fault* and *vault* was also inserted. The older pronunciation of the first of these words is indicated by Swift's "O, let him not debase your thoughts, / Or name him but to tell his faults" ("Directions for Making a Birth-Day Song").

In French loanwords like *host* and *humble,* the *h,* because it is in the spelling, has gradually come to be pronounced in all but a few words; it was generally lacking in such words in early Modern English. Renaissance spelling habits are, as we have seen, responsible for the unetymological *h* in *author, throne,* and other words, but early Modern English continued to use the etymologically expected pronunciation of such words with [t], which gradually was to give way to pronunciation based on misspelling.

There was an early loss of [r] before sibilants, not to be confused with the much later loss (not really normal before the nineteenth century) before any consonant or before a pause: older *barse* 'a type of fish' by such loss became *bass,* as *arse* became *ass,* and *bust, nuss,* and *fust* developed from *burst, nurse,* and *first;* this was not, however, a widespread change. An early loss of [r] before *l* is indicated by *palsy* (ME *parlesie,* a variant of *paralisie* 'paralysis'). Just as *l* occasionally generates an extra (svarabhakti) vowel (as in [fɪləm] for *film*), *r* has done likewise in the old form *alarum,* a variant of *alarm.*

The final unstressed syllable *-ure* was pronounced [ər], with preceding *t, d,* and *s* having the values [t], [d], and [s] or intervocalically [z], as in *nature* [-tər], *verdure* [-dər], *censure* [-sər], and *leisure* [-zər], until the nineteenth century. Though Noah Webster's use of such pronunciations was considered rustic and old-fashioned by his more elegant contemporaries, in his *Elementary Spelling Book* of 1843 he gave *gesture* and *jester* as homophones. The older pronunciation is indicated by many rimes: to mine Dean Swift once more, "If this to clouds and stars will venture, / That creeps as far to reach the centre" ("Verses on Two Celebrated Modern Poets"). Webster was also opposed to [-č-] in *fortune, virtue,* and the like, which he seems to have associated with fast living. He preferred [-t-] in such words. But many of the pronunciations that he prescribed were scorned by the proper Bostonians of his day.

The initial consonant sequences *gn* and *kn*, still represented in our spelling of *gnarl, gnat, gnaw, knave, knead, knee,* and a few other words, had lost their first elements by the early seventeenth century. Loss of [k] is evidenced by the Shakespearean puns *knack-neck, knight-night,* and others cited by Kökeritz (*Shakespeare's Pronunciation* 305).

Final *-ing* when unstressed, as in verb forms like *walking* or *coming* and in pronouns like *nothing* and *something,* had long been practically universally pronounced [-ɪn]. According to Wyld (289), "This habit obtains in practically all Regional dialects of the South and South Midlands, and among large sections of speakers of Received Standard English." The velarization of the *n* to [ŋ] began as a **hypercorrect pronunciation** in the first quarter of the nineteenth century and, still according to Wyld, "has now a vogue among the educated at least as wide as the more conservative one with *-n.*" Long before Wyld wrote these words, which would need some revision for British English today, the [-ɪn] pronunciation had come to be considered substandard in many parts of the United States, largely because of the crusade that teachers had conducted against it, though it continues to occur rather widely in unselfconscious speech on all social levels. Many spellings and rimes in our older literature testify to the orthodoxy of what is popularly called "dropping the *g*"—in phonological terms, using dental [n] instead of velar [ŋ], for there is of course no [g] to be dropped. For instance, Swift wrote the couplets "See then what mortals place their bliss in! / Next morn betimes the bride was missing" ("Phyllis") and the delicate "His jordan [chamber pot] stood in manner fitting / Between his legs, to spew or spit in" ("Cassinus and Peter"). **Inverse spellings** such as Shakespeare's *cushings* (*cushions*), *javelings* (*javelins*), and *napking* (*napkin*) tell the same story (cited by Kökeritz, *Shakespeare's Pronunciation* 314).

EVIDENCE FOR EARLY MODERN PRONUNCIATION

Our knowledge of early Modern English pronunciation comes from many sources. Fortunately not all gentlefolk knew how to spell in earlier days, which is to say that they did not know what have become in our own day conventional spellings and were pretty much so even then, thanks to the printers. So they spelled phonetically, according to their lights. What is by modern standards a "misspelling," like *coat* for *court* or *crick* for *creek,* may tell us a good deal about the writer's pronunciation. A good many such writings have come down to us.

Stress

Many words in early Modern English were stressed otherwise than they are in current speech, as we can tell especially from poetry. *Character, illustrate, concentrate,* and *contemplate* were all stressed on their second syllables, and most polysyllabic words in *-able* and *-ible* had initial stress, frequently with secondary stress on their penultimate syllables, as in "'Tis sweet and commendable in your Nature Hamlet" (*Hamlet* 1.2.87). *Antique,* like *complete* and other words that now have final stress, had initial stress; it is a doublet of *antic,* with which it was identical in pronunciation. But it is not always possible to come to a firm conclusion on the basis of verse, as the many instances of variant stress in Shakespeare's lines indicate (Kökeritz, *Shakespeare's Pronunciation* 392–8). It is likely that most of these variant stressings occurred in actual speech; it would be surprising if they had not, considering the variations that occur in current English.

Scholarly Studies

Henry Wyld in his *History of Modern Colloquial English* has used many memoirs, letters, diaries, and documents from this period as the basis for his conclusions concerning the pronunciation of early Modern English. Kökeritz relies somewhat more than Wyld on the grammars and spelling books that began to appear around the middle of the sixteenth century, which he considers "our most important sources of information" (17) on the pronunciation of the English of Shakespeare's day—works such as John Hart's *An Orthographie* (1569) and *A Methode or Comfortable Beginning for All Unlearned* (1570), William Bullokar's *Booke at Large* (1580) and *Bref Grammar for English* (1586), Richard Mulcaster's *The First Part of the Elementarie* (1582), and, in the following century, Alexander Gill's *Logonomia Anglica* (1619; 2nd ed., 1621) and Charles Butler's *English Grammar* (1633; 2nd ed., 1634), which has a list of homophones in its "Index of Words Like and Unlike." These same works, with others, provide the basis for Dobson's two-volume *English Pronunciation 1500–1700*.

There are special studies of these early Modern writers on language by Otto Jespersen (on Hart), Bror Danielsson (on Hart and Gill), and R. E. Zachrisson (on Bullokar), along with general studies of early Modern English by Wilhelm Horn and Martin Lehnert, Eilert Ekwall (*A History of Modern English Sounds and Morphology*), and Karl Luick. The first volume of Jespersen's *Modern English Grammar on Historical Principles* deals with early Modern English phonology and orthography.

The use of word-play and rime has already been alluded to a number of times. Kökeritz makes extensive and most effective use of these in *Shakespeare's Pronunciation,* a work that has been cited a number of times heretofore. There is no dearth of evidence, though frequently what we have is difficult to interpret.

EARLY MODERN ENGLISH ILLUSTRATED

Spelling

The following paragraph is the chapter "Rosemary" from Banckes's *Herball* (1525), a hodgepodge of botanical and medical lore and a good deal of sheer superstition thrown together and "impyrnted by me Richard Banckes, dwellynge in London, a lytel fro ye Stockes in ye Pultry, y^e .xxv. day of Marche. The yere of our lorde .M.CCCCC. & xxv." The only known original copies of this old black-letter "doctor book" are one in the British Museum and one in the Huntington Library in California. What became of the many other copies of the work, which went through at least fifteen editions, no one can say.

Noteworthy orthographic features of the book include the spelling y^e for *the* or *thee,* explained earlier in this chapter. Also, a line or tilde-like diacritic over a vowel indicates omission of a following *n* or *m*, as in *thē* for *them* and *thã* for *than*. This device is very ancient. The virgules, or slanting lines, are the equivalents of our commas, used to indicate brief pauses in reading. As was the custom, *v* is used initially (*venymous, vnder*) and *u* elsewhere (*hurte, euyll*), regardless of whether consonant or vowel was represented. Some of the final *e*'s are used for justifying lines of type—that is, making even right-hand margins—a most useful expedient when type had to be set by hand. Long *s* (ſ), which must be carefully distinguished from the similar f, is used initially and medially.

The statement in the first line about the herb's being "hote and dry" is an allusion to an ancient theory of matter that classified the nature of everything as a combination of hot or cold and moist or dry qualities.

Roſemary.

This herbe is hote and dry/ take the flowres and put them in a lynen clothe/ & ſo boyle them in fayre clene water to yᵉ halfe & coole it & drynke it/ for it is moche worth agaynſt all euylles in the body. Alſo take the flowres & make powder therof and bynde it to the ryght arme in a lynen clothe/ and it ſhall make thē lyght and mery. Alſo ete the flowres with hony faſtynge with ſowre breed and there ſhall ryſe in the none euyll ſwellynges. Alſo take the flowres and put them in a cheſt amonge youre clothes or amonge bokes and moughtes [moths] ſhall not hurte them. Alſo boyle the flowres in gotes mylke & than let them ſtande all a nyght vnder the ayer fayre couered/ after that gyue hym to drynke thereof that hath the tyſyke [phthisic] and it ſhall delyuer hym. Alſo boyle the leues in whyte wyne & waſſhe thy face therwith/ thy berde & thy browes and there ſhall no cornes growe out/ but thou ſhall haue a fayre face. Alſo put the leues vnder thy beddes heed/ & thou ſhalbe delyuered of all euyll dremes. Alſo breke yᵉ leues ſmall to powder & laye them on a Canker & it ſhall flee it. Alſo take the leues & put thē into a veſſel of wyne and it ſhall preſerue yᵉ wyne fro tartneſſe & euyl ſauour/ and yf thou ſell that wyne, thou ſhall haue good lucke & ſpede [success] in the ſale. Alſo yf thou be feble with vnkyndly [unnatural] ſwette/ take and boyle the leues in clene water, & whan yᵉ water is colde do [put] therto as moche of whyte wyne/ & than make therin ſoppes & ete thou well therof/ & thou ſhal recouer appetyte. Alſo yf thou haue the flux boyle yᵉ leues in ſtronge Ayſell [vinegar] & than bynde them in a lynē [c]lothe and bynde it to thy wombe [belly] & anone the flux ſhal withdrawe. Alſo yf thy legges be blowen with the goute/ boyle the leues in water/ & than take the leues & bynde them in a lynen clothe aboute thy legges/ & it ſhall do yᵉ moche good. Alſo take the leues and boyle them in ſtronge Ayſell & bynde them in a clothe to thy ſtomake/ & it ſhall delyuer yᵉ of all euylles. Alſo yf thou haue the coughe/ drynke the water of the leues boyled in whyte wyne/ & thou ſhalbe hole. Alſo take the rynde of Roſemary & make powder therof and drynke it for the poſe [head cold]/ & thou ſhalbe delyuered therof. Alſo take the tymbre therof & brūne [burn] it to coles & make powder therof & thā put it into a lynen cloth and rubbe thy tethe therwith/ & yf there be ony wormes therin it ſhall flee them & kepe thy tethe from all euyls. Alſo make the a box of the wood and smell to it and it shall preſerne[1] thy youthe. Alſo put therof in thy doores or in thy howſe & thou ſhalbe without daunger of Adders and other venymous ſerpentes. Alſo make the a barell therof & drynke thou of the drynke that ſtandeth therin & thou nedes to fere no poyſon that ſhall hurte yᵉ/ and yf thou ſet it in thy garden kepe it honeſtly [decently] for it is moche profytable. Alſo yf a mā haue loſt his ſmellynge of the ayre orelles he maye not drawe his brethe/ make a fyre of the wood & bake his breed therwith & gyue it hym to ete & he ſhalbe hole.

---

[1]The printer has inadvertently turned the *u* that was in his copy, to make an *n*.

Pronunciation

All quotations from Shakespeare's plays in this chapter are from the First Folio (facsimile ed., London, 1910) with the line numbering of the *Globe* edition (1891) as given in Bartlett's *Concordance*. Roman type has been substituted for the italic used for proper names occurring in speeches in the Folio, except for one instance in the passage cited below.

In the passage from Shakespeare's *1 Henry IV* (2.4.255–66) that follows, the phonetic transcription indicates a somewhat conservative pronunciation that was probably current in the south of England in the late sixteenth and early seventeenth centuries. Vowel length is indicated only in the single word *reason(s),* in which it was distinctive. Stress is indicated, but no attempt has been made to show fine gradations. Prince Hal, Poins, and Falstaff, who has just told a whopping lie, are speaking:

Prin. Why, how could'ſt thou know theſe men in Kendall Greene, when it
[wəɪ ˈhəʊ ˈkudst ðəʊ ˈno ðiz ˈmɛn ɪn ˈkɛndəl ˈgrin ˈhwɛn ɪt

was ſo darke, thou could'ſt not ſee thy Hand? Come, tell vs your reaſon:
wəz ˈso ˈdærk ðəʊ ˈkudst nɔt ˈsi ðəɪ ˈhænd ˈkum ˈtɛl əs yər ˈrɛːzən

what ſay'ſt thou to this?
hwæt ˈsɛst ðəʊ tə ˈðɪs

Poin. Come, your reaſon *Iack,* your reaſon.
ˈkum yər ˈrɛːzən ˈǰæk yər ˈrɛːzən

Falst. What, vpon compulſion? No: were I at the Strappado, or all the
ˈhwæt əˈpɔn kəmˈpulsyən ˈno ˈwɛr əɪ æt ðə stræˈpædo ər ˈɔl ðə

Racks in the World, I would not tell you on compulſion. Giue you a
ˈræks ɪn ðə ˈwurld əɪ ˈwuld nɔt ˈtɛl yu ɔn kəmˈpulsyən ˈgɪv yu ə

reaſon on compulſion? If Reaſons were as plentie as Black-berries,
ˈrɛːzən ɔn kəmˈpulsyən ɪf ˈrɛːzənz wɛr əz ˈplɛnti əz ˈblækˈbɛriz

I would giue no man a Reaſon vpon compulſion, I.
əɪ wəd ˈgɪv ˈno ˈmæn ə ˈrɛːzən əˈpɔn kəmˈpulsyən ˈəɪ]

In this transcription it is assumed that Falstaff, a gentleman (even if a somewhat decayed one) and an officer as well, would have been highly conservative in pronunciation, thus preferring slightly old-fashioned [sy] in *compulsion* to the newer [š] to be heard in the informal speech of his time (Kökeritz, *Shakespeare's Pronunciation* 317). It is also assumed that Falstaff used an unstressed form of *would* [wəd] in his last sentence, in contrast to the strongly stressed form [wuld] of his second sentence, and that, even though the Prince may have had the sequence [hw] in his speech, he would not have pronounced the [h] in his opening interjectional *Why,* thus following the usual practice of those American speakers of the last century who had [hw] when the word is interrogative, but [w] when it is an interjection or an expletive (Kenyon 159).

It is a great pity that there was no tape recorder at the Globe playhouse.

FOR FURTHER READING

Historical Background

Black. *A History of the British Isles.*
———. *A New History of England.*
Morgan. *The Oxford History of Britain.*

Overviews

Barber. *Early Modern English.*
Görlach. *Eighteenth-Century English.*
———. *Introduction to Early Modern English.*
Lass. *The Cambridge History of the English Language.* Vol. 3: *1476–1776.*
Wright. *The Development of Standard English 1300–1800.*
Wyld. *A History of Modern Colloquial English.*

The Great Vowel Shift

Wolfe. *Linguistic Change and the Great Vowel Shift in English.*
Zachrisson. *Pronunciation of English Vowels, 1400–1700.*

Shakespearean English

Franz. *Shakespeare-Grammatik.*
Kökeritz. *Shakespeare's Pronunciation.*
Onions. *Shakespeare Glossary.*
Partridge. *Shakespeare's Bawdy.*
Zachrisson. *English Pronunciation at Shakespeare's Time.*

Dictionaries, Usage, and Standard English

Fisher. *The Emergence of Standard English.*
Leonard. *Doctrine of Correctness in English Usage, 1700–1800.*
Reddick. *The Making of Johnson's Dictionary, 1746–1773.*
Sledd and Kolb. *Dr. Johnson's Dictionary.*
Starnes and Noyes. *The English Dictionary from Cawdrey to Johnson, 1604–1755.*

8 THE EARLY MODERN ENGLISH PERIOD (1500–1800)

FORMS, SYNTAX, AND USAGE

The early part of the Modern English period saw the establishment of the standard written language we know today. The standardization of the language was due in the first place to the need of the central government for regular procedures by which to conduct its business, to keep its records, and to communicate with the citizens of the land. Standard languages are often the by-products of bureaucracy, developed to meet a specific administrative need, as prosaic as such a source is, rather than spontaneous developments of the folk or the artifice of writers and scholars. John H. Fisher has argued that standard English was first the language of the Court of Chancery, founded in the fifteenth century to give prompt justice to English citizens and to consolidate the king's influence in the nation. It was then taken up by the early printers, who adapted it for other purposes and spread it wherever their books were read, until finally it fell into the hands of schoolteachers, dictionary makers, and grammarians.

The impulse to study language did not, in the first instance, arise out of a disinterested passion for knowledge, just as the development of a standard language did not spring from artistic motives. Both were highly practical matters, and they were interrelated. A **standard language** is one that is widespread over a large area, that is respected in that people recognize its usefulness, and that is codified in the sense of having been described so that people know what it is. A standard language has to be studied and described before it is fully standard, and the thorough study of a language has to have an object that is worth the intense effort such study requires. So the existence of a standard language and the study of that language go together.

Two principal genres of language description are the dictionary and the grammar book. Dictionaries focus on the words of a language; grammar books, on how words relate to one another in a sentence. The writing of dictionaries and of grammar books for English began and achieved a high level of competence during the early Modern English period. Several motives prompted their development.

English had replaced French as the language of government in the late Middle English period, and it replaced Latin as the language of religion after the Reformation, and particularly with the adoption of the Book of Common Prayer in 1549, which presented church services in a language "understood of the people," as the Articles of Religion put it. English was being used for secular purposes for

173

which it had not been used for nearly 300 years and for sacred purposes for which it had never been used. These revived and new uses provided a strong motive for "getting it right." In addition, English people were discovering their place on the international scene, both political and cultural, and that discovery also prompted a desire to make the language "copious," that is, having a large enough vocabulary to deal with all the new subjects English people needed to talk about.

In addition, social mobility was becoming easier and more widespread than ever before. Social classes were never impermeable in England. Geoffrey Chaucer's ancestors must have been shoemakers, judging from his surname, which is from an Old French word *chausse,* meaning 'footwear, leggings' and his father was a wine merchant, yet he became an intimate of royals and a diplomat on the Continent for the English king—talent will out. However, the later part of the early Modern period, particularly the eighteenth century, saw a significant shift of power and importance from king to Parliament, from the landed gentry to the mercantile middle class. The newly empowered middle-class English did not share the old gentry's confidence of manners and language. Instead, they wanted to know what was "right." They looked for guidance in language as in other matters. And lexicographers and grammarians were only too happy to oblige them.

THE STUDY OF LANGUAGE

Early Dictionaries

The first English dictionaries appeared in the early Modern English period. If one had to set up a line of development for them, one would start with the Old and Middle English interlinear glosses in Latin and French texts, then proceed through the bilingual vocabularies produced by schoolmasters and designed for those studying foreign languages, specifically Latin, French, Italian, and Spanish. But the first work designed expressly for listing and defining English words for English-speaking people was the schoolmaster Robert Cawdrey's *A Table Alphabeticall* (1604) ("conteyning and teaching the true writing, and understanding of hard usuall English wordes, borrowed from the Hebrew, Greeke, Latine, or French. &c.").

Other dictionaries followed in the same tradition of explicating "hard words" but gradually moved toward a comprehensive listing of English words, among them that of John Bullokar, Doctor of Physick, *An English Expositour* (1616); Henry Cockeram's *English Dictionarie* (1623); Thomas Blount's *Glossographia* (1656); Edward Phillips's *New World of English Words* (1658); Edward Cocker's *English Dictionary* (1704); and Nathan Bailey's *Universal Etymological English Dictionary* (1721), with a second volume that was really a supplement appearing in 1727. In 1730, Bailey (and others) produced the *Dictionarium Britannicum,* with about 48,000 entries. In 1755 appeared both the Scott-Bailey *New Universal Etymological English Dictionary* and Samuel Johnson's great two-volume

Dictionary, which was based on the *Dictionarium Britannicum,* though containing fewer entries than it.

The publication of Johnson's *Dictionary* was certainly the most important linguistic event of the eighteenth century, not to say the entire period under discussion, for it to a large extent "fixed" English spelling and established a standard for the use of words. Johnson did indeed attempt to exercise a directive function. It would have been strange had he not done so at that time. For most people it is apparently not sufficient even today for the lexicographer simply to record and define the words of the language and to indicate the way in which they are pronounced by those who use them; the lexicographer is also supposed to have some God-given power of determining which are "good" words and which are "bad" ones and to know how they "ought" to be pronounced. But Johnson had the good sense usually to recognize the prior claims of usage over the arbitrary appeals to logic, analogy, Latin grammar, and sheer prejudice so often made by his contemporaries, even if he did at times settle matters by appeals to his own taste, which was fortunately good taste.

The son of a bookseller in Lichfield, Johnson was a Tory by both denomination and conviction. Hence, along with his typical eighteenth-century desire to "fix" the language went a great deal of respect for upper-class usage. He can thus be said truly to have consolidated a standard of usage that was not altogether of his own making. His use of illustrative quotations, literally by the thousands, was an innovation; but his own definitions show the most discriminating judgment. The quirky definitions, like that for *oats*—"a grain which in England is generally given to horses, but in Scotland supports the people"—are well-known, so well-known that some people must have the utterly false impression that there are very many others not so well-known. It is in a way unfortunate that these have been "played up" for their sheer amusement value as much as they have been, for they are actually few in number.

Eighteenth-Century Attitudes Toward Grammar and Usage

The purist attitude predominant in eighteenth-century England was simply the manifestation of an attitude toward language that has been current in all times and in all places, as it continues to be in our own day. Doubtless there are and have been purists—persons who believe in some sort of absolute and unwavering standard of what they deem to be "correctness"—in even the most undeveloped societies, for **purism** is a matter of temperament rather than of culture.

Though very dear to American purists—by no means all of them schoolteachers—the "rules" supposed to govern English usage originated not in America, but in the mother country. Those who formulated them were about as ill-informed and as inconsistent as their slightly later American counterparts. Present-day notions of "correctness" are to a large extent based on the notion, prominent in the eighteenth century, that language is of divine origin and hence was perfect in its beginnings but is constantly in danger of corruption and decay unless it is diligently kept in line by wise men who are able to get themselves accepted as authorities, such as those who write dictionaries and grammars.

Latin was regarded as having retained much of its original "perfection." No one seems to have been very much aware that it was the culmination of a long development and had undergone many changes of the sort that were deplored in English. When English grammars came to be written, they were based on Latin grammar, even down to the terminology. The most influential of the eighteenth-century advocates of **prescriptive grammar**, who aimed at bringing English into a Latinlike state of perfection, was Robert Lowth (1710–87). He was a theologian, Hebraist, professor of poetry at Oxford from 1741 to 1753, later bishop of Oxford, then of London, and dean of the Chapel Royal, who four years before his death was offered the archbishopric of Canterbury, which he turned down.

In the preface to his *Short Introduction to English Grammar* (1762), Lowth agreed with Dean Swift's charge, made in 1712 in his *Proposal for Correcting, Improving, and Ascertaining* [that is, fixing or making certain] *the English Tongue,* that "our language is extremely imperfect," "that it offends against every part of grammar," and that most of the "best authors of our age" commit "many gross improprieties, which . . . ought to be discarded." Lowth was able to find many of the most egregious blunders in the works of our most eminent writers; his footnotes are filled with them. It apparently never occurred to any of his contemporaries to doubt that so famous and successful a man had inside information about an ideal state of the English language. Perhaps they thought he got it straight from a linguistic Yahweh.

In any case, Lowth set out in all earnestness in the midst of a busy life to do something constructive about the deplorable English written by the masters of English literature. Like most men of his time, he believed in universal grammar. Consequently he believed that English was "easily reducible to a System of rules." Among many other things, he gave wide currency, probably because of his high position in the Establishment, to those rules for *shall* and *will* as they had been formulated by John Wallis in his *Grammatica Linguae Anglicanae.*

In actual practice, the "rules," which everybody continues to think are inflexibly right, have been honored more in the breach than in the observance. Most people, only dimly comprehending their complexities, seem to think that they should observe them more conscientiously than they have actually done. But because of the deference that has been paid to these supposedly omniscient lawgivers of the eighteenth century—even though the names of many have been long forgotten—the most important eighteenth-century development in the English language was its conscious regulation by those who were not really qualified for the job but who managed to acquire authority as linguistic gurus.

One of the most influential of the late eighteenth-century grammarians was Lindley Murray, a Philadelphia-born Quaker who returned to England after the American Revolution and wrote an *English Grammar* for use in Quaker girls' schools. He was motivated by a wish to foster the study of the native language, as opposed to Latin, and by his religious piety, which "predisposed him to regard linguistic matters in terms of right and wrong. His highly moralistic outlook perforce carried over into his attitude toward usage" (Read, "Motivation of Lindley Murray's Grammatical Work" 531).

Although the grammarians who promulgated the rules for language were children of their age, influenced in linguistic matters by their attitudes toward other aspects of life, they must not therefore be thought contemptible. Bishop Lowth was not—and, heaven knows, Dean Swift, one of the glories of English literature, was certainly not. Nor was Joseph Priestley, who, in addition to writing the original and in many respects forward-looking *Rudiments of English Grammar* (1761), was the discoverer of oxygen, a prominent nonconformist preacher, and a voluminous writer on theological, scientific, political, and philosophical subjects. Like George Campbell, who in his *Philosophy of Rhetoric* (1776) went so far as to call language "purely a species of fashion," Priestley recognized the superior force of usage; he also shared Campbell's belief that there was need for some form of control of language other than that furnished by custom. Being children of the Age of Reason, both would have had recourse to the principle of analogy to settle questions of divided usage, though admitting that it was not always possible to do so.

All these men were indeed typical of their time, in most respects a good time; and they were honest men according to their lights, which in other respects were quite bright indeed. We cannot blame them for not having information that was not available in their day. And, despite the tremendous advances of linguistics since the eighteenth century, popular attitudes toward language have actually changed very little since Bishop Lowth and Lindley Murray were laying down the law. Their precepts were largely based on what they supposed to be logic and reason, for they believed that the laws of language were rooted in the natural order, and this was of course "reasonable." To cite an example, they outlawed, as far as the educated are concerned, the emphatic and still very viable double-negative construction on the grounds stated by Lowth that "two Negatives in English destroy one another, or are equivalent to an Affirmative"—in English, that is to say, just as in mathematics, though the analogy implicit in the appeal to logic was quite false. Many very reasonable people before them had spoken and written sentences with two or even more negatives: Chaucer has four in "Forwhy to tellen nas [ne was] nat his entente / To nevere no man" (*Troilus and Criseyde* 1.738–9) and four in his description of the Knight in the General Prologue to the *Canterbury Tales:* "He nevere yet no vileynye ne sayde / In al his lyf unto no maner wight" (lines 70–1). It certainly never occurred to him that these would cancel out and thus *reverse* his meaning.

Modern linguistics has made very little headway in convincing those who have not made a special study of language that language is a living thing, our possession and servant rather than an ideal toward which we should all hopelessly aspire. Many schoolroom grammars and handbooks of English usage continue to perpetuate the tradition of Bishop Lowth's *Short Introduction to English Grammar.* Indeed, the very word *grammar* means to many highly literate people not the study of language, but merely so simple a thing as making the "proper" choice between *shall* and *will, between* and *among, different from* and *different than, who* and *whom,* as well as the avoidance of terminal prepositions, *ain't,* and *It's me.* In Chapter 9 we examine in more detail the later developments of this comparatively recent tradition in England and America.

The actual grammar of early Modern English differed in only minor respects from that of late Middle English, on the one hand, and from that of our own time, on the other. There was nothing as striking as the Great Vowel Shift to mark the grammar of Shakespeare, Milton, and the eighteenth-century novelists as distinct. Yet there were many grammatical changes underway during the 300 years between 1500 and 1800.

NOUNS

As we have seen, by the end of the Middle English period *-es* had been extended to practically all nouns as a genitive singular and caseless plural suffix. As a result, most nouns had only two forms (*sister, sisters*), as they do today in speech. The use of the apostrophe to distinguish the written forms of the genitive singular (*sister's*) and plural (*sisters'*) was not widely adopted until the seventeenth and eighteenth centuries, respectively.

Irregular Plurals

The handful of mutated-vowel plurals for the most part resisted the analogical principle, so that *feet, geese, teeth, lice, mice, men,* and *women* have survived to the present and show no tendency to give way to *-s* plurals. A few *-n* plurals remained in early Modern English, including *eyen* 'eyes,' *shoon* 'shoes,' *kine* 'cows,' *brethren, children,* and *oxen.* The first two are now obsolete; *kine* continues to eke out a precarious existence as an archaic poetic word, and *brethren* has a very limited currency, confined in serious use mainly to certain religious and fraternal groups. In *kine, brethren,* and *children,* the *n* had not been present in Old English but was added by analogy with other *-n* plurals. The regularly developed *ky* and *childer,* which go back, respectively, to Old English *cȳ* and *cildru,* are current in dialect speech, or were so until fairly recently, in the north of England and in Scotland. *Brethren* (Old English *brōðor* or *brōðru*) also added an *n* by analogy and introduced a mutated vowel that did not occur in the Old English plural. *Oxen* is thus the only "pure" survival of the Old English weak declension, which formed its nominative-accusative plural with the suffix *-an.*

Uninflected plurals survive from Old and Middle English times to the present in *deer, sheep, swine, folk,* and *kind.* Analogical *folks* occurred very early in the Modern English period. *Kind* has acquired a new *-s* plural because of the feeling that the older construction was a "grammatical error," despite the precedent of its use in "these (those, all) kind of" by Shakespeare, Dryden, Swift, Goldsmith, Austen, and others. Its synonym *sort,* which is not of Old English origin, acquired an uninflected plural as early as the sixteenth century by analogy with *kind,* as in "these (those, all) sort of," but this construction also is frowned upon by most writers of school grammars, despite its use by Swift, Fielding, Austen, Dickens, Trollope, Wells, and others (Jespersen, *Modern English Grammar* 2:68). *Horse* retained its historical uninflected plural, as in Chaucer's "His hors were Goode"

(*Canterbury Tales,* General Prologue, line 74) and Shakespeare's "Come on, then, horse and chariots let us have" (*Titus Andronicus* 2.2.18), until the seventeenth century, though the analogical plural *horses* had begun to occur as early as the thirteenth. Doubtless by analogy with *deer, sheep,* and the like, the names of other creatures that had *-s* plurals in earlier times came to have uninflected plurals—for example, *fish* and *fowl,* particularly when these are regarded as game. Barnyard creatures take the *-s* (*fowls, ducks, pigs,* and so forth); and Jesus Christ, it will be remembered, distributed to the multitude "a few little *fishes*" (Matthew 15.34). But one shoots (wild) *fowl* and (wild) *duck,* hunts *pig* (that is, wild boars), and catches *fish.* The uninflected plural may be extended to the names of quite un-English beasts, like *buffalo* ("a herd of buffalo") and *antelope.*

His-Genitive

A remarkable construction is the use of *his, her,* and *their* as signs of the genitive (**his-genitive**), as in "Augustus his daughter" (E. K.'s gloss to Spenser's *Shepherds' Calendar,* 1579), "Elizabeth Holland her howse" (State Papers, 1546), and "the House of Lords their proceedings" (Pepys's *Diary,* 1667). This use began in Old English times but had its widest currency in the sixteenth and seventeenth centuries, as in Shakespeare's "And art not thou Poines, his Brother?" (*2 Henry IV* 2.4.308) and in the "Prayer for All Conditions of Men" in the 1662 Book of Common Prayer, "And this we beg for Jesus Christ his sake."

The use of possessive pronouns as genitive markers seems to have had a double origin. On the one hand, it may have arisen from the sort of topic-comment construction that we still have in present-day English: "My brother—his main interest is football." Such a construction would have provided a way in Old English to indicate possession for foreign proper names and for other expressions in which the inflected genitive was awkward. The oldest examples we have are from King Alfred's ninth-century translation of the history of the world by Orosius: "Nilus seo ea hire æwielme is neh þæm clife," that is, 'Nile, the river—her source is near the cliff,' and "Affrica and Asia hiera landgemircu onginnað of Alexandria," that is, 'Africa and Asia—their boundaries start from Alexandria.' An early example with *his* is from Ælfric's translation of the Book of Numbers (made about the year 1000): "We gesawon Enac his cynryn," that is, 'We saw Anak's kindred.'

On the other hand, many English speakers came to regard the historical genitive ending *-s* as a variant of *his.* In its unstressed pronunciation, *his* was and is still pronounced without an [h], so that "Tom bets his salary" and "Tom Betts's salary" are identical in pronunciation. Once speakers began to think of "Mars's armor" as a variant of "Mars his armor," an association doubtless reinforced by the use of the latter construction from early times as mentioned above, they started to spell the genitive ending *-s* as *his* (Wyld 314–5; Jespersen, *Modern English Grammar* 6:301–2). That such confusion did occur is shown by the occasional use of *his* with females, as in "Mrs. Sands his maid" (*OED,* 1607), and by the mixture of the two spellings, as in "Job's patience, Moses his meekness,

Abraham's faith" (*OED*, 1568). In the latter example, *his* was used when the genitive ending was pronounced as an extra syllable, and *'s* when it was not, the apostrophe also suggesting that the genitive *-s* was regarded as a contraction of *his*. Other spellings for the genitive ending were *is* and *ys*, as in "Harlesdon ys name" and "her Grace is requeste," that is, 'her Grace's request' (Wyld 315).

His (with its variants *is* and *ys*) was much more common in this construction than *her* or *their*. The *his*-genitive, whichever pronoun is used, was most prevalent with proper names and especially after sibilants, as in *Mars, Moses, Sands,* and *Grace,* an environment in which the genitive ending is homophonous with the unstressed pronunciation of *his*. Although the earliest examples of the *his*-genitive must have had another origin, those that were so frequent during the early Modern English period were certainly due, at least in part, to a confusion of inflectional *-s* and *his*. The construction has survived, somewhat marginally, in printed bookplates: "John Smith His Book."

Group Genitive

The so-called **group-genitive** construction, as in "King Priam of Troy's son" and "The Wife of Bath's Tale," is a development of the early Modern English period. The "group" in the term for this construction refers to the fact that the genitive ending *'s* is added, not to a single noun to which it relates most closely, but rather to another word that is at the end of a group of words. Though there were sporadic occurrences of this construction in Middle English, the usual older idiom is illustrated by Chaucer's "the kyng Priamus sone of Troye" and "The Wyves Tale of Bathe," or its variant "The Wyf of Bathe Hire Tale" with a *his*-genitive (in this case, *hire* for 'her'). What has happened is that a word group—usually, as in these examples, two nouns connected by a preposition—has come to be regarded as a unit; the sign of the genitive is thus affixed to the last word of what is in fact a phrase. The construction also occurs with a pronoun plus *else,* as in "everybody else's," and with nouns connected by a coordinating conjunction, as in "Kenyon and Knott's *Pronouncing Dictionary*" and "an hour or two's time." There are comparatively few literary examples of clauses so treated, but in everyday speech such constructions as "the little boy that lives down the street's dog" and "the woman I live next door to's husband" are frequent. "He is the woman who is the best friend this club has ever had's husband" is an extreme example from Gracie Allen, an early radio and television comedian noted for her confusing speech.

As a consequence of the group genitive, the morpheme we spell *'s* is now strikingly different from other inflectional endings, because it is added to phrases rather than to words. In effect it has ceased to be a member of the inflectional system and has instead become a grammatical particle that is always pronounced as part of the preceding word (an **enclitic**), although it often goes syntactically not with that word, but rather with a whole preceding phrase. Of all the Old English inflectional endings, *-es* (the origin of our *'s*) has had the most unusual historical development: it has broken off from the nouns to which it was originally added and moved up to the level of phrases, where it functions syntactically like a word on that higher level, although it continues to be pronounced as a mere word ending.

Uninflected Genitive

In early Modern English, an **uninflected genitive** occurred in a number of special circumstances, especially for some nouns that were feminine in Old English and occasionally for nouns ending in [s] or preceding words beginning with [s]—for example, "for conscience sake" and "for God sake." A few uninflected genitives, though not generally recognized as such, survive to the present day in reference to the Virgin Mary—for example, *Lady Day* (that is, Our Lady's Day, 'Feast of the Annunciation'), *Lady Chapel* (Our Lady's Chapel), and *ladybird* (Our Lady's bird). Sometimes an uninflected genitive was used as an alternative to the group genitive, as in "the duke of Somerset dowther [daughter]." The uninflected genitive of present-day African-American English (for example, "my brother car"), although of different historical origin, has re-created a structure that was once a part of general English usage.

ADJECTIVES AND ADVERBS

The distinction between strong and weak adjective forms, already greatly simplified by the Middle English loss of the final *n,* completely disappeared with the further loss of [ə] from the end of words. The loss of final [ə] also eliminated the distinction between plural and singular adjectives. Although the letter *e,* which represented the schwa vowel in spelling, continued to be written in many words and was even extended to words that had not had it in Middle English, adjectives no longer had a grammatical category of number or of definiteness. The Modern English adjective thus came to be invariable in form. The only words that still agree in number with the nouns they modify are the demonstratives *this-these* and *that-those.*

Adjectives and adverbs continued to form comparatives with *-er* and superlatives with *-est,* but increasingly they used **analytical comparison** with *mo(e)* (a semantic equivalent of *more,* though not comparative in form), *more,* and *most,* which had occurred as early as Old English times. The form *mo(e),* from Old English *mā,* continued in use through the early Modern English period, as in Robert Greene's *A Maiden's Dream* (1591): "No foreign wit could Hatton's overgo: Yet to a friend wise, simple, and no mo." It even lasted into the nineteenth century in Byron's *Childe Harold* 1.93 (1812): "Ye . . . Shall find some tidings in a future page, If he that rhymeth now may scribble moe." The homophonous and synonymous *mo'* of African-American English has a different origin but is similar in use.

The present stylistic objection to affixing *-er* and *-est* to polysyllables had somewhat less force in the early Modern English period, when forms like *eminenter, impudentest,* and *beautifullest* are not particularly hard to find, nor, for that matter, are monosyllables with *more* and *most,* like *more near, more fast, most poor,* and *most foul.* As was true in earlier times also, a good many instances of **double comparison** like *more fitter, more better, more fairer, most worst, most stillest,* and (probably the best-known example) *most unkindest* occur in early

Modern English. The general rule was that comparison could be made with the ending or with the modifying word or, for emphasis, with both.

Many adverbs that now must end in *-ly* did not require the suffix in early Modern English times. The works of Shakespeare furnish many typical examples: *grievous sick, indifferent cold, wondrous strange,* and *passing* ['surpassingly'] *fair.* Note also the use of *sure* in the following citations, which would nowadays be condemned as "bad English" in the schools: "If she come in, shee'l sure speake to my wife" (*Othello* 5.2.96); "And sure deare friends my thankes are too deare a halfepeny" (*Hamlet* 2.2.282); "Sure the Gods doe this yeere connive at us" (*Winter's Tale* 4.4.692).

PRONOUNS

Rather important changes are to be noted in the pronouns. Although they are the most highly inflected part of speech in present-day English, thus preserving the earlier synthetic character of our language in a small way, the system of the pronouns has undergone several major and a number of minor alterations.

Personal Pronouns

The early Modern English personal pronouns are shown in the accompanying table.

I came to be capitalized, not through any egotism, but only because lower-case *i* standing alone was likely to be overlooked, since it is the most insignificant of the letters of the alphabet.

In the first and second persons singular, the distinction between *my* and *mine* and between *thy* and *thine* was purely phonological (like the distinction between *a* and

PERSONAL PRONOUNS IN EARLY MODERN ENGLISH

| | NOMINATIVE | OBJECTIVE | POSSESSIVE | |
			ATTRIBUTIVE	NOMINAL
Singular				
1 pers	I	me		my/mine
2 pers	thou	thee		thy/thine
3 pers, masc.	he, a	him		his
fem.	she	her	her	hers
neut.	(h)it	(h)it		his, it, its
Plural				
1 pers	we	us	our	ours
2 pers	ye/you	you/ye	your	yours
3 pers	they	them, (h)em	their	theirs

an), as it had been in Middle English since the thirteenth century on; that is, *mine* and *thine* were used before a vowel, *h,* or a pause, and *my* and *thy* before a consonant. This distinction continued to be made until the eighteenth century, when *my* became the only regular first person possessive in attributive use (as in "That is my coat"). Thereafter *mine* was restricted to use as a nominal (as in "That is mine," "Mine is here," and "Put it on mine"), just as the "*s*-forms" *hers, ours, yours, theirs* had been since late Middle English times. Thus the distinction between attributive and nominal possessive forms spread through most of the personal pronoun system; today the only exceptions are *his,* which uses the same form for both functions, and *its,* which has no nominal function. We do not usually say things like *"That is its" or *"Its is here." (The **asterisk** before a present-day form, as in the preceding, indicates that the form does not exist, or at least that the writer believes it to be abnormal. This use of the asterisk thus differs from that before historical reconstructions, where it means that the form is not recorded although it or something like it probably did once exist. The two uses agree in indicating that the form so marked is not attested.)

When the distinction between the possessives with and without *n* was phono-logical, a confusion sometimes arose about which word the *n* belonged with. The Fool's *nuncle* in *King Lear* is due to his misunderstanding of *mine uncle* as *my nuncle,* and it is likely that *Ned, Nelly,* and *Noll* (a nickname usually associated with Oliver Goldsmith) have the same origin from *mine Edward, mine Eleanor,* and *mine Oliver.* The confusion is similar to that which today produces *a (whole) nother* from *another* (that is, *an other*).

The loss in ordinary language of the second person singular *thou* and its other forms created a gap in the pronoun system that we have not yet repaired. That loss began with a shift in the use of *thou* and *ye* forms. As early as the late thirteenth cen-tury, the second person plural forms (*ye, you, your*) began to be used with singular meaning in circumstances of politeness or formality, leaving the singular forms (*thou, thee, thy/thine*) for intimate, familiar use. In imitation of the French use of *vous* and *tu,* the English historically plural *y*-forms were used in addressing a superior, whether by virtue of social status or age, and in upper-class circles among equals, though high-born lovers might slip into the *th*-forms in situations of intimacy. The *th*-forms were also used by older to younger and by socially superior to socially inferior. The dis-tinction is retained in other languages, which may even have a verb meaning 'to use the singular form'—for example, French *tutoyer,* Spanish *tutear,* Italian *tuizzare,* and German *dutzen.* Late Middle English had *thoute,* with the same meaning.

In losing this distinction, English obviously has lost a useful device, which our older writers frequently employed with artistic discrimination, as in *Hamlet* 3.4.9–21:

Qu[een]	Hamlet, thou hast thy Father much offended.
Ham[let]	Mother, you have my Father much offended.
Qu[een]	Come, come, you answer with an idle tongue.
	. . .
Qu[een]	What wilt thou do? thou wilt not murther me?

The Queen's *thou* in the first line is what a parent would be expected to say to her child. Hamlet's "Mother, you have . . ." is appropriate from a son to his mother, but there is more than a hint of a rebuff in her choice of the more formal pronoun in "Come, come you answer . . . ," and her return to *thou* in the last line suggests that, in her alarm at Hamlet's potential violence, she is reminding him of the parental relationship.

Elsewhere also, Shakespeare chooses the *y*-forms and the *th*-forms with artistic care, though it is sometimes difficult for a present-day reader, unaccustomed to the niceties offered by a choice of forms, to figure him out, as in the dialogue between two servants, the less imaginative Curtis and the sardonic Grumio, in *The Taming of the Shrew* 4.1.101–4:

Cur[tis]	Doe you heare ho? you must meete my maister to countenance my mistris.
Gru[mio]	Why she hath a face of her owne.
Cur[tis]	Who knowes not that?
Gru[mio]	Thou it seemes . . . .

Curtis uses the polite *you* to Grumio, but when Curtis fails to understand Grumio's pun on *countenance* as a verb 'to give support to' and a noun 'face,' Grumio responds with *thou,* which a superior uses to an inferior. However, the English did not always use the two forms as consistently as the French. There is sometimes no apparent reason for their interchange.

The *th*-forms, which had become quite rare in upper-class speech by the sixteenth century, were completely lost in standard English in the eighteenth, though they have lingered on in the dialects. Our familiarity with them is largely due to their occurrence in poetry and in religious language, especially that of the King James Bible. Though less general than they once were, *th*-forms still occur in the usage of older-generation members of the Society of Friends (Quakers) when speaking to one another. In such occurrences, *thee* serves in both subject and object functions.

The third person singular masculine and feminine pronouns have been relatively stable since late Old English times. The unstressed form of *he* was often written *a,* as in "Now might I doe it, but now a is a-praying, / And now Ile doo't, and so a goes to heaven" from the Second Quarto of *Hamlet* 3.3.73–4. (The Folio has *he* in both instances.) *She* and *her(s)* show no change since Middle English times.

In the neuter, however, an important change took place in the later part of the sixteenth century, when the new possessive form *its* arose. The older nominative and objective *hit* had lost its *h-* when unstressed; then the *h*-less form came to be used in stressed as well as unstressed positions—though, as has already been pointed out, *hit,* the form preferred by Queen Elizabeth I, remains in nonstandard speech as a stressed form. The corresponding older possessive *his* remained the usual neuter form in the early years of the seventeenth century, as in Shakespeare's *Troilus and Cressida* 2.2.53–4: "But value dwels not in particular will, / It holds his estimate and dignitie." The *OED* cites an interesting American example from 1634: "Boston is two miles North-east from Roxberry: His situation is very pleasant."

Perhaps because of its ambiguity, *his* was nevertheless to some extent avoided as a neuter possessive even in Middle English times: an uninflected *it* occurs from the fourteenth to the seventeenth century, and to this day in British dialect usage. The latest citation by the *OED* of its occurrence in standard English is from 1622: "Each part as faire doth show / In it kind, as white in Snow." Other efforts to replace the ambiguous *his* as a possessive for *it* include paraphrases with *thereof*, as in "The earth is the Lord's, and the fullness thereof" (Psalm 24.1), and *of it*, as in "Great was the fall of it" (Matthew 7.27). By analogy with other possessives ending in *'s*, the present-day form (at first written *it's*, as many people still write it) began to be used instead of *his, it,* or the other options. *Its* is quite rare in Shakespeare and occurs only twice in Milton's *Paradise Lost;* but by the end of the seventeenth century *its* had become the usual form, completely displacing *his* and the less frequent *it* as a neuter possessive.

Similar to the use of the second person plural form to refer to a single person is the "regal *we*," except that here a sense of one's own importance rather than that of someone else is implied. It is still useful in proclamations by a sovereign, and in earlier times, if we can judge by the older drama, it was even used in conversation. The usage is very ancient. Queen Victoria is said to have been the last monarch to employ it as a spoken form, as in her famous but doubtless apocryphal reproof to one of her maids of honor who had told a mildly improper story: "We are not amused." The "editorial *we*" dates from Old English times. It is sometimes used by one who is a member of a staff of writers assumed to share the same opinions. It may also be used to include one's readers in phrases like "as we have seen."

In the second person plural, which became singular also, as we have just seen, the old distinction between the nominative *ye* and the objective *you* was still maintained in the King James Bible—for example, "The Lord deal kindly with you, as ye have dealt with the dead, and with me. The Lord grant you that ye may find rest" (Ruth 1.8–9). It was, however, generally lost during the sixteenth century, when some writers made the distinction, while others did not (Wyld 330). In time, it was the objective *you* that prevailed to such an extent as to drive *ye* from standard English.

Present-day nonstandard speech distinguishes singular and plural *you* in a number of ways; examples include the nonstandard, analogical *youse* of northern American urbanites (also current in Irish English) and the Inland Southern *you-uns* (that is, *you ones*), which probably stems from Scots English. *You-all* (or *y'all*) is in educated colloquial use in the Southern states and is the only new second person plural to have acquired respectability in Modern English. *You guys* is a recent gender unspecific candidate, as is *you lot* among the British, though the last has patronizing implications.

From the later seventeenth century and throughout the eighteenth, many speakers made a distinction between singular *you was* and plural *you were*. James Boswell used singular *you was* throughout his *London Journal* (1762–3) and even reported it as coming from the lips of Dr. Johnson: "Indeed, when you was in the irreligious way, I should not have been pleased with you" (July 28, 1763); but in the second edition of his *Life of Johnson,* he changed over to *you were* for both singular and plural. Bishop Robert Lowth, in his very influential *Short Introduction to English Grammar* (1762), condemned *you was* in no uncertain terms as "an enormous Solecism," but George Campbell testified in his *Philosophy of Rhetoric* (1776) that "it is ten times oftener heard." *You was* at one time was very common in cultivated American use also: George Philip Krapp (*English Language in America* 2:261) cites its use by John Adams in a letter of condolence to a friend whose house had burned down: "You regret your loss; but why? Was you fond of seeing or thinking that others saw and admired so stately a pile?" The construction became unfashionable in the early nineteenth century, but Noah Webster continued to defend it.

In the third person plural, the native *h*-forms had become all but archaic by the end of the fifteenth century, in the course of which the *th*-forms current in present English gradually took over. The only *h*-form to survive is the one earlier written *hem,* and it survives only as an unstressed form; when it is written at all nowadays, it is written *'em.* The plural possessives in *h-* (*here, her, hir*) occurred only very rarely after the beginning of the sixteenth century.

Relative and Interrogative Pronouns

The usual Old English relative particle was *þe,* which, since it had only one form, would have continued to do very well. It is a pity that it was ever lost. Middle English adapted the neuter demonstrative pronoun *that,* without inflection, for the same relative function, later adding the previously interrogative *which,* sometimes preceded by *the,* and likewise uninflected. It was not until the sixteenth century that the originally interrogative *who* (OE *hwā*) came to be commonly used as a simple relative to refer to persons. It had somewhat earlier been put to use as an indefinite relative, that is, as the equivalent of present *who(m)- ever,* a use now rare but one that can be seen in Shakespeare's "Who tels me true, though in his Tale lye death, / I heare him as he flatter'd" (*Antony and Cleopatra* 1.2.102–3) and Byron's "Whom the gods love die young" (*Don Juan* 4.12). The King James Bible, which we should expect to be a little behind the times in its grammar, has *which* where we would today use *who,* as in "The kingdom of heaven is likened unto a man which sowed good seed in his field" (Matthew 13.24) and in "Our Father which art in heaven." This translation was the work of almost fifty theological scholars designated by James I, and it was afterward reviewed by the bishops and other eminent scholars. It is not surprising that these men should have been little given to anything that smacked of innovation. Shakespeare, who with all his daring as a coiner and user of words was essentially conservative in his syntax, also uses *which* in the older fashion to refer to persons and things alike, as in "he which hath your Noble Father slaine" (*Hamlet* 4.7.4).

Case Forms of the Pronouns

In the freewheeling usage of earlier days, there was not so much concern as now with what are conceived to be "proper" choices of case forms. English had to wait until the later years of the seventeenth century for the rise of the schoolmaster's attitude toward language that was to become predominant in the eighteenth century and is still so—a relatively new thing. After a coordinating conjunction, for instance, the nominative form tended to occur invariably, as indeed it yet does, whether the pronoun is object of verb or preposition or second element of a compound subject. H. C. Wyld (332) cites "with you and I" from a letter by Sir John Suckling, as well as seventeenth-century occurrences of "between you and I," to which may be added Shakespeare's "all debts are cleerd betweene you and I" (*Merchant of Venice* 3.2.321). No doubt at the present time the desire to be "correct" causes many speakers who may have been reproved as children for saying "Mary and me went downtown" to use "Mary and I" under all circumstances; but hypercorrectness is hardly a satisfactory explanation for the phenomenon as it occurs in the writings of well-bred people from the sixteenth to the early eighteenth centuries, a period during which people of consequence talked pretty much as they pleased.

School grammar requires the nominative form after *as* and *than* in such sentences as "Is she as tall as me?" (*Antony and Cleopatra* 3.3.14). Boswell, who wrote in a period in which men of strong minds and characters were attempting to "regularize" the English language, shows no particular pattern of consistency in this construction. In the entry in his *London Journal* for June 5, 1763, he writes "I was much stronger than her," but elsewhere uses the nominative form in the same construction. The basic question for grammarians is whether *than* and *as* are to be regarded as prepositions, which would require the objective form consistently, or as subordinating conjunctions, after which the choice of case form should be determined by expanding the construction, as in "I know him better than she (knows him)" or "I know him better than (I know) her." Present-day prescriptivists opt for the second analysis, but speakers tend to follow either, as the spirit moves them.

In early Modern English, the nominative and objective forms of the personal pronouns, particularly *I* and *me,* tend to occur more or less indiscriminately after the verb *be.* In *Twelfth Night,* for instance, Sir Andrew Aguecheek, who, though a fool, is yet a gentleman, uses both forms within a few lines: "That's mee I warrant you. . . . I knew 'twas I" (2.5.87–9). The generally inconsistent state of things before the prescriptive grammarians took over is exemplified by Shakespeare's use of other pronouns as well: "I am not thee" (*Timon of Athens* 4.3.277); "you are not he" (*Love's Labour's Lost* 5.2.550); "And damn'd be him, that first cries hold, enough" (*Macbeth* 5.8.34); "you are she" (*Twelfth Night* 5.1.334). Instances of *her, us,* and *them* in this construction are infrequent in early Modern English writings. In "Here's them" (*Pericles* 2.1.67), *them* is functionally the subject, but the speaker is a fisherman.

Today also the objective form of personal pronouns continues to occur after *be,* though not without bringing down upon the head of the user the thunder of those who regard themselves as guardians of the language. There are nevertheless a great many speakers of standard English who do not care and who say "It's me" when there is occasion to do so, despite the school doctrine that "the verb *to be* can never take an object." There is little point in labeling the construction colloquial or informal as contrasted with a supposedly formal "It is I," inasmuch as the utterance would not be likely to occur alone anywhere except in conversation. Followed by a relative clause, however, "It is I" is usual, as in "It is I who am responsible," though "It is me" occurs as a rule before relative clauses where the pronoun is the object, as in "It is me that he's hunting." What has been said of *me* after forms of *be* applies also to *us, him, her,* and *them.*

The "proper" choice between *who* and *whom,* whether interrogative or relative, frequently involves an intellectual chore that many speakers from about 1500 on have been little concerned with. The interrogative pronoun, coming as it usually does before the verb, tended in early Modern English to be invariably *who,* as it still does in unself-conscious speech. Otto Jespersen cites interrogative *who* as object before the verb from Marlowe, Greene, Ben Jonson, the old *Spectator* of Addison and Steele, Goldsmith, and Sheridan, with later examples from Thackeray, Mrs. Humphry Ward, and Shaw. Alexander Schmidt's *Shakespeare-Lexicon* furnishes fifteen quotations for interrogative *who* in this construction and then adds an "etc.," though, as Jespersen (*Modern English Grammar* 7:242) points out, "Most modern editors and reprinters add the *-m* everywhere in accordance with the rules of 'orthodox' grammar." Compare his earlier and somewhat bitter statement that they show thereby "that they hold in greater awe the schoolmasters of their own childhood than the poet of all the ages" (*Progress in Language* 216). It is an amusing irony that *whom*-sleuths, imagining that they are great traditionalists, are actually adhering to a fairly recent standard as far as the period from the fifteenth century on is concerned. In view of the facts, such a sentence as "Who are you waiting for?" can hardly be considered untraditional.

Relative *who* as object of verb or preposition is hardly less frequent. For Shakespeare, Schmidt uses the label "etc." after citing a dozen instances, and Jespersen cites from a few other authors. The *OED,* along with its statement that *whom* is no longer current in natural colloquial speech, cites Edmund Spenser, among others. There are, however, a good many instances of *whom* for the nominative, especially where the relative may be taken as the object of the verb of the principal clause, as in Matthew 16.13: "Whom do men say that I the Son of man am?" Shakespeare's "Whom in constancie you thinke stands so safe" (*Cymbeline* 1.4.138) and "Yong Ferdinand (whom they suppose is droun'd)" (*Tempest* 3.3.92) would be condemned by all prescriptive grammarians nowadays; but in Shakespeare's usage, which may in this respect as in all others be taken as representative of early Modern English, such constructions stand side by side with "I should do Brutus wrong, and Cassius wrong: / who (you all know) are Honourable men" (*Julius Caesar* 3.2.128–9) and others that employ the "approved" form in the same construction. The fact is, however, that this use of *whom* occurs very frequently during the whole Modern English period. Jespersen, whose *Modern English Grammar* is a storehouse of illustrative material upon which apparently few writers of school grammars have drawn, has many examples ranging from Chaucer to the present day (3:198–9), and Sir Ernest Gowers cites instances from E. M. Forster, Lord David Cecil, the *Times,* and Somerset Maugham, all of which might be presumed to be standard English.

VERBS

Classes of Strong Verbs

Throughout the history of English, the strong verbs—always a minority— have fought a losing battle, having either joined the ranks of the weak verbs or been lost altogether. In those strong verbs that survive, the Old English four principal parts (infinitive, preterit singular, preterit plural, past participle) have been reduced to three, with the new preterit sometimes derived from the old singular and sometimes from the old plural. Comparatively few verbs that have survived can be said to show a regular development. The orderly arrangement into classes that prevailed in the older periods thus has now no more than historical relevance. Indeed, today the distinction between strong and weak verbs is less important than that between regular verbs, all of which are weak (like *talk, talked, talked*), and irregular verbs, which may be either strong (like *sing, sang, sung*) or weak (like *think, thought, thought*). In what follows, we will briefly indicate the history of the seven classes of Old English strong verbs as they have developed in Modern English, recognizing, however, that the classification is now a purely historical matter.

Class I remains rather clearly defined. The regular development of this class, with the Modern English preterit from the old preterit singular, is illustrated by the following:

drive	drove	driven
ride	rode	ridden
rise	rose	risen
smite	smote	smitten
stride	strode	stridden
strive	strove	striven
thrive	throve	thriven
write	wrote	written

Also phonologically regular, but with the Modern English preterit from the old preterit plural (whose vowel was identical with that of the past participle), are the following, of which *chide* and *hide* are originally weak verbs that have become strong by analogy:

bite	bit	bitten
chide	chid	chidden
hide	hid	hidden
slide	slid	slid(den)

The following verbs, on the contrary, have a vowel in the preterit and past participle derived from the old preterit singular:

abide	abode	abode
shine	shone	shone

Dive–dove (dived)–dived is another weak verb that has acquired a strong preterit. *Strike-struck-struck* has a preterit of uncertain origin; the regularly developed past participle *stricken* is now used only metaphorically.

In early Modern English, many of these verbs had alternative forms, some of which survive either in standard use or in the dialects, whereas others are now archaic. There is a Northern form for the preterit of *drive* in "And I delivered you out of the hand of the Egyptians . . . and drave them out from before you" (Judges 6.9). Other now nonstandard forms are represented by "And the people chode [chided] with Moses" (Numbers 20.3) and "I imagined that your father had wrote in such a way" (Boswell, *London Journal,* December 30, 1762). Other verbs of this class have become weak (for example, *glide, gripe, spew,* and *writhe*). Still others have disappeared altogether from the language.

The verbs of Class II have likewise undergone many changes in the course of their development into their present forms. Only a handful survive in modern use, of which the following have taken the vowel of their preterit from the old past participle:

choose	chose	chosen
cleave	clove	cloven
freeze	froze	frozen

Fly-flew-flown has a preterit formed perhaps by analogy with Class VII verbs.

A development of the Old English past participle of *freeze* is used as an archaism in Shelley's "Snow-fed streams now seen athwart frore [frozen] vapours," which the *OED* suggests is a reflection of Milton's "The parching Air Burns frore" (*Paradise Lost* 2.594–5). Other variant verb forms are in "This word (Rebellion) it had froze them up" (*2 Henry IV* 1.1.199); "O what a time have you chose out brave Caius / To weare a Kerchiefe" (*Julius Caesar* 2.1.314–5); and "Certain men clave to Paul" (Acts 17.34).

The following surviving verbs of Class II are now weak: *bow* 'bend,' *brew, chew, creep, crowd, flee, lie* 'prevaricate,' *lose, reek, rue, seethe, shove, sprout,* and *suck. Sodden,* the old strong participle of *seethe* (with voicing according to Verner's Law), is still sometimes used as an adjective. *Crope,* a strong preterit of *creep,* occurs in formal English as late as the eighteenth century and in folk speech to the present day.

Practically all verbs of Class III with nasal consonants that have survived from Old English have retained their strong inflection. The following derive their preterit from the old preterit singular:

begin	began	begun
drink	drank	drunk
ring	rang	rung
shrink	shrank	shrunk
sing	sang	sung
sink	sank	sunk
spring	sprang	sprung
stink	stank	stunk
swim	swam	swum

In *run-ran-run* (ME infinitive *rinnen*), the vowel of the participle was in early Modern English extended into the present tense; *run* is otherwise like the preceding verbs. In the following, the modern preterit vowel is from the old preterit plural and past participle:

cling	clung	clung
slink	slunk	slunk
spin	spun	spun
sting	stung	stung
swing	swung	swung
win	won	won
wring	wrung	wrung

A few verbs entering the language after Old English times have conformed to this pattern—for example, *fling, sling,* and *string.* By the same sort of analogy, the weak verb *bring* has acquired in nonstandard speech the strong preterit and participial form *brung.* Though lacking the nasal, *dig* (not of Old English origin) and *stick,* which at first had weak inflection, have taken on the same pattern.

The consonant cluster -nd had early lengthened a preceding vowel, so the principal parts of the following verbs, although quite different in their vowels from those of the preceding group, have the same historical development:

bind	bound	bound
find	found	found
grind	ground	ground
wind	wound	wound

Allowing for the influence of Middle English [ç, x] (spelled h or gh) on a preceding vowel, *fight-fought-fought* also has a regular development into Modern English. All other surviving verbs of this class have become weak (some having done so in Middle English times): *bark, braid, burn, burst* (also with an invariant preterit and participle), *carve, climb, delve, help, melt, mourn, spurn, starve, swallow, swell, yell, yelp,* and *yield.* The old participial forms *molten* and *swollen* are still used but only as adjectives. *Holp,* an old strong preterit of *help,* was common until the seventeenth century and survives in current nonstandard usage. The old participial form *holpen* is used in the King James Bible—for instance, in "He hath holpen his servant Israel" (Luke 1.54).

Most surviving Class IV verbs have borrowed the vowel of the old past participle for their preterit:

break	broke	broken
speak	spoke	spoken
steal	stole	stolen
weave	wove	woven

Verbs with an [r] after the vowel follow the same pattern, although the [r] has affected the quality of the preceding vowel in the infinitive:

bear	bore	borne
shear	shore	shorn
swear	swore	sworn
tear	tore	torn
wear	wore	worn

The last was originally a weak verb; it acquired strong principal parts by analogy with the verbs of Class IV that it rimed with.

Get was a loanword from Scandinavian. It and *tread* (like *speak,* originally a Class V verb) have shortened vowels in all their principal parts:

get	got	got(ten)
tread	trod	trodden

Come-came-come has regular phonological development from the Middle English verb, whose principal parts were, however, already irregular in form. A variant preterit *come* was frequent in early Modern English—for example, in Pepys's *Diary:* "Creed come and dined with me" (June 15, 1666), although Pepys also uses *came;* today the variant occurs mainly in folk speech. Variant preterits for other verbs were also common in early Modern English, as in "When I was a child, I spake as a child" (I Corinthians 13.11); "And when he went forth to land, there met him . . . a certain man, which had devils long time, and ware no clothes" (Luke 8.27); "And when he had taken the five loaves and the two fishes, he looked up to heaven, and blessed, and brake the loaves" (Mark 6.41); "And they brought him unto him; and when he saw him, straightway the spirit tare him" (Mark 9.20).

Verbs of Class V have all diverged in one way or another from what might be considered regular development. *Eat-ate-eaten* has in its preterit a lengthened form of the vowel of the Middle English preterit singular (which, if it had survived into Modern English, would have been **at*). The preterit in British English, although it is spelled like the American form, is pronounced in a way that would be better represented as *et;* it is derived perhaps by analogy with the preterit *read.*

Bid and *forbid* have two preterits in current English. *(For)bade,* traditionally pronounced [bæd] but now often [bed] from the spelling, was originally a lengthened form of the Middle English preterit singular. The preterit *(for)bid* has its vowel from the past participle, which, in turn, probably borrowed it from the present stem, by analogy with verbs that have the same vowel in those two forms.

Give-gave-given is a Scandinavian loanword that displaced the native English form. (The latter appears, for example, in Chaucer's use as *yeven-yaf-yeven.*) Variants are evidenced by Pepys's "This day I sent my cozen Roger a tierce [about 42 gallons] of claret, which I give him" (August 21, 1667) and Shakespeare's "When he did frown, O, had she then gave over" (*Venus and Adonis,* line 571).

Sit had in early Modern English the preterit forms *sat, sate,* and (occasionally) *sit,* and the participial forms *sitten, sit, sat,* and *sate. Sit* and *set* were confused as early as the fourteenth century, and continue to be. A nonstandard form *sot* occurs as preterit and participle of both verbs.

The confusion of *lie-lay-lain* and *lay-laid-laid* is as old as that of *sit* and *set.* The intransitive use of *lay,* according to the *OED,* "was not app[arently] regarded as a solecism" in the seventeenth and eighteenth centuries. It has been so used by some very important writers, including Francis Bacon and Lord Byron—for example, in "There let him lay" (*Childe Harold's Pilgrimage* 4.1620). The brothers H. W. and F. G. Fowler (49) cited with apparently delighted disapproval "I suspected him of having laid in wait for the purpose" from the writing of Richard Grant White, the eminent nineteenth-century American purist—for purists love above all to catch other purists in some supposed sin against English grammar. Today the two verbs are so thoroughly confused that their forms are often freely interchanged, as in the following description of a modern dancer, who "lay down again; then raised the upper part of his body once more and stared upstage at the brick wall; then laid down again" (*Illustrated London News,* January 1979, 61).

See-saw-seen has normal development of the Middle English forms of the verb. The alternative preterits *see, seed,* and *seen* are found in folk speech.

Other surviving Class V verbs have become weak: *bequeath, fret, knead, mete, reap, scrape, weigh,* and *wreak.*

Some verbs from Class VI (including *take,* a Scandinavian loanword that ulti- mately ousted its Old English synonym *niman* from the language) show regular development:

forsake	forsook	forsaken
shake	shook	shaken
take	took	taken

Early Modern English frequently uses the preterit of these verbs as a participle, as in Shakespeare's "Save what is had or must from you be took" (Sonnet 75), "Have from the forests shook three summers' pride" (Sonnet 104), and "Hath she for- sooke so many Noble Matches?" (*Othello* 4.2.125). *Stand* (and the compound *understand*) has lost its old participle *standen;* the preterit form *stood* has served as a participle since the sixteenth century, though not exclusively. *Stand* also occurs as a participle, as does a weak form *standed,* as in "a tongue not under- standed of the people" in the fourteenth Article of Religion of the Anglican Communion. Two verbs of this class have formed their preterits by analogy with Class VII:

slay	slew	slain
draw	drew	drawn

Other surviving verbs of this class have become weak: *fare, flay, gnaw, (en)grave, heave, lade, laugh, shave, step, wade,* and *wash.* But strong participial forms *laden* and *shaven* survive as adjectives, and *heave* has an alternative strong preterit *hove.*

Several verbs of Class VII show regular development:

blow	blew	blown
grow	grew	grown
know	knew	known
throw	threw	thrown

Another, *crow-crew-crowed,* has a normally developed preterit that is now rare in American use, but it has only a weak participle. Two other verbs also have normal phonological development, although the vowels of their principal parts are differ- ent from those above:

fall	fell	fallen
beat	beat	beaten

Hold-held-held has borrowed its Modern English participle from the Middle English preterit. The original participle is preserved in the old-fashioned *beholden.* Modern English *hang-hung-hung* is a mixture of three Middle English verbs: *hōn* (Class VII), *hangen* (weak), and *hengen* (a Scandinavian loan). The alternative weak preterit and participle, *hanged,* is frequent in reference to capital punishment, though it is by no means universally so used.

Let, originally a member of this class, now has unchanged principal parts. Other verbs surviving from the group have become weak; two of them did so as early as Old English times: *dread, flow, fold, hew, leap, mow, read* (OE preterit *rǣd-de*), *row, sleep* (OE preterit *slēpte*), *sow, span* 'join,' *walk, wax* 'grow,' and *weep.* Strong participial forms *sown, mown,* and *hewn* survive, mainly as adjectives.

Endings for Person and Number

The personal endings of early Modern English verbs were somewhat simplified from those of Middle English, with the loss of *-e* as an ending for the first person singular in the present indicative (making that form identical with the infinitive, which had lost its final *-n* and then its *-e*): *I sit* (*to sit*) from Middle English *ich sitte* (*to sitten*). Otherwise, however, the early Modern English verb preserved a number of personal endings that have since disappeared, and it had, especially early in the period, several variants for some of the persons:

	PRESENT	PRETERIT
I	sit	sat
thou	sittest, sitst	sat, sattest, satst
he, she	sitteth, sits	sat
we, you, they	sit	sat

The early Modern English third person singular varied between *-(e)s* and *-(e)th.* From the beginning of the seventeenth century the *-s* form began to prevail, though for a while the two forms could be used interchangeably, particularly in verse, as in Shakespeare's "Sometime she driveth ore a Souldiers necke, & then dreames he of cutting Forraine throats" (*Romeo and Juliet* 1.4.82–3). But *doth* and *hath* went on until well into the eighteenth century, and the King James Bible uses only *-th* forms. The *-s* forms are usually attributed to Northern dialect influence.

Third person plural forms occasionally end in *-s,* also of Northern provenience, as in "Where lo, two lamps, burnt out, in darkness lies" (*Venus and Adonis,* line 1128). These should not be regarded as "ungrammatical" uses of the singular for the plural form, although analogy with the singular may have played a part in extending the ending *-s* to the plural, as is certainly the case with the first and second persons of naive raconteurs: "I says" and "says I," and of the rude expression of disbelief "Sez you!"

The early Modern English preterit ending for the second person singular, -(e)st, began to be lost in the sixteenth century. Thus the preterit tense became invariable, as it is today, except for the verb *be.*

The verb *be,* always the most irregular of English verbs, had the following personal inflections in the early Modern period:

	PRESENT	PRETERIT
I	am	was
thou	art	were, wast, werst, wert
he, she	is	was
we, you, they	are, be	were

The plural *be* was widely current as late as the seventeenth century; Eilert Ekwall (*History of Modern English Sounds and Morphology* 118) cites "the powers that be" as a survival of it. The preterit second person singular was *were* until the sixteenth century, when the forms *wast, werst,* and *wert* began to occur, the last remaining current in literature throughout the eighteenth century. Nineteenth-century poets were also very fond of it ("Bird thou never wert"); it gave a certain archaically spiritual tone to their writing that they presumably considered desirable. *Wast* and *wert* are by analogy with present *art.* In *werst,* the *s* of *wast* has apparently been extended. The locution *you was* has been discussed earlier (185–6).

Of the other highly irregular verbs, little need be said. *Could,* the preterit of *can,* acquired its unetymological *l* in the sixteenth century by analogy with *would* and *should.* Early Modern forms that differ from those now current are *durst,* preterit of *dare,* which otherwise had become weak; *mought,* a variant of *might;* and *mowe,* an occasional present plural form of *may. Will* has early Modern variants *wull* and *woll.*

Contracted Forms

Most of our verbs with contracted -*n't* first occur in writing in the seventeenth century. It is likely that all were actually used long before ever getting written down, for **contractions** are in their very nature colloquial and thus would have been considered unsuitable for writing, as most people still consider them. *Won't* is from *wol(l) not. Don't* presents several problems. One would expect [dunt] for all forms save the third singular, for which [dəzənt] or, with loss of [z], [dənt] would be the expected form. It has been suggested that the [o] of *don't* is analogical with that of *won't* (Jespersen 1909–49, 5:431). The *OED* derives third person *don't* from *he* (*she, it*) *do,* and cites a number of instances of *do* in the third person from the sixteenth and seventeenth centuries, including Pepys's "Sir Arthur Haselrigge do not yet appear in the House" (March 2, 1660). The *OED* records a use of third person *don't* in 1670, but none of *doesn't* before 1818. It appears that *it don't* is not a "corruption" of *it doesn't,* but the older form.

An't (early ModE [ænt]) for *am (are, is) not* is apparently of late seventeenth-century origin; the variant *ain't* occurs about a century later. With the eighteenth-century British English shifting of [æ] to [ɑ] as in *ask, path, dance,* and the like, the pronunciation of this word shifted to [ɑnt]. At the same time, preconsonantal [r] was lost, thus making *an't* and *aren't* homophones. As a result, the two words were confused, even by those, including most Americans, who pronounce *r* before a consonant; and the form *aren't I?* has gained ground among those who regard *ain't* as a linguistic mortal sin. Although *ain't* has fallen victim to a series of schoolteachers' crusades, Henry Alford (1810–71), dean of Canterbury, testified that in his day "It ain't certain" and "I ain't going" were "very frequently used, even by highly educated persons," and Frederick James Furnivall (1825–1910), an early editor of the *OED* and founder of the Chaucer Society and the Early English Text Society, is said to have used the form *ain't* habitually (Jespersen 1909–49, 5:434). Despite its current reputation as a shibboleth of uneducated speech, *ain't* is still used by many cultivated speakers in informal circumstances.

Contractions of auxiliary verbs without *not* occur somewhat earlier than forms with *n't,* though they must be about equally old. *It's* as a written form is from the seventeenth century and ultimately drove out *'tis,* in which the pronoun rather than the verb is reduced. There is no current contraction of *it was* to replace older *'twas,* and, with the almost complete disappearance of the subjunctive, it is not surprising that there is none for *it were. It'll* has replaced older *'twill; will* similarly is contracted after other pronouns and, in speech, after other words as well. In older times *'ll,* usually written *le* (as in *Ile* and *youle*), occurred only after vowels and was hence not syllabic, as it must be after consonants. *Would* is contracted as early as the late sixteenth century as *'ld,* later becoming *'d,* which came in the eighteenth century to be used for *had* also. The contraction of *have* written *'ve* likewise seems to have occurred first in the eighteenth century. After a consonant, this contraction is identical in pronunciation with unstressed *of* (compare "the wood of the tree" and "He would've done it"), hence such uneducated spellings as *would of* and *should of* frequently are written in dialogue as **eye dialect** to indicate that the speaker is unschooled. (The point seems to be "This is the way the speaker would write *have* if he had occasion to do so.") As indicative of pronunciation, the spelling is pointless.

Expanded Verb Forms

Progressive verb forms, consisting of a form of *be* plus a present participle ("I am working"), occur occasionally in Old English but are rare before the fifteenth century and remain relatively infrequent until the seventeenth century. The progressive passive, as in "He is being punished," does not occur until the later part of the eighteenth century. Pepys, for instance, writes "to Hales's the painter, thinking to have found Harris sitting there for his picture, which is drawing for me" (April 26, 1668), where we would use "is being drawn."

Verbs of motion and of becoming in early Modern English frequently have a form of *be* instead of *have* in their perfect forms: "is risen," "are entered in the Roman territories," "were safe arrived," "is turned white."

Do is frequently used as a verbal auxiliary in the early Modern period, though it is used somewhat differently from the way it is used today—for example, "I do wonder, his insolence can brooke to be commanded" (*Coriolanus* 1.1.265–6) and "The Serpent that did sting thy Fathers life / Now weares his Crowne" (*Hamlet* 1.5.39–40), where current English would not use it at all. Compare with these instances "A Nun of winters sisterhood kisses not more religiouslie" (*As You Like It* 3.4.17), where we would say "does not kiss," and "What say the citizens?" (*Richard III* 3.7.1), where we would use "do the citizens say." In present-day English, when there is no other auxiliary, *do* is obligatory in negative expressions, in questions, and in contradictions for emphasis ("Despite the weather report, it did rain"). In early Modern English, *do* was optional in any sentence that had no other auxiliary. Thus one finds constructions of both types: "Forbid them not" or "Do not forbid them," "Comes he?" or "Does he come?" and "He fell" or "He did fall."

In Old and Middle English times, *shall* and *will* were sometimes used to express simple futurity, though as a rule they implied, respectively, obligation and volition. The present prescribed use of these words, the bane of many an American and Northern British schoolchild, stems ultimately from the seventeenth century, the rules having first been codified by John Wallis, an eminent professor of geometry at Oxford who wrote a grammar of the English language in Latin (*Grammatica Linguae Anglicanae,* 1653). The rule, still unrealistically included in some American schoolbooks, is that to express a future event without emotional overtones, one should say *I* or *we shall,* but *you, he, she,* or *they will;* conversely, for emphasis, willfulness, or insistence, one should say *I* or *we will,* but *you, he, she,* or *they shall.* This rule has never been ubiquitous in the English-speaking world. It has, however, been promoted through the influence of Wallis and his successors. Despite a crusade of more than three centuries on behalf of the distinction, the rule for making it is still largely a mystery to most Americans, who get along very well in expressing futurity and willfulness without it.

Other Verbal Constructions

Impersonal and **reflexive constructions** were fairly frequent in early Modern English, as they had been to a much greater extent in Middle English. Shakespeare used, for instance, the impersonal constructions "it dislikes [displeases] me," "methinks," and "it yearns [grieves] me" and also the reflexives "I complain me," "how dost thou feel thyself now?" "I doubt me," "I repent me," and "give me leave to retire myself."

Some now intransitive verbs were used transitively, as in "despair [of] thy charm," "give me leave to speak [of] him," and "Smile you [at] my speeches."

PREPOSITIONS

With the Middle English loss of all distinctive inflectional endings for the noun except for the *-s* of the genitive and the plural, prepositions acquired a somewhat greater importance than they had had in Old English. Their number consequently increased during the late Middle and early Modern periods. Changes in the uses of certain prepositions are illustrated by the practice of Shakespeare, who in this respect as in most others is representative of the early Modern period: "And what delight shall she have to looke on [at] the divell?" (*Othello* 2.1.229); "He came of [on] an errand to mee" (*Merry Wives* 1.4.80); "But thou wilt be aveng'd on [for] my misdeeds" (*Richard III* 1.4.70); " 'Twas from [against] the Cannon [canon]" (*Coriolanus* 3.1.90); "We are such stuffe / As dreames are made on [of]" (*Tempest* 4.1.156–7); "Then speake the truth by [of] her" (*Two Gentlemen* 2.4.151); " . . . that our armies joyn not in [on] a hot day" (*2 Henry IV* 1.2.234).

Even in Old English times, *on* was sometimes reduced in compound words like *abūtan* (now *about*), a variant of *on būtan* 'on the outside of.' The contracted form was usually written *a*—for instance, *aboard, afield, abed, asleep*—also with verbal nouns in *-ing—a-hunting, a-bleeding, a-praying*, and the like. The *a* of "twice a day" and other such expressions has the same origin. *In* was sometimes contracted to *i'*, as in Shakespeare's "i' the head," "i' God's name," and so forth. This particular contraction was much later fondly affected by Robert Browning, who doubtless thought it singularly archaic—for example, "would not sink i' the scale" and "This rage was right i' the main" ("Rabbi Ben Ezra," lines 42 and 100).

EARLY MODERN ENGLISH FURTHER ILLUSTRATED

The following passages are from the King James Bible, published in 1611. They are the opening verses of Chapters 1 and 2 of Genesis and the parable of the Prodigal Son (Luke 15). The punctuation and spelling of the original have been retained, except that "long *s*" has been replaced by the form of the letter generally used today.

I. *Genesis 1.1–5.*
1. In the beginning God created the Heaven, and the Earth. **2.** And the earth was without forme, and voyd, and darkenesse was vpon the face of the deepe: and the Spirit of God mooued vpon the face of the waters. **3.** And God said, Let there be light: and there was light. **4.** And God saw the light, that it was good: and God diuided the light from the darkenesse. **5.** And God called the light, Day, and the darknesse he called Night: and the euening and the morning were the first day.

II. *Genesis 2.1–3.*

1. Thus the heauens and the earth were finished, and all the hoste of them.
2. And on the seuenth day God ended his worke, which hee had made: And he rested on the seuenth day from all his worke, which he had made. **3.** And God blessed the seuenth day, and sanctified it: because that in it he had rested from all his worke, which God created and made.

III. *Luke 15.11–17, 20–24.*

11. A certaine man had two sonnes: **12.** And the yonger of them said to his father, Father, giue me the portion of goods that falleth to me. And he diuided vnto them his liuing. **13.** And not many dayes after, the yonger sonne gathered al together, and tooke his iourney into a farre countrey, and there wasted his substance with riotous liuing. **14.** And when he had spent all, there arose a mighty famine in that land, and he beganne to be in want. **15.** And he went and ioyned himselfe to a citizen of that countrey, and he sent him into his fields to feed swine.
16. And he would faine haue filled his belly with the huskes that the swine did eate: and no man gaue vnto him. **17.** And when he came to himselfe, he said, How many hired seruants of my fathers haue bread inough and to spare and I perish with hunger. . . . **20.** And he arose and came to his father. But when he was yet a great way off, his father saw him, and had compassion, and ranne, and fell on his necke, and kissed him. **21.** And the sonne said vnto him, Father, I have sinned against heauen, and in thy sight, and am no more worthy to be called thy sonne. **22.** But the father saide to his seruants, Bring foorth the best robe, and put it on him, and put a ring on his hand, and shooes on his feete. **23.** And bring hither the fatted calfe, and kill it, and let us eate and be merrie. **24.** For this my sonne was dead, and is aliue againe; hee was lost, and is found.

FOR FURTHER READING

See the list in Chapter 7.

9 LATE MODERN ENGLISH (1800–21ST CENTURY)

The history of English since 1800 has been a story of expansion—in geography, in speakers, and in the purposes for which English is used. Geographically, English has been spread around the world, first by British colonization and empire-building, and more recently by the prominence of America in world affairs. The number of its speakers has undergone a population explosion, not alone of native speakers but also of nonnative speakers of English as an additional language. And the uses to which English is put have ramified with the growth of science, technology, and commerce.

SOME KEY EVENTS IN THE LATE MODERN PERIOD

Among the events of the last two centuries that have affected the English language or its use are those in the following list.

- 1805   A victory over the French at the battle of Trafalgar established British naval supremacy.

- 1806   The British occupied Cape Colony in South Africa, preparing the way for the arrival in 1820 of a large number of British settlers.

- 1828   Noah Webster's *American Dictionary of the English Language* was published.

- 1840   In New Zealand, by the Treaty of Waitangi, native Maori ceded sovereignty to the British crown.

- 1857   A proposal at the Philological Society of London led to work that resulted in the *New English Dictionary on Historical Principles* (1928), reissued as the *Oxford English Dictionary* (1933).

- 1858   The Government of India Act transferred power from the East India Company to the crown, thus creating the British Raj in India.

- 1861–5   The American Civil War established the indissolubility of the Union and abolished slavery in America.

- 1898   The four-month Spanish-American War resulted in the United States becoming a world power with overseas possessions and thus a major participant in international politics.

- 1906   The first radio broadcast, leading in 1920 to the first American commercial radio station in Pittsburgh.

- 1914–8   World War I created an alliance between the United States and the United Kingdom.

- 1922   The British Broadcasting Company (after 1927, Corporation) was established and became a major conveyor of information in English around the world.

- 1927   The first motion picture with spoken dialog, *The Jazz Singer,* was released.

- 1936   The first high-definition television service was established by the BBC, to be followed by cable service in the early 1950s and satellite service in the early 1960s.

- 1939–45   World War II further solidified the British-American link.

- 1945   The charter of the United Nations was produced at San Francisco.

- 1947   British India was divided into India and Pakistan, and both became independent.

- 1952   The Secretariat building of the United Nations was constructed in Manhattan.

- 1961   The Merriam *Webster's Third New International Dictionary* was published.

- 1983   The Internet was created.

- 1991   The Union of Soviet Socialist Republics was dissolved, leaving the United States as the world's only superpower.

- 1992   The first Web browser for the World Wide Web was released.

THE NATIONAL VARIETIES OF ENGLISH

The two major national varieties of English—in historical precedent, in number of speakers, and in influence—are those of the United Kingdom and the United States. Together they account for some 300 million speakers of English (about 80 percent of English speakers in the world), with the United States having approximately four times the population of the United Kingdom. Other countries in which English is the major language with a sizable body of speakers are Australia, Canada, Ireland, New Zealand, and South Africa. But English is or has been an official language in other parts of the Americas (Belize, the Falklands, Guyana, Jamaica, Trinidad and Tobago, West Indies), Europe (Gibraltar, Malta), Africa (Cameroon, Gambia, Ghana, Kenya, Liberia, Madagascar, Malawi, Mauritius, Nigeria, Sierra Leone, the Seychelles, Tanzania, Uganda, Zambia, Zimbabwe), Asia (Bangladesh, Hong Kong, India, Malaysia, Pakistan, Nepal, Singapore, Sri Lanka), and Oceania (Borneo, Fiji, Papua New Guinea, Philippines). English also plays a significant role in many other countries around the globe as a commercial, technical, or cultural language.

With its vast geographical spread, the English language in all of its major national varieties has remained remarkably uniform. There are, to be sure, differences between national varieties, just as there are variations within them, but those differences are insignificant in comparison with the similarities. English is unmistakably one language, with two major national varieties: British and American.

Of those two varieties, British English has long enjoyed greater prestige in western Europe and some other places around the world. Its prestige is doubtless based partly on its use as the language of the former British Empire and partly on its centuries of cultivated products, including great works of literature. The prestige of British English is often assessed, however, in terms of its "purity" (a notion that flies in the face of the facts) or its elegance and style (highly subjective but nonetheless powerful concepts). Even those Americans who are put off by "posh accents" may sometimes be impressed by them and hence likely to suppose that standard British English is somehow "better" English than what they speak. From a purely linguistic point of view, this is nonsense; but it is a safe bet that it will survive any past or future loss of British influence in world affairs.

Yet despite the historical prestige of British, today American English has become the most important and influential dialect of the language. Its influence is exerted through films, television, popular music, the Internet and the World Wide Web, air travel and control, commerce, scientific publications, economic and military assistance, and the position of the United States in world affairs. The coverage of the world by English was begun by colonization culminating in the British Empire, which colored the globe pink, as a popular saying had it, alluding to the use of that color on maps to identify British territories. The baton was passed about the middle of the twentieth century, however, to the United States, which, as the world's only superpower by the early twenty-first century, occupied a position from which its variety of the language was exported. Although no one had planned it, English has become (somewhat improbably, considering its modest beginnings on the North Sea coast of Europe) the world language of our time.

Conservatism and Innovation in American English

Since language undergoes no sea change as a result of crossing an ocean, the first English-speaking colonists in America continued to speak as they had done in England. But the language gradually changed on both sides of the Atlantic, in England at least as much as in America. The new conditions facing the colonists in America naturally caused changes in their language. However, the English spoken in America at present has retained a good many characteristics of earlier English that do not survive in contemporary British English.

Thus to regard American English as inferior to British English is to impugn earlier standard English as well, for there was doubtless little difference at the time of the Revolution. There is a strong likelihood, for instance, that George III and Lord Cornwallis pronounced *after, ask, dance, glass, path,* and the like exactly the same as did George Washington and John Hancock—that is, as the overwhelming majority of Americans do to this day, with [æ] rather than [ɑ] as in present-day British.

It was similar with the treatment of *r*, whose loss before consonants and pauses (as in *bird* [bə:d] and *burr* [bə:]) did not occur in the speech of the London area until about the time of the Revolution. Most Americans pronounce *r* where it is spelled because English speakers in the motherland did so at the time of the settlement of America. In this, as in much else especially in pronunciation and grammar, American English is, on the whole, more conservative than British English. When [r] eventually was lost in British English except before vowels, that loss was imported to the areas that had the most immediate contact with England, the port cities of Boston, New York, and Charleston, and it spread from those ports to their immediate areas, but not elsewhere.

Other supposed characteristics of American English are also to be found in pre-revolutionary British English, and there is very good reason indeed for the conclusion of the Swedish Anglicist Eilert Ekwall (*American and British Pronunciation,* 32–3) that, from the time of the Revolution on, "American pronunciation has been on the whole independent of British; the result has been that American pronunciation has not come to share the development undergone later by Standard British." Ekwall's concern is exclusively with pronunciation, but the principle implied holds good also for many lexical and grammatical characteristics as well.

American retention of *gotten* is an example of conservatism. This form, the usual past participle of *get* in older British English, survives in present standard British English mainly in the phrase "ill-gotten gains"; but it is very much alive in American English, being the usual past participial form of the verb (for instance, "Every day this month I've gotten spam on my e-mail"), except in the senses 'to have' and 'to be obliged to' (for instance, "He hasn't got the nerve to do it" and "She's got to help us"). Similarly, American English has kept *fall* for the season and *deck* for a pack of cards (though American English also uses *autumn* and *pack*); and it has retained certain phonological characteristics of earlier British English to be discussed later in some detail.

It works both ways, however; for American English has lost certain features—mostly vocabulary items—that have survived in British English. Examples include *waistcoat* (the name for a garment that Americans usually call a *vest*, the latter word in England usually meaning 'undershirt'); *fortnight* 'two weeks,' a useful term completely lost to American English; and a number of topographical terms that Americans had no need for—words like *copse, dell, fen, heath, moor, spinney,* and *wold.* Americans, on the other hand, desperately needed terms to designate topographical features different from any known in the Old World. To remedy the deficiency, they used new compounds of English words like *backwoods* and *underbrush;* they adapted English words to new uses, like *creek,* in British English 'a small arm of the sea,' which in American English may mean 'any small stream'; and they adopted foreign words like *canyon* (Sp. *cañón* 'barrel'), *mesa* (likewise Spanish), and *prairie* (ultimately derived from Fr. *pré* 'meadow').

It was similar with the naming of flora and fauna strange to the colonists. When they saw a bird that somewhat resembled the English robin, they simply called it a *robin,* though it was not the same bird at all. When they saw an animal that was totally unlike anything that they had ever seen before, they might call it by its Indian name, if they could find out what that was—for example, *raccoon* and *woodchuck.* So also with the names of plants: *catalpa* and its variant *catawba* are of Muskogean origin. Otherwise, they relied on their imagination: *Johnny-jump-up* was inspired by a crude kind of fancy, and *sweet potato* might have originated just as well in England as in America except for the fact that this particular variety, like all potatoes, was a New World food.

On the whole, though, American English is essentially a conservative development of the seventeenth-century English that is also the ancestor of present-day British. Except in vocabulary, there are probably few significant characteristics of New World English that are not traceable to the British Isles. There are also some American English characteristics that were doubtless derived from British regional dialects in the seventeenth century, for there were certainly speakers of such dialects among the earliest settlers, though they would seem to have had little influence.

The majority of those English men and women to settle permanently in the New World were not illiterate bumpkins but ambitious and industrious members of the upper-lower and lower-middle classes, with a sprinkling of the well-educated—clergymen and lawyers—and even a few younger sons of the aristocracy. It is likely that there was a cultured nucleus in all of the early American communities. Such facts as these explain why American English resembles present standard British English more closely than it resembles any other British type of speech. The differences between the two national varieties are many but not of great importance.

NATIONAL DIFFERENCES IN WORD CHOICE

There are many lists of equivalent British and American words, but they must not be taken too seriously. On the American side of the page will be found many locutions perfectly well understood, many of them in use, in Britain. For instance, *automobile,* represented as the American equivalent of *car* or *motor car,* is practically a formal word in America, the ordinary term being the supposedly British *car;* moreover, the supposedly American word occurs in the names of two English motoring organizations, the Royal Automobile Club and the Automobile Association. And on the British side will be found many locutions perfectly well known and frequently used in America—for instance, *postman* (as in James M. Cain's very American novel *The Postman Always Rings Twice*) and *railway* (as in *Railway Express* and the *Southern Railway*), though it is certain that *mailman* (or *letter carrier*) and *railroad* do occur more frequently in American speech. Similarly, one usually finds *baggage* as the American equivalent of British *luggage,* though *luggage* has come to be very commonly used in American English, perhaps because of its frequent occurrence in "prestige" advertising. *Undershorts* is the American equivalent of British *underpants* for men's underwear, although the latter is perfectly understandable in America. *Panties* is the American equivalent of British *pants* or *knickers* for women's underwear, although the American term is known in England too.

There are many other hardy perennials on such lists. *Mad* is supposedly American and *angry* British, though Americans use *angry* in formal contexts, often under the impression that *mad* as a synonym is "incorrect," and though many speakers of British English use *mad* in the sense 'angry' as it was frequently used in older English (for example, in the King James Bible of 1611, Acts 26.11: "being exceedingly mad against them I persecuted them even unto strange cities," compare the *New English Bible*'s "my fury rose to such a pitch that I extended my persecution to foreign cities," which does not improve what did not need improvement in the first place). *Mailbox* is supposedly American and *pillar-box* British, though the English also use *letter box* for either of two things: any receptacle for mailing (that is, "posting") letters, other than the low pillar usually painted a bright red; or what American English calls a *mail slot,* a rectangular hole in a door or wall near the entrance of a house through which the postman delivers letters. *Package* is supposedly American and *parcel* British, though the supposedly British word is perfectly well known to all Americans, who have for a long time sent packages by parcel post (not "package mail"). *Sick* is supposedly American and *ill* British, though *sick,* reputed to mean only 'nauseated' in England, is frequently used in the older sense, that which is thought of as American: the actor Sir Ralph Richardson wrote, "I was often sick as a child, and so often lonely, and I remember when I was in hospital a kindly visitor giving me a book," in which only the phrase "in hospital" instead of American "in the hospital" indicates the writer's Britishness, except possibly for "visitor" where many Americans, under the impression that the subject of a gerund must be possessive, would have written "visitor's." *Stairway* is supposedly American and *staircase* British, though Mary Roberts Rinehart's bestseller from the early years of the last century was entitled *The Circular Staircase,* though *stairs* is the usual term in both countries, and though *stairway* is recorded in British dictionaries with no notation that it is confined to American usage. Finally, *window shade* is supposedly American and *blind* British, though *blind(s)* is the usual term throughout a thickly populated section of the eastern United States. There are many other equally weak examples.

There are, however, many genuine instances of differences in word choice, though most of them would not cause any serious confusion on either side. Americans do not say *coach* for *bus* (interurban), *compère* for *M.C.* (or *emcee*, less frequently *master of ceremonies*) in a theatrical or television setting, *first floor* (or *story*, which Britons prefer to spell *storey*) for *second floor* (a British *first floor* being immediately above the *ground floor*, a term also used in American English but as a synonym for *first floor*), *lorry* for *truck*, *mental* for *insane*, *petrol* for *gas(oline)*, *pram* (or the full form, *perambulator*) for *baby carriage*, or *treacle* for *molasses*. Nor do they call an *intermission* (between divisions of an entertainment) an *interval*, an *orchestra seat* a *seat in the stalls*, a *raise* (in salary) a *rise*, or a *trillion* a *billion* (in British English a *billion* being a million millions, whereas in American English it is what the British call a *milliard*—a mere thousand millions—although the American use is becoming more common in Britain). Many other differences in the use of words exist, but, as far as everyday speech is concerned, they are not really very numerous or very significant.

American Infiltration of the British Word Stock

Because in the course of recent history Americans have acquired greater commercial, technical, and political importance than any other English-speaking group, it is perhaps not unnatural that the British and others should take a somewhat high-handed attitude toward American speech. The fact is that the British have done so at least since 1735, when one Francis Moore, describing for his countrymen the then infant city of Savannah, said, "It stands upon the flat of a Hill; the Bank of the River (which they in barbarous English call a *bluff*) is steep" (Mathews, *Beginnings* 13). H. L. Mencken treats the subject of British attitudes toward American speech fully and with characteristic zest in the first chapter of *The American Language* (1–48) and also in the first supplement (1–100) to that work, which is wonderful, if misnamed, because there is no essential difference between the English of America and that of Great Britain.

The truth is that British English has been extensively infiltrated by American usage, especially vocabulary. The transfer began quite a while ago, long before films, radio, and television were ever thought of, although they have certainly hastened the process. Sir William Craigie, the editor of *A Dictionary of American English on Historical Principles,* pointed out that although "for some two centuries . . . the passage of new words or senses across the Atlantic was regularly westwards . . . with the nineteenth century . . . the contrary current begins to set in, bearing with it many a piece of drift-wood to the shores of Britain, there to be picked up and incorporated in the structure of the language" (*Study of American English* 208). He cited such **Americanisms** in British English as *backwoods, beeline, belittle, blizzard, bunkum, caucus, cloudburst, prairie, swamp,* and a good many others that have long been completely acclimatized.

In recent years many other Americanisms have been introduced into British usage: *cafeteria, cocktail, egghead, electrocute* (both in reference to the distinctively American mode of capital punishment and in the extended sense 'to kill accidentally by electric shock'), *fan* 'sports devotee,' *filling station, highbrow,* and *lowbrow.* American *radio* has superseded British *wireless,* and *TV* has about crowded out the somewhat nurseryish *telly.* The ubiquitous *OK* seems to occur more frequently nowadays in England than in the land of its birth and may be found in quite formal situations, such as on legal documents to indicate the correctness of details therein. These and other Americanisms have slithered into British English in the most unobtrusive way, so that their American origin is hardly regarded at all except by a few crusty older-generation speakers: since they are used by the English, they are "English," and that is all there is to it. Woe be it to the American who tries to convince a run-of-the-mill English person to the contrary!

The following Americanisms—forms, meanings, or combinations—appear in the formal utterances of VIPs, as well as in the writings of some quite respectable authors on both sides of the Atlantic: *alibi* 'excuse,' *allergy* 'aversion' (and *allergic* 'averse'), *angle* 'viewpoint,' *blurb* 'publicity statement,' *breakdown* 'analysis,' *crash* 'collide,' *know-how, maybe, quit* (previously regarded as archaic except in a few stock phrases), *sales resistance, to go back on, to slip up, to stand up to, way of life. Fortnight* 'two consecutive weeks,' a stock **Briticism** to most Americans, is less used nowadays by younger Britons, who increasingly are using American *two weeks.*

The convenient use of noun as verb in *to contact,* meaning 'to get in touch with,' originated in America, though it might just as well have done so in England, since there is nothing un-English about such a conversion: scores of other nouns have undergone the same shift of use. This particular conversion happened to be a new American creation. The verb was first scorned in England, the *Spectator* complaining in 1927, "Dreiser should not be allowed to corrupt his language by writing 'anything that Clyde had personally contacted here.'" But no one gets disturbed over it nowadays. By the middle of the twentieth century, it had become clear that this one word *contact* "carries high symbolic importance. . . . Mencken was wrong—there will be no American language, for the simple reason that, apart from deviations in ephemeral slang and regional dialects . . . the Queen's English and the President's English grow together" (Crane Brinton, *New York Herald-Tribune Book Review,* May 1, 1955, 3).

Actually, though, the two Englishes were never so far apart as it has been pleasing to American patriotism (which has sometimes manifested itself unpleasingly in a prideful "mucker pose") and British insularity (which has sometimes equally unpleasingly manifested itself in an overweening assumption of superiority) to pretend. "How quaint of the British to call a muffler a silencer!" "How boorish of the Americans to call an egg-whisk an eggbeater!" The most striking of such presumably amusing differences, however, are not very important, for they almost inevitably occur on a rather superficial level—in the specialized vocabularies of travel, sports, schools, government, and various trades.

SYNTACTICAL AND MORPHOLOGICAL DIFFERENCES

Syntactical and morphological differences are quite as trivial as those in word choice. With regard to collective nouns, for instance, the British are much more likely than Americans to use a plural verb form, like "the public are . . . ." Plural verbs are frequent with the names of sports teams, which, because they lack the plural -*s,* would require singular verbs in American usage: "England Await Chance to Mop Up" (a headline, the reference being to England's cricket team, engaged in a test match with Australia) and "Wimbledon Are Fancied for Double" (also a headline). This usage is not confined to sports pages: witness "The village are livid"; "The U.S. Government are believed to favour . . . "; "Eton College break up for the summer holidays to-day"; "The Savoy [Hotel] have their own water supply"; "The Government regard . . . "; and "Scotland Yard are . . . ."

The following locutions, all from British writings, would have been phrased as indicated within square brackets by American writers; yet as they stand they would not puzzle an American reader in the least:

> Thus Mgr. Knox is faced by a word, which, if translated by its English equivalent, will give a meaning possibly very different to [from, than] its sense.

> When he found his body on Hampstead Heath, the only handkerchief was a clean one which had certainly not got [certainly did not have] any eucalyptus on it.

> She'd got [she had] plenty of reason . . . for supposing that she would count in her father's will.

> He hadn't got [didn't have] any relatives . . . except a sister . . . in Canada or somewhere.

> You don't think . . . that he did confide in any person?—Unlikely. I think he would have done [would have] if Galbraith alone had been involved.

> I'll tell it you [to you].

> Are you quite sure you could not give it me [give it to me, give me it] yourself?

> In the morning I was woken up [awakened] at eight by a housemaid.

Although most of the constructions cited are not to be heard in American English, many of their bracketed equivalents are common as British variants.

There are certain differences other than *different to* in the choice of prepositions: for instance, the English householder lives *in* a street, the American *on* it; and the English traveler gets *in* or *out of* a train, the American *on* or *off* it. Other variations are equally inconsequential.

BRITISH AND AMERICAN PURISM

Perhaps because pronunciation is less important in America than it is in Britain as a mark of social status, American attitudes toward language put somewhat greater stress on grammatical "correctness," based on such matters as the supposed "proper" position of *only* and other **shibboleths**. For some people it seems to be a matter of tremendous importance—practically a moral obligation—to use *whom* where what is thought of as good grammar seems to call for it; to eschew *can* in asking or giving permission and *like* as a conjunction; to choose forms of personal pronouns strictly in accordance with what is conceived to be their proper case; to refer to *everybody, everyone, nobody, no one, somebody,* and *someone* with a personal pronoun singular in form (that is, *he, she,* or any of their oblique forms); and to observe the whole set of fairly simple rules and regulations designed for the timorous—prescriptions and proscriptions that those who are secure have never given much thought to.

Counterexamples to these supposed rules of usage are easy enough to come by. "Who are you with?" (that is, 'What newspaper do you work for?') asked Queen Elizabeth II of various newspapermen at a reception given for her by the press in Washington, D.C. Though *who* for *whom* would not pass muster among many grammarians, it is nonetheless literally the Queen's English. In the novel *The Cambridge Murders,* a titled academic writes to a young acquaintance, "Babs dear, can I see you for a few moments, please?" There is no indication that Babs responded, "You *can,* but you may not," as American children are taught to say. *Like* has been used as a conjunction—as in a comment by an English critic, Clive Barnes: "These Russians dance like the Italians sing and the Spaniards fight bulls"—in self-assured, cultivated English since the early sixteenth century but has been banned in more recent times, for purely arbitrary reasons as far as one can determine.

The choice of case for pronouns is governed by principles quite different from those found in the run of grammar books; Winston Churchill quoted King George VI as observing that "it would not be right for either you or I to be where we planned to be on D-Day," and Somerset Maugham was primly sic'ed by an American reviewer for writing "a good deal older than me." The use of *they, them,* and *their* with a singular antecedent has long been standard in English; specimens of this "solecism" are found in Jane Austen, Thomas De Quincey, Lord Dunsany, Cardinal Newman, Samuel Butler, and others. The *OED* cites Lord Chesterfield, who may be taken as a model of elegant eighteenth-century usage, as having written, "If a person is born of a gloomy temper . . . they cannot help it."

To be sure, purists abound in England, where the "rules" originated, just as they do in America. They abound everywhere else, for that matter, for the purist attitude toward language is above all a question of temperament. Moreover, the English variety are about as ill-informed and as inconsistent as their American counterparts. Most purported "guides" to English usage, British or American, are expressions of prejudice with little relationship to real use. One notable exception—the most reliable and thorough report of how disputed expressions are actually used as well as what people have thought about them—is *Webster's Dictionary of English Usage,* edited by E. Ward Gilman.

Dictionaries and the Facts

The most important and available sources for information about the facts of language are dictionaries. Since 1800, the dictionary tradition, which had reached an earlier acme in Samuel Johnson's work, has progressed far beyond what was possible for Dr. Johnson. Today English speakers have available an impressive array of dictionaries to suit a variety of needs.

The greatest of all English dictionaries, and indeed the greatest dictionary ever made for any language, is the *Oxford English Dictionary* (*OED*). It was begun in 1857 as a project of the Philological Society of London for a "New English Dictionary," and that was what the work was called until the Oxford University Press assumed responsibility for it. The principal editor of the dictionary was James Murray, a Scotsman who enlisted his family to work on the dictionary. Published in fascicles, it was completed in twelve volumes in 1928, thirteen years after Murray's death and seventy-one years after it had been proposed. But that was not the end of it. In 1933 a supplementary volume was published, largely filling lacunae from the early volumes. Then, after a hiatus of forty years, Robert Burchfield brought out four new supplementary volumes (1972–86) that both corrected overlooked history and added new words that had come into the language since the original publication. In 1989, a second edition of the dictionary was published in twenty volumes, combining the original with Burchfield's supplements and adding yet more new material. In 1992, an electronic version of the second edition was published on CD-Rom. The electronic *OED* continues to be updated and now is available online at many libraries.

What distinguished the *Oxford English Dictionary* is not merely its size, but the fact that it aims at recording every English word, present and past, and to give for each a full historical treatment, tracing the word from its first appearance until the present day and recording all variations in form, meaning, and use. Furthermore, the dictionary illustrates the history of each word with abundant quotations showing the word in context throughout its history, quotations being often the most informative and useful part of the word's treatment.

Nothing else like the *OED* has ever been done. But America's greatest dictionary is the Merriam *Webster's Third New International Dictionary*, edited by Philip Gove and first published in 1961. It is quite a different work from the *OED* but is the prime example of its own genre, an "unabridged" (that is, large and comprehensive) dictionary of current use. The Merriam Company carries on the tradition of Noah Webster's dictionaries of the early nineteenth century. Webster had peculiar ideas about etymology, but he has been called a "born definer," and his dictionaries were the best of their time in America or England. *Webster's Third* has in it nothing whatever of old Noah's work, but it carries on his practice of innovation and high quality in lexicography. Although now necessarily somewhat out of date, *Webster's Third* remains the best record of the vocabulary of recent English in its American variety.

NATIONAL DIFFERENCES IN PRONUNCIATION

In the pronunciation of individual words, much the same situation holds true as for word choices: the differences are really inconsequential and are frequently shared. For instance, in *either* and *neither* an overwhelming majority of Americans have [i] in the stressed syllable, though some—largely from the Atlantic coastal cities—have [aɪ], and others all over the country have doubtless affected this pronunciation because they suppose it to have social prestige. In any case, the [aɪ] pronunciation cannot be said to be exclusively British; and it may come as a surprise to some Americans to learn that the [i] pronunciation occurs in standard British English, probably much more frequently than the [aɪ] pronunciation occurs in American English. Pronunciation with [i] is in fact listed first in the *OED,* which notes, however, that [aɪ] "is in London somewhat more prevalent in educated speech" than [i].

The prevalent standard British English pronunciation of each of the following words differs from the usual or only pronunciation in American English: *ate* [ɛt], *been* [bin], *evolution* [ivəlušən], *fragile* [fræǰaɪl], *medicine* [mɛdsɪn], *nephew* [nɛvyu], *process* [prosɛs], *trait* [tre], *tryst* [traɪst], *valet* [vælɪt], *zenith* [zɛnɪθ]. But it is a fact that the prevalent American pronunciation of each (allowing for an interchange of [ɒ] and [ɑ] in *process*) occurs also in standard British English, as in *ate* [et], *been* [bɪn], *evolution* [ɛvəlušən], *fragile* [fræǰəl], *medicine* [mɛdəsən], *nephew* [nɛfyu], *process* [prɑsɛs], *trait* [tret], *tryst* [trɪst], *valet* [væle], and *zenith* [zinəθ]. The pronunciation [ɛt] for *ate* occurs in American speech but is regarded as substandard. For *nephew,* [nɛvyu] is current only in Eastern New England, Chesapeake Bay, and South Carolina. The pronunciation [prosɛs] is used in high-toned American speech.

The prevalent American pronunciations of the following words do not occur in standard British English: *leisure* [ližər], *quinine* [kwaɪnaɪn], *squirrel* [skwərəl] (also *stirrup* and *syrup* with the same stressed vowel), *tomato* [təmeto], and *vase* [ves]. But the prevalent British pronunciations of all of them exist, though indeed not widely, in American English—that is, [lɛžə(r)], [kwɪnin], [skwɪrəl], [təmɑto], and [vɑz].

The British pronunciation of *lieutenant* as [lɛftɛnənt] when it refers to an army officer is now never heard in American English; [lutɛnənt] was recommended for Americans by Noah Webster in his *American Dictionary of the English Language* (1828). Webster also recommended *schedule* with [sk-]. It is likely, however, that the historical pronunciation with [s-] was the one most widely used in both England and America in 1828. The current British pronunciation is with [š-].

Other pronunciations that are nationally distinctive include (with the American pronunciation given first) [šə'grɪn] / ['šægrɪn] for *chagrin,* [klərk] / [klɑk] for *clerk,* ['kɔrə̗lɛri] / [kə'rɒləri] for *corollary,* ['daɪnəsti] / ['dɪnəsti] for *dynasty,* [frən'tɪr] / ['frəntyə] for *frontier,* ['læbrə̗tori] / [lə'bɒrət(ə)ri] or ['læbrət(ə)ri] for *laboratory,* ['mɪsə̗leni] / [mɪ'sɛlənɪ] for *miscellany,* and [prə'mɪr] / ['prɛmyə] for *premier.* American *carburetor* ['kɑrbə̗retər] and British *carburettor* [ˌkɑbyu'rɛtə] are, in addition to being pronounced differently, variant written forms, as are the words *aluminum* (again, Noah Webster's choice) and *aluminium.*

As for more sweeping differences, what strikes most American ears most strongly is the modern standard British shift of an older [æ] (which survives in American English except before *r* as in *far, lm* as in *calm,* and in *father*) to [ɑ] in a number of very frequently used words like *ask, path,* and *class.* Up to the very end of the eighteenth century, [ɑ] in such words was considered lower class. This shift cannot, however, be regarded as exclusively British, inasmuch as its effect is evident in the speech of eastern New England. Present American usage in regard to such words is by no means consistent: a Bostonian may, for instance, have [ɑ] (or an intermediate [a]) in *half* (and then perhaps only some of the time), but not in *can't,* or vice versa. According to John S. Kenyon (183), "The pronunciation of 'ask' words with [a] or [ɑ] has been a favorite field for schoolmastering and elocutionary quackery" (bracketed symbols replacing his boldface ones). One cannot but agree when one hears American TV personalities pronounce [a] in words like *hat, happy, dishpan hands,* and others that were not affected by the aforementioned shift.

The use of British or Bostonian [ɑ] in what Kenyon calls the ***ask* words,** supposed by some naive American speakers to have higher social standing than the normal American [æ], is fraught with danger. With speakers who use it naturally, in the sense that they acquired it in childhood when learning to talk, it never occurs in a great many words in which it might be expected by analogy. Thus, *bass, crass, lass,* and *mass* have [æ], in contrast to the [ɑ] of *class, glass, grass,* and *pass.* But *classic, classical, classicism, classify, passage, passenger,* and *passive* all have [æ]. *Gastric* has [æ], but *plaster* has [ɑ]; *ample* has [æ], but *example* and *sample* have [ɑ]; *fancy* and *romance* have [æ], but *chance, dance,* and *glance* have [ɑ]; *cant* 'hypocritical talk' has [æ], but *can't* 'cannot' has [ɑ]; *mascot, massacre,* and *pastel* have [æ], but *basket, master,* and *nasty* have [ɑ], and *bastard, masquerade,* and *mastiff* may have either [æ] or [ɑ]. It is obvious that few status seekers could master such complexities, even if there were any real point in doing so. There is none, actually, for no one worth fooling would be fooled by such a shallow display of linguistic virtuosity.

Somewhat less noticeable, perhaps because it is more widespread in American English than the use of [ɑ] or [a] in the *ask* words, is the standard British English loss of [r] except when a vowel follows it. The American treatment of this sound is, however, somewhat more complicated than the British. In parts of the deep South, it may be lost even between vowels, as in *Carolina* and *very.* But in one way or another, [r] is lost in eastern New England, in New York City, and in most of the coastal South. Away from the Atlantic Coast, it is retained in most positions.

There are other less striking phonological differences, like the British slightly rounded "short *o*" [ɒ] in contrast to the unrounded [ɑ] in *collar, got, stop,* and the like used in most dialects of American English. In western Pennsylvania and eastern New England, a vowel like the British one can be heard in these words.

British English long ago lost its secondary stress on the penultimate syllables of polysyllables in *-ary, -ery,* and *-ory* (for example, *military, millinery, obligatory*).

This subordinate stress is regularly retained in American English, as in *mónastèry, sécretàry, térritòry,* and the like. The secondary stress is often lacking in *library* (sometimes reduced to disyllabic ['laɪbrɪ]), but it regularly occurs in other such words. A restoration of the secondary stress in British English, at least in some words, is more likely due to spelling consciousness than to any transatlantic influence. Some well-educated younger-generation British speakers have it in *sécretàry* and in *extraórdinàry.*

Intonational characteristics—risings and fallings in pitch—plus timbre of voice distinguish British English from American English far more than pronunciations of individual words. Voice quality in this connection has not been much investigated, and most statements about it are impressionistic; but there can be little doubt of its significance. Even if they were to learn British intonation, Americans (say, Bostonians, whose treatment of *r* and of the vowel of *ask, path,* and the like agrees with that of standard British English) would never in the world pass among the British as English. They would still be spotted as "Yanks" by practically everyone in the British Isles. Precision in the description of nationally characteristic voice qualities must, however, be left for future investigators.

In regard to intonation, the differences are most noticeable in questions and requests. Contrast the intonation patterns of the following sentences, very roughly indicated as they would customarily be spoken in British and American English:

BE: Where are you going to be?

AE: Where are you going to be?

BE: Are you sure?

AE: Are you sure?

BE: Let me know where you're going to be.

AE: Let me know where you're going to be.

It is usually difficult or impossible to tell whether a singer is English or American, for the intonational patterns in singing are those of the composer.

It is most unlikely that tempo plays any part in the identification of a British or an American accent. To Americans unaccustomed to hearing it, British speech frequently seems to be running on at a great rate. But this impression of speed is doubtless also experienced in regard to American English by those English people who have not come into contact with American television shows, movies, and tourists, if there are any such English. Some people speak slowly, some rapidly, regardless of nationality; moreover, the same individuals are likely to speak more rapidly when they know what they are talking about than when they must "make conversation."

The type of American speech that one now hears most frequently on national television, especially in commercials, is highly standardized and eliminates any regional or individual characteristics discernible to untrained ears. The extent of the influence and prestige of those who speak the commercials may be gauged by the astronomical sums spent on such advertising. Who can say that their standardized form of speech, based to a large extent on writing, may not in time become a nationwide dialect?

BRITISH AND AMERICAN SPELLING

Finally, there is the matter of spelling, which looms larger in the consciousness of those who are concerned with national differences than it deserves to. Somewhat exotic to American eyes are *cheque* (for drawing money from a bank), *cyder, cypher, gaol, kerb* (of a street), *pyjamas, syren,* and *tyre* (around a wheel). But *check, cider, cipher, jail, curb, pajamas, siren,* and *tire* are also current in England in varying degrees.

Noah Webster, through the influence of his spelling book and dictionaries, was responsible for Americans settling upon *-or* spellings for a group of words spelled in his day with either *-or* or *-our: armo(u)r, behavio(u)r, colo(u)r, favo(u)r, flavo(u)r, harbo(u)r, labo(u)r, neighbo(u)r,* and the like. All such words were current in earlier British English without the *u*, though most Britishers today are probably unaware of the fact; Webster was making no radical change in English spelling habits. Furthermore, the English had themselves struck the *u* from a great many words earlier spelled *-our,* alternating with *-or: author, doctor, emperor, error, governor, horror, mirror,* and *senator,* among others.

Webster is also responsible for the American practice of using *-er* instead of the *-re* that the British came to favor in a number of words—for instance, *calibre, centre, litre, manoeuvre, metre* (of poetry or of the unit of length in the metric system), *sepulchre,* and *theatre.* The last of these spellings competes with *theater* in America, especially in proper names. It is regarded by many of its users as an elegant (because British) spelling and by others as an affectation. Except for *litre,* which did not come into English until the nineteenth century, all these words occur in earlier British English with *-er.*

The American use of *-se* in *defense, offense,* and *pretense,* in which the English usually have *-ce,* is also attributable to the precept and practice of Webster, though he did not recommend *fense* for *fence,* which is simply an aphetic form of *defense* (or *defence*). Spellings with *-se* occurred in earlier English for all these words, including *fence. Suspense* is now usually so spelled in British English.

Webster proposed dropping final *k* in such words as *almanack, musick, physick, publick,* and *traffick,* bringing about a change that has occurred in British English as well. His proposed *burdoc, cassoc,* and *hassoc* now regularly end in *k,* whereas *havock,* in which he neglected to drop the *k,* is everywhere spelled without it.

Though he was not the first to recommend it, Webster is doubtless to be credited with the American spelling practice of not doubling final *l* when adding a suffix except in words stressed on their final syllables—for example, *grível, groveled, groveler, groveling,* but *propél, propelled, propeller, propelling, propellant.* Modern

British spelling usually doubles *l* before a suffix regardless of the position of the stress, as in *grovelled, groveller,* and so forth.

The British use of *ae* and *oe* looks strange to Americans in *anaemic, gynaecology, haemorrhage, paediatrician,* and in *diarrhoea, homoeopathy, manoeuvre,* and *oesophagus,* but less so in *aesthetic, archaeology,* and *encyclopaedia,* which are not unusual in American usage. Some words earlier written with one or the other of these digraphs long ago underwent simplification—for example, *phaenomenon, oeconomy,* and *poenology.* Others are in the process of simplification: *hemorrhage, hemorrhoids,* and *medieval* are frequent British variants of the forms with *ae.*

Most British writers use *-ise* for the verbal suffix written *-ize* in America in such words as *baptize, organize,* and *sympathize.* However, the *Times* of London, the *OED,* the various editions of Daniel Jones's *English Pronouncing Dictionary,* and a number of other publications of considerable intellectual prestige prefer the spelling with *z,* which, in the words of the *OED,* is "at once etymological and phonetic." (The suffix is ultimately from Greek *-izein.*) The *ct* of *connection* and *inflection* is due to the influence of *connect* and *inflect.* The etymologically sounder spellings *connexion* and *inflexion,* reflecting their sources in Latin *connexiōn(em)* and *inflexiōn(em),* are used by most writers, or at any rate by most printers, in England.

Spelling reform has been a recurring preoccupation of would-be language engineers on both sides of the Atlantic. Webster, who loved tinkering with all aspects of language, had contemplated far flashier spelling reforms than the simplifications he succeeded in getting adopted. For instance, he advocated lopping off the final *e* of *-ine, -ite,* and *-ive* in final syllables (thus *medicin, definit, fugitiv*), using *oo* for *ou* in *group* and *soup,* writing *tung* for *tongue,* and deleting the *a* in *bread, feather,* and the like; but in time he abandoned these unsuccessful, albeit sensible, spellings. Those of Webster's spellings that were generally adopted were choices among existing options, not his inventions. The financier Andrew Carnegie and President Theodore Roosevelt both supported a reformed spelling in the early years of the twentieth century, including such simplifications as *catalog* for *catalogue, claspt* for *clasped, gage* for *gauge, program* for *programme,* and *thoro* for *thorough.* Some of the spellings they advocated have been generally adopted, some are still used as variants, but many are rarely used now.

VARIATION WITHIN NATIONAL VARIETIES

Despite the comparative uniformity of standard English throughout the world, there clearly are variations within the language, even within a single national variety, such as American English.

Kinds of Variation

The kind of English we use depends on both us and the circumstances in which we use it. The variations that depend on us have to do with where we learned our

English (**regional** or **geographical dialects**), what cultural groups we belong to (**ethnic** or **social dialects**), and a host of other factors such as our sex, age, and education. The variations that depend on the circumstances of use have to do with whether we are talking or writing, how formal the situation is, the subject of the discourse, the effect we want to achieve, and so on. Differences in language that depend on who we are constitute **dialect**. Differences that depend on where, why, or how we are using language are matters of **register**.

Each of us speaks a variety of dialects; for example, a Minnesota, Swedish-American, female, younger-generation, college-educated person talks differently from a Tennessee, Appalachian, male, older generation, grade-school-educated person—each of those factors (place, ethnic group, sex, age, education) defining a dialect. We can change our dialects during the course of our lives (an Ohioan who moves to Alabama may start saying *y'all* and dropping *r*'s), but once we have reached maturity, our dialects tend to be fairly well set and not to vary a great deal, unless we are very impressionable or there are very strong influences that lead us to change.

Each of us also uses a variety of registers, and we change them often, shifting from one to another as the situation warrants, and often learning new ones. The more varied our experiences have been, the more various registers we are likely to command. But almost everyone uses more than one register of language, even in daily activities like talking with young children, answering the telephone when a friend calls, meeting a new colleague, and saying good night to one's family. The language differences in such circumstances may not be obvious to us, because we are used to them and tend to overlook the familiar, but a close study will show them to be considerable.

One variety of language—in fact, the variety that has been almost the exclusive concern of this book—is **standard English**. A standard language is one that is used widely—in many places and for many purposes; it is also one that enjoys high prestige—one that people regard as "good" language; and it is described in dictionaries and grammar books and is taught in schools. Standard English is the written form of our language used in books and periodicals; it is also known as **edited English**. It is, to be sure, not a homogeneous thing: there is plenty of what Gerard Manley Hopkins called "pied beauty" in it, more in fact than many persons realize. It is partly because of its variety that it is useful. Standard English is standard, not because it is intrinsically better than other varieties—clearer or more logical or prettier—but only because English speakers have agreed to use it in so many places for so many purposes that they have therefore made a useful tool of it and have come to regard it as a good thing.

Regional Dialects

In contrast to standard English are all the regional and ethnic dialects of the United States and of other English-speaking countries. In America, there are three or four main regional dialects in the eastern part of the country: **Northern** (from northern New Jersey and Pennsylvania to New England), **North Midland** (from northern Delaware, Maryland, and West Virginia through southern New Jersey and Pennsylvania), **South Midland**, also called **Inland Southern** (the Appalachian region from southern West

Virginia to northern Georgia), and **Southern**, or **Coastal Southern** (from southern Delaware and Maryland down to Florida, along the Atlantic seaboard).

The farther west one goes, the more difficult it is to recognize clearly defined dialect boundaries. The fading out of sharp dialect lines in the western United States is what might be expected from the history of the country. The earliest English-speaking settlements were along the eastern seaboard; and because that area has been longest populated, it has had the most opportunity to develop distinct regional forms of speech. The western settlements are generally more recent and were usually made by persons of diverse origins. Thus the older eastern dialect differences were not kept intact by the western pioneers, and new ones have not had the opportunity to develop. Because of the increased mobility of the population and the greater opportunities for hearing and talking with persons from many areas, distinct new western dialects may be slow in coming into existence.

The scholarly study of American dialects began in 1889 with the foundation of the American Dialect Society. The chief purpose of the society was the production of an American dialect dictionary. To that end, the society published the periodical *Dialect Notes* from 1890 to 1939, containing principally word lists from various parts of the country. After the hiatus of World War II, the society brought out a series known simply as *Publication of the American Dialect Society* (or *PADS* for short), which is now a monograph series. In 1925 appeared the first issue of *American Speech,* a magazine founded by three academics, Kemp Malone, Louise Pound, and Arthur G. Kennedy, with the encouragement of the journalist-critic H. L. Mencken (who was also responsible for some of the liveliest writing ever published on American English in his monumental three-volume study, *The American Language,* later combined into one revised volume by Raven I. McDavid). In 1970 *American Speech* became the journal of the American Dialect Society. During the 1960s and 1970s, work on the society's dictionary was revived by Frederic G. Cassidy; and the *Dictionary of American Regional English (DARE),* as it is now known, is being published by the Belknap Press of Harvard under the editorship of Joan Houston Hall. It is the most thorough and authoritative source for information about all varieties of nonstandard English in America.

Another project to assess the regional forms of American English is the *Linguistic Atlas of the United States and Canada*, which was originally intended to cover all of English-speaking North America but which was divided into a series of regional projects, of which three are complete: the *Linguistic Atlas of New England,* edited by Hans Kurath; *The Linguistic Atlas of the Upper Midwest,* edited by Harold B. Allen; and the *Linguistic Atlas of the Gulf States,* edited by Lee Pederson.

An engaging and informative presentation on American dialect diversity is a program originally broadcast on television but available as a video, entitled *American Tongues.* Produced by the Center for New American Media, with the advice of some of the leading dialect authorities of the day, the film presents the human side of regional and social dialects—the comedy, the angst, and the pride that can come from "talkin' different." It gives an accurate and honest portrayal of how Americans talk and of what they think about the way they and others use the English language.

Ethnic and Social Dialects

The concentrated study of ethnic and social dialects is more recent than that of regional ones but has been vigorously pursued. Among the American ethnic groups that have been most intensively studied (although not all by the same methods or with the same thoroughness) are African-Americans, Appalachians, Jews, Mexican-Americans, Puerto Ricans, Cuban-Americans, and the Pennsylvania Dutch.

The language of African-Americans, one of the most prominent ethnic minorities in the United States, has been studied especially from the standpoint of its relationship to the standard language. Two questions are involved, according to Ralph Fasold: (1) How different are the speechways of present-day blacks and whites? (2) What was the origin of **African-American** or **Black English**, that is, the typical language of African-Americans, especially as it differs from that of their neighbors?

The extent of the present-day linguistic differences between blacks and whites has often been exaggerated. There are differences in word choice through which African-American vocabulary exerts a steady and enriching influence on the language of other Americans; for example, *nitty-gritty* is a contribution from a few years ago, *jazz* is an older one, and *yam* a much older one. There are differences of pronunciation; for example, the typical African-American pronunciation of *aunt* as [ɑnt] is unusual for most other Americans (although it is the standard British way of saying the word). Blacks are also more likely than whites to drop the [t] from words like *rest* and *soft;* to use an *r*-less pronunciation of words like *bird, four,* and *father;* and to pronounce words like *with* and *nothing* with [f] rather than [θ]. There are differences in grammar; for example, blacks are more likely than whites to use **consuetudinal *be*** (uninflected *be* to denote habitual or regular action, as in "She be here everyday"), to delete forms of *be* in other uses (as in "She here now"), and to omit the *-s* ending of verbs (as in "He hear you"). Most differences—whether of vocabulary, pronunciation, or grammar—tend, however, to be matters of degree rather than of kind. The differences between black and white speech are seldom of such magnitude as to impede communication, when a will to communicate exists.

Whether such differences are increasing in importance is also controversial. As Ronald R. Butters has pointed out, studies of the subject are difficult to interpret. In some cases the language of African-Americans appears to be converging with, rather than diverging from, that of other Americans. We have no way to measure the overall similarity or difference between two speechways, so generalizations about whether the language of the two groups is becoming on the whole more different or more similar are likely to be political statements rather than linguistic descriptions.

The origin of African-American English has been attributed to two sources. On the one hand, it is said that blacks first acquired their English from the whites among whom they worked on the plantations of the New World, and therefore their present English reflects the kind of English their ancestors learned several hundred years ago, modified by generations of segregation. On the other hand, it is said that blacks, who spoke a number of different African languages, first learned a kind of **pidgin**—a mixed and limited language used for communication between those without a common tongue—perhaps based on Portuguese, African languages, and English. Because they had no other common language, the pidgin was **creolized**, that is, became the native and full language of the plantation slaves and eventually was assimilated to the English spoken around them, so that today there are few of the original **creole** features still remaining.

The difference between the two historical explanations is chiefly in how they explain the divergent features between black and white speech. In the first explanation, those differences are supposed to be African features introduced by blacks into the English they learned from whites or else they are survivals of archaic features otherwise lost from the speech of whites. In the second explanation, they are supposed to be the remnants of the original creole, which over the years has been transformed gradually, by massive borrowing from English, into a type of language much closer to standard English than it originally was. The historical reality was certainly more complex than either view alone depicts, but both explanations doubtless have some truth in them. The passion with which one or the other view is often held is probably a consequence of emotional attitudes quite independent of the facts themselves.

Stylistic Variation

Style in language is the choice we make from the options available to us, chiefly those of register. Stylistic variation is the major concern of those who write about language in the popular press, although such writers may not have much knowledge about the subject. A widespread suspicion among the laity that our language is somehow deteriorating becomes the opportunity for journalistic and other hucksters to peddle their nostrums. The usage huckster plays upon the insecurity and apprehensions of readers. ("Will America be the death of English?" ominously asked one guru.) Such linguistic alarmism does no good, other than making a buck for the alarmist, but it also does little harm; it is generally ineffectual.

The best-known of popular usage guides is the pleasantly magisterial *Dictionary of Modern English Usage* by H. W. Fowler. It has enjoyed considerable prestige in both England and America, doubtless because it makes such beguiling reading. Fowler's pronouncements on usage were often idiosyncratic, however, and frequently told the reader nothing about actual usage. They were much improved in the third edition of the book by R. W. Burchfield, the editor also responsible for the four-volume supplement to the *Oxford English Dictionary*. The best-informed and most sensible treatment of good English is *Webster's Dictionary of English Usage,* already mentioned.

One stylistic variety that is of perennial interest is **slang**, primarily because it continually renews itself. Slang is a deliberately undignified form of speech whose use implies that the user is "in" or especially knowledgeable about the subject of the slang term; it may be language (such as a sexual or scatological taboo term) signaling that the speaker is not part of the Establishment, or it may be protective language that disguises unpleasant reality (such as *waste* for 'kill') or saves the user from fuller explanation (such as *dig you* for 'like, love, desire, sympathize with you'). No single term will have all of these characteristics, but all slang shares several of them (Dumas and Lighter). Because of its changeability, slang is hard to study; by far the best treatment is the dictionary of American slang on historical principles by Jonathan Lighter, of which two volumes have been published and others are in preparation.

Variation Within British English

The British Isles had dialects from Anglo-Saxon times onward, and there has been a clear historical continuity in them. Present-day dialect variation derives in the first place from the Old English dialects of West Saxon, Kentish, Mercian, and Northumbrian—as they developed in Middle English, respectively, into Southern in the southwest, Kentish in the southeast, West and East Midland (divided by the boundary of the Danelaw, with East Midland more affected by the Scandinavian settlers), and Northern. Those dialects were affected by historical events, such as the Viking influence in the Northern and East Midland areas and the growth of London as the metropolitan center of England, which brought influences from many dialects together.

Geographical dialects are not divided from one another by clear boundaries, but rather phase gradually into one another. However, Peter Trudgill, in *The Dialects of England*, has divided present-day England into a number of dialect areas on the basis of seven features of pronunciation: *but* as [bət] or [bʊt], *arm* as [ɑrm] or [ɑːm], *singer* as [sɪŋə(r)] or [sɪŋgə(r)], *few* as [fyu] or [fu], *seedy* as [sidi] or [sidɪ], *gate* as [get] or [geit], and *milk* as [mɪlk] or [miʊk]. The sixteen dialect areas he identifies are combined into six major ones, still corresponding at least roughly to the Middle English dialects, respectively: Southwest, East (including the Home Counties around London, Kent, East Anglia, and a southern part of the old East Midland), West Central, East Central, Lower North, and Northeast (Northumberland, Tyneside, and Durham).

Trudgill concludes his study with a double glance backward and ahead (128):

The different forms taken by the English language in modern England represent the results of 1500 years of linguistic and cultural development. It is in the nature of language, and in the nature of society, that these dialects will always be changing. . . . But unless we can rid ourselves of the idea that speaking anything other than Standard English is a sign of ignorance and lack of "sophistication", much of what linguistic richness and diversity remains in the English language in this country may be lost.

WORLD ENGLISH

Although American and British are the two major national varieties of the language, with the largest numbers of speakers and the greatest impact worldwide, there are many other varieties of English used around the globe. Today English is used as a **first language** (a speaker's native and often only language), as a **second language** (in addition to a native language, but used regularly for important matters), and as a **foreign language** (used for special purposes, with various degrees of fluency and frequency). Other important first-language varieties of English are those of Australia, Canada, Ireland, New Zealand, and South Africa.

English is extremely important in India and has official or semi-official use in the Philippines, Malaysia, Tanzania, Kenya, Nigeria, Liberia, and other countries in Africa, the Caribbean, the Pacific, and elsewhere. It is the international language of the airlines, of the sea and shipping, of computer technology, of science, and indeed of communication generally. When a Japanese business firm deals with a client in Saudi Arabia, their language of communication is likely to be English.

English has more nonnative speakers than any other language, is more widely disbursed around the world, and is used for more purposes than any other language. The extraordinary spread of English is not due to any inherent virtue, but rather to the fact that by historical chance it has become the most useful language for others to learn.

In the course of its spread, English has diversified by adapting to local circumstances and cultures, so there are different varieties of English in every country. However, because the heart of its usefulness is its ability to serve as an international medium of communication, English is likely to retain a more or less homogeneous core—an international standard based on the usage of the United States and the United Kingdom. Yet each national variety has its own character and contribution to make to world English. Here we will look at only one such variety, an old one with close links to both Britain and America.

Irish English

Irish English has had an influence far greater than its number of speakers or the political and economic power of Ireland. Because large numbers of Irish men and women emigrated or were transported to the British colonies and America, their speech has left its imprint on other varieties of English around the world. The influence of Irish English on that of Newfoundland and the Caribbean, for example, is clear. In addition, many of the common features of Australian and American English may be due to a shared influence from Ireland.

Irish influence began early. The model of Irish scribes for Anglo-Saxon writing habits was mentioned in Chapter 3. In later times, Irish authors have been part of the mainstream of English letters since the eighteenth century, helping to form the course of English literature: Jonathan Swift, Oliver Goldsmith, Richard Brinsley Sheridan, Edmund Burke, and Maria Edgeworth from the earlier part of that period; from the twentieth century: William Butler Yeats, Lady Augusta Gregory, John Millington Synge, James Joyce, Sean O'Casey, and Samuel Beckett; and from more recent times, a host of new writers, some of whom will doubtless be named in future lists of major authors.

Present-day Irish English is the historical development of seventeenth-century British and Scottish English. English had been introduced to the western isle some 500 years earlier (about 1170), when King Henry II decided to add Ireland to his domain. The twelfth-century settlers from England were Normans with Welsh and English followers. Through the thirteenth century, the Middle Irish English of those settlers spread in Ireland, after which it began to decline in use.

The Normans were linguistically adaptable, having been Scandinavians who learned French in Normandy and English in Britain. When they moved to Ireland, they began to learn Gaelic and to assimilate to the local culture. As a result, by the early sixteenth century, Middle Irish English was dying out, being still spoken in only a few areas of the English "Pale," the territory controlled by the English.

Because of its declining control over Ireland, the English government began a series of "plantations," that is, colonizations of the island. The first of these were during the reign of Mary Tudor, but they continued under her successors, with English people settling in Ireland and Scots migrating to Ulster in the north. By the middle of the seventeenth century, under the Puritan Commonwealth, English control over Ireland and the position of the English language in the country were both firm.

The Modern Irish English of the Tudor and later "planters" or settlers was not a development of Middle Irish English, but a new importation. It continued to expand so that by the late nineteenth century Ireland had become predominantly an English-speaking country, with Gaelic spoken mainly in western rural areas. The independence of most of Ireland with the establishment of the Irish Free State in 1922 has intensified the patriotic promotion of revived Gaelic (also called Erse) in the south, but its use is more symbolic than practical.

Toward the northeast of the island, Irish English blends into the variety of Scots brought across the sea by settlers from the Scottish lowlands, who outnumbered English settlers in that area by six to one. Consequently, in parts of the northern counties of Donegal, Derry, Antrim, and Down, the language popularly used is Ulster Scots, a variety of southern Scots, rather than Irish English.

Among the distinctive characteristics of Irish English is the old-fashioned pronunciation of words like *tea, meat, easy, cheat, steal,* and *Jesus* with the vowel [e] as in *say* and *mate.* Stress falls later in some words than is usual elsewhere: *afflúence* and *architécture,* for example. *Keen* 'lament for the dead' is a characteristic Irish word widely known outside Ireland, and the use of *evening* for the time after noon is a meaning shared with dialects in England (from which it was doubtless derived) and with Australia and the Southern United States (where it was probably carried by Irish immigrants). *Poor mouth* 'pretense of being very poor' is another expression imported from Ireland into the American South.

Especially characteristic of Irish are such grammatical constructions as the use of *do* and *be* to indicate a habitual action (as in "He does work," "He bees working," and "He does be working") as opposed to an action at a moment in time (as in "He is working"); that construction may have been an influence on African-American English. Also, Irish English avoids the perfect tense, using *after* to signal a just completed action: "She is after talking with him," that is, 'She has just talked with him.'

Other Irishisms of grammar include the "cleft" construction: "It is a long time that I am waiting," for 'I have been waiting for a long time'; rhetorical questions: "Whenever I listened, didn't I hear the sound of him sleeping"; and the conjunction *and* used before participles as a subordinator with the sense 'when, as, while': "He was after waking up, and she pounding on the door with all her might."

THE ESSENTIAL ONENESS OF ALL ENGLISH

We have now come to an end of our comparative survey of the present state of English. What should have emerged from the treatment is a conception of the essential unity of the English language in all its national, regional, social, and stylistic manifestations. What, then, it may be asked, is the English language? Is it the speech of London, of Boston, of New York, of Atlanta, of Melbourne, of Montreal, of Calcutta? Is it the English of the metropolitan daily newspaper, of the bureaucratic memo, of the contemporary poet, of religious ritual, of football sportscasts, of political harangues, of loving whispers? A possible answer might be, none of these, but rather the sum of them all, along with all other blendings and developments that have taken place wherever what is thought of as the English language is spoken by those who have learned it as their mother tongue or as an additional language. However, the most important variety happens to be the standard English written by British and American authors—and it should be clear by now that the importance of that language is due not to any inherent virtues it may possess, but wholly to its usefulness to people around the world, whatever their native language.

FOR FURTHER READING

Historical Background

Black. *A History of the British Isles.*
———. *A New History of England.*
Morgan. *The Oxford History of Britain.*

Overviews

Algeo. *The Cambridge History of the English Language.* Vol. 6: *English in North America.*
Bailey. *Nineteenth-Century English.*

Bauer. *Watching English Change.*
Burchfield. *The Cambridge History of the English Language.* Vol. 5: *English in Britain and Overseas.*
Görlach. *English in Nineteenth-Century England.*
Gramley and Pätzold. *A Survey of Modern English.*
Phillipps. *Language and Class in Victorian England.*
Romaine. *The Cambridge History of the English Language.* Vol. 4: *1776–1997.*

American and British English

Algeo. "British and American Grammatical Differences."
Hargraves. *Mighty Fine Words and Smashing Expressions.*
Schur. *British English A to Zed.*

American English

Bonfiglio. *Race and the Rise of Standard American.*
Kövecses. *American English.*
Mencken. *The American Language.*
Read. *America—Naming the Country and Its People.*
———. *Milestones in the History of English in America.*
Tottie. *An Introduction to American English.*

American Dialects

Allen. *The Linguistic Atlas of the Upper Midwest.*
Butters. *The Death of Black English.*
Carver. *American Regional Dialects.*
Cassidy and Hall. *Dictionary of American Regional English.*
Kurath. *Linguistic Atlas of New England.*
Metcalf. *How We Talk.*
Mufwene. *African-American English.*
Pederson. *Linguistic Atlas of the Gulf States.*
Wolfram and Schilling-Estes. *American English: Dialects and Variation.*

British Dialects

Trudgill. *The Dialects of England.*
Upton, Parry, and Widdowson. *Survey of English Dialects.*
Upton and Widdowson. *An Atlas of English Dialects.*

Contemporary Dictionaries

Green. *Chasing the Sun.*
Landau. *Dictionaries: The Art and Craft of Lexicography.*

Morton. *The Story of "Webster's Third."*
Murray. *Caught in the Web of Words.*

Contemporary Grammars

Greenbaum. *The Oxford English Grammar.*
Quirk, Greenbaum, Leech, and Svartvik. *A Comprehensive Grammar of the English Language.*

International English

Bailey and Görlach. *English as a World Language.*
Bauer. *An Introduction to International Varieties of English.*
Cheshire. *English around the World.*
Todd and Hancock. *International English Usage.*
Trudgill and Hannah. *International English.*

National Varieties

Allsopp. *Dictionary of Caribbean English Usage.*
Avis. *A Dictionary of Canadianisms.*
Avis et al. *Gage Canadian Dictionary.*
Baker. *Australian Language.*
Baumgardner. *South Asian English.*
Bell and Kuiper. *New Zealand English.*
Branford. *Dictionary of South African English.*
Burchfield. *New Zealand Pocket Oxford Dictionary.*
Cassidy. *Jamaica Talk.*
Cassidy and Le Page. *Dictionary of Jamaican English.*
Chambers. *Canadian English.*
Gordon and Deverson. *New Zealand English.*
Hawkins. *Common Indian Words in English.*
Holm. *Dictionary of Bahamian English.*
O Muirithe. *English Language in Ireland.*
Ramson. *Australian National Dictionary.*
Roberts. *West Indians & Their Language.*
Romaine. *Language in Australia.*
Story, Kirwin, and Widdowson. *Dictionary of Newfoundland English.*
Turner. *English Language in Australia and New Zealand.*

10 WORDS AND MEANINGS

The sounds of a language change over a long period of time, so that even a familiar word like *night* comes to be quite different in its pronunciation from what our linguistic ancestors in the days of Alfred the Great would have regarded as normal. So too grammar has changed over a similar period, transforming English from a highly inflected language to one with few grammatical endings. Most English speakers probably have some awareness that sounds and grammar change, though they are likely to think of such change as deterioration, the lamentable effect of sloppy speech that indicates the language is going to the dogs. The kind of change that is most obvious, however, and that is consequently most interesting to the average person, is change in vocabulary. It is easy to observe, it is happening all the time, and it touches our daily lives with an unavoidable insistence.

Most people find the study of words and their meanings interesting and colorful. Witness in newspapers and magazines the number of letters to the editor, usually sadly misinformed, that are devoted to the uses and misuses of words. These are frequently etymological in nature, like the old and oft-recurring wheeze that *sirloin* is so called because King Henry VIII (or James I or Charles II) liked a loin of beef so well that he knighted one, saying "Arise, Sir Loin" at the conferring of the accolade. In reality, the term comes from French *sur-* 'over, above' and *loin* and is thus a cut of meat from the top of the loin. It is likely, however, that the popular explanation of the knighting has influenced the modern spelling of the word.

Such fanciful tales appeal to our imagination and therefore are difficult to exorcise. The real history of words, however, is interesting enough to make unnecessary such fictions as that about the knighting of the steak. When the speakers of a language have need for a new word, they can make one up, borrow one from some other language, or adapt one of the words they already use by changing its meaning. The first two techniques for increasing the vocabulary will be the subjects of the next two chapters, and the third will occupy our attention for the remainder of this one.

SEMANTICS AND CHANGE OF MEANING

Semantics is the study of meaning in all of its aspects. The Whorf hypothesis, which was mentioned in Chapter 1, proposes that the way our language formulates meaning affects the way we respond to the world or even perceive it. On a mundane level, language clearly influences our daily activities and habits of thought. Because two persons can be referred to by the same word—for example, *Irish*—we assume that they must be alike in certain stereotyped ways. Thus we may unconsciously believe that all the Irish have red hair, drink too much, and are quarrelsome. **General Semantics**, a study founded by Alfred Korzybski, is an effort to pay attention to such traps that language sets for us (Hayakawa and Hayakawa). Our concern in this chapter, however, is not with such studies, but rather with the ways in which the meanings of words change with time to allow us to talk about new things or about old things in a new light.

Variable and Vague Meanings

The meanings of words vary with place, time, and situation. Thus *tonic* may mean 'soft drink made with carbonated water' in parts of eastern New England, though elsewhere it usually means 'liquid medicinal preparation to invigorate the system' or in the phrase *gin and tonic* 'quinine water.' In the usage of musicians, the same word may also mean the first tone of a musical scale.

A large number of educated speakers and writers, for whatever reason, object to *disinterested* in the sense 'uninterested, unconcerned'—a sense it previously had but lost for a while—and want the word to have only the meaning 'impartial, unprejudiced.' The criticized use has nevertheless gained such ground that it has practically driven out the other one. That change is no great loss to language as communication. We have merely lost a synonym for *impartial* and acquired another way of saying 'uninterested' or 'unconcerned.'

Many words in frequent use, like *nice* and *democracy,* have meanings that are more or less subjective and hence loose. For instance, after relating that he had seen a well-dressed person take the arm of a blind and ragged beggar and escort the beggar across a crowded thoroughfare, a rather sentimental man remarked, "That was true democracy." It was, of course, only ordinary human decency, as likely to occur in a monarchy as in a democracy, and by no means impossible under an authoritarian government like, say, that of Oliver Cromwell. The semantic element of the word *democracy* in the speaker's mind was kindness to those less fortunate than oneself. He approved of such kindness, as indeed we all do. It was "good," and "democracy" was also "good"; hence, he equated democracy with goodness.

It is true that some words are by general consent used with a very loose meaning, and it is very likely that we could not get along without a certain number of such words—*nice,* for instance, as in "She's a nice person" (meaning that she has been well brought up, and is kind, gracious, and generally well-mannered), in contrast to

"That's a nice state of affairs" (meaning that it is a perfectly awful state of affairs). There is certainly nothing wrong with expressing pleasure and appreciation to a hostess by a heartfelt "I've had a very nice time" or even "I've had an awfully nice time." To seek for a more "accurate" word, one of more limited meaning, would be self-conscious and affected.

Etymology and Meaning

The belief is widespread, even among some quite learned people, that the way to find out what a word means is to find out what it previously meant—or, preferably, if it were possible to do so, what it originally meant. That method is frequently used to deal with borrowed words, the mistaken idea being that the meaning of the word in current English and the meaning of the non-English word from which the English word is derived must be, or at any rate ought to be, one and the same. As a matter of fact, such an appeal to **etymology** to determine present meaning is as unreliable as would be an appeal to spelling to determine modern pronunciation. Change of meaning—**semantic change**, as it is called— may, and frequently does, alter the so-called **etymological sense**, which may have become altogether obsolete. (The etymological sense is only the earliest sense we can *discover*, not necessarily the very earliest.) The study of etymologies is, of course, richly rewarding. It may, for instance, throw a great deal of light on present meanings, and it frequently tells us something of the workings of the human mind, but it is of very limited help in determining for us what a word "actually" means.

Certain popular writers, overeager to display their learning, have asserted that words are misused when they depart from their etymological meanings. Thus Ambrose Bierce (23) in what he called a "blacklist of literary faults" declared that *dilapidated,* because of its ultimate derivation from Latin *lapis* 'stone,' could appropriately be used only of a stone structure. Such a notion, if true, would commit us to the parallel assertion that only what actually had roots could properly be eradicated, since *eradicate* is ultimately derived from Latin *radix* 'root,' that *calculation* be restricted to counting pebbles (Lat. *calx* 'stone'), that *sinister* be applied only to leftists, and *dexterous* to rightists. By the same token we should have to insist that we could *admire* only what we could wonder at, inasmuch as the English word comes from Latin *ad* 'at' plus *mīrāri* 'to wonder'—as indeed Hamlet so used it in "Season your admiration for a while / With an attent eare" (1.2.192−3). Or we might insist that *giddy* persons must be divinely inspired, inasmuch as *gid* is a derivative of *god* (*enthusiastic,* from the Greek, also had this meaning) or that only men may be virtuous, because *virtue* is derived from Latin *virtus* 'manliness,' itself a derivative of *vir* 'man.' Now, alas for the wicked times in which we live, *virtue* is applied to few men and not many women. *Virile,* also a derivative of *vir,* has retained all of its earlier meaning and has even added to it.

From these few examples, it must be obvious that we cannot ascribe anything like "fixed" meanings to words. What we actually encounter much of the time are meanings that are variable and that may have wandered from what their etymologies suggest. To suppose that invariable meanings exist, quite apart from context, is to be guilty of a type of naivete that may vitiate all our thinking.

How Meaning Changes

Meaning is particularly likely to change in a field undergoing rapid expansion and development, such as computer technology. All of the following terms had earlier meanings that were changed when they were applied to computers: *bookmark, boot, copy, crash, floppy, mail, mouse, notebook, save, server, spam, surf, virtual, virus, wallpaper, web, window, zip.*

How such words change their meaning, while frequently unpredictable, is not wholly chaotic. Rather, the change follows certain paths. First, it is necessary to distinguish between the **sense**, or literal meaning, of an expression and its **associations**. *Father, dad,* and *the old man* may all refer to the same person, but the associations of the three expressions are likely to be different, as are those of other synonymous terms like *dada, daddy, governor, pa, pappy, pater, poppa, pops,* and *sire.* Words change in both their senses and associations. A sense may expand to include more referents than it formerly had (**generalization**), contract to include fewer referents (**specialization**), or shift to include a quite different set of referents (**transfer of meaning**). The associations of a word may become worse (**pejoration**) or better (**amelioration**) and stronger or weaker than they formerly were. Each of these possibilities is examined below. Another kind of meaning change results from the use of a word as a new part of speech—for example, "When you write any committee member, be sure to *carbon* ['send a carbon copy to'] the executive secretary." Because a change of meaning like this creates a new part of speech and thus a new word, it will be considered in the next chapter.

GENERALIZATION AND SPECIALIZATION

An obvious classification of meaning is that based on the scope of things to which a word can apply. That is to say, meaning may be generalized (extended, widened), or it may be specialized (restricted, narrowed). When we increase the scope of a word, we reduce the number of features in its definition that restrict its application. For instance, *tail* (from OF *teal*) in earlier times seems to have meant 'hairy caudal appendage, as of a horse.' When we eliminated the hairiness (or the horsiness) from the meaning, we increased its scope, so that in Modern English the word means simply 'caudal appendage.'

Similarly, a *mill* was earlier a place for making things by the process of grinding, that is, for making meal. The words *meal* and *mill* are themselves related, as one might guess from their similarity. A mill is now simply a place for making things: the grinding has been eliminated, so that we may speak of a woolen mill, a steel mill, or even a gin mill. The word *corn* earlier meant 'grain' and is in fact related to the word *grain*. It is still used in this general sense in Britain, as in the

"Corn Laws," but specifically it may refer there to either oats (for animals) or wheat (for human beings). In American usage, *corn* denotes 'maize,' which is of course not at all what Keats meant in his "Ode to a Nightingale" when he described Ruth as standing "in tears amid the alien corn."

The building in which corn, regardless of its meaning, is stored is called a barn. *Barn* earlier denoted a storehouse for barley; the word is, in fact, a compound of two Old English words, *bere* 'barley' and *ærn* 'house.' By eliminating one of the features of its earlier sense, the scope of this word has been extended to mean a storehouse for any kind of grain. American English has still further generalized the term by eliminating the grain, so that *barn* may mean also a place for housing live-stock or, more recently, a warehouse (a truck barn), a building for sales (an antique barn), or merely a large, open structure (a barn of a hotel).

The opposite of generalization is specialization, a process in which, by adding to the features of meaning, the referential scope of a word is reduced. *Deer,* for instance, used to mean simply 'animal' (OE *dēor*), as its German cognate *Tier* still does. Shakespeare writes of "Mice, and Rats, and such small Deare" (*King Lear* 3.4.144). By adding something particular (the family *Cervidae*) to the sense, the scope of the word has been reduced, and it has come to mean a specific kind of animal. Similarly *hound* used to mean 'dog,' as does its German cognate *Hund.* To this earlier meaning we have in the course of time added the idea of hunting and thereby restricted the scope of the word, which to us means a special sort of dog, a hunting dog. To the earlier content of *liquor* 'fluid' (compare *liquid*) we have added 'alcoholic.'

Meat once meant simply 'solid food' of any kind, a meaning that it retains in *sweet-meat* and throughout the King James Bible ("meat for the belly," "meat and drink"), though it acquired the more specialized meaning 'flesh' by the late Middle English period. *Starve* (OE *steorfan*) used to mean simply 'to die,' as its German cognate *ster-ben* still does. Chaucer writes, for instance, "But as hire man I wol ay lyve and sterve" (*Troilus and Criseyde* 1.427). A specific way of dying had to be expressed by a fol-lowing phrase—for example, "of hunger, of cold." The *OED* cites "starving with the cold" as late as 1867. The word came somehow to be associated primarily with death by hunger, and for a while there existed a compound verb *hunger-starve.* Usually nowadays we put the stress altogether on the added idea of hunger and lose the older meaning altogether. Although the usual meaning of *starve* now is 'to die of hunger,' we also use the phrase "starve to death," which in earlier times would have been tauto-logical. An additional, toned-down meaning grows out of **hyperbole**, so that "I'm starving" may mean only 'I'm very hungry.' The word, of course, is used figuratively, as in "starving for love," which, as we have seen, once meant 'dying for love.' This word furnishes a striking example of specialization and proliferation of meaning.

TRANSFER OF MEANING

There are a good many special types of transfer of meaning. *Long* and *short,* for instance, are on occasion transferred from the spatial concepts to which they ordinarily refer and made to refer to temporal concepts, as in *a long time,* and *a short while;*

similarly with such nouns as *length* and *space.* **Metaphor** is involved when we extend the word *foot* 'lowest extremity of an animal' to all sorts of things, as in *foot of a mountain, tree,* and so forth. The meaning of the same word is shifted in a different way (by **metonymy**) when we add to its original sense something like 'approximate length of the human foot,' thereby making the word mean a unit of measure; we do much the same thing to *hand* when we use it as a unit of measure for the height of horses.

Meaning may be transferred from one sensory faculty to another (**synesthesia**), as when we apply *clear,* with principal reference to sight, to hearing, as in *clear-sounding. Loud* is transferred from hearing to sight when we speak of *loud colors. Sweet,* with primary reference to taste, may be extended to hearing (*sweet music*), smell ("The rose smells *sweet*"), and to all senses at once (*a sweet person*). *Sharp* may be transferred from feeling to taste, and so may *smooth. Warm* may shift its usual reference from feeling to sight, as in *warm colors,* and along with *cold* may refer in a general way to all senses, as in *a warm* (*cold*) *welcome.*

Abstract meanings may evolve from more **concrete** ones. In prehistoric Old English times, the compound *understand* must have meant 'to stand among,' that is, 'close to'—*under* presumably having had the meaning 'among,' like its German and Latin cognates *unter* and *inter.* But this literal, concrete meaning gave way to the more abstract meaning that the word has today. Parallel shifts from concrete to abstract in words meaning 'understand' can be seen in German *verstehen* ('to stand before'), Greek *epistamai* ('I stand upon'), Latin *comprehendere* ('to take hold of'), and Italian *capire,* based on Latin *capere* 'to grasp,' among others.

The first person to use *grasp* in an abstract sense, as in "He has a good grasp of his subject," was coining an interesting metaphor. But the shift from concrete to abstract, or from physical to mental, has been so complete that we no longer think of this usage as metaphorical: *grasp* has come to be synonymous with *comprehension* in contexts such as that cited, even though in other uses the word has retained its physical reference. It was similar with *glad,* earlier 'smooth,' though this word has completely lost the earlier meaning (except in the proper name *Gladstone,* if surnames may be thought of as having meaning) and may now refer only to a mental state. Likewise, meaning may shift from **subjective** to **objective**, as when *pitiful,* earlier 'full of pity, compassionate,' came to mean 'deserving of pity'; or the shift may be the other way round, as when *fear,* earlier 'danger,' something objective, came to mean 'terror,' a state of mind.

Association of Ideas

Change of meaning may be due simply to association of ideas. Latin *penna,* for instance, originally meant 'feather,' but came to be used to indicate an instrument for writing, whether made of a feather or not, because of the association of the quill with writing. Our word *pen* is ultimately derived from the Latin word, though it comes to us by way of Old French. Similarly, *paper* is from *papyrus,* a kind of plant, and the two were once invariably associated in people's minds, though paper is nowadays made from rags, wood, straw, and other fibrous materials, and the old association has been completely lost. Sensational magazines used to be printed on paper of inferior quality made from wood pulp; they were referred to by writers, somewhat derisively, as wood-pulp magazines, or simply as the *pulps,* in contrast to the *slicks,* those printed on paper of better quality. Such "literature" has come up in the world, at least as far as its physical production is concerned, and many magazines whose reading matter is considered by serious-minded people to be of low quality are now printed on the slickest paper. They are nevertheless still referred to as "the pulps," and writers who keep the wolf from their door by supplying them with stories and articles are known as "pulp writers." Thus, because of an earlier association, the name of the physical product wood pulp has been applied to a type of periodical with reference to the literary quality of its contents.

Silver has come to be used for eating utensils made of silver—an instance of **synecdoche**—and sometimes, by association, for the same articles when not made of silver, so that we may even speak of stainless steel silverware. The product derived from latex and earlier known as *caoutchouc* soon acquired a less difficult name, *rubber,* from association with one of its earliest uses, making erasures on paper by rubbing. *China* 'earthenware' originally designated porcelain of a type first manufactured in the country whose name it bears, and the name of a native American bird, the *turkey,* derives from the fact that our ancestors somehow got the notion that it was of Turkish origin. In French the same creature is called *dinde,* that is, *d'Inde* 'of or from India.' The French thought that America was India at the time when the name was conferred. These names, like others that might be cited, arose out of associations long since lost.

Transfer from Other Languages

Other languages can also affect English word meanings. *Thing,* for example, meant in Old English 'assembly, sometimes for legal purposes,' a meaning that it had in the other Germanic languages and has retained in Icelandic, as in *Alþingi* 'all-assembly,' the name of the Icelandic parliament. Latin *rēs* was used in much the same sense and was translated by *thing.* As a result, English *thing* picked up another sense of the Latin word, 'case at law,' as one of its meanings. This meaning was subsequently lost, but because of the association, originally at one small point, the English word came to acquire every meaning that Latin *res* could have, which is to say, practically every other meaning of *thing* in present-day English. German *Ding* has had, quite independently, the same semantic history. A word whose meaning has been affected by a foreign word with partly overlapping sense is called a **calque**.

Sound Associations

Similarity or identity of sound may likewise influence meaning. *Fay,* from the Old French *fae* 'fairy' has influenced *fey,* from Old English *fǣge* 'fated, doomed to die' to such an extent that *fey* is practically always used nowadays in the sense 'spritely, fairylike.' The two words are pronounced alike, and there is an association of meaning at one small point: fairies are mysterious; so is being fated to die, even though we all are so fated. There are many other instances of such confusion through **clang association** (that is, association by sound rather than meaning). For example, in conservative use *fulsome* means 'offensively insincere' as in "fulsome praise," but it is often used in the sense 'extensive' because of the clang with *full*. Similarly, *fruition* is from Latin *frui* 'to enjoy' by way of Old French, and the term originally meant 'enjoyment' but now usually means 'state of bearing fruit, completion'; and *fortuitous* earlier meant 'occurring by chance' but now is generally used as a synonym for *fortunate* because of its similarity to that word.

PEJORATION AND AMELIORATION

In addition to a change in its sense or literal meaning, a word may also undergo change in its associations, especially of value. A word may, as it were, go downhill, or it may rise in the world; there is no way of predicting what its career may be. *Politician* has had a downhill development, or pejoration (from Lat. *pējor* 'worse'). So has *knave* (OE *cnafa*), which used to mean simply 'boy'—it is cognate with German *Knabe*, which retains the earlier meaning. It came to mean 'serving boy' (specialization), like that well-known knave of hearts who was given to stealing tarts, and later 'bad human being' (pejoration and generalization) so that we may now speak of an old knave or a knavish woman. On its journey downhill, this word has thus undergone both specialization and generalization; the knave in cards (for which the usual American term is *jack*) is a further specialization. *Boor*, once meaning 'peasant,' has had a similar pejorative development. Its cognate *Bauer* is the usual equivalent of *jack* or *knave* in German card playing, whence English *bower*—as in *right bower* and *left bower*—in card games such as euchre and five hundred.

Lewd, earlier 'lay, as opposed to clerical,' underwent pejoration to 'ignorant,' 'base,' and finally 'obscene,' which is the only meaning to survive. The same fate has befallen the Latin loanword *vulgar*, ultimately from *vulgus* 'the common people'; the earlier meaning is retained in *Vulgar Latin*, the Latin that was spoken by the people up to the time of the early Middle Ages and was to develop into the various Romance languages. *Censure* earlier meant 'opinion.' In the course of time, it has come to mean 'bad opinion'; *criticism* is well on its way to the same pejorative goal, ordinarily meaning nowadays 'adverse judgment.' The verbs *to censure* and *to criticize* have undergone a similar development. *Deserts* (as in *just deserts*) likewise started out indifferently to mean simply what one deserved, whether good or bad, but has come to mean 'punishment.' One other example of this tendency must suffice. *Silly* (OE *sǣlig*), earlier 'timely,' came to mean 'happy, blessed,' and subsequently 'innocent, simple'; then the simplicity, a desirable quality under most circumstances, was thought of as foolishness, and the word took on its present meaning. Its German cognate *selig* progressed only to the second stage, though the word may be used facetiously to mean 'tipsy.'

Like *censure* and *criticize, praise* started out indifferently; it is simply *appraise* 'put a value on' with loss of its initial unstressed syllable (aphesis). But *praise* has come to mean 'value highly.' The meaning of the word has ameliorated, or elevated. The development of *nice*, going back to Latin *nescius* 'ignorant,' is similar. The Old French form used in English meant 'simple,' a meaning retained in Modern French *niais.* In the course of its career in English, it has had the meanings 'foolishly particular' and then merely 'particular' (as in *a nice distinction*), among others. Now it often means no more than 'pleasant' or 'proper,' an all-purpose word of approbation.

Amelioration, the opposite of pejoration, is also illustrated by *knight,* which used to mean 'servant,' as its German relative *Knecht* still does. This particular word has obviously moved far from its earlier meaning, denoting as it usually now does a man who has been honored by his sovereign and who is entitled to prefix *Sir* to his name. *Earl* (OE *eorl*) once meant simply 'man,' though in ancient Germanic times it was specially applied to a warrior, who was almost invariably a man of high standing, in contrast to a *ceorl* (*churl*), or ordinary freeman. When, under the Norman kings, French titles were adopted in England, *earl* failed to be displaced but remained as the equivalent of the Continental *count.*

TABOO AND EUPHEMISM

Some words undergo pejoration because of a **taboo** against talking about the things they name; the replacement for a taboo term is a **euphemism** (from a Greek word meaning 'good-sounding'). Euphemisms, in their turn, are often subject to pejoration, eventually becoming taboo. Then the whole cycle starts again.

It is not surprising that superstition should play a part in change of meaning, as when *sinister,* the Latin word for 'left' (the unlucky side), acquired its present baleful significance. The verb *die,* of Germanic origin, is not once recorded in Old English. Its absence from surviving documents does not necessarily mean that it was not a part of the Old English word stock; however, in the writings that have come down to us, roundabout, toning-down expressions such as "go on a journey" are used instead, perhaps because of superstitions connected with the word itself—superstitions that survive into our own day, when people (at least those whom we know personally) "pass away," "go to sleep," or "depart." Louise Pound, the first woman president of the Modern Language Association, collected an imposing and—to the irreverent—amusing list of words and phrases referring to death in her article "American Euphemisms for Dying, Death, and Burial." She concluded (195) that "one of mankind's gravest problems is to avoid a straightforward mention of dying or burial."

Euphemism is especially frequent, and probably always has been, when we must come face to face with the less happy facts of our existence, for life holds even for the most fortunate of people experiences that are inartistic, violent, and hence shocking to contemplate in the full light of day—for instance, the first and last facts of human existence, birth and death, despite the sentimentality with which we have surrounded them. And it is certainly true that the sting of the latter is somewhat alleviated—for the survivors, anyway—by calling it by some other name, such as "the final sleep," which is among the many terms cited by Pound in the article just alluded to. *Mortician* is a much flossier word than *undertaker* (which is itself a euphemism with the earlier meanings 'helper,' 'contractor,' 'publisher,' and 'baptismal sponsor,' among others), but the *loved one* prepared for public view and subsequent interment in a *casket* (earlier a 'jewel box,' as in *The Merchant of Venice*) is just as dead as a *corpse* in a *coffin*. Such verbal subterfuges are apparently thought to rob the grave of some of its victory; the notion of death is thus made more tolerable to human consciousness than it would otherwise be. Birth is much more plainly alluded to nowadays than it used to be. There was a time, within the memory of some still living, when *pregnant* was avoided in polite company. A woman who was *with child, going to have a baby, in a family way,* or *enceinte* would deliver during her *confinement,* or, if one wanted to be really fancy about it, her *accouchement*.

Ideas of decency likewise profoundly affect language. All during the Victorian era, ladies and gentlemen were very sensitive about using the word *leg, limb* being almost invariably substituted, sometimes even if only the legs of a piano were being referred to. In the very year that marks the beginning of Queen Victoria's long reign, Captain Frederick Marryat noted in his *Diary in America* (1837) the American taboo on this word, when, having asked a young American lady who had taken a spill whether she had hurt her leg, she turned from him, "evidently much shocked, or much offended," later explaining to him that in America the word *leg* was never used in the presence of ladies. Later, the captain visited a school for young ladies where he saw, according to his own testimony, "a square pianoforte with four limbs," all dressed in little frilled pantalettes. For reasons that it would be difficult to analyze, a similar taboo was placed on *belly, stomach* being usually substituted for it, along with such nursery terms as *tummy* and *breadbasket* and the advertising copywriter's *midriff*.

Toilet, a diminutive of French *toile* 'cloth,' in its earliest English uses meant a piece of cloth in which to wrap clothes; subsequently it came to be used for a cloth cover for a dressing table, and then the table itself, as when Lydia Languish in Sheridan's *The Rivals* says, "Here, my dear Lucy, hide these books. Quick, quick! Fling *Peregrine Pickle* under the toilet—throw *Roderick Random* into the closet." (Early in the last century, the direction for the disposal of *Roderick Random* would have been as laughable as that for *Peregrine Pickle,* for *closet* was then frequently used for *water closet,* now practically obsolete though the short form, *WC,* is still used in Britain, especially in signs.) *Toilet* came to be used as a euphemism for *privy*—itself, in turn, a euphemism, as are *latrine* (ultimately derived from Lat. *lavāre* 'to wash') and *lavatory* (note the euphemistic phrase "to wash one's hands"). But *toilet* is now frequently replaced by *rest room, comfort station, powder room,* the coy *little boys'* (or *girls'*) *room, facility,* or especially *bathroom,* even though there may be no tub and no occasion for taking a bath. One may even hear of a dog's "going to the bathroom" in the living room. The British also use *loo,* a word of obscure origin, or *Gents* and *Ladies* for public facilities. It is safe to predict that these evasions will in their turn come to be regarded as indecorous, and other expressions will be substituted for them.

Euphemism is likewise resorted to in reference to certain diseases. Like that which attempts to prettify, or at least to mollify, birth, death, and excretion, this type of verbal subterfuge is doubtless deeply rooted in fear and superstition. An ailment of almost any sort, for instance, is nowadays often referred to as a *condition* (*heart condition, kidney condition, malignant condition,* and so forth), so that *condition,* hitherto a more or less neutral word, has thus had a pejorative development, coming to mean 'bad condition.' (Although *to have a condition* means 'to be in bad health,' *to be in condition* continues, confusingly enough, to mean 'to be in good health.') *Leprosy* is no longer used by the American Medical Association because of its repulsive connotations; it is now replaced by the colorless *Hansen's disease. Cancer* may be openly referred to, though it is notable that some astrologers have abandoned the term as a sign of the zodiac, referring instead to those born under Cancer as "Moon Children." The taboo has been removed from reference to the various specific venereal diseases, formerly *blood diseases* or *social diseases.* Recent years have seen a greater tendency toward straightforward language about such matters. No euphemisms seem to have arisen for *AIDS* or *HIV,* though the initials themselves may serve a euphemistic purpose.

Old age and its attendant decay have probably been made more bearable for many elderly and decrepit people by calling them *senior citizens.* A similar verbal humanitarianism is responsible for a good many other voguish euphemisms, such as *underprivileged* 'poor,' now largely supplanted by *disadvantaged; sick* 'insane'; and *exceptional child* 'a pupil of subnormal mentality.' (Although children who exceed expectations have been stigmatized by the schools as *overachievers,* they are also sometimes called *exceptional,* apparently because of an assumption that any departure from the average is disabling.)

Sentimental equalitarianism has led us to attempt to dignify humble occupations by giving them high-sounding titles: thus a *janitor* (originally a doorkeeper, from *Janus,* the doorkeeper of heaven in Roman mythology) has in many parts of America become a *custodian.* There are many engineers who would not know the difference between a calculator and a cantilever: H. L. Mencken (*American Language* 289−91) cites, among a good many others, *demolition engineer* 'house wrecker,' *sanitary engineer* 'garbage man,' and *extermination engineer* 'rat catcher.' The meaning of *profession* has been generalized to such an extent that it may include practically any trade or vocation. *Webster's Third* illustrates the extended sense of the word with quotations referring to the "old profession of farming" and "men who make it their profession to hunt the hippopotamus." The term has also been applied to plumbing, waiting on tables, and almost any other gainful occupation. Such occupations are both useful and honorable, but they are not professions according to the undemocratic and now perhaps outmoded sense of the term.

As long ago as 1838, James Fenimore Cooper in *The American Democrat* denounced such subterfuges as *boss* for *master* and *help* for *servant,* but these seem very mild nowadays. One of the great concerns of the progressive age in which we live would seem to be to ensure that nobody's feelings shall ever be hurt—at least not by words. And so the coinage of new euphemisms in what has been called "politically correct" language has made it often difficult to tell the seriously used term (*motivationally challenged* 'lazy') from the satirical one (*follicularly challenged* 'bald'). As the Roman satirist Juvenal put it, "In the present state of the world it is difficult not to write satire."

THE FATE OF INTENSIFYING WORDS

Words rise and fall not only on a scale of goodness, by amelioration and pejoration, but also on a scale of strength. **Intensifiers** constantly stand in need of replacement, because they are so frequently used that their intensifying force is worn down. As an adverb of degree, *very* has only an intensifying function; it has altogether lost its independent meaning 'truly,' though as an adjective it survives with older meanings in phrases like "the very heart of the matter" and "the very thought of you." Chaucer does not use *very* as an intensifying adverb; the usage was doubtless beginning to be current in his day, though the *OED* has no contemporary citations. The *verray* in Chaucer's description of his ideal soldier, "He was a verray, parfit gentil knyght," is an adjective; the meaning of the line is approximately 'He was a true, perfect, gentle knight.'

For Chaucer and his contemporaries, *full* seems to have been the usual intensifying adverb, though Old English *swīðe* (the adverbial form of *swīð* 'strong') retained its intensifying function until the middle of the fifteenth century, with independent meanings 'rapidly' and 'instantly' surviving much longer. *Right* was also widely used as an intensifier in Middle English times, as in Chaucer's description of the Clerk of Oxenford: "he nas [that is, *ne was*] nat right fat," which is to say, 'He wasn't very fat.' This usage survives formally in *Right Reverend,* the title of an Anglican bishop; in *Right Honourable,* that of members of the Privy Council and a few other dignitaries; and in *Right Worshipful,* that of most lord mayors; as also in the more or less informal usages *right smart, right well, right away, right there,* and the like.

Sore, as in *sore afraid,* was similarly long used as an intensifier for adjectives and adverbs; its use to modify verbs is even older. Its cognate *sehr* is still the usual intensifier in German, in which language it has completely lost its independent use.

In view of the very understandable tendency of such intensifying words to become dulled, it is not surprising that we should cast about for other words to replace them when we really want to be emphatic. "It's been a *very* pleasant evening" seems quite inadequate under certain circumstances, and we may instead say, "It's been an *awfully* pleasant evening"; "*very* nice" may likewise become "*terribly* nice." In negative utterances, *too* is widely used as an intensifier: "Newberry's not *too* far from here"; "Juvenile-court law practice is not *too* lucrative." Also common in negative statements and in questions are *that* and *all that:* "I'm not *that* tired"; "Is he *all that* eager to go to Daytona?"

Prodigiously was for a while a voguish substitute for *very,* so that a Regency "blood" like Thackeray's Jos Sedley might speak admiringly of a shapely woman as "a prodigiously fine gel" or even a "monstrous fine" one. The first of these now-forgotten intensifiers dates approximately from the second half of the seventeenth century; the second is about a century earlier. An anonymous contributor to the periodical *The World* in 1756 deplored the "pomp of utterance of our present women of fashion; which, though it may tend to spoil many a pretty mouth, can never recommend an indifferent one"; the writer cited in support of his statement the overuse of *vastly, horridly, abominably, immensely,* and *excessively* as intensifiers (Tucker 96).

SOME CIRCUMSTANCES OF SEMANTIC CHANGE

The meaning of a word may vary even with the group in which it is used. For all speakers *smart* has the meaning 'intelligent,' but there is a specialized, especially British, class usage in which it means 'fashionable.' The meaning of *a smart woman* may thus vary with the social group of the speaker; it may indeed have to be inferred from the context. The earliest meaning of this word seems to have been 'sharp,' as in *a smart blow. Sharp* has also been used in the sense 'up-to-date, fashionable,' as in *a sharp dresser.* But with the advent of grunge and bagginess, that use largely disappeared.

Similarly, a word's meaning may vary according to changes in the thing to which it refers. *Hall* (OE *heall*), for instance, once meant a very large roofed place, like the splendid royal dwelling place Heorot, where Beowulf fought Grendel. Such buildings were usually without smaller attached rooms, though Heorot had a "bower" (*būr*), earlier a separate cottage, but in *Beowulf* a bedroom to which the king and queen retired. (This word survives only in the sense 'arbor, enclosure formed by vegetation.') For retainers the hall served as meeting room, feasting room, and sleeping room. Later *hall* came to mean 'the largest room in a great house,' used for large gatherings such as receptions and feasts, though the use of the word for the entire structure survives in the names of a number of manor houses such as Little Wenham Hall and Speke Hall in England and of some dormitory or other college buildings in America. There are a number of other meanings, all connoting size and some degree of splendor, and all a far cry from the modern American use of *hall* as a narrow passageway leading to rooms or the modern British use as a vestibule or entrance passage immediately inside the front door of a small house. The meaning of *hall* must be determined by the context in which it occurs.

Akin to what we have been considering is modification of meaning as the result of a shift in point of view. *Crescent,* from the present participial form of Latin *cresco,* used to mean simply 'growing, increasing,' as in Pompey's "My powers are Cressent, and my Auguring hope / Sayes it will come to'th'full" (*Antony and Cleopatra* 2.1.10−11). The new, or growing, moon was thus called the crescent moon. There has been a shift, however, in the dominant element of meaning, the emphasis coming to be put entirely on shape, specifically on a particular shape of the moon, rather than upon growth. *Crescent* thus came to denote the moon between its new and quarter phases, whether increasing or decreasing, and then any similar shape, as in its British use for an arc-shaped street. Similarly, in *veteran* (Lat. *veterānus,* a derivative of *vetus* 'old'), the emphasis has shifted from age to military service, though not necessarily long service: a veteran need not have grown old in service, and we may in fact speak of a *young veteran.* The fact that etymologically the phrase is self-contradictory is of no significance as far as present usage is concerned. The word is, of course, extended to other areas—for instance, *veteran politician;* in its extended meanings, it continues to connote long experience and usually mature years as well.

Vogue for Words of Learned Origin

When learned words acquire popular currency, they almost inevitably acquire at the same time new, less exact meanings, or at least new shades of meaning. *Philosophy,* for instance, earlier 'love of wisdom,' has now a popular sense 'practical opinion or body of opinions,' as in "the philosophy of salesmanship," "the philosophy of George Bush," and "homespun philosophy." An error in translation from a foreign language may result in a useful new meaning—for example, *psychological moment,* now 'most opportune time' rather than 'psychological momentum,' which is the proper translation of German *psychologisches Moment,* the ultimate source of the phrase. The popular misunderstanding of *inferiority complex,* first used to designate an unconscious sense of inferiority manifesting itself in assertive behavior, has given us a synonym for *diffidence, shyness.* It is similar with *guilt complex,* now used to denote nothing more psychopathic than a feeling of guilt. The term *complex,* as first used by psychoanalysts about a century ago, designated a type of aberration resulting from the unconscious suppression of more or less related attitudes. The word soon passed into voguish and subsequently into general use to designate an obsession of any kind—a bee in the bonnet, as it were. Among its progeny are *Oedipus complex, herd complex,* and *sex complex.* The odds on its increasing fecundity would seem to be rather high.

Other fashionable terms from psychoanalysis and psychology, with which our times are so intensely preoccupied, are *subliminal* 'influencing behavior below the level of awareness,' with reference to a sneaky kind of advertising technique; *behavior pattern,* meaning simply 'behavior'; *neurotic,* with a wide range of meaning, including 'nervous, high-strung, artistic by temperament, eccentric, or given to worrying'; *compulsive* 'habitual,' as in *compulsive drinker* and *compulsive criminal;* and *schizophrenia* 'practically any mental or emotional disorder.' It is not surprising that the newer, popular meanings of what were once more or less technical terms should generally show a considerable extension of the earlier technical meanings. Thus, *sadism* has come to mean simply 'cruelty' and *exhibitionism* merely 'showing off,' without any of the earlier connotations of sexual perversion. The word *psychology* itself may mean nothing more than 'mental processes' in a vague sort of way. An intense preoccupation with what is fashionably and doubtless humanely referred to as *mental illness*—a less enlightened age than ours called it *insanity* or *madness,* and people afflicted with it were said to be *crazy*—must to a large extent be responsible for the use of such terms as have been cited. Also notable is the already mentioned specialization of *sick* to refer to mental imbalance.

A great darling among the loosely used pseudoscientific **vogue words** of recent years is *image* in the sense 'impression that others subconsciously have of someone.' A jaundiced observer of modern life might well suppose that what we actually are is not nearly so important as the image that we are able—to use another vogue word—to *project.* If the "image" is phony, what difference does it make? In a time when political campaigns are won or lost by the impression a candidate makes on the television screen and therefore in opinion polls, *image* is all important.

A particularly important kind of image to convey, especially for politicians, is the *father image.* Young people are apparently in great need of a *father figure* to *relate to,* just as they require a *role model* to achieve the most successful *lifestyle.* The last-mentioned expression, which has all but replaced the earlier voguish *way of life,* may refer to casual dress, jogging, homosexuality, the use of a Jacuzzi hot tub, or a great many other forms of behavior that have little to do with what has traditionally been thought of as style. *Peer pressure* from one's *peer group* is often responsible for the adoption of one "style" or another; the voguish use of *peer* has doubtless trickled down from educationists, whose *expertise* in this, as in many other matters, is greatly admired, although not always richly rewarded, by the *sponsoring society.*

Among the more impressive vogue words of the late twentieth century are *charisma* and *charismatic* '(having) popular appeal' (earlier, 'a spiritual gift, such as that of tongues or prophesy'). The original sense of *ambience* or *ambiance* 'surrounding atmosphere, environment' has shifted considerably in the description of a chair as "crafted with a Spanish ambience" and has slipped away altogether in the puffery of a restaurant said to have "great food, served professionally in an atmosphere of ambiance." Other popular expressions are *scenario, paradigm, bottom line,* and *empowerment.*

Computer jargon has been a rich source of vogue words in recent years. Although *input* and *output* have been around since the mid-eighteenth and nineteenth centuries, respectively, their current fashionableness results from an extension of their use for information fed into and spewed out of a computer. *Interface* is another nineteenth-century term for the touching surface between any two substances—for example, oil floating on the top of a pan of water; it was taken up in computer use to denote the equipment that presents the computer's work for human inspection, such as a print-out or a monitor display. Now the word is used as a noun to mean just 'connection' and as a verb to mean 'connect' or 'work together smoothly.'

Desexed Language

One of the awkward problems of English, and indeed of many languages, is a lack of means for talking about persons without specifying their sex. Apparently sexual differences have been so important for the human species and the societies its members have formed that most languages make obligatory distinctions between males and females in both vocabulary and grammar. On those occasions, however, when one wishes to discuss human beings without reference to their sex, the obligatory distinctions are bothersome and may be prejudicial. Consequently, in recent years many publishers and editors have tried to eliminate both lexical and grammatical bias toward the male sex.

The bias in question arises because of the phenomenon of **semantic marking**. A word like *sheep* is **unmarked** for sex, since it is applicable to either males or females of the species; there are separate terms **marked** for maleness (*ram*) and femaleness (*ewe*) when they are needed. If terms for all species followed this model, no problems would arise, but unfortunately they do not. *Duck* is like *sheep* in being unmarked for sex, but it has only one marked companion, namely, *drake* for the male. Because we lack a single term for talking about the female bird, we must make do with an ambiguity in the term *duck,* which refers either to a member of the species without consideration of sex or to a female. An opposite sort of problem arises with *lion* and *lioness;* the latter term is marked for femaleness, and the former is unmarked and therefore used either for felines without consideration of sex or for males of the species. The semantic features of these terms, as they relate to sex, can be shown as follows (+ means 'present,' − 'absent,' and ± 'unmarked'):

	SHEEP	RAM	EWE	DUCK	DRAKE	LION	LIONESS
Male	±	+	−	±	+	±	−
Female	±	−	+	±	−	±	+

   Lions and ducks are quite unconcerned with what we call them, but as human beings we are very much concerned with what we call ourselves. Consequently, the linguistic problem of referring to men and women is both complex and emotional. *Woman* is clearly marked for femaleness, like *lioness.* Some persons interpret *man* as unmarked for sex, like *lion.* Others point out that it is so often used for males in contrast to females that it must be regarded as marked for maleness, like *drake;* they also observe that because of the male connotations of *man,* women are often by implication excluded from statements in which the word is used generically—for example, "Men have achieved great discoveries in science during the last hundred years." By such language we may be led unconsciously to assume that males rather than females are the achievers of our species. If, as some etymologists believe, the word *man* is historically related to the word *mind,* its original sense was probably something like 'the thinker,' and it clearly denoted the species rather than the sex. In present use, however, the word is often ambiguous, as in the example cited a few lines above. The ambiguity can be resolved by context: "Men (the species) are mortal" versus "Men (the sex) are at present shorter-lived than women." Nevertheless, ambiguity is sometimes awkward and often annoying to the linguistically sensitive.
   To solve the problem, would-be linguistic engineers have proposed respellings like *womyn* for *women.* (*Wymen* would be a phonetically more adequate, if politically less correct, spelling.) More realistically, editors and others have substituted other words (such as *person*) whenever *man* might be used of both sexes. Thus we have *chairperson, anchor person* (for the one who anchors a TV news program), *layperson,* and even *straw person.* The new forms were bound to call forth some heavy-handed humor in the form of *woperson* and even more bizarre concoctions. But not all the new gaucheries have been created by jokesters; some are the products of humorless bureaucrats, such as the civil rights director for the Department of Health, Education, and Welfare who complained that he could not enforce laws against sex discrimination because of "limited person power in the Office for Civil Rights." Other efforts to avoid sexual reference, such as *supervisor* in place of *foreman* and *flight attendant* in place of both *steward* and *stewardess,* seem long-winded to the older generation, but are normal for younger speakers. On the

other hand, *housespouse* as a replacement for both *housewife* and its newfound mate, *househusband,* has a lilt and a swagger that make it appealing.

The grammatical problems of sexual reference are especially great in the choice of a pronoun after indefinite pronouns like *everyone, anyone,* and *someone.* Following the model of unmarked *man,* handbooks have recommended unmarked *he* in expressions like "Everyone tried his best," with reference to a mixed group. The other generally approved option, "Everyone tried his or her best," is wordy and can become intolerably so with repetition, as in "Everyone who has not finished writing his or her paper before he or she is required to move to his or her next class can take it with him or her."

In colloquial English, speakers long ago solved that problem by using the plural pronouns *they, them, their,* and *theirs* after indefinites: "Somebody's lost their book." Although still abjured by the linguistically fastidious, such use of *they* and its forms has been common for about 400 years, is increasing in formal English, and has in fact been recommended by progressive groups like the National Council of Teachers of English. Idealists have also proposed a number of invented forms to fill the gap, such as *thon* (from *that one*), *he'er, he/she,* and *shem,* but almost no one has taken them seriously.

Language reformers in the past have not been notably successful in remodeling English nearer to their hearts' desire. The language has a way of following its own course and leaving would-be guides behind. Whether the current interest in desexing language will have more lasting results than other changes previously proposed and labored for is an open question. Unself-conscious speech long ago solved the grammatical problem with the *everybody . . . they* construction. If the lexical problem is solved by the extended use of *person* and other gender-neutral alternatives, we will have witnessed a remarkable influence by those who edit books and periodicals. Whatever the upshot, the contemporary concern is testimony to one kind of semantic sensibility among present-day English speakers.

SEMANTIC CHANGE IS INEVITABLE

It is a great pity that language cannot be the exact, finely attuned instrument that deep thinkers wish it to be. But the facts are, as we have seen, that the meaning of practically any word is susceptible to change of one sort or another, and some words have so many individual meanings that we cannot really hope to be absolutely certain of the sum of these meanings. But it is probably quite safe to predict that the members of the human race, *homines sapientes* more or less, will go on making absurd noises with their mouths at one another in what idealists among them will go on considering a deplorably sloppy and inadequate manner, and yet manage to understand one another well enough for their own purposes.

The idealists may, if they wish, settle upon Esperanto, Ido, Ro, Volapük, or any other of the excellent scientific languages that have been laboriously constructed. The game of constructing such languages is still going on. Some naively suppose that, should one of these ever become generally used, there would be an end to misunderstanding, followed by an age of universal brotherhood—the assumption being that we always agree with and love those whom we understand, though the fact is that we frequently disagree violently with those whom we understand very well. (Cain doubtless understood Abel well enough.)

But be that as it may, it should be obvious that, if such an artificial language were by some miracle ever to be accepted and generally used, it would be susceptible to precisely the kind of changes in meaning that have been our concern in this chapter as well as to such changes in structure as have been our concern throughout—the kind of changes undergone by those natural languages that have evolved over the eons. And most of the manifold phenomena of life—hatred, disease, famine, birth, death, sex, war, atoms, isms, and people, to name only a few—would remain as messy and hence as unsatisfactory to those unwilling to accept them as they have always been, no matter what words we use in referring to them.

FOR FURTHER READING

Overviews

Goddard. *Semantic Analysis.*
Jackson. *Grammar and Meaning.*
————. *Words and Their Meaning.*
Jeffries. *Meaning in English.*
Kreidler. *Introducing English Semantics.*
Leech. *Semantics.*
Löbner. *Understanding Semantics.*
Lyons. *Linguistic Semantics.*
————. *Semantics.*
Palmer. *Semantics.*
Weinreich. *On Semantics.*

Some Semantic Categories

Allan and Burridge. *Euphemism & Dysphemism.*
Ayto. *Euphemisms.*
Mettinger. *Aspects of Semantic Opposition in English.*

General Semantics

Hayakawa and Hayakawa. *Language in Thought and Action.*

11

NEW WORDS FROM OLD

The ultimate origin of language is a mystery, but we can know a good deal about the making of words in historical times. This chapter is an examination of five processes of word making: **creating**, **combining**, **shortening**, **blending**, and **shifting** the grammatical uses of old words. Shifting the meanings of old words is considered in the preceding chapter, and borrowing from other languages is considered in the next.

CREATING WORDS

Root Creations

It is unlikely that very many words have come into being during the historical period that have not been suggested in one way or another by previously existing words. An often cited example of a word completely without associations with any existing words (a **root creation**) is *Kodak,* which made its first appearance in print in the U.S. *Patent Office Gazette* in 1888 and was, according to George Eastman, who invented the word as well as the device it names, "a purely arbitrary combination of letters, not derived in whole or in part from any existing word" (Mencken, *Supplement I* 342, n. 1), though according to his biographer a very slight association was in fact involved in his use of the letter *k,* for his mother's family name began with that letter.

Other trade names—like those for the artificial fabrics *Nylon, Dacron,* and *Orlon*—also lack an etymology in the usual sense. According to a Du Pont company publication (*Context* 7.2, 1978), when Nylon was first developed, it was called *polyhexamethyleneadipamide.* Realizing the stuff needed a catchier name than that, the company thought of *duprooh,* an acronym for "Du Pont pulls rabbit out of hat," but instead settled on *no-run* until it was pointed out that stockings made of the material were not really run-proof. So the spelling of that word was reversed to *nuron,* which was modified to *nilon* to make it sound less like a nerve tonic. Then, to prevent a pronunciation like "nillon," the company changed the *i* to *y,* producing *nylon.* If this account is correct, beneath that apparently quite arbitrary word lurks the English expression *no-run.* Most trade names are clearly suggested by already existing words. *Vaseline,* for instance, was made from German *Wasser* 'water' plus Greek *elaion* 'oil' (Mencken, *American Language* 172, n. 3); *Kleenex* was made from *clean,* and *Cutex* from *cuticle,* both with the addition of a rather widely used but quite meaningless pseudoscientific suffix *-ex.*

Echoic Words

Sound alone is the basis of a limited number of words, called **echoic** or **ono-matopoeic**, like *bang, burp, splash, tinkle, bobwhite,* and *cuckoo.* Words that are actually imitative of sound, like *meow, moo, bowwow,* and *vroom*—though these differ from language to language—can be distinguished from those like *bump* and *flick,* which are called **symbolic.** Symbolic words regularly come in sets that rime (*bump, lump, clump, hump*) or alliterate (*flick, flash, flip, flop*) and derive their symbolic meaning at least in part from the other members of their sound-alike sets. Both imitative and symbolic words frequently show doubling, sometimes with slight variation, as in *bowwow, choo-choo,* and *pe(e)wee.*

Ejaculations

Some words imitate more or less instinctive vocal responses to emotional situations. One of these **ejaculations**, *ouch,* is something of a mystery: it does not appear in British writing except as an Americanism. The *OED* derives it from German *autsch,* an exclamation presumably imitative of what a German exclaims at fairly mild pain, such as stubbing a toe or hitting a thumb with a tack hammer—hardly anything more severe, for when one is suffering really rigorous pain one is not likely to have the presence of mind to remember to say "Ouch!" The vocal reaction, if any, is likely to be a shriek or a scream. *Ouch* may be regarded as a conventional representation of the sounds actually made when one is in pain. The interesting thing is that the written form has become so familiar, so completely conventionalized, that Americans (and Germans) do actually say "Ouch!" when they have hurt themselves so slightly as to be able to remember what they *ought* to say under the circumstances.

Other such written representations, all of them highly conventionalized, of what are thought to be "natural utterances" have also become actual words—for instance, *ha-ha,* with the variant *ho-ho* for Santa Claus and other jolly fat men, and the girlish *tehee,* which the naughty but nonetheless delectable Alison gives utterance to in Chaucer's "Miller's Tale," in what is perhaps the most indecorously funny line in English poetry.

Now, it is likely that, if Alison were a real-life woman (rather than better-than-life, as she is by virtue of being the creation of a superb artist), upon receipt of the misdirected kiss she might have tittered, twittered, giggled, or gurgled under the decidedly improper circumstances in which she had placed herself. But how to write a titter, a twitter, a giggle, or a gurgle? Chaucer was confronted with the problem of representing by alphabetical symbols whatever the appropriate vocal response might have been, and *tehee,* which was doubtless more or less conventional in his day, was certainly as good a choice as he could have made. The form with which he chose to represent girlish glee has remained conventional. When we encounter it in reading, we think—and, if reading aloud, we actually say—[ti'hi], and the effect seems perfectly realistic to us. (Alison, in her pre-vowel-shift pronunciation, would presumably have said [te'he].) But it is highly doubtful that anyone ever uttered *tehee,* or *ha-ha,* or *ho-ho,* except as a reflection of the written form. Laughter, like pain, is too paroxysmal in nature, too varying from individual to individual, and too unspeechlike to be represented accurately by symbols that are not even altogether adequate for the representation of speech sounds.

It is somewhat different with a vocal manifestation of disgust, contempt, or annoyance, which might be represented phonetically (but only approximately) as [č]. This was, as early as the mid-fifteenth century, represented as *tush,* and somewhat later less realistically as *twish. Twish* became archaic as a written form, but [təš] survives as a spoken interpretation of *tush.* As in the instances cited, and in other similar ones, sounds came first; then the graphic representation, always somewhat inadequate; then finally a new word in the language based on an interpretation of the graphic representation of what was in the beginning not a word at all, but merely something in the nature of a sound effect.

Pish and *pshaw* likewise represent "natural" emotional utterances of disdain, contempt, impatience, irritation, and the like, and have become so conventionalized as to have been used as verbs, as shown by the citation in *Webster's Third* for *pish:* "pished and pshawed a little at what had happened." Both began as something like [pš]. W. S. Gilbert combined two such utterances to form the name of a "noble lord," Pish-Tush, in *The Mikado,* with two similarly expressive ones, Pooh-Bah, for the overweeningly aristocratic "Lord High Everything Else." Yum-Yum, the name of the delightful heroine of the same opera, is similarly a conventionalized representation of sounds supposedly made as a sign of pleasure in eating. These have given us a new adjective, *yummy,* still childish in its associations—but give it time.

Pew or *pugh* is imitative of the disdainful sniff with which many persons react to a bad smell, resembling a vigorously articulated [p]. But, as with the examples previously cited, it has been conventionalized because of the written form into an actual word pronounced [pyu] or prolongedly as ['pi'yu]. *Pooh* (sometimes with reduplication as *pooh-pooh*) is a variant, with somewhat milder implications. The reduplicated form may be used as a verb, as in "He pooh-poohed my suggestion." *Fie,* used for much the same purposes as *pew,* is now archaic; it likewise represents an attempt at imitation. *Faugh* is probably a variant of *fie;* so, doubtless, is *phew. Ugh,* in its purest form a tensing of the stomach muscles followed by a glottal stop, has not been conventionalized to quite the same extent when used as an exclamation of disgust or horror. As a grunt supposedly made, in pre-ethnic-sensitive days, by American Indians, it is, one hopes only facetiously, pronounced [əg].

A palatal click, articulated by placing the tongue against the palate and then withdrawing it, sucking in the breath, is an expression of impatience or contempt. It is also sometimes used in reduplicated form (there may in fact be three or more such clicks) in scolding children, as if to express shock and regret at some antisocial act. A written form is *tut(-tut),* which has become a word in its own right, pronounced not as a click but according to the spelling. However, *tsk-tsk,* which is intended to represent the same click, is also used with the pronunciation ['tɪsk'tɪsk]. Older written forms are *tchick* and *tck* (with or without reduplication). *Tut(-tut)* has long been used as a verb, as in Bulwer-Lytton's "pishing and tutting" (1849) and Hall Caine's "He laughed and tut-tutted" (1894), both cited by the *OED.*

A sound we frequently make to signify agreement may be represented approximately as [ˌm'hm]. This is written as *uh-huh,* and the written form is altogether responsible for the pronunciation [ˌə'hə]. The *p* of *yep* and *nope* was probably intended to represent the glottal stop frequently heard in the pronunciation of *yes* (without *-s*) and *no,* but one also frequently hears [yɛp] and [nop], which may be pronunciations based on the written forms.

The form *brack* or *braak* is sometimes used to represent the so-called Bronx cheer. Eric Partridge (*Shakespeare's Bawdy* 12, 83) has suggested, however, that Hamlet's "Buz, buz!" (2.2.396), spoken impatiently to Polonius, is intended to represent the vulgar noise also known as "the raspberry." (*Raspberry* in this sense comes from the Cockney rhyming slang phrase *raspberry tart* for *fart.*)

COMBINING WORDS: COMPOUNDING

Creating words from nothing is comparatively rare. Most words are made from other words, for example, by combining whole words or word parts. A **compound** is made by putting two or more words together to form a new word with a meaning in some way different from that of its elements—for instance, a *blackboard* is not the same thing as a *black board;* indeed, nowadays many blackboards are green, or some other color. Compounds may be variably spelled in three ways: solid, hyphenated, or open (*hatchback, laid-back, call back*), as explained below.

From earliest times compounding has been very common in English, as in other Germanic languages as well. Old English has *blīðheort* 'blitheheart(ed),' *eaxlgestella* 'shoulder-companion = comrade,' *brēostnet* 'breast-net = corslet,' *leornungcniht* 'learning retainer (knight) = disciple,' *wǣrloga* 'oath-breaker = traitor (warlock),' *woroldcyning* 'world-king = earthly-king,' *fullfyllan* 'to fulfill,' and many other such compound words.

The compounding process has gone on continuously. Recent examples are *air kiss* 'a kissing motion next to the cheek,' *baby boomer, date rape, downsize, drive-by shooting, ear bud* 'a small receiver placed in the ear to amplify sound, as from a Walkman,' *eye candy* 'an attractive but intellectually undemanding image,' *flat panel* 'a thin computer monitor,' *generation X (Y,* etc.), *glass ceiling, ground zero, mommy* (or *daddy) track, road* (or *air) rage, smart card, soccer mom,* and *voice mail.* The Internet has been particularly fecund in producing new terms, such as *dot bomb* 'a failed Internet business,' a pun on *dot-com* 'a company that operates on the Web' (from the domain suffix ".com"), *Internet café, laptop, pop-under* 'an ad at the bottom of the browser window,' *search engine, webcasting,* and *webmaster.*

Spelling and Pronunciation of Compounds

As far as writing is concerned, compound adjectives are usually hyphenated, like *one-horse, loose-jointed,* and *front-page,* though some that are particularly well established, such as *outgoing, overgrown, underbred,* and *forthcoming,* are solid. It is similar with compound verbs, like *overdo, broadcast, sidestep,* beside *double-date* and *baby-sit,* though these sometimes occur as two words. With the writing of compound nouns the situation is likewise somewhat inconsistent: we write *ice cream, Boy Scout, real estate, post office,* and *high school* as two words; we hyphenate *sit-in, go-between, fire-eater,* and *higher-up;* we write solid *icebox, postmaster,* and *highlight.* But hyphenation varies to some extent with the dictionary one consults, the style books of editors and publishers, and individual whim, among other things. Many compound prepositions like *upon, throughout, into,* and *within* are written solid, but others like *out of* have a space. Also written solid are compound adverbs such as *nevertheless, moreover,* and *henceforth* and compound pronouns like *whoever* and *myself.* (For a study of the writing of compounds, see *Webster's Third New International Dictionary* 30a–31a.)

A more significant characteristic of compounds—one that tells us whether we are dealing with two or more words used independently or as a unit—is their tendency to be more strongly stressed on one or the other of their elements, in contrast to the more or less even stresses characteristic of phrases. A *man-eating shrimp* would be a quite alarming marine phenomenon; nevertheless, the sharply contrasting primary and secondary stresses of *man* and *eat* (symbolized by the hyphen) make it perfectly clear that we are here concerned with a hitherto unheard-of anthropophagous decapod. There is, however, nothing in the least alarming (except perhaps to shrimps) about a *man eating shrimp,* with approximately even stresses on *man* and *eat.*

This primary-secondary type of stress in compounds marks the close connection between the constituents that gives the compound its special meaning. In effect, it welds together the elements and thus makes the difference between the members of the following pairs:

hótbèd: 'place encouraging rapid growth'	hót béd: 'warm sleeping place'
híghbròw: 'intellectual'	hígh bRÓw: 'result of receding hair'
bláckbàll: 'vote against'	bláck báll: 'ball colored black'
gréenhòuse: 'heated structure to grow plants'	gréen hóuse: 'house painted green'
mákeùp: 'cosmetics'	máke úp: 'reconcile'
héadhùnter: 'savage or recruiter of executives'	héad húnter: 'leader on a safari'
lóudspèaker: 'sound amplifier'	lóud spéaker: 'noisy talker'

In compound nouns, it is usually the first element that gets the primary stress, as in all the examples of compound nouns given above, and in adverbs and prepositions the last (*nèverthéléss, withóut*). For verbs and pronouns, it is impossible to generalize (*bróadcàst, fulfíll; sómebody* [or *sómebòdy*], *whòéver*). The important thing is the unifying function of contrasting stress in the formation of compounds of whatever sort.

Generally when complete loss of secondary stress occurs, phonetic change occurs as well. For instance, *Énglish mán*, having in the course of compounding become *Énglish-màn*, proceeded to become *Énglishman* [-mǝn]. The same vowel reduction has occurred in *highwayman* 'robber,' but not in *businessman;* in *gentleman, horseman,* and *postman,* but not in *milkman* and *iceman*. It is similar with the [-lǝnd] of *Maryland, Iceland, woodland,* and *highland* as contrasted with the secondarily stressed final syllables of such newer compounds as *wonderland, movieland,* and *Disneyland;* with the *-folk* of *Norfolk* and *Suffolk* (there is a common American pronunciation of the former with [-ˌfok] and, by assimilation, with [-ˌfɔrk]); and with the *-mouth* of *Portsmouth,* the *-combe* of *Wyecombe,* the *-burgh* of *Edinburgh* (usually [-brǝ]), and the *-stone* of *Folkestone*. Even more drastic changes occur in the final syllables of *coxswain* [ˈkɑksǝn], *Keswick* [ˈkɛzɪk], and *Durham* [ˈdǝrǝm] (though in *Birmingham,* as the name of a city in Alabama, the *-ham* is pronounced as the spelling suggests it should be). Similarly drastic changes occur in both syllables of *boatswain* [ˈbosǝn], *forecastle* [ˈfoksǝl], *breakfast, Christmas* (that is, *Christ's mass*), *cupboard,* and *Greenwich*. (Except for Greenwich Village in New York and Greenwich, Connecticut, the American place name is usually pronounced as spelled, rather than as [grɛnɪč] or [grɛnɪǰ]. The British pronunciation is sometimes [grɪnɪǰ].)

Perhaps it is lack of familiarity with the word—just as the landlubber might pronounce *boatswain* as [ˈbotˌswen]—that has given rise to an analytical pronunciation of *clapboard,* traditionally [ˈklæbǝrd]. *Grindstone* and *wristband* used to be respectively [ˈgrɪnstǝn] and [ˈrɪzbǝnd]. Not many people have much occasion to use either word nowadays; consequently, the older tradition has been lost, and the words now have secondary stress and full vowels instead of [ǝ] in their last elements. The same thing has happened to *waistcoat,* now usually [ˈwestˌkot]; the traditional [ˈwɛskǝt] has become old-fashioned. Lack of familiarity can hardly explain the new analysis of *forehead* as [ˈforˌhɛd] rather than the traditional [ˈfɔrǝd]; a consciousness of the spelling of the word is responsible.

Amalgamated Compounds

The phonetic changes we have been considering have the effect of welding the elements of certain compounds so closely together that, judging from sound (and frequently also from their appearances when written), one would sometimes not suspect that they were indeed compounds. In *daisy,* for instance, phonetic reduction of the final element has caused that element to be identical with a suffix. Geoffrey Chaucer was quite correct when he referred to "The dayesyë, or elles the yë [eye] of day" in the prologue to *The Legend of Good Women,* for the word is really from the Old English compound *dægesēage* 'day's eye.' The *-y* of *daisy* is thus not an affix like the diminutive *-y* of *Katy* or the *-y* from Old English *-ig* of *hazy;* instead, the word is from a historical point of view a compound.

Such closely welded compounds were called **amalgamated** by Arthur G. Kennedy (*Current English* 350), who lists, among a good many others, *as* (OE *eal* 'all' + *swā* 'so'), *garlic* (OE *gār* 'spear' + *lēac* 'leek'), *hussy* (OE *hūs* 'house' + *wīf* 'woman, wife'), *lord* (OE *hlāf* 'loaf' + *weard* 'guardian'), *marshal* (OE *mearh* 'horse' + *scealc* 'servant'), *nostril* (OE *nosu* 'nose' + *þyrel* 'hole'), and *sheriff* (OE *scīr* 'shire' + *(ge)rēfa* 'reeve'). Many proper names are such amalgamated compounds—for instance, among place names, *Boston* ('Botulf's stone'), *Bewley* (Fr. *beau* 'beautiful' + *lieu* 'place'), *Sussex* (OE *sūþ* 'south' + *Seaxe* 'Saxons'; compare *Essex* and *Middlesex*), and *Norwich* (OE *norþ* 'north' + *wīc* 'village'; traditionally pronounced to rime with *porridge,* as in a nursery jingle about a man from Norwich who ate some porridge; the name of the city in Connecticut being, however, pronounced as the spelling seems to indicate). The reader will find plenty of other interesting examples in Eilert Ekwall's *Concise Oxford Dictionary of English Place-Names.* It is similar with surnames (which are, of course, sometimes place names as well)—for instance, *Durward* (OE *duru* 'door' + *weard* 'keeper'), *Purdue* (Fr. *pour* 'for' + *Dieu* 'God'), and *Thurston* ('Thor's stone,' ultimately Scandinavian); and with a good many given names as well—for instance, *Ethelbert* (OE *æðel* 'noble' + *beorht* 'bright'), *Alfred* (OE *ælf* 'elf' + *ræd* 'counsel'), and *Mildred* (OE *milde* 'mild' + *þryþ* 'strength').

Function and Form of Compounds

The making of a compound is inhibited by few considerations other than those dictated by meaning. A compound may be used in any grammatical function: as noun (*wishbone*), pronoun (*anyone*), adjective (*foolproof*), adverb (*overhead*), verb (*gainsay*), conjunction (*whenever*), or preposition (*without*). It may be made up of two nouns (*baseball, mudguard, manhole*); of an adjective followed by a noun (*bluegrass, madman, first-rate*); of a noun followed by an adjective or a participle (*bloodthirsty, trigger-happy, homemade, heartbreaking, time-honored*); of a verb followed by an adverb (*pinup, breakdown, setback, cookout, sit-in*); of an adverb followed by a verb form (*upset, downcast, forerun*); of a verb followed by a noun that is its object (*daredevil, blowgun, touch-me-not*); of a noun followed by a verb (*hemstitch, pan-fry, typeset*); of two verbs (*can-do, look-see, stir-fry*); of an adverb followed by an adjective or a participle (*overanxious, oncoming, well-known, uptight*); of a preposition followed by its object (*overland, indoors*); and of a participle followed by an adverb (*washed-up, carryings-on, worn-out*). There are in addition a number of phrases that have become welded into compounds—for example, *will-o'-the-wisp, happy-go-lucky, mother-in-law, tongue-in-cheek, hand-to-mouth,* and *lighter-than-air.* Many compounds are made up of adjective plus noun plus the ending *-ed*—for example, *baldheaded, dimwitted,* and *hairy-chested*—and some of noun plus noun plus *-ed*—for example, *pigheaded* and *snowcapped.*

COMBINING WORD PARTS: AFFIXING

Affixes from Old English

Another type of combining is **affixation**, the use of prefixes and suffixes. Many affixes were at one time independent words, like the insignificant-seeming *a-* of *aside, alive, aboard,* and *a-hunting,* which was earlier *on* but lost its *-n,* just as *an* did when unstressed and followed by a consonant (135). Another is the *-ly* of many adjectives, like *manly, godly,* and *homely,* which developed from Old English *līc* 'body.' When so used, *līc* (which became *lic* and eventually *-ly* through lack of stress) originally meant something like 'having the body or appearance of': thus the literal meaning of *manly* is 'having the body or form of a man.' Old English regularly added *-e* to adjectives to make adverbs of them (108)—thus *riht* 'right,' *rihte* 'rightly.' Adjectives formed with *-lic* acquired adverbial forms in exactly the same way—thus *cræftlic* 'skillful,' *cræftlice* 'skillfully.' With the late Middle English loss of both final *-e* and final unstressed *-ch,* earlier Middle English *-lich* and *-liche* fell together as *-li* (*-ly*). Because of these losses, we do not ordinarily associate Modern English *-ly* with *like,* the Northern dialect form of the full word that ultimately was to prevail in all dialects of English. In Modern English, the full form has been used again as a suffix—history thus repeating itself—as in *gentlemanlike* and *godlike,* which are quite distinct creations from *gentlemanly* and *godly.*

Other prefixes surviving from Old English times include the following:

AFTER-: as in *aftermath, aftereffect, afternoon*

BE-: the unstressed form of *by* (OE *bī*), as in *believe, beneath, beyond, behalf, between*

FOR-: either intensifying, as in *forlorn,* or negating, as in *forbid, forswear*

MIS-: as in *misdeed, misalign, mispronounce*

OUT-: Old English *ūt-,* as in *outside, outfield, outgo*

UN-: for an opposite or negative meaning, as in *undress, undo, unafraid, un-English; uncola* was originally an advertising slogan for the soft drink 7 Up as an alternative to colas but was metaphorically extended in "France [wants] to become the world's next great 'Uncola,' the leader of the alternative coalition to American power" (*New York Times,* Feb. 26, 2003, A-27/5)

UNDER-: as in *understand, undertake, underworld*

UP-: as in *upright, upheaval, upkeep*

WITH-: 'against,' as in *withhold, withstand, withdraw*

Other suffixes that go back at least to Old English times are the following:

-DOM: Old English *dōm,* earlier an independent word that has developed into *doom,* in Old English meaning 'judgment, statute,' that is, 'what is set,' and related to *do;* as in *freedom, filmdom, kingdom*

-ED: used to form adjectives from nouns, as in *storied, crabbed, bowlegged*

-EN: also to form adjectives, as in *golden, oaken, leaden*

-ER: Old English *-ere,* to form nouns of agency, as in *singer, baby sitter, do-gooder,* a suffix that, when it occurs in loanwords—for instance, *butler* (from Anglo-French *butuiller* 'bottler, manservant having to do with wines and liquors') and *butcher* (from Old French, literally 'dealer in flesh of billy goats')—goes back to Latin *-ārius,* but that is nevertheless cognate with the English ending

-FUL: to form adjectives, as in *baleful, sinful, wonderful,* and, with secondary stress, to form nouns as well, as in *handful, mouthful, spoonful*

-HOOD: Old English *-hād,* as in *childhood* and *priesthood,* earlier an independent word meaning 'condition, quality'

-ING: Old English *-ung* or *-ing,* to form verbal nouns, as in *reading*

-ISH: Old English *-isc,* to form adjectives, as in *English* and *childish*

-LESS: Old English *-lēas* 'free from,' also used independently and cognate with *loose,* as in *wordless, reckless, hopeless*

-NESS: to form abstract nouns from many adjectives (and some participles), as in *friendliness, learnedness, obligingness*

-SHIP: Old English *-scipe,* to form abstract nouns, as in *lordship, fellowship, worship* (that is, 'worth-ship')

-SOME: Old English *-sum,* to form adjectives, as in *lonesome, wholesome, winsome* (OE *wynn* 'joy' + *sum*)

-STER: Old English *-estre,* originally feminine, as in *spinster* 'female spinner' and *webster* 'female weaver,' but later losing all sexual connotation, as in *gangster* and *speedster*

-TH: to form abstract nouns, as in *health, depth, sloth*

-WARD: as in *homeward, toward, outward*

-Y: Old English *-ig,* to form adjectives as in *thirsty, greedy, bloody*

There are several homonymous *-y* suffixes in addition to the one of Old English origin. The diminutive *-y* (or *-ie*) of *Kitty, Jackie,* and *baby* is from another source and occurs first in Middle English times. It is living; that is, it is still available for forming new diminutives, just as we continue to form adjectives with the *-y* from Old English *-ig*—for example, *jazzy, loony, iffy.* The *-y*'s in loanwords of Greek (*phlebotomy*), Latin (*century*), and French (*contrary*) origin may represent Greek *-ia* (*hysteria*), Latin *-ius, -ium, -ia* (*radius, medium, militia*), or French *-ie* (*perjury*), *-ee* (*army*). This *-y* is not a living suffix.

Many of the affixes from Old English are still living, in that they may be used for the creation of new words. Most have been affixed to nonnative words, as in *mispronounce, obligingness, czardom, pocketful, Romish, coffeeless, orderly* (*-liness*), and *sugary* (*-ish*). A number of others very common in Old English times either have not survived at all or survive only as fossils, like *ge-* in *enough* (OE *genōg, genōh*), *afford* (OE *geforðian*), *aware* (OE *gewǣr*), *handiwork* (OE *handgeweorc*), and *either* (OE *ǣgðer,* a contracted form of *ǣg[e]hwæðer*). *And-* 'against, toward,' the English cognate of Latin *anti-*, survives only in *answer* (OE *andswaru,* literally 'a swearing against') and, in unstressed form with loss of both *n* and *d,* in *along* (OE *andlang*).

Affixes from Other Languages

Those languages with which English has had the closest cultural contacts—Latin, Greek, and French—have furnished a number of freely used affixes for English words. The combination of native and foreign morphemes began quite early and has never ceased, though in earlier times it was the English suffix that was joined to the borrowed word rather than the other way round, as in Old English *grammatisc* 'grammatish,' later supplanted by *grammatical.* Since English has a lexicon culled from many sources, it is not surprising that one finds a good many such **hybrid forms**.

One of the most commonly used prefixes of nonnative origin is Greek *anti-* 'against,' which, in addition to its occurrence in long-established learned words like *antipathy, antidote,* and *anticlimax,* has been freely used since the seventeenth century for new, mostly American, creations—for instance, *anti-Federalist, anti-Catholic, antitobacco, antislavery, antisaloon, antiaircraft,* and *antiabortion. Pro-* 'for' has been somewhat less productive. *Super-,* as in *superman, supermarket,* and *superhighway,* has even become an informal adjective, as in "Our new car's super"; there is also a reduplicated form *superduper* 'very super.' Other foreign prefixes are *ante-, de-, dis-, ex-, inter-, multi-, neo-, non-, post-, pre-, pseudo-, re-, semi-, sub-,* and *ultra-.* Even rare foreign prefixes like *eu-* ('good' from Greek) have novel uses; J. R. R. Tolkien invented *eucatastrophe* as an impressive term for 'happy ending.'

Borrowed suffixes that have been added to English words (whatever their ultimate origin) include, but are by no means limited to, the following:

-ESE: Latin *-ēnsis* by way of Old French, as in *federalese, journalese, educationese*

-(I)AN: Latin *-(i)ānus,* used to form adjectives from nouns, as in *Nebraskan, Miltonian*

-(I)ANA: from the neuter plural of the same Latin ending, which has a limited use nowadays in forming nouns from other nouns, as in *Americana, Menckeniana*

-ICIAN: Latin *-ic-* + *-iānus,* as in *beautician, mortician*

-IZE: Greek *-izein,* a very popular suffix for making verbs, as in *pasteurize, criticize, harmonize*

-OR: Latin, as in *chiropractor* and *realtor*

-ORIUM: Latin, as in *pastorium* 'Baptist parsonage,' *crematorium* 'place used for cremation,' *cryotorium* 'place where frozen dead are stored until science can reanimate them'

One of the most used of borrowed suffixes is *-al* (Lat. *-alis*), which makes adjectives from nouns, as in *doctoral, fusional, hormonal,* and *tidal.* The continued productivity of that suffix can be seen in the decree of a chief censor for the NBC television network: "No frontal nudity, no backal nudity, and no sidal nudity."

Voguish Affixes

Though no one can say why—fashion would seem to be the principal determinant—certain affixes have been particularly popular during certain periods. For instance, *-wise* affixed to nouns and adjectives to form adverbs was practically archaic until approximately the 1940s, occurring only in a comparatively few well-established words, such as *likewise, lengthwise, otherwise,* and *crosswise.* The *OED* cites a few examples of its free use in modern times—for instance, *Cardinal-wise* (1677), *festoonwise* (1743), and *Timothy-* or *Titus-wise* (1876). But around 1940 a mighty proliferation of words in *-wise* began—for instance, *budgetwise, saleswise, weatherwise,* and *healthwise*—and literally hundreds of others continue to be invented: *drugwise, personalitywise, securitywise, timewise, salarywise,* and *fringe-benefitwise.* Such use of *-wise* can hardly be written off as ephemeral. Because of their economy in circumventing such phrases as *in respect of* and *in the manner of,* many such coinages are useful additions to the language.

Type has enjoyed a similar vogue and is freely used as a suffix. It forms adjectives from nouns, as in "Catholic-type bishops" and "a Las Vegas–type revue." Like *-wise, -type* is also economical, enabling us to shortcut such locutions as *bishops of the Catholic type* and *a revue of the Las Vegas type.*

The suffix *-ize* has already been mentioned. Ultimately from Greek *-izein,* it has had a centuries-old life as a means of making verbs from nouns and adjectives, not only in English, but in other languages as well—for instance, French *-iser,* Italian *-izare,* Spanish *-izar,* and German *-isieren.* Many English words with this suffix are borrowings from French—for instance (with *z* for French *s*), *authorize, moralize, naturalize;* others are English formations (though some of them may have parallel formations in French)—for instance, *concertize, patronize, fertilize;* still others are formed from proper names—for instance, *bowdlerize, mesmerize, Americanize.* This suffix became very productive around 1950, and dozens of new creations have come into being, such as *accessorize, moisturize, sanitize, glamorize, tenderize,* and *personalize* 'to mark with name, initials, or monogram' (in other senses—for example, 'personify'—this word is considerably older but is almost certainly a new creation in the sense specified). The most widely discussed of all these creations, however, must surely be *finalize,* which descended to general use from the celestial mists of bureaucracy, business, and industry, where nothing is merely ended, finished, or concluded. It is a great favorite of administrators of all kinds and sizes—including the academic.

In Greek, nouns of action were formed from verbs in *-izein* by modifying the ending to *-ismos* or *-isma*, as reflected in many pairs of loanwords in English, such as *ostracize-ostracism* and *criticize-criticism*. Several new uses of the suffix *-ism* have developed. The prejudice implied in *racism* has extended to *sexism, ageism,* and *speciesism* 'human treatment of other animals as mere objects.' Other popular derivatives are *Me-ism* 'selfishness,' *foodism* 'gluttony,' *volunteerism* 'donated service,' and *presidentialism* 'respect for and confidence in the office of president.' The suffix *-ism* is also used as an independent word, as in "creeds and *isms.*" Such use of suffixes must be rather rare, though *-ology* has also been so used to mean 'science,' as in "Chemistry, Geology, Philology, and a hundred other *ologies.*" Prefixes have fared somewhat better; *anti-, pro-, con-,* and *ex-* are all used also as nouns.

De-, a prefix of Latin origin with negative force, is still much alive. Though many words beginning with it are from Latin or French, it has for centuries been used for the formation of new words. *Demoralize* was claimed by Noah Webster as his only coinage, and it is a fact that he was the first to use it in English; but it could just as well be from French *démoraliser.* The prefix is used before words of whatever origin, as in *defrost, dewax,* and *debunk.* Other and more pompous specimens are *debureaucratize, dewater, deinsectize,* and *deratizate* 'get rid of rats.' Two other *de-* words that are more familiar nowadays are *decontaminate* and *dehumidify,* though they may seem to be merely pompous ways of saying 'purify' and 'dry out.' A somewhat different sense of the prefix in *debark* has led to *debus, detrain,* and *deplane. Dis-,* likewise from Latin, is also freely used in a negative function, particularly in officialese, as in *disincentive* 'deterrent,' *disassemble* 'take apart,' and *dissaver* 'one who does not save money.'

Perhaps as a result of an ecologically motivated decision that smaller is better, the prefix *mini-* enjoys maxi use. *Miniskirt,* first used in 1965, set the fashion. Among the new combinations into which *mini-* has entered are *mini–black holes, minicar* and *minibus, minicam* 'miniature camera,' the seemingly contradictory *mini-conglomerate* and *minimogul, minilecture, minimall,* and *minirevolution.* The form *mini,* which is a short version of *miniature,* came to be used as an independent adjective, and even acquired a comparative form, as in a *New Yorker* magazine report, "Fortunately, the curator of ornithology decided to give another talk, mini-er than the first." Despite ecological respect for *mini-,* the *minicinema* has given way to the *Theater Max,* whose second term is a mini version of *mini*'s antonym, *maxi.*

Another voguish affix is *non-,* from Latin, as in *nonsick* 'healthy' and *non-availability* 'lack.' *Non-* has also developed two new uses: first, to indicate a scornful attitude toward the thing denoted by the main word, as in *nonbook* 'book not intended for normal reading, such as a coffee-table art book'; and second, to indicate that the person or object denoted by the main word is dissimulating or has been disguised, as in *noncandidate* 'candidate who pretends not to be running for office.' Others are *-ee,* from French, as in *hijackee, hiree* 'new employee,' *mentee* 'person receiving the attention of a mentor,' *returnee* 'returner,' and *trustee;* and *re-,* from Latin, as in *re-decontaminate* 'purify again,' *recivilianize* 'return to civilian life,' and *recondition* 'repair, restore.' The scientific suffix *-on,* from Greek, has been widely used in recent years to name newly discovered substances like *interferon* in the human bloodstream and posited subatomic particles like the *gluon* and the *graviton.* Perhaps an extension of the *-s* in disease names like *measles* and *shingles* has supplied the ending of words like *dumbs* and *smarts,* as in "The administration has been stricken with a long-term case of dumbs" and "He's got street-smarts" (that is, 'knowledge about the ways of life in the streets').

New suffixes are still being introduced into English. From such Yiddishisms as *nudnik,* but reinforced by the Russian *sputnik,* comes *-nik,* generally used in a derogatory way: *beatnik, no-goodnik, peacenik* 'pacifist,' *foundation-nik* 'officer of a foundation,' and *refusednik* 'person denied a visa to enter or leave Russia.' Of uncertain origin, but perhaps combining the ending of such Spanish words as *amigo, chicano,* and *gringo* with the English exclamation *oh,* is an informal suffix used to make nouns like *ammo, cheapo* 'stingy person,' *combo, daddy-o, kiddo, politico, sicko* 'psychologically unstable person,' *supremo* 'leader,' *weirdo,* and *wrongo* 'mistake'; adjectives like *blotto* 'drunk,' *sleazo* 'sleazy,' *socko* and *boffo* 'highly successful,' and *stinko;* and exclamations like *cheerio* and *righto.* Equally voguish are a number of affixes that have been created in English by a process of blending: *agri-, docu-, e-, Euro-, petro-,* and *syn-; -aholic, -ateria, -gate, -rama,* and *-thon.* These affixes and the process through which they come into being are discussed below under "Blending Words."

SHORTENING WORDS

Clipped Forms

A **clipped form** is a shortening of a longer word that sometimes supplants the latter altogether. Thus, *mob* supplanted *mobile vulgus* 'movable, or fickle, common people'; and *omnibus,* in the sense 'motor vehicle for paying passengers,' is almost as archaic as *mobile vulgus,* having been clipped to *bus.* The clipping of *omnibus,* literally 'for all,' is a strange one because *bus* is merely part of the dative plural ending *-ibus* of the Latin pronoun *omnis* 'all.' *Periwig,* like the form *peruke* (Fr. *perruque*), of which it is a modification, is completely gone; only the abbreviated *wig* survives, and those who use it are not likely to be even slightly aware of the full form. *Taxicab* has completely superseded *taximeter cabriolet* and has, in turn, supplied us with two new words, *taxi* and *cab.* As a shortening of *cabriolet, cab* is almost a century older than *taxicab. Pantaloons* seems quite archaic. The clipped form *pants* has won the day completely. *Bra* has similarly replaced *brassiere,* which in French means a shoulder strap (derived from *bras* 'arm') or a bodice fitted with such straps.

Other abbreviated forms more commonly used than the longer ones include *phone, zoo, extra, flu, auto,* and *ad. Zoo* is, of course, from *zoological garden* with the pronunciation [zu] from the spelling, a pronunciation now sometimes extended back to the longer form as [zuə-] rather than the traditional [zoə-]. *Extra,* which is probably a clipping from *extraordinary,* has become a separate word. *Auto,* like the full form *automobile,* is rapidly losing ground to *car,* an abbreviated form of *motorcar.* In time *auto* may become archaic. *Advertisement* has become *ad* in American English but was clipped less drastically to *advert* in British English, though *ad* is gaining ground in England. *Razz,* a clipped form of *raspberry* 'Bronx cheer' used as either noun or verb, is doubtless more frequent than the full form.

Later clippings have included the nouns *bio* (*biography, biographical sketch*), *fax* (*facsimile*), *high tech* 'technologically sophisticated,' *perk* (*perquisite*), *photo op* (*photographic opportunity*), *prenup* (prenuptial agreement), *soap* (*soap opera*), and *telecom* (*telecommunications*). Clipped adjectives are *op-ed* 'pertaining to the page opposite the editorial page, on which syndicated columns and other "think pieces" are printed' and *pop,* derived from *popular,* as in "pop culture," "pop art," and "pop sociology." *Hype* is used as either a noun 'advertising, publicity stunt' or a verb 'stimulate artificially, promote'; apparently it is a clipping of *hypo,* which, in turn, is a clipping of *hypodermic needle,* thus reflecting the influence of the drug subculture on Madison Avenue and hence on the rest of us. Another clipped verb is *rehab,* from *rehabilitate,* as in "Young people are rehabbing a lot of the old houses in the inner city."

As the foregoing examples illustrate, clipping can shorten a form by cutting between words (*soap opera* > *soap*) or between morphemes (*biography* > *bio*). But it often ignores lexical and morphemic boundaries and cuts instead in the middle of a morpheme (*popular* > *pop, rehabilitate* > *rehab*). In so doing, it creates new morphemes and thus enriches the stock of potential building material for making other words. In *helicopter,* the *-o-* is the combining element between Greek *helic-* (the stem of *helix,* as in the *double helix* structure of DNA) 'spiral' and *pter(on)* 'wing,' but the word has been mistakenly analyzed as *heli-copter* rather than as *helic-o-pter* and, in addition to the independent *copter,* we have *heliport* 'a terminal for helicopters.'

Initialisms: Alphabetisms and Acronyms

An extreme kind of clipping is the use of the initial letters of words (*HIV, YMCA*), or sometimes of syllables (*TB, TV, PJs* 'pajamas'), as words. Usually the motive for this clipping is either brevity or catchiness, though sometimes euphemism may be involved, as with old-fashioned *BO, BM,* and *VD.* Perhaps *TB* also was euphemistic in the beginning, when the disease was a much direr threat to life than it now is and its very name was uttered in hushed tones. When such **initialisms** are pronounced with the names of the letters of the alphabet, they can be called **alphabetisms**. Other examples are *CD* 'compact disk' and *HOV* 'high occupancy vehicle' (*lane*).

One of the oldest English alphabetisms, and by far the most successful one, is *OK.* Allen Walker Read (in six articles available in Richard Bailey's edition of Read's *Milestones in the History of English in America*) traced the history of the form to 1839, showing that it originated as a clipping of *oll korrect,* a playful misspelling that was part of a fad for orthographic jokes and abbreviations. It was then used as a pun on *Old Kinderhook,* the nickname of Martin Van Buren during his political campaign of 1840. Efforts to trace the word to more exotic sources—including Finnish, Choctaw, Burmese, Greek, and more recently African languages—have been unsuccessful but will doubtless continue to challenge the ingenuity of amateur etymologists.

It is inevitable that it should have dawned on some waggish genius that the initial letters of words in certain combinations frequently made a pronounceable sequence of letters. Thus, the abbreviation for the military phrase *absent without official leave, AWOL,* came to be pronounced not only as a sequence of the four letter names, but also as though they were the spelling for an ordinary word, *awol* ['e‚wɔl]. It was, of course, even better if the initials spelled out an already existing word, as those of *white Anglo-Saxon Protestant* spell out *Wasp.* There had to be a learned term to designate such words, and **acronym** was coined from Greek *akros* 'tip' and *onyma* 'name,' by analogy with *homonym.* There are also mixed examples in which the two systems of pronunciation are combined—for example, *VP* '*V*ice *P*resident' pronounced and sometimes spelled *veep* and *ROTC* '*R*eserve *O*fficers *T*raining *C*orps' pronounced like "rotcy."

The British seem to have beaten Americans to the discovery of the joys of making acronyms, even though the impressively learned term to designate what is essentially a letters game was probably born in America. In any case, as early as World War I days the *Defence* [sic, in British spelling] *of the Realm Act* was called *Dora* and members of the *Women's Royal Naval Service* were called (with the insertion of a vowel) *Wrens. Wrens* inspired the World War II American *Wac* (from *Women's Army Corps*) and a number of others—our happiest being *Spar* 'woman Coast Guard,' from the motto of the U.S. Coast Guard, *Semper Paratus.*

The euphemistic *fu* words—the most widely known is *snafu*—are also among the acronymic progeny of World War II. Less well known today are *snafu*'s humorous comparative, *tarfu* '*t*hings *a*re *r*eally *f*ouled *up*,' and superlative, *fubar* '*f*ouled *up b*eyond *a*ll *r*ecognition' (to use the euphemism to which *Webster's Third New International Dictionary* had recourse in etymologizing *snafu* as '*s*ituation *n*ormal *a*ll *f*ouled *up*'). Initialisms are sometimes useful in avoiding taboo terms, the shortest and probably best-known example being *f-word,* on the etymology of whose referent Allen Walker Read published an early article, "An Obscenity Symbol," without ever using the word in question.

The acronymic process has sometimes been reversed or at least conflated; for example, *Waves,* which resembles a genuine acronym, most likely preceded or accompanied the origin of its phony-sounding source, '*W*omen *A*ccepted for *V*olunteer *E*mergency *S*ervice.' That is, to ensure a good match, the creation of the acronym and the phrase it stands for were simultaneous. The following are also probably reverse acronyms: *JOBS* '*J*ob *O*pportunities in the *B*usiness *S*ector,' *NOW* '*N*ational *O*rganization for *W*omen,' and *ZIP* '*Z*one *I*mprovement *P*lan.'

Acronyms lend themselves to humorous uses. *Bomfog* has been coined as a term for the platitudes and pieties that candidates for public office are wont to utter; it stands for '*B*rotherhood *of M*an, *F*atherhood *of G*od.' *Yuppie* is from '*y*oung

*u*rban *professional*' + *-ie*. *Wysiwyg* ['wɪzɪ,wɪg] is a waggish computer term from
'*W*hat *y*ou *see is w*hat *y*ou *g*et,' denoting a monitor display that is identical in
appearance with the corresponding printout. Another is *gigo* for '*g*arbage *in*,
*g*arbage *out*,' reminding us that what a computer puts out is no better than what we
put in it. The Internet has spawned a massive number of such initialisms used as
an esoteric code among the initiated, such as *IM* '*i*nstant *m*essaging' and *imho* '*in
my h*umble *o*pinion.'

Other initialisms are used in full seriousness and have become part of the
everyday lives of millions of Americans. For example, *CB* (citizens' *b*and radio) is
used by countless *CBers* while driving their *RVs* (recreational *v*ehicles, such as
"motor homes") or *SUVs* (sport-*u*tility *v*ehicles). Even more serious is the *SWAT*
(*s*pecial *w*eapons *a*nd *t*actics) team or force, which is deployed in highly dangerous police assignments such as flushing out snipers. When astronauts first reached
the moon, they traveled across its surface in a *lem* (*l*unar *e*xcursion *m*odule). Other
technical acronyms are *radar* (*ra*dio *d*etecting *a*nd *r*anging) and *laser* (*l*ight *a*mpli-
fication by *s*timulated *e*mission of *r*adiation). Now we are concerned with alphabetisms like *DNA* (*d*eoxyribo*n*ucleic *a*cid) and *DVD* (*d*igital *v*ideo *d*isc) and with
acronyms like *NASA* (*N*ational *A*eronautics and *S*pace *A*dministration), *PAC* (*p*olit-
ical *a*ction *c*ommittee), and *DWEM* (*d*ead *w*hite *E*uropean *m*ale).

Apheretic and Aphetic Forms

A special type of clipping, **apheresis** (or for the highly learned, *aphaeresis*), is
the omission of sounds from the beginning of a word, as in childish "'Scuse me"
and "I did it 'cause I wanted to." Frequently this phenomenon has resulted in two
different words—for instance, *fender-defender, fence-defense,* and *sport-disport*—
in which the first member of each pair is simply an **apheretic form** of the second.
The meanings of *etiquette* and its apheretic form *ticket* have become rather sharply
differentiated, the primary meaning of French *etiquette* being preserved in the
English shortening. Sometimes, however, an apheretic form is merely a variant of
the longer form—for instance, *possum-opossum* and *coon-raccoon*.

When a single sound is omitted at the beginning of a word and that sound is an
unstressed vowel, we have a special variety of apheresis called **aphesis**. Aphesis
is a phonological process in that it results from lack of stress on the elided vowel.
Examples are *cute-acute, squire-esquire,* and *lone-alone*.

Back-Formations

Back-formation is the making of a new word from an older word that is mistakenly assumed to be a derivative of it, as in *to burgle* from *burglar,* the final *ar* of
which suggests that the word is a noun of agency and hence ought to mean 'one
who burgles.' The facetious *to ush* from *usher* and *to buttle* from *butler* are similar.

Pease (an obsolete form of the word *pea*, as in the "pease porridge" of a nursery rime) has a final consonant [z], which is not, as it seems to the ear to be, the

English plural suffix -*s;* it is, in fact, not a suffix at all but merely the last sound of the word (OE *pise*). But by the seventeenth century *pease* was mistaken for a plural, and a new singular, *pea,* was derived from a word that was itself singular, precisely as if we were to derive **chee* from *cheese* under the impression that *cheese* was plural; then we should have *one chee, two chees,* just as we now have *one pea, two peas. Cherry* has been derived by an identical process from Old English *ciris,* a Latin loanword (compare Fr. *cerise*), the final *s* having been assumed to be the plural suffix. Similarly, *sherry wine* was once *sherris wine,* named for the city in Spain where the wine was originally made, Xeres (now Jerez). (In Spanish, *x* formerly had the value [š], so the English spelling was perfectly phonetic.) Similarly, the wonderful one-hoss *shay* of Oliver Wendell Holmes's poem was so called because of the notion that *chaise* was a plural form, and the *Chinee* of a Bret Harte poem is similarly explained.

Other nouns in the singular that look like plural forms are *alms* (OE *ælmysse,* from Lat. *eleēmosyna*), *riches* (ME *richesse* 'wealth'), and *molasses.* The first two are in fact now construed as plurals. Nonstandard *those molasses* assumes the existence of a singular *that *molass,* though such a form is not indeed heard. People who sell women's hose, however, sometimes refer to a single stocking, or perhaps to a pair collectively, as a "very nice hoe," and salesclerks for men's clothing have been reported as speaking of "a fine pant" instead of "a pair of pants." When television talk-show host Johnny Carson responded to a single handclap with, "That was a wonderful applaw," his joke reflected the same tendency in English that leads to the serious use of *kudo* as a new singular for *kudos,* although the latter, a loanword from Greek, is singular itself.

The adverb *darkling* 'in the darkness' (*dark* + adverbial -*ling,* a suffix that in Old English denoted direction, extent, or something of the sort) has been misunderstood as a present participial form, giving rise to a new verb *darkle,* as in Lord Byron's "Her cheek began to flush, her eyes to sparkle, / And her proud brow's blue veins to swell and darkle" (*Don Juan* 6.101), in which *darkle* is construed to mean 'to grow dark.' A few years previously, in his "Ode to a Nightingale," Keats had used *darkling* in "Darkling I listen; and, for many a time, / I have been half in love with easeful Death," where it presumably has the historical adverbial sense. This is not to say that Byron misunderstood Keats's line; the examples merely show how easily the verb might have developed as a back-formation from the adverb. *Grovel,* the first recorded use of which is by Shakespeare, comes to us by way of a similar misconception of *groveling* (*grufe* 'face down' + -*ling*), and *sidle* is likewise from *sideling* 'sidelong.' An intentional humorous assumption of -*ing* as a participial ending occurs in J. K. Stephen's immortal "When the Rudyards cease from Kipling, / And the Haggards ride no more." There is a similar play in the popular joke "Do you like Kipling?" "I don't know—I've never kippled."

There is another species of back-formation, in which the secondary form could just as well have been the primary one, and in which no misunderstanding is involved. *Typewriter,* of American origin, came before the verb *typewrite;* nevertheless, the ending -*er* of *typewriter* is actually a noun-of-agency ending (in early use, *typewriter* referred to either the machine or its operator), so the verb could just as well have come first, only it didn't. It is similar with *housekeep* from *housekeeper* (or *housekeeping*), *baby-sit* from *baby sitter,* and *bargain-hunt* from *bargain hunter.* The adjective *housebroken* 'excretorily adapted to the indoors' is older than the verb *housebreak;* but, since *housebroken* is actually a compounding of *house* and the past participle *broken,* the process might just as well have been the other way around—except that it wasn't.

BLENDING WORDS

The blending of two existing words to make a new word was doubtless an unconscious process in the oldest periods of our language. The *haþel* 'nobleman' in line 1138 of the late fourteenth-century masterpiece *Sir Gawain and the Green Knight* is apparently a blend of *aþel* (OE *æþele* 'noble') and *haleþ* (OE *hæleþ* 'man'). Other early examples, with the dates of their earliest occurrence as given in the *OED,* are *flush* (*flash* + *gush*) [1548]; *twirl* (*twist* + *whirl*) [1598]; *dumfound* (apparently *dumb* + *confound*) [1653]; and *flurry* (*flutter* + *hurry*) [1698].

Lewis Carroll (Charles Lutwidge Dodgson) made a great thing of such **blends**, which he called **portmanteau words**, particularly in his "Jabberwocky" poem. A portmanteau (from Fr. *porter* 'to carry' + *manteau* 'mantle') was a term for a large suitcase with two halves that opened like a book on a center hinge; Carroll said that the words were like that: they contained "two meanings packed up into one word." Two of his creations, *chortle* (*chuckle* + *snort*) and, to a lesser degree, *galumph* (*gallop* + *triumph*), have become established in the language. His *snark,* a blend of *snake* and *shark,* though widely known, failed to find a place because there was no need for it. The author of *Alice through the Looking Glass* had an endearing passion for seeing things backwards, as indicated by his pen name: *Carolus* is the Latin equivalent of *Charles,* and *Lutwidge* must have suggested to him German *Ludwig,* the equivalent of English *Lewis. Charles Lutwidge* thus became (in reverse) *Lewis Carroll.*

Among the most successful of blends are *smog* (*smoke* + *fog*) and *motel* (*motor* + *hotel*). *Urinalysis* (*urine* + *analysis*) first appeared in 1889 and has since attained to scientific respectability, as have the more recent *quasar* (*quasi* + *stellar [object]*) and *pulsar* (*pulse* + *quasar*). *Cafetorium* (*cafeteria* + *auditorium*) has made considerable headway in American public school systems for a large room with the double purpose indicated by it. Boy Scouts have *camporees* (*camp* + *jamboree*), and a favorite Sunday meal is *brunch* (*breakfast* + *lunch*). Other recent blends are *Ebonics* (*ebony* + *phonics*), *e-tail* (*e-* 'electronic' + *retail*), *modem* (*modulator* + *demodulator*), and *nutraceutical* (*nutrition* + *pharmaceutical*).

Blends are easy to create, which is doubtless why there are so very many of them, and they are popular. They can be found in discussions of almost every subject. Science fiction readers and writers get in touch with one another through the *fanzine* (*fan* + *magazine*). Changes in sexual mores have given rise to *palimony* (*pal* + *alimony*) for unmarried ex-partners, and *sexploitation* is the response of the entertainment industry to freedom of choice.

New Morphemes from Blending

Blending can, and frequently does, create new morphemes or give new meanings to old ones. For instance, in German *Hamburger* 'pertaining to, or associated with, Hamburg,' the *-er* is affixed to the name of the city. This adjectival suffix may be joined to any place name in German—for example, *Braunschweiger Wurst* 'Brunswick sausage,' *Wiener Schnitzel* 'Vienna cutlet,' and the like. In English, however, the word *hamburger* was blended so often with other words (*cheeseburger* being the chief example, but also *steakburger, chickenburger, Vegeburger,* and a host of others) that the form *burger* came to be used as an independent word. Compounds of it now denote a sandwich containing a patty of some kind. A similar culinary example is the *eggwich* and the commercially promoted *Spamwich,* which have not so far, however, made *-wich* into an independent word.

Automobile, taken from French, was originally a combination of Greek *autos* 'self' and Latin *mobilis* 'movable.' *Auto-* is a combining form with the same meaning in *autohypnosis, autograph, autobiography,* and a great many other words. But *automobile* was blended to produce new forms like *autocar, autobus,* and *autocamp.* The result is a new word, *auto,* with a meaning quite different from that of the original combining form. One of the new blendings, *autocade,* has the ending of *cavalcade,* which also appears in *aquacade, motorcade,* and *tractorcade,* with the sense of *-cade* as either 'pageant' or 'procession.' The second element of *automobile* has acquired a combining function as well, as in *bookmobile* 'library on wheels' and *bloodmobile* 'blood bank on wheels.'

Productive new prefixes are *e-* from *electronic,* as in *e-mail, e-business, e-commerce, e-ticket* (on an airline); *eco-* from *ecology,* as in *ecofreak, ecosphere, ecotourism; bio-* from *biological,* as in *biocontrol, bioethics, biotechnology.* Other new morphemes formed by blending are *-holic* 'addict, one who habitually does or uses whatever the first part of the word denotes,' and *-thon* 'group activity lasting for an extended time and designed to raise money for a charitable cause.' The first of those morphemes is the result of blending *alcoholic* with other words—for example, *credaholic* (from *credit*), *chocoholic* (from *chocolate*), *pokerholic, potatochipoholic, punaholic, sexaholic, sleepaholic, spendaholic,* and the most frequent of such trivia, *workaholic.* The second morpheme is the tail end of *marathon,* whence the notion of endurance in such charitable affairs as a *showerthon* (during which students took turns showering for 360 continuous hours to raise money for the American Cancer Society), a *fastathon* (in which young people all fasted for thirty hours to raise money for the needy), and a *cakethon* (a five-hour auction of homemade cakes for the Heart Association); other examples are *bikeathon, Putt-Putt-athon* (from *Putt-Putt* 'commercial miniature golf'), *quiltathon, radiothon, teeter-totter-athon,* and *wakeathon.*

Another old morpheme given a new sense by blending is *gate*. After the forced resignation of Richard Nixon from the presidency, the term *Watergate* (the name of the apartment-house and office complex where the events began that led to his downfall) became a symbol for scandal and corruption, usually involving some branch of government and often with official efforts to cover up the facts. In that sense, the word was blended with a variety of other terms to produce such new words as *Info-gate, Irangate* (also called *Armsgate, Contragate, Northgate,* and *Reagangate,* both the latter after the two principal persons involved in it), *Koreagate, Oilgate, Peanutgate,* and many another. Although use of *-gate* began as a topical allusion, the formative shows remarkable staying power. New words made with it continue to appear; for example, *Buckinghamgate* (news leaks from the royal palace) and *papergate* (the writing of bad checks by members of Congress).

Folk Etymology

Folk etymology—the naive misunderstanding of a more or less esoteric word that makes it into something more familiar and hence seems to give it a new etymology, false though it be—is a minor kind of blending. Spanish *cucaracha* 'wood louse' has thus been modified to *cockroach,* though the justly unpopular creature so named is neither a cock nor a roach in the earlier sense of the word (that is, a freshwater fish). By the clipping of the term to its second element, *roach* has come to mean what *cucaracha* originally meant.

A neat example of how the folk-etymological process works is furnished by the experience of a German teacher of ballet who attended classes in modern dance at an American university in order to observe American teaching techniques. During one of these classes, she heard a student describe a certain ballet jump, which he referred to as a "soda box." Genuinely mystified, she inquired about the term. The student who had used it and other members of the class averred that it was precisely what they always said and that it was spelled as they pronounced it—*soda box.* What they had misheard from their instructor was the practically universal ballet term *saut de basque* 'Basque leap.' One cannot but wonder how widespread the folk-etymologized term is in American schools of the dance.

A classified advertisement in a college town newspaper read in part "Stove, table & chairs, bed and Chester drawers." The last named item of furniture is what is more conventionally called a *chest of drawers,* but the pronunciation of that term in fast tempo has led many a hearer to think of it as named for an otherwise unknown person. Sometimes our misunderstanding is aided by sheer and amazing coincidence. As a child too young to read, one of the authors of this book misheard *artificial snow* as *Archie Fisher snow,* a plausible enough boner for one who lived in a town in which a prominent merchant was named Archie Fisher. In any case, Mr. Fisher displayed the stuff in his window, and for all an innocent child knew he might even have invented it.

When this sort of misunderstanding of a word becomes widespread, we have acquired a new item in the English lexicon—one that usually completely displaces the old one and frequently seems far more appropriate than the displaced word. Thus *crayfish* seems more fitting than would the normal modern phonetic development of its source, Middle English *crevice,* taken from Old French, which language in turn took it from Old High German *krebiz* 'crab' (Modern *Krebs). Chaise lounge* for *chaise longue* 'long chair' is listed as a variant in *Webster's Third,* and seems to be on the way to full social respectability. A dealer says that the prevailing pronunciation, both of those who buy and of those who sell, is either [šɛz lɑʊnǰ] or [čes lɑʊnǰ], the first of these in some circles being considered somewhat elite, not to say snobbish, in that it indicates that the user has "had" French. In any case, as far as speakers of English are concerned, the boner is remarkably apt, as indeed are many of the folk-etymologized forms that have been cited. And there can be little doubt that the aptness of a blunder has much to do with its ultimate acceptance.

SHIFTING WORDS TO NEW USES

One Part of Speech to Another

A very prolific source of new words from old is the facility of Modern English, because of its paucity of inflection, for converting words from one grammatical function to another with no change in form, a process known as **functional shift**. Thus, the name of practically every part of the body has been converted to use as a verb—one may *head* a committee, *shoulder* or *elbow* one's way through a crowd, *hand* in one's papers, *finger* one's collar, *thumb* a ride, *back* one's car, *leg* it along, *shin* up a tree, *foot* a bill, *toe* a mark, and *tiptoe* through the tulips—without any modification of form such as would be necessary in other languages, such as German, in which the suffix *-(e)n* is a necessary part of all infinitives. It would not have been possible to shift words thus in Old English times either, when infinitives ended in *-(a)n* or *-ian.* But Modern English does it with the greatest ease; to cite a few nonanatomical examples, *to contact, to chair* (a meeting), *to telephone, to date, to impact, to park, to proposition,* and *to M.C.* (or *emcee*). Verbs may also be used as nouns. One may, for instance, take a *walk,* a *run,* a *drive,* a *spin,* a *cut,* a *stand,* a *break,* a *turn,* or a *look.* A recent example is *wrap* 'a sandwich made of a soft tortilla rolled around a filling.' Nouns are just as freely used as adjectives, or practically so as attributives: *head bookkeeper, handlebar mustache, stone wall,* and *designer label,* whence *designer water* 'bottled water.' Adjectives and participles are used as nouns—for instance, *commercial* 'sales spiel on a television or radio show,' *formals* 'evening clothes,' *clericals* 'clergyman's street costume,' *devotional* 'short prayer service subsidiary to some other activity,' *private* 'noncommissioned soldier,' *elder, painting,* and *earnings.*

Adjectives may also be converted into verbs, as with *better, round, tame,* and *rough.* Even adverbs and conjunctions are capable of conversion, as in "the *whys* and the *wherefores*," "*but* me no *buts*" (in which *but* is first used as a verb, then as a pluralized noun), and "*ins* and *outs*." The attributive use of *in* and *out,* as in *inpatient* and *outpatient,* is quite old, as is their use as nouns just cited. The adjectival use of *in* meaning 'fashionable' or 'influential,' as in "the *in* thing" and "the *in* group," is recent, however. The adjectival use of the adverb *now* meaning 'of the present time,' as in "the *now* king," dates from the fifteenth century, whereas the meaning 'modern, and hence fashionable,' as in "the *now* generation," is a product of recent times.

Transitive verbs may be made from older intransitive ones, as has happened fairly recently with *shop* ("*Shop* Our Fabulous Sale Now in Progress"), *sleep* ("Her [a cruising yacht's] designer has claimed that she can *sleep* six"), and *look* ("What are we *looking* here?").

A good many combinations of verbs and adverbs—for instance, *slow down, check up, fill in* 'furnish with a background sketch,' *break down* 'analyze,' and *set up*—are easily convertible into nouns, though usually with shifted stress, as in *to check úp* contrasted with *a chéckup.* Some such combinations are also used as adjectives, as in *sit-down strike, sit-in demonstration,* and *drive-through teller.*

As with the verb-adverb combinations, change of form is sometimes involved when verbs, adjectives, and nouns shift functions—the functional shift often being indicated by a shift of stress: compare *upsét* (verb) and *úpset* (noun), *prodúce* (verb) and *próduce* (noun), *pérfect* (adjective) and *perféct* (verb). Not all speakers make the functional stress distinction in words like *ally* and *address,* but many do. Some words whose functions used to be distinguished by shift of stress seem to be losing the distinction. *Perfume* as a noun is now often stressed on the second syllable, and a building contractor regularly *cóntràcts* to build a house.

Common Words from Proper Names

A large number of common words have come to us from proper names—a kind of functional shift known as **commonization**. The term **eponym** is somewhat confusingly applied either to the word derived from a proper name or to the person who originally bore the name. From names of such eponymous persons, three well-known eponyms are *lynch, boycott,* and *sandwich. Lynch* (by way of *Lynch's law*) is from the Virginian Captain William Lynch (1742–1820), who led a campaign of "corporeal punishment" against those "unlawful and abandoned wretches" who were harassing the good people of Pittsylvania County, such as "to us shall seem adequate to the crime committed or the damage sustained" (*Dictionary of Americanisms*). *Boycott* is from another captain, Charles Cunningham Boycott (1832–97), who, because as a land agent he refused to accept rents at figures fixed by the tenants, was the best-known victim of the policy of ostracization of the Irish Land League agitators. *Sandwich* is from the fourth Earl of Sandwich (1718–92), said to have spent twenty-four hours at the gaming table with no other refreshment than slices of meat between slices of bread.

The following words are also the unchanged names of actual people: *ampere, bowie* (knife), *cardigan, chesterfield* (overcoat or sofa), *davenport, derby, derrick, derringer, graham* (flour), *guy, lavaliere, macintosh, maverick, ohm, pompadour, Pullman, shrapnel, solon* (legislator), *valentine, vandyke* (beard or collar), *watt,* and *zeppelin. Bloomer,* usually in the plural, is from Mrs. Amelia Jenks Bloomer (1818–94), who publicized the garb; one could devise no more appropriate name for voluminous drawers than this surname. *Bobby* 'British policeman' is from the pet form of the name of Sir Robert Peel, who made certain reforms in the London police system. *Maudlin,* long an English spelling for Old French *Madelaine,* is ultimately from Latin *Magdalen,* that is, Mary Magdalene, who was frequently represented as tearfully melancholy by painters.

Comparatively slight spelling modifications occur in *dunce* (from John Duns Scotus [d. ca. 1308], who was in reality anything but a dunce—to his admirers he was *Doctor Subtilis*) and *praline* (from Maréchal Duplessis-Praslin [d. 1675]). *Tawdry* is a clipped form of *Saint Audrey* and first referred to the lace bought at St. Audrey's Fair in Ely. *Epicure* is an anglicized form of *Epicurus. Kaiser* and *czar* are from *Caesar. Volt* is a clipped form of the surname of Count Alessandro Volta (d. 1827), and *farad* is derived likewise from the name of Michael Faraday (d. 1867). The name of an early American politician, Elbridge Gerry, is blended with *salamander* in the coinage *gerrymander. Pantaloon,* in the plural an old-fashioned name for trousers, is only a slight modification of French *pantalon,* which, in turn, is from Italian *Pantalone,* the name of a silly senile Venetian of early Italian comedy who wore such close-fitting nether coverings.

The following are derivatives of other personal names: *begonia, bougainvillea, bowdlerize, camellia, chauvinism, comstockery, dahlia, jeremiad, masochism, mesmerism, nicotine, onanism, pasteurize, platonic, poinsettia, sadism, spooner-ism, wisteria, zinnia.* Derivatives of the names of two writers—*Machiavellian* and *Rabelaisian*—are of such wide application that capitalizing them hardly seems necessary, any more than *platonic.*

The names of the following persons in literature and mythology (if gods, god-desses, and muses may be considered persons) are used unchanged: *atlas, bab-bitt, calliope, hector, hermaphrodite, mentor, mercury, nemesis, pander, psyche, simon-pure, volcano. Benedick,* the name of Shakespeare's bachelor par excel-lence who finally succumbed to the charms of Beatrice, has undergone only very slight modification in *benedict* '(newly) married man.' *Don Juan, Lothario, Lady Bountiful, Mrs. Grundy, man Friday,* and *Pollyanna* (which even has a derivative, *Pollyannaism*), though written with initial capitals, probably belong here also.

The following are derivatives of personal names from literature and mythol-ogy: *aphrodisiac, bacchanal, herculean, jovial, malapropism, morphine, odyssey, panic, quixotic, saturnine, simony, stentorian, tantalize, terpsichorean, venereal, vulcanize.* Despite their capitals, *Gargantuan* and *Pickwickian* should doubtless be included here also.

Names may be used generically because of some supposed appropriateness, like *billy* (in *billycock, hillbilly, silly billy,* and alone as the name of a police-man's club), *tom(my)* (in *tomcat, tomtit, tomboy, tommyrot, tomfool*), *john* 'toilet' (compare older *jakes*), *johnny* (in *stagedoor Johnny, johnny-on-the-spot,* and perhaps *johnnycake,* though this may come from American Indian *jonikin* 'type of griddlecake' + *cake*), *jack* (in *jackass, cheapjack, steeplejack, lumberjack, jack-in-the-box, jack-of-all-trades,* and alone as the name of a small metal piece used in a children's game known as *jacks*), *rube* (from *Reuben*), *hick* (from *Richard*), and *toby* 'jug' (from *Tobias*).

Place names have also furnished a good many common words. The following, the last of which exists only in the mind, are unchanged in form: *arras, babel, bourbon, billingsgate, blarney, buncombe, champagne, cheddar, china, cologne, grubstreet, guinea, homburg* (hat), *java* 'coffee,' *limerick, mackinaw, madeira, madras, magnesia, meander, morocco, oxford* (shoe or basket-weave cotton shirting), *panama, sauterne, shanghai, shantung, suede* (French name of Sweden), *tabasco, turkey, tuxedo,* and *utopia.*

The following are either derivatives of place names or place names that have different forms from those known to us today: *bayonet, bedlam, calico, canter, cashmere, copper, damascene, damask, damson, denim, frankfurter, gauze, hamburger, italic, jeans* (pants), *laconic, limousine, mayonnaise, milliner, roman* (type), *romance, sardonic, sherry* (see above), *sodomy, spaniel, spartan, stogy, stygian, wiener, worsted. Damascene, damask,* and *damson* all three come from *Damascus. Canter* is a clipping of *Canterbury* (*gallop*), the easygoing pace of pilgrims to the tomb of St. Thomas à Becket in Canterbury, the most famous and certainly the "realest" of whom are a group of people who never lived at all except in the poetic imagination of Geoffrey Chaucer and everlastingly in the hearts and minds of those who know his *Canterbury Tales.*

Some commercial products become so successful that their brand or trade names achieve widespread use. Some began as trade names but have passed into common use: *escalator* and *zipper.* Others maintain their trademark status and so are properly (that is, legally) entitled to capitalization: *Band-Aid, Ping-Pong,* and *Scotch* tape. Sometimes a trade name enters common use through a verb derived from it. In England, *to hoover* is 'to clean with a vacuum cleaner' from the name of a famous manufacturer of such vacuums. To photocopy is sometimes called *to xerox,* and a new verb for 'to search for information on the Internet' is *to google.* Verbs are not subject to trademarking, though dictionaries are careful to indicate their proper source.

SOURCES OF NEW WORDS

In most cases, we do not know the exact circumstances under which a new word was invented, but there are a few notable exceptions.

Two literary examples are *Catch-22,* from the novel of the same name by Joseph Heller, and *1984,* also from a novel of the same name by George Orwell. *Catch-22* denotes a dilemma in which each alternative is blocked by the other. In the novel, the only way for a combat pilot to get a transfer out of the war zone is to ask for one on the ground that he is insane, but anyone who seeks to be transferred is clearly sane, since only an insane person would want to stay in combat. The rules provide for a transfer, but Catch-22 prevents one from ever getting it. Orwell's dystopian novel is set in the year 1984, and its title has come to denote the kind of society the novel depicts—one in which individual freedom has been lost, people are manipulated through cynical television propaganda by the government, and life is a gray and hopeless affair.

Another literary contribution that has come into the language less directly is *quark.* As used in theoretical physics, the term denotes a hypothetical particle, the fundamental building block of all matter, originally thought to be of three kinds. The theory of these threefold fundamental particles was developed by a Nobel Prize winner, Murray Gell-Mann, of the California Institute of Technology; he called them *quarks* and then discovered the word in James Joyce's novel *Finnegans Wake* in the phrase "Three quarks for Muster Mark!" Doubtless Gell-Mann had seen the word in his earlier readings of the novel, and it had stuck in the back of his mind until he needed a term for his new particles. It is not often that we know so much about the origin of a word in English.

Distribution of New Words

Which of the various kinds of word making are the most prolific sources of new words today? One study of new words over the fifty-year period 1941–1991 (Algeo and Algeo, *Fifty Years* 14) found that the percentages of new words were as follows for the major types:

Type	Percent
Compounding	40
Affixation	28
Shifting	17
Shortening	8
Blending	5
Borrowing	2
Creating	below 0.5

Other studies have found variable percentages among the types, but there is considerable agreement that nowadays English forms most of its new words by combining morphemes already in the language. Compounding and affixation account for two-thirds of our new words. Most of the others are the result of putting old words to new uses or shortening or blending them. Loanwords borrowed from other languages (considered in the next chapter), although once a more frequent source of new words, is of relatively minor importance today. And almost no words are invented from scratch.

FOR FURTHER READING

General

Algeo and Algeo. *Fifty Years Among the New Words.*
Ayto. *Twentieth Century Words.*
Bauer. *English Word-formation.*
Cannon. *Historical Change and English Word-Formation.*
Fischer. *Lexical Change in Present-Day English.*
Hughes. *A History of English Words.*
Metcalf. *Predicting New Words.*

Word Formation

Acronyms, Initialisms, & Abbreviations Dictionary.
Adams. *Complex Words in English.*
Freeman. *A New Dictionary of Eponyms.*

Slang

Allen. *The City in Slang: New York.*
Farmer and Henley. *Dictionary of Slang and Its Analogues.*
Lighter. *Historical Dictionary of American Slang.*
Partridge. *A Dictionary of Slang and Unconventional English.*

Special Vocabularies

Allen. *Unkind Words: Ethnic Labeling.*
Friedman. *A "Brand" New Language.*
Poteet and Poteet. *Car & Motorcycle Slang.*

12 FOREIGN ELEMENTS IN THE ENGLISH WORD STOCK

Thus far we have dealt only incidentally with the non-English elements in the English lexicon. In the present chapter we make a rapid survey of these, along with some examination of the various circumstances—cultural, religious, military, and political—surrounding their adoption.

The core vocabulary of English is, and has always been, native English. The words we use to talk about everyday things (*earth, tree, stone, sea, hill, dog, bird, house, land, roof, sun, moon, time*), relationships (*friend, foe, mother, father, son, daughter, wife, husband*), and responses and actions (*hate, love, fear, greed, help, harm, rest, walk, ride, speak*), as well as the basic numbers and directions (*one, two, three, ten, top, bottom, north, south, up, down*) and grammatical words (*I, you, he, to, for, from, be, have, after, but, and*), are all native English. Nevertheless, an overwhelming majority of the words in any large dictionary and a large number of the words we use everyday were either borrowed from other languages or made up using the elements of borrowed words. So the foreign element in our word stock is of considerable importance.

When speakers imitate a word from a foreign language and at least partly adapt it in sound or grammar to their native speechways, the process is known as **borrowing**, and the word thus borrowed is a **loanword**. The history of a loanword may be quite complex because such words have often passed through a series of languages before reaching English. For example, *chess* was borrowed in the fourteenth century from Middle French *esches*. The French word had been, in turn, borrowed from Medieval Latin, which got it from Arabic, which had borrowed it from Persian *shāh* 'king.' The **direct** or **immediate source** of *chess* is Middle French, but its **ultimate source** (as far back as we can trace its history) is Persian. Similarly, the **etymon** of *chess,* that is, the word from which it has been derived, is immediately *esches* but ultimately *shāh.* Loanwords have, as it were, a life of their own that cuts across the boundaries between languages.

Popular and Learned Loanwords

It is useful to make a distinction between popular and learned loanwords. **Popular loanwords** are of oral transmission and are part of the vocabulary of everyday communication. For the most part, they are not felt to be in any way

271

different from English words; in fact, those who use them are seldom aware that they are of foreign origin. **Learned loanwords**, on the other hand, owe their adoption to more or less scholarly influences.

Learned words may in time become part of the ordinary vocabulary, even though their use may be confined to a certain class or group; or they may pass into general usage, as did *clerk* (OE *cleric* or *clerc* 'clergyman' from Lat. *clēricus* or Old French *clerc*). In the seventeenth century, *cleric* was borrowed from the same Latin source as a learned word to denote a clergyman, since *clerk* had meanwhile acquired other meanings, including 'scholar,' 'scribe,' 'one in charge of records and accounts in an organization,' and 'bookkeeper.' It was later to acquire yet another meaning, 'one who waits upon customers in a retail establishment,' in American English, the equivalent of the British *shop assistant.* The earliest English meaning has survived in legal usage, in which a priest of the Church of England is described as a "clerk in holy orders."

The approximate time at which a word was borrowed is often indicated by its form: thus, as Mary Serjeantson (13) points out, Old English *scōl* 'school' (Lat. *schola,* ultimately Greek) is obviously a later borrowing than *scrīn* 'shrine' (Lat. *scrīnium*), which must have been adopted before the Old English change of [sk-] to [š-] in order for it to have acquired the later sound. At the time when *scōl* was borrowed, this sound change was no longer operative. Had the word been borrowed earlier, it would have developed into Modern English **shool.*

LATIN AND GREEK LOANWORDS

Latin influence on English can be seen in every period of the language's history. That influence has been of a different sort, however, and with different effects from one period to the next.

Latin Influence in the Germanic Period

Long before English began its separate existence by English speakers migrating to the British Isles, while it was merely a regional type of Continental Germanic, those who spoke it had acquired a number of Latin words—loanwords that are common to several or to all of the Germanic languages to this day. Unlike a good many later borrowings, they are mostly concerned with military affairs, commerce, and agriculture or with refinements of living that the Germanic peoples had acquired through a fairly close contact with the Romans since at least the beginning of the Christian era.

Wine (OE *wīn,* Lat. *vīnum*), for instance, is a word that denotes a thing the Germanic peoples learned about from the Romans. It is to be found in one form or another in all the Germanic languages—the same form as the Old English in Old Frisian and Old Saxon, *Wein* in Modern German, *wijn* in Modern Dutch, and *vin* in Danish and Swedish. The Baltic, Slavic, and Celtic peoples also acquired the same word from Latin. It was brought to Britain by English warrior-adventurers in the fifth century. They also knew malt drinks very well—*beer* and *ale* are both Germanic words, and *mead* was known to the Indo-Europeans—but apparently the principle of fermentation of fruit juices was a specialty of the Mediterranean peoples. Roman merchants had penetrated into the Germania of those early centuries, Roman farmers had settled in the Rhineland and the valley of the Moselle, and Germanic soldiers had marched with the Roman legions (Priebsch and Collinson 264–5).

There are about 175 early loanwords from Latin, most of them indicating special spheres in which the Romans excelled, or were thought to do so by the Germanic peoples (Serjeantson 271–7). Many of these words have survived into Modern English. They include *ancor* 'anchor' (Lat. *ancora*), *butere* 'butter' (Lat. *būtyrum*), *cealc* 'chalk' (Lat. *calc-*), *cēse* 'cheese' (Lat. *cāseus*), *cetel* 'kettle' (Lat. *catillus* 'little pot'), *cycene* 'kitchen' (Vul. Lat. *cucīna,* var. of *coquīna*), *disc* 'dish' (Lat. *discus*), *mangere* '-monger, trader' (Lat. *mangō*), *mīl* 'mile' (Lat. *mīlia* [*passuum*] 'a thousand [paces]'), *mynet* 'coin, coinage,' Modern English *mint* (Lat. *monēta*), *piper* 'pepper' (Lat. *piper*), *pund* 'pound' (Lat. *pondō* 'measure of weight'), *sacc* 'sack' (Lat. *saccus*), *sicol* 'sickle' (Lat. *secula*), *strǣt* 'paved road, street' (Lat. [*via*] *strata* 'paved [road]'), and *weall* 'wall' (Lat. *vallum*).

Cēap 'marketplace, wares, price' (Lat. *caupō* 'tradesman,' more specifically 'wineseller') is now obsolete as a noun except in the idiom *on the cheap* and proper names such as *Chapman, Cheapside* (once simply *Cheap,* then *Westcheap*), *Eastcheap,* and *Chepstow.* The adjectival and adverbial use of *cheap* is of early Modern English origin and is, according to the *OED,* a shortening of *good cheap* 'what can be purchased on advantageous terms.' *To cheapen* is likewise of early Modern English origin and used to mean 'to bargain for, ask the price of' as when Defoe's Moll Flanders went out to "cheapen some laces."

Since all the early borrowings from Latin were popular loanwords, they have gone through all phonological developments that occurred subsequent to their adoption in the various Germanic languages. *Chalk, dish,* and *kitchen,* for instance, show in their respective initial (*ch-*), final (*-sh*), and medial (*-tch-*) consonants the Old English palatalization of *k;* in addition, the last-cited word in its Old English form *cycene* shows mutation of Vulgar Latin *u* in the vowel of its stressed syllable. German *Küche* shows the same mutation. In *cetel* 'kettle' (by way of West Germanic **katil*), an earlier *a* has been mutated by *i* in a following syllable (compare Ger. *Kessel*). The fact that none of these early loanwords has been affected by the First Sound Shift (78–82) indicates that they were borrowed after that shift had been completed.

Latin Words in Old English

Among the early English loanwords from Latin, some of which were acquired not directly but from the British Celts, are *candel* 'candle' (Lat. *candēla*), *cest* 'chest' (Lat. *cista,* later *cesta*), *crisp* 'curly' (Lat. *crispus*), *earc* 'ark' (Lat. *arca*), *mægester* 'master' (Lat. *magister*), *mynster* 'monastery' (Lat. *monastērium*), *peru* 'pear' (Lat. *pirum*), *port* 'harbor' (Lat. *portus*), *sealm* 'psalm' (Lat. *psalmus,* taken from Gr.), and *tīgle* 'tile' (Lat. *tēgula*). *Ceaster* 'city' (Lat. *castra* 'camp') survives in the town names *Chester, Castor,* and *Caister* and as an element in the names of quite a few

English places, many of which were once in fact Roman military stations—for instance, *Casterton, Chesterfield, Exeter* (earlier *Execestre*), *Gloucester, Lancaster, Manchester,* and *Worcester.* The differences in form are mostly dialectal.

Somewhat later borrowings with an English form close to their Latin etyma were *alter* 'altar' (Lat. *altar*), *(a)postol* 'apostle' (Lat. *apostolus*), *balsam* (Lat. *balsamum*), *circul* 'circle' (Lat. *circulus*), *comēta* 'comet,' *cristalla* 'crystal' (Lat. *crystallum*), *dēmon* (Lat. *daemon*), *fers* 'verse' (Lat. *versus*), *mæsse, messe* 'mass' (Lat. *missa,* later *messa*), *martir* 'martyr' (Lat. *martyr*), *plaster* (medical) (Lat. *emplastrum*), and *templ* 'temple' (Lat. *templum*). Since Latin borrowed freely from Greek, it is not surprising that some of the loans cited are of Greek origin; examples (to cite their Modern English forms) include *apostle, balsam, comet, crystal,* and *demon.* This is the merest sampling of Latin loanwords in Old English. Somewhat more than 500 in all occur in the entire Old English period up to the Conquest. Serjeantson (277–88) lists, aside from the words from the Continental period, 111 from approximately the years 450 to 650, and 242 from approximately the year 650 to the time of the Norman Conquest. These numbers, of course, are not actually large as compared with the Latin borrowings in later times.

Many Latin loanwords, particularly those from the later period, were certainly never widely used or even known. Some occur only a single time, or in only a single manuscript. Many were subsequently lost, some to be reborrowed, often with changes of meaning, at a later period from French or from Classical Latin. For instance, our words *sign* and *giant* are not from Old English *segn* and *gīgant* but are later borrowings from Old French *signe* and *geant.* In addition, a learned and a popular form of the same word might coexist in Old English—for instance, *Latin* and *Læden,* the second of which might also mean 'any foreign language.'

These loanwords, the later learned ones as well as the earlier popular ones, were usually made to conform to Old English declensional patterns, though occasionally, in translations from Latin into Old English, Latin case forms, particularly of proper names, may be retained (for example, "fram Agustō þām cāsere" in the translation of Bede's account of the departure of the Romans from Britain: 'from Augustus the emperor,' with the Latin ending *-ō* in close apposition to the Old English dative endings in *-m* and *-e*). As with earlier borrowings, there came into being a good many **hybrid formations**: that is, native endings were affixed to foreign words—for example, *-isc* in *mechanisc* 'mechanical,' *-dōm* in *pāpdōm* 'papacy,' and *-ere* in *grammaticere* 'grammarian'—and hybrid compounds arose, such as *sealmscop* (Lat. *psalma* and OE *scop* 'singer, bard'). Infinitives took the Old English ending *-ian,* as in the grammatical term *declīnian* 'to decline.'

Latin Words Borrowed in Middle English Times

Many borrowings from Latin occurred during the Middle English period. Frequently it is impossible to tell whether such words are from French or from Latin—for instance, *miserable, nature, register, relation,* and *rubric,* which might be from either language, judging by form alone. Depending on its meaning, the single form *port* may come from Latin *portus* 'harbor,' French *porter* 'to carry,'

Latin *porta* 'gate,' or Portuguese *Oporto* (that is, *o porto* 'the port,' the city where port wine came from originally)—not to mention the nautical use of the word for one side of a ship, the exact origin of which is uncertain.

In the period between the Norman Conquest and 1500, many Latin words having to do with religion appeared in English (some by way of French), among them *collect* 'short prayer,' *dirge, mediator,* and *Redeemer* (first used with reference to Christ: the synonymous *redemptor* occurs earlier). To these might be added legal terms—for instance, *client, conviction,* and *subpoena;* words having to do with scholastic activities—for instance, *library, scribe,* and *simile;* and words having to do with science—for instance, *dissolve, equal, essence, medicine, mercury,* and *quadrant.* These are only a few out of hundreds of Latin words that were adopted before 1500: a longer list would include verbs (for example, *admit, commit, discuss, seclude*) and adjectives (for example, *complete, imaginary, instant, legitimate, obdurate, populous*).

Latin Words Borrowed in Modern English Times

The great period of borrowings from Latin and from Greek by way of Latin is the Modern English period. The century or so after 1500 saw the introduction of, among many others, the words *abdomen, area, compensate, data, decorum, delirium, denominate, digress, editor, fictitious, folio, gradual, imitate, janitor, jocose, lapse, medium, notorious, orbit, peninsula, querulous, quota, resuscitate, series, sinecure, strict, superintendent, transient, ultimate, urban, urge,* and *vindicate.*

In earlier periods, Latin was the language of literature, science, and religion. Latin was, in fact, freely used in both written and spoken forms by the learned all over Europe throughout the medieval and early modern periods. Petrarch translated Boccaccio's story of the patient Griselda into Latin to ensure that such a highly moral tale should have a wider circulation than it would have had in Boccaccio's Italian, and it was this Latin translation that Chaucer used as the source of his *Clerk's Tale.* More, Bacon, and Milton all wrote in Latin, just as the Venerable Bede and other learned men had done centuries earlier.

Present-day loanwords with Latin etymologies are often terms that have been concocted from Latin morphemes but that were unknown as units to the ancients. The international vocabulary of science draws heavily on such **neo-Latin** forms, but so do the vocabularies of other areas of modern life. Among the recent classical contributions to English (with definitions from *The Third Barnhart Dictionary of New English* [Barnhart and Steinmetz] are *aleatoric* 'dependent on chance' (from *āleātor* 'gambler, dice player'); *circadian* 'functioning or recurring in 24-hour cycles' (from *circā diēm* 'around the day'); *Homo habilis* 'extinct species of man believed to have been the earliest toolmaker' (literally 'skillful man'); *militaria* 'collection of objects having to do with the military, such as firearms, decorations, uniforms, etc.'; *Pax Americana* 'peace enforced by American power' (modeled on *Pax Romana*); and *vexillology* 'study of flags' (from *vexillum* 'flag' or 'banner'). Latin was the first major contributor of loanwords to English, and it remains one of our most important resources.

Greek Loanwords

Even before the Conquest, a number of Greek words had entered English by way of Latin, in addition to some very early loans that may have come into Germanic directly from Greek, such as *church*. From the Middle English period on, Latin and French are the immediate sources of most loanwords ultimately Greek—for instance (from Latin), *allegory, anemia, anesthesia* (in its usual modern sense 'drug-induced insensibility' first used in 1846 by Oliver Wendell Holmes, who was a physician as well as a poet), *aristocracy, barbarous, chaos, comedy, cycle, dilemma, drama, electric, enthusiasm, epithet, epoch, history, homonym, metaphor, mystery, paradox, pharynx, phenomenon, rhapsody, rhythm, theory,* and *zone;* (from French) *center, character, chronicle, democracy, diet, dragon, ecstasy, fantasy, harmony, lyre, machine, nymph, pause, rheum,* and *tyrant.* Straight from Greek (though some are combinations unknown in classical times) come *acronym, agnostic, anthropoid, autocracy, chlorine, idiosyncrasy, kudos, oligarchy, pathos, phone, telegram,* and *xylophone,* among many others.

The richest foreign sources of our present English word stock are Latin, French, and Greek (including those words of Greek origin that have come to us by way of Latin and French). Many of the Latin and Greek words were in the beginning confined to the language of erudition, and some of them still are; others have passed into the stock of more or less everyday speech. Although Greek had tremendous prestige as a classical language, there was comparatively little firsthand knowledge of it in western Europe until the advent of refugee Greek scholars from Constantinople after the conquest of that city by the Turks in 1453. Hence, most of the Greek words that appear first in early Modern English occurred, as far as the English were concerned, in Latin works, though their Greek provenience usually would have been recognized.

CELTIC LOANWORDS

Some Celtic loanwords doubtless entered the language during the common Germanic period. Old English *rīce* as a noun meaning 'kingdom' and as an adjective 'rich, powerful' (cf. Ger. *Reich*) is almost certainly of Celtic origin, borrowed before the settlement of the English in Britain. The Celtic origin of a few others (for example, OE *ambeht* 'servant,' *dūn* 'hill, down') is uncertain.

It is likely, however, that even before the beginning of Latin borrowing in England, the English must have acquired some words from the Celts. As has been pointed out, some of the Latin loans of the period up to approximately A.D. 650 were acquired by the English indirectly through the Celts. It is likely that *ceaster* and *-coln,* as in *Lincoln* (Lat. *colōnia*), were so acquired. Phonology is not much help to us as far as such words are concerned, since they underwent the same prehistoric Old English sound changes as the words that the English brought with them from the Continent.

There are, however, a number of genuinely Celtic words acquired during the early years of the English settlement. We should not expect to find many, for the

British Celts were a subject people, and a conquering people are unlikely to adopt many words from those whom they have supplanted. The very insignificant number of words from American Indian languages that have found a permanent place in American English strikingly illustrates this fact. The Normans are exceptional in that they ultimately gave up their own language altogether and became English, in a way in which the English never became Celts. Probably no more than a dozen or so Celtic words other than place names were adopted by the English up to the time of the Conquest. These include *bannuc* 'a bit,' *bratt* 'cloak,' *brocc* 'badger,' *cumb* 'combe, valley,' and *torr* 'peak.' Just as many American place names are of Indian origin, so many English place names are of Celtic provenience: *Avon, Carlisle, Cornwall, Devon, Dover, London, Usk,* and scores more.

In more recent times a few more Celtic words have been introduced into English. From Irish Gaelic of the seventeenth century, came *brogue, galore, leprechaun, shamrock, tory,* and subsequently *banshee, blarney, colleen,* and *shillelagh.* From Scots Gaelic, in addition to *clan, loch,* and a few rarely used words that entered English in late Middle English times, came *bog, cairn, plaid, slogan, whiskey,* and some others less familiar. From Welsh, *crag,* occurring first in Middle English, is the best known; others of more recent introduction include *cromlech* 'circle of large stones' and *eisteddfod* 'Welsh festival.'

SCANDINAVIAN LOANWORDS

Old and Middle English Borrowings

Most of the Scandinavian words in Old English do not actually occur in written records until the Middle English period, though undoubtedly they were current long before the beginning of that period. Practically all of the extant documents of the late Old English period come from the south of England, specifically from Wessex. It is likely that Scandinavian words were recorded in documents that no longer exist, but were written in that part of the country to which Alfred the Great by force of arms and diplomacy had persuaded the Scandinavians to confine themselves—the Danelaw, comprising all of Northumbria and East Anglia and half of Mercia.

In the later part of the eleventh century, the Scandinavians became gradually assimilated to English ways, though Scandinavian words had been in the meanwhile introduced into English. As we have seen, many Scandinavian words closely resembled their English cognates; sometimes, indeed, they were so nearly identical that it would be impossible to tell whether a given word was Scandinavian or English.

Sometimes, however, if the meanings of obviously related words differed, **semantic contamination** might result, as when Old English *drēam* 'joy' acquired the meaning of the related Scandinavian *draumr* 'vision in sleep.' A similar example is *brēad* 'fragment' (ModE *bread*); the usual Old English word for the food made from flour or meal was *hlāf* (ModE *loaf*) as in "Ūrne gedæghwāmlīcan hlāf syle ūs tō dæg" 'Our daily bread give us today.' Others are *blōma* 'lump of metal' (ModE *bloom* 'flower') and poetic *eorl* 'warrior, noble' (ModE *earl*), which acquired the meaning of the related Scandinavian *jarl* 'underking, governor.' Similarly, the later meanings of *dwell* (OE *dwellan, dwelian*), *holm* 'islet' (same form in Old English), and *plow* (OE *plōh*) coincide precisely with the Scandinavian meanings, though in Old English these words meant, respectively, 'to lead astray, hinder,' 'ocean,' and 'measure of land.'

Late Old English and early Middle English loans from Scandinavian were made to conform wholly or in part with the English sound and inflectional system. These include (in modern form) *by* 'town, homestead' (as in *bylaw* 'town ordinance' and in place names, such as *Derby, Grimsby,* and *Rigsby*), *carl* 'man' (cognate with OE *ceorl*, the source of *churl*), *fellow, hit* (first 'meet with,' later 'strike'), *law, rag, sly, swain, take* (completely displacing *nim,* from OE *niman*), *thrall,* and *want.* The Scandinavian provenience of *sister* has already been alluded to (93).

A good many words with [sk] are of Scandinavian origin, for, as we have seen, early Old English [sk], written *sc,* came to be pronounced [š]. Such words as *scathe, scorch, score, scot* 'tax' (as in *scot-free* and *scot and lot*), *scowl, scrape, scrub, skill, skin, skirt* (compare native *shirt*), and *sky* thus show by their initial consonant sequence that they entered the language after this change had ceased to be operative. All have been taken from Scandinavian.

Similarly the [g] and [k] before front vowels in *gear, geld, gill* (of a fish), *kick, kilt,* and *kindle* point to Scandinavian origins for these words, since the velar stops became in Old English under such circumstances [y] and [č], respectively. The very common verbs *get* and *give* come to us not from Old English *gitan* and *gifan,* which began with [y], but instead from cognate Scandinavian forms in which the palatalization of [g] in the neighborhood of front vowels did not occur. Native forms of these verbs with [y-] occur throughout the Middle English period side by side with the Scandinavian forms with [g-], which were ultimately to supplant them. Chaucer consistently used *yive, yeve,* and preterit *yaf.*

As a rule, the Scandinavian loans involve little more than the substitution of one word for another, such as *window,* from *vindauga,* literally 'wind-eye,' replacing *eyethurl,* literally 'eyehole,' from OE *ēagþyrl.* Some new words denoted new concepts, such as certain Scandinavian legal terms, or new things, such as words for various kinds of warships with which the Scandinavians made the English acquainted. Others only slightly modified the form of an English word, like *sister.* More important and more fundamental is what happened to the Old English pronominal forms of the third person plural: all the *th-* forms, as we have seen (133, 145), are of Scandinavian origin. Of the native forms in *h-* (110), only *'em* (ME *hem,* OE *him*) survives, and it is commonly but mistakenly thought of as a reduced form of *them.*

Modern English Borrowings

A number of Scandinavian words have entered English during the modern period. The best known of them are *muggy, rug, scud,* and *ski,* the last of these dating from the later years of the nineteenth century. *Skoal* (Danish *skaal*) has had a recent alcoholic vogue. It comes as a surprise to learn that it first appears in English as early as 1600, though its early use seems to have been confined to Scotland. The *OED* reasonably suggests that it may have been introduced through the visit of James VI of Scotland (afterward James I of England) to Denmark, whither he journeyed in 1589 to meet his bride. *Geyser* (1763), *rune* (1685), *saga* (1709), and *skald* (ca. 1763) are all from Icelandic. *Smörgåsbord* entered English from Swedish around the mid-1920s. It is usually written in English without the Swedish diacritics. Swedish *ombudsman* 'official who looks into citizens' complaints against government bureaus and against other officials' has as yet only limited currency, though it is entered in recent dictionaries.

FRENCH LOANWORDS

Middle English Borrowings

No loanwords unquestionably of French origin occur in English earlier than 1066. Leaving out of the question doubtful cases, some of the earliest loans that are unquestionably French are (to cite their Modern English forms) *castle, juggler, prison,* and *service. Capon* could be French but was most likely taken directly from Latin. As Alistair Campbell (221) observes, "Even after 1066 French words flow into the literary language more slowly than Norse ones, and they do not occur frequently until [after 1132]."

The Norman Conquest made French the language of the official class in England. Hence it is not surprising that many words having to do with government and administration, lay and spiritual, are of French origin: the word *government* itself, along with Middle English *amynistre,* later replaced by the Latin-derived *administer* with its derivative *administration.* Others include *attorney, chancellor, country, court, crime* (replacing English *sin,* which thereafter came to designate the proper business of the Church, though the State has from time to time tried to take it over), *(e)state, judge, jury, noble,* and *royal. State* is an aphetic form; both it and the full form *estate* were obviously borrowed before French loss of *s* before *t* (Mod. Fr. *état*). In the religious sphere, loans include *abbot, clergy, preach, sacrament,* and *vestment,* among a good many others.

Words designating English titles of nobility except for *king, queen, earl, lord,* and *lady*—namely, *prince, duke, marquess, viscount, baron,* and their feminine equivalents—date from the period when England was in the hands of a Norman French ruling class. Even the earl's wife is a *countess,* and the peer immediately below him in rank is a *viscount* (that is, 'vice-count'), indicating that the earl corresponds in rank with the Continental count. In military usage, *army, captain, corporal, lieutenant* (literally 'place holding'), *sergeant* (originally a serving man or attendant), and *soldier* are all of French origin. *Colonel* does not occur in English until the sixteenth century (as *coronnel,* whence the pronunciation). French *brigade* and its derivative *brigadier* were introduced in the seventeenth century. *Major* is Latin, however, occurring first (as an adjective) in *sergeant major* in the later years of the sixteenth century; the nonmilitary adjectival use in English is somewhat earlier. The French equivalent has occurred in English since the end of the thirteenth century, its Modern English form being *mayor.*

French names were given not only to various animals when served up as food at Norman tables—*beef, mutton, pork,* and *veal,* for instance—but also to the culinary processes by which the English cow, sheep, pig, and calf were prepared for human consumption, for instance, *boil, broil, fry, roast,* and *stew.* Native English *seethe* is now used mostly metaphorically, as in "to seethe with rage" and "sodden in drink" (*sodden* being the old past participle of the strong verb *seethe* 'boil, stew'). Other French loans from the Middle English period, chosen more or less at random, are *dignity, enamor, feign, fool, fruit, horrible, letter, literature, magic, male, marvel, mirror, oppose, question, regard, remember, sacrifice, safe, salary, search, second* (replacing OE *ōðer* as an ordinal number), *secret, seize, sentence, single, sober,* and *solace.*

French words have come into English from two dialects of French, the Norman spoken in England (Anglo-Norman) and the Central French (that of Paris, later standard French). We can frequently tell by the form of a word whether it is of Norman or of Central French provenience. For instance, Latin *c* [k] before *a* developed into *ch* [č] in Central French, but remained in the Norman dialect; hence *chapter,* from Middle English *chapitre* (from Old French), ultimately going back to Latin *capitulum* 'little head,' a diminutive of *caput,* is from the Central dialect. Compare also the **doublets** *chattel* and *cattle,* from Central French and Norman, respectively, both going back to Latin *capitāle* 'possession, stock,' *capital* in this sense being a Latin loan. Similarly, Old French *w* was retained in Norman French, but elsewhere became [gw] and then [g]: this development is shown in such doublets as *wage-gage* and *warranty-guarantee.* There are a good many other phonological criteria.

The century and a half between 1250 and the death of Chaucer was a period during which the rate of adoption of French words by English was greater than it had ever been before or has ever been since. A statistical study by Jespersen (*Growth and Structure* 86–7) of a thousand French loanwords in those volumes of the *OED* available to him at the time of his investigation shows that nearly half were adopted during the period in question. Jespersen's estimate is based on the dates of earliest occurrence of these French words in writing, as supplied by the dated quotations in the *OED.* He was aware, of course, that the first written occurrence of a word, particularly of a popular word, is almost inevitably somewhat later than its actual first use. His table of the numbers of French loanwords grouped by the half centuries of their first known written appearance in English remains nevertheless a striking demonstration of the chronology of French borrowing in English.

Let us pause to examine the opening lines of the *Canterbury Tales,* written toward the end of the period of intense borrowing. The italicized words are of French origin:

Whan that Aprille with hise shoures soote
The droghte of *March* hath *perced* to the roote
And bathed every *veyne* in swich *licour*
Of which *vertu engendred* is the *flour;*

5 Whan Zephirus eek with his sweete breeth
    Inspired hath in every holt and heeth
    The *tendre* croppes, and the yonge sonne
    Hath in the Ram his half[e] *cours* yronne,
    And smale foweles maken *melodye,*
10 That slepen al the nyght with open eye—
    So priketh hem *nature* in hir *corages*—
    Thanne longen folk to goon on *pilgrimages,*
    And *Palmeres* for to seken *straunge* strondes,
    To ferne halwes kowthe in sondry londes
15 And *specially* fram every shires ende
    Of Engelond to Caunterbury they wende
    The hooly blisful martir for to seke
    That hem hath holpen when hat they were seeke.
    Bifil that in that *seson* on a day,
20 In Southwerk at the *Tabard* as I lay
    Redy to wenden on my *pilgrymage*
    To Caunterbury with ful *devout corage,*
    At nyght were come in to that *hostelrye*
    Wel nyne and twenty in a *compaignye*
25 Of sondry folk by *aventure* yfalle
    In felaweshipe, and *pilgrimes* were they alle
    That toward Caunterbury wolden ryde.

[Ellesmere MS]

In these twenty-seven lines there are 189 words. Counting *pilgrimage* and *corage* only once, twenty-four of these words come from French. Such a percentage is doubtless also fairly typical of cultivated London usage in Chaucer's time. According to Serjeantson (151), between 10 and 15 percent of the words Chaucer used were of French origin. It will be noted, as has been pointed out before, that the indispensable, often used, everyday words—auxiliary verbs, pronouns, and particles—are of native origin. To the fourteenth century, as Serjeantson points out (136), we owe most of the large number of still current abstract terms from French ending in *-ance, -ant, -ence, -ent, -ity, -ment, -tion,* and those beginning in *con-, de-, dis-, ex-, pre-,* and the like, though some of them do not actually show up in writing for another century or so.

Later French Loanwords

Borrowing from French has gone on ever since the Middle Ages, though never on so large a scale. It is interesting to note that the same French word may be borrowed at various periods in the history of English, like *gentle, genteel,* and *jaunty,* all from French *gentil*—the last two of seventeenth-century introduction. (*Gentile,* however, was taken straight from Latin *gentīlis,* meaning 'foreign' in post-Classical Latin.) It is similar with *chief,* first occurring in English in the fourteenth century, and *chef,* in the nineteenth—the doublets show by their pronunciation the approximate time of their adoption: the Old French affricate [č] survives in *chief,* in which the vowel has undergone the expected shift from [e:] to [i:]; *chef* shows the Modern French shift of the affricate to the fricative [š]. In words of French origin spelled with *ch,* the pronunciation is usually indicative of the time of adoption: thus *chamber, champion, chance, change, chant, charge, chase, chaste, chattel, check,* and *choice* were borrowed in Middle English times, whereas *chamois, chauffeur, chevron, chic, chiffon, chignon, douche,* and *machine* have been taken over in Modern English times. Since *chivalry* was widely current in Middle English, one would expect it to begin in Modern English with [č]; the word has, as it were, been re-Frenchified, perhaps because with the decay of the institution it became more of an eye word than an ear word. As late as 1977, Daniel Jones and A. C. Gimson recorded [č] as current but labeled it old-fashioned. In 1990, John C. Wells did not record it at all.

Carriage, courage, language, savage, viage (later modernized as *voyage*), and *village* came into English in Middle English times and have come to have initial stress in accordance with English patterns. Chaucer and his contemporaries could have it both ways in their poetry—for instance, either *coráge* or *cóurage,* as also with other French loans—for instance, *colour, figure, honour, pitee, valour, vertu.* This variable stress is still evidenced by such doublets as *dívers* and *divérse* (showing influence of Lat. *dīversus*). The position of the stress is frequently evidence of the period of borrowing: compare, for instance, older *cárriage* with newer *garáge, válour* with *velóur,* or *véstige* with *prestíge.*

Loans from French since the late seventeenth century are, as we should expect, by and large less completely naturalized than most of the older loans that have been cited, though some, like *cigarette, picnic, police,* and *soup,* seem commonplace enough. These later loans also include (omitting French accents except where they are usual in English) *aide-de-camp, amateur, ballet, baton, beau, bouillon, boulevard, brochure, brunette, bureau, cafe, camouflage, chaise longue, champagne, chaperon* (in French, a hood or cap formerly worn by women; in English, in earlier days a married woman who shields a young girl as a hood shields the face), *chi-chi* 'chic gone haywire,' *chiffonier* (in France, a ragpicker), *chute, cliche, commandant, communiqué, connoisseur, coupe* ('cut off,' past participle of *couper,* used of a closed car with short body and practically always pronounced [kup] in American English), *coupon, crepe, crochet, debris, debut(ante), decor, de luxe, denouement, detour, elite, embonpoint* (compare the loan translation *in good point,* which occurs much earlier, as in Chaucer's description of the Monk in line 200 of the General Prologue of the *Canterbury Tales:* "He was a lord ful fat and in good poynt"), *encore, ensemble, entree, envoy, etiquette, fiancé(e), flair, foyer* (British ['fwaye] or ['fɔɪye]; American ['fɔɪər]), *fuselage, genre, glacier, grippe, hangar, hors d'oeuvre, impasse, invalid, laissez faire, liaison, limousine, lingerie, massage, matinee* (earlier, as its derivation from *matin* implies, a morning performance), *melee, ménage, menu, morale, morgue, naive, negligee, nuance, passé, penchant, plateau, premiere, protégé, rapport, ration* (the traditional pronunciation, riming with *fashion,* indicates its Modern French origin; the newer one, riming with *nation* and *station,* is by analogy with those much older words), *ravine, repartee, repertoire, reservoir, restaurant, reveille* (British [rɪ'vælɪ]; American ['rɛvəli]), *revue, risqué, roué, rouge, saloon* (and its less thoroughly Anglicized variant *salon), savant, savoir faire, souvenir, suede, surveillance, svelte, tête-à-tête, vignette,* and *vis-à-vis.*

There are also a fairish number of **loan translations** from French, such as *marriage of convenience* (*mariage de convenance*), *that goes without saying* (*ça va sans dire*), and *trial balloon* (*ballon d'essai*). In loan translation the parts of a foreign expression are translated, thus producing a new idiom in the native language, as in (to cite another French example) *reason of state* from *raison d'état.* Such forms are a kind of **calque**.

The suffix *-ville* in the names of so many American towns is, of course, of French origin. Of the American love for it, Matthew Arnold declared: "The mere nomenclature of the country acts upon a cultivated person like the incessant pricking of pins. What people in whom the sense of beauty and fitness was quick could have invented, or could tolerate, the hideous names ending in *ville,* the Briggsvilles, Higginsvilles, Jacksonvilles, rife from Maine to Florida; the jumble of unnatural and inappropriate names everywhere?" *Chowder, depot* 'railway station,' *levee* 'embankment,' *picayune, prairie, praline, shivaree* (*charivari*), and *voyageur* are other Americanisms of French origin.

SPANISH AND PORTUGUESE LOANWORDS

English has taken words from various other European languages as well—through travel, trade, exploration, and colonization. A good many Spanish and a smaller number of Portuguese loanwords have entered English mostly from the sixteenth century on, quite a few of which are ultimately non-European, many coming from the New World. Spanish borrowings include *alligator* (*el lagarto* 'the lizard'), *anchovy, armada, armadillo* (literally 'little armed one'), *avocado* (ultimately Nahuatl *ahuacatl*), *barbecue* (prob. ultimately Taino), *barracuda, bolero, cannibal* (*Caribal* 'Caribbean'), *cargo, cask* or *casque* (perh. through MF), *castanet, chocolate* (ultimately Nahuatl), *cigar, cockroach, cocoa, cordovan* 'a type of leather' (an older form, *cordwain,* comes through French), *corral, desperado, domino* 'cloak or mask,' *embargo, flotilla, galleon, guitar, junta, key* 'reef' (*cayo*), *maize* (ultimately Arawak), *mantilla, mescal* (ultimately Nahuatl), *mosquito* 'little fly,' *mulatto, negro, palmetto, peccadillo, plaza* (ultimately from Latin *platēa,* as are also *place,* which occurs in Old English times, and the Italian loanword *piazza*), *potato* (ultimately Arawak), *punctilio, sherry, silo, sombrero, tango, tomato* (ultimately Nahuatl), *tornado* (a blend of *tronada* 'thunderstorm' and *tornar* 'to turn'), *tortilla,* and *vanilla.* Many of these—for instance, *barbecue, barracuda,* and *tortilla*—are more familiar to Americans than to the English, though they may have occurred first in British sources.

A good many words were adopted from Spanish in the nineteenth century by Americans: *adobe, bonanza, bronco, buckaroo* (*vaquero*), *calaboose* (*calabozo*), *canyon, chaparral* 'scrub oak' (whence *chaps,* or *shaps,* 'leather pants worn by cowboys as protection against such vegetation'), *cinch, frijoles, hacienda, hoosegow* (*juzgado* 'tribunal'), *lariat* (*la reata* 'the rope'), *lasso, mesa, mustang, patio, pinto, poncho, pueblo, ranch, rodeo, sierra, siesta, stampede* (*estampida*), *stevedore* (*estivador* 'packer'), and *vamoose* (*vamos* 'let's go'). *Mescal, mesquite,* and *tamale* are ultimately Nahuatl, entering American English before the nineteenth century, like similar loans in British English, by way of Spanish. *Chili,* also of Nahuatl origin, entered British English in the seventeenth century, but it is likely, as M. M. Mathews (*Some Sources of Southernisms* 18) points out, that its occurrence in American English in the nineteenth century—"at the time we began to make first hand acquaintance with the Spanish speakers on our Southwestern border"—is not a continuation of the British tradition but represents an independent borrowing of a word for which Americans had had, before that time, very little if any use.

Twentieth-century borrowings include another food term—*frijoles refritos* and its loan translation, *refried beans*—as well as terms for drinks, such as *margarita* and *sangria. Chicano, macho,* and *machismo* reflect social phenomena. *Moment of truth* 'critical time for reaching a decision or taking action' is a translation of *momento de la verdad* refering to the moment of the kill, when a matador faces the charging bull, and was popularized by Hemingway's *Death in the Afternoon.* Persons who use the expression now may be unaware of its origin in bullfighting.

No words came into English directly from Portuguese until the Modern English period; those that have been adopted include *albino, bossa nova, flamingo, lambada, madeira* (from the place), *molasses, pagoda, palaver,* and *pickaninny* (*pequenino* 'very small'). There are a few others that are considerably less familiar.

ITALIAN LOANWORDS

From yet another Romance language, Italian, English has acquired a good many words, including much of our musical terminology. As early as the sixteenth century, *duo, fugue, madrigal, viola da gamba* 'viol for the leg,' and *violin* appear in English; in the seventeenth century, *allegro, largo, opera, piano* 'soft' (as the name of the instrument, it is an 1803 clipping of eighteenth-century *pianoforte*), *presto, recitative, solo,* and *sonata;* in the eighteenth, when interest in Italian music reached its apogee in England, *adagio, andante, aria, cantata, concerto, contralto, crescendo, diminuendo, duet, falsetto, finale, forte* 'loud' (the identically written word pronounced with final *e* silent and meaning 'strong point' is from French), *libretto, maestro, obbligato, oratorio, rondo, soprano, staccato, tempo, trio, trombone, viola,* and *violoncello;* and in the nineteenth, *alto, cadenza, diva, legato, piccolo, pizzicato, prima donna,* and *vibrato.*

Other loanwords from Italian include *artichoke, balcony, balloon, bandit, bravo, broccoli, cameo, canto, carnival, casino, cupola, dilettante* (frequently pronounced as if French, by analogy with *debutante*), *firm* 'business association,' *fresco, ghetto, gondola, grotto, incognito, inferno, influenza, lagoon, lava, malaria* (*mala aria* 'bad air'), *maraschino, miniature, motto, pergola, piazza, portico,* *regatta, replica, scope, stanza, stiletto, studio, torso, umbrella, vendetta,* and *volcano,* not to mention those words of ultimate Italian origin, like *cartoon, citron,* *corridor, gazette,* and *porcelain,* which have entered English by way of French. An expression of farewell, *ciao* [čaʊ], enjoyed a period of great, although brief, popularity in trendy circles. The term *la dolce vita* was popularized by an Italian motion picture of that name; *paparazzi* are free-lance photographers who specialize in candid shots of beautiful people indulging in *la dolce vita.* Another kind of influence is attested by *Cosa Nostra* and *Mafioso,* as well as the translation *godfather* for the head of a crime syndicate.

Macaroni (Mod. Italian *maccheroni*) came into English in the sixteenth century (its doublet *macaroon,* though designating quite a different food, entered English by way of French in the seventeenth century), *vermicelli* in the seventeenth, and *spaghetti* and *gorgonzola* (from the town) in the nineteenth. *Ravioli* (as *rafiol*) occurs in English in the fifteenth century, and later as *raviol* in the seventeenth century. Both forms are rare; the modern form thus can hardly be considered as continuing an older tradition but is instead a reborrowing, perhaps by way of American English in the twentieth century. *Al dente, lasagna, linguine, manicotti,* *pizza,* and *scampi* are also doubtless twentieth-century introductions into English—most of them probably by way of America, where Italian cooking became popular earlier than in England.

GERMANIC LOANWORDS

Loanwords from Low German

Dutch and other forms of Low German have contributed a number of words to English, to a large extent via the commercial relationships existing between the English and the Dutch and Flemish-speaking peoples from the Middle Ages on. It is often difficult to be sure which of the Low German languages was the source of an early loanword because they are quite similar.

It is not surprising in view of their eminence in seafaring activities that the Dutch should have contributed a number of nautical terms: *boom* 'spar,' *bowline,* *bowsprit, buoy, commodore, cruise, deck* (Dutch *dec* 'roof,' then in English 'roof of a ship,' a meaning that later got into Dutch), *dock, freight, keel, lighter* 'flat-bottomed boat,' *rover* 'pirate,' *scow, skipper* (*schipper* 'shipper,' that is, 'master of a ship'), *sloop, smuggle, split* (in early use, 'break a ship on a rock'), *taffrail,* *yacht,* and *yawl.*

The Dutch and the Flemish were also famed for their cloth making. Terms like *cambric, duck* (a kind of cloth), *duffel* (from the name of a place), *nap, pea jacket,* and *spool* suggest the cloth-making trade, which merchants carried to England, along with such commercial terms as *dollar, groat, guilder,* and *mart.* England was also involved militarily with Holland, a connection reflected in a number of loan-words: *beleaguer, forlorn hope* (a remodeling by folk etymology from *verloren hoop* 'lost troop,' Dutch *hoop* being cognate with English *heap,* as of men), *fur-lough, kit* (originally a vessel for carrying a soldier's equipment), *knapsack, onslaught,* and *tattoo* 'drum signal, military entertainment.'

The reputation of the Dutch for eating and especially drinking well is attested by *booze, brandy(wine), gherkin, gin* (short for *genever*—borrowed by the Dutch from Old French, ultimately Latin *juniperus* 'juniper,' confused in English with the name of the city Geneva), *hop* (a plant whose cones are used as a flavoring in malt liquors), *log(g)y,* and *pickle.* Perhaps as a result of indulgence in such Dutch pleas-ures, we have *frolic* (*vrolijk* 'joyful,' cognate with German *fröhlich*) and *rant* (ear-lier 'be boisterously merry').

Dutch painting was also valued in England, and consequently we have as loan-words *easel, etch, landscape* (the last element of which has given rise to a large number of derivatives, including recently *moonscape* and *earthscape* as space travel has allowed us to take a larger view of our surroundings), *maulstick,* and *sketch.*

Miscellaneous loans from Low German include *boor* (*boer*), *brake, gimp, han-ker, isinglass* (a folk-etymologized form of *huysenblas*), *luck, skate* (Dutch *schaats,* with the final *-s* mistaken for a plural ending), *snap, wagon* (the related OE *wægn* gives modern *wain*), and *wiseacre* (Middle Dutch *wijssegghher* 'sooth-sayer'). From South African Dutch (Afrikaans) have come *apartheid, comman-deer, commando, kraal* (borrowed by Dutch from Portuguese and related to the Spanish loanword *corral*), *spoor, trek,* and *veldt.*

A number of loanwords have entered English through the contact of Americans with Dutch settlers, especially in the New York area. There are Dutch-American food terms like *coleslaw* (*koolsla* 'cabbage salad'), *cookie, cranberry, cruller, pit* 'fruit stone,' and *waffle.* The diversity of other loanwords reflects the variety of cultural contacts English and Dutch speakers had in the New World: *boodle, boss, bowery, caboose, dope, Santa Claus* (*Sante Klaas* 'Saint Nicholas'), *sleigh, snoop, spook,* and *stoop* 'small porch.'

Loanwords from High German

High German has had comparatively little impact on English. Much of the ver-nacular of geology and mineralogy is of German origin—for instance, *cobalt, feldspar* (a half-translation of *Feldspath*), *gneiss, kleinite* (from Karl Klein, miner-alogist), *lawine* 'avalanche,' *loess, meerschaum, nickel* (originally *Kupfernickel,* perhaps 'copper demon,' partially translated as *kopparnickel* by the Swedish min-eralogist Von Cronstedt, from whose writings the abbreviated form entered English in 1755), *quartz, seltzer* (ultimately a derivative of Selters, near Wiesbaden), and *zinc. Carouse* occurs in English as early as the sixteenth century, from the German *gar aus* 'all out,' meaning the same as *bottoms up.* Originally adverbial, it almost immediately came to be used as a verb, and shortly afterward as a noun.

Other words taken from German include such culinary terms as *bratwurst, braunschweiger, delicatessen, noodle (Nudel), pretzel, pumpernickel, sauerkraut* (occurring first in British English, but the English never cared particularly for the dish, and the word may to all intents and purposes be considered an Americanism, independently reborrowed), *schnitzel, wienerwurst,* and *zwieback. Knackwurst, Liederkranz,* and *sauerbraten* are fairly well known but can hardly be considered completely naturalized. *Liverwurst* is a half-translation of *Leberwurst. Hamburger, frankfurter,* and *wiener* are doubtless the most popular of all German loans (although now the first is usually abbreviated to *burger,* and the latter two have been supplanted by *hot dog*). The vernacular of drinking includes *bock* (from *Eimbocker Bier* 'beer of Eimbock,' shortened in German to *Bockbier*), *katzenjammer* 'hangover,' *kirsch(wasser), lager,* and *schnapps.*

Other words from German include *angst, drill* 'fabric,' *hamster, landau* (from the place of that name), *plunder, waltz,* and the dog names *dachshund, Doberman(n) pinscher, poodle (Pudel),* and *spitz.* We also have *edelweiss, ersatz, hinterland, leitmotiv, poltergeist, rucksack, schottische, wunderkind, yodel (jodeln),* and the not yet thoroughly naturalized *Doppelgänger, gemütlich, Gestalt, Schadenfreude, Sitzfleisch* 'perseverance,' *Weltanschauung* and its loan translation *worldview,* and *Zeitgeist. Ablaut, umlaut,* and *schwa* (ultimately Hebrew) have been used as technical terms in this book. *Blitz(krieg)* and *Luftwaffe* had an infamous success in 1940 and 1941, but they have since receded although *blitz* has reincarnated as a football term with other metaphorical uses.

Seminar and *semester* are, of course, ultimately Latin, but they entered American English by way of German. *Seminar* is probably an independent borrowing in both British and American about the same time, the late nineteenth century, when many American and English scholars went to Germany in pursuit of their doctorates. *Semester* is known in England, but the English have little use for it save in reference to foreign universities. *Academic freedom* is a loan translation of *akademische Freiheit. Bummeln* is used by German students to mean 'to loiter, waste time,' and it may be the source of American English *to bum* and the noun in the sense 'loafer,' though this need not be an academic importation.

On a less elevated level, American English uses such expressions as *(on the) fritz, gesundheit* (when someone has sneezed), *hex, kaffeeklatsch* and its anglicization as *coffee clutch, kaput,* and *nix (nichts).* German-Americans have doubtless been responsible for adapting the German suffix *-fest* to English uses, as in *songfest* and *gabfest. Biergarten* has undergone translation in *beer garden; kindergarten* is frequently pronounced as though the last element were English *garden.* By way of the Germans from the Palatinate who settled in southern Pennsylvania in the early part of the eighteenth century come a number of terms of German origin little known in other parts of the United States, such as *smearcase* 'cottage cheese' *(Schmierkäse), snits* 'fruit cut for drying,' and *sots* 'yeast.' *Kriss Kingle* or *Kriss Kringle (Christkindl* 'Christ child') and *to dunk* have become nationally known.

Yiddish (that is, *Jüdisch* 'Jewish') has been responsible for the introduction of a number of German words and minced forms of German words, some having special meanings in Yiddish, among them, *kibitzer, phoney, schlemiel, schmaltz, schnozzle, shmo, shnook, shtick,* and others less widely known to non-Jews. Other contributions of Yiddish are *chutzpah, klutz, kvetch, mavin, mensch, nebbish, nosh, schlep, schlock, schmear, yenta,* and *zoftig*—distinctly ethnic in tone, although several have become characteristic of New York. The suffix *-nik,* ultimately of Slavic origin and popularized by the Soviet *sputnik,* has also been disseminated by Yiddish through such forms as *nudnik;* it has been extended to forms like *beatnik, filmnik, neatnik, no-goodnik,* and *peacenik.*

LOANWORDS FROM THE EAST

Near East

As early as Old English times, words from the East doubtless trickled into the language, then always by way of other languages. A number of words ultimately Arabic, most of them having to do in one way or another with science or with commerce, came in during the Middle English period, usually by way of French or Latin. These include *amber, camphor, cipher* (from Arabic *ṣifr* by way of Medieval Latin; the Italian modification of the same Arabic word as *zero* entered English in the early Modern period), *cotton, lute, mattress, orange, saffron, sugar, syrup,* and *zenith.*

The Arabic definite article *al* is retained in one form or another in *alchemy, alembic, algorism, alkali, almanac, azimuth* (*as* [for *al*] plus *sumūt* 'the ways'), *elixir* (*el* [for *al*] plus *iksīr* 'the philosopher's stone'), and *hazard* (*az* [for *al*] plus *zahr* 'the die'). In *admiral,* occurring first in Middle English, the Arabic article occurs in the final syllable: the word is an abbreviation of some such phrase as *amīr-al-baḥr* 'commander (of) the sea.' Through confusion with Latin *admīrābilis* 'admirable,' the word has acquired a *d; d*-less forms occur, however, as late as the sixteenth century, though ultimately the blunder with *d,* which occurs in the first known recording of the word—in Layamon's *Brut,* written around the end of the twelfth century—was to prevail.

Alcohol (*al-kuḥl* 'the kohl, that is, powder of antimony for staining the eyelids') developed its modern meaning by generalization to 'powder' of any kind, then to 'essence' or 'spirit' as in obsolete *alcohol of wine,* and thence to the spirituous element in beverages. *Alcove* and *algebra,* also beginning with the article, were introduced in early Modern times, along with a good many words without the article—for instance, *assassin* (originally 'hashish eater'), *caliber, candy, carat, caraway, fakir, garble, giraffe, harem, hashish, henna, jinn* (plural of *jinni*), *lemon, magazine* (ultimately an Arabic plural form meaning 'storehouses'), *minaret, mohair, sherbet,* and *tariff.* Some of these were transmitted through Italian, others through French; some were taken directly from Arabic. *Coffee,* ultimately Arabic, was taken into English by way of Turkish.

Other Semitic languages have contributed little directly, though a number of words ultimately Hebrew have come to us by way of French or Latin. Regardless of the method of their transmission, Hebrew is the ultimate or immediate origin of *amen, behemoth, cabala* or *Kabbalah* (via medieval Latin from Rabbinical Heb. *qabbālāh* 'received [lore],' whence also, by way of French, *cabal*), *cherub, hallelujah, jubilee, rabbi, Sabbath, seraph, shekel,* and *shibboleth.* Both *Jehovah* (*Yahweh*) and *Satan* are Hebrew. Yiddish uses a very large number of Hebrew words and seems to have been the medium of transmission for *goy, kosher, matzo* (plural *matzoth*), *mazuma,* and *tokus* 'backside.'

Iran and India

Persian and Sanskrit are not exotic in the same sense as Arabic, for both are Indo-European; yet the regions in which they were spoken were far removed from England, and they were to all intents and purposes highly exotic. Consequently, such words as Persian *bazaar* and *caravan* (in the nineteenth century clipped to *van*) must have seemed exotic to the English in the sixteenth century, when they first became current. *Azure, musk, paradise, satrap, scarlet, taffeta,* and *tiger* occur, among others, in the Middle English period. None of these are direct loans, coming rather through Latin or Old French; later, from the same two immediate sources, come *naphtha, tiara,* and a few Persian words borrowed through Turkish, such as *giaour.*

In addition, some Persian words were borrowed in India. *Cummerbund* 'loinband' first appears (as *combarband*) in the early seventeenth century, and is now used for an article of men's semiformal evening dress frequently replacing the low-cut waistcoat. *Seersucker* is an Indian modification of Persian *shīr o shakkar* 'milk and sugar,' the name of a fabric. *Khaki* 'dusty, cloth of that color,' recorded in English first in 1857 but not widely known in America until much later, was at first pronounced ['kɑki], though ['kæki] is normal nowadays.

Direct from Persian, in addition to *caravan* and *bazaar,* come *baksheesh, dervish, mogul, shah,* and *shawl. Chess,* as noted earlier, comes directly from Middle French *esches* (the plural of *eschec*) with loss of its first syllable by aphesis, but the word is ultimately Persian, as is the cognate *check* (in all its senses) from the Middle French singular *eschec.* The words go back to Persian *shāh* 'king,' which was taken into Arabic in the specific sense 'the king in the game of chess,' whence *shāh māt* 'the king is dead,' the source of *checkmate.* The derivative *exchequer* (OF *eschequier* 'chess board') came about through the fact that accounts used to be reckoned on a table marked with squares like a chess (or *checker*) board. *Rook* 'chess piece' is also ultimately derived from Persian *rukhkh* 'castle.'

From Sanskrit come, along with a few others, *avatar, guru, karma, mahatma, mantra, swastika,* and *yoga* ('union,' akin to English *yoke*). *Swastika,* a sacred symbol in several Indian religions, whose root meaning is 'well-being,' is often thought of as a symbol of the Nazi party in Germany because they adopted the shape for their own purposes, but the term was actually little known in that country, where the name of the figure was *Hakenkreuz* 'hook-cross'; *swastika* occurs in English first in the latter half of the nineteenth century. Sanskrit *dvandva, sandhi,* and *svarabhakti* are pretty much confined to the vernacular of linguistics; nonlinguists get along without them very well.

Ginger, which occurs in Old English (*gingifere*), is ultimately Prakrit. From Hindustani come *bandanna, bangle, bungalow, chintz, cot, dinghy, dungaree, gunny* 'sacking,' *juggernaut, jungle, loot, maharaja* (and *maharani*), *nabob, pajamas, pundit, sahib, sari, shampoo, thug,* and *tom-tom,* along with a number of other words that are much better known in England than in America (for instance, *babu, durbar,* and *pukka*). *Pal* is from Romany, or Gypsy, which is an Indic dialect. A good many Indic words have achieved general currency in English because of their use by literary men, especially Kipling, though he had distinguished predecessors, including Scott, Byron, and Thackeray.

The non-Indo-European languages, called Dravidian, spoken in southern India have contributed such fairly well-known words as *catamaran, copra, curry, mango, pariah,* and *teak.* Of these, *catamaran, curry,* and *pariah* are direct loans from Tamil; the others have come to us by way of Portuguese, *mango* from Portuguese by way of Malay.

Far East and Australasia

Other English words from languages spoken in the Orient are comparatively few in number, but some are quite well known. *Silk* may be ultimately from Chinese, although there is no known etymon in that language; as *seoloc* or *sioloc,* the word came into English in Old English times from Baltic or Slavic. From various dialects of Chinese come *ch'i-kung* (or *qigong*), *feng shui, foo yong, ginseng, gung-ho, I-Ching, ketchup, kowtow, kumquat, kung fu, litchi, pongee, t'ai chi ch'uan, tea* (and its informal British variant *char*), *wok, wonton,* and *yin-yang. Typhoon* is a remodeling based on a Chinese word meaning 'big wind' of an earlier form with roots in Portuguese, Hindi, Arabic, Latin, and ultimately Greek, being a word with a very mixed ancestry. Americanisms of Chinese origin are *chop suey, chow, chow mein,* and *tong* 'secret society.'

From Japanese have come *aikido, banzai, geisha, ginkgo, go* 'a board game,' *Godzilla, hara-kiri, haiku, (jin)ricksha, karaoke, karate, kimono, miso, Pac-Man, Pokemon, sake* 'liquor,' *samurai, soy(a), sushi,* and even *Walkman* (although it is made from two English words), along with the ultimately Chinese *judo, jujitsu, tofu,* and *tycoon. Zen* is ultimately Sanskrit, by way of Chinese. *Kamikaze,* introduced during World War II as a term for suicide pilots, literally means 'divine wind'; it has come to be used for anything that is recklessly destructive. From Korean comes *kimchee* 'spicy pickled cabbage.'

From the languages spoken in the islands of the Pacific come *bamboo, gingham, launch,* and *mangrove,* and others mostly adopted before the beginning of the nineteenth century by way of French, Portuguese, Spanish, or Dutch. *Rattan,* direct from Malay, appears first in Pepys's Diary (as *rattoon*), where it designates, not the wood, but a cane made of it: "Mr. Hawley did give me a little black rattoon, painted and gilt" (September 13, 1660).

Polynesian *taboo* and *tattoo* 'decorative permanent skin marking,' along with a few other words from the same source, appear in English around the time of Captain

James Cook's voyages (1768–79); they occur first in his journals. (This *tattoo* is not the same as *tattoo* 'drum or bugle signal, (later) military entertainment,' which is from Dutch *tap toe* 'the tap (is) to,' that is, 'the taproom is closed.') *Hula* (1825) is Hawaiian Polynesian, as are *lei* (1843), *luau* (1853), *kahuna* (1886), and *ukulele* (1896). Captain Cook also first recorded Australian *kangaroo. Boomerang* (as *wo-mur-rāng*), another Australian word, occurs first somewhat later. *Budgerigar,* also Australian and designating a kind of parrot, is well known in England, where it is frequently clipped to *budgie* by those who fancy the birds, usually known as *parakeets* in America.

OTHER SOURCES

Loanwords from African Languages

A few words from languages that were spoken on the west coast of Africa have entered English by way of Portuguese and Spanish, notably *banana* and *yam,* both appearing toward the end of the sixteenth century. It is likely that *yam* entered the vocabulary of American English independently. In the South, where it is used more frequently than elsewhere, it designates not just any kind of sweet potato, as in other parts, but a red sweet potato, which is precisely the meaning it has in the Gullah form *yambi.* Hence it is likely that this word was introduced into Southern American English direct from Africa, even though there is no question of its Portuguese transmission in earlier English.

Voodoo, with its variant *hoodoo,* is likewise of African origin and was introduced by way of American English. *Gorilla* is apparently African: it first occurs in English in the *Boston Journal of Natural History* in 1847, according to the *Dictionary of Americanisms,* though a Latin plural form *gorillae* occurs in 1799 in British English. *Juke* (more correctly *jook*) and *jazz* are Americanisms of African origin. Both were more or less disreputable when first introduced but have in the course of time lost most of their earlier sexual connotations. Other African words transmitted into American English are *banjo, buckra, cooter* 'turtle,' the synonymous *goober* and *pinder* 'peanut,' *gumbo, jigger* 'sand flea,' recorded in the dictionaries as *chigoe,* and *zombi. Samba* and *rumba* are ultimately African, coming to English by way of Brazilian Portuguese and Cuban Spanish, respectively. There can no longer be much doubt that *tote* is of African origin; the evidence presented by Lorenzo Dow Turner (203) seems fairly conclusive.

Slavic, Hungarian, Turkish, and American Indian

Very minor sources of the English vocabulary are Slavic, Hungarian, Turkish, and American Indian, with few words from these sources used in English contexts without reference to the peoples or places from which they were borrowed. Most have been borrowed during the Modern period, since 1500, and practically all by way of other languages.

Slavic *sable* comes to us in Middle English times not directly but by way of French. From Czech we later acquired, also indirectly, *polka. Mazurka* is from a Polish term for a dance characteristic of the Mazur community. We have borrowed the word *horde* indirectly from the Poles, who themselves acquired it from the Turks. *Astrakhan* and *mammoth* are directly from Russian. Other Russian words that are known, though some are not yet fully naturalized, are *apparatchik, bolshevik, borzoi, czar* (ultimately Lat. *Caesar*), *glasnost, intelligentsia* (ultimately Latin), *kopeck, muzhik, perestroika, pogrom, ruble, samovar, soviet, sputnik, steppe, tovarisch, troika, tundra, ukase,* and *vodka.*

Goulash, hussar, and *paprika* have been taken directly from Hungarian. *Coach* comes to us directly from French *coche* but goes back ultimately to Hungarian *kocsi. Vampire* is of Hungarian or Slavic origin (the close linguistic contact among East Europeans making it often difficult to be sure of exact sources), but the shortening to *vamp* is a purely native English phenomenon.

Jackal, ultimately Persian, comes to English by way of Turkish; *khan* occurs as a direct loan quite early. Other Turkish words used in English include *fez* and the fairly recent *shish kebab. Tulip* is from *tulipa(nt),* a variant of *tülbend* (taken by Turkish from Persian *dulband*); a doublet of the Turkish word comes into English in modified form as *turban.* The flower was so called because it was thought to look like the Turkish headgear. *Coffee,* as has been pointed out, is ultimately Arabic, but comes to us directly from Turkish; the same is true of *kismet.*

American Indian words do not loom large, even in American English, though many have occurred in American English writings. Algonquian words that have survived are, thanks to the European vogue of James Fenimore Cooper, about as well known transatlantically as in America: they include *moccasin, papoose, squaw, toboggan,* and *tomahawk.* Others with perhaps fewer literary associations are *moose, opossum, pecan, skunk, terrapin,* and *woodchuck.* Muskogean words are more or less confined to the southern American states—for instance, *bayou, catalpa,* and a good many proper names like *Tallahassee, Tombigbee,* and *Tuscaloosa.* Many place names are, of course, taken from Indian languages. Loans from Nahuatl, almost invariably of Spanish transmission, have been mentioned already.

THE SOURCES OF RECENT LOANWORDS

English speakers continue to borrow words from almost every language spoken upon the earth, although no longer with the frequency characteristic of the late Middle Ages and Renaissance. There has also been a shift in the relative importance of languages from which English borrows. A study by Garland Cannon of more than a thousand recent loanwords from eighty-four languages shows that about 25 percent are from French; 8 percent each from Japanese and Spanish; 7 percent each from Italian and Latin; 6 percent each from African languages, German, and Greek; 4 percent each from Russian and Yiddish; 3 percent from Chinese; and progressively smaller percentages from Arabic, Portuguese, Hindi, Sanskrit, Hebrew, Afrikaans, Malayo-Polynesian, Vietnamese, Amerindian languages, Swedish, Bengali, Danish, Indonesian, Korean, Persian, Amharic, Eskimo-Aleut, Irish, Norwegian, and thirty other languages.

Latin has declined as a source for loanwords perhaps because English has already borrowed so much of the Latin vocabulary that there is comparatively little unborrowed. Now, rather than borrow directly, we make new Latinate words out of English morphemes originally from Latin. The increase in the importance of Japanese as a source for loans is doubtless a consequence of the increased commercial importance of Japan. French is the most important single language for borrowing, but more French loans enter through British than through American English, because of the geographical proximity of the United Kingdom to France. Conversely, Spanish loanwords are often borrowed from American Spanish into American English.

ENGLISH REMAINS ENGLISH

Enough has been written to indicate the cosmopolitanism of the present English vocabulary. Yet English remains English in every essential respect: the words that all of us use over and over again, the grammatical structures in which we couch our observations upon practically everything under the sun remain as distinctively English as they were in the days of Alfred the Great. What has been acquired from other languages has not always been particularly worth gaining: no one could prove by any set of objective standards that *army* is a "better" word than *dright* or *here,* which it displaced, or that *advice* is any better than the similarly displaced *rede,* or that *to contend* is any better than *to flite.* Those who think that *manual* is a better, or more beautiful, or more intellectual word than English *handbook* are, of course, entitled to their opinion. But such esthetic preferences are purely matters of style and have nothing to do with the subtle patternings that make one language different from another. The words we choose are nonetheless of tremendous interest in themselves, and they throw a good deal of light upon our cultural history.

But with all its manifold new words from other tongues, English could never have become anything but English. And as such it has sent out to the world, among many other things, some of the best books the world has ever known. It is not unlikely, in the light of writings by English speakers in earlier times, that this would have been so even if we had never taken any words from outside the word hoard that has come down to us from those times. It is true that what we have borrowed has brought greater wealth to our word stock, but the true Englishness of our mother tongue has in no way been lessened by such loans, as those who speak and write it lovingly will always keep in mind.

It is highly unlikely that many readers will have noted that the preceding paragraph contains not a single word of foreign origin. It was perhaps not worth the slight effort involved to write it so; it does show, however, that English would not be quite so impoverished as some commentators suppose it would be without its many accretions from other languages.

FOR FURTHER READING

General

Metcalf. *The World in So Many Words.*
Serjeantson. *A History of Foreign Words in English.*

Some Source Languages

Bluestein. *Anglish-Yinglish.*
Cannon and Kaye. *The Arabic Contributions to the English Language.*
————. *The Persian Contributions to the English Language.*
Cannon and Warren. *The Japanese Contributions to the English Language.*
Chan and Kwok. *A Study of Lexical Borrowing from Chinese.*
Geipel. *The Viking Legacy.*
Pfeffer and Cannon. *German Loanwords in English.*
Rosten. *The Joys of Yinglish.*

SELECTED BIBLIOGRAPHY

Works cited in the text are listed here, along with some additional books and periodicals that should prove useful in one way or another to the student of the English language. This bibliography is necessarily limited; it includes works ranging from the semipopular to the scholarly abstruse, although only a few specialized studies of technical problems have been included. A few items deal with general linguistics.

Aarsleff, Hans. *The Study of Language in England, 1780–1860.* Minneapolis: University of Minnesota Press, 1983.

Aarts, Bas, and Charles F. Meyer, eds. *The Verb in Contemporary English: Theory and Description.* Cambridge: Cambridge University Press, 1995.

Acronyms, Initialisms, & Abbreviations Dictionary. Detroit, MI: Gale, annual.

Adams, Valerie. *Complex Words in English.* Harlow, Essex: Pearson Education, Longman, 2001.

———. *An Introduction to Modern English Word-Formation.* London: Longman, 1973.

Aitchison, Jean. *Language Change: Progress or Decay?* 3rd ed. Cambridge: Cambridge University Press, 2001.

———. *The Seeds of Speech: Language Origin and Evolution.* Cambridge: Cambridge University Press, 1996.

———. *Words in the Mind: An Introduction to the Mental Lexicon.* Oxford: Blackwell, 1989.

Akmajian, Adrian, ed. *Linguistics: An Introduction to Language and Communication.* 5th ed. Cambridge, MA: MIT Press, 2001.

Algeo, John. "British and American Grammatical Differences." *International Journal of Lexicography* 1 (1988): 1–31.

———, ed. *The Cambridge History of the English Language.* Vol. 6: *English in North America.* Cambridge: Cambridge University Press, 2001.

Algeo, John, and Adele Algeo, eds. *Fifty Years Among the New Words: A Dictionary of Neologisms, 1941–1991.* New York: Cambridge University Press, 1991.

Allan, Keith, and Kate Burridge. *Euphemism & Dysphemism: Language Used as Shield and Weapon.* New York: Oxford University Press, 1991.

Allen, Cynthia L. *Case Marking and Reanalysis: Grammatical Relations from Old to Early Modern English.* Oxford: Clarendon Press, 1995.

Allen, Harold B. *The Linguistic Atlas of the Upper Midwest.* 3 vols. Minneapolis: University of Minnesota Press, 1973–6.

Allen, Irving Lewis. *The City in Slang: New York Life and Popular Speech.* New York: Oxford University Press, 1993.

———. *Unkind Words: Ethnic Labeling from "Redskin" to "WASP."* New York: Bergin & Garvey, 1990.

Allerton, D. J. *Stretched Verb Constructions in English.* London: Routledge, 2002.

Allsopp, Richard, ed. *Dictionary of Caribbean English Usage.* Oxford: Oxford University Press, 1996.

American Speech: A Quarterly of Linguistic Usage. Journal of the American Dialect Society, 1925–.

American Tongues. Video produced by the Center for New American Media, New York, n.d. Distributed by CNAM Film Library, Hohokus, NJ.

Arthur, Jay Mary. *Aboriginal English: A Cultural Study.* Melbourne, Australia: Oxford University Press, 1996.

Avis, Walter S., ed. *A Dictionary of Canadianisms on Historical Principles.* Toronto: Gage, 1967.

Avis, Walter S., Patrick D. Drysdale, Robert J. Gregg, Victoria E. Neufeldt, and Matthew H. Scargill, eds. *Gage Canadian Dictionary.* Toronto: Gage, 1983.

Ayto, John. *Euphemisms: Over 3000 Ways to Avoid Being Rude or Giving Offence.* London: Bloomsbury, 1993.

———. *Twentieth Century Words.* Oxford: Oxford University Press, 1999.

Bækken, Bjørg. *Word Order Patterns in Early Modern English: With Special Reference to the Position of the Subject and the Finite Verb.* Oslo, Norway: Novus, 1998.

Bailey, Richard W. *Images of English.* Ann Arbor: University of Michigan Press, 1991.

———. *Nineteenth-Century English.* Ann Arbor: University of Michigan Press, 1996.

Bailey, Richard W., and Manfred Görlach. *English as a World Language.* Ann Arbor: University of Michigan Press, 1982.

Baker, Sidney J. *The Australian Language.* 1966. Reprint. South Melbourne: Sun Books, 1986.

Baldi, Philip. *An Introduction to the Indo-European Languages.* Carbondale: Southern Illinois University Press, 1983.

Barber, Charles. *Early Modern English.* New ed. Edinburgh: Edinburgh University Press, 1997.

Barney, Stephen A. *Word-Hoard: An Introduction to Old English Vocabulary.* 2nd ed. New Haven, CT: Yale University Press, 1985.

Barnhart, Robert K., ed. *The Barnhart Dictionary of Etymology.* Bronx, NY: H. W. Wilson, 1988.

Barnhart, Robert K., and Sol Steinmetz with Clarence L. Barnhart. *Third Barnhart Dictionary of New English.* Bronx, NY: H. W. Wilson, 1990.

Baron, Naomi S. *Alphabet to Email: How Written English Evolved and Where It's Heading.* London and New York: Routledge, 2000.

———. *Growing Up with Language: How Children Learn to Talk.* Reading, MA: Addison-Wesley, 1992.

Bauer, Laurie. *English Word-Formation.* Cambridge: Cambridge University Press, 1983.

———. *An Introduction to International Varieties of English.* Edinburgh: Edinburgh University Press, 2002.

———. *Watching English Change: An Introduction to the Study of Linguistic Change in Standard Englishes in the Twentieth Century.* London: Longman, 1994.

Bauer, Laurie, and Peter Trudgill, eds. *Language Myths.* London: Penguin, 1998.

Baumgardner, Robert J., ed. *South Asian English: Structure, Use, and Users.* Urbana: University of Illinois Press, 1996.

Beekes, Robert S. P. *Comparative Indo-European Linguistics: An Introduction.* Amsterdam: Benjamins, 1995.

Béjoint, Henri. *Tradition and Innovation in Modern English Dictionaries.* Oxford: Clarendon, 1994.

Bell, Allan. *The Language of News Media.* Oxford: Blackwell, 1991.

Bell, Allan, and Koenraad Kuiper, eds. *New Zealand English.* Amsterdam: Benjamins, 2000.

Bennett, William H. *An Introduction to the Gothic Language.* New York: Modern Language Association of America, 1980.

Benson, Morton, Evelyn Benson, and Robert Ilson. *The BBI Dictionary of English Word Combinations.* Rev. ed. Amsterdam: Benjamins, 1997.

Benson, Phil. *Ethnocentrism and the English Dictionary.* London: Routledge, 2001.

Bex, Tony, and Richard J. Watts, eds. *Standard English: The Widening Debate.* London: Routledge, 1999.

Bickerton, Derek. *Language & Species.* Chicago: University of Chicago Press, 1990.

Bierce, Ambrose. *Write It Right: A Little Blacklist of Literary Faults.* New York: Neale, 1909.

Black, Jeremy. *A History of the British Isles.* New York: St. Martin's, 1996.

———. *A New History of England.* Stroud, Gloucestershire, UK: Sutton, 2000.

Blake, Joanna. *Routes to Child Language: Evolutionary and Developmental Precursors.* Cambridge: Cambridge University Press, 2000.

Blake, Norman, ed. *The Cambridge History of the English Language.* Vol. 2: *1066–1476.* Cambridge: Cambridge University Press, 1992.

———. *The English Language in Medieval Literature.* London: Dent, 1977.

Bliss, Alan. *Spoken English in Ireland, 1600–1740.* Dublin: Dolmen, 1979.

Bloom, Paul. *How Children Learn the Meanings of Words.* Cambridge, MA: MIT Press, 2000.

Bluestein, Gene. *Anglish-Yinglish: Yiddish in American Life and Literature.* 2nd ed. Lincoln: University of Nebraska Press, 1998.

Bolton, W. F., ed. *The English Language: Essays by English and American Men of Letters, 1490–1839.* Cambridge: Cambridge University Press, 1996.

Bonfiglio, Thomas Paul. *Race and the Rise of Standard American.* Berlin: Mouton de Gruyter, 2002.

Branford, Jean, and William Branford. *A Dictionary of South African English.* 4th ed. Cape Town, South Africa: Oxford University Press, 1991.

Brinton, Laurel J. *The Development of English Aspectual Systems.* Cambridge: Cambridge University Press, 1988.

———. *Pragmatic Markers in English: Grammaticalization and Discourse Functions.* Berlin: Mouton de Gruyter, 1996.

———. *The Structure of Modern English: A Linguistic Introduction.* Amsterdam: Benjamins, 2000.

Brunner, Karl. *An Outline of Middle English Grammar.* Cambridge, MA: Harvard University Press, 1963.

Buck, Carl Darling. *A Dictionary of Selected Synonyms in the Principal Indo-European Languages: A Contribution to the History of Ideas.* 1949. Reprint. Chicago: University of Chicago Press, 1988.

Burchfield, Robert, ed. *The Cambridge History of the English Language.* Vol. 5: *English in Britain and Overseas: Origins and Development.* Cambridge: Cambridge University Press, 1994.

———. *The New Fowler's Modern English Usage.* Oxford: Clarendon Press, 1996.

———, ed. *The New Zealand Pocket Oxford Dictionary.* Reprint with corrections. Auckland, New Zealand: Oxford University Press, 1990.

Burnley, David. *A Guide to Chaucer's Language.* Norman: University of Oklahoma Press, 1983.

Burrow, John Anthony, and Thorlac Turville-Petre. *A Book of Middle English.* 2nd ed. Cambridge, MA: Blackwell, 1996.

Butters, Ronald R. *The Death of Black English: Divergence and Convergence in Black and White Vernaculars.* Frankfurt am Main, Germany: Peter Lang, 1989.

Campbell, Alistair. *Old English Grammar.* Oxford: Clarendon, 1983.

Campbell, Lyle. *Historical Linguistics: An Introduction.* Edinburgh: Edinburgh University Press, 1998.

Cannon, Garland. *Historical Change and English Word-Formation: Recent Vocabulary.* New York: Lang, 1987.

Cannon, Garland, and Alan S. Kaye. *The Arabic Contributions to the English Language: An Historical Dictionary.* Wiesbaden, Germany: Harrassowitz, 1994.

———. *The Persian Contributions to the English Language: An Historical Dictionary.* Wiesbaden, Germany: Harrassowitz, 2001.

Cannon, Garland, and Nicholas Warren. *The Japanese Contributions to the English Language: An Historical Dictionary.* Wiesbaden, Germany: Harrassowitz, 1996.

Cardona, George, Henry M. Hoenigswald, and Alfred Senn, eds. *Indo-European and Indo-Europeans.* Philadelphia: University of Pennsylvania Press, 1970.

Carney, Edward. *A Survey of English Spelling.* London: Routledge, 1994.

Carr, Elizabeth Ball. *Da Kine Talk: From Pidgin to Standard English in Hawaii.* Honolulu: University of Hawaii Press, 1972.

Carstairs-McCarthy, Andrew. *The Origins of Complex Language: An Inquiry into the Evolutionary Beginnings of Sentences, Syllables, and Truth.* Oxford: Oxford University Press, 1999.

Carver, Craig M. *American Regional Dialects: A Word Geography.* Ann Arbor: University of Michigan Press, 1987.

———. *A History of English in Its Own Words.* New York: Harper-Collins, 1991.

Cassidy, Frederic G. *Jamaica Talk: Three Hundred Years of the English Language in Jamaica.* New York: St. Martin's, 1961.

Cassidy, Frederic G., and Joan Houston Hall, eds. *Dictionary of American Regional English.* Vol. 1–. Cambridge, MA: Belknap, 1985–.

Cassidy, Frederic G., and Robert B. Le Page. *Dictionary of Jamaican English.* Cambridge: Cambridge University Press, 1967.

Chambers, J. K. *Canadian English: Origins and Structures.* Toronto: Methuen, 1975.

———. *Sociolinguistic Theory: Linguistic Variation and Its Social Significance.* 2nd ed. Oxford: Blackwell, 2003.

Chan, Mimi, and Helen Kwok. *A Study of Lexical Borrowing from Chinese into English with Special Reference to Hong Kong.* Hong Kong: Centre of Asian Studies, University of Hong Kong, 1985.

Cheshire, Jenny, ed. *English around the World: Sociolinguistic Perspectives.* Cambridge: Cambridge University Press, 1991.

Claridge, Claudia. *Multi-Word Verbs in Early Modern English: A Corpus-Based Study.* Amsterdam: Rodopi, 2000.

Clark, Eve V. *First Language Acquisition.* Cambridge: Cambridge University Press, 2003.

Cobley, Paul, ed. *The Routledge Companion to Semiotics and Linguistics.* London: Routledge, 2001.

Corballis, Michael C. *From Hand to Mouth: The Origins of Language.* Princeton, NJ: Princeton University Press, 2002.

Craigie, William A. *English Spelling: Its Rules and Reasons.* New York: Crofts, 1927.

———. *The Study of American English.* S.P.E. Tract 27. Oxford: Clarendon Press, 1927.

Craigie, William A., and James Root Hulbert, eds. *A Dictionary of American English on Historical Principles.* 4 vols. Chicago: University of Chicago Press, 1938–44.

Crowley, Tony. *The Politics of Language in Ireland 1366–1922.* London: Routledge, 2000.

Crystal, David. *The Cambridge Encyclopedia of Language.* 2nd ed. Cambridge: Cambridge University Press, 1997.

————. *The Cambridge Encyclopedia of the English Language.* Cambridge: Cambridge University Press, 1995.

————. *A Dictionary of Language.* 2nd ed. Chicago: University of Chicago Press, 2001.

————. *Language and the Internet.* Cambridge: Cambridge University Press, 2001.

————. *Language Play.* Chicago: University of Chicago Press, 2001.

Cummings, D. W. *American English Spelling: An Informal Description.* Baltimore: Johns Hopkins University Press, 1988.

Curme, George O. *Parts of Speech and Accidence. A Grammar of the English Language,* vol. 2. Boston: Heath, 1935.

————. *Syntax. A Grammar of the English Language,* vol. 3. Boston: Heath, 1931.

Curtis, V. R. *Indo-European Origins.* New York: Lang, 1988.

Daniels, Peter T., and William Bright, eds. *The World's Writing Systems.* New York: Oxford University Press, 1996.

Danielsson, Bror, ed. *Works on English Orthography and Pronunciation, 1551, 1569, 1570* [by John Hart]. 2 vols. Stockholm: Almqvist and Wiksell, 1955–63.

Danielsson, Bror, and Arvid Gabrielson, eds. *Logonomia Anglica (1619)* [by Alexander Gill]. 2 vols. Stockholm: Almqvist and Wiksell, 1972.

Davis, Norman, Douglas Gray, Patricia Ingham, and Anne Wallace-Hadrill, comp. *A Chaucer Glossary.* Oxford: Clarendon, 1979.

Day, John V. *Indo-European Origins: The Anthropological Evidence.* Washington, DC: Institute for the Study of Man, 2001.

Denison, David. *English Historical Syntax: Verbal Constructions.* London: Longman, 1993.

Dialect Notes. Publication of the American Dialect Society, vols. 1–6, 1890–1939.

Dictionaries. Journal of the Dictionary Society of North America, 1979–.

A Dictionary of South African English on Historical Principles. Oxford: Oxford University Press, 1996.

Dimitrius, Jo-Ellan, and Mark Mazzarella. *Reading People: How to Understand People and Predict Their Behavior—Anytime, Anyplace.* New York: Ballantine, 1999.

Dinneen, Francis P. *General Linguistics.* Washington, DC: Georgetown University Press, 1995.

Diringer, David. *The Alphabet: A Key to the History of Mankind.* 3rd ed. 2 vols. New York: Funk & Wagnalls, 1968.

Dobson, Eric John. *English Pronunciation, 1500–1700.* 2nd ed. 2 vols. Oxford: Clarendon, 1968.

Douglas, Auriel. *Webster's New World Dictionary of Eponyms: Common Words from Proper Names.* New York: Webster's New World, 1990.

Dumas, Bethany K., and Jonathan Lighter. "Is *Slang* a Word for Linguists?" *American Speech* 53 (1978): 5–17.

Eggington, William, and Helen Wren. *Language Policy: Dominant English, Pluralist Challenges.* Amsterdam: Benjamins; Canberra: Language Australia, 1997.

Ekwall, Eilert. *American and British Pronunciation.* Uppsala, Sweden: Lundequistska Bokhandeln, 1946.

————. *The Concise Oxford Dictionary of English Place-Names.* 4th ed. Oxford: Clarendon, 1960.

————. *A History of Modern English Sounds and Morphology.* Trans. and ed. Alan Ward. Oxford: Blackwell, 1975.

Elliott, Ralph W. V. *Runes: An Introduction.* 2nd ed. Manchester, UK: Manchester University Press, 1989.

Ellis, Alexander J. *On Early English Pronunciation: With Special Reference to Shakspere and Chaucer.* EETS 2, 7, 14, 23, 56. 5 vols. London: Trübner, 1869–89.

Elsness, Johan. *The Perfect and the Preterite in Contemporary and Earlier English.* New York: Mouton de Gruyter, 1997.

English World-Wide. 1980–.

Evans, Angela Care. *The Sutton Hoo Ship Burial.* London: British Museum, 1986.

Faarlund, Jan Terje. *Syntactic Change: Toward a Theory of Historical Syntax.* Berlin: Mouton de Gruyter, 1990.

Faiss, Klaus. *English Historical Morphology and Word-Formation.* Trier, Germany: Wissenschaftlicher Verlag, 1992.

Farmer, John S., and William Ernest Henley. *Dictionary of Slang and Its Analogues.* 7 vols. 1890–1904. Reprint in 1 vol. New York: Dutton, 1970.

Finegan, Edward. *Attitudes toward English Usage: The History of a War of Words.* New York: Teachers College Press, 1980.

Finegan, Edward, and Niko Besnier. *Language: Its Structure and Use.* San Diego, CA: Harcourt, 1989.

Fischer, David Hackett. *Albion's Seed: Four British Folkways in America.* New York: Oxford University Press, 1989.

Fischer, Olga, Ans van Kemenade, Willem Koopman, and Wim van der Wuirff. *The Syntax of Early English.* Cambridge: Cambridge University Press, 2000.

Fischer, Roswitha. *Lexical Change in Present-Day English: A Corpus-Based Study of the Motivation, Institutionalization, and Productivity of Creative Neologisms.* Tübingen, Germany: Narr, 1998.

Fischer, Steven Roger. *A History of Language.* London: Reaktion, 1999.

———. *A History of Writing.* London: Reaktion, 2001.

Fisher, John H. *The Emergence of Standard English.* Lexington: University Press of Kentucky, 1996.

Fisiak, Jacek. *A Short Grammar of Middle English; Part One: Graphemics, Phonemics and Morphemics.* Warsaw, Poland: Panstwowe Wydawnictwo Naukowe, 1970.

Fisiak, Jacek, and Marcin Krygier, eds. *Advances in English Historical Linguistics (1996).* Berlin: Mouton de Gruyter, 1998.

Ford, Brian J. *The Secret Language of Life: How Animals and Plants Feel and Communicate.* New York: Fromm International, 2000.

Fowler, Henry W., and F. G. Fowler. *The King's English.* 3rd ed. Oxford: Clarendon, 1931.

Fox, Anthony. *Linguistic Reconstruction: An Introduction to Theory and Method.* Oxford: Oxford University Press, 1995.

Franklyn, Julian. *A Dictionary of Rhyming Slang.* 2nd ed. London: Routledge & Kegan Paul, 1961.

Franz, Wilhelm. *Shakespeare-Grammatik.* 3rd ed. Heidelberg, Germany: Winter, 1924.

Frawley, William J., ed. *International Encyclopedia of Linguistics.* 2nd ed. New York: Oxford University Press, 2003.

Freeman, Morton S. *A New Dictionary of Eponyms.* New York: Oxford University Press, 1997.

Friedman, Monroe. *A "Brand" New Language: Commercial Influences in Literature and Culture.* New York: Greenwood, 1991.

Gamkrelidze, Thomas V., and Vjaceslav V. Ivanov. *Indo-European and the Indo-Europeans: A Reconstruction and Historical Analysis of a Proto-Language and a Proto-Culture.* 2 vols. Ed. Werner Winter. Berlin: Mouton de Gruyter, 1995.

García, Ofelia, and Ricardo Otheguy, eds. *English across Cultures, Cultures across English: A Reader in Cross-cultural Communication.* Berlin: Mouton de Gruyter, 1989.

Geipel, John. *The Viking Legacy: The Scandinavian Influence on the English and Gaelic Languages.* Newton Abbot, Devon, UK: David and Charles, 1971.

Gelb, Ignace J. *A Study of Writing: The Foundations of Grammatology.* 2nd ed. Chicago: University of Chicago Press, 1963.

Gelderen, Elly van. *A History of English Reflexive Pronouns: Person, Self, and Interpretability.* Amsterdam: Benjamins, 2000.

Gilman, E. Ward. See *Merriam-Webster's Dictionary of English Usage.*

Gimbutas, Marija. *The Kurgan Culture and the Indo-Europeanization of Europe: Selected Articles from 1952 to 1993.* Washington, DC: Institute for the Study of Man, 1997.

Gimson, A. C. *Gimson's Pronunciation of English.* 6th ed. Rev. Alan Cruttenden. London: Arnold, 2001.

Gleason, Jean Berko. *The Development of Language.* 5th ed. Boston: Allyn and Bacon, 2001.

Goddard, Cliff. *Semantic Analysis: A Practical Introduction.* Oxford: Oxford University Press, 1998.

González, Roseann Dueñas, with Ildikó Melis, eds. *Language Ideologies: Critical Perspectives on the Official English Movement.* 2 vols. Urbana, IL: National Council of Teachers of English; Mahwah, NJ: Erlbaum, 2000–1.

Gordon, Elizabeth, and Tony Deverson. *New Zealand English: An Introduction to New Zealand Speech and Usage.* Auckland, New Zealand: Heinemann, 1986.

Görlach, Manfred. *Eighteenth-Century English.* Heidelberg, Germany: Winter, 2001.

———. *English in Nineteenth-Century England: An Introduction.* Cambridge: Cambridge University Press, 1999.

———. *Introduction to Early Modern English.* Cambridge: Cambridge University Press, 1991.

Gove, Philip Babcock. See *Webster's Third New International Dictionary.*

Gowers, Ernest. *The Complete Plain Words.* 3rd ed. Rev. Sidney Greenbaum and Janet Whitcut. London: H. M. Stationery Office, 1986.

Gramley, Stephan, and Kurt-Michael Pätzold. *A Survey of Modern English.* London: Routledge, 1992.

Green, D. H. *Language and History in the Early Germanic World.* Cambridge: Cambridge University Press, 1998.

Green, Jonathon. *Chasing the Sun: Dictionary Makers and the Dictionaries They Made.* New York: Holt, 1996.

Greenbaum, Sidney. *The Oxford English Grammar.* Oxford: Oxford University Press, 1996.

Greenberg, Joseph H. *Indo-European and Its Closest Relatives: The Eurasiatic Language Family.* 2 vols. Stanford, CA: Stanford University Press, 2000.

———. *Language Typology: A Historical and Analytical Overview.* The Hague: Mouton, 1974.

———. "Some Universals of Grammar with Particular Reference to the Order of Meaningful Elements." In *Universals of Language,* ed. J. H. Greenberg, pp. 73–113. Cambridge, MA: MIT Press, 1962.

Haas, W., ed. *Alphabets for English.* Manchester, UK: Manchester University Press, 1969.

Hall, Joan H., Nick Doane, and Dick Ringler, eds. *Old English and New: Studies in Language and Literature in Honor of Frederic G. Cassidy.* New York: Garland, 1992.

Hall, John R. Clark. *A Concise Anglo-Saxon Dictionary.* 4th ed. with a supplement by Herbert D. Meritt. Toronto: University of Toronto Press in association with the Medieval Academy of America, 1984.

Hanks, Patrick, and Flavia Hodges. *A Dictionary of Surnames.* Oxford: Oxford University Press, 1988.

Hargraves, Orin. *Mighty Fine Words and Smashing Expressions: Making Sense of Transatlantic English.* New York: Oxford University Press, 2003.

Harris, John. *Phonological Variation and Change: Studies in Hiberno-English.* Cambridge: Cambridge University Press, 1985.

Harris, John, David Little, and David Singleton, eds. *Perspectives on the English Language in Ireland.* Dublin: Trinity College, 1986.

Harris, Roy. *The Origin of Writing.* London: Duckworth, 1986.

Hawkins, R. E. *Common Indian Words in English.* Delhi, India: Oxford University Press, 1984.

Hayakawa, S. I., and Alan R. Hayakawa. *Language in Thought and Action.* 5th ed. San Diego, CA: Harcourt Brace Jovanovich, 1990.

Healey, John F. *The Early Alphabet.* Berkeley: University of California Press; London: British Museum, 1990.

Hendrickson, Robert. *American Talk: The Words and Ways of American Dialects.* New York: Penguin, 1987.

———. *World English: From Aloha to Zed.* New York: Wiley, 2001.

Hock, Hans Henrich, and Brian D. Joseph. *Language History, Language Change, and Language Relationship: An Introduction to Historical and Comparative Linguistics.* Berlin: Mouton de Gruyter, 1996.

Hogg, Richard M. *The Cambridge History of the English Language.* Vol. 1: *The Beginnings to 1066.* Cambridge: Cambridge University Press, 1992.

———. *A Grammar of Old English.* Oxford: Blackwell, 1992.

Holm, John A., with Alison W. Shilling. *Dictionary of Bahamian English.* Cold Spring, NY: Lexik House, 1982.

Hooker, J. T. *Reading the Past: Ancient Writing from Cuneiform to the Alphabet.* Berkeley: University of California Press; London: British Museum, 1990.

Horn, Wilhelm. *Laut und Leben: Englische Lautgeschichte der neuron Zeit (1400–1950).* Rev. and ed. Martin Lehnert. 2 vols. Berlin: Deutscher Verlag der Wissenschaften, 1954.

Hudson, Grover. *Essential Introductory Linguistics.* Oxford: Blackwell, 2000.

Hughes, Geoffrey. *A History of English Words.* Oxford: Blackwell, 2000.

Hüllen, Werner. *English Dictionaries, 800–1700: The Topical Tradition.* Oxford: Clarendon, 1999.

International Journal of Lexicography. 1988–.

Jackson, Howard. *Grammar and Meaning: A Semantic Approach to English Grammar.* London: Longman, 1990.

———. *Words and Their Meaning.* London: Longman, 1988.

Janson, Tore. *Speak: A Short History of Languages.* Oxford: Oxford University Press, 2002.

Jeffries, Lesley. *Meaning in English: An Introduction to Language Study.* New York: St. Martin's, 1998.

Jespersen, Otto. *Growth and Structure of the English Language.* 10th ed. Foreword by Randolph Quirk. Chicago: University of Chicago Press, 1982.

———. *John Hart's Pronunciation of English (1569–1570).* 1907. Reprint. Amsterdam: Swets and Zeitlinger, 1973.

———. *A Modern English Grammar on Historical Principles.* 7 vols. 1909–49. Reprint. London: Allen and Unwin, 1954.

———. *Progress in Language, with Special Reference to English.* 2nd ed. New York: Macmillan, 1909.

Jewell, Elizabeth J., and Frank Abate, eds. *The New Oxford American Dictionary.* New York: Oxford University Press, 2001.

Jones, Charles. *A History of English Phonology.* London: Longman, 1989.

Jones, Daniel. *English Pronouncing Dictionary.* 14th ed. Ed. A. C. Gimson. Rev. Susan Ramsaran. New York: Oxford University Press, 2001.

Journal of English and Germanic Philology. 1902–.

Journal of English Linguistics. 1967–.

Journal of Indo-European Studies. 1973–.

Kachru, Braj B. *The Other Tongue: English across Cultures.* 2nd ed. Urbana: University of Illinois Press, 1992.

Karmiloff, Kyra, and Annette Karmiloff-Smith. *Pathways to Language: From Fetus to Adolescent.* Cambridge, MA: Harvard University Press, 2001.

Kastovsky, Dieter, and Arthur Mettinger, eds. *The History of English in a Social Context: A Contribution to Historical Sociolinguistics.* Trends in Linguistics Studies and Monographs 129, ed. Werner Winter. Berlin: Mouton de Gruyter, 2000.

Kennedy, Arthur G. *Current English.* Boston: Ginn, 1935.

Kenyon, John Samuel. *American Pronunciation.* 12th ed. Ed. Donald M. Lance and Stewart A. Kingsbury. Ann Arbor, MI: Warh, 1997.

Kenyon, John Samuel, and Thomas Albert Knott. *A Pronouncing Dictionary of American English.* Springfield, MA: Merriam, 1953.

Kökeritz, Helge. *A Guide to Chaucer's Pronunciation.* New York: Holt, Rinehart and Winston, 1962.

———. *Shakespeare's Pronunciation.* New Haven, CT: Yale University Press, 1953.

Kövecses, Zoltán. *American English: An Introduction.* Peterborough, Ontario, Canada: Broadview Press, 2000.

Krapp, George Philip. *The English Language in America.* 2 vols. 1925. Reprint. New York: Ungar, 1960.

Kreidler, Charles W. *Introducing English Semantics.* London: Routledge, 1998.

Kretzschmar, William A., Jr., Virginia G. McDavid, Theodore K. Lerud, and Ellen Johnson. *Handbook of the Linguistic Atlas of the Middle and South Atlantic States.* Chicago: University of Chicago Press, 1993.

Kristensson, Gillis. *A Survey of Middle English Dialects, 1290–1350: The Six Northern Counties and Lincolnshire.* Lund, Sweden: Gleerup, 1967.

Krygier, Marcin. *The Disintegration of the English Strong Verb System.* Frankfurt am Main, Germany: Lang, 1994.

Kurath, Hans. *Linguistic Atlas of New England.* 3 vols. 1939–43. Reprint. New York: AMS, 1972.

———. *A Word Geography of the Eastern United States.* Ann Arbor: University of Michigan Press, 1949.

Kurath, Hans, and Sherman M. Kuhn, eds. *Middle English Dictionary.* Ann Arbor: University of Michigan Press, 1952–2001.

Kurath, Hans, and Raven I. McDavid, Jr. *The Pronunciation of English in the Atlantic States.* Ann Arbor: University of Michigan Press, 1961.

Lakoff, George. *Women, Fire, and Dangerous Things: What Categories Reveal about the Mind.* Chicago: University of Chicago Press, 1987.

Landau, Sidney I. *Dictionaries: The Art and Craft of Lexicography.* 2nd ed. New York: Cambridge University Press, 2001.

Language. Journal of the Linguistic Society of America, 1925–.

Lass, Roger. *The Cambridge History of the English Language.* Vol. 3: *1476–1776.* Cambridge: Cambridge University Press, 1999.

Leap, William L. *American Indian English.* Salt Lake City: University of Utah Press, 1993.

Lee, Penny. *The Whorf Theory Complex: A Critical Reconstruction.* Amsterdam: Benjamins, 1996.

Leech, Geoffrey N. *Principles of Pragmatics.* London: Longman, 1983.

———. *Semantics.* Harmondsworth, UK: Penguin, 1974.

Lehmann, Winfred P. *Historical Linguistics: An Introduction.* 3rd ed. London: Routledge, 1992.

———. *Proto-Indo-European Phonology.* Austin: University of Texas Press, 1952.

———. *Proto-Indo-European Syntax.* Austin: University of Texas Press, 1980.

Leonard, Sterling A. *The Doctrine of Correctness in English Usage, 1700–1800.* University of Wisconsin Studies in Language and Literature 25. Madison: University of Wisconsin, 1929.

Levin, Magnus. *Agreement with Collective Nouns in English.* Lund Studies in English 103. Lund, Sweden: Lund University, Department of English, 2001.

Lieberman, Philip. *Uniquely Human: The Evolution of Speech, Thought, and Selfless Behavior.* Cambridge, MA: Harvard University Press, 1991.

Lighter, Jonathan E. *Random House Historical Dictionary of American Slang.* Vols. 1–2. New York: Random House, 1994–7. Future volumes to be published by Oxford University Press.

Lincoln, Bruce. *Myth, Cosmos, and Society: Indo-European Themes of Creation and Destruction.* Cambridge, MA: Harvard University Press, 1986.

Löbner, Sebastian. *Understanding Semantics.* London: Arnold, 2002.

Lounsbury, Thomas R. *English Spelling and Spelling Reform.* New York: Harper & Row, 1909.

Luick, Karl. *Historische Grammatik der englischen Sprache.* 1914–40. Reprint. Stuttgart, Germany: Tauchnitz, 1964.

Lyons, John. *Linguistic Semantics: An Introduction.* Cambridge: Cambridge University Press, 1995.

———. *Semantics.* 2 vols. Cambridge: Cambridge University Press, 1977.

McArthur, Tom. *The English Languages.* Cambridge: Cambridge University Press, 1998.

———. *Living Words: Language, Lexicography, and the Knowledge Revolution.* Exeter, Devon, UK: University of Exeter Press, 1998.

———, ed. *The Oxford Companion to the English Language.* Oxford: Oxford University Press, 1992.

———. *Worlds of Reference: Lexicography, Learning and Language from the Clay Tablet to the Computer.* Cambridge: Cambridge University Press, 1986.

McIntosh, Angus, M. L. Samuels, and Michael Benskin. *A Linguistic Atlas of Late Mediaeval English.* Aberdeen, Scotland: Aberdeen University Press, 1985–.

McLaughlin, John. *Old English Syntax: A Handbook.* Tübingen, Germany: Max Niemeyer, 1983.

McMahon, April. *An Introduction to English Phonology.* Oxford: Oxford University Press, 2002.

———. *Understanding Language Change.* Cambridge: Cambridge University Press, 1994.

McMillan, James B., and Michael B. Montgomery. *Annotated Bibliography of Southern American English.* 2nd ed. Tuscaloosa: University of Alabama Press, 1989.

Macquarie Dictionary. Rev. ed. Dee Why, New South Wales, Australia: Macquarie Library, 1985.

Macquarie Dictionary of New Words. Ed. Susan Butler. Dee Why, New South Wales, Australia: Macquarie Library, 1990.

Mair, Christian. *Infinitival Complement Clauses in English: A Study of Syntax in Discourse.* Cambridge: Cambridge University Press, 1990.

Mallory, J. P. *In Search of the Indo-Europeans: Language, Archeology and Myth.* New York: Thames and Hudson, 1989.

Man, John. *Alpha Beta: How 26 Letters Shaped the Western World.* New York: Wiley, 2000.

Marchand, Hans. *The Categories and Types of Present-Day English Word-Formation.* Tuscaloosa: University of Alabama Press, 1969.

Marckwardt, Albert H., and Randolph Quirk. *A Common Language: British and American English.* London: Cox and Wyman, 1964.

Mathews, Mitford M. *The Beginnings of American English.* Chicago: University of Chicago Press, 1931.

———, ed. *A Dictionary of Americanisms on Historical Principles.* 2 vols. Chicago: University of Chicago Press, 1951.

———. *Some Sources of Southernisms.* Tuscaloosa: University of Alabama Press, 1948.

Matthews, P. H. *Morphology: An Introduction to the Theory of Word-Structure.* 2nd ed. Cambridge: Cambridge University Press, 1991.

Mencken, Henry Louis. *The American Language.* 4th ed. New York: Knopf, 1936. *Supplement 1,* 1945; *Supplement 2,* 1948; abridged and ed. Raven I. McDavid, Jr., 1963.

Merriam-Webster's Dictionary of English Usage. Ed. E. Ward Gilman. Springfield, MA: Merriam-Webster, 1994.

Metcalf, Allan. *How We Talk: American Regional English Today.* Boston: Houghton Mifflin, 2000.

———. *Predicting New Words: The Secrets of Their Success.* Boston: Houghton Mifflin, 2002.

———. *The World in So Many Words: A Country-by-Country Tour of Words That Have Shaped Our Language.* Boston: Houghton Mifflin, 1999.

Mettinger, Arthur. *Aspects of Semantic Opposition in English.* Oxford: Clarendon, 1994.

Meyer, Charles F. *English Corpus Linguistics: An Introduction.* Cambridge: Cambridge University Press, 2002.

Michael, Ian. *English Grammatical Categories and the Tradition to 1800.* Cambridge: Cambridge University Press, 1970.

Minkova, Donka. *The History of Final Vowels in English: The Sound of Muting.* Berlin: Mouton de Gruyter, 1991.

Minkova, Donka, and Robert Stockwell. *Studies in the History of the English Language: A Millennial Perspective.* Berlin: Mouton de Gruyter, 2002.

Mitchell, Bruce Colston. *Old English Syntax.* 2 vols. Oxford: Clarendon, 1985.

Mitchell, Bruce Colston, and Fred C. Robinson. *A Guide to Old English.* 6th ed. Oxford: Blackwell, 2001.

Morenberg, Max. *Doing Grammar.* New York: Oxford University Press, 1991.

Morgan, Kenneth O. *The Oxford History of Britain.* Oxford: Oxford University Press, 2001.

Morris, Desmond. *Gestures, Their Origins and Distribution.* New York: Stein and Day, 1979.

Morton, Eugene S., and Jake Page. *Animal Talk: Science and the Voices of Nature.* New York: Random House, 1992.

Morton, Herbert C. *The Story of "Webster's Third": Philip Gove's Controversial Dictionary and Its Critics.* New York: Cambridge University Press, 1994.

Mossé, Fernand. *A Handbook of Middle English.* Trans. James A. Walker. Baltimore: Johns Hopkins Press, 1952.

Mufwene, Salikoko S., ed. *African-American English: Structure, History, and Use.* London: Routledge, 1998.

———. *The Ecology of Language Evolution.* Cambridge: Cambridge University Press, 2001.

Murray, K. M. Elisabeth. *Caught in the Web of Words: James A. H. Murray and the "Oxford English Dictionary."* New Haven, CT: Yale University Press, 1977.

Nagel, Stephen J., and Sara L. Sanders, eds. *English in the Southern United States.* Cambridge: Cambridge University Press, 2003.

Names. Journal of the American Name Society, 1953–.

Nielsen, Hans Frede. *The Germanic Languages: Origins and Early Dialectal Interrelations.* Tuscaloosa: University of Alabama Press, 1989.

Nilsen, Alleen Pace, and Don L. F. Nilsen. *Encyclopedia of 20th-Century American Humor.* Phoenix, AZ: Oryx, 2000.

Nilsen, Don L. F. *Humor Scholarship: A Research Bibliography.* Westport, CT: Greenwood, 1993.

Nuessel, Frank. *The Esperanto Language.* New York: Legas, 2000.

———. *The Study of Names: A Guide to the Principles and Topics.* Westport: CT: Greenwood, 1992.

O Muirithe, Diarmaid, ed. *The English Language in Ireland.* Dublin: Mercier Press, 1977.

Onions, C. T. *The Oxford Dictionary of English Etymology.* New York: Oxford University Press, 1967.

———. *A Shakespeare Glossary.* Enlarged and rev. Robert D. Eagleson. Oxford: Clarendon, 1986.

Orton, Harold, ed. *Survey of English Dialects.* Introduction, 4 vols. each in 3 parts. Leeds, UK: Arnold, 1962–71.

Orton, Harold, and Nathalia Wright. *A Word Geography of England.* London: Seminar, 1974.

Ostade, Ingrid Tieken-Boon van, Gunnel Tottie, and Wim van der Wurff, eds. *Negation in the History of English.* Berlin: Mouton de Gruyter, 1999.

Övergaard, Gerd. *The Mandative Subjunctive in American and British English in the 20th Century.* Uppsala, Sweden: Uppsala University, 1995.

Oxford English Dictionary. 13 vols. London: Oxford University Press, 1933. *A Supplement,* 4 vols. ed. R. W. Burchfield, 1972–86; 2nd ed., 20 vols., 1989; 2nd ed. on Compact Disc, 1992.

Page, R. I. *Runes.* London: British Museum, 1987.

Palmer, Frank R. *The English Verb.* 2nd ed. London: Longman, 1988.

———. *Semantics: A New Outline.* New York: Cambridge University Press, 1976.

Partridge, Eric. *A Dictionary of Slang and Unconventional English.* 8th ed. Ed. Paul Beale. London: Routledge & Kegan Paul, 1984.

———. *Shakespeare's Bawdy.* New York: Dutton, 1948.

Pedersen, Holger. *The Discovery of Language.* Trans. John Webster Spargo. Bloomington: Indiana University Press, 1962.

Pederson, Lee. *Linguistic Atlas of the Gulf States.* 7 vols. Athens: University of Georgia Press, 1986–91.

Pfeffer, J. Alan, and Garland Cannon. *German Loanwords in English: An Historical Dictionary.* Cambridge: Cambridge University Press, 1994.

Phillipps, K. C. *Language and Class in Victorian England.* New York: Blackwell, 1984.

Pinker, Steven. *The Language Instinct.* New York: Morrow, 1994.

———. *Words and Rules: The Ingredients of Language.* New York: Basic Books, 1999.

Platt, John, Heidi Weber, and Ho Mian Liah. *The New Englishes.* London: Routledge & Kegan Paul, 1984.

Pokorny, Julius. *Indogermanisches Etymologisches Worterbuch.* 2 vols. Bern, Switzerland: Francke, 1959–69.

Polome, Edgar C., ed. *Research Guide on Language Change.* Berlin: Mouton de Gruyter, 1990.

Poplack, Shana, and Sali Tagliamonte. *African American English in the Diaspora.* Oxford: Blackwell, 2001.

Poteet, Lewis, and Jim Poteet. *Car & Motorcycle Slang.* Ayers Cliff, Quebec, Canada: Pidwidgeon Press, 1992.

Pound, Louise. "American Euphemisms for Dying, Death, and Burial." *American Speech* 11 (1936): 195–202.

Powell, Barry B. *Homer and the Origin of the Greek Alphabet.* Cambridge: Cambridge University Press, 1991.

Pratt, T. K. *Dictionary of Prince Edward Island English.* Toronto: University of Toronto Press, 1988.

Price, Glanville, ed. *Encyclopedia of the Languages of Europe.* Oxford: Blackwell, 2000.

———, ed. *Languages in Britain and Ireland.* Oxford: Blackwell, 2000.

Pride, John B., ed. *New Englishes.* Rowley, MA: Newbury House, 1982.

Priebsch, Robert, and W. E. Collinson. *The German Language.* 6th ed. London: Faber and Faber, 1966.

Prins, Anton Adriaan. *A History of English Phonemes: From Indo-European to Present-Day English.* Leiden: Leiden University Press, 1974.

Prokosch, Eduard A. *A Comparative Germanic Grammar.* Philadelphia: Linguistic Society of America, 1939.

Publication of the American Dialect Society. 1944–.

Puhvel, Jean, ed. *Myth and Law among the Indo-Europeans.* Berkeley: University of California Press, 1970.

Pyles, Thomas. *Thomas Pyles: Selected Essays on English Usage.* Ed. John Algeo. Gainesville: University Presses of Florida, 1979.

———. *Words and Ways of American English.* New York: Random House, 1952.

Quirk, Randolph, Sidney Greenbaum, Geoffrey Leech, and Jan Svartvik. *A Comprehensive Grammar of the English Language.* London: Longman, 1985.

Quirk, Randolph, and Gabriele Stein. *English in Use.* Harlow, Essex, UK: Longman, 1990.

Quirk, Randolph, and Jan Svartvik. *Investigating Linguistic Acceptability.* The Hague: Mouton, 1966.

Quirk, Randolph, and C. L. Wrenn. *An Old English Grammar.* London: Methuen. DeKalb: Northern Illinois University Press, 1994.

Ramson, W. S. *Australian English: An Historical Study of the Vocabulary, 1788–1898.* Canberra: Australian National University Press, 1966.

———, ed. *The Australian National Dictionary.* Melbourne, Australia: Oxford University Press, 1988.

Rao, G. Subba. *Indian Words in English: A Study in Indo-British Cultural and Linguistic Relations.* Oxford: Clarendon, 1954.

Read, Allen Walker. *America—Naming the Country and Its People.* Ed. R. N. Ashley. Lewiston, NY: Mellen, 2001.

———. *Milestones in the History of English in America.* Ed. Richard W. Bailey. PADS 86. Durham, NC: Duke University Press for the American Dialect Society, 2002.

———. "The Motivation of Lindley Murray's Grammatical Work." *Journal of English and Germanic Philology* 38 (1939): 525–39.

Reddick, Allen Hilliard. *The Making of Johnson's Dictionary, 1746–1773.* Rev. ed. Cambridge: Cambridge University Press, 1996.

Renfrew, Colin. *Archaeology and Language: The Puzzle of Indo-European Origins.* New York: Cambridge University Press, 1990.

Ricks, Christopher, and Leonard Michaels, eds. *The State of the Language.* 2nd ed. Berkeley: University of California Press, 1990.

Roach, Peter. *English Phonetics and Phonology: A Practical Course.* 3rd ed. Cambridge: Cambridge University Press, 2000.

Roberts, Jane, and Christian Kay with Lynne Grundy. *A Thesaurus of Old English.* London: King's College London, Centre for Late Antique and Medieval Studies, 1995.

Roberts, Peter A. *West Indians & Their Language.* Cambridge: Cambridge University Press, 1988.

Robins, R. H. *General Linguistics: An Introductory Survey.* 4th ed. London: Longman, 1989.

——. *A Short History of Linguistics.* 4th ed. London: Longman, 1997.

Robinson, Orrin W. *Old English and Its Closest Relatives: A Survey of the Earliest Germanic Languages.* Stanford, CA: Stanford University Press, 1992.

Rodríguez González, Félix, ed. *Spanish Loanwords in the English Language: A Tendency Towards Hegemony Reversal.* Berlin: Mouton de Gruyter, 1996.

Rollins, Richard M. *The Long Journey of Noah Webster.* Philadelphia: University of Pennsylvania Press, 1980.

Romaine, Suzanne, *Bilingualism.* Oxford: Blackwell, 1989.

——, ed. *The Cambridge History of the English Language.* Vol. 4: *1776–1997.* Cambridge: Cambridge University Press, 1998.

——, ed. *Language in Australia.* Cambridge: Cambridge University Press, 1991.

——. *Pidgin and Creole Languages.* London: Longman, 1988.

Rosenbach, Anette. *Genitive Variation in English: Conceptual Factors in Synchronic and Diachronic Studies.* Berlin: Mouton de Gruyter, 2002.

Rosten, Leo. *The Joys of Yinglish.* New York: McGraw-Hill, 1989.

Ruhlen, Merritt. *A Guide to the World's Languages.* Vol. 1: *Classification.* Stanford, CA: Stanford University Press, 1987.

——. *The Origin of Language: Tracing the Evolution of the Mother Tongue.* New York: Wiley & Sons, 1994.

Sampson, Geoffrey. *Writing Systems: A Linguistic Introduction.* Stanford, CA: Stanford University Press, 1985.

Schmidt, Alexander. *Shakespeare-Lexicon: A Complete Dictionary of All the English Words, Phrases and Constructions in the Works of the Poet.* 2 vols. 6th ed. Rev. Gregor Sarrazin. Reprint. Berlin: de Gruyter, 1971.

Schur, Norman W. *British English A to Zed.* Rev. Eugene Ehrlich. New York: Facts on File, Checkmark Books, 2001.

Scragg, D. G. *A History of English Spelling.* Manchester, UK: Manchester University Press, 1974.

Serjeantson, Mary S. *A History of Foreign Words in English.* 1935. Reprint. London: Routledge & Kegan Paul, 1961.

Seuren, Pieter A. M. *Western Linguistics: An Historical Introduction.* Oxford: Blackwell, 1998.

Sherzer, Joel. *Speech Play and Verbal Art.* Austin: University of Texas Press, 2002.

Shuy, Roger W. *Bureaucratic Language in Government and Business.* Washington, DC: Georgetown University Press, 1998.

Simpson, David. *The Politics of American English, 1776–1850.* New York: Oxford, 1986.

Sledd, James, and Gwin J. Kolb, eds. *Dr. Johnson's Dictionary: Essays in the Biography of a Book.* Chicago: University of Chicago Press, 1955.

Smyth, Alfred P. *King Alfred the Great.* Oxford: Oxford University Press, 1995.

Society for Pure English. *S.P.E. Tract, No. 1–66.* Vols. 1–7. Oxford: Clarendon, 1919–48.

Sørensen, Knud. *A Dictionary of Anglicisms in Danish.* Copenhagen: Royal Danish Academy of Sciences and Letters, 1997.

Starnes, DeWitt T., and Gertrude E. Noyes. *The English Dictionary from Cawdrey to Johnson, 1604–1755.* New ed. Gabriele Stein. Amsterdam: Benjamins, 1991.

Stenton, F. M. *Anglo-Saxon England.* 3rd ed. Oxford: Oxford University Press, 2001.

Stockwell, Robert, and Donka Minkova. *English Words: History and Structure.* Cambridge: Cambridge University Press, 2001.

Story, G. M., W. J. Kirwin, and J. D. A. Widdowson, eds. *Dictionary of Newfoundland English.* Toronto: University of Toronto Press, 1982.

Stratmann, Francis Henry. *A Middle-English Dictionary: Containing Words Used by English Writers from the Twelfth to the Fifteenth Century.* Rev. Henry Bradley. Oxford: Oxford University Press, 1986.

Stubbings, Frank. *Bedders, Bulldogs and Bedells: A Cambridge Glossary.* Rev. and enlarged ed. Cambridge: Cambridge University Press, 1995.

Svartvik, Jan, ed. *The London-Lund Corpus of Spoken English: Description and Research.* Lund Studies in English 82. Lund, Sweden: University Press, 1990.

————. *On Voice in the English Verb.* The Hague: Mouton, 1966.

————, ed. *Words: Proceedings of an International Symposium, Lund 25–26 August 1995, Organized under the Auspices of the Royal Academy of Letters, History and Antiquities and Sponsored by the Foundation Natur och Kultur.* Stockholm: Kungl. Vitterhets Historie och Antikvitets Akademien, 1996.

Swan, Michael. *Practical English Usage.* 2nd ed. Oxford: Oxford University Press, 1995.

Thomas, Lewis. *The Lives of a Cell: Notes of a Biology Watcher.* New York: Viking, 1974.

Todd, Loreto, and Ian Hancock. *International English Usage.* New York: New York University Press, 1987.

Toller, T. Northcote, ed. *An Anglo-Saxon Dictionary Based on the Manuscript Collections of the Late Joseph Bosworth.* Supplement with rev. and enlarged addenda by Alistair Campbell. London: Oxford University Press, 1898. Supplement 1921, Addenda 1972.

Tottie, Gunnel. *An Introduction to American English.* Malden, MA: Blackwell Publishers, 2002.

Trask, R. L. *The Dictionary of Historical and Comparative Linguistics.* Edinburgh: Edinburgh University Press, 2000.

————. *Historical Linguistics.* London: Arnold, 1996.

Trudgill, Peter. *The Dialects of England.* Oxford: Basil Blackwell, 1990.

Trudgill, Peter, and Jean Hannah. *International English.* 3rd ed. London: Arnold, 1994.

Tucker, Susie I. *English Examined: Two Centuries of Comment on the Mother-Tongue.* Hamden, CT: Archon, 1974.

Turner, George W. *The English Language in Australia and New Zealand.* London: Longman, 1966.

Turner, Lorenzo Dow. *Africanisms in the Gullah Dialect.* 1949. Reprint. Columbia, SC: University of South Carolina Press, 2002.

Upton, Clive, William A. Kretzschmar, and Rafal Konopka. *The Oxford Dictionary of Pronunciation for Current English.* Oxford: Oxford University Press, 2001.

Upton, Clive, David Parry, and J. D. A. Widdowson. *Survey of English Dialects: The Dictionary and Grammar.* London: Routledge, 1994.

Upton, Clive, and J. D. A. Widdowson. *An Atlas of English Dialects.* New York: Oxford University Press, 1996.

Upward, Christopher, Paul Fletcher, Jean Hutchins, and Christopher Jolly. *The Simplified Spelling Society Presents Cut Spelling: A Handbook to the Simplification of Written English by Omission of Redundant Letters.* Birmingham, UK: Simplified Spelling Society, 1991.

Vallins, G. H. *Spelling.* Rev. D. G. Scragg. London: Deutsch, 1965.

Venezky, Richard L. *The American Way of Spelling: The Structure and Origins of American English Orthography.* New York: Guilford Press, 1999.

————. *The Structure of English Orthography.* The Hague: Mouton, 1970.

Visser, E T. *An Historical Syntax of the English Language.* 3 vols in 4. Leiden, Netherlands: Brill, 1963–73.

Wakelin, Martyn. *The Archaeology of English.* London: Batsford, 1988.

Walker, C. B. F. *Cuneiform.* London: British Museum, 1987.

Warner, Anthony R. *English Auxiliaries: Structure and History.* Cambridge: Cambridge University Press, 1993.

Watkins, Calvert. *The American Heritage Dictionary of Indo-European Roots.* 2nd ed. Boston: Houghton Mifflin, 2000.

Webster's Third New International Dictionary. Ed. Philip Babcock Gove. Springfield, MA: Merriam, 1961.

Weinreich, Uriel. *On Semantics.* Philadelphia: University of Pennsylvania Press, 1980.

Welch, Martin. *Discovering Anglo-Saxon England.* University Park: Pennsylvania State University Press, 1993.

Wells, John C. *Accents of English.* 3 vols. Cambridge: Cambridge University Press, 1982.

———. *Longman Pronunciation Dictionary.* Harlow, Essex, UK: Longman, 1990.

Whorf, Benjamin Lee. *Language, Thought, and Reality.* Ed. John B. Carroll. Cambridge, MA: Technology Press of MIT, 1956.

Wilkes, G. A. *A Dictionary of Australian Colloquialisms.* 2nd ed. Sydney, Australia: Sydney University Press, 1985.

———. *Exploring Australian English.* Sydney, Australia: Australian Broadcasting Corp., 1986.

Willinsky, John. *Empire of Words: The Reign of the OED.* Princeton, NJ: Princeton University Press, 1994.

Winchester, Simon. *The Professor and the Madman: A Tale of Murder, Insanity, and the Making of the "Oxford English Dictionary."* New York: HarperCollins, 1998.

Wolfe, Patricia M. *Linguistic Change and the Great Vowel Shift in English.* Berkeley: University of California Press, 1977.

Wolfram, Walt. *Dialects and American English.* Englewood Cliffs, NJ: Prentice Hall, 1991.

Wolfram, Walt, and Natalie Schilling-Estes. *American English: Dialects and Variation.* Malden, MA: Blackwell, 1998.

Word. Journal of the International Linguistic Association, 1945–.

Wright, Joseph, ed. *The English Dialect Dictionary.* 6 vols. 1898–1905. Reprint. New York: Hacker Art Books, 1963.

———. *The English Dialect Grammar.* Oxford: Frowde, 1905.

Wright, Laura. *The Development of Standard English 1300–1800.* Cambridge: Cambridge University Press, 2000.

Wyld, Henry Cecil. *A History of Modern Colloquial English.* 3rd ed. Oxford: Blackwell, 1936.

Zachrisson, Robert Eugen. *The English Pronunciation at Shakespeare's Time as Taught by William Bullokar.* 1927. Reprint. New York: AMS, 1970.

———. *Pronunciation of English Vowels, 1400–1700.* 1913. Reprint. New York: AMS, 1971.

GLOSSARY

ablative   A case typically denoting separation, source, instrument, or cause.

ablaut or **gradation**   An alternation of vowels in forms of the same word, as in the principal parts of strong verbs, *sing-sang-sung*.

abstract meaning   Reference to a nonphysical, generalized abstraction like *domesticity* (cf. CONCRETE MEANING).

accent   Any of the diacritical marks: acute, grave, circumflex; *also* the prominence given to a syllable by stress or intonation; *also* a manner of pronouncing a dialect, as in *Boston accent*.

acceptability   The extent to which an expression is received without objection by speakers of a language.

accusative   A case typically marking the direct object.

acronym, *also* **acronymy**   A word formed from the initial letters of other words (or syllables) pronounced by the normal rules of orthoepy, like *AIDS* 'acquired immune deficiency syndrome'; *also* the process of forming such words.

acute accent   A diacritic (´) used in spelling some languages (like Spanish *qué* 'what?') and to indicate primary stress (as in *ópera*).

adjective   A major part of speech that denotes qualities and modifies or describes nouns.

advanced pronunciation   An early instance of a sound change in progress.

adverb   A major part of speech that modifies sentences, verbs, adjectives, or other adverbs.

æsc   A letter of the runic alphabet denoting the sound [æ].

affix   A morpheme added to a base or stem to modify its meaning.

affixation   Making words by combining an affix with a base or stem.

affricate   A stop sound with a fricative release.

African-American English *or* **Black English**   The ethnic dialect associated with Americans of African descent.

Afroasiatic   A family of languages whose main branches are Hamitic and Semitic.

agglutinative language   A language with complex but usually regular derivational forms.

311

agreement CONCORD.

allomorph A variant pronunciation of a morpheme, as the -*s* plural morpheme is pronounced [s], [z], or [əz].

allophone A variant articulation of a phoneme, as /t/ is [tʰ] in *tone,* but [t] in *stone.*

alphabet, *adj.* **alphabetic** A writing system in which each unit, or letter, ideally represents a single sound.

alphabetism A word formed from the initial letters of other words (or syllables) pronounced with the names of the letters of the alphabet, like *VP* 'vice president.'

Altaic A language family including Turkish and Mongolian.

alveolar Involving the gum ridge; *also* a sound made by the tongue's approaching the gum ridge.

alveolopalatal Involving the gum ridge and the hard palate; *also* a sound made by the tongue's approaching the gum ridge and hard palate.

amalgamated compound An originally compounded word whose form no longer represents its origin, like *not* from *na* + *wiht* 'no whit.'

amelioration A semantic change improving the associations of a word.

American English The English language as developed in North America.

Americanism An expression that originated in or is characteristic of America.

Ameslan American Sign Language for the deaf.

analytical comparison Comparison with *more* and *most* rather than with -*er* and -*est.*

analytic language A language that depends heavily on word order and function words as signals of grammatical structure.

anaptyxis, *adj.* **anaptyctic** SVARABHAKTI.

Anatolian A branch of Indo-European languages spoken in Asia Minor, including Hittite.

Anglian The Mercian and Northumbrian dialects of Old English, sharing certain features.

Anglo-Frisian The subbranch of West Germanic including English and Frisian.

Anglo-Norman The dialect of Norman French that developed in England.

Anglo-Saxon Old English; *also* one who spoke it; *also* pertaining to the Old English period.

animal communication The exchange of information among animals, contrasted with human language.

anomalous verb A highly irregular verb, like *think-thought* or *be-am-was.*

apheresis, *adj.* **apheretic** The omission of sounds from the beginning of a word, like *'cause* from *because.*

aphesis, *adj.* **aphetic**   The omission of an unaccented syllable from the beginning of a word, like *lone* from *alone*.

apocopation *or* **apocope**   The omission of a sound from the end of a word, like *a* from *an*.

arbitrary   Unmotivated, having no similarity with the referent (cf. CONVENTIONAL).

artificial language   A language like Esperanto invented especially for a particular, in this case international, use.

Aryan   An obsolete term for Indo-Iranian or Indo-European.

ash   The digraph *æ* used in Old English and so called after the runic letter *æsc*, representing the same sound.

ask **word**   Any of the words whose historical [æ] vowel has been changed to [a] in British and [a] in eastern New England speech.

aspiration, *adj.* **aspirated**   A puff of breath accompanying a speech sound.

assimilation   The process by which two sounds become more alike, like *-ed* pronounced [t] after voiceless sounds but [d] after voiced sounds.

association   The connection of one word or idea with another, so that an occurrence of the latter tends to evoke the former.

associative change   PARADIGMATIC CHANGE.

a-**stem**   An important declension of Old English nouns, in prehistoric times having a thematic vowel *a* before its inflectional endings, which include the sources of Modern English genitive *'s* and plural *s*.

asterisk   A star (*) used to indicate either a reconstructed form or an abnormal or nonoccurring form in present-day use, as Indo-European *dwō 'two' or present-day *thinked*.

athematic verb   An Indo-European verb stem formed without a thematic vowel.

Austronesian or **Malayo-Polynesian**   A family of languages spoken from Madagascar to the Pacific islands, including Malay and Polynesian.

back-formation   A word made by omitting from a longer word what is, or is thought to be, an affix or other morpheme, like *burgle* from *burglar; also* the process by which such words are made.

back vowel   A vowel made with the highest part of the tongue in the back of the mouth.

Baltic   An east-European branch of Indo-European, grouped together with the Slavic languages as Balto-Slavic.

Balto-Slavic   A branch of Indo-European including the Slavic and Baltic languages.

bar   A diacritic used in writing Polish, as in *ł*.

base morpheme   A morpheme, either free or bound, to which other morphemes can be added to form words, like *base* in *basic* or *cur* in *recur*.

bilabial   Involving both upper and lower lips; *also* a sound made with both lips, like [p, b, m].

Black English   AFRICAN-AMERICAN ENGLISH.

blending, *also* **blend** *or* **portmanteau word**   Making words by combining two or more existing expressions and shortening at least one of them; *also* a word so made, like *brunch* from *breakfast + lunch.*

borrow, *also* **borrowing** *or* **loanword**   To make a word by imitating a foreign word; also a word so made, such as *tortilla* from Mexican Spanish.

bound morpheme   A morpheme used only as part of a word, rather than alone, like *mit* in *remit.*

boustrophedon   A method of writing in which lines are alternately read left to right and vice versa in alternating lines.

bow-wow theory   The theory that language began as imitation of animal noises or other natural sounds.

Briticism   An expression that originated in Britain after American independence or is characteristic of Britain.

British English   The English language as developed in Great Britain after American independence.

broad transcription   Phonetic transcription with little detail, showing primarily phonemic distinctions.

calque   LOAN TRANSLATION.

case   The inflectional form of a noun, pronoun, or adjective that shows the word's relationship to the verb or to other nouns of its clause, like *them* as the objective case of *they.*

caste dialect   A language variety that marks its user as belonging to a hereditary class.

cedilla   A diacritic (ˌ) used in writing several languages (e.g., in French ç).

Celtic   A branch of Indo-European spoken in western Europe, including Erse and Welsh.

central vowel   A vowel made with the highest part of the tongue in the center of the mouth between the positions for front and back vowels, like [ə].

centum language   One of the mainly western Indo-European languages in which palatal and velar [k] became one phoneme.

circle   A diacritic (°) used in writing Swedish and Norwegian, e.g., in å.

circumflex accent   A diacritic (ˆ) used in writing words in some languages, like French *île* 'island'; *also* sometimes used to represent reduced primary stress, as in *elevàtor ôperàtor.*

clang association   A semantic change shifting the meaning of a word through association with another word of similar sound, as *fruition* ME 'enjoyment' > ModE 'completion' by association with *fruit.*

click   A sound like that represented by *tsk-tsk,* produced by drawing in air with the tongue rather than expelling it from the lungs.

clip, *also* **clipped form**   To form a word by shortening a longer expression; *also* a word so formed, like *soap* from *soap opera.*

closed syllable   A syllable ending with a consonant, like *seed.*

close *e*   The mid vowel [e], a higher sound than open [ɛ].

close *o*   The mid vowel [o], a higher sound than open [ɔ].

Coastal Southern   SOUTHERN.

cognate   Of words, developed from a common source; *also* one of a set of words so developed, like *tax* and *task* or English *father* and Latin *pater.*

collocation   The tendency of particular words to combine with each other, like *tall person* versus *high mountain.*

combining   Making a word by joining two or more existing expressions, like *Web page.*

commonization   A functional shift from proper to common noun or other part of speech, like *shanghai* from the port city.

comparison   The modification of an adjective or adverb's form to show degrees of the quality it denotes: positive (*funny, comic*), comparative (*funnier, more comic*), superlative (*funniest, most comic*).

complementary distribution   Occurrence (of sounds or forms) in different environments, noncontrastive.

compound   To form a word by combining two or more bases; *also* a word so formed, like *lunchbox* or *Webcast.*

concord *or* **agreement**   Matching the inflectional ending of one word for number, gender, case, or person with that of another to which it is grammatically related, like *this book–these books.*

concrete meaning   Reference to a physical object or event like *house* (cf. ABSTRACT MEANING).

conjugation   The inflection of verbs for person, number, tense, and mood.

consonant   A speech sound formed with some degree of constriction in the breath channel and typically found in the margins of syllables.

consuetudinal *be*   Uninflected *be* used for habitual or regular action in several varieties of nonstandard English.

contraction   The shortened pronunciation or spelling of an unstressed word as part of a neighboring word, like *I'm; see also* ENCLITIC.

contrastive *or* **minimal pair**   A pair of words that differ by a single sound, like *pin-tin.*

conventional   Learned, rather than determined by genetic inheritance or natural law (cf. ARBITRARY).

creating   ROOT CREATION.

creole A language combining the features of several other languages, sometimes begun as a pidgin.

creolize To become or make into a creole by mixing languages or, in the case of a pidgin, by becoming a full native language for some speakers.

Cyrillic The alphabet used to write Russian and some other Slavic languages.

Danelaw The northeast part of Anglo-Saxon England heavily settled by Scandinavians and governed by their law code.

dative A case typically marking the indirect object or recipient.

declension The inflection of a noun, pronoun, or adjective for case and number and, in earlier English, of adjectives also for definiteness, like *they-them-their-theirs*.

definite article A function word signaling a definite noun, specifically *the*.

definiteness A grammatical category for noun phrases, indicating that the speaker assumes the hearer can identify the referent of the phrase.

demonstrative pronoun A pronoun like *this* or *that* indicating relative closeness to the speaker.

dental Involving the teeth; *also* a sound made with the teeth.

dental suffix A [d] or [t] ending used in Germanic languages to form the preterit.

diachronic Pertaining to change through time, historical (cf. SYNCHRONIC).

diacritical mark(ing) An accent or other modification of an alphabetical letter used to differentiate it from the unmarked letter.

dialect A variety of a language used in a particular place or by a particular social group.

dictionary A reference book giving such information about words as spelling, pronunciation, meaning, grammatical class, history, and limitations on use.

dieresis *or* **umlaut** A diacritic (¨) used to differentiate one letter from another as representing sounds of different qualities, as in German *Brüder* 'brothers' versus *Bruder* 'brother,' or to show that the second of two vowels is pronounced as a separate syllable, as in *naïve*.

digraph A combination of two letters to represent a single sound, like *sh* in *she*.

diminutive An affix meaning 'small' and suggesting an emotional attitude to the referent; *also* a word formed with such an affix, such as *doggie*.

ding-dong theory A theory of the origin of language holding that speech is an instinctive response to stimuli.

diphthong A combination of two vowel sounds in one syllable, like [aɪ].

diphthongization The change of a simple vowel into a diphthong.

direct source *or* **immediate source** A foreign word imitated to produce a loanword (cf. ULTIMATE SOURCE).

displacement The use of language to talk about things not physically present.

dissimilation   The process by which two sounds become less alike, like the pronunciation of *diphtheria* beginning [dɪp-].

distinctive sound   PHONEME.

double comparison   Comparison using both *more* or *most* and *-er* or *-est* with the same word, like *more friendlier* or *most unkindest.*

double *or* **multiple negative**   Two or more negatives used for emphasis.

double plural   A plural noun using two historically different plural markers, like *child + r + en.*

double superlative   Double comparison in the superlative degree, or indicated by an ending like *-most* as in *foremost,* etymologically two superlative suffixes, *-m* and *-est.*

doublet   One of two or more words in a language derived from the same etymon but by different channels, like *shirt, short,* and *skirt,* or *faction* and *fashion.*

Dravidian   The indigenous languages of India, now spoken chiefly in the south.

duality of patterning   The twofold system of language, consisting of the arrangements of both meaningful units such as words and morphemes and also of meaningless units such as phonemes.

dual number   An inflection indicating exactly two; survivals in English are the pronouns *both, either,* and *neither.*

early Modern English   English during the period 1500–1800.

ease of articulation   Efficiency of movement of the organs of articulation as a motive for sound change.

East Germanic   A subbranch of the Germanic languages that includes Gothic.

echoic word   A word whose sound suggests its referent, like *plop* or *fizz.*

edh *or* **eth** *or* **crossed** *d*   The Old English letter ð.

edited English   STANDARD ENGLISH.

ejaculation   An echoic word for a nonlinguistic utterance expressing emotion, like *oof* or *wow.*

elision, *verb* **elide**   The omission of sounds in speech or writing, like *let's* or *Hallowe'en* (from *All Hallow Even*).

ellipsis, *adj.* **elliptic(al)**   The omission of words in speech or writing, as in "Jack could eat no fat; his wife, no lean."

enclitic   A grammatically independent word pronounced by contraction as part of a preceding word, like *'ll* for *will* in *I'll.*

epenthesis, *adj.* **epenthetic**   The pronunciation of an unhistorical sound within a word, like *length* pronounced "lengkth" or *thimble* from earlier *thimel.*

eponym, *adj.* **eponymous**   A word derived from the name of a person; *also* the person from whose name such a word derives, like *ohm* 'unit of electrical resistance' from Georg S. Ohm, German physicist.

ethnic dialect   A dialect used by a particular ethnic group.

etymological respelling   Respelling a word to reflect the spelling of an etymon; *also* a word so respelled, like *debt* from *dette*.

etymological sense   The meaning of a word at earlier times in its history or of the word's etymon.

etymology   The origin and history of a word; *also* the study of word origins and history.

etymon, *pl.* **etyma**   A source word from which a later word is derived.

euphemism   An expression replacing another that is under social taboo or is less prestigious; *also* the process of such replacement.

explosive   STOP.

eye dialect   The representation of standard pronunciations by unconventional spellings, like *duz* for *does*.

finite form   A form of the verb identifying tense or the person or number of its subject.

Finno-Ugric   A language family including Finnish and Hungarian.

first *or* **native language**   The language a speaker learns first or uses by preference.

First Sound Shift   A systematic change of the Indo-European stop sounds in Proto-Germanic, formulated by Grimm's Law.

folk etymology   A popularly invented but incorrect explanation for the origin of a word that sometimes changes the word's form; *also* the process by which such an explanation is made.

foreign language   A language used for special purposes or infrequently and with varying degrees of fluency.

free morpheme   A morpheme that can be used alone as a word.

free variation   A substitution of sounds that do not alter meaning, like a palatalized ("clear") or velarized ("dark") [l] in *silly*.

fricative *or* **spirant**   A sound made by narrowing the breath channel to produce friction.

front vowel   A vowel made with the highest part of the tongue in the front of the mouth.

functional shift   Shifting a word from one grammatical use to another; *also* a word so shifted.

function word   A part of speech, typically with a limited number of members, used to signal grammatical structure, such as prepositions, conjunctions, and articles.

futhorc   The runic alphabet.

gender   A grammatical category loosely correlated with sex in Indo-European languages.

generalization   A semantic change expanding the kinds of referents of a word.

General Semantics   A linguistic philosophy emphasizing the arbitrary nature of language to clarify thinking.

genetic classification   A grouping of languages based on their historical development from a common source.

genitive   A case typically showing possessor or source.

geographical *or* **regional dialect**   A dialect used in a particular geographical area.

Germanic   The northern European branch of Indo-European to which English belongs.

gesture   A bodily movement, expression, or position that conveys meaning and often accompanies language; *see also* KINESICS.

glide   The semivowel or subordinate vowel that accompanies a vowel, either an on-glide like the [y] in *mule* [myul] or an OFF-GLIDE like the [ɪ] in *mile* [maɪl].

glottal   Involving the glottis or vocal cords.

gradation   ABLAUT.

grammar *or* **morphosyntax**   The system by which words are related to one another within a sentence; a description of that system.

grammatical function   A category for which words are inflected, such as case, number, gender, definiteness, person, tense, mood, and aspect.

grammatical gender   The assignment of nouns to inflectional classes that have sexual connotations without matching the sex of the noun's referent.

grammatical signal   A word, affix, concord, order, pitch, or stress that indicates grammatical structure.

grammatical system   The patterns for combining the morphemes, words, phrases, and clauses of a language.

grave accent   A diacritic (ˋ) used in spelling words of some languages, like French *père* 'father,' and to indicate secondary stress, as in *óperàte*.

Great Vowel Shift   A systematic change in the articulation of the Middle English long vowels before and during the early Modern English period.

Grimm's Law   A formulation of the First Sound Shift made by Jakob Grimm in 1822.

group genitive   A genitive construction in which the ending *'s* is added at the end of a noun phrase to a word other than the head of the phrase: *the neighbor next-door's dog*.

haček or **wedge**   A diacritic (ˇ) used in spelling words of some languages, like Czech *haček* 'little hook,' and to modify some letters for phonetic transcription, like [š].

Hamitic   Former term for a family of languages spoken in North Africa, including ancient Egyptian.

Hellenic   The branch of the Indo-European family spoken in Greece.

Heptarchy   The seven kingdoms of Anglo-Saxon England.

High German *or* **Second Sound Shift**   A systematic shifting of certain stop sounds in High German dialects.

high vowel   A vowel made with the jaw nearly closed and the tongue near the roof of the mouth.

his-**genitive**   The use of a possessive pronoun after a noun to signal a genitive meaning: *Jones his house.*

homograph   A word spelled like another.

homonym   A word spelled or pronounced like another.

homophone   A word pronounced like another.

homorganic   Having the same place of articulation as another sound.

hook   A diacritic (ˌ) used in writing some languages like Polish and Lithuanian, and by modern editors under the Middle English vowels ẹ and ọ to represent their open varieties.

hybrid form(ation)   An expression made by combining parts whose etyma are from more than one language.

hyperbole   A semantic change involving exaggeration.

hypercorrection *or* **hypercorrect pronunciation**   An analogical form created under the misimpression that an error is being corrected, like "Do you want she or I to go?" for "Do you want her or me to go?" or *hand* pronounced with "broad" [a] rather than [æ].

ideographic *or* **logographic writing**   A system whose basic units represent word meanings.

idiolect   A variety of a language characteristic of a particular person.

idiom   A combination of morphemes whose total meaning cannot be predicted from the meanings of its constituents.

immediate source   DIRECT SOURCE.

imperative   A mood of the verb used for orders or requests.

impersonal verb *or* **construction**   A verb used without a subject or with dummy *it.*

i-**mutation**   *I*-UMLAUT.

incorporative language   A language that combines in one word concepts that would be expressed by different major sentence elements (such as verb and direct object) in other languages.

indicative   A mood of the verb used for reporting fact.

Indo-European   The language family including most languages of Europe, Persia, Afghanistan, and north India.

Indo-Germanic   An obsolete term for Indo-European.

Indo-Iranian   The branch of Indo-European including Persian and Indic languages.

inflected infinitive   A declined infinitive used as a noun in Old English.

inflection   Changes in the form of words relating them to one another within a sentence.

inflectional suffix   A word ending that serves to connect the word to others in a grammatical construction.

inflective language   A language whose words change their form, often irregularly, to show their grammatical connections.

initialism   A word formed from the initial letters of other words or syllables, whether pronounced as an acronym like *AIDS* or an alphabetism like *HIV.*

inkhorn term   A word introduced into the English language during the early Modern English period but used primarily in writing rather than speech; more generally, a pompous expression.

Inland Southern   SOUTH MIDLAND.

inorganic -*e*   A historically unexpected but pronounced *e* added to Middle English words by analogy.

instrumental   A case typically designating means or instrument.

Insular hand   The style of writing generally used for Old English, of Irish provenance.

intensifier   A word like *very* that strengthens the meaning of the word it accompanies.

interdental   Involving the upper and lower teeth; a sound made by placing the tongue between those teeth.

interrogative pronoun   A pronoun used to signal a question: *who, which, what.*

intonation   Patterns of pitch in sentences.

intrusion   The introduction of an unhistorical sound into a word.

intrusive *r*   An etymologically unexpected and unspelled *r* sound pronounced in some dialects between a word ending with a vowel and another beginning with one, as in "Cuba[r] is south of Florida."

intrusive schwa   The pronunciation of a schwa where it is historically unexpected, as in *film* pronounced in two syllables as "fillum."

inverse spelling   A misspelling, such as **chicking* for *chicken,* by analogy with spellings like standard *picking* for the pronunciation *pickin'* ['pɪkɪn].

isolating language   A language whose words tend to be invariable.

Italic   A branch of Indo-European spoken in Italy.

Italo-Celtic   The Italic and Celtic branches of Indo-European seen as sharing some common characteristics.

i-**umlaut** *or i*-**mutation**   The fronting or raising of a vowel by assimilation to an [i] sound in the following syllable.

kanji   Japanese ideographs derived from Chinese.

Kechumaran   A language family of the Andes Mountains.

Kentish   The Old English dialect of Kent.

Khoisan   A group of languages spoken in southwestern Africa.

kinesics   The study of body movements that convey meaning, or the movements themselves.

koine   Greek as spoken throughout the Mediterranean world in the Hellenistic and Roman periods; hence, a widely distributed variety of any language.

labial   Involving the lip or lips; *also* a sound made with the lip or lips.

labiodental   Involving the upper lip and lower teeth; *also* a sound made with the upper lip and lower teeth.

language   The ability of human beings to communicate by a system of conventional signs; *also* a particular system of such signs shared by the members of a community.

language family   A group of languages evolved from a common source.

laryngeal   Pertaining to the larynx; *also* a type of sound postulated for Proto-Indo-European, but attested only in Hittite.

late Modern English   English during the period 1800–present.

lateral   With air flowing around either or both sides of the tongue; *also* a sound so made.

lax vowel   A vowel made with relatively lax tongue muscles.

learned loanword   A word borrowed through educated channels and often preserving foreign spelling, pronunciation, meaning, inflections, or associations.

learned word   A word used in bookish contexts, often with a technical sense.

length   Duration of a sound, phonemic in older stages of English.

lengthening   Change of a short sound to a long one.

leveling *or* **merging**   Loss of distinctiveness between sounds or forms.

lexis   The stock of meaningful units of a language: morphemes, words, idioms.

ligature   A written symbol made from two or more letters joined together, like æ.

linking *r*   An *r* pronounced by otherwise *r*-less speakers at the end of a word followed by another word beginning with a vowel, as in "eve*r* and again."

liquid   A sound produced without friction and capable of being continuously sounded like vowels: [r] and [l].

loan translation *or* **calque**   An expression made by combining forms that individually translate the parts of a foreign combination, like *trial balloon* from French *ballon d'essai.*

loanword   A word made by imitating the form of a word in another language.

locative   A case typically showing place.

logographic writing   IDEOGRAPHIC WRITING.

long *s*   One of the Old English variations of the letter *s* (ſ) that continued in use through the eighteenth century.

long syllable   A syllable with a long vowel or a short vowel followed by two or more consonants.

long vowel   A vowel of greater duration than a corresponding short vowel.

low vowel   A vowel made with the jaw open and the tongue not near the roof of the mouth.

macron   A diacritic (¯) over a vowel used to indicate that it is long.

majuscule   A large or capital letter.

Malayo-Polynesian   AUSTRONESIAN.

manner of articulation   The configuration of the speech organs to make a particular sound: stop, fricative, nasal, etc.

marked word   A word whose meaning includes a semantic limitation lacking from an unmarked word, as *stallion* is marked for 'male' and *mare* for 'female' whereas *horse* is unmarked for sex.

Mercian   The Old English dialect of Mercia.

merging   LEVELING.

metaphor   A semantic change shifting the meaning of a word because of a perceived resemblance between the old and new referents, like *window (of opportunity)* 'brief period.'

metathesis   Transposing the positions of two sounds, as in *task* and *tax* [tæks].

metonymy   A semantic change shifting the meaning of a word because the old and new referents are connected with each other, like *suit* 'business executive.'

Middle English   English of the period 1100–1500.

mid vowel   A vowel with the jaw and tongue between the positions for high and low vowels.

minimal pair   CONTRASTIVE PAIR.

minuscule   A small or lowercase letter.

Modern English   English of the period since 1500.

monophthong   A simple vowel with a single stable quality.

monophthongization *or* **smoothing**   Change of a diphthong to a simple vowel.

morpheme   The smallest meaningful unit in language, a class of meaningful sequences of sounds that cannot be divided into smaller meaningful sequences.

morphology   The part of a language system or description concerned with the structure of morphemes into words, distinguished from syntax; morphology is either derivational (the structure of words generally) or grammatical (inflection and other aspects of word structure relating to syntax).

morphosyntax   GRAMMAR.

mutation   UMLAUT.

narrow transcription   Phonetic transcription showing fine phonetic detail.

nasal   Involving the nose; *also* a sound made with air flow through the nose.

native language   FIRST LANGUAGE.

natural gender   The assignment of nouns to grammatical classes matching the sex or sexlessness of the referent.

neo-Latin   Latin forms invented after the end of the Middle Ages, especially in scientific use.

New England short *o*   A lax vowel used by some New Englanders in *road* and *home* corresponding to tense [o] in standard English.

Niger-Kordefanian   A group of languages spoken in the southern part of Africa.

Nilo-Saharan   A group of languages spoken in middle Africa.

nominative   A case typically marking the subject of a sentence.

nondistinctive   Not capable of signaling a difference in meaning.

nonfinite form   A form of the verb not identifying tense or the person or number of its subject, specifically, the infinitive and participles.

nonrhotic   *R*-LESS.

Norman French   The dialect of French spoken in Normandy.

Northern   A dialect of American English stretching across the northernmost part of the country.

North Germanic   A subbranch of the Germanic languages spoken in Scandinavia.

North Midland   A dialect of American English spoken in the area immediately south of Northern.

Northumbrian   The Old English dialect of Northumbria.

Nostratic   A hypothetical language family including Indo-European, Finno-Ugric, perhaps Afroasiatic, and others.

noun   A major part of speech with the class meaning of thingness.

***n*-plural**   The plural form of a few nouns derived from the *n*-stem declension.

n-stem   An important Old English declension with [n] prominent in many forms.

objective form   A form of pronouns used as the object of verbs and prepositions, merging the older accusative and dative functions.

objective meaning   Semantic reference to something outside the individual, like *danger* or *pitifulness.*

oblique form   Any case other than the nominative.

off-glide   The less prominent or glide vowel following the more prominent vowel of a diphthong.

Old English   English of the period 449–1100.

onomatopoeia, *adj.* **onomatopoe(t)ic**   The formation of an ECHOIC WORD.

open *e*   The mid vowel [ɛ], a lower sound than close [e].

open *o*   The mid vowel [ɔ], a lower sound than close [o].

open syllable   A syllable ending in a vowel, like *see.*

open system   A system, like language, that can be adapted to new uses and produce new results.

oral-aural   Produced by the speech organs and perceived by the ear.

organ of speech   Any part of the anatomy (such as the lips, teeth, tongue, roof of the mouth, throat, and glottis) that has been adapted to producing speech sounds.

orthoepist, *also* **orthoepy**   One who studies the pronunciation of a language as it relates to spelling; *also* such study.

orthography   A writing system for representing the words or sounds of a language by visible marks.

ō-stem   An important class of Old English feminine nouns.

overgeneralization   The creation of nonstandard forms by analogy, like **bringed* for *brought* by analogy with regular verbs.

OV language   A language in which objects precede their verbs.

palatal   Involving the hard palate; *also* a sound made by touching the tongue against the hard palate.

palatalization   The process of making a sound more palatal by moving the blade of the tongue toward the hard palate.

palatovelar   Either palatal or velar.

paradigmatic *or* **associative change**   Language change resulting from the influence on an expression of other expressions that might occur instead of it or are otherwise associated with it, as *bridegum* was changed to *bridegroom.*

paralanguage   The vocal qualities, facial expressions, and gestures that accompany language and convey meaning.

parataxis   The juxtaposition of clauses without connecting conjunctions.

part of speech   A class of words with the same or similar potential to enter into grammatical combinations.

pejoration   A semantic change worsening the associations of a word.

personal ending   A verb inflection to show whether the subject is the speaker (first person), the addressee (second person), or someone else (third person).

personal pronoun   A pronoun referring to the speaker (I, we), the addressee (you), or others (he, she, it, they).

phoneme, *adj.* **phonemic,** *or* **distinctive sound**   The basic unit of phonology, a sound that is capable of distinguishing one meaningful form from another, a class of sounds that are phonetically similar and in either complementary distribution or free variation.

phonetic alphabet   An alphabet with a single distinct letter for each language sound.

phonetic transcription   A written representation of speech sounds.

phonogram   A written symbol that represents a language sound.

phonological space   The range of difference between sounds expressed as the articulatory space in which they are produced or a graph of their acoustic properties.

phonology   SOUND SYSTEM.

pidgin   A reduced language combining features from several languages and used for special purposes among persons who share no other common language.

pitch   The musical tone that marks a syllable as prominent in some languages.

place of articulation   The point in the breath channel where the position of the speech organs is most important for a particular sound.

plosive   STOP.

pooh-pooh theory   The theory that language began as emotional exclamations.

popular loanword   A word borrowed through everyday communication and often adapted to native norms of spelling, pronunciation, meaning, inflection, and associations.

portmanteau word   BLEND.

postposition   A function word like a preposition which comes after rather than before its object.

prefix   An affix that comes before its base.

pre-Germanic   The dialect of Indo-European evolving into Germanic, as it was before the distinctive Germanic features developed.

pre–Old English   The language spoken by the Anglo-Saxons while they lived on the Continent.

preposition   A function word often preceding a noun phrase, relating that phrase to other parts of the sentence.

prescriptive grammar   Grammar mainly concerned with prescribing the right forms of language.

present tense   A form of the verb that represents time other than the past; Germanic languages like English have only two tense forms, the present tense being used for the present, the future, and the timeless.

preterit-present verb   An originally strong verb whose preterit tense came to be used with present-time meaning and which acquired a new weak preterit for past time.

preterit tense   A form of the verb that represents past time.

primary stress   The most prominent stress in a word or phrase, indicated by a raised stroke (') or an acute accent mark.

principal part   One of the forms of a verb from which all other inflected forms can be made by regular changes.

pronoun   A function word with contextually varying meaning used in place of a noun phrase.

pronunciation   The way words are said.

pronunciation spelling   A respelling that suggests a particular pronunciation of a word more accurately than the original spelling does.

prosodic signal   Pitch, stress, or rhythm as grammatical signals.

Proto-Germanic   The Germanic branch of Indo-European before it became clearly differentiated into subbranches and languages.

Proto-Indo-European   The ancestor of Indo-European languages.

Proto-World *or* **Proto-Human**   The hypothetical original language of humanity from which all others evolved.

purism   The belief in an unchanging, absolute standard of correctness.

qualitative change   Change in the fundamental nature or perceived identity of a sound.

quantitative change   Change in the length of a sound, especially a vowel.

rebus   A visual pun in which a written sign stands for a meaning other than its usual one by virtue of a similarity between the pronunciations of two words, as the numeral 4 represents *for* in "Car 4 Sale."

received pronunciation or **RP**   The prestigious accent of upper-class British speech.

reconstruction   A hypothetical early form of a word for which no direct evidence is available.

reflexive construction   A verb with a reflexive pronoun, especially a redundant one, as its object, as in "I *repent me*."

regional dialect   GEOGRAPHICAL DIALECT.

register   A variety of a language used for a particular purpose or in particular circumstances.

relative pronoun A pronoun at the front of a relative clause.

retarded pronunciation An old-fashioned pronunciation.

retroflex Of the tongue, bent back; *also* a sound produced with the tip of the tongue curled upward.

rhotacism A shift of the sound [z] to [r].

r-**less** *or* **nonrhotic speech** Dialects in which [r] is pronounced only before a vowel.

Romance language Any of the subbranch of languages developed from Latin in historical times.

root An abstract form historically underlying actual forms, as IE *es- is the root of OE *eom, is, sind* and of Lat. *sum, est, sunt; also* a base morpheme without affixes.

root-consonant stem A class of Old English nouns in which inflectional endings were added directly to the root, without a stem-forming suffix of the kind found in *a*-stems, *ō*-stems, *n*-stems, and *r*-stems.

root creation Making a new word by inventing its form without reference to any existing word or sound; *also* a word so invented.

rounded vowel A vowel made with the lips protruded.

RP RECEIVED PRONUNCIATION.

r-**stem** A minor Old English declension characterized by an [r] from rhotacism of earlier [z] in some forms.

rune One of the letters of the early Germanic writing system, a letter of the futhorc.

Samoyedic A group of Uralic languages spoken in northern Siberia.

satem language One of the generally eastern Indo-European languages in which palatal [k] became a sibilant.

schwa The mid-central vowel or the phonetic symbol for it [ə].

scribal -*e* An unpronounced *e* added to words by a scribe usually for reasons of manuscript spacing.

secondary stress A stress less prominent than primary, indicated by a lowered stroke (ˌ) or a grave accent mark.

second language A language used frequently for important purposes in addition to a first or native language.

Second Sound Shift HIGH GERMAN SHIFT.

semantic change Change in the meaning of an expression.

semantic contamination Change of meaning through the influence of a similar-sounding word, especially one from a foreign language.

semantic marking The presence of semantic limitations in the meaning of a word; *see* MARKED WORD, UNMARKED WORD.

semantics   Meaning in language; *also* its study.

Semitic   A family of languages including Arabic and Hebrew.

semivowel   A sound articulated like a vowel but functioning like a consonant, such as [y] and [w].

sense   The referential meaning of an expression.

shibboleth   A language use that distinguishes between in-group and out-group members.

shifting   Making a new word by shifting the use of an expression.

shortening   Of vowels, changing a long vowel to a short one; of words, making new words by omitting part of an old expression.

short syllable   A syllable containing a short vowel followed by no more than one consonant.

short vowel   A vowel of lesser duration than a corresponding long vowel.

sibilant   A sound made with a groove down the center of the tongue producing a hissing effect.

sign   Any meaningful expression.

Sino-Tibetan   A group of languages spoken in China, Tibet, and Burma.

slang   A deliberately undignified form of language that marks the user as belonging to an in-group.

slash   VIRGULE.

Slavic   An east-European branch of Indo-European, grouped together with the Baltic languages as Balto-Slavic.

smoothing   MONOPHTHONGIZATION of certain Old English diphthongs.

social change   Language change caused by change in the way of life of its speakers.

social dialect   A dialect used by a particular social group.

sound system *or* **phonology**   The units of sound (phonemes) of a language with their possible arrangements and varieties of vocal expression.

Southern *or* **Coastal Southern**   A dialect of American English spoken in the eastern part of the country south of Maryland.

South Midland *or* **Inland Southern**   A dialect of American English spoken in a narrow strip on the Atlantic seaboard but stretching through the Appalachians and westward.

specialization   A semantic change restricting the kinds of referents of a word.

speech   The oral-aural expression of language.

spelling   The representation of the sounds of a word by written letters.

spelling pronunciation   An unhistorical pronunciation based on the spelling of a word.

spelling reform   An effort to make spelling closer to pronunciation.

spirant   FRICATIVE.

sprachbund   An association of languages, which may be genetically unrelated, spoken in the same area, sharing bilingual speakers, and therefore influencing one another.

spread vowel   UNROUNDED VOWEL.

square bracket   Either of the signs [and] used to enclose phonetic transcriptions.

standard language, *specifically* **standard English,** *also* **edited English**   A prestigious language variety described in dictionaries and grammars, taught in schools, used for public affairs, and having no regional limitations.

stem   A form consisting of a base plus an affix to which other affixes are added.

stop *or* **explosive** *or* **plosive**   A sound made by completely blocking the flow of air and then unblocking it.

stress   The loudness, length, and emphasis that marks a syllable as prominent.

stroke letter   A letter that, in medieval handwriting, was made with straight lines so that it could not be distinguished from other stroke letters when they were written next to each other: i, m, n, u, v.

strong declension   A Germanic noun or adjective declension in which the stem originally ended in a vowel.

strong verb   A Germanic verb whose principal parts were formed by ablaut of the stem vowel.

style   The choice made among available linguistic options.

subjective meaning   Semantic reference to something inside the individual, such as a psychological state like *fear* or *compassion.*

subjunctive   A mood of the verb for events viewed as suppositional, contingent, or desired.

substratum theory   The proposal that a language indigenous to a region affects a language more recently introduced there.

suffix   An affix that comes after its base.

superstratum theory   The proposal that a language recently introduced into a region affects the language spoken there earlier.

suppletive form   An inflectional form that is historically from a different word than the one it has become associated with, like *went* as the preterit of *go.*

svarabhakti *or* **anaptyxis**   The insertion of a vowel sound between consonants where it is historically unexpected, like [fɪləm] for *film.*

syllabary *or* **syllabic writing**   A writing system in which each unit represents a syllable.

symbolic word   A word created from sound sequences with vague symbolic meanings as a result of their occurrence in sets of semantically associated words, as *gl* in *gleam, glitter, gloss, glow* may suggest 'light' and in *gloom,* its lack.

synchronic   Pertaining to a point in time without regard to historical change; contemporary (cf. DIACHRONIC).

syncope   The loss of a sound from the interior of a word, as in *family* pronounced *fam'ly.*

synecdoche   A semantic change shifting the meaning of a word because of a metonymic association of part and whole, species and genus, or material and product, like *hired hand* 'worker,' *cat* 'any feline (lion, tiger, etc.),' *iron* 'instrument for pressing.'

synesthesia   A semantic change shifting the meaning of a word by associating impressions from one sense with sensations from another, like *warm color.*

syntagmatic change   Language change resulting from the influence of one unit on nearby units before or after it, like assimilation or dissimilation.

syntax   The part of a language system or description concerned with arranging words within constructions, distinguished from morphology.

synthetic language   A language that depends on inflections as signals of grammatical structure.

system   A set of interconnected parts forming a complex whole, specifically in language, grammatical, lexical, and phonological units and their relationship to one another.

taboo   The social prohibition of a word or subject.

tempo   The pace of speech, in which the main impression is of speed, but an important factor is the degree of casual assimilation versus full articulation of sounds.

tense vowel   A vowel made with relatively tense tongue muscles.

thematic vowel   A vowel suffixed to an Indo-European root to form a stem.

thorn   A letter of the runic alphabet (þ) and its development in the Old English alphabet.

tilde   A diacritic (˜) used in writing some languages, as in Spanish *señor.*

Tocharian   A branch of Indo-European formerly spoken in central Asia.

transfer of meaning   A semantic change altering the kinds of referents of a word as by metaphor, metonymy, etc.

translation   The representation of the meanings of the words in one language by those in another.

transliteration   The representation of the symbols of one writing system by those of another.

trigraph   A combination of three letters to represent a single sound, as *tch* in *itch* represents [č].

typological classification   A grouping of languages based on structural similarities and differences rather than genetic relations.

ultimate source   The earliest etymon known for a word (cf. DIRECT SOURCE).

umlaut *or* **mutation**   The process of assimilating a vowel to another sound in a following syllable; *also* the changed vowel that results; *also* DIERESIS.

uninflected genitive   A genitive without an ending to signal the case.

uninflected plural   A plural identical in form with the singular, like *deer.*

unmarked word   A word whose meaning lacks a semantic limitation present in marked words, as *horse* is unmarked for sex whereas *stallion* and *mare* are both marked.

unreleased   Of a stop, without explosion in the place of articulation where the stoppage is made.

unrounded *or* **spread vowel**   A vowel made with the corners of the lips retracted so the lips are against the teeth.

unrounding   Change from a rounded to an unrounded vowel.

unstressed   Of a syllable or vowel, having little prominence.

Ural-Altaic   A hypothesized language family including Uralic and Altaic.

Uralic   A family of languages including Finno-Ugric and Samoyedic.

usage   The choice among options when the choice is thought to be important; *also* the study of or concern for such choice.

Uto-Aztecan   A language family of Central America and western North America.

velar   Involving the soft palate or velum; *also* a sound made by touching the tongue against the velum.

verb   A major part of speech with the class meaning of acting, existing, or equating.

verbal noun   A noun derived from a verb.

Verner's Law   An explanation of some apparent exceptions to the First Sound Shift.

virgule *or* **slash**   A diagonal line (/) used in pairs to enclose phonemic transcriptions.

vocabulary   The stock of words of a language.

vocalization   Change from a consonant to a vowel.

vocative   A case typically used to address a person.

vogue word   A word in fashionable or faddish use.

voice   The vibration of the vocal cords and the sound produced by that vibration; *also* a grammatical category of verbs, relating the subject of the verb to the action as actor (active voice in "I watched") or as affected (passive voice in "I was watched").

VO language   A language in which objects follow their verbs.

vowel   A speech sound made without constriction and serving as the center of a syllable.

Vulgar Latin   Ordinary spoken Latin of the Roman Empire.

weak declension   A Germanic noun or adjective declension in which the consonant [n] was prominent.

weak verb   A Germanic verb whose principal parts were formed by adding a dental suffix.

wedge   HAČEK.

West Germanic   A subbranch of the Germanic languages including German, Dutch, and English.

West Saxon   The Old English dialect of Wessex.

Whorf hypothesis   A proposal that the language we use affects the way we respond to the world.

word order   The sequence of words as a signal of grammatical structure.

world English   English as used around the world, with all of its resulting variations; *also* the common features of international standard English.

writing   The representation of speech in visual form.

wynn   A letter of the runic alphabet (ᛈ) and its development in the Old English alphabet.

yogh   A letter shape (ȝ) used in writing Middle English.

yo-he-ho theory   The theory that language originated to facilitate cooperation in community work.

INDEX OF MODERN
ENGLISH WORDS
AND AFFIXES

INDEX OF PERSONS, PLACES, AND TOPICS